D1377861

STONEWALL INN EDITIONS
Keith Kahla, General Editor

Buddies by Ethan Mordden
Joseph and the Old Man
by Christopher Davis
Blackbird by Larry Duplechan
Gay Priest by Malcolm Boyd
Privates by Gene Horowitz
Conversations with My Elders
by Boze Hadleigh
Epidemic of Courage
by Lon Nungesser
One Last Waltz by Ethan Mordden
Gay Spirit by Mark Thomspson, ed.
God of Ecstasy by Arthur Evans
Valley of the Shadow
by Christopher Davis
Love Alone by Paul Monette
The Boys and Their Baby
by Larry Wolff
On Being Gay by Brian McNaught
Living the Spirit by Will Roscoe, ed.
Everybody Loves You
by Ethan Mordden
Untold Decades by Robert Patrick
Gay & Lesbian Poetry in Our Time
by Carl Morse & Joan Larkin, ed.
Personal Dispatches
by John Preston, ed.
Tangled Up in Blue
by Larry Duplechan
How to Go to the Movies
by Quentin Crisp
Just Say No by Larry Kramer
The Prospect of Detachment
by Lindsley Cameron
*The Body and Its Dangers and Other
Stories* by Allen Barnett
Dancing on Tisha B'Av by
Lev Raphael
Arena of Masculinity by Brian Pronger
Boys Like Us by Peter McGehee
Don't Be Afraid Anymore by Reverend
Troy D. Perry with Thomas L. P.
Swicegood
The Death of Donna-May Dean
by Joey Manley
Sudden Strangers by Aaron Fricke
and Walter Fricke

Profiles in Gay & Lesbian Courage by
Reverend Troy D. Perry with
Thomas L. P. Swicegood
Latin Moon in Manhattan
by Jaime Manrique
On Ships at Sea by Madelyn Arnold
The Dream Life by Bo Huston
Sweetheart by Peter McGhee
Show Me the Way to Go Home
by Simmons Jones
Winter Eyes by Lev Raphael
Boys on the Rock by John Fox
Dark Wind by John Jiler
End of the Empire by Denise Ohio
The Listener by Bo Huston
Labour of Love by Doug Wilson
Tom of Finland by F. Valentine
Hooven, III
Reports from the holocaust,
revised edition
by Larry Kramer
Created Equal by Michael Nava
and Robert Dawidoff
Gay Issues in the Workplace
by Brian McNaught
Sportsdykes by Susan Fox Rogers, ed.
Long Road to Freedom
by Mark Thompson, ed.
Sacred Lips of the Bronx
by Douglas Sadownick
The Violet Quill Reader
by David Bergman, ed.
West of Yesterday, East of Summer
by Paul Monette
The Love Songs of Phoenix Bay
by Nisa Donnelly
*I've a Feeling We're Not in Kansas
Anymore*
by Ethan Mordden
Another Mother by Ruthann Robson
Pawn to Queen Four by Lars Eighner
Coming Home to America
by Torie Osborn
Close Calls by Susan Fox Rogers, ed.
How Long Has This Been Going On?
by Ethan Mordden

ALSO BY ETHAN MORDDEN

NONFICTION

Better Foot Forward: The Story of America's Musical Theatre

Opera in the Twentieth Century

That Jazz!: An Idiosyncratic Social History of the American Twenties

A Guide to Orchestral Music

The Splendid Art of Opera: A Concise History

The American Theatre

The Hollywood Musical

Movie Star: A Look at the Women Who Made Hollywood

Broadway Babies: The People Who Made the American Musical

Demented: The World of the Opera Diva

Opera Anecdotes

A Guide to Opera Recordings

The Hollywood Studios

The Fireside Companion to the Theatre

Medium Cool: The Movies of the 1960s

Rodgers & Hammerstein

FICTION

I've a Feeling We're Not in Kansas Anymore

One Last Waltz

Buddies

Everybody Loves You

A Bad Man Is Easy to Find (as M. J. Verlaine)

How Long Has This Been Going On?

Some Men Are Lookers

FACETIAE

Smarts: The Cultural I.Q. Test

Pooh's Workout Book

HOW LONG

HAS THIS BEEN

GOING ON?

Ethan Mordden

HOW LONG HAS THIS BEEN GOING ON?

St. Martin's Press ❧ New York

Library of Congress Cataloging-in-Publication Data

Mordden, Ethan
How long has this been going on? / Ethan Mordden.
p.   cm.
ISBN 0-312-16867-5
1. Gay men—United States—Fiction.   I. Title.
PS3563.07717H68   1994
813'.54—dc20   93-11746

First published in the United States by Villard Books, a division of
Random House, Inc.

First Stonewall Inn Edition: October 1997

10 9 8 7 6 5 4 3 2 1

TO THE MEMORY OF

RIPLEY SMITH

1946–1989

ACKNOWLEDGMENTS

To my advisers on geographical and professional arcana David Brisbin, Cinda Holt, and Rex Knight; to my brilliant copy editor Benjamin Dreyer and my expert proofreader Sybil Pincus; to the once-and-future Bob Gottlieb; to Helen Eisenbach, Jerrett Engle, Erick Neher, and Robert Trent; and to my vastly overworked and intrepid secret agent Joe Spieler.

HOW LONG

HAS THIS BEEN

GOING ON?

PART I

Los Angeles, 1949–1950

IN THE DAYS when men were men and women adored them, there was a club called Thriller Jill's on a side street off Hollywood Boulevard. It was one of those late-night places, didn't get going till ten or even eleven. Bouncer at the door, tiny stage for the acts, one toilet marked "Men" and the other marked "Queens." The walls of the Queens' Room drew a lively business in graffiti—mostly a name, a phone number, and a brief statement of intent ("Mona, La Brea 6-8738, I'll suck you silly"), observations on fellow habitués ("Delissa is a scheming cunt," answered in green lipstick by "I am *not* scheming!"), and the occasional poll, with names constantly rubbed out and replaced, on such topics as "The Worst Lay in Hollywood," which became so popular that its list of names ran along three sides of the room, especially after somebody thought to cross out "Hollywood" and write in "the World." The walls of the Men's Room were relatively bare, although directly over the urinal someone had written, "I have killd six fagots so far number sevin get reddy."

The question is, Was there really a Jill? Some of the older crowd, the johns who'd been coming as long as anyone could remember, would tell you that there certainly had been a Jill, way back before the war, and she was some thriller, all right. A few claimed to have known her. Over an Angel's Tip or a Seabreeze they'd spill their curious stories, about how Jill said this and they snapped right back with *that,* or how she threw some fresh-mouthed hustler boy right out onto the street on his pretty little bum, just right out there. *Bonk!*

But the truth of it was that the club had changed its name about as often as a queen changes her shade of eye shadow. It had started as a tidy Italian cafeteria catering to rank-and-file technicians in the picture business, degenerated to a hash joint during the Depression, reasserted itself as a nightclub—three of them, Alfonso's, Club Morocco, and the Happy Palace, growing more sullen at each resuscitation—and finally went to the Other Side as Dirty Ginny's, then the Glass Slipper, Long Jim's, Easy Mary's, the Diadem, and at last Thriller Jill's, with the little platform of a stage and the blundering pianist and the gloomy bouncer and a pair of *incredible* bartenders in tight black T-shirts and Lois, the manager, her eyes always on the move to keep the place legal. "Stay clean," she'd warn the aggressive johns, the ones who treated Jill's like their personal bordello. Look, what they did outside the club was none of her business. Once they were through the door and thirty feet from the entrance they could bang a zebra for all she cared. But inside Jill's everything was strictly G.I.: no dancing, no kissing, no fondling. "Fancy stuff," Lois called it. "Fancy stuff's for your bedroom," she liked to say. She hated being touched—you know, the way some guys can't talk to you without putting a hand on your arm or something, like they're going to fall on their ass if you don't hold them up. All these guys running around touching each other while they talk. It's some fancy thing they're doing. Course, they don't touch women, but Lois dressed like a guy, talked like a guy, and moved like a guy. So they treated her like one. Fine. Just keep your hands to yourself.

Monday night. Slow. But slow even for Monday. Place is so dead the Russians could fill it with spies and no one'd notice or care. That's why Derek Archer's here, with the usual starlet beard. Where do they all come from? Week after week, Monday after Monday, this half-baked movie star slips over to the Other Side in Thriller Jill's; and this week the starlet is Charnay, next week it's Adrienne, then Sheree, Brenda, and Carelle. Beard after beard helping that faggot convince himself that No One Knows About Him. Sure. Like I don't know Truman's daughter sings crummy opera.

Movie star, Lois thought, watching him at his table, the same one every week, way in the back at the corner—watching him stare deeply into the eyes of this week's starlet, talking about "the contract" and "Mr. Mayer" and "You know what Hedda says?" Who is he lying to? is what I want to know—the rest of us or himself? Funny thing about it, he's got real sure taste in starlets. Lois tried to date Sheree, but Sheree was playing it cool. Okay, honey. You think you're getting something out of life letting a famous pixie take you out to a pixie club where you and I are just about the only biological women on the scene? Fine. But can I say this? One night with me and you would have a whole different picture of what the world calls pleasure, whether you like it or not. And, Princess Sheree, I believe you would like it once we got going.

Starlets. You know what a starlet is? A hooker in bugle beads.

Look. Mr. Derek Archer's eye wavers briefly as one of the hustlers lazily stretches, drawing the bottom of his shirt from out of his belt and catching Archer honest. The john at the table with the hustler is so entranced that he touches, and Lois strides by in her usual way.

"Stay clean," she tells them, hustler and john. The hustler takes off, unconcerned, while the john pats it down with Lois.

"He's so skittish," the john tells Lois. "Such an unruly boy."

"You'll figure him out," says Lois, starting to move on.

The john tries a smile; it looks carved, as on a jack-o'-lantern. "He's so trampy, wouldn't you say?" he calls after Lois. "A deliciously trampy boy."

Hustlers and johns, Lois thought, watching the room. That's the sex that shows. You're young, you trade; you're old, you pay. Then there's the sex you don't know about: the queens, living entirely on the Other Side but keeping their dignity; and the double-jointed, like Derek Archer, who lives on both sides. There are the tourists, too, who come in every size from starlet to plainclothes cop. But, hell, the starlets dress the place up and the dicks don't hassle you except before an election as long as they get their dough.

That's where I fit in, Lois thought. Money for fuck and actors going into their dance and the queens taking in everything that happens. And me: I pay off the cops. Someday some crazy broad'll wander in here by accident, look around, turn to Lois and say, "I'll take *you*." And the whole fucking homo world can drop dead on itself.

No, she thinks, heading backstage. No, this gig's okay. It's just that everyone you meet in it acts like a conga line of himself, you know? Like, trade is so *tough*, and johns are such *squares*, and the cops are so nun-fucking *corrupt*. Funny, they call it law enforcement—but they're so busy raking in their percent they couldn't arrest Sinatra for being thin.

Yeah, and what about *you*, in your man's pants and the greasy T-shirt?, she adds. Backstage, the boys second the thought with their eyes—Jo-Jo the emcee, Desmond the pianist, and Johnny the Kid, the club's singer and all-purpose cutie-pie. More purposes than Lois liked to think about, because one wrong foot—even one overheard comment—and the cops could close her down like snap-your-finger.

"Hey, Lois," said Jo-Jo, sewing a button onto his jacket. "When are we going to get these dead bulbs on the mirror replaced?"

"When lesbians own poodles."

Jo-Jo shrugged. "It's just lightbulbs, lady. So we can see what we're—"

"You want million-dollar showbiz, join the *Follies*. This joint is Skid Road."

"No, it isn't," said Desmond, in his gentle way. "This is a nice place."

"Empty tonight?" asked Jo-Jo.

"Yeah, but watch yourself. There's two guys I don't recognize. I'm not saying it's J. Edgar Hoover honeymooning with Clyde Tolson exactly, but let's don't beg for trouble, okay?"

"Gotcha."

"Johnny the Kid," Lois said. "Like, why do I constantly regret having taken you among us here? Why do I not trust you? Why do you look so sweet yet give airs of treachery on a scale of, like, some pirate in the *Arabian Nights*?"

Johnny the Kid beamed at her, and did he have a smile.

"Why do I suspect that you are underage, carrying false papers, and lying about everything except the color of your eyes?"

"He's a nice boy," said Desmond. "He sings the most beautiful 'What's the Use of Wond'rin'?' I ever played for."

"Gatti-Casazza has spoken," Jo-Jo put in as he smoothed his hair, staring into the mirror.

"He's good for the club," Desmond went on, rising to look at himself over Jo-Jo's shoulder, Desmond the woeful player of a thousand songs and the master of none. "He brings the customers in clamoring, with his fresh looks and appeal."

Jo-Jo looked at Desmond in the mirror, shook his head, turned to him, and straightened Desmond's bow tie.

"What good is it checking the glass," said Jo-Jo, "if you don't *fix* what you *see*?"

"Got a new number for you tonight, Lo," said the Kid. "Desmond and me're putting in 'So in Love.' "

Lois, looking over some papers at her desk in the corner, nodded absently.

"Come on, Lo. Don't we get points for working so hard? *Brownie* points, Lo? 'So in Love'—that's the masochists' national anthem." The Kid sampled a bit of it for her, emphasizing its "taunt me" and "hurt me." Jo-Jo hummed along, and Desmond helpfully mimed his accompaniment, his fingers pattering along the edge of the makeup table.

"What are you wearing tonight, Johnny?" Lois asked, looking up.

"This."

The Kid was in a summer-weight cotton dress shirt, open to the belt, and black slacks.

"He always dresses so nice," said Desmond.

"Last night," Lois corrected, "he sang the closing set wearing nothing above the belt but a funny-looking vest!"

"It was paisley," said Jo-Jo.

"I don't give a fuck it was Fauntleroy chartreuse. You know how borderline that stuff is." She took two envelopes out of her desk, locked it, and, as she passed, told the Kid, "Don't dress like a whore when you sing in my club, okay?"

"You're the boss," said the Kid.

"He's a fine young fellow," Desmond called out as Lois left. "He brings them in, panting."

"They'd come in, anyway," Jo-Jo observed. "What else are they going to do—stay home and listen to the A & P Gypsies?"

Back in the club room, a few more tables had filled and the smell of liquor and smoke was asserting itself. First Monday of the month—payoff night. Lois stuck the two envelopes into her back pocket, checked her watch, leaned against the bar.

One of the johns—one of the younger ones, always unobtrusively well dressed and soft-spoken in a confident way—came up as if he'd been waiting to speak to her. Lois braced herself.

"The show's getting better and better," the guy begins, toasting his beer at her. "Really fine singer, that boy."

The guy pauses, waiting for Lois to respond.

"So?" she says.

"That boy-next-door look is, uh, really nice to see. And he's so young, too. When he sings he seems so, uh, smart and experienced, and yet he can't be much over, what, sixteen?"

"You want to talk, talk. You want to ask questions, find a school."

"Wait, I . . . Sorry, I just wanted to know if he maybe . . . like, if he needed an older friend to help him, you know. . . ."

Lois plays it real easy. She's certain the guy is no plant, because he's one of the regulars. And she's not unsympathetic to his problem, because she and he both know that Older Friends meeting young men to Help is the reason for Thriller Jill's in the first place. The entertainment and socializing are fun, but the sex is what's true.

Still, Lois hates it when they try to use her to get to the Kid, or even to the hustlers. It's like getting touched. It's taking more than they got a right to.

"I'm a barkeep and a dyke," she tells the man. "I'm not a pimp. Got it?"

He nods and moves away as one of the bartenders signals to Lois—the law is here—and the lights go down for the show. Lois pats her envelope pocket and hits the street.

Nothing is said at these transactions. No one ventures an opinion—even, apparently, has one. It's not a matter of attitude. It's a matter of fact: If you're outlaw, you pay off. You pay in full, on time, and without a face. No expression. Don't provoke them. Think of it as Other Side tax. Think of it as a bank deposit without the hello. Some cops joke it around a little, especially when they see a woman. Lois's cops don't say anything. They just sit in their unit and the guy in the shotgun seat takes the dough and that's it.

Tax. Lois thinks, Everybody pays it somewhere along the line. Your gender. Your race. Your looks. Moving up in business, you'll pay certain kinds of tax. Your wife and kids and mortgage—that's a tax, too. That's a "Don't hate me, I'm like everybody else" tax.

Back in Jill's, Lois stands against the bar during the entertainment, as always admiring how easily Jo-Jo creates a wholly different show every night by varying his jokes and bouncing off the news.

"It seems that F.D.R. left Harry S. two sealed letters," Jo-Jo is telling them, "the first to be opened in grave need and the second in gravest need. So there was the railroad strike, and Harry opens the first letter. It reads, 'Blame it on me.' So everything's fine. Then Miss Alger Hiss comes to trial."

A few titters.

"Communists and pumpkins and it's terribly embarrassing for Harry. So he opens the second letter. It reads, 'Start writing two letters. . . .' "

Well, they laugh. But, shit, they're not here for Jo-Jo's views on newspaper stuff. They want him way over the fence, with the secret words and the jokes nobody else gets. And they want the Kid, because he's a looker. Even Lois kind of felt a little something, watching him in the vest. He had oiled his chest, too, the sneak.

The Kid's doing a lot of nostalgia tonight: "Let's Do It," "Lucky in Love," "Make-Believe." Are they really listening to him, or are they just watching, drinking him in? The all-American looks with the busy green eyes: Everybody loves a scamp. Anyway, they know what's good around here, and the Kid knows he's it.

Larken's here, too, Lois notices—the only regular she truly likes. Strange guy. He doesn't hustle, he's too young to be a john, and his style's too jam for a queen. He's like the nice-looking young guy in a war movie who gets blown up about reel three. Sandy hair, slim, smart-looking. Remember high school? Larken was the boy you pretended to be crazy about when what you really wanted was for Mary Beth Taggert the Head Cheerleader to rub against you, saying, "How about I eat your muff?"

As the show ends and the lights come up—about thirty-five seconds late because the bartenders are asleep again—Lois joins Larken at his table.

"What do you say, my friend?" is her opening.

"Hi, Lois. Dandy show."

"With Bob Hope and that Dead End Kid of a Buddy Clark, how can I go wrong?"

Larken smiled. "You always tear down whatever you build."

"What do I build?" Lois caught the eye of one of the bartenders and cocked her head at Larken. The bartender nodded.

"You've got a whole little world in here," said Larken. "Self-contained. Neat-like."

Desmond the pianist shuffled by in hunt of praise. Larken waved at him, and Desmond asked, "Did you like the Jeanette-Nelson medley? We worked so hard on it."

"I could tell. But you sneaked a little Jeanette-without-Nelson in at the end."

"*The Love Parade!*" Desmond exulted. "You noticed! But life is one great parade of love, isn't it?"

The bartender put Larken's drink on the table, a glass of draft. Larken started to say something, but Lois made a quick gesture: You're welcome and say no more.

"Yes," Desmond went on. "Love parades through this bar. Now we sense it, now it's gone. It's just like music, because all of us respond to it, yet not all of us can sing."

Larken thought that over. "Desmond, that's . . . that's pretty deep."

"It's quite a thought," Desmond eagerly admitted. "It just came out of me."

"Desmond, Desmond," said Larken, nearly laughing.

"Look," said Lois, "it isn't love parading through anywhere, because love is in hiding. As for this place—"

"It's a nice place," said Desmond. "They come from miles around."

"It's a joint," said Lois.

"The music and the fun," Desmond cited. "The jests and surprises of this bar."

Larken and Lois looked around: at the johns silently aching; at the glowering hustlers lined along the back wall; at the queens dishing everyone in sight, in history, in the imagination. This was the world. All it contained, besides your day job, and maybe your cover marriage, was here.

"It's a joint," Lois insisted. She turned to Larken. Her eyes said, Right?

"Well, yes, it's a joint," Larken agreed. "But a necessary joint."

Desmond, feeling ratified, wandered off.

Lois shrugged.

Larken shrugged, too, smiling at her.

"I wonder why you come here," Lois told him. "You're not like the others. You're too . . ."

"Uh-oh."

"No, it's not an insult. You're too gentle for this place. Look at them."

Lois nodded her head at the crowd, not taking her eyes off Larken.

"What do you see?" she asked him.

"My friends, I guess."

"Your *friends*? The queens gabbing away there like exotic birds in some rain forest? And those saphead johns? Your friends? The hustle boys are your friends?"

"They're my kind, somehow or other."

"Christ."

"Well, why else are we all here? See, that's why you put on these shows for us. The comedy and song. Because we've got this . . . this thing in common."

"You could sell it, you know that? You're cute enough."

"Queens only go with trade, Lois. They want a handsome piece of trash."

She nodded. "You guys sure know how to make it tough on yourselves."

Larken nodded. "It's kind of hard to fall into step with each other when we're so invisible in the real world. I mean, how are we supposed to know who we *are*?"

"We aren't. That's why they call it the Other Side."

"They don't call it that. *We* do."

"Yeah." She looked at him pointedly. "Funny how that works out."

"So how do you get along, Lois? What's your story, anyway?"

"Yeah," she said. "Right," as she rose. "I'll tell you someday."

Derek Archer was satisfied with the stir he made when he took his first-ever visit backstage at Thriller Jill's. This is Hollywood, after all, and a star is a star, even a star as yet on the rise who'll still be a second-rater when and if he does get there. Jo-Jo played it smooth but grand, Desmond genuflected, and the Kid let the star pay him court. The Kid, after all, was the reason for Archer's visit in the first place, and the Kid knew it. You don't grow up constantly getting slurped by your cousins and rammed by your schoolmates without developing a certain perception about your marketability. You watch the eyes, read the codes. You begin to figure out that they are starving and you are cake.

The Kid has perfected a way of flirting that is not flirting, whereby he is dreamily attentive, technically fixed on you but drifting. He finds that it draws people closer to him, because while everyone is grateful for attention most of them are dying to know exactly *what kind* of attention they are getting. So the Kid gives them attention, but the kind is kept secret.

"I love your movies," Desmond was telling Archer. "They are so elegant and profound." Thrillers and weepies. "I wouldn't miss one, except for a death in the family."

"Which is your favorite?" Archer foolishly asked.

Desmond, stumped for a title, sweats for a bit till the Kid steps in for him.

"Who could choose?" the Kid says—confides, really, in a tone meant for one of those quiet little tables for two that he's always singing about.

"Don't *you* have a favorite?" Archer asked, moving closer.

"I don't have favorite movies. I have favorite people."

"That's so true of all of us!" Archer turned to his starlet date. "Isn't it?"

"I—"

"Don't you think he has amazing eyes?"

"Some of us have favorite movies," Desmond put in, having thought of a Derek Archer film to praise: *It Happened in Monterey.* "Rather than favorite—"

"And what about his singing?" Archer, staring at the Kid, asked the starlet.

"I—"

"Simplicity," said Archer. "Honesty. Youth. It's exciting to be around such talent in its . . . its beginning time. Uncompromised. Unmarked."

"You sound like one of your posters, Hollywood," said Lois, striding up and eyeing each of them in turn, commanding Archer, warning the Kid, and, briefly, sifting the starlet, who sifted right back.

"Someone's been around the block, I see," Lois half muttered to the starlet. Then to Archer she said, "What's her name this week? Nippla? Muffina?"

The starlet guffawed.

"Lois, I am your convinced fan," Archer told her. "Oh, totally. Because I *love* this club," as he's taking her with an arm around the shoulders for a walk away from the others. Shit, another toucher.

While Lois's back is turned, the starlet smiles at the Kid, carefully holds a finger to her mouth—carefully, so that he will comprehend the advanced level of discretion that he is being asked to maintain, because this is very high-contract Hollywood and we don't want anything to go amiss, do we?—and whispers, "When do you get off?"

The starlet? But the Kid is game, because he is in his beginning time, and who knows where he might end, if he can only continue right.

"A little after two," the Kid tells her, his voice low.

"He'll send a car. Two blocks down the Boulevard. *That* way." She points. "What is that, east? Anyway, ask the driver for 'Mr. Nougat.' "

The Kid plays it easy, wry. "Mr. Nougat?"

The starlet shrugs. "His little joke, I guess."

"It suits him," says the Kid.

She had been turning to go; she stopped, one eye on Archer and Lois. "Careful what you say, you hear? Like, no irony. Got it, baby?"

"Irony. Lady, you're *literary*. Where've *you* been, huh?"

"Where? Toured by experts and coming home for a rest. Roger wilco?"

"And out."

Archer merrily signaled to the starlet, who told Lois as she passed, "Not Muffina. Latwata. Latwata B. Tasty."

"I'm free most afternoons," said Lois, playing along.

Archer cut in with "Oh, the atmosphere is so dense here. Dense. You know, I play a cabaretier in my next film, *Broadway Lullaby*. What a challenge, you're thinking. But that's why I love to come here. To breathe in the . . . Don't you think the color of the place," he asked the starlet, "is truly—but I mean sincerely now—*positive*?"

"You—"

"It's so useful coming here, I can't tell you," Archer told Lois, and he and the starlet left.

Jo-Jo, who had witnessed, and relished, every detail, piped up with "He's one part Cary Grant and one part Audie Murphy, but who's the third part?"

"Ann Blyth," said Johnny. The Kid.

Lois grimaced and Jo-Jo made no-no fingers at Johnny.

"You know," says the Kid, "I only describe what everyone sees."

The black Duesenberg was waiting for Johnny, the capped chauffeur as stiff as an extra in the movies.

"I ask for Mr. Nougat," the Kid told him as he slid inside, describing rather than taking part in the espionage. He felt a bit less ridiculous that way.

The chauffeur said nothing the whole trip, never even glanced at the Kid through the rearview mirror.

That's okay, as long as you plush me. Do it to me, the works. Movie stars and limousines and a date with Mr. Nougat. Not bad for a kid from Placentia who spent high school sweating it out in the principal's office for being a wise guy when he wasn't being cornered by bullies.

Chauffeur's a sharp driver, too. Fleet but smooth. Derek Archer obviously hires right and pays well. That's good news.

Johnny the Kid, how old are you, really?

Well, that depends on who's counting. My mother, if she cared, would say, "Too old for his age." Precocious. You know: twelve going on Dorothy Parker.

Jo-Jo, who doesn't know everything, would guess, "Jailbait till the next remake of *Beau Geste*."

Lois figured it out. "You're seventeen and don't tell me about it," she said. "And don't show me your doctored I.D.s. Just keep it clean for the cops, *versteh*?"

Keep it clean, sure, as I ride into the Hills for my dance with Mr. Nougat. Give a boy looks and moxie and he's going to keep it clean? What planet have you been living on? Because the Kid's going to make out, see? He's going all the way up there, see? Top of the world, Ma! *Exposure*. Meeting the kingpins. Oozing to the heights in a limo where a chauffeur knows the protocols and you're getting hot for your date with Mr. Nougat.

Unless, of course, you're no more than a night's lay in a Hollywood mansion. Grr, whirr, thank you, sir.

Well, we'll see about that. I'll just have to be too memorable to be forgotten.

The car docked in a circular driveway before an ornately designed but surprisingly compact house.

Size isn't everything, the Kid told himself, as the chauffeur held the door for him and the Kid got his first good look at the guy.

"Why didn't you tell me you were so tall?" the Kid asked. "What else have you got?"

The chauffeur said nothing, didn't move. Behind them, a ray of light broke along the stonework of the drive; the Kid turned, and there, in the open doorway, stood Derek Archer in a dressing gown and, apparently, nothing else.

"Mr. Nougat, I presume?" said the Kid, flirting with danger despite the starlet's warning about No irony. "Hard on the outside and soft in the center?"

"Come in and shut up," Archer replied, drawing the Kid into the house with a hand on his collar as the car hummed off to the garage. "Quickly, now. No stalling."

The Kid wants the adventure, but he does not like being ordered around, and he balks. He's not angry; he just stops moving.

Suddenly, Archer changes his tone. "Please," he says. "I'm sorry I was so abrupt, really. But I have to move fast. Don't fight me."

"Okay, Mr. Nougat, sir. Or can I call you 'Candy'?"

"And please don't joke. Not till it's over."

The Kid bowed.

"Come."

Archer led the Kid upstairs to a bedroom. "Take a shower first," he said. Gesturing toward the bathroom, he added, "Everything you need is there. Use it all. Take your time. Spoil yourself."

He smiled at the Kid for the first time, a flash of the movies' Derek Archer, the endearingly fumbly good guy, well-intentioned but unsavvy. An American type.

"Okay, now? Don't feel hurried or under any pressure. When you're finished, go through that door there. It connects to another room. I'll be waiting for you."

Archer went to a closet and pulled out a blue-and-green tartan bathrobe of the kind worn mainly by adolescents in Pasadena.

"It's so me," said the Kid.

"Don't . . . joke. Please? Don't say anything at all. Take your time in the water, get all nice and clean, and come visit me in your robe. Make sure you wash your hair, too—and don't dry it. I like to see a young boy all fresh and sloppy at night, getting ready for bed."

Fifty gleeful spoofs occurred in the Kid's head, but he kept his face straight and simply nodded.

"Good," Derek Archer said, and he stood there, smiling again and gazing contentedly at the Kid for a bit. "I'll see you soon," he added, leaving through the connecting door.

Huh, thought the Kid, with a double Huh for the bathroom, a boutique's worth of unnecessary accoutrements from "bath champagne" to "facial gel." Is this what keeps a young boy fresh and sloppy?, the Kid thought, stepping out of his clothes and exploring. Soap stamped out in cunning animal shapes? Cologne in bottles so elaborate they look like Sinbad's hookah? Nobody uses this stuff, so why is somebody manufacturing it?, he wondered. How would anybody even know where to buy it?

Soaping up in the spray, the Kid started to put it together. Apparently, Derek Archer, America's up-and-coming romantic hero, has a thing for the teenage boy-next-door type. And he likes the picture of a raw kid blundering around in a faggy bathroom; it tells him how unspoiled I am. Yeah. Well, maybe I'm not too far off the type, he thought, getting a load of Kid in the biggest mirror he had ever seen in a private home, running along three sides of the room. Boy next door. Well, I look the part; I just don't want the insides. Can't use them.

Dry and robed, the Kid took a last look, mussed up his hair, and walked into the next room, where he found Archer sitting at a table, smoking. Something caught the Kid's eye, and he turned to find the starlet in bed.

Archer stubbed out a cigarette. "Let's have a look at you, young fellow," he said, rising. "Johnny's your name, right?"

On his guard, the Kid nodded slightly.

Archer clamped him by the shoulders. "*Johnny.* Well. Let's see what sort of fine young boy we have here. A little confused and unsure about things. Out of his element." Opening the robe and gently pushing it back on the shoulders. "Spent the afternoon playing . . . what? Football's in season, isn't it? Fine young fellow here," tracing the pec line. "Trim and . . . manageable," teasing the nipples. "Turn slightly to the . . . yes," as he guides the boy. "That's very Johnny." Taking the robe off him and tossing it onto the floor. Kneading his neck and sides. Shaping the cheeks of his butt. "Beautiful fan. A very *winning* boy, wouldn't you say so?" he asked the starlet.

The Kid exchanged a look with her; his grinned and hers reminded him *no.*

Archer tore open his own robe and held the Kid close. "Tight around me, young man," he directed. "Let me feel the warmth of you. Tight and tight and now and tight. Yes. Yes, harder." Keeping his hands on the Kid's shoulders, Archer gently disengaged from the embrace and looked at the Kid for a while, stroking his hair now and again in an absentminded way. One month short of eighteen—so now we know—and at the height of his sexual majesty, the Kid had been hard for some time; but Archer had pointedly been gazing at his eyes all the while, as if . . . well, dismissing the rest of the Kid. Only now did Archer take in the whole of the boy, as he set him faceup on the bed, knelt before him, and launched what was by far the most splendidly coaxing and teasing slurp operation the Kid had enjoyed in his life. To be fair, most of the Kid's partners heretofore had been frenzied amateurs or opportunistic dilettantes, while Derek Archer was clearly a cultist. Still, it says something that even as the Kid went with it, passive and deep into delight, he was trying to memorize Archer's technique for his own use in the future.

However, Archer abruptly abandoned the Kid and, throwing his robe to the floor, walked around the bed to the starlet, mounted her, and, gasping and shouting, moved his ass off. He came much earlier than the Kid thought respectable, and immediately leaped up, staggering back against the wall and holding himself and nodding over and over while staring at the Kid. Panting, he held up the flat of his hand—Silence? *Ave?* Cut? He smiled at the Kid. And then Derek Archer left the room, spent, his eyes vacant, as the Kid and the starlet shared another look. It was over, that fast. Her look said, *C'est la vie,* and the Kid's look agreed.

The starlet waved at the Kid as an oblivious butler helped the Kid back to the shower and into his clothes, then through the house to the kitchen, where the chauffeur was waiting for him. The butler gave the Kid an envelope—cash, you could see right through it—and the chauffeur led him out to the car.

Some plush, the Kid thought. Some exposure. This is breaking in? He opened the envelope and counted—two hundred bucks. Well, Archer may not bring you off, but at least he's no mean cheese with the tip. Stuffing the envelope into his pocket, the Kid leaned forward and took a look at the chauffeur. The chauffeur ignored him.

"How about if I hop in the front seat with you?" the Kid asked. "It's so lonely in the back here."

The chauffeur said nothing and the Kid jumped up front. He stared at the chauffeur for a bit, then: "First you're real tall, then you've got a beautiful nose. I really notice noses on men, you know? There are cute noses, and arrogant noses, and stupid noses. I like a nose that's not too small, very straight, and perched in the middle of a really handsome face, like yours."

The chauffeur waited two counts, turned to look at the Kid, then returned to his driving.

"Boy, you're some top number. I don't mean to pry, but are you planning to fuck me inside out tonight? I think I have a right to know."

Alone in the sitting room next to the bedroom, Derek Archer was listening to music. The long-playing 33⅓ discs had been introduced a year ago, but Archer prized his many volumes of 78s, ten-inchers, the spines carefully labeled, because Archer's a careful man. There were volumes on "Russ Columbo," "Fats Waller," "Hollywood Medleys," "Ballroom Smooth," "Kern-Gershwin," "Artie Shaw," and one labeled "Special," with Archer's particular favorites—Buddy Clark's "It's a Big, Wide, Wonderful World," Hildegarde's "I Worship You," Russ Case's "If This Isn't Love," and the disc he was playing now, the Merrymakers' "Jukebox Romance," another of the many close-harmony, tamed-bop numbers that came out of nowhere, conquered, and then vanished in the years after the war:

> The record started playing,
> The song urged, "Take a chance!"
> Our eyes began to fox-trot
> In a love-enchanted trance.
> We made the introductions;
> I asked you for a dance
> And a one-night jukebox romance.

As the car pulled up at the Kid's boardinghouse, the Kid made a shh finger at the chauffeur. "My landlady thinks I go to U.C.L.A.—'You Can't Learn Anything.' And U.S.C. is 'You Still Can't.' Anyway, we have to be prudent. Because I'm not supposed to have guests, especially late at night, when anything can happen and might interfere with my studies. So, easy on the shoes, Ivanhoe."

Being careful in the Derek Archer way means, for instance, hiring an all-gay staff to preclude the possibility of blackmail: because then they're vulnerable, too. Careful means staying out of the Y.M.C.A., which Archer dreams about, it sometimes seems, from moment to moment, because that's where all the Johnnys are, showering and wandering around saying "Yes, sir" in that incredibly *innocent* way. Careful means following the studio line on cover dates and conniving at the absurd "sweethearts" flashes in the columns and, eventually, marrying. If Robert Taylor can, he can.

> What a swingtime!
> What joy!
> What a night for a girl and a boy!
> What heaven for two!
> What a dream that may almost come true!

Sometimes I wonder if there might be two people inside me—the man I am and the man I'm chasing. Because I know him so well. I could play him, in the right movie. I could be my own lover.

> The melody surrounds us,
> The crooner hums and chants.
> The couples sway around us,
> We don't give them a glance.
> We'll sit the next set out, dear,
> But save the last dance
> For our brand-new jukebox romance.

The Kid was leaning against the bed, the chauffeur nested up to the hilt in his ass. The visitor started slowly, then increasingly picked up the tempo till he was roughing the Kid, and the Kid was loving it. He came first, but the chauffeur wasn't far behind. Pulling out, he grabbed a towel, dried off, and got back into his uniform, available but unconnected.

"Next time," said the Kid, "let's do it on skates."

Frank Hubbard didn't get into law enforcement to get stuck on the Vice Squad, trapping hookers and homos when the city was full of real crooks. Frank hated Vice, hated arresting people after making nice to them, and most of all he hated his partner, Jack Cleery. Well, maybe he didn't hate Jack, exactly. Jack wasn't the most compassionate or well-intentioned guy on the force, but he wasn't vile, either. It's just that everything that came out of his mouth was stupid or, at best, irrelevant. Now, the thing is, when you're a cop the most important thing in life is your grasp of procedure, staying alert and doing it by the numbers. And the most stimulating thing in life is the thought that, every day, you can do at least something to improve the world. But the most constant thing in life is your partner's conversation, and Jack's talk was one fucking problem. Frank couldn't figure which was worse, the idiotic content of the words themselves or the all-the-way *seriousness* with which Jack uttered them. It was like Winston Churchill reading the lines of Goofy. He'd repeat things, too—eighteen, nineteen times, each time with this gruesome, self-discovering wonder, as if he hadn't already battered you to death with "If I had to choose between Betty Grable and Esther Williams, you know who it would be?" or "My dad had a lousy war."

"A real lousy war, you know?" he's going. "I mean, from Pearl Harbor to V-J Day, one big aggravation. Like—"

"Listen, okay?" Frank puts in. "*Everybody* had a lousy war."

Jack looked stung; he could do this even in the dark. "So what are you so jumpy about? I'm just telling you what he told me."

"A quartermaster in a little port outside New York City has a lousy war, huh? How about all the guys in the *infantry* getting shot up while we took Italy and Berlin, okay? If you're talking lousy wars—"

"Fort Totten happens to be one of the significant, the major—"

"Jesus, who cares about your fucking father and his fucking war, already? What are you *talking* to me, Jack?"

Jack clammed up, drumming his fingers on the steering wheel. Good, let him sulk and we'll have some peace. It was late in the watch, maybe an hour to go, in the old-faithful fishing ground of Griffith Park. Vice did a lively business there, a never-miss commerce in the taking of souls. No one's armed. Everyone's scared. So fucking easy. That's why you joined the force, right? To arrest frightened faggots in a park. You and Jack Cleery. What a team. And that's your contribution to the public good.

"Time to hit the trail," said Jack, breaking the silence. He never stayed hurt long. You couldn't listen to him, you couldn't correct him, and you couldn't offend him. He was indestructible.

"Yeah, yeah, yeah," said Frank, not moving even after Jack had opened the door and put his feet on the ground.

"What's with you?"

Frank didn't answer for a bit. Then: "Why do I always have to be the lure? How about you do it for once here?"

"I told you that already, boy. It's because you're the looker. No one's going to follow me down any magic pathway to ecstasy, are they?"

Frank flung the door open and leaped out. "Yeah, right, let's get out there and *move* those fruiters, huh? Let's find one guy who wants to fuck around in the woods with another guy, and let's destroy his life, okay?"

"What destroy? So they get collared—"

"And fired from their job. Or, like, it's the third offense—you know what they do to them then?"

"Man, suddenly, you're all . . . I don't know about you, boy, I really don't. Because all of a sudden—correct me if I'm wrong—you're doing a Let's Feel Sorry for the Homos routine."

They were each standing at the side of the unit, in the open doors, staring at each other across the roof.

"Don't you ever . . . You don't feel something for these guys? Picking them off like . . . like pool scum in a net?"

"Shoot, I didn't make them that way, did I?"

" 'Shoot,' " Frank repeated. "Right, *'shoot.'* "

"Well, did I? Was it my idea they come down here pushing it around Griffith Park?"

Jack pronounced it "Griffiss." Another of his many charms. Griffiss Park.

"These faggots keep on living different from us," Jack went on, "something's going to happen to them. They know the rules. You break the rules, you pay."

They stood staring at each other for a moment. Then Jack added, "Now, look, already. We going to argue the philosophy of life or are we going to do our job?"

They were on the edge of the part of the park that was known—not to them—as "Garboland." No one knew when the name had come into use, or why. Perhaps because it was a place of avid fantasy, of romance to death, you might say. Every night, from sundown nearly to dawn, men would populate Garboland, sitting, strolling, lurking, and looking: cruising. The results were variable. Most nights, only the most determined would score, and scoring was often no more than a fast grope or a blowjob behind the trees. The more romantically inclined held out for something more sociable and less furtive—an exchange of phone numbers for a dinner date, perhaps, or walking out of the park together, then car trailing car through the city to whoever lived nearest, or whoever felt like playing host, or whoever wasn't married.

On "hunting nights," Frank and Jack would split up, Jack following Frank at a distance till Frank parked himself on a bench and waited. Twenty-one years old and, as Jack always reminded him, a looker, Frank never waited long. A man would pass, gazing at Frank. Frank would gaze back. The man would pause, perhaps look at his watch or pretend to spot something fascinating in the distance. Frank called it "punctuation." The man would back up, sit next to Frank, and open it. "Nice evening." "You alone tonight?" Or maybe he'd just nod.

This man was the fish.

Going by the book, Frank would offer neither encouragement nor resistance. The fish would keep talking, getting closer and closer to it, always riding on those strange make-believe phrases, like "Would you like to take a walk?" or "Could we go somewhere and get to know each other better?"

Finally, Frank would ask the guy, "What exactly do you want to do?" This was the hook.

Some guys shied away at that point. Frank never knew why. Some of them, the smart ones, might have read him as a cop. They were the ones that got away. But some of them told him exactly what they wanted to do.

And that was the bite.

So Frank would stand and tell them they were under arrest as Jack stamped up with the cuffs.

That was fishing, and that was Frank's life, to his despair. He told himself that it was going to happen anyway, that if he didn't, somebody else would. He figured that at least with him doing it nobody ever got hurt, which was not usual when Vice cops went fishing. There was a detective named Ragdon who was known as "Filthy Bill." Six-footer. Face like one of Dick Tracy's villains and the heart of a bank president. Ragdon had worked his way up from Vice, and they say that for his entire career every fish he brought in was a bloody wreck. Resisting arrest, right? Some little slob who couldn't call Lou Costello "Fatso" resisted Filthy Bill Ragdon. Right.

Something else. Maybe it didn't matter in the long run. But whenever Frank saw a man who looked . . . well, like a good guy . . . Frank would put him off, glance away and shake his head and never reel him in.

Like tonight. Frank's on his bench, alone in the dark except for Jack hiding behind Frank's left shoulder, way back in the greenery. There's enough moonlight to catch the outlines of moving figures here and there. Twigs crackle, leaves whish against something. Every now and then a whisper floats over from somewhere. It could be a scene from a movie, Frank thinks. Dark lighting, all this atmosphere, then A Doomed Stranger enters.

It never took long. Two or three minutes after Frank took up his post— four minutes, absolute tops—some guy would come wandering up the path, the fish all set for the hook. You never knew what you'd get— young, old, athletic, out of shape, shy or so practiced they could have been working from a script. Some of them could be movie stars. Some of them could be Frankenstein's Uncle Cy.

This guy, tonight, seemed like a grown-up version of your kid brother, and Frank tried to freeze him off by turning away. But the guy plopped down on the bench and said, "I think I've seen you here before, haven't I?"

Frank turned to him, real slow, not too friendly. I don't want to hook you, okay? Why don't you just trot along? Be smart and go home.

"My name's Lark. Larken, really. Dumb name, huh?"

The guy held out his hand; Frank took it without answering.

"I really hated it when I was a kid. All the other boys had regular names. Steve, Bob, Jim. There was a Cornelius in my third-grade class but everybody called him Neil. What's your name?"

Frank looked at the guy, his eyes tight, his mouth a line drawn by a ruler, trying to show him that this is no place for kid brothers. The guy's smile had dimmed, but he was no quitter. Moving closer and gently taking Frank's hand, he said, "Want me to tell your fortune? A Gypsy taught me."

He brushed Frank's palm lightly, once, twice, again. He looked at Frank. "Actually, it was an entertainer I know. He goes by the name of Gypsy Pete."

The guy brushed Frank's palm again, sweetly tingling the skin.

"Feels good, doesn't it?" the guy asked.

Frank nodded.

"Except you really have to relax for this. Just put yourself in the hands of Gypsy Pete." The guy laughed nervously. "It's quite a routine that he has. Quite a routine. See, he sort of mesmerizes you while he's telling your fortune. I don't do it as well as he can, but then he's part Gypsy. He *says.* And Gypsies always know more about the world than anyone else, I hear. They have to, because everybody hates them, so they learn how to defuse that hatred and persuade people that—"

"I'm waiting for somebody," said Frank, as the guy, Larken, kept brushing his hand.

"I was hoping you were waiting for me."

Frank leaned in real close to the guy and said, "I want you to walk away from this bench right now. Don't make me get up."

The guy gulped and moved a bit away from Frank, but he didn't leave, didn't even let go of Frank's hand.

"Why do I have to walk away?" he asked.

"Because I . . . I don't want to hurt you."

"You're hurting me now."

Frank turned his wrist so that now he was holding Larken's hand. He brushed Larken's palm, once, twice. "Gypsies." Again. "I know Gypsies, too. Know what they told me?"

Larken shook his head.

"The law is on your homo tail, and they're going to catch you if you don't run for it."

Larken got up, staring at Frank. He clearly wanted to say something, but suddenly turned and walked quickly away.

Frank's heart was pounding. He leaned hard against the bench, ran a hand through his hair, exhaled, threw his arms back.

"You let him go," said Jack, coming up.

Frank shrugged.

"How come you let him go? How come, Frank?" Jack sounded almost hurt.

"He didn't break the rules."

"He was perfect."

Frank looked at Jack. "What do you mean, perfect?"

"You talked all that time and he didn't bite? What are you waiting for, some guy to drop his pants and bend over?"

Frank stood up. "Hey," he said. "Jack?" for emphasis. "You *can* that stuff, *right*?"

"Just don't be so busy with the next one, huh? It's a collar, not a marriage bureau. It's no vacation hanging around back there in Sherwood Forest."

"What are *you* beefing about? I'm the one who does the . . ." Dirty work.

"Yeah, well, pick up one of the Merry Men and let's get the shit out of here. I'm getting hungry."

The next guy up the path was a fat old scrounger in a baseball cap who called Frank "Dollface" and felt up his ass and then, irritated at Frank's bland reticence, told him, "You're not the only slice of loin on the meat rack, honey."

Rising to signal Jack, Frank thought, This is going to be a pleasure.

Elaine wrote letters to herself on legal pads. Some began "Dear Elaine," others "Dear Mrs. Denslow," and every so often she would address one to "Dear Homemaker." She wrote as an artist paints fruit, standing apart from her life and looking at it. Its textures, colors, light. For instance:

Dear Elaine:

You married a fine man. Everyone told you so at the time, and they were right. He was a nice-looking boy, right up there in the main crowd in school. "The Echelon," they called it, in the yearbook: Most Likely to Own U.S. Steel, Most Humorous, Most Promising Star. Jeff was Most Popular. All the girls were wild for him, I suppose because he was so gentle. It was the wrong award; he should have been Most Shy. Once he saw Elaine and two friends whispering about him and staring at him. You might say they were penetrating him, and he blushed and locked his eyes on the floor so hard he almost shivered. Elaine thought that was the sexiest thing she had ever seen.

Elaine liked to smoke cigarillos while she wrote, and she tanked in black coffee. It was a quiet-afternoon thing, writing the letters, a task but a pleasing one. It made her appetitive. Sometimes she topped off the smoke and caffeine with sucking candy—butterscotch squares or green mint drops.

Jeff lost something after graduation. At first, I thought it was his sense of belonging, his prominence on the team sports and his popularity. No: his shyness. Somehow or other, he managed to get used to himself, to take himself for granted as a fine man who always does the right thing. That's why I feel so guilty not worshiping him any more. He not only needs it—he deserves it. He really does. And I'm twenty-seven and drying up.

Driving to the Meeting, Larken kept berating himself for not being aggressive enough. That's how you connect, isn't it? You *push* for it. You let that man in Griffith Park go, like a fisherman throwing one back, you know that? Just gave him up. He was such an attractive fellow, too. You don't see a hell of a lot of them there, for some reason. It's mainly a ghoul party, in fact. I don't blame anyone for how he looks, but is that all I get?

Following instructions, Larken parked on San Mateo and walked the three blocks to the address on Knowland. Security compelled them to hold the Meeting at a different member's address each time, and to disperse the cars in order to keep neighbors from getting a read on the Group. A bunch of cars at a single house disgorging an all-male coterie would look suspicious.

I still don't understand why he seemed friendly and then suddenly turned on me. Maybe he thought I was a cop?

Reaching the address of the Meeting, Larken took a long look at himself at one of the little windows that bordered the upper half of the front door. He ran a hand through his light hair, pulling it back to see how it would look shorter. Then he tilted his chin and put on a more or less steely gaze, trying to sample himself as a Vice cop.

Ridiculous, he told himself. No cop looks like me. Of course, that would be the best kind of Vice cop, wouldn't it? Undetectable.

Suddenly the door swung open and "Paul," the man whose house it was, stood glaring at Larken.

"What are you doing, you truly vicious fool?" Paul said, under his breath so the neighbors couldn't hear. "You want to bring all the nosey parkers out to—"

"Just get him inside, for Chrissakes!" a second man cried.

Paul literally pulled Larken into the house and carefully closed the door. The other men had all arrived, and were standing in the living room looking at Larken.

"Why do you think we use fake names and change the meeting place every time?" Paul went on, advancing on Larken as Larken backed into the room. "Why do we park our cars blocks away? Why do we stagger the arrival times twenty minutes apart?"

"All right, Paul," said one of the men. "You've made your point."

"Not to him, I haven't! Not to him!"

"Jesus."

"I'm sorry," said Larken. "I was just . . . I wasn't thinking."

Paul threw up his hands in disgust.

"If we're going to turn on each other like this," said another man, "Alfred," "how can we possibly hope to start a movement for homosexual rights?"

" 'The Liberation of the Homosexual from the Oppression of the American State'!" snapped Paul, really upset now.

"Goddamnit, Paul," said yet another man, "Jake." "You cut it out or I'm leaving."

"We'll all leave," said Alfred.

"Well, why can't he get it right?" Paul complained; but his tone was already changing from fury to mild irritation as he surveyed the faces in the room.

"Let's just sit down and start the—"

"No," said Paul, very calm now. He looked away from everyone and sighed deeply. "I have to apologize," he said, turning back to them. "I'm scared and I'm nervous and I flew off the handlebars. I'm scared, that's all. Maybe about nothing. Maybe about the old biddy across the street who spends the whole day peering at everyone through her window curtains. I don't know. Maybe she's blind. Maybe the police will be in here in five minutes."

Yet all we do is talk, Larken thought. Six homosexuals, some married and some not, all lonely for another man to talk to and love, but we scarcely even *socialize*.

Larken wondered what it would be like if they suddenly decided to pair off. It was hard to think of any of these men sexually. But Jake was pretty nice-looking, dark-haired, short and trim in a T-shirt and slacks. And Alfred was rugged in a kind of nondescript way, big without power. Paul was definitely the least imposing of the group. He was its founder and leader, but he was half-bald and very overweight.

Paul went up to Larken and extended his hand. "I'm sorry," he said. "I've even forgotten your name."

"Lark," came the reply as they shook hands.

Paul's face clouded, and Jake chuckled.

"I mean 'Russ,' " Larken quickly added.

"Come on, boys," said "Terry," guiding them into the living room with a hand on each shoulder. "Let's conspire."

Dear Elaine,

You had the most wonderful reunion with three of your classmates this afternoon. A gossip lunch. You remember Sally Lankston. Made the All-State Cheering Squad because she had the most spectacular breasts in Santa Ana? Anyway, I thought so. Last time I saw her, she was engaged to a Quaker from Whittier. She's a hooker now—afternoons, when her husband's at work. She *loves* it. I asked her how she got through a date with some coarse galoot, and she said it's no problem at all once you realize that all men are the same. Because what distinguishes people *as* people is their feelings, and of course men don't have any. So what's the big deal?, she says.

And Marjorie Thomas was there—that sort-of-troublemaker who ran around with bikers and greaseballs? Marjorie said that Sally had a pretty good theory going there, because a woman's approach to lovemaking had many variations, whereas men were strictly "Shove in and spend."

Sally said, "Absolutely," nodding her head over and over just the way she used to do. Remember how she would say "Absolutely" at least once every two minutes?

Marjorie will only wear men's clothes. Suits and so on. And her hair looked great chopped short like that, straight black hair flopping around to *just* below her ears. I offered her one of my cigarillos, but she said she prefers a substantial cigar, and only after dinner.

Sarah Wild was there, too—my dearest friend at Santa Ana High. Boy, has she changed! Swears like a trucker and looks you right in the eyes to speak her mind and she killed her husband. She says it was an accident. He had bashed the car up putting it in the garage, and Sarah said, "Well, that's so typical," and he got offended and impossible, the way men will. So she clonked him on the head with the skillet in which she was going to fix a chili dinner, and he sort of died. So, after dark, she dragged him out to where the car was stuck into the side of the garage and put him in the driver's seat. Then she cooked the chili and ate it and called the cops. So they think he got killed in a car accident.

Sally said that was probably the best way out for all concerned. "A clean break," she called it. "Absolutely." And Marjorie asked if she could go through his closet.

It was really nice seeing the girls again, even if I am making the whole thing up—because I have been thinking a lot about them, about what they look like now, and even dreaming of them, of having long talks and taking naps with them.

Larken was hardly listening to the Meeting. He kept getting distracted by that guy in the park, going over the conversation and trying to see where he had made the wrong move. Some of the queens at Jill's claimed that you could get anyone as long as you played it right. Larken didn't believe that. But there was, he was certain, a science of cruising, a *discipline,* and if he could only reckon it he wouldn't have to go home alone all the time.

I've got to *clamp down,* Larken was thinking. I need to be more sure of myself—at least, I have to seem it. But how do you *seem* sure of yourself if—

Everyone was looking at him, Paul with annoyance.

"I what?" said Larken.

"I *asked* you," said Paul, "if you would be willing to host the next meeting."

"Oh. Oh, sure. Of course."

"Write down the address and directions north and south, navigating by the Freeway," said Paul, handing Larken paper and a pencil.

But Larken was already back in the park, rehearsing his patter for the hundredth time. I really liked that guy a lot, Larken kept thinking. Sometimes you just know about someone.

The Meeting broke up with staggered departures to match the staggered arrivals. Two of the men left by the back door and cut through an alley to gain the street. Larken, waiting his turn, wondered what they were accomplishing. Sure, it had to start somewhere, and talking about the problems of being a homosexual in an anti-homosexual society relieved some of the tension. Still, in the long run, what were they but a bunch of frightened men hoping for the impossible?

It was dark by the time Larken, last of the guests, was counting off for his departure, and Paul said, "Don't be in such a hurry. Sit down. Relax. There's more beer and—"

"The thing is," said Larken, "that all this secrecy is probably the opposite of what we need. We have to become visible and . . . regular. Like soda pop or blond hair. If they keep thinking of us as—well, if *we* keep thinking of—"

"The Meeting's over, so calm down," Paul urged him, guiding him to the sofa, a great old monster patched here and there with black tape. "Next time we can raise any issue you want."

"And it shouldn't be behind closed blinds like this," Larken went on, as Paul sat next to him.

"We need the security," Paul purred, a hand kneading Larken's shoulder. "We want to outwit them, don't we, hmm?"

"No, see, that's just the—" Paul's hand moved to Larken's thigh, and Larken jumped to his feet. "We have to be open about what we are," he said, backing away as Paul advanced. "They say it's shameful, and we say it isn't. But if we meet in all this"—Paul had Larken backed against the front door—"this darkness, then it's as if we're agreeing that it's shameful."

"But it's such an advanced approach. So *bold*."

Larken threw the door open.

"I have to go," he said. "I have to be open. I have to go to the park and find that guy and be more aggressive. That's always been my problem, not being self-assertive and Dale Carnegie and everything."

Paul stood well back from the door, very irritated. "Running out on me

like this." He looked at his watch. "And it's long, long before your time."
Larken ran to his car.

Frank's father had known that Frank was going to be a cop before Frank
did. Frank's father was a cop, and he told Frank's mother that they had a
little cop on hand when Frank was born. Frank's father held the infant in
his arms in the hospital—that early on—and solemnly announced, "This is
the next cop. He's going to save the world, watch."

They named him Winston Peter Hubbard, Jr., and called him Little
Pete. But in June of 1933, after the "Hundred Days" Congress that
launched the New Deal, when the boy was five, his father decided to
rename him Franklin Delano Hubbard.

So now they called him Frank, and because they had both wanted a son,
and because he was their only child, they petted him and heartened him
and protected him. Frank's father would settle Frank on his lap and tell
him stories, especially "The Dog On the Quicksand":

"When I was no bigger than you are right now," Frank's father would
begin, "there was a quicksand pit on the edge of town. There was a sign
there reading, 'Stay Away.' No one knew who had put the sign up, but
everyone knew about it, and about the quicksand, which is, like, at first
you think you got stuck a little, but soon you're sinking, and then you're
swimming, and at last you're drowning. That's how quicksand works.

"Now, it happened that the town needed to repave its roadways, and
there was a crew working right where the quicksand was. And it happens
that a homeless dog lived round about there in a dump, and he would lope
up at lunch hour to see if any of the workers would share a piece of his
lunch with a harmless and friendly old dog like himself.

"Well, one of the workers was a low sort, never had a kind thought for
man or beast, or for wife or child. He had a liverwish sandwich for lunch
there. And he waved it at the dog, kind of luring him over. So then he
pulled off a good-sized bite of liverwish sandwich and tossed it atop the
quicksand, right in the center of the pit there.

"Now, the dog had some idea about this quicksand, because that's how
dogs are. They couldn't tell you what quicksand is, or analyze up the way
of how it sucks you in. But they know enough to stay off it.

"Still, that dog was hungry, because strays are always hungry. There's
nobody putting out a bowl of dog food for them, so they're on the
lookout for a chaw of something day and night. Never know when it'll
turn out to be the last for a while, you see. And there's this thing about

dogs that you have to know about, that they're always hoping to find a person they can trust. That's how they are, dogs. They need someone to believe in.

"So the dog's looking at this guy with the sandwich, trying to figure out what a dog should know about him, and he's also looking at the hunk of liverwish sandwich sitting there on the quicksand. Meanwhile, the man's wheedling him, like, 'Go on, little doggie, scoop up that liverwish, now.' The dog thinks that is a pretty corny routine, but it's the usual thing that people do when they're cozying up to dogs. So the dog mistakes the man's motive. And even though he doesn't like the way this guy smells, the dog's judgment is getting overwhelmed by the liverwish.

"So the dog's guard is down, and that is a big mistake. You never let your guard down except with people you know. But finally the dog can't figure it out any more. All he knows is, he had just better collect that piece of liverwish there. So he lets out one good loud bark and hops over to the food and goofs it down. Then he turns to the man and wags his tail and barks again.

"By this time, the dog is already sinking. And he can see that something screwy is going on, and he starts to move out of there. But he can't. The more he struggles, the faster he's going down. And all the workers are standing there watching him. A few of them are thinking, Well, this is a serious and interesting thing, to watch a living creature die with the full knowledge that it is dying. But to most of them it's a joke. And not one of those guys moves to rescue the dog. They could easily lean over and pull it out with no risk to themselves. But no, no. They don't even try to. They stand there watching this thing that is happening. And there's the dog, fighting to keep his poor old head above the ooze, bravely pumping away but sinking all the same, probably wondering why nobody's helping him. At last he's all gone, and the men pack up their stuff and go back to work."

When Frank was very young, his response to this story was "Did the dog come back later?"

When Frank was a little older, his response was "Did that really happen?"

And when Frank was a teenager, he asked his father, "How come you told me that story?"

Frank's father had been waiting quite some time for that question. He said, "Because I wanted you to see what's missing from that story. What it doesn't have that it needs."

"A smarter dog?"

"Don't be a wise guy," said Frank's father, tousling Frank's hair.

"I give up."

"Don't give up. Think about it."

Frank did. But at every try his father would say, "Good guess, but no," or "Keep trying, son."

And Frank would reply, "Do you have to call me 'son'?"

"What'll I call you, 'Uncle'?"

"How about *Frank*?"

Frank's father called Frank 'son' because simply uttering the word emphasized their bond, and kept the boy close to him, and expressed his love. It was Frank's father's way of holding and kissing Frank when Frank was too old for it.

Frank hated it, especially when his friends were around, so Frank's father offered a deal: He'd call Frank by his name when, as, and if Frank figured out what was missing in the story of the dog and the quicksand.

So now Frank thought hard on the matter, because you can't go on being a son forever. And one Saturday when he was fourteen, he went outside to talk to his father, who was giving the Ford a water-and-wax.

Frank said, "What's missing from the story is a cop."

"How so?" said Frank's father, working on the window on the driver's side.

"Because a cop is there to keep guys from drawing decent people into the quicksand."

"You got it, Frank."

Frank had a crush on his father, much more than most boys do. But since Frank's father was a great guy and because Frank had no siblings, it seemed like the most natural thing to both of them that they would hug each other and roughhouse around all the time. And Frank's mother thought it was cute.

Still, it was an odd thing, this crush, because Frank was always thinking about his father, and admiring him, and comparing other men with him, even past the age when boys grow apart from their parents and concentrate their attention upon their coevals, especially girls. Yet, to the casual glance, Frank was enjoying the standard high-school life of his place and time. He played ball and surfed, dated for movie shows or dances, and got into endearingly minor trouble with his pals. He was a handsome but serious boy with a somewhat sluggish sense of humor—but this made him wonderfully mysterious to the girls. To each other, they called him "deep," a word of highest praise among kids in that era.

Like many a word tossed about by high-schoolers, "deep" bore a number of meanings. In its pure form—which must have lasted for all of two months during the summer of 1944, when it was introduced on the beach by a waggish junior from Pasadena High—it meant "intense in an *intelligent* way." But it quickly became almost meaninglessly complimentary, denoting anything from "cute" to "dangerous." Frank used it, privately, when he would lie on his bed thinking, to describe men of quiet determination, fearless men with a purpose in life, like his father. Like Mr. Hillingson, the tenth-grade history teacher; or Skip Deroyan, Frank's father's bowling-team captain; or Lieutenant Peterson, the Homicide detective with whom Frank became friendly when he was first assigned.

Frank had had crushes on all of them, one after the other. They weren't sustained crushes, like the one on his father, and of course Frank never thought of them that way. Crushes were for girls mooning over some boy they had spotted in the grocery store. Frank was a man. A cop. A "hard rower," as his father liked to phrase it. Men didn't have crushes. Men fell in love with women, whom they married.

Anyway, there was nothing wrong with looking up to impressive men, or in wanting to be like them and hanging around them. Right? What was wrong in Frank's life was the Vice Squad, though so far the Chief was rejecting Frank's requests for a transfer.

"A right-looking guy like you is too important to the work" was the Chief's assessment.

Lieutenant Peterson was sympathetic, but there wasn't much he could do, because he didn't get along with the Chief himself. Frank and the Lieutenant were standing in the parking lot next to the station, cops coming and going around them, and Frank was running on at sixty words a minute, letting it out of his system to a guy he trusted. Before he left, Peterson—this towering big character with the shoulders of a linebacker—puts an arm around Frank and gives him a squeeze. You know, just to hearten him up. But Frank plays and replays that moment for a week, shivering with relish.

The Kid was up in the front seat with Derek Archer's chauffeur again, riding to Archer's house.

"This beats the bus," the Kid was saying. "This is plush and I am Johnny the Kid. And you're what, Blue-veined Joe the Driver?"

Silence.

"Limousine Lou, the Sizable Sheik?"

Silence.

"Jeanne Crain as Pinky?"

The chauffeur, staring straight ahead, said, "Tom Visco."

"Long Tom Visco," the Kid amended, "the Chauffeur Who Does."

Silence.

"Gee," said the Kid, "can't anyone else get a word in someday?"

Silence.

"Chatterbox."

The chauffeur smiled.

This was purely a social event, Archer had assured the Kid on his land-lady's phone. Archer was taking the Kid to an "afternoon," as they were called then, at the home of a retired but well-heeled and even vastly re-spected director noted for the glamour of the all-male gatherings around his pool. It was a mutually advantageous date, for the Kid would have the chance to meet important Hollywood people and Archer could show up with something stunning in tow and thus not have to feel he was turning into a hapless old queen like dreary George Cukor, sitting off to the side with the other aunties, talking shop while their eyes drilled the doings at the pool.

"Want some lunch before we go?" Archer asked when the Kid hit the house, keyed up for an exciting and possibly life-changing day. "Or would you—"

"I want everything," said the Kid. "I want lunch, I want sex, I want fame, I want surprise, I want admiration, I want a cookie."

"Lesson number one on breaking into Hollywood," said Archer, amused. "Never interrupt anyone more powerful than you are."

"Lesson number two," the Kid countered. "Get to know the chauf-feur."

Archer, not catching on, or perhaps rising above it, guided the Kid into the kitchen, where the butler, his sleeves rolled up, was cleaning an elabo-rate coffeepot.

"Swenson," said Archer, "could we rustle up some bacon and eggs for this young man?"

"Certainly, sir."

"Yeah," said the Kid, "the butler."

Ushering the Kid into the living room, Archer said, "I can see you're planning to become known as a raffish and unpredictable charm boy. That'll go well today, I expect. Don't go too far, though, will you? For instance, when you meet Mr. Cukor, address him as—"

"*Mr. Georgette, sir!*"

Archer ran his hand through the Kid's hair and around his ear. Archer gazed upon the Kid, serenely aching to own the boy from top to toe.

Archer said, "You're an arresting young fellow, because you look like one thing and you act like another."

"Yes," the Kid agreed. "I'm Judy Garland rolled into one."

"Come see the grounds."

Archer led a marveling Kid past pool, gardens, tennis court.

"Am I supposed to be inspired by all this, and hungry for it," asked the Kid, "or doesn't it matter?"

"Do you play?"

"Play what? Chauffeur bingo?"

"Tennis."

"Sure, after you teach me."

"It's not something you pick up, tennis. You sort of know it already."

"Everyone starts somewhere, don't they?" said the Kid. "You weren't born playing tennis. Anyway, I dressed smart, didn't I? It's not like you're bringing a piece of trash to this party, is it?"

"You look fine."

"Don't just say that. Did I dress right or not?"

The Kid looked perfect, in fact, in a button-front white Mexican dress shirt and navy pants, and Archer put his arms around the Kid, who reciprocated. Archer held him for a while, not moving, till the butler strode up with the Kid's lunch on a tray and Archer slowly eased out of the embrace, surveying the Kid as the butler set up lunch on a wooden barbecue table.

"I brought you coffee, too, sir."

"Thank you, Swenson."

"I don't get what side you're on," said the Kid, tucking in as the butler returned to the house. "Like, first you're discreet and then you're open. Or one minute you're down on my cock and the next you're screwing Miss Sadie Thompson."

"I'm double-jointed," Archer said.

"What's that mean?"

"I like it both ways."

"On your back and on your stomach?"

Archer sipped his coffee and sighed. "Don't you ever feel the need to be with a woman?"

"No," said the Kid. "Nor do you, is my guess. Because, if you did, you wouldn't have had to boil yourself up for it by eating my cock. The need you feel, Mister, is to fool yourself into thinking you're jam."

"Jam?"

"Normal and boring. You'd call it heterosexual. Isn't it funny how not one of us knows *all* the terms? 'Double-jointed'? 'Jam'?"

Archer sipped his coffee.

"There's this myth," the Kid went on. "This myth about jam occasionally going to the Other Side for fun or profit. The guy who does it tells himself he likes women. But what he *really* is is a closeted homo. He's the lady in the no-way mirror. So half his life is what he thinks he's supposed to be. And half is what he really is. That's not double-jointed. That's lying."

"I'd call it protection."

The Kid shrugged.

"How do you know so much so young?" Archer asked.

The Kid slathered butter onto his toast and nodded. "Looks like I've been keeping my eyes open." Gulping down the toast, he said, "All you guys with your women covers and your double-jointed. How come I never hear about a homo being double-jointed in the other direction? It's always jam out hunting for boy ass."

Archer shook his head. "Your mouth," he said.

The Kid's mouth served him well at the afternoon, because he's bright and quick and pretty and that's an odd package; usually it's bright and quick *or* pretty. At pool parties, age decides dress—the young and trim don trunks and the aged and powerful remain tastefully clothed. This rule is observed as strictly as Ramadan in Baghdad, especially by the aged; but the Kid put his twist on it by keeping his pants on and simply opening the front of his shirt. I'm not in any of the classified groups, he seemed to say. I'm a new kind.

Archer introduced him to their host, and their host took the Kid around from group to group of the old boys, letting him stay put just long enough to dazzle, and then leading him on to the next group.

I'm a star, the Kid thought. These directors and writers are *listening* to me.

Archer, who spent this time chatting about neutral topics with a British actor who was married and the father of three children and even hungrier for young boys than Archer was, finally joined the Kid at the laden table, where the Kid was suspiciously discovering artichoke vinaigrette.

Archer put a hand on the Kid's neck, lightly, lightly. "Just scrape off the bottom with your—no, the other side."

"Neat-o."

"They liked you."

"You weren't there, so how do you know?"

"I was watching. The sight of older men enchanted by a teenager is unmistakable even at fifty yards, no matter how cautious or self-protected the men may be."

"Who's Mr. Whale? Does he have a first name?"

"James. Everyone defers to him because he's English."

"Who is he?"

"Has-been director. Some of his films were major, though. I'd call him eminent but irrelevant."

"He didn't like me."

"No?"

"Sometimes you can tell they're thinking, like, Shut up and be cute, you know? Such as I'm their private dumb bunny."

"Surely not."

"Well, that's what *you* want, isn't it?"

Startled, Archer blinked at him.

"Isn't it?"

"I . . . I need something of a particular kind, that's all. I don't think of you as a . . . a dumb bunny, was it?"

"What are those guys like?" asked the Kid, nodding at the trim-and-tan brigade hanging around the pool, the famous and indispensable Young Men of Hollywood afternoons. "They're dumb bunnies," the Kid went on. "They have to be. Their names are, like, Ted and Steve and Billy—"

"Well, you're Johnny."

"Johnny the *Kid*. The mouth. The surprise boy of truth is Johnny. Whereas Ted and Steve are not surprising. Ted and Steve are just beautiful. Some may be content with that, but I give more."

"If you want to make it in show business, you'd better concentrate on being beautiful."

"What are you concentrating on today, by the way?" the Kid asked. "Don't you want to meet those guys at the pool?"

Archer glanced at them mildly. "I've met them."

"Well, I haven't and I'm going to. See you after?"

"Without question," said Archer, smiling.

Ted, Steve, and Billy were easy to meet, though they weren't altogether what the Kid expected. For one thing, they were Griff, Phil, and Bram. Griff had a deep voice, Phil shook your hand in a grip of iron, and Bram's eyes were so intense you had to converse with his left ear.

"I'm Johnny the Kid," he told them. "I sing down at Thriller Jill's."

"What do you sing, Johnny?" Phil asked.

"Old and new," the Kid replied. "Sad and silly. High-hat and low-down."

"Would that include 'Smoke Gets in Your Eyes'?"

"Yes," admitted the Kid, surprised at Phil's knowledge and a bit resentful.

"I like medleys," said Griff.

That sounded good and dumb to the Kid. "Why medleys? They're just a bunch of songs instead of one."

"Not the best ones. A really sharp medley will play one number against another, kind of develop it."

And Phil was nodding along with this.

"Kate Smith did a really interesting medley on her show a few weeks ago," Griff went on. "Did you happen to hear it, Johnny?"

The Kid shook his head.

"She sang 'Falling in Love with Love' and then went right into 'This Can't Be Love' before the first song was over. So you got two different sides of the question, you know? The sorrowful side and then the side that's joyful. It was like the musical equivalent of losing a boy friend and finding a new one in the same day."

As Molly Goldberg liked to say, This I had not anticipated.

"We ought to come down and hear you sometime," said Bram. "Are you on every night, Johnny?"

"I'm on twenty-five hours a day. But I *sing* Monday through Saturday."

Griff and Phil laughed appreciatively, and Bram said, "We'll be there."

"You wouldn't like it. It's not like this."

"This?"

The Kid gestured at the lawn and the pool and the Beverly Hills mansion. "This."

The boys were perplexed and the Kid felt a surge of power. Just then, however, a fourth pool boy loomed up out of the water, a dark-haired Viking with an expert smile. The Kid stood back a bit as the boys greeted the newcomer affectionately, hugging and patting him.

"Come and meet Johnny," Griff told him. "Johnny, this is Mark."

"Hi, Johnny," said Mark, proffering his smile and a giant hand.

"Yeah," said the Kid, taking it. "You're Dumbbell Mark of the Jungle and Gym."

"Johnny's a wild card," Phil told Mark.

"Hey, Mark," said the Kid. "Joan Crawford wants her shoulders back."

Mark, his arm wrapped around Griff's waist, grinned.

"Just because you're a big monster beauty and I'm a little guy," said the Kid, "does not mean that I couldn't stuff your ass and have you howling with delight."

Mark said, "I'd love that sometime, Johnny."

The Kid had had enough. Quitting while he was behind and furious with himself and not having the faintest idea why he had taken them on so ferociously, he abandoned the field of contest and looked for Archer.

He found him sitting with some of the older men. The Kid perched on the grass and said nothing until one of the guests playfully observed, "The young man is strangely silent."

The Kid looked at Archer. "Whither thou goest," he said, "I will go. As soon as possible."

Archer smiled and rose. "On that note, gentlemen . . ."

It took forever to get out of there, as Archer diplomatically worked his way through the luminaries and the Kid dully moved with him. And when they got into the car, all that the Kid said was "I made a wreck back there."

Archer asked what he meant, but the Kid didn't want to talk.

"Your first Hollywood party, and you look as if you'd lost all your best friends."

They pulled off and rode back to Archer's house.

The Kid was breathing hard, really upset. "Mr. Archer," he began, and stopped.

"Surely you'd be calling me Derek by now."

The Kid said, "I really blew my top. I . . . Somehow, I lost my place. I don't know what I did."

Derek pulled him closer and caressed him. "I told you this was a social event, but you're rather putting me in a romantic mood. Do you mind that?" He brushed back the Kid's hair. "Just you and me? No Sadie Thompson?"

The Kid nodded.

"What? No jokes about my chauffeur?"

The Kid glanced into the rearview mirror to see if the chauffeur was looking at them.

"Tom's been with me for three years now. He takes it all in his stride."

The Kid said, "I made the ultimate mistake today: I showed my vulnerable side."

"Come here and let me hold you," Derek urged. "Come on. Was it the boys at the pool?"

"It was me," said the Kid, holding on to Derek, his head on the older man's shoulder. The Kid started to weep, and Derek, rubbing his back, whispered, "I love you like this."

•   •   •

Elaine's right rear tire went flat just after Sycamore, and for the first few minutes she simply sat there hating cars, having to drive to the grocery store and the laundry, and her life. Then she said, "All *right!*," and got out to see what was in the trunk, such as a genie.

Well, the necessary parts were there—spare tire, crank, the gizmo that unfastens the tire bolts. However, as Elaine had put it in one of her letters, "I am a very thorough maid and an unadventurously competent cook, but I know nothing about Equipment."

Glancing from the stuff in the trunk to the cars sweeping past on the road, Elaine wondered if she should stand there looking helpless but game so that some chivalrous guy would stop and change the tire for her. Isn't that how Claudette Colbert always handled it? Trouble was, Elaine had never been listening when her mother was giving her the helpless lessons.

Because where do you stand? How do you hold yourself? Hands on hips?: bewildered. Giving car dirty look?: adorably unable. Waving gizmo at passing cars?: demented. What exactly did Colbert do? Didn't she flash a bit of leg at them? Rogue that she is, Elaine tried that for a second or two. And, lo, a car did slow down and pull over. And Lois got out.

"Flat tire, huh?" she said, coming over.

Elaine nodded.

Lois was already poking into the trunk.

"A cinch," she called it. "You know? Some women can't change a flat. But some men can't, either."

Lois handed Elaine the gizmo. "Hold that? Yeah."

She winked at Elaine.

"Now, the whole thing: Crank it up, pull it off, push it on, crank it down. A cinch. Excuse me here."

"Much obliged," said Elaine, giving her room.

Lois permitted herself a smile as she passed.

"Thing is," said Lois, cranking up the rear of the car, "sooner or later everyone gets a flat. So everyone's got to learn how to switch tires."

Lois looked back at Elaine. Elaine nodded.

"My name's Lois."

"Elaine."

Lois nodded.

"Elaine the wife of Jeff."

"Good man?" Lois asked, working away.

"The best, unfortunately."

Lois gave Elaine a look.

"We have lovely memories. You know where we went on our honeymoon?"

"Hand me the wrench?"

Elaine gave it to her, saying, "We went to a bungalow village near Bakersfield. I have no idea why. There was nothing there but . . . bungalows. And couples like us. We'd say Howdy to each other whenever we'd pass, which, given the nature of the bungalow village, was much too often. And what I noticed was, everyone said Howdy in exactly the same way. *Amiably*. So I tried bringing up the personality in my Howdy. I'd say it tensely, or mysteriously, or flirtatiously. But all I ever got back was the same amiable old Howdy. What does that mean?"

Lois grunted.

"Down the road from the bungalows was a barbecue spot. So every evening we'd all troop down to this one place and have barbecue. So it was Howdy all over again. Except this time it was 'Howdy, you having the chicken?'; 'Why, Howdy, no, we're trying the ribs'; 'You go for the steak tips, Howdy?'; 'No, we're up to the combination Howdy dinner, with fries, slaw, and pickle choice.' But you're not married, are you?"

"Nope."

"Who are you not married to?"

"My job at Thriller Jill's."

"Thriller Jill's. Is that a sophisticated nightclub?"

"Well," said Lois, fitting in the spare, "no one says Howdy."

"*Very* sophisticated. Got it. Tuxedos and movie stars."

"We get a few."

"I shouldn't be so flip. It's very nice of you to help me out."

"Spare's a little flat, too," said Lois, testing it. "You'd better get this into the shop before long."

"Lois."

After a moment. "Yeah?"

"What's it like at . . ."

"Thriller Jill's."

"Yes."

"Dandy. It's on the Other Side, in case you're wondering. And so am I."

Elaine was thinking.

"Yep," said Lois, working away with the wrench. "The Other Side is where I live."

"Where is Thriller Jill's?"

"West end of Hollywood. Just off the Boulevard, between Davis and La Forma."

"*Is* Jill a thriller, in fact?"

"Jill . . . Jill's a satisfier. I'm a thriller."

Elaine was thinking.

Lois got up. She said, "I'm the deepest thriller this side of the Valley," and held out her hand. Elaine took it, smirking as one might at a school-child's prank. The two women shared a long look of the eyes, auditioning feelings, attitudes. Men want a shape; women want an idea.

"You should come down sometime and see the show," Lois told Elaine, as they broke. "We've got Jo-Jo there, our emcee, and a real sweet-voiced kid named Johnny. Bar discount for all unaccompanied females."

"Half off my Pink Lady?"

"Everything off and we'll go all the way."

"My. Something tells me I oughtn't bring my husband."

"Oughtn't," Lois echoed, shoving the flat into the trunk. "Right."

"Thriller Jill's."

"That's the place." Lois looked at Elaine, long and true. "I'll tell you this, and I'm telling it honest. I'd like to see you there. Any night of the week, it's always me. Lois Rybacher. Any night. Thriller Jill's."

"The west end of Hollywood."

They shook hands.

"Thank you again," said Elaine, now feeling truly helpless: helpless to express her gratitude, and interest. "I really mean it!" she called out.

"I know you do," Lois replied as she got into her car.

Well, that was . . . that was very odd, Elaine is thinking.

Wasn't it?

Larken, driving to Griffith Park, kept thinking of him as That Guy on the Bench. It had become a mission now, something Larken had to complete in order to retain his self-respect. He would find that guy if it took the rest of the year, and collar him, and make him say *either* I don't like your face so get lost or I do like you so I'm taking you home.

I should be good at cruising, Larken told himself. I do enough of it. I should know how to let down in a very gentle way the guys I don't care about, and how to make a quick connection with the guys I do. I should; and I don't. Somehow it always gets confused. Or it starts out fine and then . . .

I've got to get better at this.

Larken was prepared to sit on That Bench for two or three hours, waiting for That Guy. Sometimes you have to. But That Guy was there when Larken came up the path.

Larken smiled and quickened his pace and sat down and told Frank, "Just listen to me. I'm twenty-three years old and a nice guy. I've got a good sense of humor and I'm considerate of other people and I'm very lonely. I came here from Salt Lake City almost two years ago, and I'm all by myself. I've met people, but it never gets past that first night. You know, how you exchange phone numbers because you had a really fine time and they did, too? All this enthusiasm, and this great hug at the door. Then you call him a few days later and he doesn't know who you are."

Larken paused, searching Frank's face for directions. There was nothing there—nothing, at least, that Larken could read.

"It's Friday night," Larken went on, "and I'm supposed to have my whole life before me. But I'm losing hope, and that's putting it honest."

Some moments passed, as the two men looked at each other, then Frank put his hand on Larken's shoulder, just touching him. Feeling suddenly welcomed, Larken leaned his head against Frank, and Frank, startled, leaped to his feet.

"What did you have to do that for?" Frank shouted.

Larken was speechless.

"That isn't . . ." Frank began, without knowing where to take it. *That isn't what?*

Larken rose and tried to take Frank's arm, but Frank pushed him away and called out, "No!," to someone behind him. "He didn't bite!"

"Screw that," said Jack, shoving Larken against the bench to pat him down. "How long are we supposed to stand around and—*hands on the bench,* cocksucker! So what are *you* looking at?" Then, to Frank: "You put him under arrest yet?"

"He's not under arrest," said Frank.

Jack was cuffing Larken.

"Jack, he didn't bite."

"He bit, you stood, so I say he's made."

Larken was staring at Frank.

"He *didn't bite,* Jack!"

"He bit. I heard him, pretty much. Yeah, he said, 'I want to blow you, big boy.' " To Larken: "You said that, didn't you, sweetie-pie?"

Larken wouldn't take his eyes off Frank.

"We can't bring him in, Jack."

Jack was hustling Larken down the path to the unit.

"Jack!"

Jack stopped and turned to Frank. "What are you, anyway, Hubbard?" he said. "Are you a cocksucker or are you a cop?"

I'm not a cocksucker, thought Frank later that night, lying fully dressed on his bed in the house he grew up in, his parents' house. But I'm probably something close to it. Some kind of reluctant homo, right? Don't want to do it, wouldn't know *how* to do it, yet I think about it all the time. Think about Lieutenant Peterson and his wife, or about Skip Deroyan and the date he told me he had with the twin redheads where they divided him up at the navel and one worked his top half and the other his bottom. Now I'm being honest, right? Now I'm saying who I am and I still don't know what it means: because, if I'm not a cocksucker, what kind of homo am I?

Frank's bedroom hadn't changed since he'd been fifteen—*Hardy Boys* books and minor sporting trophies on the shelves, world globe on the desk, hiking boots at the foot of the bed. The Great American California Teenager's Lair. Normal room, normal guy. Right? And there's Frank beating off, night after night, to a dream of Lieutenant Peterson walking in on Skip Deroyan's little trio and trying one of the twins, then the other, and then Skip Deroyan himself. It is as if Frank were directing a movie and got stuck on one scene and is running it over and over till they get it right.

Christ, next thing you know I'll be in that movie, too.

They booked that guy in the park. Larken Young, of 2030 Abigail, in Burbank. And that's *wrong*. That's a dirty case. In the unit going back to the station, Jack, driving, kept telling Frank to cool off, meaning Shut up. Frank tried to visualize telling the Sergeant that they have a bad arrest on their hands. Sure: Jack's hauling the crook in and Frank's going to pipe up and announce to all and sundry, This is a bad arrest and Jack Cleery is a bad cop.

That just isn't the way it works, especially when you're a rookie and your partner's logged eight years on the force. Frank was as trapped as Larken was.

Technically, Larken had not been trapped but *entrapped*, meaning he never said anything incriminating and therefore shouldn't have been taken in and shouldn't have been booked. The whole time, the whole ride back and all through the booking process, Larken never said anything except in answer to the Sergeant's questions. And he never took his eyes off Frank.

There was a soft knock at Frank's door, and Frank said, "Come in, Dad."

"I saw your light on," said Frank's father, coming in and pulling up a chair. "Anything wrong?"

Frank shook his head.

"Your mother's having a difficult time. She's always like this before one of her visits, I guess."

There are three ways to die of cancer: the quick way, whereby one day you feel a little odd and three weeks later you're gone; the slow and steady way, whereby the pain gradually outwits the anodynes until, instead of the illness becoming part of the body, the body has become part of the illness; and the slow, mysterious way, whereby medicine is unable even to prescribe an effective anodyne from the onset. Frank's mother was dying the third way. She had to go in and out of the hospital for tests and further tests. These the Hubbard family euphemized as "Mother's visits."

Frank and his father talked for a bit, touching upon the usual matters—how glad Frank's parents were to have him with them at such a Difficult Time, how proud they were of this son of theirs, how Frank was happy he could help out. Frank and his father used to have more colorful conversations; the gap in their ages and interests was beginning to separate them.

"Sure there's nothing wrong, Frank?"

Frank shrugged. "Everyone has something wrong, right? I'll work it out."

"If it's something you're uneasy about telling me—"

"Look, it's just not—"

"Because there's nothing you couldn't tell me, you know that."

"How can you *say* that?" Frank almost shouted. "There's plenty of things I couldn't tell you and we both know it!"

"All right, now, simmer down, Frank."

"Jesus!"

"Don't wake your mother. Let's—"

"Parents . . . Please stop. . . . You don't . . ."

Frank's father got up, sat on the bed next to Frank, and put a hand on his arm. "If you've got to talk about something, son," he said, "talk about it. Straight out, now. Maybe there's someone better than me to tell it to, I don't know. Just let it out and off of you."

Frank was thinking, If I tell him I'm in on a bad arrest and I'm a homo, which would kill him first?

"Talk to me, Frank."

"No, Dad."

"You can at least say you're sorry you hauled off on me. Makes me feel funny, having my own kid dressing me down."

Frank's father was smiling, but he was probably serious, too.

"Yeah, I'm sorry."

"Son—"

"You're not supposed to call me that."

"I'd better get back to your mother." At the door, he said, "Maybe think it over about whether there's anything you could throw at me that I couldn't catch. Your old man's done right by you so far, hasn't he?"

Frank nodded.

"Good night, now."

Alone again, Frank kept going over the choices he had, choices of many kinds. He kept wondering what he was, kept rephrasing the answer. But he knew what he was.

He was the bait on the quicksand.

Frank was usually off on Saturdays, but after a few hours of fitful sleep he went in and told Lieutenant Peterson about the arrest. Frank glossed over Jack's blatant disregard of procedure, pretending that his partner misheard the conversation and made the grab too soon. Frank also pretended that he himself had been unsure about what had been said, and naturally had felt inclined to side with his partner. But now, Frank told the Lieutenant, he was certain that the crook had been entrapped, however accidentally, and Frank would be letting the force down if he didn't speak up.

The Lieutenant heard all this in a not abundantly friendly silence. He thought about it awhile, glancing over at the Chief's office as if considering how *he* would take it.

"The arrest was made last night?"

"Yes, sir."

"So it won't go to the D.A.'s office till Monday. Where's the crook now?"

"Released O.R." On his own recognizance.

The Lieutenant nodded and thought some more.

"You weren't sure what you heard last night?"

"Not entirely, sir."

"But *now* you're sure, that it?"

"Yes, sir."

The Lieutenant paused, probing this inconsistency simply by looking unconvinced, but Frank held to his story by keeping his expression neutral.

"Where's your partner now, Hubbard?"

"He's probably at home, sir. I haven't . . . He doesn't know about this."

The Lieutenant stared at Frank for a while, then nodded. "Let's talk to the Captain," he said.

The Kid's sitting backstage, waiting to go on for the early show that same Saturday evening. The Kid's in black and feeling keen. Black slacks, black silk shirt, black string tie; and he's keen because you can learn from your mistakes. It's smart to make little ones, like blowing up at a party, because then you won't make big ones, like blowing up at a producer.

The Kid's okay, he tells himself, checking the view in the mirror. The Kid's superb, oh yes, because he now knows the Three Rules of Dating Etiquette:

Rule 1: Never wear what everyone else is wearing.
Rule 2: Never get mad because there are better-looking guys than you. The potential for better-looking is infinite, so even Griff, Clonk, and Pec have that problem.
Rule 3: Never let your boy friend see you cry.
Oh, and here's a tip for you younger boys: Stay younger.

"Johnny, I still don't understand the cue for the new song," said Desmond, pattering up in his usual good-natured fog.

"Desmo," says the Kid, taking the music from him and looking for a pencil. "It's simple. I do three minutes on the Contessa Dooit and this sailor she picked up the night before. Then I go"—marking the music— " 'And this is what she said to him,' and I'll start right in. Just remember to pick up with me. No piano intro, *comprende?*"

Desmond fussed. "I hate these last-minute changes. And the Contessa Dooit, Johnny, it's so *strange!*"

"Desmo, how many different ways are there to say 'And now, an old favorite'? I'm just spicing up the patter, is all."

"Yet who *is* this Contessa? And what would a sailor be doing in her palace?"

"Desmo, just study your music, will you?"

"It's such *strange* music, Johnny."

"Come on, it's some old pop tune. Fanny Brice sang it. I thought I'd try a comic number for once."

Derek Archer had given it to him, antique sheet music adorned with a photo of Brice looking surprisingly glamorous in an evening gown. The song was called "Cooking Breakfast for the One I Love," from an early talkie, *Be Yourself,* and the oxymoron of an affable grotesque coming off as a movie star charmed the Kid's imagination.

"What's it like out there?" he asked Desmond. "Empty?"

Desmond struck a pose, left hand on hip, right limply fanning the air, trying to imitate the queens. "It's men, men, everywhere. And me without my Kotex!"

"Don't make fun of women, Desmond. Something tells me they're our natural allies."

"Who's the enemy, then, Johnny?"

"Derek Archer's coming tonight," said Lois, brisking in and heading for the desk. "His butler phoned. Made a big deal about it. Second show, Mr. Archer's favorite table, if I please."

Nosing around in the desk, shuffling papers, inspecting, staying *on* top and *in* charge: That's Lois.

"Imagine having a favorite table in this dump," she said.

"Especially that one," the Kid put in. "He's so far back from the stage, he's halfway to Hawaii. Derek in the dark."

"Well, you know these Hollywood boys. They think they're the world's best-kept secret." She looked up. "Meant to tell you. Jo-Jo isn't coming in tonight. You'll have to introduce yourself."

"Fine by me. New song tonight, Lois."

"What do you get, a medal?"

"No, appreciation."

"Nice crowd out there for a nine-thirty show. Sing nice and you'll get all the appreciation you want."

Bustling back into the club, Lois found Larken looking tired and sad.

"What's with you?" she asked, sitting with him.

He didn't speak at first, though he seemed to be working on a sentence. Finally: "I got arrested last night. Griffith Park."

She slowly shook her head, mad.

"It's a cheat, too, Lois. I mean, I never even got to come on to the guy and everything. They just clapped me in irons and dragged me away."

"The bastard fucks."

"Yes, I guess they are."

"You going to fight it?"

Larken made a helpless gesture. Judges and straights?

"You know what's funny about it?" he said. "The guy they used as a lure. The cop? I could've sworn he was . . ."

"A fag?"

"I thought I saw something gentle in the way he looked at me. Just gentle and calm and strong."

Too bad I'm not a toucher, Lois thought. He could use a little fancy stuff right now.

"You don't have family here, do you?" she asked.

"I don't have family. I'm an orphan. Alumnus of the Second Foundling Hospital and Orphanage of the Latter-day Saints, class of '44."

"Shit, you poor kid!"

"It wasn't so bad. Everyone's terribly nice to you and everything, in a sort of generically charitable way."

Lois was just looking at him. Funny, the stuff you find out about people when they're ready to spill it.

"That's why my surname is Young, you know. Half the kids are named Smith and the other half Young."

"Any reason?"

"They're kind of like Mormon Number One and Mormon Number Two."

"Lois," said one of the bartenders as he passed, gesturing toward the bar. "Someone to see you."

Lois turned to look; it was Elaine. Lois blinked at her, and Elaine came forward, smiling.

"I had a free evening," Elaine began. "And I thought, Well, I believe I'll just make my way over to the Thriller Jill club and see what the world of Lois is like."

Lois got up, stunned, thinking this new thing over.

"Not in your wildest dreams?" asked Elaine.

"Sit," Lois replied. "What'll you drink?"

"I'll drink with you," said Elaine, settling in. "Whatever you're—"

"This is Larken Young. Elaine . . ."

"Denslow."

"Last names don't matter," said Larken, shaking Elaine's hand. "It's all Betty and Bob around here."

"Yeah? Where's Betty?" said Lois, holding three fingers up to the bartender.

"You *are* surprised, aren't you?" Elaine asked, as Lois turned back to join them.

"Nothing surprises me," said Lois, knowing that she was glad about this yet feeling a bit encircled.

"What would surprise you?"

"I'll tell you someday," and the lights were going down and Johnny the Kid came out to a nice hand and the bartender dropped off three beers and Lois was off on a private tour of her life to that point.

Describe yourself.

Twenty-nine, dark blond sort of wavy hair—at least, *I* call it wavy; the kind that, like, half of it hangs there and the other half is always going *cloing?*—and a nice figure. What do I mean *nice*? I call it slim, with good breasts—round, solid, just this side of big, with sharp, dark buttons that get really out there when I'm onto something. Pleasing skin tone. I bite my nails and I walk tough.

What do you hope for?

Survival, independence, and no shit from men, especially cops and touchers.

What else?

Nothing else.

Be honest, Lois.

A friend.

What kind?

Close friend.

Close how? Close who would it be?

Close like how, I could talk to her and she can get me all the way home. Like, we could construct a world and move into it, just us. A smooth world, very smooth and knowing. Separate from everyone else. A refuge, like. Close like who, that's anyone's guess.

Elaine?

The lights came up as Johnny the Kid gave Desmond his bow and they walked off together. The applause was strong.

"It's getting better and better," said Larken. "It really is, Lois. Whose idea was it to put in that old Fanny Brice number?"

Lois shrugged. *Songs.*

"You know what I really liked?" said Elaine. " 'So in Love.' I know it from the radio, but it's amazing to hear someone so youthful perform love songs, isn't it? He looks so sweet and yet so . . . knowing. . . ."

"That's his charm," said Larken. "His act is the precocious kid playing the sophisticate."

Elaine raised her beer with "Here's to Thriller Jill's," and Larken touched his beer to hers, and they looked at Lois.

"I hate that fancy stuff," she said. "But *hell,*" and she hit their glasses so hard she nearly broke them.

" 'Cooking Breakfast for the One I Love,' " Larken mused. "It's an ironic statement in a place like this. Because everyone . . ." He stopped, mindful of what Elaine might represent to Lois, and how little she might know about the place.

"Talk free," Lois told him.

"Well. Here, it's all quick dates. Thirty minutes or so. It would take you longer to bring your partner home than to have the sex. But that song is about . . . well, housekeeping. And all that preamble about a Contessa picking up a sailor just—"

"It was dumb," said Lois.

"No. *No,* Lois. It was more irony. It's the Kid's analysis of what's on every mind in the room. It's the ultimate queen picking up the ultimate trade. *Passion.* Then the Kid goes into the music. *Deflation.* I think it's neat."

Elaine caught Lois's eye and said, a touch apologetically, "I liked it, too."

Lois shrugged. "You've the right."

"No, listen, Lois, you've got something here," Larken went on. "The Kid's working up his own style of act. Something new. He could easily have turned himself into another Mickey Rooney, the way they all do. But instead—"

"What difference does it make?" Lois countered. "Look around and say what you see. A joint, huh? So who cares if we got Mickey Rooney or—"

"You care. Because it would make the club more successful if the act became an attraction instead of part of the furniture, the way it is in every other club like this one. You could move to better quarters, maybe."

"Huh. You mean, like, have a real place? Cross back over to—"

"No, no! We need this place as it is, *our* place. But you could up the tariff a bit. Go a little Hollywood."

"Business advice from Mormons, now," Lois told Elaine.

"Mormons run a sound church, Lois," Larken told her with a smile. "It's just their sex that's problematical."

"The imp is here," Lois announced, as the Kid pulled up at their table.

"They liked the new song," the Kid said. "You heard them, Lois."

"Larken liked it."

"Yeah?"

"I'd say you should turn your whole act around," Larken explained. "Build up the Contessa patter and do more of those old comedienne specialty numbers instead of the current hit parade."

"Lois?" the Kid asked her.

"Listen to him," said Lois, and Larken talked to the Kid while Lois talked to Elaine.

"All right, like, first," said Lois, "where's Mr. Denslow?"

"On the road."

"What is he, *Oklahoma!?*"

"A salesman."

"Okay . . ."

"I don't," Elaine began, and stopped. Then: "Please tell me, just . . . very directly . . . if I did the wrong thing . . . or, let's say, an impetuous thing . . . in coming here."

Her defenses penetrated, Lois managed to force herself to grunt out, "I'm glad you came."

"That's Dewey telling Truman, 'I'm glad you ran.' "

"Shit," said Lois, "why can't I just be . . . Hell. Look, I really am, chick. Glad you're here. Question is, are you?"

"I've never seen anything like it! Everyone's so *interested* in everyone else!"

Meanwhile, Larken was giving the Kid a fast lecture in the discography of Sophie Tucker, Ruth Etting, and other top mamas of the torch-and-novelty-song circuit, and the Kid was drinking it in.

" 'My Friday Man Is Busy Saturday Night'?" he echoed. "Where can I get a copy?"

"You'll have to get an arranger to take down a lead sheet from the record," said Larken. "This was specialty material, written on commission for the singer herself and never published."

"How do you know so much about these dead songs?" the Kid asked him, genuinely curious.

"I don't know. Listening and watching, I guess."

"But this stuff is *old*. It's gone. Where did you find it? There isn't a club you can join, is there?"

"I wish."

Lois had some managing to do and the Kid had to get ready for the second show. Larken decided to go home early. Now that the music had stopped, he was back to confronting what was happening to him, getting arrested and looking toward a trial and being found guilty of his life. Anyway, he hadn't gotten much sleep last night.

"Yes," said Lois. "Okay. Don't be . . ." What do you say in a case like this? "Look, it's your dues. It's dues we all have to pay."

Lois was giving Elaine the details as Larken left; he turned and waved at them at the door, but it was a very depressed wave. It was funny how just being in Jill's could cheer him up, though he never put it to use the way everybody else seemed to, the johns morosely chatting with the hustlers, the queens sizing them up, and the hustlers making their deals. Twenty to twenty-five bucks was the going rate, and Larken usually had it to spare. But he didn't want sex with a stranger: He wanted love with a friend.

It was after ten o'clock by the time Larken reached his semi-attached hacienda, Los Angeles's single-story equivalent to the urban apartment building. All he could think of was This New Trouble, and That Guy in the Park, and having to go to court, and he sat in the armchair and fretted—nothing doing, no radio, even. Just Larken and his worries as the night drew on.

There came, then, a knock at the door. Larken glanced at the clock: 11:12. Who would visit so late when Larken didn't know anybody in the first place?

Larken ignored the knock, but there came another, so he got up and looked out one of the side windows at the door. It was his neighbor Todd, the sun-crazed masseur and bodybuilder with the white blond hair and Little Boy Blue eyes. Larken couldn't imagine when Todd got around to earning his living giving massages, as he was always at the gym or, especially, the beach. You had the impression that even his shit had a tan. However, Todd had been kind to Larken the night he lost his job in the record store and helpful when Larken locked himself out; so Larken was responsive to Todd's occasional visits.

"Sorry to stir you, man," said Todd, with his habitual sly smile. "I ran out of milk just when I felt the most *intense need* for a banana-fruit-hypo shake, so I—"

"Let me look in the—"

"Energy. When you got to have it, you *need* to really *got* to have it."

"Here you go, Todd."

"Thanks. Hey, you okay, man?"

Larken was desperate to talk, but "I'm fine," he said, because Todd just wouldn't get it. "It's late."

"Yeah, sorry about that, okay?"

Back in the armchair, Larken tried looking at his life. This is hard to do at his tender age. Assessments and projections at twenty-three? Premature. Unnecessarily anxious. Misleading.

Another knock at the door.

"Todd!" Larken cried, nearly jumping out of his chair. "Will you please stop running out of things while I'm having a crisis?"

He pulled the door open and froze, because it wasn't Todd. It was That Guy in the Park.

The Kid knew he'd been onto something, he *knew*! But, okay, we'll take it slow. We'll examine. I'm good at that. They think I'm a dumb-bunny sweetheart, but no, guys, I've a head on me. Larken saw it. I've got direction. Oh, and look who's here: Enter Derek backstage with . . . I *think* this one's Tresa. Very redhead and stacked. I'll bet he can get hard for her even without my help.

"You sang *our* song," Derek told the Kid.

"Yeah, your sheet music."

"You don't think you made yourself too . . . open?"

"Too open what?"

"The sailor material was on the touchy side. And, well, a man singing a woman's song?"

The Kid shrugged. "It's how I feel, so why shouldn't I?"

"Because people will take the wrong idea from your actions."

"They'll *take* the right idea, actually," said the Kid into Derek's face in the Kid's mirror. "They'll find out who I am, which is the thing that is important. And didn't I handle the emcee stuff well? I don't need an announcer. I'm my own act."

"You're so headstrong," Derek purred. "You know I love you like that."

"No, you love me crying. Remember?"

"Can I come in?" Frank asked Larken.

"You're the police."

"I'm off duty."

"No."

"I just want to talk to you. Personal, it's a personal matter. Look, your case has been dropped. And . . . and I'm the guy who got it dropped. They'll call you Tuesday or Wednesday. I thought you'd like to know now, get it off your heart."

Larken stepped aside.

"Thank you," said Frank.

"Why is my case dropped?"

"Can I sit down?"

Larken, still in a whirring confusion, nodded.

Strictly procedural, deadpan, take-no-sides Frank said, "There were ambiguities."

"About what?" said Larken, sitting on the other side of the room from Frank.

"About the arrest and my feelings and your way of living. About how I should handle this. Even about whether I should have come here."

From Larken, nothing.

Frank said, "Please don't make this tough on me. Because—"

"Cops don't visit the people they arrest, do they? And how about you making it tough on me? How do you think *my* ambiguities feel after . . . And *handcuffs*! That's how dangerous I am!"

Larken got up.

"Get out of my house, you cop," he said.

Frank slowly got up and told Larken, "Look, I understand how you feel and I don't blame you and I'm very sorry it happened to you, right? But I did get you off and I didn't have to do it. And I think that means you should listen to me."

"You entrapped me in the first place, so getting me off—"

"Please—"

"No, you get out."

"I need to talk to—"

"I don't *want* to—"

"Please," Frank begged. *"Please hear me.* You're the only one I know. The only . . . the only one like me and I please I have to talk about this to someone *please.* To talk to about who I am."

Larken backed away, considering. "You *don't* know me."

"Well, give me a chance, kind of. Like, what do you do?"

"Huh?"

"You know. I'm a cop and you're . . . what?"

"A waiter. Just now. Usually, I can get better work than that."

Frank blinked at him.

"Well, what did you take me for?" Larken asked. "A diplomat?"

"No, but . . . what's your goal in life? I mean, what are you working towards?"

"To become happy, I guess."

"That's all?"

"That's *all*? If I were a doctor and I were going to save the world, would that make me a better person? Or a cop—that's best of all, isn't it? Doing good with my handcuffs."

"I just thought you were . . . In the park, I figured you were a teacher."

"You can sit down, anyway. It's ridiculous for us to stand staring at each other as if we were boxers starting a match."

As they sat, Larken went on, "First, I don't like being taken for a teacher, because I don't know what that means that you think about me, but it probably isn't flattering. And, second, I don't know why you're here."

"Why? I'll say why right now, okay? Because I date women. Right? And it's pleasurable, as you might expect."

Larken just looked at him.

"Well, so I . . . I have these other feelings. Okay, now, why I'm here?"

"Feelings for men?"

Frank couldn't quite bring himself to nod. "I guess it's silly," he said. "I don't even know what I'd do with a man."

"Kiss him?"

Frank, genuinely revolted, said, "What the hell do you take *me* for, now? Do I look like a . . . a sissy shadow boy who just—"

"Don't shout at me in my house!"

"Well, what do you—"

"Why does it have to be me that you talk to?" Larken asked, jumping up. "Do you have any idea how badly I wanted to know you before? I would have given anything to get you, just about. But after what happened I don't believe I should like you any more. So talk to someone else!"

Frank sat there, looking at him. He said, "Larken . . . Is that what they call you?"

"Lark."

"Frank." He stood and held out his hand, but Larken didn't move.

"I don't want to shake your hand," Larken told him.

"Okay. That's fair. Just . . . just tell me what happens. After the park, when you go home with someone. What do you do?"

"You don't want to know."

"Probably not, but I kind of have to. Lark? I want to be honest, and you're the only man I can be honest to."

"Oh? Then you be honest, right now. Who do you have a yen for? Go on. This is your moment."

I guess it is, Frank thought. It really, really is. "Well," he began. Am I going to do this? "There's this . . . this detective at the station. He's in Homicide. Lieutenant Peterson."

"What does he look like?"

"He's a big guy. Nice guy. Tough-edged, kind of, because of the work. Real hard rower . . ."

Frank went on and Larken listened, occasionally asking a question or reshaping the saga when Frank doted upon trivialities. It was a long talk, for it was Frank's moment and he was going to do this, and when it was over, he felt a lot better for having had it. Because someone, somehow, has to know what you are, or you'll never know it yourself.

It was very late. Frank asked Larken if he could come back again and talk some more.

"You know," Frank added, "it can be handy to know a cop."

"I'm not sure about that."

"You're pretty sore, I guess."

"How would you like to be taken downtown in handcuffs?"

"If you'll let me be your friend," said Frank, "I swear I'll make that up to you."

"Like how?"

"You tell me."

They looked at each other for a while, Frank pleading and Larken trying to be obdurate, though it was not in his nature.

"All right," said Larken.

"Home sweet home," said Lois, holding the door for Elaine.

"It's wild."

"No, it isn't. What do you mean, wild?"

"Well, isn't that where you sleep?"

"Sure."

"A mattress on the floor?"

"Who passed a law about beds?"

"No flowers in the room, she sleeps on the floor, and she doesn't wear a bra."

"You finally noticed."

"I noticed when you stepped out of your car that day I—"

"Who made bras? Men. Why? To hold women in, am I wrong? To hide the sight of their wives' buttons from other men. Arabs hide their women's faces. You ever hear of a society where men have to hide any-thing?"

"You're scary."

"How so, chick?"

"You're so convinced about everything." Elaine moved closer to Lois. "I like that. I think what drove Jeff and me apart was . . . You'll think this absurd."

"Try me."

"It's that he never has opinions." Elaine put her hands on Lois's shoulders, just resting there. "He takes the shape of his container. For instance . . . Is it indecorous of me to be talking of my husband now?"

"Don't ask me, talk!"

"Well, this weekend he's in Tucson on a convention."

"Of like what?"

"Of computer integrators."

"Of *what*?"

"Don't laugh. I hear it's the coming thing." Elaine was playing with Lois's hair, smoothing it out, trying the strands. Lois had taken Elaine by the waist. "Anyway, he's away, so I'm here, and I imagine that right now he's out drinking with some of the other computer integrators, agreeing with everything they say, because that's how he is. He just . . . *agrees* with you. He respects your opinion so much that he adopts it, instantly. That's Jeff. But I like . . . I want to be . . ."

Lois kissed Elaine.

". . . challenged . . ."

More kissing.

"Yes," said Elaine.

After a bit, she said, "Yes."

Then, "Exactly like that."

She looked at Lois. "Except . . . what else? Because this is very . . . wild."

"Just come here and lie down," Lois told her. "On your stomach, and just relax. Just . . . I'm not always so rough. I can be sweet. Yes, that's right. Easy, now."

"My husband calls me Ellie when he—"

"I'm calling you Elaine. See, just a . . . Right, a massage like this. Let me just get this off you and . . . No, I'll do that."

"Do you—"

"Don't say anything," Lois urged her. "Just let me. I know how it works."

"And I'm a fast learner," Elaine started to say, but what came out of her was a gasp.

"Don't talk, Elaine. Don't talk. Don't talk."

Elaine moaned.

"See?"

After a bit, Elaine whispered, "Lois, that feels so wonderful."

"And I'm not even doing anything illegal yet."

Frank and Larken had an arrangement by which they met every Saturday at Larken's apartment at lunchtime, going out for burgers, then returning to Larken's for a talk. Sometimes they talked about police work and how uncomfortable Frank felt on Vice. At other times they spoke of the men Frank admired, and Larken would chime in with some thoughts on the men he knew. Once, Larken told Frank what it was like being raised by the state as an orphan. They shook hands at the beginning and end of each of these dates, and after the third one, at night, Larken started pretending that Frank was in bed with him. Larken hugged his pillow as if he were holding on to Frank.

At the next Meeting, which was held at Larken's house, Larken told his comrades of his arrest and of how the charges were dropped, but he did not bring up Frank or mention that one of the arresting officers was now a friend of his.

"Should you fight it, I wonder?" mused Paul. "Sue them for false arrest or something the like? I think . . . Mind you, I *think* I see an issue here."

"Forget it, Paul," said Jake. "He couldn't win a case like that. They might reinstate the charges to cover themselves."

"It's so frustrating. We can't win if we fight, but if we never fight—"

"Who's *we*?" Larken said, abruptly. "I mean, what are we supposed to even call ourselves? Because this has been bothering me for a long time."

"What do you mean, Russ?" asked Alfred.

Larken made a face; I mean, come on, these fake names. "The idea," he said, "is that someday we're going to be able to identify ourselves. Aren't we? That's what we're working toward with this Group. And when that day comes, what *word* do we use?"

There was a pause as the others thought this over, and Paul saw his grip on the Meeting slipping. So he ups and says, " 'Homosexual' isn't good enough for you?"

"It's too long. It's some professor's word."

" 'Homo,' then. Short and sweet."

"That isn't sweet," said Larken, a touch annoyed that he would have to point this out.

Alfred agreed. "It's too much like 'fag' and 'queer.' "

"What word do you use?" Larken asked Jake.

"Well, if I'm describing someone *to* someone, I might call him 'a cousin of ours.' "

"There's that phrase the old-timers use," said a newcomer to the Group, "Mervyn." "You know, 'a friend of Dorothy'?"

"Too long again," said Larken. "And it sounds coy. Who's Dorothy, anyway?"

"The movie people," said Jake, "call it 'gay.' "

"Preposterous," said Paul.

"It does sort of trivialize us," said Alfred.

"Besides," Paul added, "it already is a word, with a meaning all its own."

"It's kind of fallen out of use, though, hasn't it?" asked Larken. "The only time you hear it nowadays is when the Civic revives an operetta."

Jake nodded. "I hear the word 'homophile' more and more now," he said.

"Yes," Alfred agreed.

"Who cares what we call it?" cried Paul, his patience, as usual, quite run out.

"I care," Larken answered. "Because we'll never have rights in this world till the straights know about us. And they can't know us till they know what to call us. Besides derogatory slang words, I mean. As long as we're homos or faggots we'll never be anything legitimate. We'll be like . . . highbrows. Even Communists. Nothing but a mystery and a threat and a disgrace."

Paul clapped sarcastically, but Alfred told Larken, "I agree with you there."

They all did, except Paul—and Frank, of course, who was utterly bewildered when Larken told him about the Meetings the following Saturday after lunch. What are you going to do, change the language around because you don't like the words we already have? What do you have those Meetings for, anyway?

"What *for*?" Larken asked him, readying the percolator for coffee. "What for do you keep coming over here to see me?"

"That's different," Frank replied, leaning on the refrigerator door. "We're not planning anything."

"Those Meetings aren't about planning, really, though Paul thinks they are. And that's only because he likes to think he's in charge of some great movement and everything. The real reason we go there is to talk to other men who will understand us, sympathize with our problems the way no one else ever will. Isn't that why you and I are friends, Frank?"

"You and I? That's because . . . I don't know. Because I'm a homo. I'm Frank the homo cop."

"You're whipping yourself. Don't—"

"Could you do me a favor?" said Frank, taking Larken's arm and pulling him into the living room. "Come here with me, okay?"

"No, first tell me what you—"

"I just want to . . . Just sit with me, Lark."

They were on the couch, not facing each other. Frank was tense, so Larken got tense, too.

Suddenly, Frank stood up. "Forgot about the blinds." Drawing them to, he sat down again. Then he said, "I want to put my arm around you, okay?"

"Yes."

"You can look at me, all right?"

Larken did; and Frank took his hand.

"This is going to sound funny," said Frank. "I would like to do it with you, but I don't know what to do."

"The first time I did it—back in Salt Lake—I didn't know anything about it, either. The other man was much older, and—"

"Who was he? How did you meet him?"

"Oh, he was a Church elder. They generally take you out to dinner for a special treat on your eighteenth birthday. Just hamburgers and everything, but still it's . . . Anyway, this man was . . . Somehow he had managed to stay a bachelor all that time, which is not easy if you're a Mormon Church elder. As you've probably heard, we marry early and often."

"So he . . . what?"

"So instead of taking me out to dinner, he invited me to his house for a cookout. And later, inside, he . . ."

Larken looked at Frank.

"It feels naked telling you this."

"Do I have to call you Lark? Don't you have another nickname?"

"Just Lark."

Frank rubbed the back of Larken's neck. "Okay, it's Lark, it's Lark. So what did this guy do to you?"

"Well, I was very shy and totally inexperienced. I knew some of the kids in the house fooled around—kind of, oh, jacking off and everything. But I had never taken part. And this man saw that somehow, so he eased me into it."

"How?"

"He stretched out with me on the bed, both of us still dressed. And he talked to me. He held me, stroked my hair. You know. Getting acquainted. Then we got undressed and he gave me a massage. To relax me, I guess."

Larken paused.

"You don't want me to keep going on about the details, do you?" he asked.

Frank said, "Yes, okay, I do."

"Look, how about if you just lie full-length on the couch, and I'll lie on top of you? We can get used to each other, and then . . ."

Frank was already moving, and Larken flowed along with him till they were head to head and toe to toe, holding on to each other. It was like Larken's pillow game, only now he was grasping Frank.

"Are you okay?" Larken asked.

"Fine. Once I get the sex part of it down, I can be a juicy homo like everyone else."

"Do you have to use that word?"

" 'Homo'? Why? Is there some secret club term you can teach me? Because, while you're at it, there's the walk and the wrist thing. . . ."

Thinking of the Meeting, and deciding that it has to start somewhere, Larken said, "We call it 'gay.' "

"You call *what* gay?"

"This. You and me, now. And everything between us that could possibly come out of our being together." Larken shifted his grip and moved his head, brushing Frank's hair with his own.

"Let me see how this works," said Frank. "You're not a homo, you're gay, right?"

"Right."

"And getting arrested and losing your job and everybody spitting on you all the time is gay, too, right?"

"Frank," said Larken, using the name as a caress. "You hurt my feelings when you talk as if all we do is cruise Griffith Park. There's a lot more to it than that."

Frank was silent, drawing his hands slowly across Larken's back, running them up and down his sides, sifting his hair with Frank's upraised cheek. Frank was hard, and Larken started to get hard, too.

After a long while, Frank said, "Tell me what more there is to it than that. Tell me, Larken, okay?"

"It's hard to explain. It's something you just know about, like . . . these unusual aptitudes we have. A collection of exciting and colorful things in our lives, like music and the theatre and the movies. . . ."

"That's a real World Series you have there. Who wins the pennant, the Rockettes?"

All this while feeling each other, rubbing cheeks against each other, moaning between the lines.

"You should see something of our gay life," Larken said. "You should get a better idea about it."

"No, I have an idea about you, Larken boy."

Larken sat up next to Frank, taking Frank's hand in both his own. "Listen. There's this place I can take you to, and I don't mean Griffith Park. But you can't go around arresting everyone in sight."

"What would I arrest them for?" asked Frank, smiling, reaching up to Larken's face with his free hand.

"Everything. Because everything we do has been outlawed by the people you work for. *Everything* we do."

Frank sat up, taking Larken by the shoulders. "All right, don't get sore. I didn't make the laws and I hate working Vice. And I'll go anyplace you point me at. But right now we both have hard-ons and where we're going is the bedroom. Right?"

"Are you nervous?"

"Hell, yes. I don't even know what we're going to do in there."

"We'll take it slow. We can leave out any parts you don't like."

"No kissing," said Frank. "Okay?"

"Okay."

"Let's go." Frank was on his feet and moving. Larken followed slowly, and paused at the bedroom door.

"Frank?" he said. "I really like you."

The Kid, Jo-Jo, and even Desmond had been *begging* Lois to throw a real New Year's bash in Jill's at the end of 1949, just like the fancy restaurants along the Strip.

"Come on, Lois," the Kid urged her. "You'll make a mint. A five-dollar door fee will cover food, drink, and funny hats."

"Five bucks for food, party favors, and one glass of champagne," said Lois, considering the deal. "Drink is extra and the bar cleans up."

"Is that a yes?"

"I could fashion duotone crepe-paper streamers," said Desmond, a handsome offer.

"We should hold a raffle," said Jo-Jo, "and the winner gets Desmond and the streamers."

"That's second prize," said the Kid. "First prize is the streamers alone."

"I'll leave you boys to plan it," said Lois.

The three men cheered.

"You've got a budget of exactly twenty-five dollars."

So that was a yes, though Lois didn't quite see it until she told Elaine.

"It's just another chore for me, is how I work it out," Lois groused. "They're the ones who hang the streamers—I'm the one who has to weigh in the champagne, and coax that mutt of a cook into coming up with the food, and tip the cops . . . for what? A New Year's party, for junk's sake?"

"First of all, stop complaining," said Elaine, straddling Lois as she massaged her neck and shoulder muscles. "Your whole body tenses up."

"Chick, that feels so good you have *no* idea."

"I love to make you sigh with pleasure. It's the first positive act I've committed since I quit the Santa Ana High School Pep Squad."

After some silence of massage and no more sighing from Lois—she was withholding the reward for a prank—Elaine said, "Second of all, I think it would be nice to have a party. Why don't you let me help, with my housewife skills?"

"I wasn't thinking of serving rib roast."

"I meant my *festivity* skills, my dear."

"I love when you talk dirty. It's like Eleanor Roosevelt leading a conga line."

"How about those dainty little open-faced sandwiches? The kind where extraordinarily antagonistic ingredients are mixed in a blender, spread upon innocent bits of white bread, and served as a breathtaking novelty surprise?" Elaine got up, giving Lois a sharp pat on the butt.

"Like what foods?" asked Lois, turning over.

"Oh, peanut butter, tuna, cling peaches . . ."

Lois got up, took Elaine in her arms, tickled her ear, and predicted, "Suburbia is doomed."

Actually, this New Year's Eve wasn't like any night of the year, or even like any other New Year's Eve, for the country had reached a new decade, and its midcentury point, and a marking of sorts in what was for many the first Era of Good Feelings after an age of Depression and Wartime. It

promised to be one of the great New Years, and, as Jo-Jo assured the Jill's
crowd, night after night, this club was certain to give one of the great New
Year's celebrations. People were actually buying tickets in advance, Jo-Jo
had wheedled an actor friend into lending him a dinner jacket, the Kid was
putting in new songs and comic business complete with lines for Desmond
(from the piano), and Desmond had learned, or at any rate was using, a
new word: "festooned."

As befits a gala, Jill's didn't open till nine o'clock that evening, staying
shuttered as the bartenders readied the fizz and the new glasses; Elaine
assisted the chef; Jo-Jo, the Kid, and Desmond polished the act; and Lois
stormed around, crabby and content. By nine-thirty, a few johns and two
or three of the more diffident queens had taken positions at the back and
sides. By ten-thirty or so, the showier queens were sweeping in in groups
of three and four and nabbing the tables of prominence, and the bouncer
was deciding which of the hustlers to let in for free. By eleven, the place
was packed, the bar was doing land-office business in extra glasses of
champagne, and Desmond had ruined his tie with one of Elaine's finger
sandwiches. The joint was jumping.

"Who's the new boy?" asked a thin, dyed blond queen named Donny,
indicating to his party one of the hustlers lined up at the bar.

"They call him Trey," said a queen named Lanning, holding his cigarette way out and blowing his smoke. "They say he's from Georgia and
talks like *thee-yuss*."

"He looks sharp," said Otis, the fat queen of the group, big fat ugly
Otis, and he knows it. "A very, very sharp-looking boy."

"Carlotta took him home," said Lanning, his voice low and his grin sly.
The others glanced over at Carlotta—Carl—and his friends, at a neighbor-
ing table. "Trey plays it very slow and quiet, so the story runs. You know
trade—don't want to spoil their possibilities. Comes on real *man*. Well
. . . they get to it, and Carlotta's all set to go into her dance. Suddenly"—
Lanning stubs out the cigarette in one quick gesture and leans in to the
others, sudden himself—"Miss Trey flops on his back and his Georgia legs
go sky-high!"

Donny giggles; Otis is silent with hunger.

"Fluttering," Lanning concludes, "like flags in the breeze. Poor Carlotta. Thought she'd cut herself a real hunk of jam and all she gets to eat is
another flimsy like the rest of us!"

Lighting up another, Lanning says, "There's more. At the moment of
beauty, Georgia Trey breathes out, 'I'm fixin' to come.' "

Gales of laughter from Donny and Lanning as a john comes up to Trey and offers to buy him a drink.

Trey takes a beer, the john nursing his champagne. Of course, they look odd together—the tall, sullen, restless-calm youth in jeans and white T leaning down to hear the anxious prattle of a bald little pear of a man in a suit. Of course: because this is the land of odd, so secret and tactless, so needful and denied. For some reason, the man never gets down to business. After launching a number of conversational tacks he more or less subsides, just stands there now, next to but remote from Trey.

Trey decides to make the move himself. "Well, now," he says, turning to the guy, "What exactly do you got in mind, Saul?," thinking, What kind of name is that, *Saul*?

"I just never know somehow," says Saul, not daring to look at Trey. "I *thought* I knew earlier tonight. I *thought* I did."

The queens at Lanning's table are watching this, and as Saul stumbles away and Trey shrugs, Donny comments, "No sale."

A big-shouldered, veteran hustler in a black turtleneck leans over to Trey and says, "It takes practice."

"Huh?"

"How to handle these fags. You're new here, ain't you?"

"I'm new everywhere," says Trey, glancing around, seeing what's up, looking available. He has a habit sometimes of breaking into a smile just before he speaks, and there are more than a few men who find this infinitely fetching. It is not clear whether Trey is aware of this habit.

"Keep on pitching," the older hustler advises him. "You'll get there." Two beats, then: "My name's Cord."

"Trey."

They shake.

"Yeah, Carl told me about you," says Cord.

"Carl?"

"Over at the big fag table there. Where everyone's wearing pretty colors."

"Oh, yeah." Trey keeps it cool. He flashes his smile and says, "That was some easy gig."

"Carl's okay, when you learn how to handle him. I guess all fags are. Just make sure they know who's in charge, is how it works."

"Yeah."

"Don't let 'em slip away, boy. You nail 'em. They come up and talk,

you tell 'em how it'll be. They like that, 'cause they're fags. It's not like
bein' with a woman.''

"Yeah.''

The two of them scanning the place, leaning back against the bar,
stretching out. They've got boots on, heavy belts, rough mouths, and
they're in charge.

"The real thing," says Trey, "is I gotta get me a gig tonight, 'cause I
been thrown outta where I was puttin' up.''

"Hell, if it comes down to that," says Cord, looking the boy over nice
and full, "you can sack with me.''

Jo-Jo is peering out at the crowd through the black curtains that hide
backstage from the club room.

"How does it look?" Desmond asks.

"It's a capacity crowd, Desmond, old boy.''

"No, how does it *feel?*''

"Beg pardon?''

Desmond hugs himself. "We're going out there and we'll put it over!
That's the show business!''

"Desmond," says Jo-Jo, looking over at the Kid as he primps, "don't
get ecstatic on me.''

The Kid's in white sailor's pants, a baggy red silk shirt with all the
buttons taken off, and a navy silk tie.

"Dashing," says Jo-Jo. "You look almost legal.''

"You're irked at me for putting on a great new act, I'm afraid.''

Jo-Jo keeps forgetting how honest the Kid can be. It's as if he were
kicking your leg and you fell down: because *then* what do you say? No,
I'm not irked. I'm not nervous because you're so ambitious and energetic
and talented and cute.

Jo-Jo says, "You're afraid?''

"I don't want you angry at me. I'm going to put on the best show I can,
but it's not because I want to crab your act.''

"Then don't crab it," says Jo-Jo, angry but contained. "Let me be who
I am, too.''

"There's room for everyone, Jo-Jo," the Kid replies.

A john named Ray was telling Saul, "I saw you talking to the new boy.
What's he like?''

"Mysterious. You never know what he'll say next.''

"Did you set it up with him or not?''

"Oh, dear, no. He's so—''

"Maybe he likes the more aggressive type."

Ray stared intently at Trey. Trey felt it, looked at Ray, and, before their eyes locked, casually looked away.

"He doesn't like anyone," said Saul, bewildered. "I don't know what he wants in the world."

The three queens at Carl's table have determined to drive Lanning's gang from the club by scorning them. "Look, look, look," says Carl's second-in-command, Arkel. "Just look and look and never touch. All that toothsome trade going to waste." He's staring straight at Lanning for this. "Who may they be, the daughters of Bilitis?"

"They're the Cherry Sisters," says Carl.

Arkel's voice rises. "Is that Otis I see, or a camping tent wearing Laird Cregar?"

"Trash," Donny calls him.

"Goons," cries Arkel.

"Trolls," says Lanning. "Get back under your bridge!"

"Better cool it down, girls," one of the bartenders tells both tables as he races by with a laden tray.

"Who wants us to?" Arkel calls out.

For an answer, the vigilant Lois silently manifests herself in direct view of the warring tables, and both parties immediately turn in to themselves.

"It's astonishing," says Elaine, coming up from behind with a tray of sandwiches. "You can even be testy without saying a word!"

Lois runs her hand along Elaine's back as she passes. "Mr. Husband on the road again?"

"On the road *still*." Dropping the tray onto the bar.

"Huh. And you don't think he's wondering—"

"If I'm seeing a man? Surely he does, because he's got plenty of girl friends. But don't ask me if he suspects that there's a woman." Elaine filled the tray with empty plates to take back to the kitchen. "Don't waste your breath on that one. Because to men like Jeff, lesbians simply do not exist. Even to men not like Jeff."

Lois is staring intently at one of the tables.

"What?" Elaine asks.

Nodding her head at a group way up in front of the stage, Lois says, "Some of those women aren't women."

"What do you mean?"

"Drag's against the law, and I *don't* allow drag in my club," says Lois, starting off to do what she does best, namely settle someone's hash.

"Wait," says Elaine, gently touching her arm. "You mean those are men dressed as . . ." Elaine takes another look at the table. "That's called 'drag'?"

"Yep. And it's catnip for cops."

"But . . . why do they *do* that?"

"Search me."

"Though it's sort of cute, in a goofy way. And, as I look now, I'd say that *all* of those women aren't women."

"Right. And they're *all* taking a flying leap straight out of—"

"Lois, it's New Year's. Let them stay. For me?"

Thinking it over, Lois smiles and, going behind the bar, says, "Got something to show you, Miss. Bought it this afternoon in a very exclusive shop on Redondo."

"I tremble."

Lois opens a paper bag and pulls out a metal rod.

"What's that, I dread to ask?"

"Massage toy." Lois winks. "You run it up and down and back and forth along the skin."

Elaine puts a hand to her mouth. "Now I really do," she says. "Tremble."

"They used to make these out of wood. Very sanded down, of course. Maybe they're mass-producing them now."

"Exactly how much experience have you had?"

"I'll tell you someday."

"No," says Elaine, thoughtfully, as she hands the tray to one of the bartenders to take into the kitchen. "Tell me now."

Lois hates being challenged, except—she suddenly discovers—by Elaine. Lois tells.

At the drag queens' table, one seat is empty, and those already in place—Milady Darla, Faye Sylphides, and the Duchess of Topsy—take turns scanning the door as if awaiting a Major Entrance. Lanning and his coterie pass a few remarks.

"Who's the empty chair for, girls?" Donny asks, leaning confidentially toward the Duchess of Topsy. "Superman?"

"No," says Lanning. "P. T. Barnum. He has a few vacancies in his freak show."

Lightly fanning herself, Milady Darla languidly asks, of no one, "Dear, who *are* these guano riffraff?"

Faye Sylphides says, "I dread to think."

"We can all see that," Lanning snaps back.

"I know who they're waiting for," Otis begins, then breaks off as a piece of trade passes their table: tall and tight, with an absurdly fetching gap in his upper front teeth, wearing a black leather vest over a cowboy shirt. "Oh, Lord," Otis moans.

"Who is that guy?" Donny asks, following him with his eyes.

"His name's Eli," says Lanning. "White, white skin and tattoos everyplace."

"Oh, heaven, set me free," Otis pleads.

Ray is talking to Woody, a versatile and accommodating hustler whom Ray has taken home a number of times. Many hustlers look annoyed or disgusted when talking to johns, but Woody tries to appear interested in them. He feels it's part of the service.

"Do you know anything about the new guy?" Ray asks.

"Not much. People are talking, but that's about it."

"Is he . . . difficult?"

"He doesn't do a lot."

"That way he lights up as he speaks, as if he thought of something incredibly wonderful to say."

While Ray fills his eyes with Trey, Woody gazes off at something or other and lets a businesslike pause set in before he turns back, his arms folded to show off his biceps, his body rocking slightly from side to side, his mouth welcoming. "So what are you looking for tonight, Ray?" he asks. "The usual, or something special for the holiday?"

Over at Lanning's table, Otis is a wreck and Lanning is lecturing him. "If you're going to make a scene," he says, "you'll have to leave the table."

"I just . . ." Otis starts. "I don't know what to . . ."

"You can see he's available, silly. If you want him, get him."

"Oh, sure, he's really going to come home with a big, fat horror like—"

The three drag queens have burst into applause and now they rise, still clapping, as a fourth drag queen makes her way to the table, tastefully imperious, blowing kisses at a couple of wags who play a fanfare on their New Year's noisemakers.

"Shit," says Lois.

"Jesus, it's *Arnold!*" cries Lanning.

This stops the queen dead. Slowly she turns. "No," she tells Lanning, touching at her wig, smoothing out her Empire gown, raising a tiny bejeweled mirror (attached to her bodice by means of a dainty chain and a cunning faux-emerald clasp) to check her beauty spot. "No," she repeats, to one and all: "The Empress Leticia," which she pronounces, in four syllables, as "Le-*ti*-ci-a."

"And we are her court," adds the Duchess of Topsy, as the other two make the most gala of curtsies.

Thriller Jill's is packed and dense with expectation. Carl's table sends drinks to the Empress and her courtiers. The kitchen is running out of everything. The line of trade along the back wall scowls and mutters. The johns take out their wallets and count their money. Elaine sneaks up on Lois and steals a kiss. Trey tells a joke and Cord laughs; the joke is stupid, but everything a sexy boy does is wonderful. Eli takes one last parade through the room, now wearing the vest without the shirt. "I want to be held," Otis whispers, watching him. "I want to be kissed, I want to be fucked, I want to be loved." Backstage, the Kid takes a fleeting last look in the mirror, Desmond prays, and Jo-Jo cries, "Overture and beginners, friends."

Larken and Frank were standing outside Jill's, and Larken said, "We've gotten this far and you are not changing your mind now. So work those feet and—"

"Just give me a chance, right, Lark? It's a heavy step to take."

"Stop seeing it as a historical moment in your life and just glide in with me."

"Boy, oh, boy," said Frank, shaking his head as they walked up to the door.

"Here goes Frank," said Larken.

The bouncer told him, Sorry, they're full up; but Lois waved them in, momentarily noting that Larken had a date. The lights were going down for the act, so Larken caught two beers at the bar and then joined Frank, standing at the back, and that worked all right till one of the hustlers ran the flat of his hand along the crack of Frank's ass; just then, luckily, a john and one of the younger hustlers got up to leave, and Larken grabbed their table. By the time Frank had finished giving the offending hustler a vigorous critique of back-wall cruise-bar etiquette and joined Larken, Jo-Jo had already brought the Kid on.

"Now, I'm a big believer in dating," the Kid was telling the crowd. "Because dating is where love begins, and love is our truth." Heading for the piano, he said, "Desmond, can I ask a personal question?"

Desmond, nervously reading from a script propped up next to the music, answered, " 'Why sure, Kid,' " sounding like a constipated robot.

"Folks, this is Desmond, the deaf maestro of Thriller Jill's. Let's give him a hand."

" 'Desmond bows,' " read Desmond off his script.

The Kid elegantly rose above it—nobody was clapping, anyway—and said, "Now, Desmond, in your vast dating experience—tell the truth, now—have you ever dated a man?"

" 'Pshaw,' " replied Desmond, pronouncing the *p*—" 'none of them were men.' "

Scattered laughs, as the Kid returned to the stage, muttering, "I don't know what I'd do without him, but I'd rather."

"Kind of informal for a show, isn't it?" Frank whispered to Larken.

"So," the Kid was saying, "I figured I ought to set up my dear friend, Miss Coty de Tramp—the 'Voom' girl—with this guy I know, James Shortzaroff. But when I told her, Miss Coty said, 'Oh, I couldn't possibly—I just had twins!' "

Looking mildly scandalized, the Kid nodded at the crowd.

"That's right," he said. "She picked them up on Hollywood Boulevard!"

"It's odd, the way he tells them," Elaine murmured to Lois.

"What way?" she answered, helping the bartenders wash an overflow of champagne glasses.

"He's so quizzical with all those double meanings. He doesn't act as if he's performing blue material. He acts like a high-school student doing campus takeoffs at the annual talent show."

Carl's table was so busy dishing Lanning's table that they became a nuisance during the Kid's first two numbers, "Find Me a Primitive Man" and "Do It Again." Naturally, Lanning's table clapped furiously after the songs, leading what for Thriller Jill's had to count as something of an ovation. Larken even put in a whistle, and Elaine cried, "Bravo!"

"I don't see what's so great," Frank told Larken. "To me, it's some kind of freak show."

"See, what I think we need," the Kid was telling them all, "is a superhero of our own. A Superman or Batman for *our* kind, not so much to save us from physical danger as to rescue us from our unique curse of death by romance. And I have the hero all picked out—Transvesto. Gender: unknown. Dress: to kill. Life's goal: to make sure that those who love true, love well and long."

Frank snorted.

"Desmond, you believe in Transvesto, don't you?"

" 'Desmond nods.' "

"Well, I'd like to dedicate the next number to Transvesto—"

The Kid abruptly stopped and sought Lois, who was already signaling to one of the bartenders to up the lights: Two cops had walked into the club.

"And I'd like to thank Father Murphy," the Kid announced, "for teaching me the lovely devotional hymns I sang for you tonight. God bless America."

He put down the microphone and left the stage.

Habitués of clubs on the Other Side know the drill, and newcomers do what everyone else does: You go into suspended animation and hope it isn't a raid.

Lois talked with the cops briefly, held up the flat of her hand to Larry, the head bartender, and left the club with the cops.

"Do you know those guys?" Larken asked Frank.

Frank shook his head. "Different station. How come everyone gets so quiet? The call looks routine to me."

"Patrolman, in this world, the appearance of a cop is never routine."

"*Transvesto*. Now I've heard everything."

"You're not having a good time, are you?"

Frank looked at him. "What do you think?"

Backstage, Desmond was in a state.

"It's the new act, Johnny," he wailed, wiping his brow with a paper napkin. "I told you it was too daring."

"Relax, Desmo." To Jo-Jo, the Kid said, "She showed her palm to Larry."

Jo-Jo nodded.

"Is that good?" Desmond asked.

"The act's playing really well," said Jo-Jo. "Something tells me you're going places."

You wish, the Kid thought.

Lois was back in the bar in no time, nodding at Larry. As the lights went down, Lois murmured to Elaine, "Believe it or not, it was trash on the sidewalk. Someone must have overturned the cans."

The Kid trotted out and went right into "He's So Unusual," the old Helen Kane number about a boy who refuses to make out. Frank got so irritated that he began to work his glass around the tabletop.

"They have *songs* about this, too?" said Frank, as Larken confiscated Frank's glass.

"Why shouldn't they? Would you prefer a song about cops coming in where they aren't needed simply because they're vicious, slimy pricks?"

Frank's eyes blazed at Larken in the darkness.

"Now, the problem with Bombasta," the Kid was explaining, "is that she thinks she has all the answers. She doesn't listen enough. For instance, just the other day I was telling her about this dance I attended. Sweet lights and soft music. Such a romantic scene. Miss Coty de Tramp—the 'Voom' girl?—was there, doing the peabody with Transvesto. And, I must admit, I was feeling pretty randy. And Bombasta said, 'Oh, Randy isn't that pretty.' "

Lois, at the cash register, told Elaine, "I hate to admit it, but we broke the bank tonight."

"It's so exciting here," said Elaine, taking it all in, from the back wall to the stage, from the hustling to the act. "It's a world with entirely new rules."

"Yeah," Lois agreed. "Be sure to tell Jeff all about it."

"That Bombasta," the Kid was saying. "What a caution she is. You know what she calls the other kind? *Joes.* As in 'Joe Doakes' or 'Eat at Joe's.' See, Bombasta has this theory that what sets them apart from us is that they're nothing but dreary, disgusting, boring, vile idiots." The Kid shook his head. "The *phrases* that Bombasta will utter! The *furies* she contains!" The Kid was gleeful, but now he grew temperate, even solemn. "Yet she is on a holy quest. I know this about her. Bombasta seeks but one thing on this earth, and that is a pure and perfect love. Yes. Yes, it's true. One pure and perfect love is what Bombasta seeks." One beat, then: "So she seeks it with one guy on Monday, another guy on Tuesday . . ."

Desmond swung into the finale of the act, one of the Sophie Tucker numbers that Larken had put the Kid onto, "Cheatin' Charlene."

Frank was staring at Larken and Larken was staring at the stage, two icebergs about to have a crash.

Cord was standing behind Trey, holding him by the waist and methodically licking his way around Trey's ears.

Saul was watching this, transfixed.

Lois was whispering to Elaine. "Chick," she said, "I have plans for you."

The Empress Leticia and her court were beating their fans against their glasses in time with the music.

Lanning's and Carl's tables had forgotten each other. The Kid had them enthralled. Even Otis was beaming.

Winding up solid for the coda, the Kid sang:

Say, she's got a sofa
And a 'lectric fan.
Why, she's got everything
But one good man.

That no-repeatin',
Permanently cheatin'
Charlene!

The crowd erupted in cheers, and the Kid, waving them down, said, "Desmond and I had timed this *perfectly* so that it would have been twelve midnight just this second. Thanks to the surprise visit of Jane Law, it is already 1950 plus four minutes. So hit the noisemakers, kiss your boy friend, and, from Lois, Jo-Jo, Desmond, and myself, have a wonderful new year!"

Thriller Jill's enjoyed the most uproarious few hours in its history—but riding back to Larken's in Frank's car made for a very silent night. Larken decided to get right out without a word and let Frank drive off, but Frank parked the car and followed Larken to his door.

"We'll call it a night," said Larken. "Please, Frank?"

"Oh no, you don't," said Frank, pushing Larken inside and following him. "You're not getting out of this one," he said, snapping on the lights.

"No, Frank, because—"

"Look, fella, don't tell me *no,* right?"

"You just want to fight."

"You're damn *straight* I want to fight!" Frank shouted, slamming the door behind them and giving Larken a shove that sent him sprawling back onto the couch. "What the fuck kind of *place* is that, will you tell me? *Joes'?* He calls the others *Joes'?* Who's that faggot to call people names?"

"You apologize to me for using that word or you get out of my house," said Larken, getting up, "and I mean it."

Frank, surprised, said, "What word?"

" 'Faggot.' "

Frank looked at Larken and saw that he meant it.

"Just a minute there," said Frank. "That guy's allowed to use words on my mother and father, and I'm not allowed to use words on *him?*"

"*Now* you've figured it out. Apologize or get the fuck out!"

"Look—"

"No, *you* look, *buster!* Because *you're* wrong! And you know what else? You're still a joe! You don't just dress like a joe and talk like one—you think like one! It's still us against them to you, and gay people are *them,* aren't they? And Johnny or Bombasta or whoever he finally decides he's going to be is perfectly in the right to call your parents 'joes' and you're not going to give him 'faggot' back! Because you and your kind have been giving us 'faggot' for many, many years! From now on, it's our turn. Your parents are *joes* and you can *stand* there and *take* it!"

Stunned by Larken's unaccustomed fire, Frank was silent—but now Larken changed his tone. "These stupid vases, you know?" he said, calmly regarding two matched green glass pieces that stood upon the coffee table. There was never anything in them; they just sat there. "Why did I buy them? I guess . . . they must have seemed like a bargain at the time. Now I'm tired of them. They annoy me, you know?"

Larken picked one up and sent it smashing to the wall just to Frank's right. By the time Frank looked from the broken glass back to Larken, Larken was holding the other piece and looking grim.

"This goes straight at your head, I swear to God," said Larken, "if you don't apologize to me for your disgusting attitude. And if you call the cops on me, when they get here I'm going to tell them that you've been screwing my ass and letting me blow you, and this is not a bluff."

Frank stared at Larken.

"You have five seconds."

At three, Frank said, "Okay, fuck it, I'm sorry, Larken, *okay?*"

"And stop shouting at me in my own house."

"Right. *Jesus.*"

Larken put down the vase.

"Neat," said Frank. "Because you throwing that vase is like . . . you know, the wife is angry."

"I'm not your wife, Frank. I'm a man, just like you."

"How come you let me cram your ass, then?"

"Frank, to tell the truth, I don't know. Because I don't even like getting screwed. I have much more fun on top."

Frank snorted, as if to say, Fat chance, buddy.

"You won't understand this, Frank, but I go along with it because I like the thought of you taking that . . . that right over me. It's not the physical sensation. It's thinking about what you look like, all of you, and having you moan inside me—"

"Hell, you make noises, too."

Larken sat on the couch.

"It's a contest, isn't it, Frank? That's how you see it. The winner is the one who shows the least need for the other man, the least affection. I moan less, so I win, is that it? That other guy, he's just a piece of ass."

"That isn't true," Frank growled, but he sat next to Larken and took his hand. "I'm always affectionate with you."

"You don't like being gay."

"Of course I don't. Who would, with all the hard time you get from . . ."

"Joes."

"You say that to hurt me."

"Because you think you're a joe. Somewhere deep in Frank is a voice telling you you're better than me. You're more of a man. You won't kiss, you won't suck, and you won't get fucked. You're like the trade in Jill's. You think you're straight."

Frank shrugged.

"This," Larken announced, taking his hand back, "is not a sensible way to have an affair. Because—guess what?—I think we just broke up."

"I'll ignore that last bit while you tell me what a sensible way would be."

"I have no idea, Frank."

"Well, what's the usual way?"

"That's just it. There is no usual way because what we're doing isn't usual. Where would you go to . . . to inspect the models? You ever hear of a book about two gay men in love? A movie?"

"Are we in love?"

Larken looked right at Frank. "I think one of us is."

Frank put his arms around Larken, pulled him close and petted him. "Come on," he said. "Fighting is stupid. And I was stupid, because I started it. We don't . . . understand each other yet. You meant to do the right thing by taking me to that place, but I have to tell you that it's the biggest collection of cranks and goofies I've ever seen. If that's what gay is, then you're right: I'm not gay. And neither are you."

Larken said, "I want to fuck you."

He felt Frank freeze and pull away, but Larken held on to him. "If you can fuck me," he reasoned, "why can't I—"

"Why do you worry about it, when you give such beautiful beak?"

"Beak?"

"It's cop talk. *Head.* Give head."

"Well, why do I have to be the one who—"

"Because *you like* it! You told me you did."

"I don't like it, Frank, I love it. And I'm not even a size queen."

Frank paused. "A who what?"

"A size queen."

"Uh, do you suppose you could help me out here, because I seem to have mislaid my dictionary of weird homo terms."

Larken looked at him.

"Sorry—weird *gay* terms."

"A size queen is especially attracted to extra-big-hung men, like you. You *have* noticed that you're kind of heavy in that department?"

"Yeah, but why a *queen*?"

"Frank! You can't be that dense! Haven't you heard me use the word 'queen' a thousand times?"

"But why not . . . oh, size *hound*? Size *fan*?"

"Frank, you keep wanting to stick Nelson Eddy and the Mounties in there to sing 'Stouthearted Men.' But if you fuck guys—as you have been fucking me—not somnolently or with a gun to your head but gratefully and with noisy abandon . . . Oh, you're blushing; that's cute."

Larken got up.

"Anyway," he went on, "if you do all this, then you are gay. And if you're gay, you're a queen. You want some coffee and everything?" Larken went to the fridge. "Or maybe a toast to welcome the new—"

"A size queen," Frank muttered.

"There are other kinds, too," said Larken, readying the drinks. "Like for what you're interested in . . . theatre queens, toe queens—they go to the ballet. Or for what you want sexually. Tart queens only go with hustlers, for instance. Rice queens like Orientals."

"Rice queens . . ." Frank echoed, with a slight air of desperation.

"There's also snow queens, but I forget what they do."

"And what kind of queen are you?"

"I'm a Frank queen," said Larken, handing Frank his drink. "But you're going to have to be more tolerant and accepting. You want to be a joe, fuck women. You want to be with me, stop pretending you're a joe. In fact . . . did you ever think of coming out on some small scale? Like to your parents?"

"Coming out?"

"Of the closet."

"*What* closet?"

"Frank, you're so literal it's almost sweet. What closet? I guess the . . . the closet you've been hiding your secret self in. The closet with your dresses, in a way."

"My . . . *what*?" Frank jumped up. "Now I'm a *dress* queen, right? Pull open Frank's closet and what do you see? All *I* see, Lark, my boy, is my uniform gear and the white T-shirts and jeans for days off and my dark suit from graduation and maybe a sweater. What's in your closet? Some . . . I don't know, velveteen gown with a blue thing on it, what are they called, a sash? And your silk . . . step-ins? And your scarlet jumper with the, what? matching lunch box of iodine red? Is that what's in your closet, Larky? Right?"

The Kid opened the door and pulled out hanger after hanger of new costumes for the act—a beaded silk number, the body in fir green and the beads avocado and corn; a black sheath with a white organdy bow in the back and matching turban; and a sensational outfit in red satin with Carmen Miranda rumba ruffles on the arms and a red velvet snood; along with jewelry, barrettes, clips, bags, and shoes.

Arranging them on the bed, the Kid thought, the silk is Contessa Dooit and the black is definitive Bombasta. The red satin would work for Miss Coty de Tramp. But Transvesto . . . Or maybe Transvesto shouldn't actually appear. Once you're in drag, any allusion to a drag character would be redundant.

"You can't," Derek told the Kid. "You can't, you can't, you can't."

"Wait till you see the wigs."

"My boy—"

"What do you think of the name Jerrett Troy?"

Derek took a sip of his drink. "I don't believe I think anything of the name. Who is it?"

"Me, when I crash out of Thriller Jill's and hit the circuit."

"What circuit?"

"There are other cities besides L.A., you know," said the Kid, holding the green silk against himself and studying the effect in the mirror. "There are other clubs besides Thriller Jill's. I'm thinking of taking this play on the road."

Derek dropped his head and covered his eyes.

"Well," said the Kid, "I can't wait around for you to break me into the movies, can I?"

"I *can't,* Johnny, you must know that." Derek went over to the Kid—crossed to him, really, as an actor moves across a stage, with Timing and Profile and an Air. "Certain agents do get away with that, but for an actor to bring his boy friend into his career . . . It starts people talking."

Laying the dress down and not looking at Derek, the Kid said, "I thought you were going to help me. That was the whole point of this, wasn't it?"

"Money. Advice. Introductions. I *am* helping you."

The Kid looked at Derek sadly. "Yes, you really are, in your way. But it's possibly not a way I can all that terribly much use."

"A fine young American Y.M.C.A. lad in these ridiculous getups! It's disheartening. And that risible patter, Johnny!"

"What should I do?" said the Kid, smoothing out the beaded silk. "Tell Truman jokes like Jo-Jo?"

"But the very look of you is smooth, simple, smiling—"

"*Derek.* That fantasy of yours about clean-limbed, cocky little Penrods is *so* off the track! I went to high school with them, remember, in the very recent past, and they were basically a bunch of dirty stupid cunts. These are the guys who grow up to beat their wives and kids and put on bellies, and if they can get a prostitute to nag their wiener into a semi-boner, they strut home as if they'd just fucked their way through a harem."

"Johnny—"

"So stop talking about the Y as if it were some sort of paradise."

"Oh, it's forbidden paradise. If I got caught there—"

"They caught Robert Taylor there two months ago and it never made the papers, did it?"

"They buy the *big* stars out of trouble. Not the also-rans, like me."

The Kid, trying a cameo here and there against the black sheath, said, "I thought you were doing okay."

"I was," said Derek, lighting a cigarette, crossing his legs, and looking debonair. "I was doing brilliantly, for someone with looks, style, and no talent whatsoever. It appears that it finally caught up with me."

The Kid turned to him. "All of a sudden?"

"No." Puff. "For a while now. Rather a long while, actually. The last grosses are not good, and the wait outside Mr. Weber's office has grown from ten to fifty-five minutes, and they're loaning me out on the next one, to Paramount."

"Well, that's not—"

"For a western."

"Paramount makes westerns? Like, Tonto's wearing a tuxedo?"

But when the Kid smiled at Derek, the actor looked genuinely upset, *this* close to breaking down.

"I'm sorry, Derek. I figured you were just . . . floating along."

"Nobody floats along in this business, as I'm sorry to say you will soon learn." Puff. Derek the wise. "Those who try to float soon crash down, my so very young friend. Float? One doesn't float." Puff. "One *surges*. One roars and lies and manipulates, and I've never been good at that sort of behavior. It's probably my one good quality. *So.*" Sniff. "I'm not really taking root here, you see, and they . . . quite possibly . . . won't renew my contract."

The Kid looked at him for a bit. "Does this mean . . . no more chauffeur?"

Derek laughed and stubbed out the cigarette and held his arms open. "Beamish boy, come and cheer me. Sexlessly. Patiently. Lovingly. Faithfully." Holding the Kid and sighing, Derek said, "I really would help you if I could. I don't have the power. I can't help myself, in point of fact. I'm in debt to my temples and I don't know what comes next in this career."

The Kid was set with another chauffeur joke, but Derek quickly said, "Don't jest with my life, Johnny, please."

"Won't jest."

"They screened a rough cut of *Broadway Lullaby* last week. And they're saying, Don't worry. The inserts. The color prints. The publicity. Well, *lullaby* is right, because ten minutes into it, everyone's asleep. The projectionist's asleep, the page is asleep, the security guards at the front gates are asleep. It's Sleeping Beauty's castle. One wave of my fairy wand and an entire kingdom is bored into coma."

The Kid was looking at him.

"What?" Derek asked him, lighting up again. "With the disapproving face?"

"You shouldn't use the word 'fairy,' Derek."

"You use it."

"For fun. You use it for anger. But what do you think?" the Kid asked, modeling the turban. "For Bombasta? Can you believe I paid ten bucks for the whole outfit?"

Now it's Derek with the disapproving face. "You will never break into the movies if you go on stage in those things."

"In those *clothes*."

"In those *dresses*."

"Dresses. Yes. I *will* go, Derek. On stage. In those. Dresses."

Derek shook his head. "Oh, there are rules, Johnny."

"Rules," says the Kid, "are what I humiliate."

"They're going to get you. You think they'll let you—"

"Derek, my man, you already sound like your Paramount western. *Who're* going to get me?"

Annoyed, Derek stubbed out the cigarette and started pacing.

"Who's going to get you?" he echoed. "You have to ask?"

"It's not against the law for a performer to—"

"It's against *nature!*"

"Derek, nature isn't clothes. It's acorns and blue jays and rainbows. Nature is just there. Clothes are an invention. And who are you to judge me by my clothes? Some would say that it's against nature for a romantic movie hero to be played by a man who blows little boys."

"Not little boys. Young *men*. Fine, handsome, young . . . You make it sound disgusting."

"I make it sound great. You think it sounds disgusting. That's because you've been playing by their rules."

"Their?"

"The joes." The Kid in the beaded silk, the material hugging his skin; the Kid in the mirror, posing, turning; the Kid humiliating the rules.

"Johnny, you'll . . . you'll pay for this, I'm warning you. It's the wrong . . . emphasis. . . ."

The Kid says, right into the mirror, as if the words could bounce off the glass, "Probably." He gets into the shoes, tries the bag. "What do you think—hanging off the shoulder? Swing it by the chain?"

Derek is horrified but somewhat in awe. "You're ahead of your age, Johnny."

"No, I'm right on time. The age is behind me."

Dear Elaine,

Tonight, at last, you told Jeff about Lois, and that you were leaving him. He took it convivially. Perhaps it suits his own plans. Ray Milland couldn't have played the scene more sleekly, though I admit I goaded him a bit, just to see.

"She's tougher than you," I told him. "Lois."

"I was never tough enough, I know," he said. "I was half-tough."

"You were patient, hopeful, my bright young man."

"Really? I wanted you to revere me."

"And I did, you idol."

"Can't you *ever* be serious?"

No, I'm lying. He beat me. At the suggestion that he could be replaced—by a woman, at that, though I must say he was angry rather than shocked—he turned upon me the terror of an imperfect man defied. He brutalized me; I let him. I uttered no cry. I wanted our parting to be conclusive, irredeemable.

No, wait. He was neither calm nor furious, simply perplexed. But he has been away a great deal on those business trips, and I am a neglected wife. I have my yens. I am not stable, not a machine, not an employee. I am a disappointed partner.

That is when Elaine's husband walked in. Suitcase, cigarette, weary, half smiling; and Elaine looking up at him from her notebook, gently putting down the fountain pen.

"Jeff," she said.

Putting down his suitcase and shaking his head.

"I'll never get used to that," he told her.

"Jeff," she murmured lovingly.

"It's not my *name,* Elaine."

"Oh, Rex, darling."

"Rex was last year, remember? And Charlie was the—no, it was Giacomo the year before, Charlie before that, Tony somewhere in there—"

"Jeff!" Elaine rose as if delighted. "Jeff, what *is* your name?"

"It's so dumb when you act silly, Elaine. You've got a steel-trap brain and X-ray eyes, so drop the bull doody, please."

Elaine stood there, smiling. "Waiting for the name," she said.

"Elaine, you *know* the—"

"Yes, but to hear you say it, my love."

He sighed, stabbing out the cigarette. "Elaine . . ."

"Just to appreciate the force of your baritone," Elaine went on, "wrapping itself around the gravity of your personality."

He nodded and went into the bedroom. She followed him.

"You're tired," she said.

"Yes."

"You're not willing to fight with me," she said.

"That's right."

"You're Keith," she said.

"Yes, Elaine, finally. I am Keith, your husband, and you are toying with me, and you . . . you want to sack me, is that it?"

"More or less."

"I've been expecting it." Keith unpacking. "Marriages don't smash like windows, do they? They . . ."

"Melt!" Elaine cried. "Like icicles in May."

"Thanks. Yes. They melt. Finally, one or the other says, You're fired, I want a divorce."

"Or simply," Elaine offered, "I quit."

Keith nodded.

"Some guy?" he said.

"No. Some time. Some time between high school and now. Some realization. Some I don't know thing, because you have been the kind of husband my mother was hoping I'd have. A just husband—like a judge, I suppose. Granted, a long-distance husband, too. But it's not as if I missed you. Some emptiness in what we are together. It's possibly a trite notion, but you deserve someone better . . . well, *other* than a wife who gets whimsical and irreverent when her marriage melts, instead of turning passionate and terribly betrayed by it all."

"Well, I don't blame you, Elaine, and I hope you don't blame me."

"Yet you might at least stop sorting out your socks while I steal out of your life."

"How do you want to do it?" he asked. "Legally, I mean."

"Actually, I'm planning to go lesbian, so technically speaking I don't even need a divorce."

He smiled wanly as he closed the sock drawer. "You and your ridiculous jokes, Elaine."

Lois said, Who needs movers? She could truck Elaine into Lois's place without any help. But Elaine said Lois had enough to do, and this exchange took place in Thriller Jill's with Larken at their table, and Larken said, As long as he's out of work, why can't he and his boy friend do it, and Lois and Elaine, simultaneously to the nth, said, "What boy friend?" So Larken did three minutes on Frank and how he's still on the jam side but we're working on that, and Elaine said, "I want to date him," a joke Lois didn't enjoy.

She also had mixed feelings about Elaine's new job, as secretary to an attorney. Lois didn't like lawyers. "But wary Lois doesn't like almost everyone," Elaine explained. "Anyway, it's mostly writing letters, and I'm a whiz at that."

"Why don't you write stories and sell them to the magazines?" Lois challenged her. "That'd be a job to be proud of."

"Stories?" Elaine asked.

"Well, you're always making things up, anyway, aren't you?"

"Stories," Elaine repeated, thinking about it.

Now, Larken felt great, because everything was going to work out for him, even if he had gotten fired again.

And Lois felt great, because Elaine's decision to domesticate their relationship looked to be the most interesting thing to happen to Lois in many years. Yeah, it has its drawbacks. They get rain in heaven, as Lois's mother used to say. Well, that's fine, says Lois. Let's try heaven for a while.

And Elaine felt great, because, for the longest time, she had been wanting something desperately without knowing its name. Now she knew.

And Johnny the Kid felt great, because when he walked on stage in the black sheath as Bombasta, the whole place gasped and stared at him like children awed by an incendiary disciplinarian.

So he turns to Jo-Jo, who is just making his exit, grabs his arm, and says, "Hold it, fullback. Have you heard tell of the nun and the blind man?"

"Come to think of it, Bombasta," Jo-Jo replied, playing along, "I haven't heard of the nun and—"

"The *nun*," Bombasta begins, "is in the *bath*! So. Well. Comes a knock at the door. 'Who's there?' she cries. Guy yells, 'Blind man!'

"Nun thinks, I'm ever so proud of my endowment. Here at last is my chance to show it off *without committing a sin*! Then. So. She calls out, 'Come in!' The blind man enters. Do you know what he says"—turning to Jo-Jo and eyeing him from top to toe—"you cabaret cavalier?"

"No, Bombasta. What does the blind man say?"

"He says, 'Nice tits, lady. Now, where do I hang the blinds?' "

Desmond had his hands over his eyes and Lois was muttering, "Fancy stuff." But Larken thought to himself that the Kid was right. *This* is what it should have been, right the way along! This was gay comedy. And, help!, did he look sharp in those clothes. He didn't mince or swish. He didn't imitate women. He played it like a tough but feminine man—like some of the dames who starred in musicals. It took itself entirely for granted, yet it was turning the familiar inside out, saying, What you find familiar has always been strange. You just never noticed because everyone's so busy playing roles.

"What a masquerade!" Larken called it, later, telling Frank. Of course, Frank thought the whole thing repulsive, but out of respect for Larken he just grunted.

"A dress and some makeup," Larken went on, "and there is this . . . this new invention. Right there before you, someone we never met before. You know, Frank, I think the Kid does that so well because all gay people learn to be actors almost from birth. Because we have to pretend to be like everyone else even while we *know* that we're different. We ape them, you know? Perform a version of them and everything."

Frank grunted.

And, frankly, Frank's not much of an actor. Because on moving day he and Larken pulled up to Elaine's in a little rented van. Elaine's husband was gone, and she gave them coffee, and then Lois drove up. So Frank met everybody, and he took charge of the whole thing, getting very inventive about filling the van precisely, to take advantage of the space and fit everything in. So Elaine was transported and she unpacked and became Lois's roommate and everything was peachy keen.

But while Frank and Elaine were dollying her bureau inside, Lois went up to Larken and said, "I ought to cuff you up and down the avenue."

"Huh?"

"That boy friend of yours is a cop."

Larken blinked at her.

"Don't *do* that to me, boy!" Lois told him. "You got a cop in tow, you give a body warning!"

"Lois, I'm sorry. It never occurred to me to . . . How did you know?"

"How did I *know*? With those eyes rolling around all over hell like he's checking the house for clues? And that tight little air of morality he's got on, like he knows what trash everyone really is but he's too tired to chew you off just now. You tell me, what's that but a cop?"

Larken couldn't help laughing. "Gee," he said, "it's that obvious?"

"It's that obvious."

"Funny," said Larken. "The first time I met him, he sure fooled me."

Frank's in his car, driving to Larken's, and he is in one great mood, okay? Because he is *out* of Vice and *into* Homicide. That fucking Chief and his "we need men like you" crap! I marched into that office, and I was polite and smart and crisp. Pure Academy style, right? Like some rookie so fresh that the Kodaks his father took of his graduation are still on the line drying. I told the Chief, straight out, that I can't see any future in this particular type of work, and if I can't transfer into another division I'm reluctantly going to have to resign from the force.

Not that he cares, the son of a bitch. But he knows my father would drag himself into it, and he knows about my mother, too. We've got enough travail without him adding to it, okay? So he gave me no grief.

Frank liked that phrase in this context so much that he said it aloud: "He gave me no grief." And if he had given grief, Frank would have resigned right there, right then. That's how he felt about it.

Homicide! Now, that's a section of law enforcement that a man can fit into. That's police work, law and order, *prevention*. Catching killers is keeping the dog off the quicksand.

You know what's funny? Until Frank met Larken, he had no one who would understand how wonderful this news was. Okay, Lieutenant Peterson gave him a fine, true, man's handshake on it at the station. And Frank's father will be glad because Frank is glad. But only Larken is going to know how much it means to Frank not to have to do harm to his own kind any more. Hell, that Griffith Park cruising is just . . . It's the only way those guys have of finding a friend.

Because, look, if you asked me where Larken fit into my life, I'd say, He's my real good friend. I wouldn't say I'm crazy about him or I love him. That's for a man and woman. This is different. It's a new kind of best friends.

Larken wasn't there, so Frank let himself into the apartment with his key; almost immediately, the doorbell rang.

"Hi," says this beachboy. "I'm Todd. I saw you pulling in and I hoped I could cut some sweet-and-hot stuff off you."

"You could what?"

"Borrow some honey? Because I've been on the run all day and my pantry is, like, decimated?"

Frank was looking at him.

"I need it for my banana-carob shake," said Todd.

"Oh. Yeah, help yourself," said Frank, stepping aside to let him in.

Real big boy we have here. Barefoot in swimming trunks. Incredible stomach muscles. Frank watched him as he carefully measured the honey into a metal cup he'd brought along.

"Larken doesn't mind," said Todd, concentrating on the operation. "I'm always running out of stuff, but he knows if he was in trouble I'd dash right over here."

"Where do you . . . I mean, what kind of . . . How did you get that size?"

"Oh, me? In the gym, mostly. A little biking, of course, and my surf laps. But I have pretty good genetics in the first place." Finished, Todd put the honey away. "Then there's my cals and isos."

Frank stared at him.

"Calisthenics and isometrics. You can spend just so many hours in the gym, and there's all that time at home. You got to put it to work. You know, I can press a hundred pounds while standing still, say, talking on the phone. *Equivalently,* I mean. I can iso a hundred pounds, is what I'm saying here, man."

Frank wasn't listening; Frank was looking. This is what they mean by "dumb blond." Now I get it. Stupid is sexy because you figure anything that empty has nothing to hold it back in bed. No mind to ask himself, Am I good at this?

You're beautiful, Frank wanted to tell him. You are a fucking big-built beautiful man. He couldn't utter that any more than he could bring himself to hunker down, sucking, on Todd's nipples, though he felt an insidiously newborn desire to. You don't just come out, Frank thought. You actually become gay by degrees. It's like school.

"Tell Larken thanks," said Todd, moving out. "See you in the sun."

"Right," said Frank. "The sun."

Todd, he's thinking. Todd is a Greek demigod who lives next door and comes over periodically to borrow things. Larken has mentioned him. Todd, *right.* Todd is nearby and something to see.

Keyed up with the news about his assignment to Homicide, Frank paced the apartment. He was so eager for Larken's return that he couldn't even turn on the radio. But listen. When Larken came in at last, loaded up with grocery bags and suddenly smiling at the sight of Frank, all Frank could say was "Who's Todd?"

"The gay surfer? Next door?"

"Well, he . . . Todd is gay, too?"

"Didn't I tell you that every gay man like me has a gorgeous gay neighbor like Todd who comes and goes like the good fairy in *Pinocchio* and drives everybody crazy?"

"How do you know he's gay?"

"How do I *know*?" Unpacking groceries, Larken had the curious habit of putting anything anywhere—rice in the fridge, grapefruit in the pantry—and only eventually correcting the assignments. Talk about driving you crazy. "How could Todd not be gay?"

"How like *what,* if you'd kindly?"

"That body, for starters. Joes just don't look like that."

"There are plenty of—"

"And they're all gay," said Larken, his left hand on a box of Corn Flakes, his right hand opening the fridge.

"No, Larky, in the pantry."

"Oh, of course. With the Shredded Wheat. Anyway, no heterosexual has tits like Todd's."

"Anyone can—"

"No, Frank, these have been worked on. You know, the way they stick out like that? Women don't do that to their boy friends. Guys do it. You see nipples like Todd's, you say, That man is a lively gay flyboy just like you and me. Listen, though, I want to tell you about the Meeting today."

Frank smiled, because he would wait for the right moment and hit Larken with the news and stun him.

"You want a beer?" Larken asked.

"Hit me."

Larken cut his beer open, then tossed Frank the church key. Frank grabbed a beer in his left and caught the church key in his right.

"What a guy," said Larken.

They settled on the couch, Frank's arm around Larken's shoulders, Larken playing with Frank's free hand.

"Now, here's the thing," Larken went on. "Tonight we tried group therapy, where each of us had to face the others and find out what they held against him, like his personal qualities and everything. Naturally, everybody jumped on Paul, because he's so pushy and whiny and—"

"What did they say about you?"

"Nothing. They like me. Why? What would you have said?"

"Just that you're sort of a slob."

There's a moment or two, then Larken, with this funny look on his face, goes, "Huh?"

"Well, you are, right?"

"A . . . sort of a . . ."

"You leave your stuff all over the place, don't you? Clothes on the floor and towels thrown around the bathroom any old way. Soap lying right in the sink. Well, don't look surprised, because—look, I'm just being honest with you."

Frank reaching for Larken, and Larken, bewildered, pulling away.

"Hey, what did I do?" says Frank. "I'm sorry, okay? I thought I could be straight with you about things like that. Look, we practically live together now. I'm over here so much my father thinks I'm shacking up with some . . . Jesus, Lark, don't *cry* on me!"

"I know I'm not tidy. It doesn't bother me, and you never said anything, so I—"

"Aw, shit it to hell, Larken. Crying over a little—"

"It's just when you call me a slob right out like that . . . A blunt thing like that . . ."

"It's just words, so don't cry, now. Larken. Don't cry."

Frank is holding Larken, rubbing his cheek against Larken's shoulder and back and neck. Frank starts saying "Don't cry" over and over as if they were magic words, or poetry, or some kind of caress for the third hand. Frank says, "You didn't cry when you got arrested."

"Later I did. When I got home."

"Stop crying and I'll take you out someplace."

Larken's head bobbed up. "Could we go to the movies?"

"Two guys on a date? It looks funny."

"Frank—"

"We've been around the block a hundred times on that one, right?"

"We can't go to the movies and you won't go to the theatre. What are we supposed to do for recreation? You won't even go to Jill's with me."

"That fag parlor?"

"Boy, you're really loaded with words tonight."

"I offered to take you to the ball game how many times? If you won't try that, why should I go to *your* places?"

"Wouldn't it be great," said Larken, getting up to wash his face, "if there were someplace we could go dancing?"

"What, together?"

Larken in the bathroom. "No," he called out. "You'd go one night and I'd go the next night." Toweling, he reappeared. "Of *course* together. Isn't that what dancing's for?"

"Yeah, when it's boy-girl."

"Frank, Frank, Frank." Larken sat back on the couch. "You bought every line they handed you. Everything in you resists what you are. Everything, do you realize that? Who says two men shouldn't dance together?"

"Everybody."

"That's my point. You were taught to be like everybody, and everybody says it, so you say it, too. It's not a decision you came to, after thinking the matter over. There's no thought in it. You just accepted it like . . . like a commandment. So think about it now, just for itself. Who would be harmed if two men who like each other were to get up on a dance floor, hold each other, and—"

"I got my transfer today. I'm out of Vice and over to Homicide. I'll never have to arrest another gay man for cruising as long as I live."

Larken froze. Well, not quite *froze*. But he was very still and staring at Frank.

"Congratulate me, right?" Frank said.

"Is it true? *Gee*. And look at you, so smug."

Well Frank might be: for his job had been the stone in their wine, so ruinous a topic that they had been afraid to speak of it to each other.

"Frank!" Larken cried. "You are such a *hero* to me now!"

"Well, come on . . ."

"How did you do it?"

"I just . . . I insisted. I *made* them."

"Boy, you did good. You'll be writ up in the book."

"What book?"

"That's what our teachers used to tell us when we did good."

"One thing," said Frank. "Don't cry when I'm around, okay? It really hurt me to see that."

Larken turned away. "Oh, I wouldn't normally have wet my sockets like that. It's just . . . Well, I got fired again today, and I knew you'd bark at me."

"Why would I—"

"Well, they're such dinky little jobs, and I can't even hold them."

"Why'd they fire you?"

"Same as last time. I keep getting the orders mixed up. Like, is it two waters and an anchovy for Table Three or three Cobb Salads and two napkins for Table Sixteen? Besides, who knows which Table is Three and Sixteen and everything?"

"Fired."

"Fired. But look. We're on the verge of something, us two. Aren't we? I mean, true, I did cry, but I promise I won't any more, and now you're out of Vice—which I really, really hated; and I'm glad I can finally say that—and, all right, we can't go dancing, but we'll figure something out. I'll try to be neat if it matters to you. I really will. Because you and I are going to make history."

"For what?"

"As the first gay couple that becomes famous and lives forever."

"That's funny," said Frank. "Because we haven't even figured out the sex yet."

"I got you to like kissing, didn't I?"

"You got me to do it. I don't know if I—"

"It's like olives—you'll get there. Now, if I could only lure you into letting me switch—"

"Forget it, buddy. No rear-entry on this baby."

"Well," said Larken, "we'll have to work on that."

Frank was all ready with Oh no, we won't, but he caught Larken's quiet mood, and was silent. He sensed Larken saying, I love you—conveying the words, really, as Larken wouldn't have verbalized the thought out of respect for Frank's reticence—and Frank did his best to transmit a comparable report back to Larken.

"They'll put us in the indexes," said Larken, "in History, Homosexual, See under Gay Life in Postwar America. Maybe they'll print a photo of us. We should take some, in any case."

"Who'll hold the camera? No one knows about us. We're history's secret."

"Todd."

"Huh?"

"Todd'll hold the camera. He has a Polaroid. You know, where you pull it out after you snap? He has me shoot him from time to time, so he can check his progress with the weights. Frank."

"What?"

"I'm so lucky. Even if I am a slob and I can't hold down a job, at least a guy as fine as you likes me."

"No, Larken," says Frank, looking straight at him. "I love you." Frank is terrified of those words, but he believes he means them, and the history meter just clicked on.

PART II

Los Angeles, 1952–1961

YOU KNOW WHAT'S wrong with Homicide? You know why Homicide's not that much better than Vice? You know what's probably wrong with the whole fucking department?

The *cops* are what's wrong! Jesus, the fucking assholes they give you for partners! Frank was actually starting to miss Jack Cleery. It's crazy how you can get on more or less okay with a guy but then he'll maybe use a word here or there that you can't stand hearing. You can't ask him not to, because he'll ask you why the fuck he shouldn't. What are you supposed to say then? Especially since they're such common words. Like "cocksucker." And "faggot." And "queer." One guy came up with a new one, "fairy doodles." As in "That's one real fairy doodles crossing the street in the sandals, see, right there?" I mean, *fairy doodles?*

Frank's getting sensitive, okay. But it's this enveloping thing. For instance, he doesn't even like the word "nigger" any more. He used to use it, thought nothing of it. It's not derogatory; it's descriptive. White, French, Methodist, nigger: words that tell who you are. Suddenly, Frank hears the meanness in one of those words. He walks into the cop shop, first day on Homicide, lasts two hours with his first partner and the rest of the week with his second partner, runs through four more partners in the next three months, cruises alone for a while, then hooks up with a guy who seems okay because, right at the top, he tells Frank he doesn't like "racial slurs." Turns out the guy is part Indian, though he doesn't look it, and his name's O'Brien. O'Brien works out fine for four days. On the afternoon of the fifth, they're taking a Code Seven at the donut place on North Vermont, and O'Brien cranks down the last of his coffee, blissfully belches, and says, "You hear the one about the shitpacking faggot and the lurid lisping lesbian?"

Frank finally landed with John Luke, a Chinese American who was as uncomfortable with generic tags as Frank was. John overused the term "M.O."—for *modus operandi,* "method of procedure," meaning everything from a crook's habits to the speediest way to open a bottle of beer when you can't find the church key. All right, every cop overused it. But with John it was chronic, almost moment to moment. Still, better "M.O." times without number than "cocksucker" anytime.

What a stupid notion, anyway—sucking cock. Frank was a full-fledged gay man now, even if he couldn't stand Thriller Jill's and was utterly mystified when Larken told him that Judy was "a high priestess of the cult." (First, Frank didn't know whom "Judy" referred to; second, he said, "What cult? And why not Joanne Dru?") Still, no one can make rules for you to be what you are. You make your own rules; and, by Frank's rules, Frank was gay. Yet he had never as much as lapped at Larken's cock and had no intention of trying to. Larken was a devotee of sucking, and that was okay, because getting blown is just about the easiest *satisfying* thing to do sexually, all men will agree. And if Larken enjoys it, well . . . fine. But to call all gay men "cocksuckers" is to . . .

Aw, fuck it.

Oh, but you know what's funny? Coming into this world of Larken's, you really do start to see things differently.

Like your parents. It's almost as if you were an actor in a play, and one night you go on and, without warning, all the other characters are spouting lines from some other script. You *know* these people—I mean, the guy's your father, right? Yet he's coming off as a stranger.

Look, it's the same room, the same bed, the same father coming in to talk nights. And I feel the same way about him, don't I?, and I very clearly feel the burden he's carrying. Yet suddenly I don't think he can hear what I'm saying. It's the wrong script for what he knows.

Like this trouble I had settling on a partner. I tell him about these guys and the stupid things they say, and he just looks at me.

"It's no big deal, Frank," he goes.

"It is to me."

"They're good guys, are they not? Stand-up guys, sticking by you?"

"I . . . Sure, but—"

"That's what matters. The rest is words. Words is nothing, Frank. You keep your eye on the main things—how a man carries himself. Is he *righteous*? That's what to know."

"Words do matter, Dad. Words are the . . . the proof of what we're thinking. If a guy uses crummy words to knock everyone else down, what does that tell you about how he thinks about people? How's he supposed to protect them when he can only think of them as dagos and yids and bitches?"

"Don't use that word."

"Huh? What word?"

" 'Bitches.' With your mother in the house and all. . . ."

"The other words are *all right*?"

Frank's father gave his son a good hard look. "Frank," he said, "just what in hell are you getting so beefed over?"

See, he can't hear what I'm saying. Maybe I should bring Larken over to explain the world to him.

Or John Luke. Frank's new partner was one sharp talker. An analyst. You give him a situation, he *figures* it, right? Any situation at all.

Like this: John's driving. There's this three- or four-minute pause. And John suddenly says, "We think of ourselves as law and order. You know, that's why we got into this. We're going to be so good for the world. But where do they get us from, anyway? We're mostly from the working classes—the most stubbornly intolerant and suspicious group in the job pool, if I may say."

"So what does that mean?" asks Frank.

"It means that the legislative entities don't really have to pass laws limiting the freedom of troublesome people, because the police will suppress them informally. Paralegally."

John has a nice voice, too. A coaxing voice.

" 'Legislative entities'?" Frank echoes. "You go to college, John?"

Blushing, John says, "I do a little reading."

"Legislative entities, right."

"Just think about it, Frank. The way we treat the non-groups . . ."

"What are the—"

"Negroes. The poor. Unclaimed women. Foreigners. Homosexu—"

"What unclaimed women?"

"Single women, Frank. Women unprotected. You ever take in a rape report?"

"No."

"I'd like to think you'd be a lot more sympathetic than most of our blue brothers. A cop taking a rape complaint is not unlike a rabbit taking a complaint from a carrot."

"I don't get that."

"What does the rabbit want, Frank? He wants to eat the carrot, doesn't he?"

Frank grunted; but he was impressed enough to adopt John Luke's ideas and to pass them off as his own in conversation with Larken, and with his father, and even with Todd, who had taken to dropping in so often lately that Frank was starting to regard Todd as Frank's "other" gay friend.

Larken said that the idea of the police recruiting from the least tolerant social class was a historically significant perception that would have to be raised at the next Meeting, and he loved that line about the carrot, and he was proud of Frank to have come up with it, and he hugged Frank, and he suddenly seemed so happy that he almost wept.

"Yeah," Frank said, babbling out of embarrassment. "Yeah, he would be inclined to eat the carrot right up there."

Frank's father said that no Good Woman could be raped. Had Frank no respect for his dying mother?

Todd said that Frank was really nifty-looking, and he should consider what a solid gym program could offer a guy like him.

John Luke would erupt with these analyses without provocation—not in a cop bar after work, when law officers typically waxed philosophical, nor even in the middle of a Code Seven, when a recent encounter with some piece of human garbage would lead to a wry look at the way of the world, but while the two partners were riding in the unit. They could be resting, cruising, or even responding to a call, John breathlessly pouring out his views as they screeched around corners in pursuit of a crook.

"You notice about parents," John said, "that they keep saying they only want you to be happy, when what they *mean* is that *you* have to make *them* happy."

"Shouldn't you?" answered Frank. "After all they've done?"

"What if they don't like the girl you picked out?" said John, smiling at the wheel. He was all ready for this. Oh, was he ready. "What if they want you to be a doctor and you want to be a cop? Who gets to be happy, you or them?"

They had made a coffee-and-donut shop, sipping and dunking in the black-and-white, eyes roving the street for Signs of Something.

"See," John went on with his wry smile, "my parents are really more Chinese than American, so they make no pretenses about wanting me to be happy. They want me to be obedient. That's the M.O., see? Now, they don't like the girl I'm going to marry, and they always wanted me to be a doctor. But it's not that I haven't chosen wisely in love and work. . . . What's so funny over there?"

"Just the way you put it," said Frank. " 'Love and work.' "

John shrugged. "They're the two main things in life, no? You get a 95 or the like on those two tests, you've made it, Frank, old sport."

"That's a good thing to know. Love and work, right."

"So, anyway, my parents tell me the girl is wrong for me and doctor is better than cop. But you know what it really is? Carol doesn't make kowtow to them, and they want *my* career to reflect *their* ambitions. Ha! I'm more American than Chinese, so I said, Nuts to them."

It had been four months since Frank and John had partnered up, and Frank liked John enough to count him as a friend. True, Frank couldn't relax with him and speak freely, as he could with Larken, or even with Todd. But John was another intelligent human being to communicate with, and there aren't that many of those. Good sense of humor, too. A sensible, fair, direct kind of guy.

"My parents never tried to tell me what to do," said Frank, not realizing—it's a common error—that his father had been directing him from birth. "But I'm not as solid with them as I used to be. I don't know. I'm . . . growing away, or something."

Frank's mother's condition had deteriorated so rapidly in the last few weeks that it was she who was growing—dwindling—away. Consequently, Frank's father was becoming harder and harder to reach, as if he had to turn himself to stone in order to weather it.

"Growing away," said John, like a teacher, or a mayor, as if he were announcing the next topic. "Yes," said John—which was so odd to Frank, because every other cop in the world said "Yeah." "It can happen in three ways, I've noticed," John continued. "You grow apart at about fifteen and never reconnect with them, or you just start to notice that they're this whole other generation with a whole different way of looking at the world. That would happen in your twenties. *Or* you become so fed up with them at thirty-five or so that you—"

"Whoa, I couldn't do that. Your parents are . . . well, like sacred beings who—"

"They're just people, Frank," said John, smiling his quiet smile; and his eyes do something, too, something friendly and at ease. "Sure, you're related to them by a cry of blood, as some Chinese put it. But you didn't marry them. You have a free choice about it. You can walk out of any-thing, Frank. Anything at all. A romance. A job. A family, if you have to."

There were times, in these discussions, when Frank felt that he could tell John that he was gay and John would have said no more than "Good for you." Frank would get shuddery at these moments, teasing himself with the possibility yet knowing he must never do it. Never.

Yet Frank very nearly . . . came out (Larken and that stupid image of a closet!) to his father a week or so later. Frank suppressed the urge as soon as he felt it, but he was shaken all the same. Where does an urge like that even come from? Christ, why do I have to *tell* someone I'm gay? Why can't I just *be* gay?

It's like there's this . . . *thing* in you, stirring and trying to get out. You can *feel* it.

Frank felt it so palpably that it was as if the word "gay" were rising inside him at the very sight of his father; and just as it hit air, Frank changed it to "I don't want to be a cop any more, Dad."

His father, boiling the water for Frank's mother's evening cup of tea, went on wiping the goo off the honey jar, then finally said, "Yeah, Frank. Yeah."

"No, Dad, I mean it. It just doesn't—"

"It's *not* the *time,* Frank," his father growled, so sharply that Frank in-stinctively grabbed him: to soothe, help, reassure. Frank's father turned away, almost shaking his son off.

"It's never the time," said Frank, quietly.

His father went on cleaning the honey jar.

So the very next thing that Frank said to Larken was "What do you say we set up a moving business? You and me."

"Moving?"

"Why not? The two of us managing it, with a small fleet of vans and some guys to . . . you know."

Larken, grinning, said, "What happened to law enforcement?"

"Too much quicksand everywhere you look."

"Huh?"

Lightly punching on Larken's arm, Frank said, "At least this way you couldn't be fired. And we'd be our own bosses."

"You're serious?"

Frank nodded.

"We moved one person's things across town and suddenly . . . You're not turning joe on me, are you, Frank? I mean, surely you realize that gay men aren't usually movers."

Frank was standing there, holding Larken by the shoulders, looking at him.

Larken might have asked, What, Frank?, but he read the answer in Frank's eyes, and they held each other close then, and Larken whispered, "Please move in with me."

Frank immediately broke the embrace. "What?"

"I want us to live together, Frank. Like real . . ."

"Boy friends."

"Gay *lovers,* Frank. You and me, from dawn to . . . star time. . . ."

"I *told* you, I have to stick by my folks. I couldn't duck out on them now that . . . It's my *mother,* Lark."

"Well, let me ask you this one thing. What about after? I mean, after she . . ."

"I know what you mean."

"Well, could we live together then?"

"I guess so."

"Gee, what enthusiasm."

"It's just—"

"I know what it's just. One day your father will call and I'll answer. And he'll say, 'Frank, who is that guy?' Is that it?"

"Right," said Frank, quite promptly.

"That's it."

"Yeah," said Frank. "Because I don't know how far . . . *out* . . . I'm ready to go, you know? I'm not as brave as you."

Larken gave him a look. "Frank, I'm the world's biggest coward."

"No, you're not. Being so open about yourself, and so unapologetic to the world. You're *honest.* You're like a . . . maybe a warrior of some kind."

"You think that, Frank?"

"No, Lark. I know it."

Frank took Larken's hand, wrapped his own hands around it, then pulled Larken close. "You sort of inspire me," Frank told him.

"When you talk like that," Larken replied, "I just don't care about anything else in my life. I mean, you praising me like that. Respecting me for what I am."

"Well . . . I guess you're going to have to forge the way, kiddo. For both of us."

"The trick," said Larken, "is just to be as honest as you can."

.   .   .

Frank quit the force, pooled some money with Larken (and with Lois and Elaine, their sole investors), and bought a very used moving van. Add in a dolly, cushion pads, a huge supply of flat cardboard boxes, the legal papers, print and radio ads, Alfred (from Larken's Meetings, to assist on the big jobs), and Move For Your Life was in business. After five hauls, the van broke down and they had to replace it. Nine hauls after that, Alfred quit and they hired Jake. Twelve hauls after *that,* Frank's mother died, and Frank's father burrowed so deeply into that death, and the life that had preceded it, and the sharing absolutism of their marriage, that he was no longer listening to anything at all that was said to him. A world that could live on, when his companion had passed beyond, had nothing to tell this man.

Nevertheless, Frank decided to inform his father that he was no longer in law enforcement—and on the day of the funeral, too. But all that Frank's father said was "That's not true, Frank. So let's skip it."

They had just come back from the funeral home, still in their dark suits and armbands, sitting at the kitchen table while Frank's father sipped at a glass of whiskey.

"Dad, listen, I just don't feel righteous about it any more. I know it was always this sacred thing between us. . . ." His father was looking at him with something between irritation and loathing. "Dad, what can you possibly mean by 'It's not true'? Obviously, it's true if I'm—"

"Frank, it just isn't true, and it *isn't,* so why go on with it?"

"Dad—"

"*Enough,* Frank."

Suddenly tense, Frank said, "No, it is *not* enough!"

"You talk to me like this?" Leaping up, Frank's father tried to loom magnificently, but he was weaving too much to pull it off. "With your mother's body warm in the ground?"

Frank quietly said, "You've been using her as a weapon against me for years."

Wham!, as the glass of whiskey flew past Frank's ear to shatter on the wall.

"Oh, a *weapon,* you say?" Frank's father was screaming. "That sainted woman in her pain, and all our loss—"

"Why," Frank virtually whispered, "are you never listening when I talk? I always listened to you."

"*Get out, then!* Out of this *house* with you and we'll *see* who *listens!*"

Surprised but realizing that he was ready to take this step, Frank slowly got up, went to his room, packed a valise of essentials, took one final look around him at the place of the Frank that had been, walked out of the house past his father, who had poured a fresh drink and did not look up to answer Frank's "Good-bye, Dad," and drove to Larken's. Because that is where Frank could go to be listened to, and that is what builds friendship: more than looks, charm, and laughter. These matter, but what matters most is: Listen to me. Comprehend me. Share my discoveries and delight and sorrow.

Larken wasn't home, so Frank made himself a drink and sat down to wait, with the valise standing very noticeably in the center of the living room. Frank hoped that Larken would see it, figure it out, and jump for joy.

Larken didn't show up at first, but Todd dropped in. Crazy Todd.

"Look, my mother has died," said Frank. "Finally. I mean . . . she was in a lot of pain and it's . . . Where's Larken, do you know?"

"Calm, Frank," said Todd, coming up and putting his hands on him. "Calm. Watch."

"No, don't—"

"Sit, Frank. Easy."

"No, Todd, because I don't need anyone giving me instructions right now. . . . Okay, okay."

Todd's grip was reasonable, compassionate, and Frank let Todd guide him to the couch like a kindergarten teacher soothing a crybaby.

"You're upset, Frank. Something has happened."

"Well, of course something has happened! I told you, my—"

"Now, calm, man, gently does it . . . see?"

Todd was rubbing Frank's neck rhythmically, humming along with the motion, sneaking in pacifying adverbs. Nicely. Softly. Uhm, lovingly, Frank.

"You have a wonderful touch," Frank told him. "But please don't keep saying my name."

"I do this professionally, you know. Massage. Sure. To relax guys like you, who are tense and brooding."

"Look, I'm not brooding, right? As a matter of fact, I feel free for the first time in . . . Skip it."

Some moments passed as Frank responded to the pressure of Todd's fingers.

"Come with me, Frank," Todd said. "Let me put you on my rubbing table."

Todd was pulling him out of the apartment, and Frank was letting him. The moment they got into Todd's place they were both so hot they didn't even bother to pretend that this was anything about a massage.

Derek Archer reasoned that since most people didn't know where you lived but everyone knew what you showed up in, he could move into a little duplex and retain the Duesenberg. It was a little like going barefoot to keep your shoes snazzy, but it saved a fortune in rent.

For the first time since his modest rise as a modest star had begun, Derek was, as the term quaintly visualized it, "strapped." Like so many of his colleagues, he had overspent to appear prosperous, therefore successful.

I'm all the go, he had told himself. I do *seem* to be the thing.

But *Broadway Lullaby* had finally come out and exploded like a sodden bomb. Derek blames the writers, the director, those hurdy-gurdy songs, and, somewhat, himself for agreeing to do a musical in the first place. But Hollywood blames a flop on the star, and Derek's in trouble.

Tommy, Derek's new boy, is reading the Sunday comics while Derek chain-smokes and thinks it through. The Paramount western he's doing on loan-out—action parts never hurt a man's image. The Regency-rakes costume bio he's up for—Derek's right for it, and though it's only a supporting role it's solid romantic stuff with no-fail potential. The pizza restaurant he has a chance to invest in—vulgar as it sounds, the sponsors swear they can make their nut back within three months, and from then on it's a free ride.

Tommy is looking at Derek. He has just said something, and Derek wasn't listening.

"Sorry, Tommy."

"I said, this *Alice in Wonderland* comic isn't funny. It's just the story of the Disney cartoon. So why is it in the funnies?"

Derek never knew what to say to Tommy. Sometimes they're just *too* young, or too unlettered, or . . . something. Curse me for the pederast that I am. Why isn't my type George Cukor?

"It's like *Prince Valiant*," Tommy went on. "That isn't funny, either. No one even talks in it."

Live-in boys like Tommy were rather thin on the ground when Derek first hit L.A. But those nights at the Y! Sauntering down the hall from your room, an unknown with no reputation to imperil, into the showers and gazing about one. A long look. Someone nods: Yes. Then the two of you racing back down the hall to your room. Cops were everywhere, of course, but the aficionado plumed himself on being able to tell the cop from the all-American boy, the pure, unhaunted wonder kind of—

"What are we doing today?" asked Tommy, gathering the papers into a neat pile, each section squared off and facing up. Derek preferred a boy who didn't care how the papers looked. A lazy, unconcerned boy. They always turned human at length, though. There was always some concern.

"We're entertaining," Derek told Tommy. "Someone I'd love you to meet."

"Okay."

They listened to records till they heard the car pull up, and Tommy leaned out of a window to watch Derek greeting the Kid, just back from his first professional jaunt out of town, to San Francisco.

The chauffeur—Derek's only servant now—started off, but the Kid grabbed his arm.

"Stay handy," he stage-murmured, "and keep the Campho-Phenique on ice."

"To hold you," said Derek, as they embraced. "Yes. My Johnny boy." Then: "Now. How was it?"

"Oh, Derek, I wish you'd been there. They really bought it, dressing up and all! They bought Bombasta, the Contessa, Transvesto . . ."

The Kid saw Tommy looking down at them.

"You baby-sitting Margaret O'Brien's kid brother?" he asked Derek.

"That's Tommy." Whispering, Derek added, "You won't be rough on him? He's so raw and tender."

"Oh no, Derek. I'm elegant now. I transcend. No more crying around the pool when beauties confront me." They headed inside, Derek waving at the still-watching Tommy. "Besides," the Kid went on, "I've had a very heady time up north. I'm in demand, Derek. Everybody wants this body!"

"Because you're so handsome, jailbait."

"Because I'm in *drag*. Those evil queens want to fuck pussy, my friend. Like, what *is* this heterosexual fantasy that impels so many of our more fashionable studs? You ought to know. . . ."

Coming upstairs, Derek and the Kid met Tommy, coming down.

Derek introduced them. Tommy, Johnny.

"No," the Kid said. "I'm Jerrett Troy now, Teller of Tales, Master of Truths, and Cupbearer to Transvesto, god of all that is taboo and beautiful in the secret world. It's a D cup, by the way."

"Hi," said Tommy.

The Kid paused, turned to Derek, and said, "I was never this dumb."

"Go gently, Johnny."

"I've played Broadway!" the Kid cried, racing up to the landing, then parading downstairs in a spoof of Old-Time Theatrical Entrances.

"San Francisco," Derek told Tommy.

"Well, they call it Broadway," Johnny told them. "And Tommy is very nice-looking but I'm not going to get peeved about it."

"That's my good Johnny."

"I'm not anyone's good Johnny, Derek. I'm trenchant and reckless, dancing on a tightrope, and so I always mean to be."

"I don't follow a lot of this," said Tommy.

"Will we see you back at Thriller Jill's immediately," Derek asked the Kid as he steered the youths upstairs, "or will you take a holiday to gloat on your triumph?"

"Jill's will seem pretty dead after San, but a boy has got to live."

"Johnny the Star!" said Derek, leading them to his room.

What was the Kid's status with Derek, now that Tommy was the official boy friend? As so often happens in these younger man–older man relationships spooled on a thread of money, gifts, or favors, after the first few dates it wasn't clear to either of the participants precisely how they were joined. Tommy was now the Boy on Call as well as resident in the house: but that did not preclude the Kid's reassuming a pride of place—nor was it certain that Derek and the Kid had lapsed into a strictly platonic association, or that Derek would never again tip the Kid for a showy evening.

Certainly, Derek was as demonstrative with the Kid as with Tommy, ruffling hair and sneaking hugs from behind with both the boys like a scampy fay prancing through a high-school locker room.

"I would love to come upon you two boys in the showers at the Y," Derek purred, taking a cigarette out of a silver case, tapping it, and lighting up.

"Ugh, that awful smoke of his," said Tommy.

"It's part of his act," said the Kid. "Everybody's got an act, and mine is the best act of all."

"The two of you would be so busy staring at each other," Derek went on, rapt in his fantasy, "that you wouldn't notice me. I would watch you lathering up . . . mechanically, dreamily . . . the soapy water running down your splendid skin as you become so engrossed that you move toward each other as if you were . . . you were . . ."

". . . going into the Continental?" the Kid asked.

Derek sighed, and Tommy said, "I heard all about the Y."

"What," prompts the Kid, "did you hear?"

Tommy shrugged. "Guys go there to date. You know, they take a room and then hit the showers."

"I would love to watch you two together," said Derek quietly. "Tommy's strictly a bottom and Johnny is versatile," he reasoned, "so Johnny can do the honors."

"Go easy on me," Tommy told the Kid.

"I'll bang you halfway to Lourdes," Johnny snapped back, "you Humorette."

"No joking, now," Derek ordered. "It's a sacred moment. Two all-American boys coming in from wrestling practice. It's a . . . a soft afternoon-like picture."

Derek's voice took on lilt and wonder as he glided into another of his idylls.

"The gym is empty," he intoned. "The two boys strip and stretch their young muscles and head for the showers. Accidentally, the leg of one brushes the leg of the other. Thighs touch. They halt . . . Johnny, will you *please* stop giggling?"

"Derek, you make it ridiculous when you go into that play-by-play. You sound like Lowell Thomas narrating a fertility rite."

"Do it in your own way, then," said Derek, gesturing surrender.

Tommy was nervous as the Kid approached him.

"I love to see a boy very easily aroused," said Derek, mildly reproaching Tommy's quiescent member. "A boy who bursts out of his pants."

"Pretend," the Kid told Tommy. "You're the Contessa Dooit's chauffeur. Big strapping guy, really fits his coat. Heavy beard, huge jaw, chest hair curling up at his collar, moves slow and secure. Really *solid* guy, you know the kind?"

Tommy was staring at the Kid.

"Now, the Contessa's feeling horny and she sends for the chauffeur. A knock at the door. He enters."

The Kid had his hands on Tommy, massaging his back and shoulders.

"He walks in, two hundred fifty pounds of sizzling stew, and the Contessa is ready for it. She's ready."

"Yes," said Derek, opening his pants. "Yes, Johnny."

"The Contessa doesn't say, 'Hello.' The Contessa doesn't say, 'How are the carburetors?' The Contessa says, 'Take off my blouse.' "

Derek, working himself, began to breathe heavily, his eyes roaming up and down Tommy's body.

"Then the Contessa says, 'Take off my skirt.' "

Tommy, with a little help from the Kid's right hand, was growing out nicely.

"Then she says, 'Take off my bra and panties.' "

"Oh, Johnny. . . . Tommy boy."

"Then she says, 'If I ever catch you wearing my clothes again, *you're fired!*' "

Derek was too deeply into his dream to react, and Tommy didn't get it. He turned around and put his arms around the Kid and whispered in the Kid's ear, "Aren't you going to fuck me?"

"Go on, Johnny," Derek urged as he fell back into a chair, pulling at his shirt buttons. "Like two cornfed boys who don't know anything except how to be sweet to each other."

"On his tummy, or legs high?"

"Johnny, just *do* it. You're the Contessa, aren't you? The Contessa makes the rules."

"So I do," said Johnny, laying Tommy on his back on the bed, and kissing him from top to toe. "The stuff still in here?" he asked, pulling open a drawer. "Ah, so. K-Y in the tube, a boy's best friend."

"Don't hurt me," said Tommy.

"Be very, very kind to him," Derek insisted. "Make him fall in love with you."

"Just by fucking him?" asked the Kid, loosening Tommy up. "It takes more than that, Derek."

"Oh, Johnny, no. Boys fall in love with the man who makes the cream flow free."

"Say that three times fast," said the Kid, sliding inside Tommy's asshole.

"I never like this part," said Tommy.

"And I wish you were Sterling Hayden," the Kid replied.

"Oh, Lord," said Derek, beating off with an enthusiasm he never showed as an actor. "The beauty of the boys! Tommy! His ass upraised like that of some primeval sacrifice to greet Johnny's swollen portion—"

"—and his face about as sour as June Haver's," said the Kid, working away with Tommy, "when the Fox commissary served her a mere half portion of their primeval Green Goddess salad. . . ."

"This hurts!" Tommy cried.

"Go on, Johnny!"

"You little shit!" the Kid murmured, picking up the tempo.

"Well, you're hurting me!"

"Partner me, princess!"

Derek, spending, gasped out, "Don't . . . fight . . . please . . . boys . . ."
but the Kid was in a rather gung ho mood just then, lost in the abandon of
his pleasure. Tommy was silent now, moving with it, and perhaps secretly
content. They say it's an acquired taste; this may have been the moment of
acquisition. Johnny's head slowly rose, eyes closed and teeth sharp, and he
made it to Go. As so often in sex of this kind, the top came and the bottom
didn't; but the night is young.

Lying on top of Tommy, panting and holding him tight and, when the
boy tried to pull free, tighter, the Kid said, "Listen, boys, I am the Green
Goddess."

Todd was only the second man with whom Frank had had sex in his entire
life, and he was surprised at how different Todd was from Larken, more
demanding, a coaxing and intrepid partner. Larken was soft, romantic.
Todd was sin itself, a thing of such certain satisfaction that God has to
outlaw it or the world will consist of little else. Not only did Frank get a
lesson in kissing in places he hadn't known you were supposed to kiss in:
He felt himself nearly enjoying it. And where Larken was a reluctant bottom, Todd was avid, a tensely possessive and wildly elated partner who
sustained a cascade of dirty pep talk and who, after Frank came, jumped up
to finish himself off by hand, his head nodding from left to right and his
eyes alight, whistling through his teeth when he shot. It was wicked,
shameless, grotesque, and wonderful. Frank felt so treacherous that he
didn't dare go back to Larken's even after showering. He hopped into his
car and sped off to Elysian Park to sit and think it over.

Now, Frank could come to terms with his guilt at having cheated on
Larken, and his anger at his father for not listening, and even the realization that not too many people have been listening to him at all for his
entire life, which is, what?, twenty-three years, okay? But what you don't
come to terms with so easy is, How come sex is suddenly so *incredibly*
terrific—and with someone I scarcely even know?

That crazy Todd. It's as if he wrote the handbook. What doesn't he
know? He showed me this thing he called "Around the World," where
you just lie there and he does it all, licks your skin every which way from
your head all the way down, blows you real solid with your legs strung up
over his shoulders so he can stroke your thighs while he's sucking, and
then pushes you back so you're bent double, parts the cheeks of your
ass—you're not going to believe this, right?—and licks you up there, too.

Scary, Frank thought, as he drove to the park. Indefinably scary. Something new in this old world. I mean, who in a hundred years would think of putting his mouth on someone's behind?

Where did Todd learn all this stuff, anyway? Around the World, no less! If I showed it to Larken, would he guess about Todd? Would it hurt him? Because I owe the guy too much now to risk that.

The midsummer sun was an hour or so from fading when Frank rustled into the park, hands in his pockets and eyes canvassing the many paths that lay ahead of him. He didn't know this park well, and simply let chance beckon to him. It took him up a hill, around a bend, then to a bench where he sat to watch the sky blur into its reds and gold. Frank thought, Getting out of law enforcement—that was right. Taking up with Larken—that was right. Sounding off to my dad—that was not right. And Todd—

"Hello, handsome," said a stranger, sitting next to Frank. "Know any ritzy jokes?"

"What do you call it," Frank asked, "when some guy licks around in your ass?"

"Heaven."

"No, the technical for it. What's the name of that act?"

"Rimming."

Frank didn't catch it. "Hit me again?"

"I rim, you rim, he shall have had to rim. *Rimo, rimas, rimat.*"

"Rimming," said Frank. "Okay."

"I don't, by the way," said the stranger, a pleasant-looking chap with heavy shoulders and a crew cut wearing a white T-shirt and jeans. He could have been a cop on his day off. "The medical penalties are a little—"

Frank, suddenly alert, said, "You a cop?"

"Man, are you kidding?"

Frank quickly asked, "What's 'deuce'?"

"Huh?"

The guy seemed genuinely bewildered, and Frank relaxed. A deuce is a drunk driver, and any cop would have given something away at the question—a flicker of the eyes, a split second's pause. Anyway, cops know cops, right? This guy was either John Q. Public or one hell of an actor going to waste in Vice.

"Look," said the stranger, "I don't rim and I don't have leather sheets or a closet full of racy costumes. But if you're interested in some conventional sex . . ."

"But what's conventional?" Frank countered. "Everyone is different, so who decides what's conventional, right?"

"You're really handsome. Do people continually tell you that?"

"I cheated on my boy friend today."

"Me, too. All the time."

"Well, don't smile about it," Frank chided him. "Don't you feel bad?"

"I hang my head," said the stranger, rather neutrally. "But one indiscretion here and there won't change the way I feel about him. Will it?"

". . . Well . . ."

"For instance. Now, I could spend a very nice hour or so with you. And I could give everything I have to it. But then we'll say ta-ta and go back to real life. So what's bad? Who's hurt?"

"I keep thinking that something's rotten about it."

"While they're counting the votes," said the stranger, dryly, "shall we give it a whirl? My name's Don, by the way."

"Frank."

They shook hands.

"You're very thoughtful, Frank. Besides handsome. Your boy friend must be very happy."

"He's a very intelligent guy. He's sensitive and yet he's fearless. I like him, but also I admire him."

Don was looking at Frank with an odd expression. "Frank," he said, "I have the most awful premonition that you're one of those unbearably nice guys who destroy everyone with their niceness."

"Huh?"

Don got up. "I had one of you last fall. One hour with him and I was devastated for three months. I couldn't think about anything but how sweet and strong he was."

"Well, see?, it isn't just ta-ta and—"

"I won't go through that again. Sorry."

And off he went.

Fine, Frank thought. *Perfect.* All I need now is, like, a bottle of something, and I'm slobbering drunk and Larken is tending to me and never guessing what's been going on. Rejected for being unbearably nice in Elysian Park. I would have done it with that guy, too. He fit the bill.

Walking back to his car, Frank thought, So Larken's too basic and Todd's too crazy and I'm blurting out come-ons to guys on park benches.

That's some world I have here, huh?

Frank pulled into Larken's after dark with a bottle of vodka all set to flow. One look at the living room told him that Larken had returned, for there was junk all over the place, an unpacked grocery bag on the kitchen counter, and Larken's baseball cap peeking out from under the sofa.

Frank looked inside the bedroom and found Larken deep in a nap. He had supervised one move early that morning, then crossed town to the Valley to run a haul all the way to Long Beach, so the guy must have been pretty tuckered out.

Frank lay down beside Larken and held him and stroked his hair till he awoke, slowly, easily, with a whimpering "Hmuuh?"

"Hey."

"I saw your bag," said Larken, not yet turning to face Frank. "Are you here to stay?"

"Yeah. I had a fight with my dad."

"You'll make it up, I guess. But I want you to stay here anyway. Promise?"

"I love you so much, boy."

Now Larken turned to Frank, and the two held each other, dozing and breathing and nuzzling like puppies.

Larken said, "Sometimes I think I like this better than actual sex."

"It's nice like this," Frank agreed. "But I feel so fucking guilty, Lark. If you only knew."

"About your dad?"

"At least this way I'll feel too compromised to chew you out for sloppiness."

"What did I do now?"

"You didn't put the groceries away."

"Oh, that."

"Well, the milk and the eggs will . . . Never mind, I took care of it."

"I wish we could stay like this forever. No apologies to anyone."

"No apologies."

"No worries."

"No worries," Frank agreed, throwing his arms around Larken and still feeling horribly guilty about Todd, with whom he had a date for that night, when Larken would be out on a job.

"Just us," Larken said.

No doubt about it, Lois was thinking: Jill's needs the Kid. Not that business fell off while he was in San Francisco—they don't come for the music. But the Kid does give off some wonderful feelings, and it spreads through the place.

"What is it that Johnny gives the club?" Lois asked Elaine.

"A theme," Elaine replied, after some thought. "He centers its sense of identity and soothes its worries. Lois, I want to come back to Jill's to work."

"No."

"The lawyer is . . . not relishable."

"There's other jobs."

"All with men saying, Give me."

"It's not good for us to spend all day together, chick. I need room. I need someone to miss and come home to, not a shadow."

Elaine looked doubtful, so Lois said, "Look, are you with me or against me?"

She said the same thing to the Kid upon his return from San Francisco. Jill's had been getting by in his absence with a closeout-sale matinée idol with so little left of whatever he might once have had that he was forced to turn his act into one huge medley to hide the fact that no one was clapping.

"I'm for everybody in this club, one way or another," the Kid told Lois. "But I've got a career to set up, don't I? I wasn't put on earth to play Thriller Jill's for life."

"I just don't see keeping you on here if you're going to duck out on me all the time."

"Want me to quit?"

"Nope."

The Kid was getting into his Bombasta outfit, the black sheath. "I'm going to have to find another of these," he was muttering. "The laundry bills are killing me."

Lois said, "I want you to sign a contract. So we always know where you are."

The Kid thought it over for maybe three seconds. Then he said no.

"Why not?"

"Freedom."

"Yeah, freedom to drive me wild annoyed with, like, are you here next week or not?"

"Tell you what," said the Kid, staring into the mirror as he painted his lips. "You cast around for someone good enough to replace me. You find him, let me know. Then we'll discuss whether I'll sign a contract or take off. But as long as I'm the best piece you can show, I feel I should keep myself liquid, you know?"

"That's a deal."

Elaine was in Jill's that night, and when Lois came out front, Elaine announced that she would chain herself to the bar in the manner of the English suffragettes if Lois didn't free her from the lawyer and let her return to barmaiding at Jill's.

" 'Barmaid,' " Lois scoffed. "The word is 'waitress.' "

"Is that a yes?"

"Why don't you stay home and write stories like I asked you?"

"I intend to write," Elaine replied. "But I need a job, too."

"Shit," Lois said.

The beauteous Laura Robertson knew that nothing mattered as much as breaking hearts at the dance. Laura lived to dismay and dismayed to live; she fed off the envy and admiration of others as a crocodile feeds, and she felt no more guilty. She knew how the angles of the tango showed off her calves, and how expertly the lindy flattered her rippling

"Garbage," said Elaine aloud, tearing the page out of her notebook.

Jeremy was the ideal young man—handsome, shrewd, and determined. The girls fluttered like buttercups in a zephyr when he passed, wondering which he would choose, and when.

But Jeremy was unusual. He said he wanted a prima donna, and would wait as long as he had to.

Everyone wondered what this must portend.

Then Elvira came to town, with her

"Oh, Christ," Elaine shouted, ripping the page out and crumpling it to join the pile of crumpled pages in the wastebasket. "Jesus, this is cockeyed!"

Lawyers are crafty, and this lawyer—fat, ordinary, and satisfied—made the fox look like Br'er Bear. Oh, this lawyer! He bides his time. He waits for you to accustom yourself to his rhythms—his entrances, his summonses, his pacings as he shouts out a letter. He waits for months.

But he doesn't pounce. Nor does he seduce. This one *alludes*. He alludes to dinner, to a motel, to

This is closer, Elaine thought. This I believe.

.   .   .

In fact, Elaine and Lois developed this new way of Being Together in which Lois knocked around the house, neatening, cleaning, and even repainting while Elaine transcribed her longhand first drafts onto her Remington.

"Read me some of that," Lois would say, to encourage Elaine.

"When it's finished," Elaine would reply.

There was silence then, a densely occupied pause of some kind, and Elaine turned around to find Lois just sitting and watching her.

"You look so cagey," Elaine said.

"I like seeing you like that."

"Like what?"

"Creative. What's that book?"

"It contains the names of the staff and the addresses of all the publishers in—"

"So you *will* send this story out!"

"I maybe will."

After much thought, Frank decided that Around the World was his favorite thing to do. Fucking was great, but a lot of guys wouldn't let him top them. They often seemed surprised that he would even ask. This one really sharp-looking guy—a real gent in a suit, whom Frank met when Move For Your Life hauled a small realty office from Glendale to downtown—told Frank with a suave sneer, "That's for animals."

It wasn't easy to find a good Around the Worlder, either. Jake turned out to be a complete bust at it. "I have to lick your *what?*" he said. Frank told him he could skip that part, but Jake wasn't much of a sucker, either.

Of course, there was this much larger problem, that Frank found himself turning into a pickup addict. This, Frank knew, was not good. There was the legal danger, first off; and sooner or later you were bound to come down with something. Besides, most of the encounters weren't all that satisfying. So why did Frank keep feeling drawn to the hunt?

Not that there were that many places to hunt in. Larken occasionally made joking references to the "T-rooms," latrines where gay men sought each other out: but Frank found the idea utterly disgusting.

Then Todd suggested that Frank join a gym.

"I get enough exercise hefting furniture."

"No, man, no: for the guys. First you do the early-morning routine, okay? So when you run through everyone at that slot, you start showing up after work and there's this whole new crowd. *Yum!* Then you try the late-afternoon boys. Then the lunchtime cast, see?"

Frank grunted.

"You have the altogether *really* genetics for it, too, you know? You'd build out real sweet, man. *Real* sweet."

"You never use my name."

"Huh?"

"When you talk to me. You never call me Frank."

"What do I call you?"

"You don't."

"So, anyway, you won't have this chasing-around stuff hemming you in, bo. Because once you fill out and get a load of yourself in the magic glass, you aren't going to be so available. You'll think, I'm too good for just anyone. I'll wait till the *champs* show up. That's how it goes."

Frank was thinking how funny it was that while he had already tired of sex with Larken and couldn't seem to get enough of crazy Todd, once they had both come Frank and Larken would lie in bed talking for hours, whereas he and Todd had nothing to say except So long.

"Course," Todd went on, "you might prefer the real serious gym over on Santa Cruz and Romero." He was mixing up another of his repulsive banana–milk–wheat germ concoctions; Frank kept thinking about how relieved Todd seemed when he offered to make Frank one and Frank declined. Todd was a little stingy. Selfish. "What's your type, anyway?"

"My type?"

"Yeah. What kind of guys are you after?"

"I don't know. . . . A solid guy, right? A heavy rower. He knows what he wants out of life and . . . Something funny, Todd?"

Laughing as he washed some strawberries, Todd said, "That's not a description. What does he *look* like, man?"

"How do I know till I meet him?"

"Like Larken?"

Frank shrugged.

"You go for them slim and pretty?"

"Larken isn't pretty. He's . . . handsome."

"Same thing," said Todd, dicing the strawberries expertly.

"No, it isn't. Women are pretty. Men are handsome."

Todd took a look at Frank and set the blender spinning. "So what *do* you go for? Musclebod? Rough stuff? Big joint? Faraway boy?"

"Whoa, there. Hold it off a bit." Frank was shaking his head, resisting this. All these labels for your appetites, this fully ordered and structured world that had existed all these years beneath his notice. It was as if a colony of Martians had settled here centuries ago, blithely passing for human but constantly retreating into their own company to speak Martian and throw Martian-style parties and have Martian sex. Men from Mars. Now he was one of them, yet they baffled him. They gave him what he couldn't use and lured him with what ultimately wasn't worth the having. If only Larken had Todd's hungers; if only Frank could find someone smart and fun who was also wild in bed. Was there such a person?

"One thing I want to hear," said Elaine, "is when you realized that you were a lesbian."

"That word."

"What word instead, I wonder?"

"I always use 'on the Other Side,' " said Lois. "Or 'dyke.' "

"Can't we call it what it is?"

" 'Lesbian.' It's like something you'd hear in a hospital."

"Anyway, when did you know?"

"Always, I guess." Lois shrugged. "It's built into you, isn't it?"

"You don't think it could be directed by something? Introduced?"

"By what?"

Elaine was thoughtful. "Because I . . . I don't think I knew what my feelings were till quite some years along. Or maybe I didn't have the feelings till then."

"Wasn't there some girl in high school that you—"

"A number of them, in fact. But I never thought I wanted them. I thought I admired them. Because they were so sharp and cute and popular. I wanted to be like them, accepted by them. I never thought I'd be nibbling on their breasts or . . ."

"Never?"

"Did *you*?"

"All the time."

The two were lying in bed in the afternoon, talking in the dark, holding each other, occasionally brushing limb with limb or altering their positions.

"Tell me more about 'directed,' chick," Lois urged. "Let me in on that one."

"It's just a theory."

"Like if a man rapes you, that would direct you to women?"

"No. It would happen younger. And I don't believe it's a specific occurrence that does it. It's psychological. . . ."

"Like what? Crazy parents?"

"Maybe."

Lois snorted. "Who doesn't have crazy parents?"

"You never talk about yours."

"I don't like parents," said Lois. "I like kids."

"It's picturesque imagining you liking anything."

Lois laughed.

"I quit the lawyer today," Elaine suddenly said. "No notice. I just left."

"Without telling me?"

"I don't need your permission."

After a bit, Lois said, "True enough. But it affects me."

"More than you know."

"What does *that*—"

"I'm writing a story about it. I can explain it better that way."

"Fancy stuff," said Lois. But Elaine could tell that she was pleased.

Frank joined Todd's gym, and the bigger Frank got the more time he put into it. After three months he was getting grand; after six months, he was opera. It was funny how the gym sneaks into your life as a hobby and suddenly becomes a marriage. It's inviolable and always there, part of the rhythm of your week, which now ran something like: Larken, gym, hauling; Larken, gym, hauling; Larken, cheating with Todd, hauling; and so on.

Or is it *cheating*?, Frank wondered. Lark and I are good friends, not . . . Look, we passed the first anniversary of my moving in with him and neither of us noticed till weeks later. And then we just had a laugh over it.

What Frank found *really* interesting was how everyone in Frank's world reacted to the new gymmed-up Frank. Larken tried to understand and respect it. That was Larken: thoughtful and loyal. Todd just kept egging Frank on and calling him "Stud." Frank's father, nursing his grudges and drinking like a man in a desert, accepted Frank's apology for their fight without even a handshake and turned away from Frank. He never noticed a thing.

No one else had much to say, but then Frank hardly knew anyone else. When he was in high school, his friends were students. When he was on the force, his friends were cops. Now that he no longer belonged to an institution, he had a very small circle of acquaintances.

Unless you counted the guys at the gym, the *types*. First, the serious bodybuilders, eyes on ice and as routined as clockwork. Then the sociables, who gab up and down the weight room from the bench press to the sit-up inclines, some never getting in more than a set of curls and a push-up. Then the flirts, who stalk their favorites, asking for training tips and admiring their "serious" arms. Finally the clunks, who wear the waistband of their shorts too high and who get on everybody's nerves by changing the weights on a bar while someone's between sets.

When Frank told Larken about all this, Larken annoyed him by saying that the very notion of a clunk was very gay thinking.

"You're coming over to the Other Side for sure, Frank," Larken warned him, enjoying the irony. "Categorizing guys by their style is what we do. Once you buy the idea that some people are exciting and some people are drab, you're a homo."

"I thought you didn't like that word."

"I can use it," Larken blandly rejoined. "You can't."

"I sold that story," Elaine told Lois.

"Hey?"

"The one I was writing. I went to this place where they run each page through a big wet machine that makes extra copies and—"

"For money? Like the *Reader's Digest*?"

"*The New York Review.*"

"What's that? Some famous magazine?"

"I don't know what it is. But they sent me a check for twenty-five dollars."

"That's great, chick. That's *lavish*."

"Lois! Imagine you thinking something was lavish."

"When do I read it?"

Elaine handed over her carbons. Lois nodded but didn't move. "Here and now?"

"When else? We're home, it's quiet, we'll contemplate the characters and the themes. We'll ask, What is this about?"

"What'll you do while I read?"

"Listen."

"I have to read it *aloud*?"

"How else can we share it? To hear you discovering me!: It will be a new form of making love."

"Sure, now I'm an actress," said Lois, stroking the papers, stalling, bemused. "What's it about?"

"An amorous lawyer."

Lois looked at Elaine.

"Or maybe not amorous. There was no love in him. Oh, an *appetitive* lawyer. Yes!"

Lois peered hard at the first page and began: " 'Lawyers are crafty, and this lawyer—fat, ordinary, and satisfied—made the fox look like Br'er Bear.' "

Lois stopped. She asked, "What's the title of this story?"

"That's not the question you mean to ask."

"You're right. Whose story is this?"

"All fiction is true."

"What happens if I go on reading?"

"You will learn about life."

Lois, on strike, dropped the pages onto the floor.

"But it's not my job as a writer to make you happy," Elaine explained. "It's my job to make you think."

"The lawyer's out of your life now, no? You're back at Jill's, whether I like it or not."

"You have to understand how it felt at the time. For me, for a woman. And for us."

"How about understanding how I might feel reading this?"

"Yet read on."

"Don't you *ever* talk like anyone else?"

"Never. Why would you wish me to?"

Lois snorted.

"Read," Elaine urged. "Find out."

"What happens?" asked Lois dangerously.

"I strongly regret that dark look," said Elaine, sitting next to Lois to hold her and lean against her and press her, head to head, almost rocking her. "Don't be angry yet," Elaine cooed.

Lois retrieved the story and read on, with Elaine still weighing against her. The appetitive lawyer made advances to his secretary, and Lois stopped reading.

"Why does it have to be about you?" she complained.

"Some fiction is necessary," said Elaine, picking her head up.

"Am I in it?"

"No fiction is complete."

"Does the secretary give in? Is that what happened, in fact?"

"We must read to discover."

Lois grimly read three more pages, and when the lawyer and the secretary left work for the rendezvous—"an overbuilt hotel with a turret," Elaine had written, "reserved, she fancied, for the most adulterous, the most disgraced, the most hungry, and the least denied"—Lois threw the pages into the air and jumped up to visit the kitchen. There she banged around with the Savarin and the percolator, a certain sign that she was angry.

After some while, Elaine appeared in the kitchen doorway. "Somehow," she said, "I pictured you reading doggedly to the end."

Lois, buttering toast, said nothing at first. Then she put down the knife—carefully, like a hostess whose tea is going badly—turned to Elaine, and asked, "What are you telling me here? Something about men and dicks? Answer straight!"

"I don't need their fucking," Elaine replied, also carefully. "But I need to wonder about it."

"Wondering's okay. But writing it isn't."

"Writing *is* wondering."

Lois grunted and turned back to the toast.

"Is that our afternoon coffee and toast?" Elaine asked.

"I *feel*," Lois said, "that it should be coffee for one."

"In that big percolator?" Elaine glided up behind Lois and embraced her. "Don't be angry at me for being honest, I beg you," Elaine urged. "Don't freeze me out for airing our worries."

"They're not *my* worries, Miss."

"We share worries. We share work. We share perceptions."

"Never in a hundred years will I get used to how you talk," said Lois, her body relaxing in Elaine's arms. Going with it, Elaine nuzzled Lois's ear and said, "You released the madcap in me."

Lois put down the knife and let Elaine work on her, arching her back and then pulling off her sweater so that Elaine could finger her breasts, working her way from the bottom of the globes to the tip of the nipples with a slow, confident pull. Lois breathed in rhythm with Elaine's touch, and gasped at the high points, so it was a bit like trashy music, some Broadway tango or something.

"Oh, it's so much easier to quarrel with a woman," said Elaine, finally. "Men scream at you, but with a woman it's a little grumbling and then caresses."

"Tell me how the story ends."

"It's avant-garde for 1951. They gain the turret room, but the sex is terrible, and there is an earthquake and the hotel collapses, and only the turret is left intact. The couple is amazed, three stories high, nude in the clouds. It's a wee bit symbolic, you see."

"Did that happen?"

"The earthquake?"

"The sex."

It must have been a whole minute before Elaine moved to the stove, turned the heat off under the percolator, then poured them cups of coffee. Handing Lois hers, Elaine said, "It happened to someone, surely."

"Stop," said Lois. "What's the title of this story?"

"The title of this story is 'Ambivalence.' "

I'm not worried about the girls; this looks to me like Love for Life. But in fairness I must report that it was not long after this confrontation that Lois got stomach cramps one evening, packed it in at Jill's, and came home to find Elaine on the couch with an unknown man.

Oh, they were fully dressed and just sitting there; but all the same Lois went nuclear, screaming and cursing and running to the kitchen for a weapon all at once. She came out with a rolling pin—remember those? the woman's baseball bat—but by then the man was out the door and headed for the hills, so Lois kept yelling at Elaine and then threw the rolling pin at the wall so hard it broke.

Lois is tough, loving, absolutely honest and reliable, humorless, bossy, incredibly sensualistic behind closed doors, and a totally supportive guy: but right now all she is is *mad*. She wants to tear at Elaine for all her affected, fruity airs, just rip her right down from her stage; but something holds Lois back. "Who was that?" she cries, spitting the words out. "You tell me, and now and here! You *speak to me!*"

Elaine is quick, doing those hand things with the plams down and the fingers splayed, the calm-down things. "Our neighbor, borrowing a cup of sugar?"

This is not a calming thing to say, however, and Lois screams, "God-*damn* you to *hell!*"

Elaine, it's serious. But she pursues her line of defense:

"My long-lost brother, with the long-awaited concessive message from crabby Aunt Sally?"

Lois, by now absolutely blazing, takes a step forward that is meant to threaten.

"The pumpkin man?" Elaine suggests.

"You *Judas!*" Lois shouts, not advancing now but backing away, in tears. *"Get out!"* She screams. *"Pack up!* It's *enough!* Do you hear me? It's *over!* It's *over!* It's *over!* It's *over!"*

Elaine stands there, takes this in, and says, "I used to be ashamed of my body. All women are, I think, no matter how beautiful they may be. How . . . supple. Firm. The skin tone. So strong and sweet. But ashamed. I'd blush at the very mention of the word 'body.' What it . . . what it brings up. All women. You wonder. It's something they do to us. Men aren't ashamed—hairy, rumbling things on the beach. Some fat horror passes a sleek and trim young one of us and he grins at her. He has no shame of what he is. Somehow they're idols and we're freaks. My husband stamped the house naked, but I always had to be wrapped in something, like a ballerina.

"But I don't—no, listen, I don't *feel* that with you, Lois. That shame. I won't be wrapped. The way you make love to me tells me that we both are lovely, that our bodies are wonderful. Your eyes, Lois. Your touch. You drink me in. My husband . . . Well, he . . . You redeem me. You turn me free. You make of me an explosion of feeling that is amazing, and ecstatic, and virtuous. This is the only honest, plain speech I've made in my life, and I hope you appreciate that."

Lois had stopped crying. "What about ambivalence?" she asked.

"That's all in my head. My art, ha. In what little I can admit of reality, there is only you."

Lois took a deep breath, nodded, asked, "So who's the pumpkin man?"

"Oh, you know the old song:

Do you know the pumpkin man,
The pumpkin man,
The pumpkin man?
Do you know the pumpkin man
Who dwells in Shady Lane?"

Lois—stunned and admiring and stubborn and thrilled—got out, "I don't know that song."

·   ·   ·

Frank had had one of those unpredictable days: He and Jake showed up for a haul from San Gabriel to Inglewood to find that the contract had found a more attractive lease two blocks away, and the whole thing was over in less than two hours. So Frank lost some money but gained some free time, and even at the mature age of twenty-four that can't be such a bad thing.

Feeling light and humorous, Frank stopped the van at the donut place near Cahuenga that Jack Cleery had said had the best whole-wheats in L.A. Frank handpicked an assortment box and sneaked into Larken's to surprise him and found him and Todd lying in bed as wrapped as a burrito, wet and hot and just sliding down from their climax.

Now, this is strange: because all that Frank felt then was relief. It was as if he'd been carrying a great weight on his back without knowing that it was there, and suddenly it was lifted off him. He was laughing as he tossed the box of donuts onto the bed, and he winked at Larken and said, "Yeah, me, too."

Then Frank went into the living room and sat and waited. Todd would pass by, presumably, as soon as he got dressed—no, here comes Todd *carrying* his clothes; but that's crazy Todd. "Got to run," said Todd, as if scurrying out of a party. "I'm late for my malted."

"Right," said Frank.

Larken followed presently, dressed and miserable.

"I never did that before," he said.

Frank patted the sofa. "Come over here."

Larken didn't move. "To make up?" he asked, his voice so unsteady that Frank felt a surge of guilt for what he was about to do.

"Just come over here, okay?"

Larken sat next to Frank, tense and wary, though he melted when Frank put his arms around him. In fact, he wept. He said, "Don't, Frank. Please . . ."

"We're going to split up, Larky."

"Frank, *no*. Not because of this!"

"Of course not because of this." Larken frantically shaking his head, Frank trying to soothe him, chuckling, feeling easy. "But think about it, my friend. This place is too small for—no, just *listen*, Lark. You're a good listener, and you're going to hear what I say, right? Right, Larky boy? Shh. Shh, now. Listening to me, listening, Lark . . ."

"Frank, I *knew* you'd been with Todd all this time and I never—"

"Lark, it isn't that. I need room, and people haven't been giving it to me. Not ever in my life. I want . . . well, I—"

"No, Frank. Because *you* listen now." Larken rose, too anxious to sit. "I don't want to go back to being alone. I'm too used to you, and this is all I want. I don't care how many times you and Todd—"

"It's not—"

"*Frank, I don't even like him!* He's just some blond sex baby. *You're* the real man that I know of!"

Frank was smiling, still free but now a bit bewildered.

"What does that *mean*, Lark?"

"It says that you've got stuff inside you Todd will never even know about!"

Larken began to sob, but as Frank rose, Larken backed away and held up a hand.

"*No,*" Larken told him. "No emotional blackmail. I'll get over this in a second."

"Shoot, why are you always crying, Lark?" Frank asked, holding him tight but already feeling the wonderful release of going off on his own.

"I'm crying," said Larken, "because I'm afraid there's only going to be one of you in my whole life."

"Larken, you're twenty-five! There'll be . . . What do I have inside me that Todd won't know about?"

"Fairness. You care about other people's opinions. You stop and say to yourself, Maybe they're right."

"What's the big deal about that?"

"*Frank.* You just don't see it, do you?" Another wave of tears flooded Larken's face, and Frank had to steer him into the bathroom and help him wash up, then steer him back to the couch saying sensible but unavailing things like "This would have happened eventually, anyway."

"It isn't just you who needs understanding and everything," said Larken. "I need that, too."

"But I'll go on understanding you, Lark. I just won't be around every second."

"Understanding is a round-the-clock occupation."

Frank had to laugh at that. "Come on," he said. "You'll always have me to talk to. Maybe sometimes by telephone, but so what? I'll be there, is the thing. I'm not getting rid of you—we owe too much on the vans for that."

"Very funny."

"I need to cut out and feel my strength, okay? See what I'm like as a citizen. You know . . . find out the reason I was put on earth."

"I know what you're like," said Larken, but Frank cut him off with a hand on his mouth.

"All my days," Frank told him, "people have been telling me what I'm like. My father says I'm a cop. The Captain told me I'm irreplaceable. The Lieutenant told me I'm promising. Todd told me I'm . . ." Frank stood up. "It's funny," he said. "I was going to spend the rest of the day loafing, not making life decisions."

"I'd take a shower," said Larken, "only I'm afraid you'll slip off."

"Look, I'm not escaping from you. We're just—"

"Totally dead as a couple."

That stopped Frank for a bit. But wait. "What's a couple, Lark? Do we have to sleep in the same bed to be close?"

"It's a well-known fact on the Other Side that when a guy moves out on you he vanishes forever."

"Tell me something. What do you think of Todd sexually?"

"Oh, for gosh sakes!"

"Tell me."

A pause.

Larken said, "At least he let me fuck him."

"Yeah, he's a real yes queen."

"A yes—"

"I can't invent terms? I have to take all my technicals from you and Todd?"

"Boy, if you're making up lingo, you're a practicing gay man for certain." Larken's forced smile gave way then, and he said, "Too bad we never took that photograph of ourselves for the history books. Frank . . . please don't go."

"Turn me loose, Larky, and we'll talk every day and run the business together and stay real close. We'll just . . . figure out a different kind of loving. Can we do that?"

They have to: because the sense of destiny that Frank's father had laid upon him from birth impels Frank to *do*. Frank was not put on earth, as he phrases it, to keep Larken company. Frank has bigger work in store, he believes, dog-on-quicksand work. As for Lois and Elaine, they excite our confidence. They seem to know how to shape a relationship, making the periodically necessary forgivenesses better than men do. True, Lois isn't sure what, if anything, she had to forgive in Elaine. No one knows what Elaine has done except Elaine, and she's telling stories.

It is late autumn, 1953. Dwight Eisenhower is the president, peace negotiations on Korea are completed, and Joe McCarthy is yet one year ahead of his downfall. The gay history meter is running, and we're looking for signs of life. Let us drop in on our several friends, and meet some new ones.

Oh *damn*, Derek Archer was thinking as he put the phone down for the seventh time that evening. Johnny's still out.

Everything's gone to total *hell*, and Derek has run out of cigarettes because now that he has no servants he has to do it all himself and over the seven years of his contract he had accommodated himself to having forgotten the timing and logistics of laying in supplies.

Derek is desperate to talk to someone. He even called Tommy, that greedy little slug, but Tommy couldn't talk because "this big producer's assistant from . . . Columbia, I think? . . . but, anyway, so he's going to take his girl friend and me out dancing and I got to get ready."

I built my house of straw, Derek thought as he hung up. Damn Johnny to pieces! He doesn't work tonight, and he *told* me he wasn't seeing anyone.

The phone rang.

We're suave, Derek told himself. Collected. Sophisticated. Think: Ronald Colman.

"Derek, it's Jerrett Troy."

"Johnny, how fine to hear your voice. Hang on while I light up."

"Derek, don't sly me, because the tale's all over town."

"Twenty years old and such a know-it-all. The tale?"

"They canceled you, didn't they?"

"Well, of course, if you . . . It's . . . it's all over—"

"Want to come see me?"

"Oh, hell. They got me, didn't they? The *tale's* over the *town*. Well, it'll take me a bit. The chauffeur's really gone, finally. I've still got the car, but I can't quite master the gears and I bump into things every now and again."

"Never mind, Derek. I'll come to you."

"How?"

"I bought a used Studebaker. It's wonderful. I never realized what definition it gives your life to have your own wheels."

"Come quickly? And, do you think, could you *possibly* pick me up some cigarettes?"

"Now, there's the tone I like in you. That's the real Derek, a scared guy with feelings. How I respect you this way. You have no idea."

"Don't talk nonsense."

"I've got a tale for you, too. Some big news for me about New York. Though mine isn't industry gossip, unfortunately."

"Is it really . . . *Everyone* knows?"

"If I do, who doesn't? I'm not exactly a Hollywood insider."

"Well, they'll never hire me again, will they?" asked Derek, his voice breaking. "I'll have to live on that . . . *ridiculous* investment in that scabrous little *pizza parlor!*"

"Stay put. I'm on my way."

Griffith Park is the Planet Moon. It's the beyond and it's weightless. Lean over its edge, look down, that's the rest of the world parked way below. You, you're flying.

Up here is do what you like. Now, I like to fool the freeks. Get them to feel they know this Walt Disney boy in the spotless white T and the jeans so fresh they squeak. Friendly is the style, for I withhold not manna from them. I squeeze their shoulder or rub their back while they make their representations. Yeah, this friendly boy. Freek eyes go all sunny because they got an *easy* one this time. Sure, Pop. I'll be easy. See, I like to go Surprise! with the knife. Just the few seconds there when I flourish it and they note it, before anything else in the world happens, puts the two of us on the higher plane. I don't know how Pop is doing, but I get hard then, in anticipation of delight. It's a lovely moment. Transfixing, is what it is. But you have to do them quick, or the moment grows tawdry. Cloying. You grab that freek hair and yank back to expose the throat and slice across there straight and clean. I find it advisable to turn them slightly to the side and to cut from far to near. Otherwise they mess on you. Boy, I like the freek noise they make while I'm walking off, a jack-in-the-box springing naked on the Planet Moon and wailing.

"Come on, Lois, it was bound to happen!" said Larken, getting a bit annoyed. "Don't be so sensitive."

"He's a cheat, isn't he?"

The Kid, she means.

Larken shrugged. "He got a good offer and he took it."

"How am I supposed to keep this place together? Aren't we talking about a whole world here? This little world that we . . ." Lois made a defeated gesture. "What about loyalty?"

"Maybe it's a sign," said Elaine.

"Of *what?*"

"Don't bite my eyes out, but maybe Johnny goes and an era is over and everybody finds something else to be."

"Bullheap!"

"I knew she'd be understanding about it," Elaine told Larken.

They were in Thriller Jill's on a Sunday morning, waiting for the first auditioner to arrive: to replace the Kid. Word had gone out along the underground circuits of communication about this handsome, virile young man doing comedy and song in drag, and the Kid had gone on accepting so many out-of-town dates—San Francisco again, Las Vegas, Houston, Chicago, and now, apparently, New York—that Lois had told him to choose between a steady job at Jill's or freedom forever. The Kid took freedom, as the Kid congenitally must, and now Jill's had to find a new act. Larken, Lois felt, was just the man to help her do it.

"While we're at it," she said, "can we get rid of Jo-Jo and Desmond, too?"

"Why would you want to?" Larken replied. "Sure, Jo-Jo's a little bland, and Desmond is the worst pianist west of the Mississippi. But they're familiar figures by now. Welcoming, relaxing. Look, what have your customers spent all day doing? Placating the joes and hiding from them, right? Then they come here, to be among their own kind. The people they're used to and can trust, okay?"

"I can see that," Elaine put in.

"They want fuck," said Lois. "That's why they come."

"Lois," Elaine countered, "how many of them actually pair off each night?"

"Who cares a bushel?"

"I've been with you here till the wee hours time and again. And I can't say that all that many people go out as a couple."

"So what?"

"So that's not why Thriller Jill's is here," said Larken. "That's a side effect. The real reason is so we can take it easy and be what we are."

A noise at the door, and all three turned to find that the first auditioner had arrived: a measly-looking middle-aged man in a toupee.

"Oh, brother," said Lois.

The ad had asked for a "male singer, Broadway, swing, and Your Hit Parade. Youth, looks, and charm a must."

"My accompanist had to fill in as emergency shortstop in a father-son softball game," said the auditioner. "But if someone can handle 'Walking My Baby Back Home' in B-flat, we'll be all set."

Lois was looking at him as if sighting her first roach. "You don't know that number from *Oklahoma!,*" she asked, " 'Sappho Will Say We're in Love'?"

The auditioner looked confused. "Not in B-flat," he finally said.

" 'Youth, looks, and charm a must,' " Elaine quoted gently. "I placed the ad myself, I'm afraid."

"Yes. Ah. Though I was hoping you'd consider the looks and charm of the more seasoned artiste." He pulled some paper out of a briefcase. "As my résumé will attest, I was in the original revival touring company of *Nina Rosa.* Sigmund Romberg's masterpiece?"

Lois started toward him in battle trim, so Elaine quickly interposed herself. "Youth is essential for this job. A young man is the star of Thriller Jill's, and it seems that nothing ever will change that."

"I could throw the Kid into a cement mixer," said Lois. "Happily, I mean."

"It's evolution, Lois," said Larken. "Roll with the wave."

The auditioner stood staring at them for a moment, then snapped to. "Yes. Well. I appreciate your attention," he said politely, leaving his résumé on a table. "Just in case," he explained, backing out.

"There you have it," said Lois. "Thriller Jill's is over."

"Lois, it's ten twenty-two in the morning," said Elaine. "Who knows who will appear?"

Who appeared was, fundamentally, one buffoon after another. One of these was a near miss, a lively (or maybe nervous), strapping (if overly boyish) baritone who apparently sang nothing but operetta rousers.

Because he opened with "The Riff Song," and when Lois asked for something else, the guy—Hudson Something—sang "Your Land and My Land."

"Didn't we just hear that?" asked Lois, when he had finished. "Let's try something different."

So Hudson launched into "My Sword and I," and Lois stopped him after maybe fifteen seconds.

"Look," she said. "Something soft and tender?"

"How about a ballad?" said Larken, from the piano.

"Oh," said Hudson. And he sang the first ten seconds of "Every Lover Must Meet His Fate," from Victor Herbert's *Sweethearts,* whereupon Lois explained, *"Out!"*

"No, wait a minute," said Larken, jumping up. "I'm Larken and you've got a very nice voice, but you . . . you're kind of military. Do you know 'Lover, Come Back to Me' or 'Indian Love Call'?"

Lois cried out, "How about something from the Siegfried Romberg masterpiece *Nina Rosa*?"

"I'm sorry," said Hudson, stepping off the stage and marching out. "I'm not what you want."

"It's doom," Lois remarked to Elaine, as Larken ran after Hudson. "You see this?"

"We could pack it in, you know," Elaine replied. "Move on. Some new place we would love."

Larken was on the sidewalk by the time he caught up with Hudson.

"Don't be angry," Larken told him. "It's just that your repertory—"

"They always say that."

"Hudson, are you—forgive me for saying this, but I just broke up with my boy friend, so I'm acutely aware of . . . well, of the possibilities when someone kind of crosses my path and everything, so . . . I'm sorry, what was your last name?"

"Smelki."

"You don't want to change that?"

"Thank you for listening to me," said Hudson, turning away.

"Wait, Hudson!"

Hudson turned back.

"I mean . . . Don't get mad if you don't like this, all right? But I . . . Did you catch that last thing about my boy friend?"

"It's not my business."

"I know I'm way out of line here," said Larken. "But you're not unlike my boy friend, at least physically. And I . . . *Smelki?*"

"You want to date me, is that it?"

Suddenly self-protective, Larken hesitated.

"No, you do, don't you?" Hudson went on. "You're not one of the world's outstanding accompanists, but you're nice-looking and you thought—"

"I like your voice, to tell the truth," said Larken. "And I like you."

"If you like my voice, how come I don't get the job?"

"How come you only sing marches?"

Hudson looked surprised. "I sing . . . the operetta greats. It didn't do Nelson Eddy any harm."

"Nelson sang a love song every now and then. Or maybe it's your name."

"Is 'Nelson Eddy' such a great name?"

"Consider what it was when he started."

"Nelson Eddy was born with that name," said Hudson, with immense confidence.

"He was born Eddy and *then* named Nelson, yes. So the legend tells. But in the Metro vaults are documents proving that Nelson had changed his first name."

"From what?"

"Miriam."

Hudson didn't laugh.

"I'm not getting anywhere," said Larken. "Right?"

Hudson shifted his posture a bit, looked here and there. "You want to have dinner sometime?" he said.

"Yes."

Hudson kept looking around, and he said, "I don't handle auditions well. I'm the only one who thinks I'm great." Then he put his hand on Larken's arm and sort of smiled.

Larken exhaled. "You know, I really did like your voice."

"Thank you."

They did the usual exchange of the phone numbers, and Larken rambled back into the bar like a mooncalf to find Lois and Elaine talking to a young woman.

"I sing everything," she was telling them. "Old, new. Waltz, Latin. Hot, sweet. Torch, cheer-me-up. I'm a catalogue of song."

"Larken," said Elaine.

"Don't we only run male singers?"

"Yes, I saw the ad," the woman said. "But what do you want, gender or talent? I'm talent. Couldn't you at least hear me? I mean, what else is happening here, V-J Day?"

Lois nodded at Larken, Larken went to the piano, and the young woman sang. Slim, straight brown hair with Colleen Moore bangs, big eyes, full-bosomed, tight-waisted, great legs, weirdly cute face.

And she could sing. She could *really* sing.

She gave them a jazzy "Cuddle Up a Little Closer" and a comically frantic "Who?" and a magnificent "Bill," and Larken shot up from the keyboard and said, "Hire her."

Freeks run wild on the Planet Moon: I soothe them. They find my smile gratifying, my touch heartening. It is a rare thing in their lives, for they are obscene freeks, angry, anxious fat wavering losers you wouldn't throw your garbage out in. No one misses them when I put forth my hand and they are cut. Sometimes the newspapers sing a little song, but there it ends, and all are glad. I maketh the storm calm.

On the Planet Moon, I am one of a kind. I am the birthday boy at a party given by uncles. Yeah. I see other twenty-year-olds sometimes, right-looking fellows, and I wonder why they're here. Could they be cutters, like me, with all my reign and dominion? Here's this guy strolling along, full and tall like me, really put together. I like to follow a man like that and see what he's up to. He's walking around. Every time he passes under a lamplight you see how straight and strong he is. You would almost never cut a guy like that. Then he bumps into this other young fellow and they go into a surprise and laugh, because it seems they know each other.

"Jake!" said Frank.

"Hey, the boss," says Jake.

"Funny, right?"

"It's . . . different."

"How often," Frank muses, "do you run into someone you know here?"

"First for me."

Pause. Is something supposed to happen now?

"Well, okay," goes Frank, his body rearing to chug. "See you tomorrow."

"Sure thing."

Frank takes off down the path. Because of his days in Vice, he knows the park so well he could map it, and he decides to favor the culs-de-sac this afternoon. Larken says, "I don't see why the whole thing has to take place in the Black Forest." So what does he want instead? A dance hall! Two guys doing a fox-trot, right? Who'd lead?

Frank walks on, grinning inside himself about Jake, when he comes upon Something Deep. One of those outgoing blond guys, tall and bosomy. An overgrown Eagle Scout leaning against a tree, his eyes parked on Frank.

"Hey," says Frank.

"Hey, yourself."

"You look happy."

"I'm okay."

"What else?"

"Oh . . . a little hungry, maybe."

It's quirky how fast you invent patter, falling into this new world. "What are you hungry for?" says Frank, pulling his arms back in a body stretch to emphasize the gym chest.

"You tell me."

Odd answer.

"Just what do you like to do?" Frank asks.

"Whatever you like. Give me an idea what you got in mind."

Frank looks at the guy. Something's not working.

"You want to do me?" the guy asks.

Frank just looks at him.

"You want to blow my tool?" the guy asks.

"No."

"*No?* How come?"

"You're a cop," says Frank.

"No kidding," says the guy, his expression now changed to disgust.

"I just left the force. I worked Vice, too."

"So what are you doing *here?*"

"Force of habit?" Frank joked.

"Jonesy!" the guy calls out. "My partner," he tells Frank.

Fat Jonesy looms up from the usual nowhere.

"Hook 'em up," says the blond.

"Pleasure," says Jonesy, coming forward.

"Hey, look," says Frank, backing away. "I'm a cop. I know the drill. You don't have anything on me."

"We'll have cuffs on you for starters."

"Fairies in the park!" a high-pitched voice chants from somewhere deep in the trees. "Fairies in the park!"

Frank, still backing off, says, "This is false arrest. You'll never make it stick."

"Don't give me lip, asshole," says Jonesy, having a spot of trouble freeing the cuffs and starting to breathe hard at the exertion. He is really obese, well past the weight limit set by the L.A.P.D.

"You're not a cop," says Frank, as the high-pitched voice sails out from the distance again. "You're a fat horror."

"Fairies in the park! All the cops are fairies!"

"Hey, *fuck you,* somebody," the blond shouts.

"Jonesy," says Frank, "you're letting your partner steer you into a bad—"

Everybody ducks as a good-sized rock thunks against a tree about three inches from the blond's head.

"*Shit!*"

"Blond cops are fairy cops! Fairy cops hate fairies!"

A second voice chimes in with "Who's the fairy *now,* cops?" and both join in for a chorus of this, over and over.

"That's it!" the blond cries, stalking off toward the singing.

Jonesy has the cuffs out at last, but Frank backs around behind a tree, timing it to the blond's passage: Four seconds more, three . . . and as the blond disappears from sight, Frank suckers Jonesy with a right feint and a hard slam with the left. Frank grabs Jonesy's baton and gives him a good one for luck, throws the guy's gun into the trees, and runs. He's in his car, he's on the road, he's at Larken's door—it's twenty minutes later but in his mind he's still running—and he's banging on that door like a refugee.

When the door opened, Frank leaped inside and grabbed on, saying, "Hold me, just hold me."

"Who are you? Un*hand* me!"

Frank took a look. It wasn't Larken.

"Lark?" Frank called out.

The toilet flushed and Larken appeared. "Frank!"

"Who *is* this, Larky?" the stranger asked.

" 'Larky'? *I* invented that," said Frank.

Smiling nervously, Larken said, "If you'd kept up with me the way you promised, you'd know what's going on in my—"

"We're on the phone all the time!"

"About the *business.* Then you always jump off."

"So this is Frank," said the stranger. "I'm Hudson."

"What the fuck kind of name is that?" said Frank, trying to look taller.

"Wait till you hear the rest of it," said Larken. "Hudson's my new boy friend. Would everyone please sit down?"

"Boy, you moved fast," said Frank.

"What was I supposed to do, take the veil? At least he looks like you."

"Not that much," said Hudson.

"You mean," said Frank, "I get *replaced*?"

"Complimented is how I'd put it."

"I thought you were just going to . . . be here," said Frank. "That was dumb of me. And selfish." Frank sat on the couch, then jumped up, pulling a wet towel up after him. "Damn it, Lark! You've always got something in the wrong place here!"

"I've been meaning to mention that," Hudson began—but Frank was already through the door—for he had thought of something he had needed to do for a long time, and had best do it now.

His father. Frank was thinking about the two cops, reckoning that only the most vindictive man would try to seek him out through the precincts of L.A., even assuming that he bought Frank's story. The blond seemed like the kind who gets really dedicated to his personal causes, okay; but it was Jonesy whom Frank flattened and disarmed. Taking a cop's weapon is about the worst thing you could do to him short of castration. Okay, it *is* castration. But Jonesy looked too fat to pursue it.

Still, if it came to looking through the precincts for Frank, it would help to have his father in on it. No one has ever figured out how a false arrest against a resisting arrest is supposed to play if the guy who's getting arrested is a cop himself . . . *was* . . . but it was dollars to donuts that any Chief would throw it out on the spot. Cops just don't lock up cops.

When Frank moved into his apartment in West Hollywood, he formally returned to his father the key to the house he had grown up in. Now, on Frank's visits, his father had to let him in.

"*Rootie Kazootie*'s on," said his father at the door.

"Oh yeah?"

"Poison Zoomack's trying to steal Polka Dottie's polka dots," his father went on, the way you'd say, "Eisenhower's telling that egghead Stevenson where to get off."

Visiting Frank's father nowadays meant plonking down in the den and waiting till he tired of the doings on the tiny television and finally started talking. Visits also meant not commenting on the slovenly way Frank's father was dressing now, or on the booze he lapped up straight out of the bottle.

"Dad," said Frank once *Rootie Kazootie* had ended, "we have to talk, okay?"

"That's my boy, Frank," said his father, rubbing Frank's shoulder. "Next is cartoons."

"Dad, we just saw cartoons."

The bottle again. "That was puppets."

Frank got up and turned off the television.

"Dad, I want to talk to you. I'm in trouble."

"You'll work it out, Frank. No male of the Hubbard name has ever failed to square up."

"I brained a cop, I ran from an arrest, and I fuck men up the ass."

"Not in uniform, I hope, Frank?"

"Dad, look at me, will you? I got into trouble in Griffith Park this afternoon. I may need your help, and I need you to listen to me just once in your whole life, will you, please?"

Frank's father stopped drinking and looked at Frank.

"Will you?"

Another swig out of the bottle.

"Yeah, keep drinking," said Frank, "and don't listen."

"I always enjoy having you over here, son."

"Do you know what a homosexual is, Dad?"

"Sure. Your Uncle Felix."

"Huh?"

"Sang on the radio. You recall. 'Softly Within the Morning Sunrise' and such. High notes, like opera. Of course, we didn't call it 'homosexual.' We called it 'faggot,' or 'fairy.' We'd say a guy like that is some fucking worthless fairy brown-ass and he deserves the worst he got. He'd get it, too, most often."

"There was someone calling out stuff like that today," Frank mused. "About fairies in the park, and the fairies are coming."

"They're always somewhere."

Big swig this time. *Real* big taste of the whiskey.

"They're sitting next to you, Dad. They're in your house."

"Yeah," said Frank's father, wiping his mouth, wiping it all away.

"Mother's dead and I'm a fairy and you're watching cartoon shows. That's your life."

"Right, Frank."

"I can't figure out what reason anyone had for shouting in the park when I was about to be arrested. I'd have been all hooked up and down at the station being booked but for that. It was another bad arrest, too. Just like . . . Dad, do you realize how many major things happen by accident? I mean, even if it looks as if they were interconnected, they're just a series of mistakes. They're just . . ."

Frank's father was looking right at Frank, but Frank got up and switched the television back on.

"Thanks for your help, Dad," said Frank, on his way out.

"She was a saint, just remember that. A fucking *saint,* bless her immortal memory."

The Kid called Derek Archer long-distance from New York, where the act had had a great success. Derek was not doing so well. He was drinking, and kept babbling about someone killed in Griffith Park, his throat slashed, so terrible, another homo going out the way they all go out.

The Kid said, "Derek, what do you mean *they* all go out? Who do you think *you* are?"

"Oh, don't, *don't* chastise me," Derek answered. "I'm falling apart."

"Derek, you're drunk."

"A bit . . . something like . . ."

"Damn. You won't hear a word I say now. Do they at least have a suspect in this park murder?"

"Police baffled, citizenry apprehensive."

"It was probably the police who killed him."

"Johnny, really!"

"Derek, have you ever been stopped by a cop? Do you have any idea what kind of power they wield?"

". . . Johnny boy . . ."

"You're sloshed."

"I want to go out. I want to visit the Y."

"If that's what you want," said the Kid, "do it."

"No, Johnny."

"Don't play games."

"The guy in the park, Johnny. The police call it pure robbery, but it was the gay section of—"

"I've got to go, Derek. Anything I should bring you from New York?"

"Some spotlight," Derek cried.

He really was drunk. He staggered around his apartment, wondering and singing. Gesturing. Dramatizing. Head bobbing and knees sinking.

He's considering, What have I to lose? When I had a career and an income and property, I had something to protect. I had a *name*.

Fumbling with his 78s, Derek upends an album, and a few discs fall onto the floor. Swaying, he stares at them. They don't seem to be damaged, but he can't quite reach them. They keep slithering away and giggling. Derek wanted to play Doris Day's "Papa, Won't You Dance With Me?" but maybe this isn't even the right album.

When Derek's agent bid him farewell, he assured him that Derek would always find *some* work. "It may not be a lead, or Metro, or even anything you'll be proud of," the agent said. "But you won't starve."

That's *good* to know, Derek thinks, fussing with the records. I won't go hungry—except for the perilous clarity of the Beauty Palace known as the Y.M.C.A. Oh, why do they build places like that if not to delight the eye and savage one's resistance? I have so tried—so and so and so and *so* very much tried—to free myself of this humiliating need. I have sat around a Saturday-afternoon pool rampant with handsome boys; and I played it so smooth, scarcely looking. I have watched colleagues pressure toothsome and impressionable newcomers into bed for a role, a test, even a *single word of dialogue* in a mob scene; and I knew that was wrong and never tried it myself.

But I cannot stand back from the Beauty Palace when my life is caving in. There is no reason to save myself now.

The phone rang, and Derek made a helpless sign with his left hand. Ridiculous. Nobody makes calls to a loser in *this* town.

The phone kept ringing, so Derek made his way to it, crunching a few records as he passed.

"Yes?"

"Derek, it's Johnny again. You'd better talk to me and stop drinking so much."

"Johnny. You're so kind to call me back. So kind."

"Cut it out, Derek. Sober up."

"I can't find the music I need. The Doris Day—"

"Damn you, Derek!"

"—a Columbia red label . . ."

Derek grabbed at another album, and all twelve 78s tumbled onto the floor.

"Derek, listen to me. *Derek!*"

"Yes, Johnny."

"You're supposed to be the father figure, and here I am taking care of you!"

"Such a fine boy, my Johnny. The only one who became my friend. You like me even when I can't give you . . . I can't . . ."

"This is hopeless. Look. I'll be back there in four weeks. Don't do anything foolish while I'm gone."

". . . never foolish, Johnny . . ."

"Derek, will you *please!* We can get you into shape again, if you'll—"

"Johnny, won't you dance with me," Derek sang. "Please dance with me—"

"Derek, you birdbrain!"

"Oh, dance with—"

"Get a pencil or something. Hear me? Do it now!"

"Johnny—"

"Get a pencil!"

About a minute of bumping and falling noises followed, then the Kid heard Derek's voice again.

"Okay," said the Kid. "Now write—and do it neatly, so you can read it tomorrow when you're back among the living. Write 'What do I want from life? What are my priorities? Is it work? Is it love? Is it fantasy?' "

"... 'What do I ...' "

"Derek, you asshole! You're going to break the rules and throw it all away!"

"... 'You're going to break the ...' Johnny boy?"

The Kid had hung up.

By now it's New Year's Eve, heading into 1953, and Larken has invited everyone he knows to Thriller Jill's to see the new act. There have been a few problems. First, the new girl singer objected to Desmond, the deaf pianist. (Lois said, "It'll be Desmond, or Larry the bartender on that stupid harmonica," and Larry, cleaning up at the bar, called out, "Any time, Lo.") Second, Larken told Lois he needed a backdrop of fir trees with snowy branches so the audience could believe in the *Nutcracker* effect he was going for. (Lois said, "I can get that nutcracking effect without a backdrop; and Elaine said, "Lois!," in a merry warning manner; and both Larken and Lois shrugged.) Last, part of the stage collapsed. ("Cancel the future," said Lois, as everybody raced around.)

Maybe there should be a few problems: for then you will appreciate the results all the more. You have to earn your title.

So the show goes on. Larken is there with Hudson, but Frank has brought some guy, too. They're all at one table, and Frank is trying to figure out how this is supposed to work, with all these rivals within punching distance.

Aw hell, be nice about it, he thinks.

The lights are dimming.

"I staged this whole thing," Larken whispered, "and I helped choose the songs, and I ... This act is my baby." Hudson darted an admiring look just as Frank did, but Larken was beaming at the stage, rapt, gone into the art, as the singer walked out in simple black, leaned against the piano, and broke into "Sam and Delilah." It was Larken's re-creation of the moment in the Gershwin musical *Girl Crazy* when Ethel Merman became a star.

"It was splendid, Lois," said Elaine, later that night. "It was renewal."

"I could dump the club," Lois told her. This was something she had been thinking about for a while now. "We could move on."

"To another club?"

"Another place, I mean."

"Good heavens."

"Would it scare you to leave Los Angeles?" Lois pronounced her hometown's name with the hard *g* that, even as late as the early 1950s, marked descendants of the immigrants who settled the area in the century's first decade. Elaine thought it sexy, a kind of symbol of what Lois was, set in her ways yet wild, unlike.

"I'm not sure about starting all over somewhere," Lois went on, "seeing as how I got it all set up locally already. But see what it says in the article here." Lois passed the *Reader's Digest* to Elaine, indicating a line with her thumb. "Yeah, right there. Read it up."

"You mean, read it aloud?" said Elaine, putting down her novel, Nancy Mitford's *Love in a Cold Climate*.

"Yeah."

" 'Studies indicate that Lois Rybacher has scored a hundred percent on her sexitivity test, tracing the electromagnetic emendations from her lips, muff, nipples—' "

"Tell what it *really* is!"

"When I tell what something really is, people become upset at me. All my life, Veronica."

"Look, just read it, huh?" Lois snorted. *"Veronica."*

They were in bed, late, as usual getting in their culture after the mild storm and intense sunshine of their lovemaking. Married straight couples do this, too, I understand, with matching lamps at each side of the bed. Or sometimes the male dozes while the woman reads. Frank and Larken, when they lived together, tended to cap their day with the sex alone, exhausting themselves till, panting, one or the other doused the light. Then they would reach for each other, stretch out, and sleep.

Lois and Elaine, however, observed what we might call a neutral period between lovemaking and rest. An intellectual period. Sometimes Elaine launched it by slipping into the shower, and sometimes Lois came along. "Boy, what I can do with a soap," Lois would announce in her low-key yet intent Lois way; and sometimes Elaine said something like "Oo, I can't wait," and sometimes she was silent.

The article Lois had handed to Elaine to read from was "Moving Saved My Life," by someone who claimed to have redeemed himself by moving first from one part of town to another, then out of state, then by kicking off all traces and heading for the metropolis of Evanston, Illinois. Elaine gave a relatively somber account of the indicated passage, then, more warmly, told Lois, "I've always wanted to see Evanston. The lights! The people! The Jell-O with bits of fruit inside!"

"Okay, make fun."

"Keep your Paris Opéra, your Prado," Elaine went on, "when I can applaud the sandwich makers at the Evanston Fourth Street Diner."

Lois shook her head. "Lady of the wisecracks. It doesn't have to be Illinois, does it? The *Reader's Digest* knows *something,* or they wouldn't print it, and they're saying that a change of scene perks you up."

"Does crabby Lois need perking, hmm?"

"I *hate* that baby stuff. But, yes, I am ready to pack it in with Thriller Jill's. Singers and acts and New Year's parties. Even the stage is coming apart! I could sell the place and be free."

"I thought you just managed the club. You *own* it?"

"Sure. My parents left it to me."

"Veronica!"

"Lois to you, Miss Fancy."

"Your *parents* owned a nightclub?"

"It was an eatery when they opened it. Italian-style, because spaghetti was a real craze then. Christ, all those movie people coming in from all over the country! Raised on beans and eggs and cheese sandwiches. Suddenly, pow!, Italian food, and they were babies in my parents' arms."

"But you're not Italian."

Lois shrugged. "You figure out a need and you fill it. That's the rule. And that was them and now it's me. I could sell it. What do you say?"

"Wait. Where were you in all this? The toddler running under the tables and crawling under everyone's legs? The little darling?"

"Oh . . . something like that." Lois was grinning.

"But then what? After the restaurant, before you opened Thriller Jill's. Where were you then?"

"Teaching second grade."

"Surely not."

"What do you know about it, Miss Smarty?"

"You were a grammar-school teacher?"

"I told you, I like kids. Now—"

"I'm trying to see this. Miss Rybacher leads the class in the Pledge of Allegiance . . ."

"What do you say to New York? We throw it all behind us and light out. Have an adventure."

"What will we do?"

"Open another club, maybe." Lois shrugged. "It's what I know, at least."

"So," said Elaine. "There is no Thriller Jill per se?"

"Nope. Just Hazel and Mike."

"Your parents?"

Lois nodded.

"Nice ones?" Elaine asked.

"Did the job" is all Lois would say.

"Where does the name Thriller Jill come from, then?"

Lois laughed. "Named it after a dildo some sly Frisco lizzy tried to use on me in 1944 or so."

"A *dildo*?"

Elaine looked at her. "Haven't I mentioned that ever? A rubber dick. You strap it on and—"

"Sheer terror!"

Lois chuckled. "It doesn't get used much. Women have such a . . . what? A graceful . . . construction . . . down there. I mean, why spoil it with this vile thing bobbing around? What do you want to bet some man invented it? They're the ones who are so fascinated with dicks."

"They're not the only ones, Veronica."

"Look, I'm not Veronica."

"And I'm not Elaine. They named me Joan. But so what? A name is like an address. You change it."

"Then how do you feel about moving?"

"Very ready, I expect. Because everything about L.A. is what I was. Every street leads to my former lives. New York . . . New York would be transformation, a rehabilitation of my genre."

Lois gave her a funny look.

"Poetry," said Elaine.

"If I sell Thriller Jill's," Lois reasoned, "it could easily go off the Other Side. The guys will have other places to go, but not as nice. You see what I mean?"

Elaine nodded.

"Can I let them down? is what I'm asking."

Elaine replied, "Look at it so: You started them off, gave them the model. They can copy it, can't they? It's not your job to be the Statue of Liberty forever."

"Larken could start a new place up . . . or Jo-Jo . . ."

"How do *you* feel about New York?"

"Curious, I guess. Except I hear you can't run a car there."

"How ever do they get around?" Elaine wondered.

"They don't have to. It's all right there, in the center. You walk to everything."

"It sounds like Evanston."

They've been up for so long that Lois is moved to have some more of Elaine, a little coda to the symphony earlier. She sucks on Elaine's nipples, which always drives Elaine wild, because Lois is very determined and takes her time. Then they hold a pussy-tasting contest, and it's a draw, and the light goes out, and they sleep. Lois dreams about cities with boats instead of cars, and Elaine dreams that men are fucking her with dildos.

Derek Archer checks into the Y and heads for the showers, because he has nothing to lose now. The place looks hot tonight, and Derek is handsome and trim and barely thirty-two. Everything is going to belong to him.

Oh, I am a roving man, and find the Planet Moon anywhere. Tenderly I take out the book of confession for the Midnight Queer to sign. I will find him in the showers, and bring him to my room for a chat. Some hot-blooded freek, you'll see. Surely I have known the blood of freeks, for I have caused it to flow.

Derek made contact quickly, which disappointed him. He liked to shop at first, lose himself in the scene. His partner was a sailor who said, "I need to score a ten off you, Mister." Derek offered him five and the sailor said okay, but he isn't going to do a heck of a lot for five.

Frank closed his door as the guy left. Some guy he picked up cruising Hollywood Boulevard. The sex was okay, but Frank missed Larken. Missed talking to him.

Lois took four books out of the library, all on New York. While Elaine wrote stories, Lois studied. Occasionally she would read a passage aloud and Elaine would smile.

Derek waited three days, then slipped into the Y again. Walking into the showers, he found two nondescript, oblivious strangers and Griffin Finlay, one of the outlaws from Derek's loan-out western. Except for the tiniest start when he spotted Derek, Finlay played it cool till the two other men left. Dripping like some torpid walrus and rubbing himself all over with the most irritating pleasure, Finlay came up to Derek with an ironic smile. Derek hated that look.

"Well! And here we thought you had too much class for this place, Archer. You're coming down in the world."

"Research for my next picture."

"Oh? What picture is that, I wonder?"

Finlay's one of those big hairy numbers that some people mysteriously find attractive. Derek thinks of them as great horrid dogs.

"It's a detective thriller," said Derek, turning off the water and going for his towel. Finlay followed him. "Very *Lower Depths*. Everyone's either a creep or a pervert. I should probably interview you to authenticate my characterization."

"It's a date," said Finlay, strolling off, unperturbed. "I'll meet you on the unemployment line."

Jill's new singer walked in with her own pianist and promised to quit if they didn't replace Desmond.

Lois and Elaine shared a look.

Jo-Jo said, "We're family in this club. We don't go around replacing each other."

"Nevertheless," said the singer, as Desmond looked dismayed and the singer's accompanist loitered in a blasé manner.

"California," Lois murmured, "here I go."

Frank's father, on his way to the kitchen in the splendor of his cups, takes a shortcut down the stairs—ass over teakettle—and is put into traction. Frank visits in the hospital, and, after the salutations, the two of them have not a word to share between them.

The Showers Moon is hopping tonight. Freeks are everywhere. I like the furtive ones. They think they know a secret about you. Yeah. I'll be opening the book of confession tonight, and some geezer will sign in, drooling.

The guy at the shower next to mine is staring.

I tell him, "Relax."

He says, "You're so green and incomplete. I could help you."

I tell him, "I don't need any help. I do it all myself."

He's young and smart-looking. He would be nice to talk to. I can go to work later.

Derek finds it charming that the young man doesn't towel off before they visit Derek's room, just picks up the neatly folded terry cloth and carefully wipes himself here and there. He's a shy youth, Derek's favorite kind.

Derek's room is early-middle Spartan: brass bed, wooden table and chair. The boy sits on the bed, his towel, still folded, next to him. Derek, towel around his middle, sits at the chair and lights a cigarette. They sit in silence, Derek smoking, smiling.

The boy asks, "Are you an actor?"

Startled, Derek says, "Why? I mean, what—"

"The way you do that. The match and your legs crossed. It's like on a stage."

"I just made a western for Paramount."

"A *movie* actor. That's great."

"Yes, I cleaned up a lawless town."

"How'd you do it?"

"Well, I . . . I got all the black hats together in a room and sucked them off, one after the other, and with such thorough *pull* that there was nothing left inside them. They became harmless zombies."

The boy is silent.

Derek laughs. "Let's talk about you, shall we? What sports do you like?"

The boy cocks his head as if conferring with distant voices.

"You have a beautiful body," Derek observes. "Such white, white skin."

Their voices are low in the room. Traffic noise drifts up from the street. Two men laugh as they pass in the hall.

"I thought you were different," the boy says.

"From . . . what?"

"We were going to talk for a while. Friendly talk, like brothers, or strangers. Now you seem like a freek."

"Oh, I'm a freak all right," Derek agrees, killing the cigarette.

The boy gets up and approaches Derek, taking his towel along. He is hard, brazen, pensive. He places the towel on the table and stands behind Derek, rubbing his shoulders.

"Do you like that?" the boy asks.

"Oh, yes."

"Stand up, please, sir."

As Derek rises, the boy gently unfastens Derek's towel and lets it fall. The boy's outstretched cock nudges Derek from behind, and Derek arches his back, moaning, as the boy holds him.

I didn't mean it to be him, but he opened up the book and wrote his name there without I even asked him to, and he was going all dippy while I sizzled him up, the way they all do. He was just another Midnight Queer, and I took my time. Got him rubbing his cheek against my palm while I eased the knife out of the towel. It was all so smooth that I didn't pull his hair back, and I cut real light along the throat so he would flop around all quick and creepy-like.

Derek made a larger headline than the man in Griffith Park had; but again the police had no leads and no suspects. The funeral, held at the graveside, was as sparsely attended as Derek's last pictures: a sister and brother-in-law and two men whom the Kid took for reporters, though they asked no questions of anyone. The sole other mortal on hand, besides the gravediggers, was the rabbi.

Derek, the Kid was thinking, you tricky devil.

Derek had never mentioned his family, and the Kid had long assumed that Derek was one of those who had none. I'm like that, the Kid thought. Self-contained and born out of me.

The rabbi had a supply of little white caps for the men to wear. (The reporters declined.) Then, after intoning the traditional prayer for the dead, the rabbi signaled to Derek's kin, and they each took a bit of the earth heaped up at the grave and tossed it onto the coffin. When the Kid moved to share in this ceremony, the rabbi gently waved him back.

"I was more his family than any of you guys," the Kid told them, taking an ample helping of dirt and letting it dribble into the grave as slowly as possible.

He was crying.

Lois had no trouble unloading Thriller Jill's, because the L.A. club scene was on the boom and there were plenty of offers. She did try to isolate a buyer who would keep Jill's the way it was, or at least a place welcome to those on the Other Side. But everyone had plans to make it over.

"They aren't landlords," Lois observed. "They're entrepreneurs. They want to do something personal with the place."

She shrugged, and the rest of them tried to look philosophical—Elaine, Larken, Jo-Jo, Desmond, the bartenders, and a very few regulars, who had gathered for a spaghetti dinner and closing party on Lois's final night as the Mistress of Thriller Jill's.

"I always thought the place was personal as it was," said Desmond. "Especially with our wonderful new singer."

"She wanted me to fire you."

"Great artists are always difficult," Desmond replied, extending his hands to add, What can you do?

"She *was* good, Lois," said Larken. "In a way, she was more appropriate here even than Johnny."

Lois snorted.

"The customers loved her," said Jo-Jo. "They shut up when she came out, and they never did that for Johnny."

"They wanted other things from Johnny, okay?" said Larken.

"You know," Lois told Larken, "you're getting to sound like that cop boy friend of yours."

"Ex–boy friend."

"Oh, I forgot about Smelton."

"*Hudson.* He's my *current* ex–boy friend."

"You broke up?"

"Well . . . I have a kind of closing announcement to make, too. I'm moving to San Francisco."

"*What?*"

"Larken!"

"Hey, that's—"

"Congratulations, boy!"

They were crowding around him, beaming, forgetting the loss of their clubhouse for a moment, and Larken thought, I guess they always liked me.

"So how come?" said Jo-Jo.

"It was Johnny, really. I helped him put an act together, and when—"

"The Kid actually *collaborated* on something?"

"Well, it's hard to direct your own show. You need someone to look it over, tell you where it plays and where it goes off, so you're free to dive down into the *performance* part of it. Anyway, they held him over at the Trocadero, you know—"

"So he's really good?" Lois asked. "Not just Thriller Jill's good, but the whole world good?"

"He'll take some getting used to, but yes, he is that good. Smart, too. He was such a hit he became the thing to see, and he wanted fresh material so when people came back and brought their friends they'd feel they got their money's worth. So Johnny needed new stuff and a co-director in a hurry, and I went up there and . . . I liked it." Larken smiled. "It's so surprising all the time—the streets going up and down . . . and the weather can change from one neighborhood to another. And this incredible thing. You're walking along, and you turn a corner, and there's beautiful water in front of you. Not on the beach, like Malibu—right there, in the city!"

"What's the big deal?" said Lois. "Didn't you have views of Salt Lake when you were growing up?"

"Oh, Salt Lake City isn't on the water. It's seventeen miles away. Didn't you know that?"

"It must be one of the better-kept secrets," said Lois dryly.

"Well, anyway," Larken concluded. "I'm moving for my life."

They gave him three cheers, and Desmond, at the piano, tried (and failed) to pick out "For He's a Jolly Good Fellow" by ear; so everyone sang it instead as Jo-Jo hammered out the rhythm with forks on glasses.

"Everybody's so nice and everything," said Larken. "Now I'm sorry to leave."

"Speech! Speech!"

"No. No . . . speech. It's just that I think people like . . . well, like *us* need a city to get things done in. We're special people. Sophisticated and knowledgeable. Seeing San Francisco, I realized that I've been living in big small towns all my life. What have I been here, I mean? A fired waiter and a fired store clerk, then a mover—and that only because my boy friend started the business. Now I've got a job as producer of acts for the Troc. Okay, it's only part-time. But it's a start, right?"

"And this," said Jo-Jo, raising a glass and urging the others to join him, "is an end. I don't know about you, but for me this closes an era. I know everyone's got other work lined up. Except Desmond, of course."

One of the bartenders cried, "Hooray for Desmond!," and Desmond, blushing, said, "I can always go back to the A & P."

"Where you have been sorely missed, I feel almost certain," said Jo-Jo. "But we will be sorry to lose our two bosses, Lois Rybacher and Elaine Denslow, to the Emerald City of the East, where we wish them health and prosperity forever. To the girls!"

"To the girls!" came the answering salute as they all drank. Then it was *"To Larken!"* and *"To Jo-Jo!"* and even *"To Desmond!,"* who got so drunk by the end of it that Jo-Jo had to drive him home.

Frank insisted on buying Larken out of the business, though Larken only agreed to take it in I.O.U.s. "That way," he said, "you'll have to stay in touch." Together, they loaded a van to haul Larken to San Francisco, the first time Move For Your Life had ventured north of Santa Barbara.

They decided to take it easy and enjoy the drive, making plenty of rest stops and investigating curious places, such as—for Larken had always wanted to see it—William Randolph Hearst's castle at San Simeon, opened to the public since his death two years earlier.

It was one of the happiest days in Larken's life, possibly the longest time he had ever spent in Frank's company, with no Todd, no gym, no law enforcement, no Frank's family to distract Frank. At one point, just north of Watsonville, Frank said, "How come you and I never run out of things to talk about?"

"What do you mean?"

"Other people, after a few hours they've gone through everything they have to say, so the rest is fadiddle. I ought to know, logging all those hours in black-and-whites, okay? But you and me, pal . . . I don't know, it's as if we could keep going forever."

"I wish we could—just ride the highway and never have to get there."

"Yeah, but, I'll tell you, I'm pretty pooped."

Nevertheless, when they got to Larken's new place on Polk Street they immediately began unloading, and by one A.M. they were finished, halfing a bottle of beer and doing an Alphonse-Gaston routine over who would shower first. Finally, Frank took Larken into the bathroom, and they played around in the water and kissed and got hot, so they ended up making love all night, and now they were very confused: because have they broken up or not?

This is what Larken would have said if he could have been in grasp of all the contours of his thoughts:

I am one of the people with the knack, or the skill, or the luck, that enables me to pair off infinitely. As soon as one romance ends, I happen upon another. And I don't choose badly. This may be the result of my origins, among a brood without family. Foundlings, orphans, and foster kids learn to recognize certain qualities in people—tolerance, patience, and above all forgiveness. Whatever the reason, I know that I can go on mating up, but I only want you. I know that the sex went from satisfactory to perfunctory pretty soon, because you're accomplished and driving and I'm not. And I know that we can't couple up if we're not sexually attuned. But I also know that I am going to be in love with you for the rest of my life. That's a definite. Because of those qualities you have, that I recognized. I recognized them from the first moment, way back in Griffith Park, when I talked to you on that bench and then you arrested me. And I hereby forgive in advance every hasty or inadvertent offense you make, because I know that, at rock bottom, you respect me and enjoy my company and like to hear me talk. What more can a man give another man on this green God earth?

This is what Frank, free of his armor, would have said in reply:

I love you back, but how come I can only get off with other men? When you're away, I want you around; but when I'm hot, I need some new guy. How could we live together, with me always hunting a catch and you feeling left out?

LARKEN: I guess it would be strange, living together asexually. It would be like your parents.

FRANK: Don't bring them into this.

LARKEN: Okay, that's fair.

FRANK: I'm afraid to leave San Francisco, you know that? Because this means you're out of my life.

LARKEN: If I thought I could, I'd drag you up here with me.

FRANK: Leaving L.A. would be admitting that I've failed.

LARKEN: At what?

FRANK: At living up to my [father's] expectations. Keeping the dog off the quicksand.

LARKEN: Frank, whatever happens, please, please keep me in on it. Remember, we were going to be this great historic couple.

FRANK: Speaking of that, what happened to your Meetings?

LARKEN: Oh, they broke up when Jake was arrested. They convicted him, too.

FRANK: Shit.

LARKEN: Yeah.

FRANK: So, tomorrow morning, I'll just get up and . . . get out?

LARKEN: And we'll be hesitating in the doorway, and trying not to be solemn. . . .

FRANK: I really do love you, Larky.

LARKEN: I know that much.

FRANK: I love you because you don't judge me. You accept me.

LARKEN: I delight in you, actually. Except when you were mean about how sloppy I am.

FRANK: I'm sorry, Lark.

LARKEN: That's why I love you. When an issue comes up, you don't defend yourself no matter how wrong you may be, the way most people do. You don't attack. You soften.

FRANK: Keep in touch, Larken. Promise?

What they did in fact say to each other that night was a jumble of some of these and other ideas in tones as supportive as they were ambivalent. Unfortunately, the two were unable to see that they should stay together not as lovers but as best friends. That didn't sound like a couple to them: but we were hoping that they would invent a new kind of couple—"a different kind of loving," as Frank once phrased it. Apparently, they didn't see that they had invention in their power.

It's funny. The main thing in Frank's life when Larken was around was cruising. Now the main thing in Frank's life was his phone calls to Larken in San Francisco—every one of them answered, Frank might have grumbled, by some lunkhead boy friend. Obviously, Larken had expounded upon the wonders of Frank to them, and they were jealous, suspicious, reluctant to call Larken to the phone and expose him to more of the man they couldn't be. Once, one of them announced that Larken was napping and mustn't be disturbed.

"Just get him," said Frank.

"I certainly will not. We all need our beauty sleep."

"Oh, fuck you, you girly twit," said Frank as he hung up, wondering where on earth he had picked up that phrase. It sounded British—maybe he'd fucked an Englishman somewhere.

Frank's father died, and Frank thought, Okay, right: because it turned out that, indeed, parents are not sacred beings. They can alienate you—particularly if you undergo some major change in style that causes you to consider the world rather than simply inhabit it.

.   .   .

In late 1955, a rival moving firm jolted Frank with an immensely hand-some offer for Move For Your Life—far less for its equipment than for its name and its boss. "We want you with us," they told Frank, "not against us." Never in his life had Frank had enough money to feel truly free, so he jumped at the deal, not realizing that absolute autonomy lay at the center of his freedom. As an employee, Frank became disaffected and difficult. His co-workers began to refer to him, sarcastically, as "Charm boy." There was an incident, directly followed by one of those moments in which one quits and is fired simultaneously.

But Frank had a bank account, so he tried eating of the lotus for a while. He spent more time in the gym—three or four hours a day, till many in the weight room mistook him for staff. He bought a television. He moved across town. He dated women. He was restless, experimenting but not expanding. When he ran into his former partner John Luke at the movies, John said, "Frank, you were one good hell of a cop. What are you doing off the force?"

There was John and his wife and their two little girls kind of hanging on to their mother, the four of them dressed up as if a movie show were some sort of treat. And there was Frank in his jeans and sweatshirt, because why dress up for a movie, right?

Still, he felt odd in some incomprehensible way.

He thought, then, of moving to San Francisco, of starting over, maybe reorganizing a hauling outfit with Larken. But there was an air of surren-der about that, of looking needy. Moving was a good idea, maybe. Los Angeles had kind of dried up for Frank: Like many a gay man and woman, he had become too rich for the place he was accustomed to.

Yet he continued to float, ham-and-egging his way through the days on odd jobs. A Hollywood agent discovered him—in southern California this happens to somebody every twenty seconds—and for a while Frank pur-sued a movie career, putting out for extra work here and a bit there. Sex-for-casting turned Frank on, especially since it mostly boiled down to Frank doing a performance with himself. It seemed that he liked showing off. Still, these ventures never came together into a career, somehow. In 1957, a certain amount of highly committed greenroom fucking landed him a job as a sailor in *South Pacific*—no lines, but what they call "good screen placement." That led to nothing. Two years later, acting on a tip, Frank reamed and wanked his way through eight people to get to a well-placed producer, who told him, "The show business can't use you—you're too big all over."

Frank floated some more, gymmed, cruised, voted for J.F.K. in memory of his father, who would have wanted it so, and wondered what else there might be in the world for Frank.

One night, for fun, Frank packed a bag. What belonged in it, besides his elemental wardrobe of jeans, T's, and gym shorts?

Look around the room: Nothing belongs. None of this is necessary. Freedom has a catch, then—you lose your ties.

The bag of clothes sat, packed, in Frank's living room for some time. Every now and then he raided it for a clean shirt, which he would replace when he picked up his laundry. It was June of 1961. Frank was thirty-three and floating.

Then his apartment lease and gym membership came up for renewal within a month of each other, and Frank called that a sign. He sold his car and television and took the bag down to the bus station. When the ticket clerk asked, "Where to?," Frank replied, "As far from here as possible."

"Well," said the clerk, unwrapping a stick of gum and looking Frank spang in the eye, " 'bout the furthest you'd get from here and still talk American'd be New York City, U.S.A."

Frank said, "I'll take it."

PART III

Gotburg, Minnesota, 1967–1968

WHEN MARK VAN Bruenninger married Mary Ellen Reid, they were the ideal couple in all respects but one. They had youth and looks; and he was smart and she was loving. As an apportioning of virtues, that's not as common as one might think. Many a man goes through life unseeing, unlearning; many a woman is unfit to nurture children, assume though she may the indicated duties.

But Mark was atheist and Mary Ellen a churchgoer. Moreover, Mark was Jewish and Mary Ellen a Baptist, a true believer. "Sin" was a word she used often and not lightly, and all that was beautiful in Creation, she believed, spilled from the cup of Revealed Religion.

That was the respect in which Mark and Mary Ellen were not the ideal couple. But Mark figured it all out, and while they were engaged he pored over the map of their native state of Minnesota to find a certain kind of place that he had in mind for them to live and raise their family in. It would lie far from the urban centers, with their divisive churches and synagogues. It would stand defended from opinionated relatives. It would be so small and so isolated that it would function entirely on the human scale, whereby each person is judged by his or her personal qualities and not by the isms that he or she belonged to. Mark was particularly keen on finding a town without a Baptist or Jewish congregation, so that their children could be brought up in what Mark saw as the perfect compromise: no Baptism and no Judaism. No religion whatsoever. No superstition, no hatred of outsiders, no terror, no rules about sex practices. Only children brought up on love and care, children who would therefore rise up hale and well intentioned and full of the world's happiness.

The homeland that Mark chose for his family was Gotburg, far to the west of the state, almost to Big Stone Lake, a town founded by Swedes in 1878, when it was called New Göteborg. Over the years the "New" dropped off and the old-country pronunciation gave way as the children and grandchildren of the founders accustomed themselves to the American style of saying things. Mark and Mary Ellen moved into a Gotburg made of Maple Avenue and Birdsong Lane, a bright, fair little Scandihoovian town where kids came crashing around the street corner, pedaled right up on the lawn, jumped off the bicycle, and let it fall as they hit the ground running to shout, "Hey, *Luke*!"

Luke was the only child of Mark and Mary Ellen, Luke de Maupassant Van Bruenninger, the most elaborate name in Gotburg. Mary Ellen had insisted upon the first name, Luke being her favorite book of the Gospel, so Mark had insisted upon the middle name, after the French author. Mark had expected Mary Ellen to withdraw "Luke" from consideration upon confrontation with "de Maupassant." But the lack of a proper church— Mary Ellen occasionally sat in with the Methodists, but all her life she nursed a powerful inference that the religious life of Gotburg was beneath her notice—led Mary Ellen to demand that her son be given, as she put it, "a name in Christ."

"Then," said Mark, "he will also have a name in French literature."

Mary Ellen snapped, "Amen"; and what can you say after that?

So Luke grew up with a weird middle name, as an only child with a best friend in the house next door, Tom Uhlisson, exactly Luke's age and also an only child with a weird middle name (Gösta). The two boys became inseparable so early on that they were known townwide as "the Twins." And, you know, they somewhat resembled each other. For by the early-middle 1960s, when they were in high school, both Luke and Tom were tall, lively, wide-shouldered kids with bouncy dark hair and heavy jaws, popular joking boys with a lot of energy, and stars in team sports. They were distinguishable: Tom was broody, given to outrageous ethnic jokes, and easy to anger; Luke was vivacious and soft. Who would come up to you humming some old tune? Luke. Who scandalized the town by wearing hip-hugger bell-bottoms to school? Luke—and shaded glasses, too, be it said, like that country singer Roy Orbison. Well, looks count and grades don't.

The girls were annoyed, because you never dated Luke or Tom: you dated the Twins, in the company of another girl. These boys studied together, showered together, bunked together. When they—so seldom—got into trouble, they were punished together. In fall, they were cheered for their pass combinations; in spring, they excelled in double play. Come summer, they went to fishing camp in the Lake of the Woods region and cast their rods as a unit. Over Christmas vacation, they co-captained the (invariably) victorious side in the annual War of the Ice Forts in Lindbergh Park. They were the Twins.

The Van Bruenningers lived at 124 Wild Rice Street and the Uhlissons at 126. At 128 lived the Lundquists, whose youngest daughter, Christine, had been nursing a crush on the Twins ever since Trudy Eckerstrom's fifth birthday party, when the ice cream fell out of Chris's cone and Luke and Tom sorrowfully and simultaneously offered her theirs. A few months later they were all in kindergarten, right there spang in a room, day after day, and by then Chris was hopelessly in love. You may wonder which of the two boys she preferred; but could one choose? There were those in Gotburg who said that Luke was on the nutty side, or that Tom could be grudging. Well, Chris had no favorite. It was the splendor of the two boys' bond that fascinated her more than the boys themselves. The perfection of their marriage awed her—the ease with which they communicated, and the respect with which they treated each other.

They are surrounded by themselves, she thought. Who else can get in?

The Twins made room for Chris, more and more as the years passed and the three entered high school as leaders of their class. Chris headed the bohemian set, the ones who smoked and shared pints of booze at parties and knew who Allen Ginsberg was and got terribly involved in the Class Play. The Twins were the jock senators, smoothing over the volatile relations between the athletes and the rest of the world and helping the class hold together as a unit.

By tenth grade, they were ubiquitously a trio. They even attended the Junior Prom that way, and, in a small midwestern town in the late-middle 1960s, two boys taking one girl to a dance was enough to set off a controversy, with the authorities Taking Steps and various parent groups furiously debating our Ancient Liberties and exactly where kids fit into them. But the Twins were so well liked, and so trusted, that but for a few murmurs here and there, their threesome became the prize of the prom. You know what Alice Thorsten—head of the Decorations Committee—said? "Our crepe-paper garlands are *nothing* next to those three!" Look, if some people are so outlandish that they make a terror of everything they do, others can, by the very command of their nature, make aberrant acts tolerable, even basic. So it was with Chris and the Twins.

The Twins did not normally date Chris. They seemed to favor dumb girls, pretty things concerned with charm bracelets and eau. Sometimes Chris wondered what it might be like to date, even marry, one of them. But she knew them too well for that. Didn't she? Imagine dating your brothers. Splashing around in Connie Dawson's parents' pool with them, going to lunch with them at Wendy's, playing championship Sorry with them in the basement (it was known as "the rec") at Tom's, then finishing off the afternoon with them in the tree house that Luke's father had built the year that Luke was born, Chris thought that never in a million could she possibly consider being physically involved with Luke or Tom, and that never in a million was she likely to meet a boy as handsome, bright, and kind. This suggested that Chris's romantic life was going to run downhill from here on, and she hadn't even had sex yet.

Luke and Tom were napping, stretched out side by side in the late-August sun that beamed in through the tree house's one great window.

Chris was taking little bites out of a slightly unripe peach, extra-hard. She hated the juicy ripe ones that leak on your clothes.

Tom exhaled, shivered a little, and turned over. Luke did the same. They were both still asleep.

Chris opened up a paperback of *Pride and Prejudice,* the last of her vacation books. Each summer, every student returning to high school had to read three novels, of the student's free choice, then report on them viva voce in English class. "*Pride and Prejudice,*" Chris saw herself saying, "is about getting past the art of a person to reach his soul."

Tom was shivering again. His free arm suddenly thrust out, came to rest upon Luke, then bent to Luke's form, holding him by the waist.

Chris put down her book, fretting about the burdens of being born midwestern in a country that makes its history on its seacoasts. Born to be uprooted, is how Chris saw herself. It wasn't an unpleasing notion, and, applying another coat of 6-12, so the blackflies wouldn't eat her for summer, she ceased to fret.

Tom stirred again and drew closer to Luke, both arms around his friend now; and the two still slept.

Chris watched them, thinking, in awe, They even breathe as one. And I'll be famous one day, one of those actresses who play the daring roles— *Of Human Bondage* in some new adaptation for the stage, seething so persuasively that the audience will become distressed. It will be said that there are walkouts during the scene in which I destroy the paintings, because of the intense satisfaction with which I go about it. Oh, yes. The New York interviewer will ask me, "Who did you love?," and I'll reply, with my secretive half smile, "The Twins." And the interviewer will say, "Ah, but where are they now?"

Hunching her shoulders up in delight, Chris returned to her book.

I wish I could tell you how it is to spend one's youth in a small town where half the families are related to the other half. The kind of town that has somehow managed to evade the plagues of business depression and natural disasters such as floods and dust. The kind that has two thousand bicycles and no bicycle locks, the kind where everyone has somewhere to go on Thanksgiving. Yes, there is the rigid winter and the greasy, bug-infested summer. Nevertheless, it is privileged to grow up in such a place, for there are no worries besides making the team or figuring out how dating works: pure childhood.

Luke was awake, sitting cross-legged, blinking at Chris. Tom always awoke instantly, eager to be Tom again; Luke came to slowly, as if thinking over his choices. He said, "I don't want summer to end because I don't know what happens, next thing."

Chris put her book down. "That's easy. I'm going to Bennington to major in drama, you're going to Dartmouth, major as yet unknown, and Tom'll get his scholarship to Rutgers or State."

Luke grinned, smoothing out his disorderly hair. "Is that an official Chris Predicts?"

Chris shrugged. She occasionally prophesied, but only when she was sure of her materials—and she doesn't know what happens, next thing, either.

"The idea is," Luke went on, "this is the first kind of major experience that's ever come upon us. College. The three of us splitting up."

Chris nodded.

"There are kids all over the country just like us," Luke went on. "Most of them don't even go to college. Or they do a year or two at State and come back home." Luke thought of that. "Home," he repeated. *Home,* knowing what it means: the safe place. "But we're spreading out. Dispersing."

"We've been Guinevere and the two Lancelots all our lives," Chris observed. "Every show closes sooner or later."

"Yeah. It's just . . ." Luke looked over at Tom.

"Is this something Tom shouldn't hear?" Chris asked.

"Chris, I have to say something. I mean, something happened. Between Tom and me."

Luke paused. Chris waited. "Shoot," she said.

"Yeah. Well." Luke looked at Tom again.

"He's sawing a log," Chris assured him.

"Last week," Luke began, "we were up and at 'em nonstop. Remember? Because first it was the touch-football play-offs and then the swim meet and the dance that night. We were both pretty tightened up, Tom and me. And you know how we might give each other a rub, to ease off the tightness? We've always been doing that. Some jockological thing. And . . . well, Tom was stretched out on his bed and I was tending to him there . . ." He looked at Chris, as if to ask, Can you bear to listen to more? She nodded as if she'd heard him speak.

"Well, I . . . I guess I went . . . a little far. Because while I was working on his shoulders I just . . . I dropped my head and rubbed my cheek against his. Because he is such an incredible friend of mine. It looks like I was trying to tell him that. Chris?"

She nodded.

"You hear me, don't you?" he said.

"I hear you."

"Okay. Well, Tom didn't like it. He shook me off and got into the shower, and when he came out it was as if nothing . . . Chris, do you know what I am saying?"

"Yes."

Luke watched her for a bit. "Golly, you're not even shocked?"

"Say!" came a voice from below. "Is my cousin up there?"

Chris went to the window. "Yes, Walt, he's up here."

"Well, I'm coming up, too. Dexter, you wait here."

Walt was Tom's eleven-year-old cousin, and Dexter was Walt's dog, a rowdy Irish setter. From his dearest youth, Walt had been enchanted with Tom. Somehow, their being cousins made Tom wildly exotic and Walt's personal property at the same time. Walt had plenty of cousins—Gotburg was loaded with Uhlissons, all of them related—but Tom was old enough to be inspiring, and imposing enough to be necessary. Walt lived just across the street from Tom, and when Walt had a nightmare he would run over to Tom's house, Dexter in relatively hot pursuit, and climb into Tom's bed. Walt simply adopted Tom, and, extending the logic, Chris and Luke as well.

Tom was sitting up when Walt gained the tree-house interior. "Hey, chief," Tom said, rubbing his eyes, then shaking his head to throw the hair back.

"Oh, Cousin Tom," said Walt. "I just hate that summer's over now."

"But what do you mean by that?" Tom cried, fake-angry, reaching up for the kid and pulling him into his lap. "Aren't you looking forward to getting on in school? What sports are you planning to go out for, anyway?"

"I'm going out for the Hershey squad."

"Well, I never heard of that team."

"It's when you break up into the plain Hershey side and the side with almonds. That's the two sides. Then you face each other across the net and eat, like, eight Hershey bars each. Then you run around all over and the fans go crazy."

Luke and Chris, thus gentled back from the abyss they had both been looking into moments before, laughed. Tom nodded sardonically and released Walt, who leaped up and danced around the tree house like Elvis at a prom.

"Hey," said Luke. "Fancy footwork."

"It's the Hershey bar shuffle," Walt announced, still moving. "We do that to warm up, and also to win over the little people up there in the stands."

"Their hearts and minds?" asked Chris.

"Yet it is a totally passionate game," said Walt, suddenly still, "and so it has no mind at all." He grinned at them, the adolescent drunk on attention from big kids. He's going to go for it now.

"Imagine the scene," says Walt. "It is the eighth round, and the Hershey bars are brought in. There is no tie in this sport, so only *one team can leave the field in victory!* Which will it be? The crowd is mumbly and unsure as the candy is passed out. The wrappings are torn off. *Yes!* And then—"

Ferocious barking from below drew them all to the window in time to see Dexter take off after a rabbit.

"Yikes!" said Walt, jumping onto the rope ladder. "Say, Dexter, wait for me!"

The others left the tree house soon after, to finish off the afternoon at Tom's with a typical Scandihoovian teenager's tea: refrigerator-raid sandwiches and (as the adults were nowhere about) beer at the kitchen table. The boys pulled out the meat and cheese and fish, the bread and condiments, as Chris settled down with the local paper, a weekly made mainly of shopping coupons and editorials. A town as small and incestuously derived as Gotburg gets its news more directly than by gazette. Still, every-body took the *Press,* perhaps out of tribal solidarity. Chris liked to read aloud from it. She was fascinated by how much the paper found to be reportable in a repressed little place like Gotburg.

"Oh!" she cried, settling in with the movie column. "*Blowup*! At last!"

"The biggest sandwich in the world," said Luke, dumping the sweet mustard, the tomato chutney, and the horseradish sauce onto the table while fighting off Tom's headlock, "is called a Dagwood."

"No, let's consider foreign film," said Chris. "It's daring, it's worldly, and it's naked."

"I'm in favor of that," said Tom, battling Luke into a corner of the room, twisting his arm, holding him close. "There should be Naked Days for seniors. Fridays, say."

"Listen to this dolt," Chris went, engrossed in the review. "Golly: 'The pseudo-sophisticate tone is underscored in a tennis game *played without balls!*' " She turned to the scuffling Twins. "But that's the whole point!"

"I'll say," said Luke, getting the better of Tom with a half nelson. "Where would we be without balls?"

"I knew I'd find you here," said Walt, coming in briskly, masterfully. "Now for a cheese sandwich with stuffed olives, ever so finely sliced."

"Well, I'm getting sliced," said Tom, wrestling with Luke.

"Now, here's something odd," said Chris, caught by a story.

"Takedown!" cried Luke, as he and Tom crashed to the floor.

"*Ow!*"

" 'GOTBURG MAN ARRESTED IN TWIN CITIES PERVERT BAR RAID,' " Chris read. "Listen—"

"I appeal to you," said Luke, holding Tom in a scissor-lock, "as a gen-tleman and a jock." Then he spoke for Tom, in Yogi Bear's voice: " 'You don't appeal to me.' " As himself, Luke replied, "Oh, yeah?"

"All right," said Tom, panting. "All right, I'm bushed, all right."

" 'Richard Engquist, 34 years old, of 82 Salmon Lane, was one of twenty-eight patrons of the Green Thursday Bar in Minneapolis who were taken into custody by the police shortly before midnight on August 18. According to authorities, the bar was known to be a den of deviant activity and had been under surveillance for some months before the raid. All twenty-eight men were charged with public drunkenness and lewd and lascivious conduct, misdemeanors carrying maximum jail terms of six months and three years and a day, respectively.' "

The Twins were resting it off on their backs on the linoleum; Walt was searching the fridge. It was his habit to supply the voices for the various foods he was interested in, the milk as a ho-hoing Santa and the cake as Julie Andrews but the cheese as rebellious, a subversive in the food chain.

" 'That greedy boy is back again. Quick, I'll pretend I'm cauliflower!' "

" 'Mr. Engquist was relieved of his position at the Hancock law firm of Edeson and Engquist, and local police were called to remove him from the Salmon Lane house at the request of his wife, Sheila Engquist, to protect their sons, Stephen, 6, and Harvey, 4.' "

"Oh, yes, I *will* eat you, you silly cheese," said Walt, clutching the long yellow Velveeta box.

"The police were called to remove him?" Chris asked the Twins. "As if he were trespassing in his own house?"

Tom shrugged. "Well, what do you expect, anyhow? Some faggot."

Chris looked at Luke; but he was deaf and grinning.

"You want another round?" Tom asked him. "Or do you give up?"

"*Give up?* I had you tooth to nail!"

"Huh," said Chris, closing the paper. "Life is a cabaret."

" 'Will you cut that Broadway stuff out?' " said Luke, in Tom's voice.

"I wouldn't say that," Tom objected.

"Yes, you would, you anti-intellectual ape-man."

"That's fighting words!"

"En garde!"

Chris made a face as the Twins rejoined the battle and Walt bit into his sandwich. "Velveeta tastes so nice in August," he observed.

Happy days. But Chris had chores to do and Walt had to find Dexter, so the party broke up. Luke was last to leave, and seeing him to the door, Tom grabbed his arm and looked at him.

Luke said, "What?"

"Well, it's this one thing, pal. You say too much."

"What do you mean?" Luke asked.

"You should be more smooth, not telling the world what's in you."

Luke dreaded this yet had to get close to it. "You heard me when I—"

"Don't share your secrets," Tom urged him. "Just be cool."

"I told Chris. I couldn't—"

"Well, Chris is solid, anyhow." Tom made a "Come on and join the team, boy" face. "But you really ought to keep it wrapped, buddy. Okay?"

Tom's arm barred the doorway, meaning, You better.

"Okay, Tom."

Up goes the arm.

"That's my fella. If I were a girl, I'd kiss you."

. . .

All his life, it seemed, Luke had been dreaming of Tom. Yet *what* had he dreamed, beyond the two of them flying in each other's arms or floating in mystical green seas? A homosexual teenager in America in the 1960s could not know what his dreams were because there was no reality to tether them to. Luke Van Bruenninger had always known that he Liked Men, and he had no problem with this. But he did presume that it was his unique secret, that he belonged to a company of one. His subterfuges were the momentous swindles of a ghost, terribly important to him but invisible to all others: pretending to tighten the laces of his sneakers in the gym while eyeing Danny Vorisek's torso, affecting the most casual interest in *Surfside 6* and *Cheyenne* and the other television private-eye and western shows that habitually unshirted their heroes, assuming a precocious interest in *Esquire* magazine only to comb its back pages for the Parr of Arizona bathing-suit ads of big lean blond boys who smiled as if they had an angle on something. There were times when Luke believed that at least some of this was not fortuitous—that certain people in charge of television shows and bathing-suit ads were aware of Luke, and his life, and his secrets. Perhaps they were aware of Tom as well.

Sharing everything with Tom to the point of being virtually a part of him was Luke's paradise; but then, such sagas were occurring in every town in the nation. There were many thousands of Lukes and Toms, with their secret that had the power to draw them close or sunder them absolutely. But this pair is especially intriguing, I think, because the two pals were so intent on each other, and because they were the Twins, and because Luke had reason to suspect that Tom was . . . well, how do you describe it when you scarcely know what to call it? . . . that Tom was like Luke.

One can become too close, of course. "Stop thinking so hard!" Tom would tell Luke, for instance during a ball game when Luke went into a reverie. Then Luke (catcher) would rush up to Tom (pitcher) to confer on a protocol, and Tom would grab Luke in some crazy, swaggering way, as if nothing mattered but that Tom got his hands on Luke in front of everyone.

Yet no one thought of them as homosexuals. What, two stalwart young athletes? Football team co-captains, no less? Besides, they were always dating, sometimes even spotted at parties making out in some dark corner, or even Getting to Second Base (that's a kissy-face and feelies, topless but with skirt and pants on) with notable girls of the class or one class below. Anyway, this was 1967, when there were no homosexuals in America except Liberace, and no homosexuals in Minnesota whatsoever.

Both boys were virgins, because of the time and the place. A small town like Gotburg, with its magnificent social and religious controls, did not give teenagers the scope for much sexual experiment, certainly nothing like what their counterparts in the freewheeling urban environments enjoyed. Oh, there were cracks in the system even in Gotburg—impromptu circle jerks in the showers, say, or a very determined young couple who would take advantage of her baby-sitting gig and tear off a quickie on the couch. And there was that legendary night in June of 1965, when Connie Dawson gave the first pool party of the season and right in the middle of it word came that Connie's little brother Ben had been hurt on his bike in a collision with a car. So Mr. and Mrs. Dawson rushed to the hospital, leaving the party without parental supervision, and within three minutes, in the pool house, behind the pool house, on top of the pool house (and even in Connie's bedroom, though Connie not only fiercely denied it but is planning to go to her deathbed with her view of the story), a goodly fraction of the party were graduated from boys and girls to men and women.

Where were Luke and Tom during this, you ask? Typically, they had wandered off for a neighborhood walk with Chris, the three of them wet and happy in their bathing suits, whapping towels at each other. Just walking along, talking and joking and singing. Oh, the purity of such times! The innocence, friends! By the time they got back to the Dawsons', Dickie Horton's parents had shown up as substitute chaperons and had organized a bunny hop. Given the tenor of the evening, there was speculation for weeks afterward as to the nature of the Luke-Chris-Tom relationship; but then their classmates had been wondering about them for years. When Chris's friends would ask for the story, she would only smile like Ethel Barrymore; and when they wanted to know which of the two she really liked, she answered, "Someday I'll know." At the time, she probably thought that was true.

On the last Sunday before their senior year, Connie Dawson and her boy friend, Sven Bjornson, called to ask the Twins and Chris over for the Final Swim Before School, and Luke's mother went outside and got them out of the tree house and over to the Dawsons'. Connie was trying to tell Sven the plot of *The Three Musketeers,* one of his summer books for English class. But Connie was getting it all wrong, so Tom and Luke helped out till Sven felt reasonably secure.

"How come you picked a longie like that?" asked Tom. "It's just more work."

"We had the *Classics Illustrated* in the basement," said Sven. "But my unbelievably gross older brother burned it before my eyes."

Sitting at the edge of the pool, paddling her legs in the water, Connie said, "This whole year isn't going to matter, anyway, since we both got into State early-acceptance. All we have to do is pass."

"Yeah," said Sven.

"You guys make your mind up yet?" Connie asked the others. "The way you've been talking, it's like you're applying to every school in the country."

Luke shrugged. Chris was silent. Tom said, "Oh, they've made their minds up, all right. They're going to fancy places." He looked at his two best friends. "Tell them, go on."

"Dartmouth," said Luke.

Sven gave a low whistle.

"Anyway, that's my first choice."

"And Chris has a Dartmouth for girls," said Tom.

"Bennington," said Chris. "If I make it."

There was a pause, everyone looking at Tom.

"*Well?*" said Connie, at last.

"Who knows?" said Tom. "Who knows about me? Because what I need here is a scholarship. And my grades aren't so hot and my S.A.T.s are lousy."

"You didn't cheat?" Sven asked.

"No, I didn't cheat," said Tom, a little annoyed.

"Who proctored when you took them? We had Mrs. Russell, and the whole room was eyeballing every test paper within a radius of like five desks. I mean, she's such a—"

"Well, I didn't have Mrs. Russell, anyhow, and, besides—"

"State isn't expensive," said Connie.

"My parents don't want to . . . They don't have the . . ." Suddenly he turned to Luke. "Are you guys going to college if I can't, too?"

"Of course we are," said Chris, splashing up to stand with Luke. "We've been planning our whole lives around college."

"All *three* of us," said Tom. "That's what it was, wasn't it?"

"Look out, the whole world!" came the voice of Walt, running over the lawn to the pool followed by Dexter. "I'm going to do the cannon-ball!"

Leaping into the air, Walt folded arms and legs around himself, making a ball as he crashed into the water. Dexter more or less did the cannonball, too, showering the party.

Annoyed cries of *"Walt!"* and, from Sven, "What is this, National Dog in the Pool Month?," welcomed Walt to the pool.

"Dexter," he said, "you'd best sit this one out," and Dexter climbed up the steps, shook himself, and lay down to nap and pant. Luke hunkered down in the water so that Walt could ride around on his back. It was this thing they would do; when Luke got tired, Tom would take Walt.

"Listen," said Tom. "The last time they gave a party for the family, my parents made this real public announcement about how Tom can't go to college. The whole basement's full of Uhlissons, and they're going to take up a collection or something, so poor Tom's dreams won't get wrecked. With me right there, too! Now everyone's making speeches about what they should do. Uncle Alf, Uncle Gustav, Cousin Dave, Uncle Harald, Aunt Frelinda. They're all drinking beer and laying plans. Uncle Alf—'Now I don't want to make like I know more than the rest of you,' while he waves his ludicrous cigar in the air. Uncle Gustav—'The family got to stick together.' And it's just a lot of hot wind, anyhow. Uncle Harald even says college would spoil me."

"Quel rat," said Chris, borrowing from *Breakfast at Tiffany's,* her favorite movie.

"My daddy's name is Harald," said Walt, from Luke's back.

"I want Chris Predicts," said Tom, turning to her. "What's going to happen?"

"No," said Chris.

Connie looked at Sven.

"You two are going to leave me behind, is that it? Tell me, Chris."

"Tom—"

"They can't leave you behind," said Walt. "Never in a million. We're all in this together!"

"Chris Predicts," Tom demanded.

"Tomorrow, Tom. Not now. Today is too lovely to—"

"Well, what's lovely about it?" Tom asked. He was getting away from them all, stabbing at the water with the flat of his hand. "The whole rotten family of them! They're good for scorning you when your voice changes. But try *passing* the *hat* to send poor Tom to *college!*"

"What are you going to do about the draft?" Connie asked, and Tom stopped moving. He was looking away from them, at the water and then the sky, pointlessly, as if he were alone.

"I haven't figured that out yet," Tom said, quite suddenly, turning to face them. "Maybe my friends have an idea."

He looked at Luke and Chris.

Walt, half-asleep on Luke's back, murmured, "First I'm in the pool, then I get all hungry."

"Why don't you tell them you're a homosexual?" asked Luke. "That'll get you off."

"Oh, brother," said Sven.

"Luke!" cried Connie, mildly outraged.

"It doesn't have to be true," Luke continued. "It's a moment in your life, a trick you play on someone. It's nothing that matters and no one will know. Ask yourself what matters and what everybody knows. Ask yourself, Tom."

"Ask what *you* know," said Tom.

"Far too much. Right?"

"I don't want to be left behind."

"You don't want to be known."

There was a pause.

"What is this?" asked Sven. "*The Twilight Zone?*"

Walt, suddenly awake, slid off Luke's back into the water with a neutral plop. Coming up for air, he cried, "Say, Dexter! We'd better get back for dinner!"

Dexter looked up, rose, and luxuriously stretched himself from tail to snout. The humans were staring at him as if they'd never seen a dog before, except Walt, who was frantically drying off. "And it's make-your-own B.L.T.s tonight, too!" he explained. Dropping the towel, he added, sotto voce behind his hand, "Of course Dexter just gets dog food, but you put a slice of Dole pineapple on it and *he* thinks it's Polynesian meat loaf."

Everyone was still looking at the dog, or at Walt.

"What's the matter?" Walt asked. "It's very quiet in the pool."

"We're just not used to seeing the most famous friendship in town unraveling before our eyes," said Luke.

"Luke," said Connie, "you are so exasperating!"

"Hey, don't be crude, man," Sven put in.

"I don't want to be left behind," said Tom, almost weeping with frustration. "I'm the only one who isn't going anywhere."

Chris started toward him in sympathy, but Tom moved away, wading into the deeper end of the pool.

"Tom!" she cried.

Tom slid below the surface and swam underwater to the far end of the pool.

" 'Nobody sees me cry,' " Luke said, for Tom.

Walt, standing there stunned with his towel and his dog, said, "What's happening to my cousin?"

Tom climbed out at the far end and started off, dripping wet, walking home.

Chris forced her way through the water and out of the pool and after Tom.

Luke watched them for a bit, then followed Chris, pausing to pick Walt up and drop him into the pool.

"I sincerely hope that was meant as a friendly gesture!" Walt indignantly called after him upon resurfacing.

Sven and Connie looked at the retreating, celebrated trio of Tom and Chris and Luke; or of Chris with TomLuke; or of the Twins plus Chris; or however it goes.

Walt grumbled at having to dry off from scratch again, then hurried off after them, and when he got there it was, from left to right, Tom and Chris and Luke, their arms around each other in a slow, pensive flying wedge.

"Far out," said Connie, back at the pool, following them with her eyes till they disappeared in the summer green.

They could always patch it up, those three. They had never really fought over anything, because nothing worth fighting for had ever been at stake in those lives in that transcendent place. Historically, of course, it was an era of upheaval—Luke was regarded as daring simply because he was applying to the roiling University of California at Berkeley, as well as Dartmouth (his first choice), Williams, and Reed (his safety); and Chris hit upon Bennington precisely because she felt it would be liberal yet not revolutionary. But then, Gotburg did not generally produce complaining kids. In the great cities of our civilization, nothing works but everything is possible. In Gotburg, very little was possible but everything worked: and, for those raised in that system, who had no idea what else the world might contain, this seemed eminently sensible. So Luke was a little nervous about Berkeley; and Chris felt that Bennington was as dangerous as she dared get.

Sensible is a powerful notion to lay upon children. So much of the world does seem sensible, even when it may impede or even destroy our sense of self-esteem. Sensible looks easy because everyone claims to be doing it. But sensible, really, is some grown-up telling you that you can't have what you want.

So it seemed sensible to Tom that he could not voyage off with his friends to college, and power, and liberty. If his family could or would not pay and he had no money himself, then he must remain behind. It seemed sensible to Tom but unfair to Luke and Chris, and that was in their minds as the two of them walked Tom home. Then Walt and Dexter caught up with them, and Walt began to sing his usual mishmash of *Sgt. Pepper* numbers. The album had come out just before the summer's start, and no matter where Walt happened to be—in Tom's room, brushing up on the sports news; or at Luke's for a post–tree-house snack of crullers and cocoa, regaling Mr. Van Bruenninger with the doings in Walt's latest *Dr. Doolittle* book; or at Chris's, quietly watching her helping Tom with his Biology— the *Sgt. Pepper* record was playing. Lines from "She's Leaving Home" intertwined with those from "When I'm Sixty-four" to the tune of "A Little Help from My Friends." As they walked and Walt sang, Tom put his arm around Walt's shoulders.

"You like me, right, Cousin Tom?" said Walt.

"Golly, we should have thought of this before," said Luke. "Is there maybe some way we could raise the money? Kind of invent our own scholarship so—"

"It would make a fool of me," said Tom. "I would look hungry to the entire town."

Walt sang

What do you see when you don't go to school?
Well, I'm certain that I'll dance a little jig

and Tom knelt and grabbed Walt and held on, really weeping now as he had nearly wept in the pool. Walt was startled, but he said, "That's all right, Cousin Tom," and patted his back. Luke gave Chris a stern look that said, We cannot leave our friend behind.

Then Tom took to saying "No, I'm getting used to it" and "I can live with it." He seemed to mean it.

"There are these inevitable things," he would say. "And me not going to college is inevitable. We wouldn't have been together, anyway, at these different colleges. It was a weirdo plan in the first place."

"We would have been doing the same thing at the same time," said Luke. "That was the plan."

They were in the tree house and they didn't know what the outcome of their lives was going to be. Well, who does? Okay: They didn't know how they were going to feel about each other by the end of the year. It was getting scary.

"Well, I was wrong to cry," said Tom. "That day, you know."

"Especially near the Dawsons' pool," Walt put in. "Though I have to say that if my Cousin Tom did so, there has to be a reason for it."

"Nobody feel sorry for me," said Tom. "I have my own plans, and besides I'm tired of school."

"I have this idea," said Luke, "that colleges shouldn't go by money but looks. They would see Tom's big shoulders and how smooth and full he all is, and how handsome. And every one of them would jump at him."

Two beats. Then Walt said, "He's my favorite cousin of all time, I don't mind telling you."

Tom ruffled Walt's hair and said, "It's just because I take care of you that you're soft on me."

"I'm soft on you, too," said Luke. "And if it means anything, I'll stay back here with you after we graduate, if you want me to."

"I don't."

"Yes!" said Walt. "Chris?"

"Look, I could hang around here," Luke insisted.

They sat there in silence, Tom glancing at Luke now and then. Finally, Tom said, "Yeah, I can almost imagine that." Luke couldn't tell whether Tom was relishing the prospect or mocking it.

Chris thought the topic was smoldering a bit much for safety's sake but that they had to work it out honestly sometime. Now was the time. She took Walt away on some insidiously plausible pretext—Walt complaining all the way down—and left the two boys to deal with it. It was early evening in late October, very near dark. Tom's eyes were shining like cigarette tips in a movie balcony.

"You've got a lot on your mind," said Tom in a leisurely manner. "So tell me, Luke. Blurt it out to me."

"What are you going to do when I tell you?"

Tom smiled. "Gamble and see."

"I meant it about staying behind with you."

" 'Staying *behind*'? How do you think that makes me feel? 'Staying *behind*'!"

Luke tried another tack. "Golly, how can I be honest with you when you act so insecure?"

"Well, who's *asking* you to be honest?"

Luke sitting up, leaning against the wall. Tom across from him, lying supine, hands behind his head as the darkness falls on them.

Luke said, "My father told me he built this place so I would always have a refuge. Even from him, he said. From anyone. It's my own place, and it's where I am honest whether anybody asks me or not."

Tom made a gun of his hand and shot Luke, blowing off the smoke.

"Tom?"

Tom was silent.

"Tom, I have to do this."

"Well, you *don't,* in point of fact."

"I've been in love with you my entire life."

"Yeah, and now you said it."

The silence must have lasted six or seven minutes.

"That's all?" Luke finally asked.

"Well . . . yeah. I guess if I'm smooth and full and handsome—whatever that means—then it's no big surprise. I never thought of it that way my-self."

"I think you have."

Tom looked keenly at Luke. "Yeah?"

"That's right. It takes two to lindy."

"What do you mean, buddy?" said Tom, sitting up. "Well, you just tell me, now."

"Not as much as me, I admit. But there's—"

"*Nothing*. There's *nothing*. You want to turn into a freak, *fine*—don't try to sneak me in there with you! Anyway, you're all set to move out of town, so what do you even—"

"Tom! I've been *saying* I'll stay with you if you—"

"Stay *behind* with me, like the kiss of death! I heard you say that! Well, you don't have to stay behind, pal. I'm letting you off, all right? You and Chris, you go off to your future lives. You leave me alone, and I mean it, anyhow. No one's going to be my friend out of charity!"

Another pause. A short one. Luke ended it by jumping up, scrambling down the ladder, and slamming the door on his way inside.

"Faggot," said Tom, contentedly.

.   .   .

They actually started avoiding each other. Chris shamed them into shaking hands, but Tom stopped coming around to visit; and in winter, as usual, the two boys separated as lanky Tom went out for basketball and the heavier Luke favored wrestling. Further to distance himself from Luke and Chris, Tom turned Romeo, entrancing the available belles by means of the study date, usually in the library, followed by a delicious walk home, idling along the avenues and being sure to be seen.

"I know why he's mad," Luke told Chris. "And okay, he's got a right, I guess. But how can he break us up after all those years?"

"We're breaking up anyway, come June. He thinks *we're* the culprits."

They were walking home from school on a February afternoon, one of those heartlessly gray days that the northern Midwest specializes in, when it seems as if every tree in the world is dead and birds haven't flown south but become extinct.

"How come we never thought this would happen?" Chris asked. "Pals forever? What did we expect, to all go away to school and then . . . what? Come back to Scandihoovia? This is where you grow up. It isn't where you live."

"Our forefathers did."

"That's what forefathers are for," said Chris.

They walked on for a bit in silence. Then precocious Chris sighed, "Moscow, Moscow," *Three Sisters*–style.

"I meant it about staying here with him, you know," said Luke. "I'm not like you—I don't need to break out anywhere and become . . . some new version of myself."

"You don't want to learn what else there is in the world? This place won't look half so interesting after Dartmouth."

"I could skip college. Except my parents would be awfully disappointed. Or let's just say my father would, and I don't even know why. If he's so hot dog about college, why doesn't *he* go?"

Walking home from school and talking things over. Once, the three friends would have made this trip, Walt and Dexter tailing them, sometimes openly and sometimes hiding behind trees like footpads. Now, of course, Tom had broken away, and Walt, unable to shadow this new dating Tom, was off on other adventures, perhaps forging relationships with people of his own age.

"Chris, what if I didn't go to college?" Luke asked her. "What would become of me?"

"How do I know, on a street in Minnesota?" She's a little fed up.

"Chris Predicts?"

She shook her head. "Not enough to go on. And if you're asking, Do I see you and Tom in a little white house?, that would be pushing it."

Luke nodded. "Because what I want is what nobody gets?"

"Because Tom can't handle it. You're opening him like a can of beans. He doesn't want to be opened."

Connie Dawson stalked by, turned to them—without stopping—and said, "Sven Bjornson is a gross juvenile delinquent who thinks the whole world is sex!" Without missing a step, she faced front and marched on.

"Do you think I'm right about him?" Luke asked Chris. "Is he . . . like me?"

"Connie!" Sven called out from behind them. Muttering a curse or two, he came abreast of Luke and Chris.

"Look, what'd I do?" he asked them.

"We have no idea, ectu'lly," said Chris in her Noël Coward voice.

"I put my hand down her bra. Big deal!"

"In this weather?" asked Chris.

"No, in the gym. No one was there, and I was mostly joking, anyway."

"Don't let us keep you," said Chris dryly. Now she was Eve Arden.

"Connie!" Sven shouted. And off he ran.

"You didn't answer my question," said Luke as they turned into Wild Rice Street. "About Tom."

"I don't know about Tom. I don't know what Tom knows."

"How could . . . Look, you know what you're attracted to, don't you? You may pretend it isn't true, but inside you, you'd know. It's factological."

Chris shrugged—not an easy feat when bundled against a Gotburg winter.

"For instance," Luke pursued, "are *you* confused?"

"No, I've always known what I wanted."

"See?"

She was thinking, These two boys of mine are so beautiful, and so sweet, and so wondrous, and no one will ever know them as I have known them, for I got to them when they were pure and vulnerable and their insides were showing. No one will see them up close as that for the rest of their lives.

They had reached number 128, the Lundquists'. Chris went inside, and Luke trudged on home, looking up at Tom's room as he passed. It was no more than a glance, I assure you.

.   .   .

By March the snow was piled up so densely that a foreigner—as natives of this part of the state term outlanders—would have thought the weatherman must be reporting "winter for the rest of your life." These were the days on which Walt and Dexter would turn stone-still during Walt's consumption of Cream of Wheat when the radio turned to the question of whether or not the schools would be open.

Gotburg had only two schools, Minnewaska Science and Grammar and Sawtooth High; on snow days they functioned as a unit. When one closed, the other closed; and Walt's mother (Tom's Aunt Frelinda, as it happens) would undergo a mild heart attack and Walt and Dexter would don their snow clothes. (Dexter had a woolen doggy coat with his name sewn into it surrounded by fruits, the gift of an elderly widowed Uhlisson aunt with little to do but collect pension checks and make things.) Walt and Dexter would then race outside to build a fort and stockpile ice balls. In years past, Tom, Luke, and Chris would have turned up for a snow fight, the two Uhlisson boys against Luke and Chris, with all, at length, repairing to Luke's house for grilled-cheese sandwiches and hot chocolate with marshmallows floating.

This year, Walt and Dexter were on their own, and Walt was—let me tell you—pretty chagrined. What a relief when April melted the earth down to ordinary again and everyone came out to play. But Tom was still keeping his distance from Luke.

This was the month of college acceptances. For our folk, it was less acceptances than replies, for Bennington turned Chris down and Dartmouth rejected Luke. Nevertheless, they got packages from, respectively, N.Y.U. and Berkeley, and that's where their future was going to take them.

Tom didn't get in anywhere, and when he told his parents, they said, "Oh." They were off to Redwood Falls for a dynastic interaction with Tom's mother's relatives, and planned to make it an overnight.

"Do your homework," they said as they left.

Sure. As if that were the difference between he does or he doesn't do it. After twelve years of school he needs them to say Do your homework. Sure.

He could drop out of school tomorrow; what difference would it make? He had his job lined up, starting the first Monday in July, as a carpenter's assistant, minimum wage plus ten bucks bonus every week. He'd commute to Caledon, two towns over, with Mr. Kjellin, who ran a chain of hardware stores and a lumber yard. In the thrifty Swedish tradition, Mr. Kjellin would be paid off in work time, one hour per week of "S and H"—sawing and hauling—at the yard, to be sustained every Monday afternoon.

Seventeen years old and I'm in chains, Tom thought. I'm all given over. I'm accounted for. Really, I'm finished for life. Get the church stone ready: Here Lies Tom.

Now I know why so many young men get into trouble and end up in the pokey. They're just trying to bust out. They don't want to hurt anybody—they're just shaking their chains.

Tom has gotten into his parents' liquor locker and he's getting—as his coevals like to put it—"swacked." What an elegant word for teenage boys puking their guts out around eleven P.M. of a party, getting clear of the living room just in time.

"I'm *swacked,*" Tom told Luke on the phone. "Come on over."

It was late on a Saturday night. Luke hadn't heard a word out of Tom in quite some while, but Tom sounded real bad, a depression masked in a good-time mouth.

So Luke went over and took the bottle away from Tom and said maybe he should eat something.

"No," said Tom, sloshing around. "Because . . . No . . ."

"Shit, Tom, you're so pissed you can't stand!"

"So what about a cheese sandwich?" said Tom. "That's eating. Okay? On . . . toast."

"First, sit down, will you?"

Tom sat at the Formica-topped, L-shaped kitchen counter—the Uhlissons couldn't send their son to college but their house boasted all the trendy renovations—as Luke rustled up the grub.

"Not *well-done* toast," said Tom. "*Medium* toast."

"Okay, Tom."

"Funny you came over when I called, after how tough I've been. You must be some real great guy."

"Mustard, Tom?"

"Butter."

"Do you want lettuce? Tomato?"

"I want you."

Tom had gotten up and was weaving again.

"I want you to tell me it's all right, what I did."

Luke, supporting Tom, got him back on his stool at the counter.

"Just stay there," Luke told him.

"No, tell me it's okay," said Tom, holding Luke's arm. "I've been real wrong to you, cutting you off like that. Tom is a mean son of a bitch."

Luke paused, then turned to Tom. "You know," Luke said, "telling me this doesn't count if you're drunk. Because you don't know what you're saying and tomorrow you'll have forgotten it."

Luke poured hot water over the latest suburban miracle—freeze-dried coffee chips—and put a cup of it in front of Tom.

"Come on, Tom, sober up."

Tom was humming "See You in September," a ballad from 1962 that became a hit single in an up-tempo version by a group called the Happenings in the summer of 1966. It was popular all over the country, but for some reason it especially swept the Midwest, where it became the number every band played at proms when the chaperons announced the Last Slow Dance. Tom and Luke had danced it with Chris at their Junior Prom, the three of them bent to each other, head to head, reckless of everyone; and, as all the girls said later, that was when romance came to Gotburg.

Tom was humming and Luke was working on the sandwich. Occasionally Tom tried filling in the words, though he was almost as approximate as Walt at balladeering. But Tom did get the last line right. "Will I see you in September?" it runs, "or lose you to a summer love?"

Luke, at the counter, put down the knife and stood right there, his back to Tom; Luke was shaking, trying to regain his composure. He tried thinking of the three of them dancing to that song at the prom, the boys in their rented black-and-whites and Chris in that snazzy red thing she was so proud of. He remembered how smoothly they danced, even if a couple of three should have been awkward; and how they made that moment theirs alone, their eyes shut and dreaming as they touched brows.

Luke turned back to Tom, who had dozed off, his head resting on folded arms. Or no: because he suddenly said, "Where's my cheese sandwich, Luke?"

Tom looked up. His dark hair, long in front, had tumbled into his eyes. He brushed it back and smiled craftily.

"You ate my sandwich," he said. "Right?"

Luke, stricken with love for his friend—aching, passionate, terrified, guilty, best-friend-hungry love—thought that no one he knew of made so imposing a picture as Tom. The colors of him—the blank skin and black hair. The sharp angles—all jutting out when he ran for a pass; or tilted, surprised, when he considered what you said. No one equaled Tom, not even Bill Oxley, who had been graduated the previous year and whom

Tom had watched grow from a quiet, serious youth into a rambunctious football star with the torso of Zeus. Not even Garrett Oleson, a tight-assed, slit-eyed icon who liked to look as if he'd been caught doing something wicked. Not even Clint Walker.

"I've got your sandwich right here," said Luke.

Tom imitated the laugh of a mad scientist in a Saturday-afternoon thriller. "Give me, give me," he chanted, reaching for the plate.

Luke watched Tom eat the sandwich.

"People don't realize how important a cheese sandwich can be," said Tom between bites. "They want steak or caviar. French stuff. Roast lamb where they put a little white paper hat on it for no goodly reason. But it's simple things that work best. Basic things."

He put down the sandwich, his head falling and his eyes clouded. He said, "I figure I've got about thirty seconds before I lose consciousness." Smiling at Luke, he slowly got to his feet and began to move.

Luke grabbed Tom just before he fell, and helped him struggle upstairs to his room. By the time he hit the bed, Tom was totally out, and Luke started pulling off Tom's clothes. Shoes, pants, shirt. Tom was down to shorts and socks, faceup, and Luke was trying to get him under the bed-clothes, but Tom was so dead he was too heavy to move. Luke sat on the bed and looked at his friend. Stroked his hair, his arms, his legs. Pulled Tom's shorts off, thinking, I'm really doing this. Jumped up and threw his own clothes off till they were both down to socks, keeping an eye on Tom, fearful that he would suddenly wake.

"Tom?" he whispered, coming close to him. This is very close. This is Luke parking himself on the bed, line for line with Tom, and taking him in his arms, and making love to him.

Luke had pictured this countless times; he knew exactly what he wanted to do. His hands were all over Tom, fondling details he had memorized sometime long before: for instance, the hairs that had begun sprouting along Tom's chest, so fine they were virtually invisible unless you broke the rules and got this close; or the slight suggestion of an arrowhead in the tip of Tom's cock.

Luke was not shy. He kissed Tom's dead lips, his eyes and chest, and he ran his tongue over Tom from top to toe. Then he got down at the very center of Tom, hiked Tom's legs up to rest on Luke's shoulders, and began to swing on Tom's cock like the first pope happening upon the first altar boy. It wasn't one of your precedent-shattering dates, perhaps, nothing for the *Kama Sutra*. But it was close, very close; and for a small-town teenager who had never had all-out sex, much less nonconformist sex, it went rather well. By the end of it Luke was rubbing himself against Tom, terrified to see that Tom's eyes had opened but too caught up in his passions to back off; and Tom had his hands on Luke, expressing passions of his own, the two of them raging hard against each other, wet and gasping; and the two of them came.

Panting, winding down, thinking about it, Luke stared at Tom as near to unblinking as can be. But Tom's eyes were unwaveringly closed. He had done his homework and he was really asleep.

Luke got a towel from the bathroom and cleaned both their bodies of semen and sweat. Taking his friend by the sides and very gently turning him over, Luke managed to pull down the bedding and cover them both. Summer nights can be cool in that part of the world, and it felt fine under the covers with Tom, like so much of what they did and said a secret thing for them alone. Luke permitted himself the luxury of whispering Tom's name as he held him and nuzzled the back of his neck. He felt protective toward his friend, though he had taken advantage of him—cheated, perhaps even raped, him. In truth, the guilt that had begun to seep into him just after climax was now a flood. Yet it made Luke hold Tom all the more tightly: for he felt guilty not because he loved Tom but because he was abandoning him.

It must have been between ten and twenty minutes that the two boys lay so. Then Luke said, "Tom?," and gave him a little shove. He was feeling braver, and a bit whimsical. He was feeling close; that made him happy.

Tom was clearly out for the night, so Luke got up, showered, dressed, and, just before he left the house, stood over Tom and said, "I won't let you down, buddy," and "You sleep well, now," and "Good night, Tom."

Now, directly after that night, three things occurred that altered forever how the three friends saw themselves and each other.

First, Tom became very changeable in his humors, sometimes so ebullient it seemed a performance, but more often withdrawn, almost inert.

Second, Luke told Chris, in end-of-the-world confidence and under the direst penalties if she told even an animal or a stone—an oath the three had respected since childhood—that he was planning to go back on the letter of acceptance that he had mailed to Berkeley.

Third, Tom dropped out of school.

He said, What difference did it make? Because he had the job all set up, and why wait? For a diploma? What was that to Tom at this point? "It's no big deal," said Tom, with a face so straight you thought he might be losing his mind.

In the tree house, Luke told Chris, "He's not talking to me again. He's always busy, or just about to go."

"It's not like before, though, is it? Before he was sulking. Now he's *evading.*" A thought struck her. "Something occurred between you two, didn't it?"

Luke nodded.

"Something . . . *physical?*"

"Sex," Luke told her.

"At last! And?"

"Oh . . . we . . . got together. I don't know, it just . . . sort of . . . came about. . . ."

Chris was in no mood for coaxing and working up to it. She said, "Choose one of the following. A, It was an adolescent mistake. B, It was fun but impractical. C, I am his devotee, his slave, the dust in his road."

Luke laughed. "It's D," he said. "I scared him off."

"So what did happen?"

"I don't want to say in so many words. He was drunk and he passed out and I . . . got to him. That's all I'll say. Except for one detail that I know you will enjoy: His eyes were open."

"The whole time?"

"No. For a moment. Somewhere in it all. I'm not sure when. So he knew what was going on and he didn't stop me. But he must have drunked it away by now, blocked it out. It never happened, in a manner of speaking."

Chris felt an exquisite wave of longing pass over her. She wondered if sex could be as good as the dreams you have of it. Like that perfume ad with the male pianist leaping up to to kiss the female violinist. Is it possible, Chris wondered, that they'd be better off sticking to Mendelssohn?

"Oh," said Walt, no more than a head peeping at them from the door, the rest of him standing on the rope ladder. "I came up here to cry where no one would see."

"Come in and tell us about it," said Chris.

"And cry?"

"If you need to."

"My cousin won't play with me any more," said Walt, hefting himself inside the tree house. "There I was on President Street, wondering what to do till my piano lesson, when I see Cousin Tom heading up from Mayo

Street. So I ran up to him, thinking we could try a fast game of Trade a Punch or maybe just talk things over, man to man. Well, sir, he just told me to buzz off, and he never did that before."

Walt was getting tearful, but he didn't cry.

"He would always at least trade punches with me. He's becoming very foreign all of a sudden, and I don't know why."

Chris held Walt, said, "He's upset," and Walt held back real tight. "He's got a lot to deal with."

"He's not going to college, right?" said Walt.

"No," said Chris, releasing him. "Right."

"Do they have piano college?"

"Why?"

Walt made a face. "It looks like my parents are going to try to send me to one, because all they ever say is 'Practice, practice.' It's nothing but scales, though. It's not even songs yet." In his passion, Walt turned to Luke for support. "It's not the real thing," Walt cried. "It's not music."

"Do you like music, Walt?" Luke asked him.

"I like the Beatles and Bob Dylan. Of course, I'm very ahead of my generation. Mr. Engborn said so."

"Who's Mr. Engborn?" said Luke, smiling.

"My teacher at Minnewaska Science and Grammar School." Walt looked up at Chris. "He said I'm so bright, they should name a dessert after me."

Chris shared a look with Luke.

"You want some advice?" said Luke to Walt. "Don't get caught in a dark corner with Mr. Engborn."

"Don't you guys have anything better to do than hang around jawboning in that stupid tree house?" Tom shouted from below.

Luke, Walt, and Chris (in that order) leaped to the window and gazed down.

"He's drunk again," Luke whispered to Chris. "He's swaying."

"I know what you're saying about me," Tom called up. "And it isn't true."

"It's true," Walt cried, "that you are not so friendly."

"Yeah," Tom agreed. "That may be true."

"He is drunk," Chris murmured.

"And I'm not going to the prom, you hear that?" Tom added. "I'm *over* school. And all the things connected to it."

"What could that *mean*?" Walt breathed out.

No one in the tree house said anything more. Tom contented himself with pointing a finger at them, this waving finger, and staring at them, then more or less marching off.

"My cousin is drunk!" said Walt, amazed. "At three o'clock on a sunny children's afternoon! And did you notice he didn't apologize to me for being so rude on President Street?"

Chris said, "We notice many things."

Tom didn't go to the prom, but he glided into the post-prom party—a secret party, one of those unknown-to-all-but-the-elite things, where the presence of parents, however earnest and dramatic, does not entirely preclude a couple's finding a spot in which to get to know each other better. Tom was drunk again. Happy and sloppy, with his shirttail hanging out, grinning sideways at everybody, and winking at Connie Dawson's parents: for of course we are once again at the Dawsons'.

Is every party the same party, every summer setting the Dawsons' pool? That's small-town life. So there's Sven Bjornson showing off his swan dive, and Butch "Gross-out" Thorson stalking around like a man who must get laid or else—fat chance—and Susanna Hohner radiating up and down the patio because she had been anointed Queen of the Prom. Another of those Sawtooth High parties.

Something new happened at this one. Tom pulled Chris close and asked her why they hadn't ever done it together.

Our Chris is very sad at this, very disappointed in her Tom and very irritated at his hypocritical bravado. Chris's tragedy, for life, is that she knows the truth about everyone, including herself.

"Stop it, Tom."

"No, I'm serious." The ridiculous young hero, running his hand along her back as if he were too hot to behave. "Why don't we do it?"

"Because you only do it with boys," says Chris.

Tom's look hardens as he grabs Chris's arm. "What'd he tell you?"

Chris carefully reclaims her arm, her face as worried as a mother's. "You shouldn't drink, Tom," she says, "because you can't hold it and it makes you angry at your friends."

"My friends aren't so great," he said; to be fair, we note that he was so embarrassed to say something so dishonorable that he mumbled it.

"Luke wants to give up college and stay home with you. Give up his *future,* Tom! Everything that—no, you *look* at me now!"

"Why don't *you* stay?" Tom asked.

"Because getting out of this place means everything to me."

"I thought *I* did."

They looked at each other, and Tom leaned his head against hers, dropped his glass onto the lawn, and held her lightly by the shoulders.

"I thought we were the friends of forever," Tom went on, rubbing his forehead against hers, shifting his grip on her over and over, as if seeking a foolproof hold. "We were such champs here."

"Tom," Chris said, putting her arms around him only now, at this moment, "that's just high school."

Now comes life, she would no doubt have added if Tom had not, very gently, pressed his lips to hers. He kissed her beautifully, with an attack so tender and giving that she immediately regretted never having asked for this before.

This is what it's like, she thought. To see the hidden side of a wonderful boy. He is wonderful not because he is handsome and sweet, but because he is sorrowful and no one knows but me. I love that part of him because I can carry his pain with me.

"We were the pride of the town," Tom was saying, even as he kissed her. "We're giving that up."

"Who's we, Tom?"

"You know."

"But say it."

"You," he replied, between kisses, "and me," rubbing foreheads again, "and Luke."

Then he held her close, just stood there holding her, perhaps thinking over their wonderful history, and she held him for a long time.

"I'm so sorry," he said.

" 'Strawberry fields forever,' " sang a quavery voice, Luke's voice. He was watching them, and Chris and Tom parted and made this kind of welcoming gesture and he came in there with them, the trio of old together now as they always should be, Chris and her Twins, who's we?, the friends of forever.

"I saw you two kiss," said Luke, swaying in their arms, "and it was so lovely I wanted to be part of it."

"What was the prom like?" asked Tom, mournfully.

"Impoverished. Everybody asked, 'Where's Tom?' "

Tom's head reared back, and he was laughing. "They really did that about me?" he said.

"They really did, Tom."

The three of them together in joy. I love them like this.

"Anything special happen?" asked Tom.

"The band started playing 'Lonely Boy' and we went into the stroll," Luke told him, "and just as Earl Kohnecker and Sheila Forling began making their pass down the lane, Earl cut loose with one of his whoppers . . ."

"Earl *farted* at the prom?"

"Right in the middle of the thing."

"That's Earl!"

"Yeah, but Suzy Dunbar and Gail Hansson screamed 'Oh, gross-out!' at exactly the same moment, kind of like a singing group, and Mrs. Erlandsson came over and chewed us out for Unworthy Behavior and she disbanded the stroll on the spot."

Tom shook his head slowly. "She banned the dance?"

"Threw us right off the floor."

"Wow!" Tom cried, clapping and dancing like a wild man. "I should have *viewed* that! Should have been there with you!"

Luke and Chris shared a look.

Now Tom was shadowboxing. "Who won Cutest Couple?"

"Connie and Sven."

"Yeah," Tom agreed, calming down. "They should. They go so neat together."

Now Tom is pensive, in that advanced stage of drunkenness wherein the mind shakes off all trivia and flattery and is just about to clear. Chris sees that this is the moment when Tom must open up to Luke. She adored that moment when Tom kissed and held her; she would give anything to know how it would feel to be his lover, and everything not to have to know it. She is afraid of his power. Luke is easier, softer. Luke she could handle. Tom would break her.

So Chris tells Luke to take Tom home. Tom does not object. Clearheaded, he sees that the party's over. Luke takes Tom back the long way, along Madison Street, the two boys looking up at the summer sky and kicking stones out of their way and making a pointless and excessive racket because that's how they know they're alive.

"Come on," Luke told Tom, who was lagging. They were cutting through what the town referred to as "the little woods," a stray bit of park that had somehow been left undeveloped during Gotburg's construction boom in the 1950s.

"Tom!" Luke called again.

Tom wasn't moving, and Luke went back to him. In the moonlight, he saw a bottomless sorrow flash across Tom's features before coldness settled there.

"What did you tell Chris about that night?" Tom said.

Luke was silent.

"You had to tell her, didn't you?"

"Tom, your eyes were open."

"Well, I'm really sore at you now, pal."

Luke folded his arms across his chest. "You're not the only one around here with a grievance, you know that? I was going to throw college away for you and what do you do? Cut me off right out of your life!"

"I'm going to beat you up, Luke."

"No, you're not," Luke immediately replied. Then, after a moment: "How would you even *say* that?" And, after another moment: "Why would you . . . That's just so . . ."

"Because of that night."

"Tom, I . . . I did that because I feel so . . . I *need* you in some terribly painful way that is different from . . . what is usual. That night, I thought . . . maybe . . . you felt that way, too."

"I don't," said Tom, in a voice as mean as a file.

"It would be stupid to fight about that now. Besides, you've been fighting me all summer."

"That wasn't fighting. That was time-out. Now it's fighting, *now,* because it's been eating at me that you . . . pulled me in along with you."

"Okay," said Luke, angry now, and eye to eye with his friend of forever. "But you know what? I'm not fighting you, Tom. Because you're *drunk!*"

"No," said Tom, strangely calm. "I *was* drunk. But now I'm very ready."

"You saphead! You think hitting me is going to change what you are?"

"It's going to show you that you're wrong about what I am," said Tom, his body English squaring off. Luke tried to grab him, but Tom struck out sure and fast at Luke's jaw, and Luke went down.

Tom was shaking his fist in pain. "Get up for more," he said, plain as plain.

Dazed, Luke scrambled up, backing away from Tom.

"I won't let you do this," said Luke, his voice low.

"Come here, now, Luke," said Tom, advancing. "Come to me like this."

Still retreating, Luke suddenly changed direction and plowed straight into Tom with a head butt, and now Tom went down.

This is war, with two sides and swiftly shifting fortunes, as Tom rears back and charges into Luke and Luke whirls to the side and makes a grab.

The boys were really scrapping now, furious and determined. They tried to trip each other up, slam each other down, sock each other silly—all because Tom thought he could kill the thing he hated by hurting what he loved. Oh, he loved Luke, all right. He loved that they were the Twins. He even loved knowing that something in Luke responded to what Tom was as no one else—not even Chris—could comprehend. He just didn't like knowing that something in himself responded to Luke in kind. Comedy is easy: *Love* is hard.

Luke was heavier but Tom had the advantage of height and speed and the added intensity of one who shatters a mirror. By the end of it, he had Luke flat on his back, and Tom was pounding him, and sobbing, and holding him, and petting him, and hating him.

Luke was trying to get away, but Tom wouldn't release him. "Listen," Tom kept saying. "Listen."

"Let me go!" Luke gasped out. "Your eyes were open!"

"Listen!" Tom insisted, but then he tore himself away and staggered up a little hill. At the crest he turned and watched Luke carefully get to his feet. The two boys looked at each other for a moment.

Tom said, "I know, you'll never forgive me for this. Well, that's fine, anyhow. Because in point of fact I want you to leave me alone."

"I will leave you alone, Tom," said Luke.

They lived next door to each other. Yet Tom went off in one direction and Luke took himself home in another.

See you in September.

"He has to be drunk to love me and drunk to hate me," Luke told Chris the next day. He wasn't badly hurt—physically—but he was vastly bruised, and he had to invent some story about some stranger in a ski mask attacking him in the woods. Some stranger.

"Probably one of the sophomore jocks," Luke told his father. "They're always trying to prove something."

His father and mother were both greatly aggrieved, and it took all of Luke's strong young sense of independence to persuade them not to call the police.

"If you do, I'll say I fell down a ravine somewhere," Luke told them. "I'll swear to it."

Luke's mother was simply bewildered, but Luke's father, remember, was smart, and he knew that people sometimes have solid reasons for making apparently airy decisions. He may even have been wise enough to figure out more or less what had happened, or at least who was involved. In the end, it came down to ailing joints and black-and-blues for a week or so, then Luke was free of it, except in his heart; and now when he and Chris shared a look, their eyes were a bit older and clearer; and Tom was virtually never around.

It was not till much later that they learned that Tom had actually been called up for his Army physical. He got off somehow, and came back on the bus from Fort Johnson so high on relief that he was seen passing out dimes to the little kids hanging around the President Street Amusement Palace, for the playing of Pokerino and Mini-Bowling and the taking of eccentric photographs, four for a quarter. When anyone asked Tom *how* he'd gotten out of the draft, he just said, "Flat feet," and grinned.

I will apprise you of what really happened: Tom told the Army doctor that he was a homosexual. Amazing? But Tom's reasoning was irreproachable. He didn't want to chance Vietnam and he couldn't see himself living in Canada. There was no alternative but this big little lie, one that many young men of the day were considering and, almost all, rejecting out of masculine pride—including many who really were homosexual.

Yeah, it's a lie, Tom told himself. It's a moment in your life. Some guidance counselor would wave you away from it, saying, It's going to be on your record forever. But what's your *record*, huh? Consider this: It's a file somewhere amid miles and miles of cabinets no one ever goes into. So I won't be president. I'll live.

Tom was not much of a student, but he was no fool. He remembered Bill Hedstrom's older brother Ken's experience at trying to dodge the war in just this way, and Tom learned from Ken's mistake. For when the Army doctor asked Ken if he also had sex with girls, Ken saw a chance to restore his mortified self-esteem and replied enthusiastically in the affirmative.

This was what the doctor was waiting for. "That proves you're not homosexual," said he, smiling as he signed Ken's death warrant—for Ken blew up with a Vietcong mine after being In Country two days.

I can't say that Tom got the same doctor, or even that this doctor was smiling. But he did quiz Tom on his sexual habits, and Tom, who had had the whole of Ken's saga from Bill, was prepared.

"I like girls well enough personally," Tom told the doctor, "but not at all physically."

The doctor went "Mmm" in a kind of tune that lay low, then suddenly jumped for a high note. "But where do you find partners for your . . ."

"Habits?"

"Mmm." *Very* low this time, with a tight, almost wailing high tone at the end. A real Aïda, thought Tom, tense at the immensity of fate that he was trying to buy off but pleased at the way things were going.

"There are some guys in town," said Tom. "They know what to do."

The doctor got creative. "Are you the aggressor in bed, or are you . . ."

"In the kitchen."

". . . the . . ."

"Kitchen, that's where. Beds are out. Kitchens are the place. Because of all those appliances."

"*Mmm,*" all low notes down in the brass section, and short, stifled. Something Beethoven might have liked.

"Now, you take the toaster oven," said Tom, as the doctor stared at him in consternation. Make the nine yards, Tom was thinking; so he winked at the doctor.

The doctor did a little pencil work, and Tom was free.

I lied, he kept thinking; it's in a good cause. Maybe I should have gotten into college and Luke should have gone to the physical, because he wouldn't have had to lie to get out.

Tom continued to make himself scarce and avoid his comrades. Not once the entire summer did he enter the Dawsons' pool or put in an appearance at Sorenson's Lotta-Burger (known to the kids as the "Not-a-Burger" or the "Lotta-Nothing"). He was early off to work and late back, having added a part-time assignment helping Mr. Kjellin renovating Victorians in Caledon's up-and-coming West End.

Sometimes Tom would phone Chris out of the blue and talk about nothing for a bit, then abruptly get off. There were three topics he never mentioned: college, his work, and Luke.

So the summer passed for our friends, and so their forever was put on ice.

"It's over," Tom told Chris on the phone one night. "Summer's over now."

"That's not all that's over," she told him, getting a bit exasperated at having to broker this increasingly strange relationship from the middle position.

"Yeah," Tom said, drawing it out, and adding "well" as slow as it goes. "That's how the pigskin bounces."

"I'll tell you something, Tom," she said. "Hang up on me if you need to. Lounging around at the Dawsons' pool is over, yes. Football and the drama club are over. But you and Luke are not over, Tom. Not by a long haul to Racine."

"Never in a million," Tom laughingly said, hanging up.

Luke, that night, was in his room packing for Berkeley, as his mother came in and out with Things: Things Maybe to Take, on one hand, and, Things That Could I Please Throw Out After All These Years? on the other. Every third trip up to Luke's room, his mother was weeping, but she was so happy for him that the tears felt like a rain of candy.

"I remember when you were about to make your first visit to Grandma Compton's in Middlefort," said Luke's mother, Mary Ellen Reid Van Bruenninger, "and how intrigued you were about visiting another town. You thought everything was going to be the opposite of Gotburg."

She was sewing elbow patches onto Luke's corduroy jacket, because— she said—that was the new sophisticated look in the cities.

"Remember, Luke? You kept bringing us your storybooks and your magic-show tricks and asking us if Middlefort was going to be like that."

"Golly, Mom, I was four years old."

"Then when it was time to leave for Middlefort you locked yourself in the cellar. Remember?"

Luke, trying to decide whether to pack his old book bag or invest in something native when he hit the Berkeley campus, said, "I did that?"

"Uh-huh. *There.*"

Luke's mother proudly held up the jacket.

"Mom, I don't know if they wear a lot of jackets at Berkeley. It's pretty nonconformological there."

" 'Look well to date well' is how they put it when *I* was your age, young man. Mark me, women always go for a dressy fellow. I've probably told you a thousand times how your father swept me into his heart in that black pin-striped suit of his—the only one of its kind, I'm certain, in all Saint Cloud. With the red-and-gray tie and the gray handkerchief falling out of his pocket."

"You *have* told me a thousand times."

"Well, the more you tell it, the truer it gets."

"Time for the men to talk," said Luke's father, coming in.

"Mark?" Luke's mother asked Luke's father, holding the patched jacket against her son.

"Whatever he wants," said Luke's father.

"Luke?" she asked.

"It's fine, Mom. Don't make a big scene."

"Needless to say," she replied, weeping again. "One day they're lock-ing themselves in the basement because they're afraid of Grandma Comp-ton and the next day or so they're going to California, and all they can tell you about that is, Don't make a scene."

"I'm still afraid of Grandma Compton," said Luke.

"Me, too," said his father. "What does it for you, Luke? Her whiskers, or the gigantic biting teeth of doom?"

"I can take the patches off, Luke, if you so wish."

"They're *fine*. Just stop *doing* stuff, please?"

"Food," said Luke's mother, raising a forefinger to demonstrate the wisdom and efficiency of the motherly arts. "Sandwiches and snacks for the bus."

"Mom, it's a three-and-a-half-hour ride."

"Yes, but you're making an early start, and you won't eat before, and there's the plane, and suddenly . . ." Now she was really crying, and she turned to Luke's father, who held her with a sadly wry smile. He winked at Luke, but he was somewhat broken up about this, too, for, as all upper-middle-class parents know, they belong to you till ten or eleven, and they share themselves with you till seventeen or so; but when they leave for college, you lose them absolutely.

Luke's mother went downstairs to rustle up the road food, and Luke's father indulged in what was bound by rules of tribal taboo to be the last embrace in his and Luke's lives. Mr. Van Bruenninger gave light hugs, with his body well apart from yours; a pat on the back and it was over, though the smile he gave you could last for days. Usually, Luke simply endured these hugs, like all teenage boys, but this time he held on to his father for a long time, as if the touch of this strong and unquestioningly loving man could relieve for a bit the regret that Luke felt about Tom.

"You want to tell me about school?" Luke's father asked, as they parted. "You want advice on what to major in? You want to hug me some more?"

"No, I'm okay now," said Luke, moving to the desk. "I'm going to show you the college catalogue and how I picked out my courses."

Luke and his father sat on the pleasantly worn-out couch and pored over the Berkeley catalogue as Luke outlined his strategy.

"First, no classes that start before ten o'clock," he said. "Second, extra-heavy in language and history, because that could come in very handy someday."

"Take plenty of math."

"*What?* I hate math! That was my only weak subject all through high school!"

Luke's father shrugged. "I hate it, too. It just struck me as sound advice, somehow. Isn't this the moment when I give you sound advice?"

"It's okay, Dad. Give me time and I'll figure it out for myself in my plodding way."

"Did you make your village good-byes? Exchange secret vows with Tom and Chris?"

"Chris and I had dinner at Pagano's."

"Fancy place."

"We just had lasagna."

"No Tom?"

"Well . . . it was a college dinner sort of thing. Just this sacred grotty thing we were doing. Because Chris and I have this secret side to our lives, a privacy only for us. I've never told you about it."

Luke talking fast to confuse and evade. Luke on his feet, pacing.

"It was a fare-thee-well sort of thing," he goes on, "and very, very honest. We forced each other to admit things we thought we'd never share with anyone mortal, in our frantic teenage way. And of course we're both very grateful to our parents for making it possible to see the world and get an education. In fact, we had a grateful contest right there at the table, to see who was the more appreciative that we were being permitted to leave this dumb town and forge ahead with our life's work. So I say to you now . . . and I know Chris backs me up all the way in this; yep, all the way . . . I say, let it happen. He's leaving home with his lonely hearts club band of one, and he's going and he's not afraid. In fact, he's excited, Dad. He's not going to cry no matter what. You just watch."

"It was Tom who hurt you that night, wasn't it?"

"Yes," and of course Luke *was* crying, and his father pulled him close and held him again, and let him cry and hold on, till his father was rocking him and humming to him as if Luke were three and three quarters and had just gotten stung by a bee.

"Why did Tom hurt you, Luke? Was it because of Chris? A rivals thing?"

Luke paused for no more than a second. "Yes."

Luke's mother came in. "Oh, that's sweet," she said. "The sandwiches are in a brown paper bag in the fridge. There's chicken-salad and cream-cheese-and-jelly, with Almond Joy and a Granny Smith . . ."

"And a Granny Compton," Luke added, his voice muffled against his father's shoulder.

"Luke, are you *listening* to me?"

"No."

"What about seeing the boy off?" she asked Luke's father.

"Mom, don't be a crank," said Luke, brisk and all pulled together, getting up and taking command of the room. "It's bad enough that I have to get up at dawn. Let's not add to it."

"I can't even watch my own son depart for—"

"Mom, it's a bus to Minneapolis."

"It's a bus and a plane, young man, to be fair about it, and then, Our Lord willing, we won't see you till Christmas."

"If we're lucky," Luke's father joked.

"It's a crazy idea," said Luke. "Picture us all standing there when the bus pulls up. It's so . . . Why would you even *dream* of doing a thing like that?"

"Because we treasure you," said Luke's father.

"It sounds funny to say that," said Luke, after a long moment.

"Yes, well," said Luke's mother, bustling out.

Luke's father nodded. He got up and handed Luke the catalogue. He was about to leave. "You prefer things felt but not said," he told Luke. "I understand that. I'm like that, too."

"I'm not like that. I want things said. I mean, if they ought to be. I like honesty, I think."

Luke's father extended his hand and they shook.

"Dad, you have ridiculously big hands."

"Your mother likes them."

"They're the hands of a strangler. But I like them, too."

"So long, son."

"Night, Dad."

Luke couldn't sleep. However one looked at it, it was an exciting—a promising—step to take, and despite his misgivings Luke was ready to take it. Lying in bed, thinking about this impossible but potentially wonderful and in any case almost certainly necessary step in his life, Luke finally dropped off at about three-thirty, and two hours later, when the alarm went off, he hit the floor like a fireman.

He thought, It's today and this is really happening.

It was still dark when he left the house to walk the three blocks to the bus stop. Gotburg was too small to maintain a proper bus station, so there were simply two corners, in the east and west ends of town, where the buses stopped if you waved. It was cool and, when the sun rose, clear, the start of what Minnesotans call a "no weather" day, meaning no clouds, no rain, no tornadoes, no floods: just the earth, trees, birdsong, and lone Luke trudging along the road. Passing Tom's house and Chris's house, Luke looked resolutely in front of him, but a few paces on he put down his bag and looked directly across the street at Walt's house.

Fired by an idea, he ran over, slipped inside, and sneaked upstairs to Walt's bedroom, where Walt lay on his back, his head at the foot of the bed, tangled half in and half out of the blanket.

Dexter, perched atop the pillow with Walt's teddy bear, Claude, clamped in his jaws, raised his head and wagged his tail.

Luke made a shh finger at him.

"Walt," Luke whispered. *"Walt."*

"Mhnum," Walt breathed out.

"It's Luke. Listen."

"Okay," said Walt, his eyes closed.

Dexter released Claude and watched all this with great interest.

"Walt, I want you to give a message to Tom. Walt?"

"Hmunh."

"Walt."

"Okay."

"Tell him I don't forgive him, but I wish him well all the same. No— tell him I even forgive him."

Walt's eyes were still closed, but he said, "Yes," and Luke, feeling released in some obscure but powerful way, sneaked back outside, holding the door for Dexter, who had followed him through the house.

Dexter proceeded to pee up and down Wild Rice Street as if it were the last day of his life. Between occurrences of lifting his leg, he managed to patter after Luke, because Dexter was friendly and Luke was familiar and the curious business with Walt suggested that there was some exploit in the offing.

Waiting for the bus, Luke and Dexter split the chicken-salad sandwich and the Almond Joy, but in the silence Luke began reviewing everything and he felt halfhearted again in no time.

"Oh, boy," he sighed, as Dexter stared at the lunch bag, wondering what else was in it.

"Dexter," said Luke, "did you ever feel that you've done your best and not only is it not enough, it's totally terrible?"

Dexter pounded his tail against the ground and recommenced staring at the lunch bag.

"My best friend on earth," said Luke. "My whole life of feelings is bound up in the guy. I can't help it."

Dexter barked politely and nodded at the lunch bag in case Luke had forgotten about it. No! He's picking it up . . . *oh,* and putting it into his valise. Dexter whimpered, and the bus hove into view around the corner.

Luke patted Dexter. "Good-bye, pal. Take care of Walt for me."

Dexter barked, and the bus door opened.

"I just want you to know," Luke told the driver as he paid his fare, "that I'm leaving everything that matters to me behind in this town."

"Smoking in the rear," said the driver. "Have a good trip."

Dexter watched the bus curl away down Chickasaw Street and sat, wondering if the bus would come back and Luke would come out of it and share some more of his lunch bag. After a while of nothing, however, Dexter rose, stretched, peed some more here and there—you never know—and trotted back home, parking himself patiently by the front door till Walt's father banged out on his way to work. Gliding inside, Dexter went up to Walt's room and licked Walt's face.

Walt, startled awake, shot bolt upright and shouted, "What happened?"

PART IV

New York City, 1969

FRANK WAS THE head bartender and assistant manager of Hero's, and he opened it every Friday through Wednesday at 3:45 in the afternoon to set up. It was easy work. Hero's was a no-frills bar for virile-looking guys in their twenties, thirties, and forties. The lighting was low, the pool table always busy, the jukebox locked into heavy metal and blues, the dress plain. So was the drinking: Nine out of ten customers would take a can of Bud, and the rest vodka or scotch. You didn't have to worry about setting up for Bloody Marys or Screwdrivers, not to mention Rusty Nails and Coronados and the rest of that uptown nonsense. The Hero's gang didn't come to show off some kicky new style or to impress a date; they came to talk things over and think about who they were and sometimes make a connection to go home and fuck.

It's like this, right? The hottest men are here to seek out the other hottest men—heavy-shouldered, long and lean frames pumped up at Sheridan Square or one of the Y's to the proportions of a high-school quarterback. They're the A's.

Then come the next-hottest guys, the B's, with a minor flaw here or there—a just-missed-it face or unambitious definition.

Then come the borderlines. They do all right if they know how to cruise aggressively and they hang around long enough.

Then come the I-don't-knows, because no one ever takes them home, but they're always around.

What's left are the D's, total rejects. Sorry, buddy.

And that is life as Frank sees it.

It's winter, but the heating is perfunctory, for Hero's offers no coat check, and many of the customers stand around in their jackets. Nevertheless, Frank is shirtless, a big gleaming wolf of a guy with a slow smile and a waiting list from here to next Flag Day. Forty years old and he still has it; he's legend, in fact, from the piers at the western end of the Village to the boardwalks of Fire Island Pines. He's Frank the Bartender.

Who made Bodies Unlimited *the* hot gym just by accepting a free three-year contract? Who flashed Bloomingdale's? Who danced as if he were Pan? Who drove This Year's Trendiest Model to tears at a Pines tea dance by saying, "I won't sleep with you because you're a selfish guy"—not to the point of tears, but to the tears themselves, in public and before the world, as eight dish queens ran home to phone the news all over town? Frank's bright, kind eyes, no-apologies attitude, lurid mustache, imposing nipples, and giant cock have made him a walking magic. What he wants, he is given; he doesn't even have to ask for it. He is a force of nature, a fixture of the scene, and a master of the revels. They call his type a "hot daddy": the expert older man, very loving but with a touch of danger about him. He dates around a lot, but hasn't had a lover in some twenty years. Everyone knows about him and nobody knows him.

Unlike most gay bars, Hero's fills early, possibly because it runs on a strong social energy. This isn't strictly a cruise bar, like Keller's, way down below Christopher Street; or a show-off-your-latest-sweater bar, like Harry's Back East, far uptown on Third Avenue. Hero's is an everything bar, perhaps the one of its kind. There is no emphasis on youth—the twenty-twos are less common than the forty-odds—and, truly rare, there is no air of "whites only." Few of the regulars are wealthy, or even well-off. The atmosphere is almost relaxed, where most of the other bars are studied, presentational. Men come here to cruise, sure—but also to identify themselves and commune and feel what it's like to be gay without asking for permission.

The first hours drag by. At nine o'clock or so, the bench along the wall is filling and the names on the pool table's chalkboard are backed up for three or four rounds. Everyone's still, standing or sitting and looking, mainly at Frank. Jim has arrived. He's one of Frank's most devoted customers—a Bud, with an ingratiating tip. Frank likes Jim: not sexy but pleasant-looking and pleasant-acting, too careful to look hungry. Frank likes guys who nurse their pride.

Then there's this old guy, Paul. He bustles, as if Hero's were his clubhouse. He's over here, he's over there, chatting, declaiming, lecturing. He reads from a notebook. Frank used to be pretty fast at putting people into slots, judging and sentencing them. He moves easy now. It takes all kinds, right? It even takes Paul, one of those touchy guys, quick to quarrel. But he means well. He's political, progressive: Gay Liberation. He's not only old but totally out of shape; but Hero's finds a place for everybody—and what's funny is, Paul's from L.A., too.

Those were the days, huh? Twenty-one and crash out of the fucking closet. The whole thing then was where could you find a guy to shack up with and how many of the possible lewd acts would either of you refuse to do? Think of it: It was actually hard to find a guy who was willing to get fucked. Nowadays, you get a guy every night you want it and you do everything, including a couple of maneuvers that haven't been invented yet. So you invent them: It's today. You invent yourself, with the gym and the clothes and the look. Everyone has a type, but, also, everyone *is* a type—preppy, twinkie, actor-model, leather man, street kid, trucker, loose teen, tight end, Alice in Wonderland . . . The list grows every week.

Now, that is a world for you, Frank thinks, running his eyes over the place—not in case of trouble, because there never is any: just to keep track of things.

Andy's here. Now, there's a sweet guy. Likes to sit at the bar and chat you up about the movies. "Have you seen *Wild in the Streets?*" he goes. Frank says, "Seen it? I *am* it," and Andy laughs and the skin around his eyes crinkles up. Makes him look like a little boy. Must have had a real secure home life to turn out so pleasant.

Henry enters the bar, shrugging off the chill outside, and he and Frank catch eyes and point at each other. (Frank grins and snaps his thumb and middle finger as the index points.) Henry's what Frank's mother would have called "a caution." This means that he's his own man. He doesn't care what you think. If he doesn't like what you're saying, he'll pipe right up about it, and if you give him grief, he'll bounce it back at you, right between the eyes.

Henry gets in there and looks around. He thinks, Is this going to be the same place forever? Same beauties, same drips, same Paul and Jim and Andy and that incredible bartender? Another harangue from Paul about the Historical Possibilities; Jim I know so well I can get his news just by looking at him; Andy is dear, fine, ordinary Andy; and the bartender is death by hunger, so you don't get too close to him if you're smart.

Henry doesn't get too close to anyone in Hero's, actually, because all he turns on to is trash. Street trash, especially the lone, drifting hustlers of Third Avenue, are Henry's fascination. "Wild boys," he calls them. Another type. He likes to think of them as a force of revolution, blithely dismaying the fascist marital system, throwing closeted patriarchs into quandaries and exploding the traditional American hypocrisy about sex. Alas, all he's found thus far is a bunch of kids on the make.

No revolution, Henry thinks. They just are. Paul keeps saying that Gay Liberation means having an agenda. Indeed, Henry and Paul have one. They belong to Sacred Acts, a political group with an agenda so passionate that it is still being hammered out as the mechanics scream at each other. We've got sixteen male and three female members. And if you can find a topic on which any two of these people agree, you're a better man than I am, Errol Flynn.

This is going to be a *very* slow revolution—like when the women wanted a consensus on pornography, which degrades women, and Paul snapped out, "Well, it *exalts* men!" Sacred Acts did two and a half hours on that, and still the genders disagreed.

What's Frank the Bartender's agenda? Henry wonders. What's he after? He seems such contented trash, so amiable with his decision to live without the approval of the Great White Father, of the System, of families, the law, respectability. Is that where our rank and file will come from, or is that our charismatic prince of outlaws? Our president?

"*Henry!* You *dashing* tall and cool white boy, which is my second favorite kind—the hesitant, too-young-for-it frightened little white boy being my *most* favorite—well, now, how be you today?"

This was Jezebel, a black queen with the fastest snap and the biggest chest development in the East Village. Jezebel's love-to-shock-you style was a test even in the everything-goes atmosphere of Hero's. "I'll stuff the tightest ass in the house!" he'd scream, working his hips and showing his fist on the chance that someone was about to retort disrespectfully. "I'll ream some pretty honky boy!" he'd shout, just when the jukebox had finished a side and conversation had dropped to murmurs. Jezebel enjoyed being heard, like it or (even better) not. "I'll fuck all the cops and marines!" he'd bellow, doing his walk and giving the finger to those who were so dainty as to be amazed. "I'll make them do the dance of joy! Teach them *snap jive!*" Turning to a stranger, Jezebel would ask, "Will they *do* it, you say? Hey, ain't you dig my *tell* here? You hear me calling at your door, white?"

That was Jezebel's way of deciding whom he could live with. He had his catalogue of types, like anyone else, and they were but two: those who were part of the Liberation and those who were not. "There go some moderate douche bag, I guess," he'd say, as someone, fearing Jezebel's patter, made himself scarce. "Raised him from a puppy, too."

Then he'd flash out with, for instance, "Who gonna blow on my magic stick? Marilyn Monroe? Deal. Tyrone Power? Too beautiful. I in the mood for some street bish. Who gonna get *on* me, now?"

So, that night in Hero's, Jezebel asked Henry, "You gonna eat me or beat me?"

Henry grabbed Jezebel by the arms and said, "I'm going to hear you and fear you."

"Yeah," Jezebel replied, flexing his stuff. "Yeah, you know what it is."

They pulled each other close for a moment, because they were gays who had already been with each other and had had a nice time and didn't need more—what was known as "getting it out of the way." They were equals, colleagues, and friends.

"Remind me," said Jezebel, lowering his voice and following Henry to the bar, where he bought a can of Bud from Frank. "Did I fuck you tough or easy?"

"We just fooled around a little. At the Everard."

"Oh, the baths? Well, I don't do much *there*. I like a intimate format, you know? Bed and some cushions in pastel colors. Do it family-style."

Henry nodded, distracted by the comings and goings of the men, the types, the possibilities.

Jezebel tapped Henry on the shoulder. "Everyone say you a good catch, upward mobility and such. Next time, you give me six or seven minutes' warning and I gonna bust you head to sideways with my ream. I give you the black boy *landslide* fuck."

Henry grinned. "Jez, you're a man of many moods."

"I got but the one mood in me, and that be meanness. What I am is a man of many personalities."

Henry gulped at his beer; he was about to get moving.

"Now, for instance," Jezebel went on, slipping his hands into his pockets and leaning against the wall in a collegiate manner, "just the other night someone asked me for a recommendation as to which integral recording of the holy Beethoven Nine he should buy." Jezebel smiled, relishing the game. "I told him von Karajan Two. His first set was expert, but the sonics are outdated and of course mono LPs are rather hard to come by except in the specialty shops. Besides, the Berlin Philharmonic plays so beautifully on the newer set."

"Gotta walk, Jez."

"It has been nice to see you, Henry."

Standing in the huge picture window that fronted the bar, Jezebel watched as Henry headed off for the Stud and the Strap. This was Henry's regular tour, combing the streets of Chelsea and the West Village in a sweep running way south and then northward again, from the chummy Hero's down to the cruisy, anything-can-happen Stud, up again to the severe, leather-and-western Strap. All the way, Henry was hoping that he might run into some really nice, attractive, middle-class guy—but *really* nice, and smart, and funny—so he could be detoured from his socially, culturally, and politically ridiculous (and probably dangerous) quest for the Hottest Man Alive.

Life as Henry sees it? The whole thing is Control, and it's Sweethearts versus Wild Boys. Sweethearts are guys you could have gone to high school with; their idea of a great time in bed is to lie with their head against your chest holding on to you and talking intimately. Wild Boys are from another planet; their idea is to fuck their brains out, and they wouldn't know intimately if it fell on them.

Control is what it is. See, with Sweethearts, Henry is . . . well, on top. They respect and want to please him. With Wild Boys, who are by nature out of Control, you become the respecter, even the buffoon. Sweethearts root you in social norms. Wild Boys take you out of this world.

It's a problem: because Henry would like to own the Control, but then he'd have to forgo experiencing the magnificent clarity that Wild Boys bring to sex. It's a terror: because you cannot truly go all the way till you've gone too far. It's a choice: between dignity and ecstasy.

Sweethearts are, like, Jim and Andy. They're good guys, but they're so . . . wide-eyed and fumbly. Henry once spent the night with Jim. It was the right Saturday and the right drugs, and they tried a marathon. Henry made of Jim's body a veritable engine of sin; and Henry came three times and Jim twice; and they did everything; and Jim even got a little abandoned. (Well, what he did was whisper, "Fuck me till I shoot!," which is abandoned for Jim.) But they were both performing, and Henry's looking for something hotter than that, more wired up. Yes, you have your various missions in life. You have friends, leisure, and brunch. But, without the perilous honesty of ground-zero, no-one-gets-out-of-here-alive sex, what is life?

The Stud is oddly dead this Sunday evening, so Henry moves on, watching carefully for the hunters, the teenagers who patrol the empty streets of the dock area, looking for gays to assault. It is nearly midnight when Henry reaches the Strap, the most famous leather bar in the gay world. Everyone's dressed as a biker or cowboy or, like Henry, as an eclectic derivation: brown bomber jacket over jeans, a flannel shirt, and heavy western boots.

Icons, Henry thought as he stepped inside. We worship ourselves.

"Hey, Tex, you live with your folks?" someone breathed in Henry's ear.

"Martin. You missed the meeting."

"Hold this."

Henry took Martin's can of Bud as Martin struggled out of *his* bomber jacket.

"You realize," said Henry, "that the day they declare that the world's supply of used bomber jackets has been exhausted, life as we know it will come to an end."

"To your right, at the corner of the bar, in the blue shirt. Yes? No?"

Henry looked. "Handsome but sexless."

"Look again."

Henry did. "Nice arms," he admitted.

"I love the way the sleeves are rolled *just* halfway up the biceps."

"If you want him . . ."

"Listen, three teenagers were attacked this evening on Eleventh Avenue."

"What?"

Martin nodded. "With a baseball bat, apparently. The whole bar's buzzing about it. Looks like another bashing."

"You mean they were *gay* teenagers?" Henry cried. A couple of men turned around to look at them. The Strap was very strict on style: and real men speak low when they speak love.

"It's not clear who was what, exactly," said Martin. "I don't even—"

"Excuse me," said a younger man, in sailor's blues, behind them. "I happened to be passing the scene when the police were there."

"Yeah?" said Henry.

"They had identified the victims by their wallets, and they all live in the projects on Eighth Avenue."

Martin said, "Hunters?"

The sailor shrugged. "Looks like."

"Who bashes hunters?" asked Henry.

"Maybe we should," said the sailor.

"You're cute," Martin told him. The sailor smiled.

"Catch you later," Henry said as he began a slow tour through the bar.

Control. You're the giver of blessings. The man of note. Decisive and formidable, Henry's second and third favorite adjectives. His first was *dominating*. That's why he kept trying to find a middle-class boy to work with, someone like himself, a Sweetheart.

And that's why he really preferred a Wild Boy: because only the man who wrested Control from the Controller could teach Henry its value. Henry cannot respect what he has: He respects what he fears.

It was cold and Henry was tiring. Still, he took the E train uptown to Third Avenue to see who was Wild tonight.

You wonder how certain locations are singled out for use by gay people. Who chooses the men's rooms that will become hotbeds of furtive activity? Who claims a bar for our crowd? Who decided that the east side of Third Avenue from Fifty-third to Fifty-fourth streets was where the hustlers would hold their fire sale?

Wild Boys. You know what Henry wants? Some fierce and fearless being who doesn't regard the world but simply inhabits it. Someone intrepid—no: *natural*. Like many intellectuals, Henry reckons that his advanced states of conjecture and analysis have denied him access to the life force.

Not too many kids out tonight. Some of the regulars are huddled in doorways, one very doped-looking and slightly older fellow sways in the window of Clancy's Bar, a couple of *objets trouvés* guarding the subway entrance mutter near each other like escaped zanies. Oh, and here's someone new. Someone very young, underdressed for the cold, tall and stocky, with white blond hair. He has a smile, and a way of standing. Oh, yes. Standing like *Everything's okay* and a nice real heavy solid *I am* sort of smile.

Henry isn't wealthy, but he makes a good living, and he occupies, by illegal sublet, a rent-controlled apartment that costs him pin money. He has the spare twenty, twenty-five, for this.

After the standard "How are you doing?" opening and a bit of blather, the blond rejects Henry's offer. "Forty," he says.

"I don't have forty."

"You could get it fer me if you needed it."

But the blond doesn't turn away with a *Keep it moving* attitude. The blond keeps looking at Henry, smiling.

"Everybody finds what they need," he tells Henry.

"Are you southern?"

"Well, now, sure I am."

"Carolina?" Henry asked, for the hell of it.

"West," says the blond, "Virginia."

"That's just below Pennsylvania," says our Henry, meaning to give the boy welcome. "It's almost the North."

"No, it ain't," the boy contentedly replies.

"It's cold," says Henry, wrapping his arms about himself. "Have you a place to go tonight?"

"Didn't ask to stay over, did I?"

Henry, taking a deep breath, asks, "Is the rest of you as breathtaking as what I see? And could I get away with thirty? I think I could swing it that far."

"Well . . . thirty-five then."

"Come on." Henry looks down the avenue. "Here's a bus, even as we speak."

Henry pays for both of them, as custom demands, then joins the boy on the seats at the back.

"Much obliged," says the boy. He looks even nicer in the light. Nice skin.

"My name's Henry."

"Blue."

They shake.

Blue smiles again. "How much do you like me?" he asks. "A whole piece of a lot, or some?"

"Thirty-five dollars' worth, anyway."

"How much is that fer you?"

"A whole piece of a lot."

"Yeah. Okay. Where to, now?"

"East Seventy-fourth Street. Not far from the bus stop."

Blue nods amiably.

"Pardon my lack of expertise in southern folkways, but are you *named* Blue, or did you pick it up because of . . . the eyes?"

"No one is *named* Blue," the boy replies, as if telling a very small child, That face in the moon isn't *really* a man. "But that's all I been called ever. Or Whitey Blue, originally. Shortened it, see?"

On this bus are some vacant old men, a dating boy-and-girl or two, a few weary black women riding home after custodial work, three teenage music students—you can tell by the odd shapes of their black cases and the excited, confidential way they huddle together, as if trading aperçus on some wildly intoxicating subject, such as Pachelbel—and a smartly dressed woman with a boy just big enough to walk.

"No, Cal," she keeps saying, as he stares at a neighbor or starts staggering down the aisle. She carries a toy bag and offers him objects of fascination. He chooses a little plastic tuba, repeatedly blowing into the wrong end, then staring at the piece as if to say, They don't make these toys right.

Blue, sitting two seats away, reaches over, takes the tuba, turns it around, and hands it back to the boy.

"Now it'll really sing," says Blue.

"Cal," goes the mother, for no apparent reason.

Cal blows and the tuba sounds, a deep and absurd little bay. Cal glows at Blue.

"Told you," says Blue. By then Henry has risen to stand at the exit and Blue is with him.

"Bye, Cal," says Blue, as he leaves.

Cal waves. "Bye, bye," he says.

"That was a nice kid," observes Blue as they walk to Henry's building. "Headstrong and clever, I bet. He'll have fetching ways when he's a tad older."

That's right, Henry is thinking, as he unlocks. Get to me, guy. Dazzle.

Henry's apartment is early-middle have-not intellectual, a little den halfway up a brownstone, at the rear. Blue looks around with mild interest, moving here and there.

"The view is good," Henry tells him, pulling off his coat. "In the back?"

Blue obligingly samples it. "Yeah," he agrees, looking out. "Got yer own personal tree right there. A tree in the city."

"It's lovely when it snows. Early on a weekend morning, shimmering white, and . . . It's like one vast snowflake."

"Yeah?"

"Can I get you anything?"

"Glass a water?"

Blue's taking off his autumn-weight coat, his ratty sweater, his two T-shirts, his wacked-out old boots and socks, his pants, his shorts: one flowing rhapsody as Henry, in the tiny kitchen, looks on spellbound.

"Cold in here," says Blue, nude and grinning. "Snappy."

"I was just . . . some ice," says Henry, coming over with a glass.

"Much obliged." Blue takes the whole glass down, nice and slow, then bites off a piece of ice and chomps.

Henry stares at Blue. There's this slogan kind of thing that Henry likes to think of, even say out loud to himself when he's beating off—"a tight-naveled big-hung boy with a beautiful set of tits." It's a phrase of incantatory power; Henry can mesmerize himself with it. It's on his mind now.

"Yeah, I can see you like me, huh?" says Blue, putting down the glass. "Now, what do you need here? Want me on top of you, deep and smooth? You want to blow me? I'm willin' to please you. I can see by the surroundings here that you don't have a lot of dough to throw around. It's a sacrifice fer you, maybe. Not like those guys that pull up in limousines."

"Limousines?" says Henry, tracing lines on Blue's torso.

"We get a few."

Kissing. Henry's attack is slow and tender, moving around the mouth to the neck and cheeks and ears. Blue concentrates on the mouth. Neither one uses a lot of tongue.

Blue smiles. "You fixing to do this clothes-on?"

Henry quickly steps out of his clothes.

"All so fine and trim," says Blue—but he is looking straight into Henry's eyes, not assessing him. "Most of the gentlemen on the street are pretty much past their proper time."

The kissing has made them hard, and Henry dives down for a little cock worship. He doesn't like sucking all that much—after thirty seconds or so it gets tiresome—but he sees it as part of the panorama. It places one by role, as god or acolyte. With a boy friend, Henry emphasizes his intelligence and talents and charm and wit and he plays god to them. With Wild Boys he needs to be taken over, taught, amazed.

Suddenly, Blue pulls Henry up and guides him to the bed, the two of them holding and kissing and grabbing, encouraging each other to up the stakes. Henry is taking out the Vaseline and pulling back the bedclothes and Blue is moving right along with him. It's not business: It's a date. It's sex. It's some real thing they're doing.

"Just go easy on me," Henry warns.

"Ain't supposed to be easy, kimo sabe," says Blue, winking as he greases Henry up. "Yer tight."

"I don't do this all the time."

Blue, helping Henry onto the bed, says, "Get on your back fer me, now. I'm going to do you knees-to-ears." Positioning Henry. Easing him. "You got to pull your shoulders back and kind of throw yer feet way out, and then you'll work real well. You got to really want it, like I really want to give it to you."

"You don't have to perform for me," Henry tells him. "Just be what you are."

"That's not so easy," says Blue, forcing in.

Henry gasps.

"Hurtin' you?"

"No, it's just . . . No, go ahead."

"You're almost ready. I can see that you're hot now."

"I'm thinking all about you," Henry tells him. "About everything you are."

"Bend up to it. Look at how my body's moving. That's the rhythm of it. Yeah. . . . Come with me, now. . . . That's the ticket."

"I hate this," says Henry, "but I need it."

A bit of silence, then, and the steady sawing truth of what Henry is undergoing. Staring at Blue above, he reaches for him, to pull him near, but Blue shakes his head.

"Can't get too close," Blue tells him cheerfully.

More silence.

"Some guys like it rough and yellin'," Blue says then, "but I think this is best. Smooth-style, real fuckness. You like me, right?"

"Yes."

"You feel me in there, right in the center a you?"

"Yes."

"I respect you fer saying that."

Out of his mind with fuckness, Henry grabs at Blue, crying, "Hold me, please. Hold me while you do this."

Blue hunkers down, shrugging Henry's legs off his shoulders so they can close up together.

"You don't want to be fucked," Blue tells Henry. "You want to be loved."

"Needed," says Henry.

"Can't always get that," says Blue; then he hears Henry moan. "Does it feel that good? I never understand that part." Building it, panting, straining. "Whether guys moan because they can't help it or because they just think they should."

"It's kind of . . . *Blue,*" Henry breathes out, caressing the back of the young man's neck, right at the hairline. "Blue, I'm not moaning."

"You are and it's nice." Blue nuzzles Henry's ear, cheek on cheek. "It's nice to get that out of a guy. Make him wild for it. Doing it to you. Let's really start."

"Blue!"

"Yeah, that's . . . Oh, Blue is fucking . . ."

"All the way! Fill me!"

"Yeah. *Yeah.*" Head back and eyes closed. "Oh, that's yeah for me right down to yeah, boy."

". . . Blue . . ."

Gasping, slowing, eyes heavily lidded, Blue let it run down, then rolled over to the side and laughed and patted Henry's chest.

"Good guy," Blue told him. "Real good guy."

Panting and wondering. The two of them, wet and hot. Scary, necessary. Without sex, what is art?

"Bit cool in here on our bodies," said Blue. "Pull up the blanket?"

Henry lay there for a while, then forced himself up to grab the blanket and cover them.

"You didn't get there?" Blue asked him.

"I don't come when I'm fucked."

Blue nodded. He was used to this. Only the most seasoned and exultant bottoms can ejaculate simply by being fucked. The myth that two men screwing leads directly to two men coming is an invention of the writers of porn.

"You want me to split?" Blue asked.

"No."

"You want me to talk?"

"How old are you, anyway?"

"Old enough to love."

"Do they card you in bars?"

"Don't go to bars."

Henry nodded. "Nineteen? Maybe twenty?"

"Seventeen."

"Wow."

"I look older, don't I? Twenty, I always figure."

"It's because you're so tall, I guess." Henry shoved back the covers and gazed upon Blue. "You're a very beautiful man."

"Thank you."

"So . . . smooth and flowing. But you don't go to a gym, surely?"

Blue shook his head.

"So where'd you get those shoulders from?"

Blue thought it over. "Willpower."

Henry laughed. He said, "You're a natural man. What were you like as a teenager?"

"I still am."

"I mean, as a kid, in school. Your parents. Your siblings. Your friends."

Blue considered this, looking at the ceiling, then turned to Henry. "I'd call that a funny thing to talk of with a stranger."

"Just to pass the time?"

Blue laughed. "You want to hear about the Parris boys?" he asked, grinning.

Henry nodded.

Blue stirred a bit, as if seeking a position fit for storytelling. "Well," he began, "this is about Billy Boy and Andy Lee Parris. That was the family farmed the spread just north of us. Sizable place. No back forty or anything, but roomy. Parrises had been workin' that ground so long that they'd moved the farm around over the years. Took this crop over from *there,* and that crop over *here,* you know? A number of wrecked old buildings was standin' in odd places where nobody'd bother with them any more, and one of these was the Old Barn. Basically just a deserted place for kids like Billy Boy and his younger brother Andy Lee to play in. Swing on a rope, hide-and-seek in the hay. Now, I will tell you that Andy Lee was a sweet guy in many certain ways. But Billy Boy was a tyrant to all. He was a bully, and yer friend Whitey Blue was one of his favorite targets."

Speaking at length, Blue's drawl grew thicker and more picturesque. Henry longed to put his arms around Blue as he listened, but he was fearful of vexing the mood.

"Well, Billy Boy Parris made it a rule that anytime I was found on the Parris land, he and Andy Lee could take me to the Old Barn and punish me for trespass. Course, they'd have to catch me first. But the Parris place was situated plumb between *our* place and school. It woulda made every trip longer by fifteen minutes if I'd walked around the Parris spread. I *had* to go across.

"So they'd be lyin' in wait for me, at Billy Boy's direction, and they'd jump me when I passed and waltz me up to the Old Barn. This wasn't mornin's, now, when you had to get on to school, and it was too cold then, anyway. But a spring afternoon would be the perfect occasion. Billy Boy and Andy Lee would get me in that barn and lock the door, and then they'd shuck down my pants, spit me up back there, and each take a turn doing the honors.

"It was this regular thing after a while, with me always trying to fight them off. And failing, what with there was two of them, even if I was big fer my age. So yer saying, How come this Blue here doesn't just go around the long way and avoid the Parris boys? Well, that was partly 'cause of my plain old bullheadedness, and partly because I kind of hankered after Andy

Lee. Now, that was one handsome West Virginia boy, I can tell you, with the dark hair fallin' over his eyes and the smile comin' up so slow you think yer watchin' the sun rise. Billy Boy? He was as pure and stupid a piece of trash as ever I knew. But Andy Lee was someone you might take any way you could get him.

"Anyway, this was all goin' on for a number of years with them and me. They'd catch me and ream my butt out, Billy Boy hasty and pushy and Andy Lee kind of slow and dreamlike. Then, one day, it was Andy Lee to catch me there all by hisself, because Billy Boy was took up with a flu. And that Andy Lee, he didn't grab on to me and run me up to the Old Barn the way he would when Billy Boy was with him. No, Andy Lee took hold of me almost gentlelike, and said I didn't have to go with him unless I wanted to.

"I said, Sure, I'll go."

Blue paused there. He seemed pensive. Then he smiled at Henry and said, "You like this story?"

Henry nodded.

"Don't usually tell such a thing to customers. But you seem finer than most. You suppose I could have some more water?"

Henry went to the kitchen, refilled Blue's glass, and returned to find Blue standing in the middle of the room, looking around.

"Lotta books here. You a writer?"

Henry shook his head, handing Blue the glass. "Editor. Magazine."

"*Life*?"

"*Aficionado*."

Again, Blue downed the water quickly. "Thank you kindly," he said, returning the glass.

Henry just stood there with it, looking at Blue.

"You're not sayin' too much," Blue observed. He took the glass from Henry, put it down, yanked up the blanket, and guided Henry to the couch, where they lay together under the coverlet.

"Comfy like that?" Blue asked.

"Yes."

"So, now Andy Lee led me to the barn real quiet, instead of 'I'll teach you to come snoopin' around' and such similar remarks as Billy Boy liked to make at these times. And, lo and true, what if Andy Lee don't lock the door, drop *his* pants, and bend over like he's going to take instead a give it!

"Well, I give it to him, real friendly-like, the way he always give it to me. Because I truly liked that Andy Lee. But first I moved him over to the hay so we could lie down for it. And then, while it was goin' on, I thought a turnin' him onto his back, to do him that way and get the most out of him, knees-to-ears. So smooth and slow like that. I don't know, it just occurred to me. So there we were, facin' each other and holdin' on, and I started feelin' love for him, and I took up kissin' his mouth.

"Well, that Andy Lee became furious and started shoutin', and he threw me off him and ran out of there, cussin' me out for a devil-son. He must have told Billy Boy of it, later on, because from then on they never waited to nab me for trespass, and word spread through school, and no one would talk to me again. All because I kissed Andy Lee instead of just screwin' his ass and sayin', Huh, that's okay. Things got so tough on me that I decided to drop outta school and work full-time on our land, maybe add a new crop.

"But my father said, No, yer goin' to join the service.

"I said I didn't feature such a fixed term of employment, and he told me there ain't no choice in the matter. The Navy's where I'm goin', or the Army, or somethin'. And that's it."

After a pause, Blue said, "Seems funny that someone else would have such a powerful opinion about how you are goin' to lead yer life, don't it?"

After another pause, Henry piped up with a statement he had made so often he had it down cold: "We were not put on earth to fulfill other people's expectations. We're here to fulfill our own."

"Well, now," said Blue, giving Henry a playful punch. "Hear the trumpet blow."

"I'm dead serious," Henry insisted, sitting up to face Blue. "Do you realize how many people don't know that? Who spend their lives taking orders from authority figures who have only their own interests in mind?"

"Give you no quarrel there, son. 'Cause I sure didn't stick around fer any more of that from my dad, as you can see."

"What made you come to New York, though?"

Blue had gotten up and was starting to dress. He seemed not to have heard the last question.

"If you'd like to take a shower . . ."

"No need," said Blue, hauling on his T-shirt. "Get that done later."

Henry watched Blue dress for a while. Then he said, "You're really something, you know that?"

"Guess I do, more or less."

Henry rose, found his pants, dug out his wallet, and paid up.

"Thank you kindly," said Blue, stuffing the bills into his pocket without counting them.

"I wish it were five hundred."

"You want to take my phone?"

"Sure."

Henry handed Blue a slip of paper and a ballpoint.

"You're not like the other gentlemen on the street," said Blue as he wrote. "Why're you so young, first of all? And a fair-looking guy, certainly. You don't need to pay."

"I'm looking for something."

"Was I it?"

They were at the door, Blue fastening his jacket, Henry nude and shivering.

"It's cold for those clothes," Henry said.

"I'm still new in town. Haven't collected all my northern wardrobe."

Blue had his hand on the doorknob; Henry put his hand on Blue's.

"I have to say this to you," said Henry. "You're . . . you're an incredibly hot guy. The way you did that was just . . . totally wild and true."

"Uh-huh."

Blue got the door open, and as he passed through he said, forgivingly, "But I kinda believe that you didn't enjoy it the way you should."

Chris had been out all day, so she hadn't picked up her mail till well after one A.M. Rehearsal had run long and then she had gone out for a beer with some of the actors, and she knew she shouldn't stay for more than a half hour because she had that asinine paper on *Tristram Shandy* to write *and* a truly vicious Soc exam in three days. But Chris was still working on shucking off her Scandihoovian ways in order to become a New York Woman, and hanging out in a bar for two hours seemed very sophisticated after swatting blackflies in the Dawsons' swimming pool or playing ghost in the family basement.

The mail included a letter from Aunt Brenda, another of her round-robins written for everyone in general—family news, local gossip, and personal items addressed to specific people. This is the kind of letter that begins, "Well, all I can say for *this* winter is no one has suffered frostbite. (So far—ha-ha.) And that deadly Pastor Lagerborg has mentioned marijuana in his last three sermons in a row. He pronounces it 'marjewna,' and the third time, Aunt Greta broke into a giggle fit." There was one line aimed at Chris, by name: "That Uhlisson boy you liked so much has moved to Minneapolis, to work for a firm that renovates old houses. Margit Uhlisson told me he said he never wants to see Gotburg again, and I wonder what *that* means!"

Aunt Brenda and Uncle Carl, Chris thought. Those unbelievably heavy hooded winter coats. Seaweed in the lakes, proms, and "Golly!" All that is behind her. She is Chris de Manhattan, and she knows her choices now.

The other letter is from Luke, at Berkeley. Luke can't compete with Aunt Brenda for news gathering, but he's got feelings. Aunt Brenda strips a culture of its cover-ups; Luke bares himself. He tells Chris about the guys he is drawn to and how absurd he feels taking part in their bull sessions about girls. He yearns for Chris, for someone to whom he can speak himself fairly. "I miss you," he writes. "I love you," he adds. "I know you."

"This is true," Chris murmurs, in her New York Woman way.

Luke and Tom. That Uhlisson boy you liked so much. When they were home from school, Chris and Luke would catch glimpses of Tom from time to time. He would nod and keep moving. So now he was off to the city and out of their lives forever. Was he really as wonderful as she always thought back then, or just beautiful and strange? Luke never fails to mention Tom when he writes, wistfully and with a profound regret that Chris cannot fathom.

Chris is directing Bertolt Brecht's one-acter *The Elephant Calf* with a cast of students and a few East Village N.Y.U. hangers-on. (They're known as "lurkers.") The boy who plays the title role, a ringer from the Drama School, is cute and endlessly charming. His eyes are, like, *very,* and his name is Ty.

Paul enters observations in his notebook. "Sacred Acts is without promise," he writes. "All these boys want to do is go out and have sex. No agenda, just fun. Try to show them how the historical possibilities are opening up, how the times may be ready for a national organization to fight for gay rights, and all that's in those pretty heads is weekends at the beach or making an entrance into Kingdom Come, this year's trendy dance club. At least in my day, the places we frequented welcomed a gay clientele. Kingdom Come is a mess of celebrities, bohemians, tourists, and probably a squad of undercover cops. I gather that one night a week the place is packed with gays, but no one will tell me which night."

Paul has to get up at seven-thirty tomorrow morning. Another dreadful Monday at his dreadful nothing job. God, what would it be like to do something amusing for a living? It's late, yet Paul goes on brooding and writing. "Civilian foot patrols in the West Village?" he writes, underlining it. "Whistles?" he adds, along with "Liaison with straights in the neighborhood?"

Another ten minutes and he calls it a night. He is fastidious in his hygiene, cleaning his teeth, showering, and donning fresh shorts before getting into bed. About to kill the light, he looks about him, at the tiny apartment, the graying walls, the finders-keepers furniture, the collection of paperback novels devoted to the lurid doings of the homosexual underworld. *Lusty Friends, Villa of Forbidden Desire, Swish Beach, Mister Madam:* lavender ménages and nonstop tricking.

Where was all this taking place, Paul wonders, as he gets into bed, during my pathetically ascetic life? Who was holding the orgies? Everyone was so *serious* back then.

Or maybe only Paul was. Anyway, he missed it all. He never had a lover, not even a casual boy friend. Heavens, in those days one scarcely ever heard of two men living together. Although there was that very sweet young chap in the Meeting Group back in California who was always teaming up with somebody. Lincoln? Lester? Or was that his code name? Paul tries to tell the younger gay men how it was. He tells them he isn't really Paul. It's his alias; that's how scary it was. But they aren't listening.

It's the age thing, of course. The gay world used to be about fighting for honesty. Now it's about being good-looking.

Andy's in bed, too, in his little one-bedroom on Grove Street. He has had a very difficult Sunday evening; but he always does, because Sundays he spends with his family, around the corner on Bleecker Street.

It's a full house: Andy's two older sisters and their husbands, Cecilia's two little girls, Gianna's infant boy, and Andy and his parents. It's also very Old Country, not just like stepping into a different world but a different century. The senior Del Vecchios inhabit—in fact, rule—a medieval duchy in which daughters are married off for sociopolitical gain and sons serve in the family army. So:

"Adreiano," Andy's mother announced over the pasta, "I ran into Teresa Lo Gatto outside Café Figaro, and her little Rose Annette has no date for the school dance that they have—"

"I know what's coming," Cecilia put in.

"You shut up, Cecilia. So naturally I told Teresa that my Adreiano would take Rose Annette to the dance. Because it's no good that a pretty girl like that should be left out of a major social event at her school." In an aside directed to Andy, she added, "Probably every boy is crazy to take her, but most boys today are too rough and Teresa tells them no."

"Mama," said Cecilia, "let *him* decide."

"You shut up, Cecilia. So, Adreiano, you'll call Rose Annette, I have the number here for you, and think how grown up and fancy she'll feel, Rose Annette, to be taken to the dance by a handsome young man of twenty-three!"

"Mama," Cecilia urged. "Look at him. He doesn't—"

"You shut up, Cecilia." Turning to her husband, Andy's mother asked, "Carlone?"

Spooning up the noodles, Mr. Del Vecchio paused long enough to say, "He will call Rose Annette and take her to the dance."

"Adreiano, you hear?" said his mother.

Andy said, "I don't want to."

"Why wouldn't you?" his mother cried. "A pretty girl to a dance?"

"It's just that I don't want anyone arranging my—"

"I'm *very close* to Teresa Lo Gatto, and her daughter is like *my* daughter. Can you imagine how I would feel if Rose Annette had to stay home on the night of—"

"Mama, that's ridiculous."

"You shut up, Cecilia. Anyway, it's all arranged, and Teresa and Rose Annette are probably pinning up her wonderful new dance gown *at this minute.*"

"Gianna?" Cecilia pleaded.

"Twenty-three is too old to date a high-school girl, Mama. It looks funny."

"You shut up, too, Gianna. I know what's best. Carlone?"

"She knows what's best."

Andy said, "Mom, I don't even know Rose Annette. We'd both feel very awkward."

"But you'll buy her a heart box of candy when you pick her up, and tasting the candy will break the ice."

"I wouldn't even know what to talk about with her."

"So talk about the candy."

"High-school girls don't eat candy nowadays, Mama," said Cecilia, pulling one daughter's hands away from the oil-and-vinegar tray. "They're all dieting."

"One piece of candy couldn't hurt," said Andy's mother.

"If Andy doesn't want to," said Cecilia, "then Andy doesn't have to." She poked her husband. "Sal?"

"Yeah."

"No, *say* something, you lunk!"

"He doesn't have to."

Andy said, "Actually, Rose Annette and her dance are much less important than the news I have for you all."

"There is *nothing* more important," said Andy's mother with immense decision.

"Mom, I've found a really nice apartment and I'm going to be—"

"No!" Andy's mother shouted. *"Never!"*

"It's still occupied, so I can't move in until—"

"Carlone! He's moving!" Then, fixing Andy with narrowed eyes: *"Where?"*

"I found this really neat studio in a high-rise on East Fifty-sixth Street." Here, Andy's mother let out a terrible gasp, something like the Pietà as rendered by Mount Vesuvius. "It's very affordable, and there's a twenty-four-hour door security, and a sunny terrace on the roof with flower boxes, and—"

"No!" said Andy's mother.

"Mama, let him—"

"Shut up, Cecilia!"

"No, *you* shut up!"

"Gianna, I appeal to *you!*"

"Why can't he live where he wants, Mama?"

"Carlone!"

"No moving."

"Especially so far," Andy's mother reasoned, changing her tone as she collected the empty pasta dishes and nudged Cecilia to serve the salad. *"Sciocchezze,* eh! All the way across the city you'll move! Who knows what kind of people live there? What's the matter, the neighborhood isn't good enough for you, big fancy assistant manager of a clothing store?"

Andy said, "You forced me into that job, remember? I wanted to—"

"Never mind what you want. When it's time for you to move, your mama and papa will find the right place for you, here in the neighborhood."

Andy looked beseechingly at Cecilia, who set down the salad bowl and turned to her mother.

"You shut up, Cecilia," said her daughter Tina, age nine, deftly beating Nonna to the punch.

"Eh, the kid can move if he wants to," said Sal. "Right, kid?"

"Look who's talking," said Andy's mother. "The big-shot auto mechanic."

"If Cecilia ain't complaining—"

"*Everything* he got to fight about," Andy's mother declared. "He don't like the *soup,* he don't like the *talk,* and now he's telling Adreiano to turn against his own mama!"

Andy said, "I'm not turning against anyone. But I'm old enough to make these decisions for myself, and I'm going—"

"You're old enough to take Rose Annette to her dance, and that's all we're gonna to say!"

"Mom," Andy pleaded, starting to lose control, "when are you going to stop throwing these girls at me? I've told you and told you that I can run my own—"

"You *told* me? *You* told *me? Vergogna! Pazzìa!* A snotnose like you is gonna *tell?* Carlone, speak to him!"

"Eat your salad, Adreiano."

Andy's mother had become so exercised at the general air of mutiny that she began to weep, wiping the corner of her eyes with her apron.

" 'Now see what you did,' " said Cecilia ironically, citing a family cliché. " 'You made your mama cry.' "

Roused, Andy's mother gave Cecilia a whopping cuff at the nape of the neck and a good, solid, deeply satisfying *"Shut up!,"* and Cecilia, rising, said, "Sal," and gathered up the kids to shove them into their coats, punctuating the operation with "Sal!" and *"Sal!,"* because he wasn't moving fast enough.

"What?" Mr. Del Vecchio kept saying. *"What?* Cecilia! What's she so hot about? *Luisa!* Make her sit! What is this?"

"She can go, it's fine with me," said Andy's mother.

This was a routine as central to the Del Vecchio Sunday dinner as *The Ed Sullivan Show.* If it wasn't Cecilia, it was Gianna. If Mama didn't start roaring about something, Papa did, especially at Sal. (Stan, Gianna's husband, was half Polish and therefore beneath Carlo's contempt.) The only one who virtually never made or took part in trouble was Andy, the exceptional event being the four months just after his twenty-second birthday, during which he first announced that he had to have a place of his own, and insisted on this, and finally—with an astonishing show of will—did indeed move out, although he abided by the conditions that he let his mother select an apartment within screaming distance of his parents, that he bring his laundry over every Friday, and that he always remain within telephone reach, no matter what he was doing. At that, he was summoned to the Del Vecchios' so constantly that his mother could justify his little place on Grove Street as vaguely unreal, like a lease's no-sublet clause that you have every intention of ignoring. If Andy happened to be unavailable when she called his place of business, she would leave the message "Call home." To her mind, a home is not something you establish. Home is where your mother lives.

Sunday dinner eventually dwindled into Sunday television, with everyone fighting over what to watch, and Andy on the rug playing with his two-year-old nephew. The toys were generic, basic: the simple oval of a wooden train set, a tiny one-octave piano, alphabet blocks. They were bruised but whole, for they had been manufactured at a time when things were built to last. Mr. Del Vecchio had played with them, then Andy, and now baby Keith. A horizon seemed to stretch out to the view as Andy and Keith played, but it lay not before Andy but behind him.

And he *was* going to move, he told himself, as he tossed in bed that night on Grove Street. I already paid the deposit and signed the lease. Besides, this place is much too small. Andy's mother had chosen it precisely to discourage him. She had even chosen the décor, collecting his furniture from various family members; and one day, shortly after Andy had moved in, his mother showed up with a shopping bag full of wall hangings—two paint-by-numbers views of Venice executed by his Cousin Lina, a dynastic family photograph, and a poster for Club Med of some girl in a bikini that she had cadged from his Uncle Ferruccio, who ran a travel agency. Andy tolerated everything but the poster. He pulled it down as soon as his mother left, and replaced it with a group shot of the Rolling Stones. The next time Andy's mother visited, she ripped it off the wall, as she did with each succeeding poster on each successive visit.

In my new apartment, Andy promised himself, everything will be new. The furniture, the stuff on the walls . . . He fell asleep and dreamed that he was being shown a series of homes that became ever larger and more glamorous, till finally he was being toured around a palace: and the realtor was Henry.

Jezebel generally had to step over bodies to get home—drunks, bums, and the various forget-me-nots of the deep East Village, including people conked out in the stairwell of his building. By the time he reached his tiny box, fourth floor rear, he was exhausted with contempt for the world and its inmates. Why don't they get a job and a decent place to sleep? was half his cry; Why aren't job and place provided when so obviously necessary? was the other half.

Grumbling, Jezebel invaded his space, spicy and bitter. No wonder he's always changing voices, personae: Any life would be easier than this life. Anyone else would have more room, that's for sure. Shit, they didn't have any more room uptown, where Jezebel . . . Howard Tynes . . . grew up. Yet, uptown, there was no sense of being caved in on. No sense of your life being measured in inches.

That was maybe because of his family, for they knew how to spread themselves out in limited space. This included such little miracles as Grandma Maggie's giving you change to take your sisters downstairs for ice cream cones when the population count was about to tell on your father.

Grandma Maggie was something. Christmas Eve, she would marshal the crew—her daughter and her daughter's children, Deneera, Howard, and Maureen—and squire them to the toy store to pick out their presents. Grandma Maggie was strict: You were allowed three silly little things and one main thing. Jezebel's sisters would fritter their rights away on trifles and some idiotic doll; Jezebel ran to the forts and gas stations. Grandma Maggie was a grumbler, too, and she deeply resented having to have the kids out so late—past nine or ten or even eleven. But that's when Harlem did its Christmas shopping.

Jezebel greatly missed those days, because Grandma Maggie's thorny wisdom helped him make sense of the absurd white view of the world. When the rules are all aligned against you, it eases the oppression if some-one smart and loving is close by, telling you that the rules are stupid. But "Don't break the rules," Grandma Maggie warned. "Walk aroundside of them. You break the whites' rules, they going to break you."

Trouble is, there is no aroundside of the rules. They're everywhere—where you school, where you work, where you just stand around waiting for a bus. Even if there isn't a white within a mile's radius, his rules are still in force. Money? That's white rules. Television? Cops? You name it, it's white or it's something nobody wants.

Another bit of wisdom that Jezebel learned from Grandma Maggie was the therapeutic effect of a bath before bedtime. "Water's about the one thing whites don't attach a penalty to," she observed, "so use plenty of it." But she mainly thought it a necessity for one's well-being, to rest at the end of a day all nice and clean, lay one's troubles aside, and commune with the inner self. "Don't even have to wash, if you don't feel you need to," said Grandma Maggie. "Just float and think."

Toweling off in front of the full-length mirror on the closet door, Jezebel admired himself, ran his hands over his huge muscles, and gloated.

One thing I got they can't penalize, he thought, is this *heavy* gym on me. Whites, gaze and wish.

Jezebel habitually intoned a litany while getting into bed. He'd say, "Hate my job, hate my poverty, hate most of the people I know. But I am *never* giving up."

Frank, so amiable when on the job behind the Hero's bar, goes sad when he trudges home. He can get through the empty hours before work well enough, listening to the radio or taking walks; and tending bar does keep one busy. But once he locks up and heads downtown to West Tenth Street, he starts wondering about what chances he missed.

I blew it, he keeps thinking. Everything just came to me, right? Jobs, friends, sex. I never needed anything, so I didn't work for anything. Now I have nothing.

What am I? I've been a cop, a mover, a movie extra. I acted off-Broadway now and again, when they needed a guy with a build. I had a shot at fashion modeling and I hustled when I had to. I'm a solo kind of guy, I guess, though I had Larken, didn't I? There was a good man. A man who knew what was right—except, mostly, in boy friends. Where did he find all those schmucks? It finally drove me away, fighting with them on the phone all the time. But I never could replace Larken. I've tried to. You meet some guy who seems more special than the others, get him to stay over, and make him breakfast, smiling at him, trying to get to know him. But you can see him fading out on you even before the toast is browned. Everyone wants to get in my bed but nobody wants to *talk* to me.

I blew it is a rough thing to face at forty-one, but is Frank the best possible Frank he could have been? Or is he a gorgeous hunk of waste?

Eric is sitting on Frank's stoop, shivering in the cold, as Frank arrives.

"They throw you out again?" asks Frank, coming up the steps. Eric rises, nodding, and as he turns to come inside, Frank puts an arm on the kid's shoulder.

"Wait a minute," says Frank. "You hungry?"

Eric nods again.

"Let's stop at the deli."

A bit later, Frank is cooking bacon and eggs in his kitchenette—half-size fridge, one cabinet, no counter space. Eric is sitting in the armchair, silent and upset. Like all teenagers, he dresses total slob: T-shirt hanging out, holes in the sweatshirt, a jacket he must have found in Mammy Yokum's garbage can. It's one of the many things his parents don't like about him. Every now and then they give him a lecture on what a disgrace he is, and they get so impressed with their grief that they kick him out. A pretty teenager walking Village streets at night can usually find some obliging stranger hoping to trade favors: my bed, your body. But Frank knows that this is not good. Besides, as far as Frank can make out, Eric is straight.

The kid is ravenous, scarfing down everything on his plate plus three apples for dessert. The phone rings, and Eric glances quizzically at the clock on the night table: 3:27. But many a New York phone rings that late, especially when the guy you need to speak to works till 2:30 A.M.

Frank picks up with "Yo," a usefully neutral greeting, fit for everyone from a long-lost boy friend to an anonymous fan who wants to close down his day with a jack-off session.

The caller, Bart Stokes, is something between a colleague and a pardner, an old trick Frank occasionally bumps into along the bar, street, and beach circuit.

"Hey, Bart."

"Frank, this is a business proposition."

"Shoot."

"Okay, this guy I know. He's got a loft and a camera and some lighting equipment. He's a commercial photographer or something, but now he's branching out. He wants to make a sexy movie."

"Stag films, you mean?"

"For *our* kind, yes sir. And *real* sex, he says—not that Athletic Model Guild stuff where they just stand around."

"What for?"

"Seems he's going to show them. In a *theatre,* pal."

"You're kidding."

"This place on Eighth Avenue in the Forties. He's run three of them already. Claims to be cleaning up."

"Bart, I'm nuts even to ask this, but where do I fit in?"

"Looks like it's your big showbiz break, my friend. You ready to turn pro?"

"What do I have to do and how much?"

"It's good bread—three hundred smackers for four or five afternoons' work. Three, maybe, the way you heat up a room. What you do . . . Well, you show up, I show up, Phil Neil shows up—"

"The blond with the . . . "

"That's the one. Guy's shooting silent, so there's no script to worry about. There's a story line, but it's . . . you know, some bunch of excuses to get two guys together and then the next two guys. So on, so forth. Like, I'm the plumber working in Phil's apartment and my clothes get all wet, so . . . " Bart chuckled.

"Who am I?" Frank asked.

"You play a cop."

Silence.

"Frank, you there?"

"Yeah, I'm there."

"So are you in or out? He's shooting this week, so I've got to . . . See, he's kind of unhappy with the quality of the talent he's been using. I promised to assemble a more, uh—"

"What the hell."

"That's yes?"

"Sure. Yeah."

"Great. Keep your afternoons open. I'll get back to you with the details"

"I could be crazy."

"Way I see it is, it's nothing you wouldn't be doing anyway. And think of how you'll brighten the dreary lives of our less distinguished cousins. Seeing us in action will inspire and bless them."

"Bart, you are a gentleman and a slut."

"Too kind of you, too kind. See you, Frank."

As Frank pensively put down the phone, Eric asked, "What was that all about?"

"Bedtime for you, youngster."

A typical New York walk-up, the apartment is cold by now, with the radiators dead till dawn. But Frank has stripped and now he peels Eric to the skin and steers him to the shower.

"I'm already clean," Eric complains. But when Frank holds him, under the running water, the boy leans back into the embrace, whimpering for affection—and later, in bed, he says it's Frank's choice, anything he wants.

"I don't go with straight kids."

"Other guys make me," says Eric, complacently.

"That's why I told you, Always come to me. Kid like you loose on the streets, getting into all kinds of . . . Move your arm. Right. There you go."

Eric shifted a bit, then settled his head on Frank's chest. Stroking Eric's hair, Frank said, "If you were gay, I'd sure take you for a ride. But fair is fair."

"Frank? Do you know about a job that I could get?"

"Sixteen, no experience, and—sorry—not the smartest guy in sight?"

"I'm seventeen."

"I'll ask around."

"Frank," Eric went on, taking hold of the big guy, heavy pleading, genuine distress, "please, please help me."

"I will, okay?"

"Frank." Holding on.

"Look, I told you, right? So stop sighing or I'll screw your ass."

"I just wish I could be like you."

"The hell you say."

"Because you're so independent. With your own place, for instance, and if you feel like breakfast, you just dish it up no matter what the clock says."

Eric snuggled up closer to Frank, who growled, "Stop trying to get me hot for you."

"I'm not. Anyway, you are hot now. I can tell."

"Yeah?" Frank took Eric's hand under the blanket and guided it down for a tour. "You ready to take that up your tail?"

"Come on," said Eric with adolescent bravado. "You couldn't get that up the Lincoln Tunnel."

"I'll say one thing for you, you don't scare easy."

"You scare me? Come on, you're this big cream puff."

"Well, three creeps lying unconscious on Eleventh Avenue don't think so."

"What does that mean?"

"That means I went over to my buddy Gordon Niles's place on my break tonight, to pick up his house keys so I can feed his cats while he's in Key West next weekend. Coming back, I turned the corner on Eleventh and saw three guys with a baseball bat jumping two leather boys."

Eric whistled, No kidding!

"Right. Well, I'm not about to walk away from that, so I did a little jumping on my own. Those fuckers were so happy in the act of cornering their victims they didn't hear me coming up behind them. They're shouting away. They're like . . . like vampires. 'We're going to kill you faggots!' Suddenly I've got the bat from them and I'm doling it out. First one in the stomach, second sharp on the knees—boy, does he scream—third on the side. Down they go, a perfect strike."

"Are they dead?"

"I doubt it. But sure as shit those guys have something in them leading them to kill. Tonight it was gays. Tomorrow it's blacks. I say, Kill them first. Then the only ones who die are the ones who deserve to."

"What did the gay guys do?"

"Took off like rabbits."

"You're making this up."

"Sure I am."

After a pause, Eric said, "My brother does that. With his friends. Going after gay guys. They call it 'hunting.' "

"So do we."

"Boy."

"There's this war going on," Frank explained. "But one side doesn't know it. Hunting, right. Hunt them from their jobs and their apartments. Deny them. Jail them. And, for the sportsmen among you, hold a miniature Tet Offensive with baseball bats on Eleventh Avenue."

Frank grunted. "Had a dear friend," he said. "He was murdered in Central Park last year by your brother and his friends. Great guy, he was— smart and funny and generous. A man like that leaves a hole in your being that you never refill. Why's he dead? Defending his country? Battling a fire? He's dead for somebody's *fun!*"

Eric was asleep.

Frank gently moved the kid to the side to give himself some room. Yeah, he'll find the boy a job, and he'll see about getting him a place to stay in, maybe share the rent with some good-humored gay guy with a spare couch. Frank will work on it, though he's got a lot on his mind as it is. He has the Failure of Frank to ponder. He hears the history meter ticking away while he dicks around tending bar and amounting to nothing more than being one of the town's most essential lays. He has middle age to face; once, he had planned to have made Captain by then. Captain Frank the Cop.

What is he instead? He'd say, *Nothing;* but he's wrong. Frank is the Saint of Christopher Street.

Elaine was early. Her editor's assistant had called to reschedule the lunch date from one o'clock to one-thirty, and Elaine said fine. But she couldn't bring herself to accommodate any change in plans, having spent over a week revving up for this day, deciding when she would get up, what she would breakfast upon, when she would start dressing, and how she would enter the Russian Tea Room.

"Abashedly," she said, miming for Lois how that would look, "as if to present the writer at bay amid the fleshpots?"

Or: "Guardedly, out of fear that that close a relationship with one's publishers must impair one's freedom in negotiating the next contract?"

Then: "Commandingly, as the purveyor of chic, bittersweet romances for women, regally condescending to my cult as I enter the temple of luncheon?"

"Fancy stuff," said Lois. "Just do it."

Elaine had had a number of literary lunches in the past, but never one this grand. When her first novel, *A Woman of Some Renown,* was accepted, in 1960, the aging editor had asked Elaine to a quietly pleasant French restaurant in the East Thirties; and they met again in the same place to celebrate the salutary reviews. "You have been *beautifully* launched," the editor told Elaine. With no agent and no writer friends to advise her, Elaine had no idea how to shape her career, but her editor encouraged Elaine's knack for the spinning of stylish yarns about attractive women prospering as they juggled their romantic and professional lives. Her second and third books were in fact entitled *How She Prospered* and *Love and Money.*

I'm trendy, Elaine told herself as all this was going on, not without relish. It's amusing to think of oneself as taking the pulse of a readership. I know everything, Elaine gloated.

"Why do you always tell who made the clothes and the sheets and the cigarettes?" Lois asked. "A sheet is a sheet, no?"

"My readers like to read *la dolce vita*'s labels."

Elaine made a turn with her fourth—the present—book. *Me and Mister Right* incorporated a new and bolder Elaine into the fashionable popcorn Elaine; and she had changed publishing houses. She had been stolen, even: through a letter that, neither euphemistically nor playfully but resolutely, scorning any who would think it ethically questionable, praised Elaine's work and offered her a place in a more prestigious and high-powered house "should you ever want a divorce from your present publishers."

"They really like you" was Lois's very satisfied observation.

"It's lovely to be lured," said Elaine; and she went for it. The much higher advance that her new house offered—on the basis of an outline and the first chapter—enabled Elaine and Lois to turn their savings into a mortgage on a country place. Moreover, Elaine felt a bit relieved to abandon her old house, a tweedy place whose editors were all in their sixties. Her new house had an air of youth and daring, as did her new editor, Johnna Roberts: trim and quick and tense and pretty, with evaluating eyes.

Lois would go for that, Elaine thought, the first time she and Johnna met.

But Johnna was very much a hands-on editor, Elaine discovered. Her former editor had given her absolute freedom, but Johnna, upon receiving the manuscript, sent Elaine a series of letters mistrusting and disputing what Elaine had written, as in "Chapter 4—I don't know what any of these people look like," or "p 183—Won't yr readers loathe daughter's bitter tone?"

She's a good editor, Elaine reckoned. I can see that in her keenness for detail. But she is encircling me, and she is incorrect. Chapter 4—You can tell what these people look like by the way the other characters treat them and speak of them. And p 183—Many a mother has stubbornly earned and thus deserved her daughter's bitterness.

Three books were wish-fulfillment. The fourth one will be documentary.

That, of course, was what this lunch was to be about. New author and editor, new book, new turn in the career. Which way does she go?

"You be the judge," Elaine told Lois, twirling at the front door to show off her outfit.

"Chick, you're *punishment!*"

"The blouse is virtuous, the skirt determined, and the coat"—as she put it on—"is arrogant."

"That's it," Lois approved. "The whole nine yards."

"I shall travel by cab," said Elaine, taking up her green tartan scarf, "for that touch of omnipotence. Oh!" She turned to Lois. "You don't think the scarf is concessive?"

"What do you mean?" cried Lois, who had given it to Elaine one Christmas. "That's cashmere!"

Elaine smiled. "Of course."

"Go on, you goof."

In the doorway, Elaine paused. "How long has it been?"

"Don't mawk at me!"

"Just say, because I'm certain you know."

"Nineteen and a half years."

Elaine blew a kiss and Lois snorted.

Celebrity, in New York, often favors anonymity, and how to enter the Russian Tea Room, Elaine decided, was artlessly. She was shown to one of the front tables—ominous, she thought, as these were the A-list seats and this meant that Elaine's new editor really did have a lot of power.

Oh, well. As long as she had nothing to do but wait, Elaine munched on black bread and scrutinized the company. She saw fame, money, style—exactly what she had been writing about for three novels. Inside one minute, before her gaze passed two television newscasters, a legendary stage actress in foxtails, a splendid-looking couple muttering their way through the fight of their lives, a man so important he employed two bodyguards, one fore and one aft, and a young woman apparently named Snow. At the end of that minute, Johnna Roberts appeared, unapologetically late—another sign of the powerful. Elaine asked for potage Saint-Germain and blinis with caviar, and she had poppy-seed cake in mind for dessert; Johnna was content with some light salad thing, yet further evidence that she had clout and used it because she Knew What Things Were.

But even the people who run the world can't control it, and Johnna started right in on her infuriating boy friend. Books she knew; love she messed up somewhat, it seemed.

"It's familiar," she explained, "but it's incredible. You wouldn't dare try it in a book. Worldly older woman and transparent young man. So it's all about sex, but what isn't?"

"Politics isn't," said Elaine. "Music isn't. Train sets aren't."

"Too real," said Johnna, giving Elaine a once-over. "So your novel. Let's talk."

Elaine took a guess. "You don't like the lesbian sequence."

"I don't dislike it. It worries me, though."

"Ah."

"Do you want to be beloved or bold?"

"Neither, actually," said Elaine, dipping into her soup.

"Everyone in fiction is one or the other. It's better if you choose it yourself. Anyway, your first three novels were all . . ."

"Girl gets *boy*."

"I meant the style."

"Romantic, carefree, upmarket?"

"Yes."

"Suddenly this one," Elaine went on, "is uncertain yet determined. Ambivalent nevertheless ever so hungry. Comic, yes, but psychotically so."

"*Dark,* is how I'd put it. Your readers are used to a sunnier view of the world. Long engagement in heavenly apartments with heroines named

Francesca who own sets of Le Creuset cookware in blaze, or whatever they call that shade of orange. . . . And now—"

"It's about sex."

"And everyone's named Grimma and their kitchens are all pots and pans. This isn't the book you outlined. Even the pages you showed us have been totally rewritten. Nobody has parents or an address." Johnna shook her head as if dazed. "What color is their hair, even? Where have they been?"

"It is not of concern," said Elaine. "I have caught my characters at the moment of decision in their lives. Where they have been doesn't matter. It's solely a question of where they are going." There was a pause. "It's about choices."

Johnna considered this.

"Tell me about your boy friend," Elaine said. "How young?"

"Much too."

"How transparent?"

"Selfish and deceitful. A little light-fingered, too."

"He *steals*?"

"Little things. Candy bars and comic books."

"How young did you say?"

"He's a drama student. Who ever knows how old they are? And who knows why I'm doing this? He's just . . . very . . . seductive. You know that way some men have of focusing on you as if they were a camera and you're the movie? Closing in?"

"Well, I've been with Alicia for so long now that I must have forgotten."

"Alicia? The woman who sometimes answers the telephone?"

"Yes."

"Wonderful name—like one of your characters."

"I really do think," said Elaine, "that most women only pretend to be startled by women who . . . 'love women,' I believe, is the hardy old term for it. They wonder about it, just as a few lesbians wonder about men. So if I slip a lesbian into my novel, I think my readers will be more intrigued than anything else."

"Actually, I wasn't worried about startling anyone. I'm just asking if it's fair to treat lesbianism as a . . . sequence."

"Thank you," Elaine murmured, as the waiter took away her soup plate.

"Your first three books were bewitching. I have to use the word."

"All those Francescas were bewitching, and I was their puppet," Elaine said. After a moment, she added, "It's a good book, isn't it? This one?"

"We don't say good or bad about books. We say, It reads well."

"Does it?"

Johnna looked dead-on at Elaine. "In my opinion, this book will not sell well in its present form. I would want a major rewrite, sequence and all. I would like to see the elegance and charm restored. Of course, we have to consider that you may prefer it the way it is, which would put us in a very awkward position."

"Because if I was adamant about it," Elaine asked, "you wouldn't want to publish it?"

Johnna shook her head.

"It's the old Elaine," said Elaine, "or no Elaine at all?"

Johnna said, "It's about choices."

"I'll mull it over. Now let's have more about your boy friend." Inside, she was thinking, I am forty-seven, relatively sure of myself, a success, and ambivalent. I claim valuable things, particularly: my energy, my byline, and my Lois. I have a gift. I have an audience. I have a great new deal with a major house. But if I don't tell all of you what I have learned of the world and its people, no one will ever know: including me.

This is life as Elaine sees it.

At dinner, Jim was telling Henry, "The trouble with you is, you think gay life is a religion. I mean, *really* a religion. Not the going-to-church-on-Sunday-morning-and-forget-it-till-next-week religion, but a *cult*. To everyone else, it's musicals and dressing right and maybe some dating. To you, it's death and rebirth every day of the week."

"It's all that I am," said Henry.

"See?"

At Williams College, where they were both in Psi U, they had been acquaintances, making "mystery loaf" jokes on the dinner line, blithely grousing about calculus, and faking heterosexual frenzy on "road trips" to Bennington. A few years pass. Then, as so often happens, the two meet up on a street in the West Village on a Saturday night. A bit of miscellaneous nostalgia is framed by warm greetings and slightly warmer farewells. Each then thinks, I wonder. Henry notes that Jim was in a black leather jacket; Jim is almost certain he saw Henry staring Very Pointedly at the humpy blond number leaning against a mailbox just before Jim said hello. They meet again, this time at the theatre—a revival of *Brigadoon*—but each is with a group and they do little more than wave. But next time they meet in a gay bar, Henry grinning and Jim doing a mock take because now the jig is up, and they clasp hands in a good, solid grip, because this time they are going to work on a very different kind of nostalgia—whom they had crushes on in college, who else *was,* when exactly they themselves knew they were—the conversation, in short, that marks the two men's passing from acquaintances to comrades. One hour of such talk and you can be intimates for life.

Every gay man with a number of gay friends in a big gay city has one person to whom he tells more or less everything. This person is not his lover or roommate; it is more likely someone who lives at some remove, someone you telephone rather than say good morning to, or Who finished the milk? It is, in fact, most often a friend from the past, because he already knows a lot of your secrets, and for Henry it was Jim and for Jim it was Henry. They were well suited: middle-class in background, a year apart in their late twenties, relatively eager players on the burgeoning gay scene, smart, articulate, and good-natured. One completely unimportant differ- ence between them was that Henry was in the arts-and-media world, as an editor on the staff of *Aficionado* magazine, while Jim was an attorney. Also—as Jim kept reminding Henry—Jim was prudent in all things (espe- cially sex), while Henry was a berserker.

"You're going to tear yourself apart someday," Jim was saying, "with this ritualization you make out of the erotic. And that hustler stuff is really . . . Look, it's a dangerous scene, you know that. What are you looking for with those creatures, anyway?"

"God in Her wisdom tell me, because even I don't know." Fresh out of fries, Henry reached over to take one of Jim's. "And I wish I could figure it out without having to get reamed all the time."

Jim winced. "Doesn't that hurt?"

Henry snatched another fry. "It's more like uncomfortable."

"You know what you could do?" Jim began. Then he stopped, the way people will when they're about to give you advice and want you to agree in advance to take it.

"What could I do?"

"Give Andy Del Vecchio a call. He's such a nice guy, and he has a real case on you."

"Yeah, I know. *Nice.*"

"What's wrong with nice? Andy would be the perfect lover. He's cute, he's affectionate, he's incredibly loyal."

"What are you selling, a boy friend or a beagle puppy? If he's so fabulous, why hasn't he been snapped up?"

"Fabulous is the *dream,* Henry. You can't live a dream. Anyway—well, take the whole plate if you're that hungry—Andy hasn't been snapped up because he just came out a few months ago."

Henry looked at Jim. "So how do you know so much about him?"

Jim tried on a crooked smile. "I took him home last November."

"And?"

"Well . . . he mostly talks."

"So I figured."

"He just needs someone to show him the ropes. We don't all start in by raping our college roommate, you know."

"I didn't rape him. We got drunk and he got curious. Besides, if I'm that advanced a sportsman, I should stick with the men who can play at my level. I'm not a teacher, Jim. I'm a gay desperado."

Jim checked his watch. "You coming to the meeting?"

"Let's go."

A young man walks up Third Avenue in the Seventies, trying to master his anxiety. He has taken this walk for the past three nights, each time becoming so unnerved as he reaches his destination that he walks right by it, cursing his risible shyness. At Seventy-ninth Street, he crosses to the west side of the avenue, his feet slowing as he nears Eightieth Street. A few more doors and he's there: Harry's Back East, the gay bar that this man has chosen as the first he will enter in his life. For the fourth time, aching with fear, he walks past it.

Tomorrow, he says.

The Kid was holding a tech run-through in Café Tremendo, where he would presently be performing. That evening, in fact, was more or less his opening, though of one of his old acts. He was readying a new one to be unveiled four weeks later, with Heavy Invitations to the press and a summoning of every Major Queen in town.

"Okay," said the Kid, moving a chair from one side of the miniature stage to the other. "This. Yes." He picked up another chair, surveyed the stage, put it down. "All right, forget the chairs," he told the lighting man. "Just pick me up with a spot for the *Camelot* medley, when Bombasta breaks into 'Before I Graze On You Again.' That's the warning for the iris out. I only do sixteen bars, I fade pathetically, and the medley is over. You'll see Bombasta turn upstage in a resigned yet regal pose. *Blackout.* Got it?"

Henry and Jim had wandered in, for Sacred Acts held its meetings in Café Tremendo with the indulgence of Paul, a close friend of the café's owner.

"Hi," said the Kid. "I'm Jerrett Troy."

"It will be marve, it will be ripping, it will be"—this was Paul, bustling in with shopping bags in tow—"*utterly making.* Say hello to Johnny, boys."

Hellos all around.

"Okay, Paul, when does your chum the manager get the piano tuned?" asked the Kid, on the tough side.

"Now, now, Johnny, I knew you when you were hustling—"

"I may have hustled, fat stuff, but you never knew me."

"Please!"

"This guy wants decent talent, he should treat it decently. The piano's a wreck, the lights are a scandal . . . Yes, *you*," he threw at the lighting man. "And the cook refuses me even a plate of something. I am owed better treatment. Is this my life, Paul?"

"Look around you, Johnny. It's a tiny—"

"He's charging heavy cash for me, isn't he? He's trendy, and I'm one reason why!"

The door crashed open, and everyone turned to look.

"Hi," said Andy. "Sacred Acts?"

"Andy!" said Jim. "Right. So you know Henry. And this is Paul and *that's* Jerrett Troy, the boy wonder of cabaret."

"Hi," said everyone.

"Johnny's running his tech for the show tonight," said Paul, motioning the others to a table as far from the stage as possible, which in Café Tremendo was about ten feet. Tremendo was a Village coffeehouse that had gone theatrical, upping its prices while paying the help in food and the performers in exposure. It was a delicate economy, selling the avant-garde at a discount and counting on the artists' need to be heard simply to break even. No one ran a café theatre for the money. Paul's friend wasn't anyone's idea of a good time, but—do him justice—he put it together and he kept it together for subsistence profits, simply because someone had to or the gay world wouldn't have any art besides Tennessee Williams plays and Joshua Logan musicals.

"Sigh," said Paul, taking out his notebook as they all sat. "Should we wait for the others?"

"Andy," said Henry, "it's nice to see a new face here. Are you planning to become permanent?"

"Well, I . . . I guess."

Jezebel paraded in and threw off his overcoat to reveal a jumpsuit and a feather boa.

"Do I or don't I?" he purred. "That *is* the question."

"I know that butt," said the Kid, behind him.

Whirling, Jezebel cried, "Look who's in town! The Mad Duchess of Telegraph Hill!"

They rushed to each other, but, just short of the promised raucous embrace, all they shared was a solid handshake.

"Good to see you, Johnny," said Jezebel warmly, dropping his ghetto intonation.

"You with this group?"

"Yeah, we're going to mash the rules up a bit here."

Martin arrived, still in the suit he had worn to work as a junior vice president in an architectural firm.

"Wow, that sailor," Martin told Henry, drawing up a chair. "Actually," he added to Andy, who was gaping a little, "just a boy in a sailor suit." Back to Henry: "Well, the great thing was, he lived only a block away from the bar, so I went right back after, and that guy from the Red Party was there. Remember?"

"The Red Party?" Paul asked. Something else he got left out of.

"Two in one night?" said Jim. "Martin, are you going for a record, or what?"

Martin looked bewildered. "*Two* is a record?"

"Martin," Henry told Jim, "is our Gold Medalist in cruising."

"I've heard of people spending a whole night at the baths and doing something or other with a slew of people while they were drugged out of their mind," Jim replied. "I've *heard* of it, I mean, the way you hear of the Lost City of the Incas or something. But surely it isn't—"

"*Two* is a *record?*"

"I look around," said Paul. "And all I see is youths. Isn't somebody here at least thirty?"

"I might be thirty-three," said Jezebel. "But who can tell age on a black people?"

The three women in Sacred Acts always arrived (and left) together, as they did now. Dorothy was tall and angular with a lilting southern accent; Tatiana was Ukrainian and supposedly had a great sense of humor that none of the men had ever seen the slightest shred of; and blond, over-weight little Cora wore her hair plaited into the longest braid in the Western world. All three were serious about feminism and oblivious of everything else.

"Here come the Andrews Sisters," said Jezebel. "Pull up the love seat, ladies. I gots the BarcaLounger."

The women settled in, and Dorothy gently said, "Last time, we were discussing the use of social means to better our relations with the police department. Cora has prepared an agenda, and will now share it with us."

"Uh-oh," said Jezebel. "This gone be as long as *War and Peace*."

"It *is* war," said Dorothy.

"And you a piece," Jezebel snapped back. "Pretty piece, too, don't think I ain't notice."

Cora and Tatiana looked questioningly at Dorothy, who shook her head: No, we won't walk out yet.

"Actually," Henry put in, as two other men came in and joined the group. "We've got some pretty lively ideas already here. Paul suggests a basketball game in the—"

"All-male, of course," said Dorothy.

"Well, the police are all-male."

"My point exactly," said Dorothy.

"How about a dance?" said the Kid, coming over. "You want to loosen up the relations, you move to music."

"A dance!" said Henry. "*That's* what we'll ask the police to!"

"That's it!" Martin put in.

"Maybe you should choose a club song, too," the Kid suggested. "I recommend 'Night and Day.' " He sang a sample for them:

Dwight is gay,
So is his son . . .

"Cora will present her agenda now," said Dorothy.

"If Cora would present her hair to the pillow industry," said the Kid, "an entire generation of geese would breathe a whole lot easier."

"That is a chauvinist comment," said Cora, instinctively touching her braid.

"Look, Rapunzel—"

"Shut up, Johnny!" Paul cried. "Go back to your rehearsal!"

"His master's voice," said the Kid, shrugging as he made himself scarce.

Cora and Tatiana looked questioningly at Dorothy: No, not yet.

"A dance would be neat," said Jim. "We'd attract a lot of business, that's for sure."

"Yeah," said Henry. "Can you imagine selling tickets to a basketball game?"

"Where do we hold it?" asked Paul.

Henry said, "How about Kingdom Come? It's at least half gay as it is, and it's gay-owned."

"Really?"

"Well, gay-managed. No one really knows who owns the places we go to."

"It's the Italian boys, isn't it?" said Martin, as Andy reddened.

"Was that true back in the old days, Paul?" Henry asked.

Thrilled to be given the chance to expound, Paul managed to get out "Well" when Dorothy interrupted with "This is another male-oriented activity."

"Dancing?" said Jim.

"The men will dance with men, won't they?"

"So? The women—"

"What women? Ah, *yes,* you see? These festivities are always set up for, run by, and attended by men."

"What are they supposed to invite the police to?" the Kid called over from the stage. "A quilting bee?"

Cora and Tatiana looked questioningly at Dorothy, and Dorothy nodded. *Now.*

"Thank you so much," said Dorothy as the three women rose, "for another sympathetic meeting of the genders."

"Dorothy," Henry began.

She held up a hand as Cora and mute Tatiana, already in their coats, awaited her at the door. "One thing I know," she said, "is that before there can be homosexual liberation, there must be feminism. And the more of these meetings I attend, the more I believe that I cannot make feminism with men."

Dorothy joined her friends, and the three of them walked out of Café Tremendo.

"Damn," said Henry. "God*damn.*"

"Cheer up," said the Kid, fussing with some music sheets at the piano.

"Thirty years from now you can invite them back and give it another shot."

Jezebel said, "Trouble is, you white honky-tonks always seeing things from your side, never recollect that there's anyone else around. Basketball? Sure! Kingdom Come? That my usual place! Funny hair on a lady? That gotta be *aberrant!*"

"So how would you handle it?" the Kid asked.

"Jerrett, my man of stage and screen, I would stop thinking that what I'm used to is all there is. Basketball? Women don't feature that—plenty men, too. Kingdom? Some people do not *care* to dance. Funny hair? Well, maybe you light skin look funny to *me.*"

"Jez, you are raising my consciousness."

"No, I ain't, and that's the pity of it. Because you the most forward person of us here. You do your stuff even on television, 'cause I saw! And movies. You the famous queen of the time. And even *you* don't stop to consider what's being ignored or deliberately left out by 'stablishment masters of the realm."

The Kid sang, "I'm in the nude for love . . ."

Dropping his black voice, Jezebel turned back to the group at the table. "Look, a dance is probably best, since those who don't actually dance at least would have a place to socialize in. But it really has to be coed. It has to. Now, the police have their wives, don't they? We have our boy friends, or some trick of the evening. Is that the whole world? What about our sisters-in-arms?"

"That's a good point," said Andy.

"Anybody know of a very young, very hot man who wouldn't be afraid to play a nude scene?" the Kid asked. "I've got to come up with one in three weeks."

"Go on, Andy," Henry urged him.

"It's just . . . I know the girls come on pretty strong when they get political, but that's just to make you take them as seriously as you take other men. And the dance probably *will* be all-male, won't it?"

"High-school dances aren't," said Jim.

"Yes, but high schools are boy-girl, boy-girl in just about everything except sports. When you go beyond that time in our lives, people start to break up into . . . you know . . . closed groups. . . ."

"Cliques," said Martin.

"And we're just as bad, aren't we?" Andy went on. "That's what the girls are pointing out. Look at us. We're almost all young, white, middle-class. . . ."

Henry liked this bold, sound criticism from quiet little Andy. Jim caught Henry's eye and winked. But Paul, the only older person in the group, stared at his hands; and Jezebel went back into his ghetto tones. "Who say the *police* gone even *attend* a gay dance?" he asked.

"We've got to start somewhere," said Paul, who had been saying that for over twenty years.

So they pushed and pulled at it as one molds warm taffy, and at length they settled on scheduling a dance at Kingdom Come, the men of the police precinct house on West Tenth Street to be their guests and a genuine effort to be made to welcome lesbians. Henry said he'd serve as liaison with the dance hall and the police, and Andy said he'd help Henry and make it a committee; and Jim gave Henry another meaningful look.

"I'm still looking for a sexy guy for my new act," said the Kid as the meeting broke up. "If anybody's got a name and number . . ."

"What exactly is the role that you're casting?" Jim asked.

"A combination cowboy, sailor, and Mountie. I do almost all the talking, so no experience required. The whole thing is looks."

"Is this, like, for a play?" Andy asked.

The Kid looked at him for a bit. "Who's cute but dumb?" the Kid finally said, and Andy blushed again.

"Come on, Committee," said Henry, putting an arm around Andy's shoulder. "I'll walk you home."

"If you think of anyone, gents," said the Kid. "Someone hot who'll do anything for money. Remember, not nice-looking. *Explosive.*"

"Oh," said Henry, stopping. "I know someone."

Blue, wearing the sweater he had bought that afternoon in a thrift shop, was idly looking out the window of his tiny fourth-floor walk-up in the East Village, thinking about Henry. Sometimes, as you're leaving a trick's apartment, you say to yourself, Well, that was nice and okay; but later you start to feel that it was considerably better than that, and you get to wondering what else there might be in it.

"Let me grind the beans here," Andy was telling Henry, "and heat the milk. It'll take just a second."

Henry said, "Relax."

"The secret to having a good day is a perfect cup of coffee whenever you want it. That's why I'm so careful about it."

"It's because you're Italian, probably. Italians are very aware of good food and the like."

Andy looked at Henry like a kindergarten child trying to decide whether the teacher was admiring or reproaching.

"I'm not all that Italian, actually," said Andy, over the electric grinding of the beans. "I'm rebellious. So they tell me."

"Stifling family?"

"Well, not *stifling*. But they're a little . . ."

"Yeah, I have one of those myself."

As Andy opened the coffee grinder, Henry grabbed it, his hand over Andy's hand, and pulled the machine close to sniff the beans. They smiled at each other.

"Yeah," said Henry. "I haven't spoken to my parents for four years now."

Blue loved watching the streets of New York. You could see more in an hour than in all of Blue's hometown on all your birthdays stuffed together. It was like the movies—people kissing, people fighting, people cutting capers. It was the whole world, and a new one to Blue.

He was wondering just now if maybe he should have taken Henry's phone number, instead of just giving his to Henry. He could call and say, What about getting a bite of something in some New York place a yers? I want to hear more a yer talk.

Trouble is, once you're on the footing of buyer and seller, everything you try to do is going to look monetary. Calling up this guy for a meet like that—even a young guy like this Henry—is going to get translated into, You can treat me to dinner and then give me work right after, for the usual fee.

Blue has pride and he does not like to be misperceived.

Blue says, aloud, "I got the lonely boy blues," as he stares down at the street.

Andy whimpers like a puppy when you kiss him. He's in very nice shape, full and round, and Henry is where he wants to be, in command. It's so easy to fall in love, Henry tells himself. But he knows he's performing for the boy. He's not intoxicated: He's expert.

Still, there's nothing like being on top and feeling the rise of the sap inside you, flying straight on high to that *clongg* of delivery, and then

Henry's all over Andy, kissing him and thanking him and holding him and trying not to realize that a man who has just come would be as grateful to Whistler's Mother as to his real object of desire. "A hard cock has no conscience" was a favorite intelligence of this era—but, more nearly correct, it would have run, A freshly exploded cock loves whomever it's lying next to.

Then ask the guy to take you out next Thursday, and see how far you get.

Johnna's boy friend is on the phone, saying, "Lady, why do you not trust me?"

"Because you're young, gorgeous, and a devastating lay. And you know it, unfortunately."

"So you bewitch me, what can I tell you?"

"Cut the bullshit!"

"You *taunt* me."

"Am I seeing you tonight or not?"

"As soon as the rehearsal's over, darlin'."

Nothing on Johnna's end.

"Anybody home?" he asks.

"I'm here," she says, grimly. "I'm trying to recall how many times I've heard you play that as-soon-as-something's-over jazz."

"Aw, don't go schoolteacher on me. You know I'm a crazy man on fire when it comes to you. Thinking about you? I burn."

Silence.

"Break out the sirens, and the spotted white dog."

"All right," she says.

"Forgive me, lady?"

"Only since I have to."

"An apple for the teacher."

A voice calls out, "Ty! Get your butt over here and stop holding up the show!"

"Got to go," he says, hanging up.

As he joins the group, Chris is getting everyone spread out into the improv circle, to put them through games and enactments designed to loosen them up yet make them edgy as well, like horses about to race. Chris knows that improvs make her look a bit faddish, but faddish behavior can be endearing in a twenty-year-old bumpkin who is transforming herself into a sophisticate. Besides, the improvs encourage her troupe to experiment. She keeps telling them she wants everything "weirder, bolder, sillier." It suits *The Elephant Calf*'s dourly comic tone, and its theme, which states, You can prove anything with an argument. *Anything.*

Improvs. Chris has them do goblins, then fat bankers eating themselves to death, then casts half the gang as elephants and the other half as mice. She has them mime their worst fears, their happiest memories; but these aren't effective.

"We're getting far from Brecht," she tells them. "It's a little too Living Theatre."

Someone makes a face, but Ty says, "Hey! Let's do a nude improv."

"That was last year," says the actor playing the Moon. "Every show we put on, there were nude improvs before each performance."

"No kidding."

"It kind of helped with *The Bacchae,* but it was distracting on *Carousel.*"

"Let's get our books," said Chris briskly, pleased that she could handle them with finesse.

As a director, Chris was more concerned with understanding the play than with creating pretty pictures. She was not a dedicated blocker, for instance. She concentrated on readings, talking character with the actors, then letting them try their own moves when they put a scene on stage and simply cleaning up what looked sloppy. Student-directed plays were the pumping blood of the undergraduate drama club, the evenings of three or four one-acts exciting more interest—because of the unconventional repertory and performance style—than did the major productions, such as the drearily sock-and-buskin *Bacchae* (for all the nude improvs before the performances, once the lights came up everyone was standing under a ton of mask) or the ruthlessly leaden *Carousel.* Chris had fallen into the drama club with her typical energy and patience, working her way in by handling props on *The School for Scandal,* running publicity on the winter evening of one-acts, and emerging in the spring of her freshman year as the Widow Quin in a student-directed *The Playboy of the Western World.* Chris's subtext was that she was Mrs. Bjorlind (her sixth-grade teacher) and that the Christy Mahon, the Playboy himself, was Tom (who, everyone knew, was teacher's pet). Chris was a sensation, and she consolidated her rep the following autumn as a daringly campy Gwendolen in *The Importance of Being Earnest.* Chris became a Person of the Campus, at least among the drama students. She was now Heard Of. To Luke she wrote:

Looking back on our youth, I am amazed to see how different my life and society and interests are at this point. Was I ever that moony little

Bobbie Sox who stopped the prom cold simply by dancing with two boys at once? Though it was lovely, the three of us. (Remember?) It was easy to stand out in Minnesota, not so easy here! Wait till summer, dearie—in my short hair, clutching my Greek bag, exploiting an ethnic demeanor—well, you won't recognize me.

Luke responded:

Oh, I'll recognize you, kid. They have short hair on girls and Greek bags in Berkeley, too, you know. Though—what's an ethnic demeanor? Never mind, you'll teach me. How's Tom? Any news?

That was my past, she reflected: the odd sister of two beautiful boys. The one holding the camera for their pictures. Chris was glad to notice that she had departed their story and was developing her own. With her testy, loving, desperate Widow Quin, her intrepidly facetious Gwendolen, and now her direction of *The Elephant Calf,* Chris was on her way to stardom as the American university knows it. In her mind, the immediate future held three things that she must accomplish: to fulfill the science requirement, join her militant friends on the demonstration lines, and lose her virginity.

The rehearsal went well. The play is short, fleet, and picturesque, and cagey Chris had brought a pianist into the company, encouraging him to work out the score through improvs with the singers. "Brecht always plays better with music," Chris, the compleat thespian, assured her cast. Her lighting man—man! a myopic seventeen-year-old who went everywhere in the same hooded red sweatshirt, jeans, and saddle shoes—was a genius, and the costume people were combing the flea markets.

"It's going to be splendid, my dears," Chris told them all, and she was right. What makes a director? A keen understanding of the human character, a sense of structure, and an appetite for the sheer sensuality of theatre, of voices and faces and pageantry. "Think 'Pomp and Circumstance,' " Chris told the actors playing British soldiers, when arranging their entrance. "You're merry kids trying to look solemn!" Or "Watch your timing, everyone," she told them. "Some of you are dragging your lines and some of you are rushing. Keep it crisp and even, *almost* as if you were declaiming—except the Banana Tree. *You* are the center of the show, so you can vary your delivery." And Chris's freezes, four of them at surprising moments, immobilizing the entire cast for five seconds each time, were going to be the talk of the campus.

She was young and untried, but she had *it*. Why? The understanding of character came from her exposure to, her observation of, the Twins; her sense of structure from the ordered upbringing of small-town life; her sensuality from dreams of what Chris might be.

"I'll see you tomorrow at eight," she tells her actors. "And, remember, everyone's off book!"

Rehearsals break up quickly, because the lives of university students are replete and everyone's always eager for the next thing. But Ty dawdles, sitting at a table, chin on hand, gazing at Chris.

"What?" she says, amused.

"Just wondering, boss."

Chris is packing.

"Don't you want to know what I'm wondering?"

Chris considers her answer—flip? bemused? direct?

"Tell me," she says. Direct.

"I'm wondering what you would be like the next morning."

Be cool, Chris. "Aren't all women the same the next morning?" she says. "Radiant and thankful?"

"Well, yes, the first time," Ty concedes, getting up and coming toward her, half smiling, maybe stalking her. "But later . . ."

"What are you like, the next morning?"

"Guess."

"Sinister, my dear. Playful, maybe. Or lazy, yawning. These pictures of you."

"I couldn't be all those things at once, now," he said.

"You're actor enough to play a lot more than that at once," Chris replied, taking up her things.

"Feel like a bite of something?"

"Sure."

They started out together. "I feel like a bite of you, actually," said Ty.

Chis laughed and said, "You're exceeding the speed limit." Flip.

"It's because I'm older than the guys you're used to. High-school boys and college men. I'm twenty-six."

"You're kidding."

He shook his head. "I didn't jump right into grad school after college. That would be, like, homework for the rest of your life. Kind of bummed around for a while first. So there are a couple of lost years in my résumé, and that's a nice feeling. Odd feeling. Nicely odd."

Thinking, Go ahead and stare at his smile, that's what it's there for, Chris said, "You really are a sharp actor. Most of the drama club is just more of the Senior Play kind of thing from high school. As soon as they graduate, they'll be out of the theatre. But you—"

"Well, that's the drama club. *School* of Drama's a different thing. We're the real actors."

"*You* are, anyway."

They turned into the dinky little coffee shop on Greene Street and settled into a booth.

"Whoa," said Ty, opening his jacket and pulling off his scarf. "Winter." He gestured at the waitress for coffee, adding, "And cheeseburgers extraordinaire." Grinning at Chris, he said, "Who'd look at a menu in a place like this?" A bit of consultation, and he called out, "That's one medium rare but not too red and one very, very, very well done."

"One rare, one well," the waitress told the cook.

"Dig New *York,*" said Ty. "Where you can't get what you need. Except the perfect haircut."

"Where are you from?" Chris asked.

"Washington State. Tacoma."

"That's far."

"From *here,* maybe. To itself, it's close, real close."

"Tell me, sexy, are you naturally out of control?" Chris asked. "Or are you just playing it?" Bemused.

"Like how?"

"Oh . . . the bobbing head and the undress-me eyes and so on. Is that shtick or is that you?"

"It's always me."

The waitress brought the coffee.

"We could be real nice friends," Ty went on. "I'd love to get to know you, Chris."

"Can a man and a woman really be friends? Like two men?"

"Aw, men can't be friends. No possibility." He leaned forward. "One guy lets another guy into his confidence, and suddenly it's a boxing match. They'd kill each other."

"Why?"

Ty shrugged. "Jealousy? Insecurity? Poetry?"

They laughed.

"Well, I knew two men," said Chris. "Boys, really. Friends. And they did end up fighting. But for years and years it was . . ."

"Almost a love affair?"

She nodded.

"Yeah, I've seen that. Were they gay?"

And do you know that Chris had never heard the word before in this context? Stunned, she figured it out at once, and considered it as well. It was a bizarre choice of word, yet appropriate, because it was short and meaningless, beyond the windy, academic noise of "homosexual," a quiet little word that you never heard any more. *Gay.* Luke was gay. And Tom . . .

"No, yeah, that happens," Ty went on. "More than you'd think."

"How do you know about this?"

"My friends tell me the truth." Ty laughed. "The gay ones, anyway. Because they know we're hunting different fields. No competition." He lit a cigarette. "Or maybe the gay guys are more easygoing or something. No boxing matches." He laughed again. "No, I don't want to be friends with women. Friends is, like, lend me five till Tuesday. Woman and man is . . ." His free hand mimed a rocket taking off. "Something special."

"Those two boys I knew were special."

"Yeah, just not to me."

Ty had four no-fail smiles—toothy little lost boy, game young man with hidden pain, playful but dangerous-when-wet Eagle Scout, and guy utterly engaged by the woman he's with right now. Moreover, Ty had an infallible instinct for using the right smile at the right time. He crossed the game young man with the guy utterly engaged and brushed Chris's hand several times.

"Oh, Ty, come on," she said, very in charge in her director's voice.

And Ty was thinking, She'll fall easy.

Johnna did not fall easy; she was one of Ty's toughest cases. But then Johnna was very self-protected, because, for all her power and note as a major editor in a major house, she had had little education and was fiercely aware that all her colleagues and authors knew more than she did. The only child of tremendously wealthy philistines, she had leaped to prominence at Macmillan in the early 1960s by fostering three authors of fiction who each cracked the *Times* best-seller list by their second or third book. Then a publisher with Heavy Lit Prestige made Johnna an offer, and she brought her three authors to her new house, where she discovered Elaine.

It was a neat little bio, triumphant and apparently effortless. Johnna had Made It, but she worried the knowledge as a puppy tears into a slipper that stubbornly refuses to come apart. I'm brilliant, she thought—but am I *desirable*?

So of course she told Ty, "I could clobber you," when he finally showed up at her apartment at something like 11:10 that night.

"I'm an actor, darlin'," he told her, smoothing his way into the apartment as she resentfully backed up. He kicked the door closed behind him, still advancing upon her and not entirely smiling. "Actors rehearse, you know."

She was going to melt right down as soon as he reached for her, of course. You knew that and she knew that. She's right about him: He's a two-faced make-out artist. But he's got something that many women cannot resist: confidence. It reminds them of their fathers: for, to a young girl, her father's salient quality is the ease with which he uses her—picks her up, asks and tells her about things of no importance to anyone but her, tucks her into bed. Very young daughters are perhaps the only women that a man—however slippery his sense of command—can feel absolute mastery over.

So Ty can enchant Johnna as her father could, wholly and easily. He especially loves women who have misgivings about giving themselves to him, and he doesn't care why. In Johnna's case, it is because she knows that she is rocking her precarious self-esteem by letting him take her for granted. Ty prefers a woman who fears him physically, fears the humiliating erotic abandon he's going to inspire in her. The younger girls are good for this, despite their bravado; this cornfed Chris kid will work out real nice that way. It's why Ty calls them "darlin'," you know: He finds it wondrous that there is this entire race of people that he can accommodate as naturally as if they were two cuts of jigsaw, and with pleasure unbounded. Ty loves women of many ages, shapes, and coloring; but he has a weakness for smallish and perfectly rounded breasts, long, long, *long* white calves, and terror.

"You tell me one thing," Johnna begins, gently trying to break Ty's hold. "Am I the only—"

Ty quiets her with kisses. He says, "Let me coax you, now. You know I love to coax you." Drawing her into the bedroom. "Give you the slow treatment, deep and tender, and that is so coaxy."

"Ty—"

"Shh." He held a finger to his lips, against the playful but dangerous Eagle Scout smile. Could he get away with this if he weren't young, slim, and handsome? Of course. Women are taken in not by his looks but by his characterization. He is beautiful to them because he concentrates on them, intent and knowledgeable as he is. He *understands* them: and how many other men have bothered to?

•　　•　　•

Bart Stokes's directions for the porn shoot led Frank to a loft in the wilds of SoHo, and Bart himself opened the door. The place was one great room without subdivisions, the bedroom furniture in one corner, the kitchen along a wall *here* and the couch and other leisure pieces grouped around a rug *there*. A skylight let in a hefty share of winter sun, which an assistant was trying to concentrate with the use of great white umbrellas, and the photographer, checking the camera, looked up as Bart brought Frank over.

"Great," said the photographer, as they were introduced. "We got us a King Clone."

"King what?" said Frank, taking off his jacket.

"Perfect. Jeans, cowboy flannel shirt, the boots . . . I could have ordered you from a catalogue."

"What's he saying?" Frank asked Bart.

Bart shrugged. "Some term he uses. A leather-and-western guy with dark hair and a mustache is a clone." He asked the photographer, "Right?" Back to Frank, as the photographer nodded: "Because there are so many of us."

"A *clone?*"

"A copy," said the photographer. "A double."

"Well, that's wrong, because I'm one of a kind."

"So Bart assures me," said the photographer, openly admiring Frank.

Phil Neil came out of the bathroom. "Hey, Frank."

"Phil."

"It's funny seeing everyone shake hands," said Bart, "when we're all going to be fucking in three minutes. Take a look at your costume, Frank." Crossing to some clothes laid out on a couch: "It's the real thing here."

"So am I," said Frank, following him. Under his breath, he muttered, "Say, what's this *clone* bit, okay?"

"Search me where it comes from. But you do hear it here and there." Handing Frank the cop costume. "And it does sort of describe the look of Village guys, stalking around lean and mean." Frank started stripping. "I mean, it's kind of funny when a cab pulls up in front of the Eagle and out steps a cowboy. . . . You're going to be some stuff in those duds, chum."

"So it's just us three in the whole movie, or is there—"

"Yeah, there's a neighbor and a painter. They're coming in tomorrow."

"We're all fixed up with the lights," the photographer called out. "Why don't you all get into costume, and I'll describe the first scene? That's the plumber and the man in the suit. Ready on the set!"

"Real Hollywood," Frank observed sarcastically, and Bart began changing into workingman's attire.

As Bart had warned Frank, it was a silent, a movie so primitive that all it needed was visuals. The day's shoot comprised the film's opening segments: Working alone in an apartment, a plumber accidentally gets his clothes sopping wet, takes them off, and masturbates in a full-length mirror; enter then the tenant, a fancy-dan professional whom the plumber artlessly seduces; whereupon a cop comes in because of a complaint about excessive noise.

"Wait a minute," said Frank. "*What* excessive noise? Those guys have been fucking, not holding a rumba contest."

"The scenario is a little shaky by the standards of Alfred Hitchcock, perhaps," said the photographer, airily. "But this is a fantasy, after all. A dream."

"Your costumes are real enough," said Frank.

"Yes, to strengthen the dream. The clothes tell us who has the power. The man in the suit has the least power, because he's the most civilized. So the plumber has his way with him, and then the cop . . ." Here the photographer faltered, but his three actors were standing there listening to him, their faces blank, taking it in. The photographer went on, "You see, it's a dreamworld populated exclusively by very hot and very available men. It obeys its own rules."

It was an odd grouping: the fat, sweatered photographer and his lighting man, nondescript in jeans and turtleneck, the two of them encircled by the implausibly handsome plumber, fussing with the zippers on his many pockets; and the shirtless cop, his pants resting unfastened on his hips; and the dazzling man in the suit, readjusting his tie before pulling on his jacket: as if fantasy were edging around reality, trying to hem it in.

Frank was saying, "I just think it should make sense."

"Hey, Frank," said Bart, "this isn't *Bonnie and Clyde.* It's a sex flick. Think Forty-second and Eighth."

"Yeah, but it's this . . . this kind of knightly thing we could do," said Frank. "All those guys out there who want to see what it's like when really hot guys get together, right? We can give them something to be a part of, in a way. It isn't just a sex flick. It's like the ancient Greek tales, where they—"

"Frank," said Bart, "it's a movie."

"Anyway," humphed the photographer, "the cop comes in, and of course he's straight, but the other two lure him into a threesome, so first—"

"What do you mean, *of course* he's straight?" cried Frank. "You don't think there are gay cops?"

"Thousands, and I'm sure you've had them all," said the photographer dryly. "But the straight cop who is nevertheless available is a favorite imaginary figure."

"Why can't he be available and gay? Isn't that more inspiring? Because someday you might actually meet one and—"

"*Inspiring!* And *Greek myths!* What do think this is, big stuff? All you're supposed to inspire is a cannonload of jism!"

Frank's eyes got tight and he put the cop shirt down on the couch; but before anything else happened, Bart got to him and was rubbing his back and shoulders and whispering to him. And, though Frank was in a fighting mood, he let Bart subdue him because it felt good, and feeling good was about all that Frank had been working on for the last fifteen years. He'd tell you that himself, straight out. He has lived for pleasure, any way it comes to him. Bart runs his hands up and down the sides of Frank's famous torso, then fiddles with his fly like a pickpocket and tugs down the pants to reveal Frank's shocking erection, a legend of the town.

"See, Frank," Bart whispers to him. "That's all it is here. No story, sport. It's a dream of Frank. That's what this whole fucking thing is about."

How do you forge a long-lasting, meaningful relationship? Easy: You collaborate on a spaghetti carbonara dinner. Henry was the geneticist and Andy the gosling, in Henry's apartment. Henry was teaching life to Andy. Browning the bacon, chopping the cheese, cooking the pasta, readying the egg.

Henry said, "As soon as the pasta is drained, pop it in the pot, beat in the egg, and add the cheese all at once. It happens in a blink, like all the great things in life."

"Yes," said Andy, madly in love with Henry, the first man he'd known who treated him with respect.

"So we have Kingdom Come for the dance," Henry went on, stirring the pasta. "The third Saturday in May. Saturday's the gay night there, anyway." Stirring. "Do you know of an opening somewhere? For a job?"

"Who for?"

"Oh, this kid, one of Frank the Bartender's protectees. Frank's always trying to . . . No, grate the cheese the long way so it . . . That's right. . . . That guy's always got some charity case he . . . I think the pasta's done."

"How does it come about that a dance hall can be gay on a certain night? Who spreads the word?"

"I always wondered. Now, quick, throw it all back in the pot and I'll do the egg. . . . Yes. . . ."

"Is Frank Italian?"

"I have no idea. Why do you ask? See how you thrust it all around till it melts all . . . Looking good, pardner."

"Well, it's sort of Italian to watch out for each other. That's why I thought—"

"Ha! Gays should be like that," said Henry. "Clannish and defensive."

"And do I stir it now?"

"Why can't we . . . Yes, stir it quickly. It's supposed to fall all over itself and melt into—"

"This total mess?"

"Exactly," said Henry, reaching for the plates. "Keep stirring, it'll come."

The phone rang.

"Oh, hell!" said Henry, struggling to get the dinner onto the plates. "We'll take control and ignore it."

"I'll get it," said Andy, leaving the stove.

"No, just—"

"It's no trouble."

"*Leave* it," Henry insisted, grabbing Andy's arm with his free hand.

"Well, it might be . . . See, I gave my parents this number, in case of an emergency."

Henry put down the plates and stared at Andy.

"What emergency?" Henry finally said, his voice like nails ready for a crucifixion.

"It's still ringing," said Andy, moving to the phone—but Henry got there first, picked up, and said hello. Two beats. Then he held the receiver against his chest and told Andy, "In this apartment, there are no parents. By which I mean to say, There are no archons of the system that destroys anyone who insists on living his own—"

"Is that my parents?"

Henry said, "I don't let anyone interpose heterosexual biology into my life." Andy could hear a buzzing through the receiver dots; Henry pulled the phone back as Andy tried to grab it. "You really *have* to talk to your parents now?"

"Is it them?"

Into the receiver Henry said, "Your son is a real sweetheart, lady."

Turning the shade of white of the monument to Vittorio Emanuele in Rome, Andy tried to grab the phone, but Henry added, "He's so tasty, I can see why you're after him, too," and, with a wry look, gave Andy the phone. Control.

Andy had the devil of a time placating his mother, while Henry saw to the carbonara. He chuckled as Andy tried to pass off Henry's remarks as the joking of an outrageous friend. Setting down the pepper mill, Henry murmured, "You have ten seconds to get off that phone," and Andy quickly promised to call back the next day, and hung up.

Andy told Henry, "I can't believe you did that." He wasn't angry—just a bit hurt—and he made the best of it because he knew that Henry was his hook shot into a happier life, quick and true. Henry was all set to chide Andy for allowing his parents to encroach upon Henry's existence, but Andy's undemanding charm touched Henry. He said, "I really am sorry, but I've got this thing about parents pushing in where they don't belong."

Andy said, "That's because you're not Italian."

"That's because I'm not taking orders from anyone. Anyway, let's eat." It was plates on laps, and Henry said, "Was your mother terribly shocked at what I said? I guess I really went overboard, Andy." Henry got up and moved the plates out of the way and pulled Andy up and held him. That's sweet: their first little quarrel-and-make-up.

"Actually," said Andy, as they broke, "she doesn't know what anything you said means. She thought you were one of my rougher friends from high school—they were always using sex talk that way. Like, it wasn't I'll beat your brains in but I'll ream your ass out."

As they sat back down to eat, Andy said, "You know, this pasta is *wonderful*"; and they went on to other things. But I'm worrying, because Henry does not realize how tightly Andy's parents have bound him to them, and Andy does not understand how profoundly Henry mistrusts the motivation of parents. I hope these two will talk it out and work up a game plan before there is another incident. But I also think Andy is old enough not to have to leave a number Where He Can Be Reached every time he leaves a six-block radius surrounding his place of birth, nurture, religious instruction, and high-school graduation. Everyone, at some point in her or his life, has to tell the monitors, *Hold it!*

Pulling up the blanket and folding his arms behind his head, the Kid said, "There was no one like you in the old days."

"Like me?" Blue asked him.

"Generally, when you paid for it—even, I have to say, very often when you didn't—you got a straight or some facsimile. They'd just stand there with you on your knees sucking their insides out. As if, if you got enough of them, you'd turn straight, too. There wasn't that much fucking then, and even guys who were out didn't like to screw. Of course, almost no one *was* out, except me."

"Boy, I hear that."

"Let me show you something," said the Kid, scrambling over Blue to get to the little leather writing case he always took when traveling. There he kept essential documents, and perhaps most essential of all was a photograph that he now handed to Blue, of the Kid at nineteen in a bathing suit standing on a lawn somewhere.

"That's you, huh?"

"That's me."

"Jailbait," said Blue, with the smile of the ace meeting the spade. They were in the Kid's temporary Village sublet after Blue's first rehearsal as the . . . well, the straight man, really, of the Kid's act: in which the Contessa Dooit, Bombasta, and some newer of the Kid's inventions enjoyed characteristic encounters with Blue, whose attire gradually grew skimpier as the Kid's grew more baroque. The Kid invited Blue out for a bite, and halfway through the food Blue said, "I want to date you." He didn't mean malteds at the soda fountain, and the Kid took him home and they got right to it. Blue said it was on the house, but the Kid insisted on paying him something. "Never ask a pro to work for free," he said.

Now they were resting and talking, grinning and caressing each other during lulls. The Kid snapped on the radio, and they listened to a few cuts of Bob Dylan's *John Wesley Harding* till the Kid shut the music off.

"Maybe I'm getting old—no, I'll never be old, for I am the Green Goddess," said the Kid. "But I won't listen to it if Jo Stafford wouldn't sing it."

"Who's he?"

The Kid laughed.

"How old are you, anyway, come to that?" Blue asked.

"Guess."

"Thirty and a piece, I'd say. Thirty-two?"

The Kid was glad. "Pushing thirty-eight, and nobody knows but us."

"You're real trim, though. Young skin, like me. I like to date you, you know that? But how come a nice-looking guy like you dresses up to be a woman on the stage like so?"

The Kid sighed, stroking Blue's corn-silk hair, tracing the lines in his face. The Kid thinks, There's nothing like young, and he says, "You'd think I'd have an answer to the Drag Question after all these years. Something keen that slashes right out when they ask me why I want to play a woman."

"Leave me be," said Blue, shaking off the Kid's touch; unperturbed, honoring the request, the Kid went on, "See it this way—there are two fundamental characters in gay art, the raving diva and the gleaming stud. Like *A Streetcar Named Desire,* or Mae West and the musclemen."

Blue smiled. "Don't know what that all stuff is."

"That's partly what makes you so attractive, unfortunately."

"Is one of those two characters you're talking about like the funny ladies you were playing tonight? The Duchess that does it—"

"The Contessa Dooit."

"I was scared a her."

"It's just an act, handsome."

"And what's that other character again? The man?"

"You. And you're pretty scary yourself."

"No, I ain't."

"Yes. Yes, because you've got it all and you pay no penalty."

"What about all the regular people? Like Henry—he's not one of your two characters, is he? So where does he fit in?"

"In the audience. This is gay art I'm talking about, not gay life."

"Shouldn't the art be about the life?"

The Kid was looking at Blue. "Well," he said at last, "if you want to get serious about it. Yes, the art should describe the life. But who knows what the life is like, since it's all underground? Where did Henry meet you—on Third Avenue, right?"

Blue nodded.

"So someone's going to write a story or a play about a magazine editor picking up a prostitute? Who'd read it? Who'd put it on? I get around the whole thing by treating the myths of the homosexual rather than the everyday. Because we all know what the myths are. One is the camp queen, beautiful in her rage—what we *are.* The other is the redeeming hero— what we *want.*"

"All you're talking about is a good-looking guy, and he won't necessarily be any kind of hero. Heroes is hard to come by."

Suddenly, Blue grinned and shrugged, as if embarrassed at venturing an opinion on something so irrelevant. He said, "You really do this for a living, huh?"

"More or less," the Kid replied. "Someone left me money a long time ago, some crazy investment he had made before he died. So when I moved to San Francisco, I liquidated the assets and bought a house. I occupy part of it, and rent out the rest, and that's what I live on. Nobody earns much doing gay cabaret."

"Could you act, maybe? In a movie?"

"Oh, I've done Hollywood. They still call me from time to time, but only to play fag roles so all the joes in the house can feel superior to gays, which is about the only thing they're good at, besides embezzling from banks and declaring wars and having faces only a mother could sit on. No thanks. I'll stick with my kind, on the margins of the known world, and that is my honesty and my choice."

"Politics," said Blue, dismissing this.

"No," the Kid told him. "My life."

"You want to give me a bit of a rub?" asked Blue. "My back is sore or somethin'."

"Turn over, you heavenly thing."

The Kid worked in silence for a while, enjoying the contact with Blue's heavy shoulders and the sloping V of his torso.

"Feels real good," Blue murmured.

"You heartbreaker. I can see you driving a hell of a lot of men out of the closet. Or maybe back into it."

The Kid gave up the massage and lay prone atop Blue, letting the boy fold his hands around the Kid's.

"Lovely," the Kid breathed out. "I'll have quite a case on you before the run of the show is over."

"You like me that much, maybe you'll take me back to Frisco with you, let me live on the high in your house there."

"Would you really like that?"

"Sure."

"You take it easy, don't you? No passions is the style."

"I'll bet *you* got passions, huh?"

The Kid rolled off Blue's back, rose, and pulled on a T-shirt and shorts.

"What's wrong?" Blue asked, lazily turning over.

The Kid shook his head.

"I meant it about goin' with you, if you'd have me. This place is too cold by far."

The Kid shrugged.

"Now you're real silent. You sore at me?"

The Kid turned on the radio again, fishing the stations till he found one for "easy listening." There was a snatch of Nat King Cole in something the Kid couldn't place, then Doris Day came in with "Papa, Won't You Dance with Me?" The Kid turned the radio off.

"Don't like that one, huh?" said Blue.

"Have you ever loved anyone, Blue, young as you are?"

"Guess not."

"I've never loved anyone, me. It was not my choice. Some people don't, and that may be their loss but it's not their fault."

The Kid sat on the edge of the bed, looking down at Blue.

"But there's this one thing. Many years ago, before you were even old enough to swim bare-ass in the crick or rape a cow or whatever southern adolescents do for a hobby—before you were born, maybe—I knew a somewhat older man who paid me for sex and took me to fancy parties and . . . well, sort of liked me and regarded me as his friend. He was a phony and a jerk and a loser, and though I liked him I couldn't respect him, so we were never . . . Anyway. He died—died horribly, in fact—and it turned out that he had left everything to me. He didn't have much, just this little interest in a firm that built pizza parlors all over Los Angeles. That's the investment that enabled me to buy my house. So I felt really lucky, and very grateful to this man, even though I didn't think much of him. But, you know, as the years passed I began to miss him. I wanted him to see me breaking through in this absurd and glorious, however tiny, career I've invented. I was the first to do what I do and I'm still the best, even if showbiz in general couldn't care less about a man who performs in drag in seedy clubs in the Tenderloins and West Hollywoods and Villages of America. I was the first, and he would have been impressed, and I really miss that man now."

"You're cryin'," said Blue.

"No, I'm not."

"You ain't got tears, but it's cryin' just the same. So come here." Blue made room for the Kid and patted the bed. "Lie down, son. Whitey Blue's gonna fix you up."

"No."

"Come on." Blue gently pulled the Kid down to lie beside him. "I want to date you some more."

A few blocks to the west, along the river, a youngish man in jeans and bomber jacket strides up Eleventh Avenue, hands in pockets because of the heavy wind. (He has plenty of gloves and scarves at home, but bourgeois accoutrements look sissy in the Strap, whither he is headed.) As the man crosses Eighteenth Street, he sees two teenagers armed with baseball bats coming toward him from the northern side of the street, and he instinctively turns to run south. But no sooner has he whirled around than two more teenagers come up on his rear, similarly armed. As they close in, one of them says, "This'll even the score for last week, faggot."

Paul was on the phone with Henry, moaning and lecturing. "It's hopeless," Paul said. "In the last six months, we've picked up exactly two new members. How can we accomplish anything until we're a *crowd?*"

"Calm down, Paul. That's the point of the dance—to get a whole gang of us together to—"

"*Dancing?* We're going to change the world by *dancing?*"

"Dancing is the *introduction,* Paul. Political organization is the goal, but we've got to start somewhere. We're having flyers printed up to hand out at the door, and of course if the dance turns out to be hot, everyone will want to join the group so they can—"

"A *dance!*" said Paul, seething. "How could a dance lead to sociopolitical *awareness?*"

"Paul, we're not registering voters. We're trying to institute the notion of a community."

"I only agreed to this dance in the first place because I wanted *some* event that I couldn't be left out of."

Henry laughed. "I'm sorry, Paul. But you know there's a generation gap here."

"Gay boys are so heedless of mature men. We're invisible."

"Paul, American youth in general is heedless of mature people."

"And what *was* the Red Party, anyway, since nobody told me about it?"

"Same old thing. Somebody hired a loft and invited all the circuit beauties and everybody wore red."

"Red suits? Red shoes? It's ridiculous!"

"I can't say I noticed any suits, Paul. It was more like a black top over red shorts and then you'd take the top off. Jezebel came in a red ball gown with an orange whatever-it-may-be around his shoulders. He was pretty stunning."

"I don't see the *aim* of it, and I'm getting impatient."

"I've got to go. I'll see you later."

Henry hung up and went on to Andy, who had been listening to the whole thing with a smile. They were in Andy's apartment after a long day of living their lives, and Andy was tired and happy.

"Poor Paul," Andy said, as Henry dropped next to him on the couch, holding him, in control. "He's always cranky."

"He's annoyed because he missed out on all this. They didn't have gay dances when Paul was twenty-two. Or gay plays."

The two had just been to gay plays, in fact, on a double bill entitled *Geese*, about the sexual relationships between, first, two young men and, next, between two young women. "Relevant" theatregoing was part of Henry's program to construct his relationship with Andy, to create an emotional bond using the available social norms. They went to movies and off Broadway, sampled cookbooks, did the grocery shopping together, took exploring walks in odd parts of town with guide in hand, caught the same cold together: in short, mated.

The sexual component was less easy to maintain than the rest of it, but Henry was imaginative and Andy was willing. They experimented. They made love in the shower, or partly dressed. They pretended to be strangers picking each other up in the A & P; frat brothers coming out to each other in their room after months of nursing a secret crush; two sailors on leave, with Henry cooing redneck come-ons into Andy's ear, such as "We're gonna shack up tonight, see?" and "You know what it means to be asshole buddies?"; a nervous john (Andy) picking up a hustler (Henry, who modeled his part on Blue). They tried a threesome with Martin, who directed them in a "fuck sandwich": Henry screwed Andy on his stomach, then turned him over so Martin could blow him. Andy said it was interesting but he wouldn't do it again for all the rice in China; and Henry rather liked hearing that. He knew that he was not born to be monogamous, that the excitement of the multiplying possibilities in gay life would always inveigle him. But he resented the loss of control; he felt like a lion having to hunt for dinner every day; Henry wanted to have it right there, like a container of cottage cheese. There were certain hazards to worry about as well. He actually knew someone who had had syphilis—which, to Henry, was like knowing Nana or Doctor Pangloss: fantastical. Henry wanted everything plain and true. He was twenty-eight and contemplating the future. He fancied the image of the settled-in, middle-class gay—could there be such a thing? He would give up bars for brunches, cruising for homesteading. He didn't like the idea of becoming a man whose address is the street.

"You want a nightcap?" Henry asked Andy, heading for the fridge. "There's some white wine left from last night."

"I'm pretty beat. I was going to shower and hit the sheets."

Henry smiled. "Go on. I'll have a glass and then we'll . . ."

"Okeydokes."

They had come back to Andy's place right after the show, and, while Andy went to the bathroom, Henry had unplugged Andy's phone, just in case Andy's parents tried to horn in. Sipping the wine, Henry glanced at the phone—yep, still neutralized. Control. Andy's family was going to break this habit of checking up on him whether they liked it or not. More important, Andy was going to have to do the breaking.

This is easy, Henry thought, lounging and drinking, listening to the running water. It's comfortable. It flows. And it's very pleasant absorbing Andy's admiration. The kid has seen so little of life that attending the theatre is his Book of Revelation. I could learn to love his style, couldn't I? He has the makings of something.

Andy came out of the shower lazily toweling himself, his hair a mop and his eyes dreaming. He started to grin at Henry, but broke into a yawn, like a child kept up on Christmas Eve. Henry got up and undressed, and they moved to Andy's little bed. Tonight, Henry decided, the sex was going to be conventional: kissing and stroking, sixty-nine, then some buddy-up penetration, Henry on top, with Andy on his stomach first and then flipped over for the climax. They were still blowing each other when Andy's buzzer rang.

"Ignore it," said Henry; but it kept ringing, a series of long and insistent buzzes, a rest, then the buzzes again.

Andy scrambled up to answer as Henry said, "It's some drunk"—but listen to what Henry heard Andy say after hello:

"Well, it's probably just disconnected."

"I don't *need* to check it now. I'm in bed. I'll check it tomorrow."

"No, you can't, I *told* you, I'm in bed."

Then Andy turned helplessly to Henry with his hand over the speaker and said, "It's my father. He wants to come up."

"Let him," said Henry, stroking himself. "Let him right in here."

"Jesus, what do I do now?"

"Tell him that if he doesn't back off and leave you alone, you will cut him and the rest of your fucking family off for one full year, no less. And if he makes any attempt to contact you during that year, you will double it and start counting all—"

The buzzer interrupted Henry, ringing over and over, longer and longer, demanding and pushing and taking and mashing. *I own you,* it said. You *give* me what I *want!*

Andy was hugging himself and weeping as the buzzer continued to sound. The tenant next to Andy, disturbed by the noise, was banging on the wall.

Henry bounded up and held Andy, comforted him. "Let's call the police," he said. "I'll get dressed and leave, and when the cops arrive—"

"You can't call the police on your father," Andy sobbed. "They're all fathers, too. They'll arrest *me*!"

"Have we any molten lead? No, right, it's a rear apartment."

"Oh, thanks for joking at a time like this."

But you know what? The buzzing had stopped.

"We won," said Henry.

"Yeah." Andy wiping his eyes, poor kid.

"Listen," said Henry. "When you move—I'm dead serious now—you *must not tell them your address*. You hear me, Andy? The only reason they can do this to you is, well, you let them. You empower them to—"

Now it was angry knocking on Andy's front door.

"Adreiano! Open to me or I will break it down!"

"Who is that?" said Henry. "Mussolini's gardener?"

"He has a slight accent."

Andy's neighbor was banging wildly on the wall.

"Adreiano! You *open*!"

"You can't go on like this, Andy," said Henry.

"Adreiano, who is talking?" Kicking the door, slamming into it, the father who is God.

"Andy, I swear to you, if you don't lay down the law to these disgusting idiots, I'm through with you."

"*No*, Henry! You know how much I count on you! You shouldn't even joke about that!"

"Adreiano! What voices I hear?"

"I'm not joking, Andy. Just . . . just *look* at how you live!"

Henry gestured at the door, at Mr. Del Vecchio's continued assault and the neighbors' infuriated reactions—besides the hammering on Andy's wall, two people were shouting at Andy's father in the hall.

"Look at how you let them trap you. He'll keep that up until you let him in."

"Adreiano! Adreiano! Adreiano! Adreiano!"

"And if you do let him in, he'll see me and figure out what you are."

"No! You're a friend who is visiting."

"In the nude?"

"Well, let's get—"

Henry grabbed Andy's arm. "You can lie about it. I won't."

The banging had stopped, and other voices were heard talking in the hall: Apparently someone had called the police. Andy was jumping into his clothes, calling out "Just a moment, please!" over his shoulder at the cops' summons, a sharp rap and "Open up, police." Henry just stood there, to let it be what it is, as Andy opened the door so slightly a fleeing mouse would have passed it up. Slipping outside, Andy talked to the cops, who had to restrain Mr. Del Vecchio from attacking Andy. The law made short work of the incident, sending Andy back inside after he declined to press charges and warning Mr. Del Vecchio that if they were called back this night he'd spend the rest of it as a guest of the city.

"Got me, pal?" said one of the cops, in closing.

Mr. Del Vecchio muttered something, the cop rapped again on Andy's door, called out, "G'night, there, kid," and the hall was empty.

Henry and Andy were immobile, staring at each other, Henry serious and still naked, Andy miserable and clothed (with his pants on backward). Henry shook his head.

"Tell me what to do," said Andy, "and I'll do it."

"No, you won't. They've got you. You're not their helpless victim. You're their enthusiastic dupe."

"Tell me the cure," Andy pleaded. "I want to live the way you do, Henry. Can I put my arms around you?"

Henry was silent, and Andy stayed put.

Then Henry said, "I can't respect someone who accepts this . . . this unspeakable terrorism. Sacred Acts wants the world to grant legal protections to the most despised people on earth, and one of its members can't even get his father and mother off his back for one night. What a worm you are, Andy."

Henry reached for his shorts as Andy came up behind him.

"Henry, how can you be so hard with me?"

Henry shrugged. "You like it when your parents do it."

"I *don't* like it."

"If you didn't like it, you wouldn't let them do it. You don't try to stop them, so you must like it."

"I've told you and told you, they're like an octopus. You get some tentacles off and they wrap more around you." Andy started crying. "Just hold me."

"No."

Andy moved away and sank onto his couch. He wiped his eyes and watched Henry finish dressing.

"Henry, please talk to me."

Henry seemed to be weighing the next move in his mind. Leave? Not leave? Say something?

"Tell me what to do, Henry" came out of Andy with such quiet decision that Henry immediately responded.

"All right," he said. "Listen. One, first thing tomorrow you change your phone to an unlisted number. Two, call your parents. Tell them you won't be over for the Sunday dinners for a month, because of what happened tonight. Tell them you will institute these boycotts every time they impose on your privacy. Three, you'll say, My phone is now unlisted and out of your reach. I will not give you the number until the day dawns when you stop telling me what to do."

"What if there's an emergency?"

"There, see? You *are* their slave. You've internalized their propaganda so devotedly that you can spout the party line for them when they're not around." He laughed. "Andy, my friend, there are no emergencies."

"Someone could die."

"So? You can't raise the dead."

Andy was silent.

"There are no emergencies," Henry repeated. "There is only their desire to crush you, and your willingness to let them. I can't take this poison into my life."

"No. I'll do it. I will, Henry."

"Maybe you shouldn't." Pensive Henry. "The way you live, you'll only be exchanging one tyrant for another. Frankly, I don't see myself as a tyrant."

"You're my *hope!*"

"Really? Because I'm Give Me Liberty or Death, and you're—"

"I want it, too, Henry. Liberty."

Henry blinked at him.

"I'm going to write all this down right now." Andy fussed at his desk, actually a little table with a span of books and neat piles of paper and notebooks.

"One more thing," said Henry. "When do you move?"

"In six weeks. April first."

"Whatever happens, don't give them the address, because that's your ace in the hole."

"Oh. But—"

"These people would kill you before they'd let you loose."

Trying a smile, Andy said, "They're not that terrible."

"Yes, they are," Henry replied, with immense conviction.

It wouldn't be the 1960s without an anti-war demonstration—or, to put it as Chris's friends put it, "Testing the barricades is part of your education." But I must tell you that for Chris—and for Ty, who accompanied her—the demonstration in Washington Square Park was something between a go-see and a lark. Chris was young, rather entranced with herself, and a bit in love with Ty. Wherever he was, that place became a romantic rendezvous. Besides, there was very little sense of confrontation about the outing: The police were obviously disgusted but keeping their distance, and bystanders ranged from the neutral through the amused to the firmly supportive.

"Where are all the pro-war people?" Chris asked Mark, the bearded grad student who was in charge of their section of the rally.

Mark shrugged. "Just keep warm and look clean," he said, whereupon Ty and Thompson appeared with the brown paper bags of take-out coffee without which no demonstration could be called idiomatic. Thompson and his dorm roommate, Chase, who was also on the line with Chris, held a major place in Chris's coterie, as fellow stalwarts of the drama club, as natives of cities (Chicago and Washington, D.C., respectively) and thus models of urbanity to small-town Chris, and as (she suspected) gay boys, possibly lovers, which made them especially enticing.

I wonder if Chris has noticed that her friends tend to be male, whether straight or gay?

Chris was closer to Thompson than to Chase, because Thompson seemed to have an endless supply of pot and was always in a mood to toke up. Smoking was rampant on the campus, of course—but most students couldn't afford the habit and more or less bummed off each other. Thompson, however, was a rich kid: also tall and phlegmatic, almost wooden, where Chase was short and energetic, with busy eyes and flailing gestures. Chris wondered what they were like at night together. Quiet Thompson would surely be in charge of Chase. Picturing them, she would flash back to Luke and Tom. Who'd be in charge there, if her two boy friends of the tree house could be reconciled, if the past could be corrected? Tom said he never wants to see Gotburg again.

Well, Chris thought, I probably don't, either. How could one return to that drably pristine world after having directed plays and stood on the barricades? College wasn't more school, as Chris had anticipated. School was a normalization of the familiar. College was a penetration into the exotic.

For instance: getting fucked by Ty. Because Chris had no doubt that this was where the two of them were headed. It was wild—well, really amusing . . . or possibly the tiniest bit alarming—to see such dreamily calculating aggression in a man. In high school, it meant he expected to get his hands inside your bra. With Ty, it meant you are going to surrender to him the very center of your body. She had thought about this very carefully, and was very satisfied to give in to Ty, because he'd want it to feel beautiful to her out of his vanity: the actor pleasing his director.

Ty got on well with everyone, Chris noticed, watching him bantering with Thompson and Chase and listening almost respectfully to Mark's occasional notes on the Issues. It wasn't all *that* cold, the sunlight was plentiful, and the kids were enthusiastic. It would have been a highly fulfilling event but for a bunch of frat galoots who came barreling into the park on skateboards, deliberately steering as close as possible to the edge of the line of demonstrators. Immediately, the rally monitors—readily discerned by their orange sashes and clipboards—were converging upon the police, cool and polite but quick, fervent. The police shrugged; twenty years younger and they'd have been on the skateboards, too.

So the protesters started shouting at the goons as they tooled back for another run. The cop in charge, a lieutenant, was halfheartedly trying to signal the goons to ride off, but he had also told his men to stay in formation. Let it happen, was his idea: If these candy-ass lefty bullshitters get physical, the cops can break the whole thing up and clear the park.

Chris said, "I don't like this."

"Are we allowed to leave," Chase asked, "or do we have to be dismissed? Because—"

"Whoa, this is nothing," said Ty. "It's local color. A challenge match. Playing chicken on skateboards."

Mark and the other monitors were conferring with two students who were not part of the protest.

"They're from the paper," said Thompson. "The tall one is the deputy editor."

The other one had a camera. After shooting the demonstrators and the cops, he paused, watching the frat goons spinning their wheels and smirking. Then he raised the camera and took them into the story, even as the monitors rejoined the students and told them to leave the park and stay cool and avoid contact with the goons. There would be an editorial in the paper tomorrow and a fresh demonstration the following day, this time not in defiance of the war but in defense of free speech.

"Don't give them anything to play with," the monitors urged as the demonstrators dispersed. "Say nothing and leave immediately."

Thompson and Chase were happy to get out of there, however, and Ty, looking over the scene, gave a shrug and started moving. But Chris was staring at those frat goons, smug and self-righteous as Crusaders mounted before some defenseless town. She paused as the student with the camera had paused; like him, she was realizing something. This is where the violence in the world comes from, she was thinking. These aren't simply the odious jocks that students in the arts majors joke about. (For instance: A jock picked his nose—and his head caved in.) No. These are the men who beat and rape women, who most enthusiastically subscribe to the conventional bigotries because everything different from them is hateful, who spoil freedom for everyone else.

The field was so cleared by now that Chris, with Ty pulling on her arm, stood out. One of the goons, showing off, glided by on his board, his body planted sideways so it directly faced Chris, his arms thrown out to the sides, his face lit with a merry grin.

"Hey, honey box!" he called as he sailed past.

Chris stared at him, Ty gently telling her to give it up. He said, "It's all over, boss."

Hitting a dead end, the goon reversed and flew back before Chris, shouting, "Hey, leave the faggot and meet a real man!"

The other goons laughed and hooted and made various tribal signs.

"Darlin'," Ty began; Chris said, "Hold this," handed him her attaché, and walked over to the police, immobile in their line. She looked up and down the file, looked them right in the eyes. She said—not all that loud, but they surely heard her—"Where I come from, the police are heroes. They are courageous and kind. They do amazing things like trekking out at night in blizzards to search for folks who haven't been accounted for and may be stuck on the road. They comfort injured children on the way to the hospital. They attend to the grief of survivors at a time of death. We call them police, but they're really guardians. They see their job as protecting the innocent, whether against Acts of God or a predatory creep."

Without shifting her gaze to the goons ranged to her right, Chris went on, "There's a gang of predatory creeps right over there, and you're on their side. You're not like the police in Minnesota. You're no one's guardian. The only difference between those frat rats and you is that you're in blue coats."

Chris really expected to be arrested, and this was a frightening proposition, now that all her confederates had gone. Everyone knew that getting arrested in a group as part of a political manifestation was routine, a process, almost a joke—because, if nothing else, the television film was running, and cops generally don't like to be filmed while they're beating the citizenry.

Anyway, nothing happened to Chris. The goons went on making their noise, and the cops—probably more baffled than offended—just stood there regarding her. Chris turned, walked back to Ty, retrieved her attaché, and let him lead her to the coffee shop on Greene Street. Ty said nothing for a while, then: "Darlin', you daunt me."

The joint was jammed with kids from the rally in exactly the way that Chris's teenage haunts in Gotburg would be after a prom or a football game, everyone—won or lost—stimulated and commentative. It was fun wading into the gang, waving the attaché that was one of your distinguishing features as a Person of the Campus, a star in the place where you belonged. It was great.

Chris and Ty found Thompson and Chase, and crawled into their booth with a few semi-strangers. Chris looked around: Someone was explaining the *facts* of Vietnam to one of the waitresses, who did not look impressed; kid after kid upon kid was thrashing out the Issues; monitors were Considering in the center of the room, occasionally slapping a shoulder as a comrade passed. (Chris noticed that they never slapped a girl.)

"Something's happening," Chris announced. "I don't even think it's political. But there will be changes."

The coffee arrived. Ty's fingers dawdled on Chris's. Mark the graduate student loomed above them. "The system's flowing along," he said bitterly. "They'd be happier if we shot someone instead of protesting federal policy."

"Let's shoot Doctor Rodinis," said Chase. "He gave me a D on my—"

"Because, look at it, criminals are as much a part of the system as your parents are," Mark went on. "They've got the apparatus to handle crime—judges, jury duty, prisons. Crime's okay—run it through the system. But a *group of people* standing in a *public place* to *refuse to accept* this *business-as-usual governmental war* on . . ."

Mark was so upset that his voice broke and he started to cry. "We're nothing," he got out. "We're such trash, they don't even have the apparatus to deal with us. We're less than the most lurid, murdering pieces of criminal garbage that . . ."

"Whoa, Mark," said Ty. "It's cool, give it time."

"A couple of skateboards and we run. What's lower?"

"A couple of fags, maybe," said Chase.

Chris, startled, looked sharply at him. "The word is 'gay,' isn't it?"

Chase shrugged.

Mark left.

"Who do you think you are, junior?" Chris went on, getting angry. " 'A couple of—' "

"He's sorry," said Thompson. "He's wrong and he will improve."

Ty was smiling and shaking his right hand: Watch out, she's perilous.

"I mean, what do you think you're separating yourself from?" Chris went on, still annoyed at Chase. "Something's happening, can't you see that? Something's going to open the whole thing up, finally. From Berkeley to Yale, kids are saying no to the lies—has that *ever* happened before? I'm not even a political, but I can see the potential, so why can't you? 'A couple of faggots'! And who do we think those faggots are, may I ask?"

Chase looked at Thompson.

"This lady means to change the world," said Ty.

"Right, first thing after rehearsal, which starts in twenty minutes, so I might as well . . . Yes, thank you, gentleman Ty, and my coat is . . . ? Yes, and . . . "

So Chris had had it with that section of the day, and she was off to *The Elephant Calf,* to her cast, to her belief in herself. She led a sternly invigorating assault on the play, loaded with improvs and insights; and when it was over she felt exhausted and unhappy. Alone with Ty, she wept a little as she packed up, and Ty took her in his arms.

"Oh, I'm all right," she said.

He shook his head.

"It's . . . the frustration, I suppose. . . . "

Ty kissed her, long and deep and slow.

Chris responded in kind. Good, she thought.

He kept on kissing her, and she thought back twenty months to the party after the Senior Prom, when Tom kissed her. He was gentle, boyish; Ty is elaborate, probing, a man.

"Come on" says Ty. "This is our special time."

"Where?" she asks. He doesn't answer, just smiles. Anyway, she knows where. Good, good, good. Now I find out about this. Some women probably think this is a great step in their lives. What, because it's the first time? Getting hired to direct *Love's Labour's Lost* at the Old Vic—*that's* a great step. This is . . . homework.

Ty took Chris's hand as they crossed Sixth Avenue; neither was wearing gloves despite the nippy weather, and Chris felt a pleasurable tingle as she looked at Ty and he smiled (the game young man with hidden pain). Chris smiled back; something's happening. Of course, a woman's first time is always awkward on one level, if only because it types her as a novice. But this belief that one must yield up her virginity only to That Special Someone is silly. If such a One does indeed happen along, one wants to be ready for him, broken in and practiced and well beyond the so-this-is-what-it's-like stage. This is sex as Chris sees it.

Ty lived in a dour old mid-rise on Christopher Street, just west of Seventh Avenue. Here is the Village at its most urban, the narrow sidewalks and even the roadway crammed with people, some scurrying off to some opulent new thing in their lives, some lounging, waiting for the thing to come to them. Chris was so keen to take it all in that Ty had virtually to propel her inside; once they gained his apartment, she became fascinated anew.

"It's so roomy," she said, exploring.

"One life, many rooms," said Ty, as Chris peered into a bedroom filled with books and records. "My roommate," Ty explained. "He's never around when I am, so it works out pretty well. It's his place, mainly. I'm kind of the guest artiste here. A sublet. Real New York–style."

Chris was staring at a black-and-white print, framed on the wall, of two gigantically built men in some sort of struggle. One of the two was nude, wrestling the other out of his clothes, an outfit of motorcycle leather from cap to boots, and both sported impossibly vast erections.

"Some stuff, huh?" said Ty, drawing Chris into the room. "Take a look around, my roommate won't mind. He's kind of a show-off about his stuff, you know? Everything's rare in here. Records you can't find in stores, antique books . . . not to mention the under-the-counter stuff. *Erotica,* he calls it. Pretty word, huh? He's got these magazines that—"

"Are these two men fighting or joking?"

"What, on the wall there?" Ty came over. "Yeah, that's . . . Who knows? It's some real contest, but they're smiling at the same time. Look at the whoppers on them, though, huh?"

"Pardon my nose, but are many men that . . . big?"

"Oh, babe, it's a fantasy thing. You're not sore that I kissed you back there, are you?"

"Not sore."

"Come on, we'll have a cup of tea and relax. Herbal tea, to make us all smooth after the excitement today."

Chris was relieved that Ty didn't start in seducing her just then. Five minutes after you've entered the man's apartment is much too soon; it makes the girl feel Easy. Twenty minutes is almost flattering; but, ideally, there should be thirty to forty minutes of humorous socializing during which sex is never alluded to *in any way whatsoever*. Then the man and woman have a chance to establish themselves as intimates. This does nothing for the man, but it does allow the woman to get a grasp on the interaction of personality that is, for her, the reason to have sex in the first place. To put it another way, the man is horny and needs to get off; the woman wants to meet the father of her children.

These are, of course, strictly heterosexual guidelines. Among male homosexuals, it is generally believed that the more you talk first, the less hot you'll prove to be. Frank, a master of style in this age, favored very short conversations at the moment of the pickup and getting right to it upon entering the suite of the act. Many a trick, having taken Frank home, was startled by the grip of Frank's strong hands before the door was closed, or even being grabbed and kissed in the elevator going up. Henry, too, liked to cut the red tape and get physical quite, quite soon. But Luke, we notice, nourished powerful yearnings for a man he had been speaking to all his life; and Larken liked to get acquainted before he buddied up.

Lesbians, when courting, offer even greater variety in the matter of timing. With gay men, there are some rules but many exceptions; with gay women, there are no rules. Lesbians can be great talkers, socially rigid, caperers, on the shy side, all for action, poignant phonies, uncertain navigators, easy riders, truculent Donna Juans, and two-fisted Queen Elizabeths. You never know what you'll get. "Butch in the streets, femme in the sheets," runs the chant. Yet sometimes two women will meet, talk a bit, go to one or the other's home, and mate for life.

In the kitchen, as Ty brewed the tea, Chris decided that she felt very comfortable with him. Bluntly, she asked, "You don't mind having a gay man for a roommate?"

"Why mind it? He's got a right."

"There's no awkwardness?"

"The trick with tea is lemon in the *pot,* so it expands into the tea as it's forming. See? Awkwardness about what?"

Chris shrugged quizzically.

"Like, he'd want to score me?" Ty asked.

Chris nodded.

Now Ty shrugged. "It hasn't come up. Anyway, I like gay guys, I told you. They're show people, like me. And you."

"Arty."

"They know about performance. Life is a craft, darlin', you know it is. It's style. And without style . . . Well, for instance, how would you like to be your parents? Grossed out by everything that's lively, and disapproving of everyone who's free. Lady, that's *dead*."

"I wonder what you'd think of my friend Luke. Because he's . . . gay. But he's no show people. He's a plain country-town schoolboy, and very, very honest."

"Tea's getting there," said Ty, checking the pot.

"Honesty," said Chris, "can be—"

"Tricky. I prefer style."

"What's your roommate like?"

"He's this sort of lovable sourpuss. Got a weakness for suits."

"Suits?"

"That's what he calls them. Lawyers, bankers. Tie at the throat and carrying a case like the one you've always got. His dream is, some suit takes him to a real luxurious apartment like on Sutton Place and sticks him across the knee for a good old-fashioned spanking."

Teased, startled, Chris roared with laughter.

"No, that's his serious hope," said Ty.

"He told you that?"

"Why shouldn't he?" said Ty, pouring the tea into mugs. "We're pals. I tell him my life, so why wouldn't he tell me his?"

Thinking it over, Chris said, "Valid point."

"The lady agrees."

"Look, just how cool are you with homosexuality? Can I ask that? Because that's a rare tolerance."

"I'm a rare guy. No, don't drink it yet, it needs to relax."

"Would you . . . have sex with a man?"

"That's not my bag. I dig a true babe, roger and out."

"Golly, what if . . . There's this major part on Broadway. The director likes your reading. Callback. He likes you even better. Your chances look good. Then he says he'd like to . . . ."

Ty chuckled. "Get to know me real close."

"Okay. What would you do?"

"First, it's this: I'd say no. Don't want to do it and don't need to, because there's other parts for our boy Ty. But let's just say. It's years later. Ty needs that big jump. Now comes a part and it's the *one*. Gay director makes his offer. . . . Well, that one I'd have to think about. That's a definite maybe, because the stakes would be too high to scorn. But this year I am still my own man, playing as I prefer. Try the tea."

"Lovely."

"Yeah, lovely." He grinned at her over the cups. "Now, tell me how much you like me—a little this-and-that or stay-the-night?"

"Wow. You don't fail on the big scene, do you?"

"Come on, anyway, and see my room. Take your tea along."

Fine and dandy. Ty's room is the living end, painted black from ceiling to floor and marked only by careless piles of books in one corner, an open trunk of clothes with a laundry bag leaning against it in another corner, and, at stage center, a mattress dressed with a colorful Amish coverlet and two pillows encased in fire-engine red. Balancing their mugs, the two perched cross-legged on the edge of the mattress, Chris quietly laughing at the ease with which she was taking this major step.

"Most girls would feel funny at this moment," she blurted out.

"Now, wait a bit here, since I just want to make you happy," said Ty, flashing a million dollars' worth of little-boyness at her as he took her mug and set it down with his. "Maybe do a little coaxing. Do you like to be coaxed? Huh?" His face close to hers. " 'Cause I love to do coaxing."

He started kissing her puppy-style, steady, rhythmic, in an upward motion, no hands. He kissed her deep, hands on. He bent her to him. He nuzzled her, nibbled her ears, slithered along her neck, whimpered into her hair, brought her chin up in his hand, smiled at her, and started in again.

She was wondering if his roommate kissed like this, or Luke, or Tom.

He said, "Is there anything you don't like, darlin'?"

"Uh-oh," Chris replied. "Why?"

"Oh, 'cause I do it all."

"Well, I haven't done all that much of any of it, actually, so take a free hand."

"Lovely," he said, starting to undress her. He did this idiosyncratically, undoing a button up here and then taking off a shoe, darting to another button and then loosening her blouse. He looked at her, as if he were an artist studying his canvas.

"This will take forever," said Chris.

"What do you want, now, a dog race?"

"I want you," she said, thinking of Luke and Tom running through the woods. Are they sorrowful or glad?

"No, *I* want *you*," Ty corrected her. "It starts with me, and begs for your sweet attention. I would quote Shakespeare now, but I don't recall the fitting lines."

Now he moved quickly, separating her from her clothes and somehow finding the odd second in which to strip off his own things. He took quite some time examining her breasts, plumping and very, very gently licking at the tips of them with an expression of the utmost seriousness. Chris was concerned. Doesn't he like me?, she thought. But now he was smiling, running his hands down her arms, and sighing.

"Oh, darlin'," he murmured, burying his head between her breasts, smooching the sides of them, then up and around the nipples, first one, then the other, back and forth, his eyes half-closed, intoxicating himself as Chris arched her back and moved with the pull of his lips and tongue. She imagined Tom doing this to Luke, and when her head tilted and she felt for his neck, she was Luke knowing Tom, although she called Ty's name.

"Yes," he answered, "in the rhythm of love. Like that, now." His hands guided her, at the hips, on the ass, stealing back up to her breasts, his head moving down to her clit as his arms held and lovingly forced her backward. She watched in some alarm as his mouth drew toward her insides; she hadn't realized that the foreplay was going to last so long, and she was afraid she might climax too early in the fucking section. She grabbed for him, caught his arm, a shoulder, but he was oblivious, gone from her head and heart to her flesh, licking at the folds of her cunt with a systematic abandon. His deep, really rather rapturous moaning flattered her, and she was charmed by his habit of glancing upward at her face without moving his head as he lapped away. He was simply lovable; she had known he would be. A New York Woman chooses carefully. But he was more than lovable, she began to feel, as he slowly worked his way up her torso to her breasts again, to the part of a woman's body that men most delight to savor. Chris had forgotten about Tom and Luke. Watching Ty, letting Ty, having Ty, had powerfully focused her interests. No one should be this good at it, she thought, mesmerized, desperate, as he nibbled on her neck while stroking her hair and emitting little humming notes of almost unendurable pleasure. "Coaxing you, darlin'," he whispered, lifting her legs, and she was alert now, wary. How much will it hurt, and is he going to say something skeptical when he realizes how brand-new she is?

Trust Ty, that master. He was exceedingly gentle, and seemed quite palpably honored that he was the first to break in. He had scarcely begun when Chris rose to her pinnacle, her head thrust back and her legs straining to take him, more of him, all. She gasped. "Oh, my certain darlin'," he called her, moving, smiling, "you're sure getting there now." They were kissing, her hands mauling his neck, his hair, and she watched in wonder as he blasted off, head high and eyes sheer slits through which power radiated like the aura of an enchanted gem.

He fell on her, sighed, suddenly slid away to lie on his back staring upward, turned to her, then away again. They reached for each other, held on as the panting subsided, and Chris idly fancied herself as Wendy flying to Never Land with Luke and Tom. But then she saw herself tumbling, and wanted Ty to save her. That's why they call it "falling" in love.

Jezebel says nothing when Lester joins him at a booth in the back of Hero's. Jezebel doesn't like Lester, a very fair-skinned, effeminate young black man with Caucasian features who—Jezebel has decided—suffers from a lack of Race Commitment. Lester is a clerk in a law firm, an opera queen, a circuit socialite, a conservative dancer—things that Jezebel associates with Going Uptown and Leaving That Other Trash Behind.

"Everybody's buzzing about the dance you're giving, you and your political coterie," says Lester. "Buzzing like bees in a praline factory, yes, indeed. Has a name been chosen yet? For the dance?"

Jezebel just stares across the table at Lester.

"And May, too, such a perfect month for it," Lester goes on. "I already know what I'm wearing, but I'll never tell. And the dance is called?"

Jezebel fakes a look behind him, as if wondering whom Lester might be addressing. Then Jezebel says, "You must be at the wrong place, Miss Mayonnaise Wish-I-Was. This ain't no opera box. We got no bankers and heirs and such. So why you want to pick on me?"

"You have me so wrong," says Lester, touching Jezebel's hand; Jezebel eyes this maneuver with loathing. "I would even help you with the dance. Organization and so on?"

"I'll speak to the Crepe-Paper Committee."

"Always so hard with me, you luscious big meany. Won't even whisper me the name of the dance."

"Ain't it enough we *giving* a dance? Gotta have a *name* for it, too?"

"All the truly top dances have titles now, oh yes," says Lester, gently pulling the bottom of his right ear between thumb and forefinger, a habit Jezebel despises. "Last year there was 'Smiles of a Summer Night,' remember? And 'Angel Skin'?"

Jezebel snorts.

"Have you seen Henry?" asks Jim, suddenly looming over them.

"Not yet," Jezebel replies, glad about anything that puts Lester at a distance. "Anything major?"

"The police have, uh, declined our invitation to the dance. They didn't even bother fabricating an excuse. It's basically just, Fuck you."

"I hope you're not surprised."

"Well—"

"It was a drippy idea from the start. Can you imagine this cop coming home and telling his wife, Circle May seventeenth in your date book, honey, because that's the night we're going to a faggot dance?"

Jim thought it over. "Well. When you put it like that . . ."

"What we need to mix in with the *police* for? How many times do you have to learn that the *police* are the enemy? How many times are they going to whop a fag or laugh when we report a bashing before you white boys learn *what is the truth on this earth?*"

"That's because we've been demonized by the culture they're raised in. The idea was to show them that we're human beings just like—"

"Jezebel, introduce me to your handsome friend here," said Lester.

"Oh, shut your hole, white bread."

Jim gave a smiling little shrug on Lester's behalf, told Jezebel, "Later on," and skedaddled as Louis joined the table, sitting next to Lester.

"Now, here's a man," Lester cried, "who knows how to spread his charm."

Louis, a shortish, stocky, bearded black man in his late twenties, was the bridge between Jezebel and Lester—indeed, between any two gay people, of whatever race or class. To Louis, it was simply: us against them. Us was all the gay world and them was everyone else. The trouble with Jezebel, Louis thought, was that he was too judgmental, and Louis said so now. "You always harp on a person's less good qualities," he observed, after Jezebel had let loose another barb at Lester. "You ignore the better sides."

"Is *this* got a better side?" Jezebel snarled, indicating Lester.

"He's a tasty fuck, for starters. Can't have tops without bottoms." Louis put an arm around Lester's torso and winked at him. "Right, honey cake?"

"Oh, my man," sighed Lester, his head dropping onto Louis's shoulder.

"See the harmony?" Louis asked Jezebel. "That's what I call gay-style living. All the different kinds in harmony together. Look at us, how each is different. Besides being gay, all we have in common is that we're black."

"Some of us," said Jezebel, with a beady eye on Lester, "ain't even got *that* in common."

"Jez—"

"Man, we have major things to deal with. Oppression, waste, discompassion. I can't be troubled by these Miss Dainties and their uptown ways."

"If tolerance doesn't start with us," Lester reasoned, "where's it ever to come from?"

Jim had been sitting at the bar, meanwhile, talking to Frank.

"Something funny happened," said Frank, cracking open a can of Bud for a man to Jim's left and parking the money in the cash drawer. "That kid whose family threw him out? Eric? I've been trying to find him a place to stay and a job, and what do you know but Paul took him in. You know, the fat old guy from Before."

"Before what?"

Frank shrugged. "Before us. Before Hero's."

"Isn't Paul a little difficult, though?"

"I figure it's safe and secure compared to the street, and old Paul's kind of tickled to have a cute kid living in. Makes him feel like he's part of the scene, right?"

Jim nodded again, the very picture of an attorney considering a case, examining it from root to branch—the homeless boy, the frustrated senior citizen, the confrontation of youth's spark and age's ashen languor. Inside, however, Jim was simply being dazzled. God, this man is hot, he was thinking. He's . . . *powerful*. It isn't just the opulent sturdiness, the devil's eyes. It's his personality, the strength of his belief in himself. He's so fucking *man*. What kind of life, Jim wondered, has this chap enjoyed?

"Of course, Eric is straight, more or less," Frank went on, after pouring Vodka Collinses for a trendy-looking couple, East Side gays going Village. "But he seems to like putting out, for some reason."

"I never know how to take that—straight boys having gay sex. Doesn't that make them gay boys doing what they secretly want to do?"

Frank shrugged. "Who knows with kids? There's probably a streak of hustler in Eric. He gets off on being desired."

Henry joined them.

"Andy's attending his nephew's birthday party," he said. "So I've got the night off."

"Eric's moving in with Paul," said Jim.

"With strict instructions," Frank put in, "not to fuck up."

"Paul's the one who'll fuck up," Henry replied.

"Let's hear the trial before we slap down a verdict, okay?" said Frank.

Henry said, "What we could do is, once the summer gets going someone should take Eric out to the Pines and set him up with one of the money gays. I mean, if he's cute enough, he could be houseboy-for-life."

"He's a stunner," said Frank, "if you like street meat with his shirt hanging out and holes in his jeans. You know that type?"

"Terribly well," said Henry.

"Two aging dykes, two male cats, and a charge account at the local knitting boutique," said Lois. "Chick," she told Elaine, "we've become a cliché."

"What if I changed the title of my book to *A Psychotic Episode Called Her Life*?"

The two were relaxing at their little "weekend place" in Sea Cliff, Long Island. Lois's dance club, Kingdom Come, was closed Sundays and Mondays, so the couple could take off late Saturday night and enjoy the country through Tuesday afternoon. Monday, today, was usually the nicest, for some reason.

"What psychotic episode?" Lois challenged.

"It's so peaceful out here," said Elaine. "That's what I love, after the eternally imploding city, and talking too fast, and double vision. Do you know, I think I'm starting to see the same people over and over? The same *exact* people, as if they were models issuing out of . . . I don't know, duplicating pipes in some factory. There's one—I swear I've seen her five or six times now. Sometimes she strides past me as if she couldn't care less. But *sometimes* she's staring at me, very seriously, as if she . . . I don't know. It's such a *bamboozling* city."

"Maybe she recognizes you. It's the price of fame, chick."

"This isn't recognition. It's . . . hunger."

"Should I make a fire?"

"Yes, please."

Elaine, watching Lois build the woodpile, said, "Everything's so simple out here. What if we moved to Sea Cliff for good?"

"Who'd run my dance hall?"

"Ah." After a bit, Elaine said, "A lot of money's coming in. From my books. We could . . . relax?"

"No one's putting money in my pocket, chum. Except me." Lois sparked the blaze. "You talk as if my dance hall didn't matter like your books."

"Truth to tell, I thought you might be tired of it."

"Can't be," said Lois, rising and dusting her hands on her knees. "Because it's necessary. It's a needed thing." She sat again, in the armchair that faced Elaine's armchair. "I used to see Thriller Jill's as a gig. My job, that's all. Yeah, there was some family attachment in the building, maybe. But the club itself was a club, period. People told me different, I said, *Huh*. That joint? With Tiger and Biff guzzling beer-in-the-can on one side of the room and Alistair and Marshall quaintily sipping their Pink Ladies on the other side?"

Elaine sat there listening to Lois. The cats, who as a rule amused her with their strolling and lunging, their ferocious battles with croissants they had raped off the kitchen table, or their attempts to hitch a ride on the stereo turntable, could not distract her now. For Lois to analyze her past—to analyze anything—was rare, cherishable. Elaine was thinking, You fascinate me as much today as you did back then. How could I possibly have dwelt in carnal treaty with a man, when you I love forever?

Lois had grown wonderingly silent, so Elaine prodded her. "What changed your mind? The shows?"

Lois snorted. "Took the *dancing* for me to see homo clubs in a new way. All the wild energy these young boys spend on it, that pack of them pulling off their shirts and pounding the floor like a tribe in some ceremony, discovering an identity in that . . . shared thing. The straight boys' energy is put into throwing things out of cars at bike riders or looking for a black kid to harm. Or one of ours. And the girl dykes, the way they go for a slow dance! The boys only like a heavy beat. Put on a fox-trot, they'll clear the floor. The d.j.'s so used to it, when he spins a slow tune he'll say, 'Now here's one for the ladies.' And out they come, taking each other by the hand, and the heads go together and the cheeks touch. It's so romantic."

"I never thought I'd hear you praise anything with that word," said Elaine.

"Anyway, it taught me that we need our own place, even if we only use it one night a week."

"Do you think Kingdom Come will be all-gay every night someday?"

Lois shook her head. "Dance halls are permanently temporary. Transitory. None of them's ever lasted more than a few years. Hate to say it, but I could be out of business before long."

"Transitory," said Elaine, teasing Lois to make her blush a little. "I'm feeling somewhat transitory myself."

"Why, babe?"

"It's my book."

One of the cats, annoyed at the lack of attention, did a samba around the couch. The other cat turned its back in disgust.

"I'm rather in a quandary," Elaine went on. "I want to . . . take a step forward. Join the dancing, you might say. My editor opposes me."

"Get a new editor."

"It doesn't work that way, and, anyway, her reasoning is sound. She says, Why trade away a prepared readership for a readership that may not even exist? My book could fail."

"Why?"

"It's . . . very woman."

"Fem-lib stuff?"

"In a way. There's a feminist viewpoint, at least."

Lois looked skeptical. "Should a story be feminist? A story is a story."

"A story should be what its author needs it to be, whatever that ultimately is." Elaine sighed. "It may be that my editor simply isn't in touch with the women's movement. She's very apolitical."

"Why don't you invite her to the dance?"

"The dance?"

"The big one, in May. Down at the hall. The fund-raiser for the gay political group. Let her see for herself, your editor."

"See . . . what?"

"What I was speaking of. The wonderful spirit of this new world that is beginning to come into the open. Remember when we called it the Other Side? Have you noticed that we gave that up years ago? Because it isn't . . ."

"Applicable."

"Right, any more. Thank you, Miss."

"Lois, it sounds ingenious and strange, a combination I've always doted on. But will it appeal to Johnna Roberts? Ah."

"Don't give me ah. Invite her up and let her see how we are."

"Yet this isn't a book about gay life. Most of the characters are joes. Johnna could easily say, Lovely dance but what has it to do with selling your book?"

Lois shrugged.

"Of course," Elaine reckoned, "it is a way of proving to her that new cultures are evolving."

"And new readerships for the new cultures, no?"

"The dance has color, range, and my characters—"

"Call the fucking editor!" Lois ordered, as she went off to snoop around the kitchen and plan dinner.

Checking her watch, Elaine calculated that Johnna would probably have just returned from lunch, a good time to try her. Johnna's assistant said the editor was on another line, so Elaine asked for a callback, grabbed a sweater, and walked outside to think some more. What if Elaine refused to revise her book and peddled it elsewhere? What if every other editor felt as Johnna did? But then, how will Elaine feel if she pulls all the truth out of her book and—

"Hey, you!" called Lois, at the door. "It's Johnna Roberts!"

As Elaine approached, Lois asked, "And who the hell is Alicia, huh?"

Johnna was leery of the dance, but Elaine made it sound glamorous, stimulating, and illustrative, and Johnna said yes at last.

Elaine told her, "Bring your wild boy friend."

"Now, Ty," said Johnna, "is always a maybe."

Hanging up, Elaine announced, "The editor will come."

" 'Alicia,' she called me. Can't you come up with something that fits?"

"Like what?"

"Hank."

Elaine laughed.

"I'm just getting tired of all that fancying up of what's real," said Lois, taking Elaine in her arms. "You know?"

"Yes," said Elaine, head to head with her lover, sister, ally. "The funny part of it is, I am, too."

"Oh, don't ask me about the play," Chris told Luke on an emergency phone call a few hours after the opening night of *The Elephant Calf.* "My life is rags."

"Talk."

"Ty finked out on me, the cad. For the last week I've virtually been living with him, and right in the middle of the cast party he just slips out with Ta-ta and It's been a learning experience and . . . No, he didn't *slip out,* what am I trying to get away with here? I ran after him and practically made him fight his way out. You would have liked me, though—very Barbara Stanwyck, you know? With just a *hint,* the slightest sachet whiff, of Susan Hayward."

"All right, let's reality-test. Perhaps he's just—"

"No, no, no, you gentle boy. I know the fuck-'em-and-forget-'em type when I have one."

"You've had so many."

"Very funny. The tragic side of it is, at first I thought *I* was using him. You know, to, uh, forfeit my pathetic virginal state."

"Yikes."

"Well, I swore I could protect myself from getting involved. And now look!"

"At?"

"I'm in love with him!"

"Really?"

"Or at least in crush. I know I feel terribly let down. Terribly . . . Oh, gee, I'm *not* going to cry, oh, please, am I? No. No, I'm not. Okay."

"Now, *that's* my New York Woman."

"Quite so. La, my first love affair, gone with the wind."

"Tell me something. What's it like?"

"What's *what*—"

"Getting . . . possessed."

"You mean, How does it feel to get fucked?"

"She's tender, she's direct, she's our Chris."

"Our Chris—that's what I mean. Like, the only men I can stay solid with are . . ."

"Homosexuals like me and Tom."

Chris sighed. "Just what do I do now? Take an oath of spinsterhood and get out the chic yet strangely dowdy outfits that I'll wear to countless gay brunches and Oscar parties?"

"Is that what the gay boys do in New York? They have a party and watch the—"

"In the presence of certain ladies who, I believe, are known as 'fag hags.' "

"Wow."

"Brother, we're talking about *doom* here."

"Boy. A guy stands you up and suddenly . . . You were always talking about the exciting life you'd create. *Destiny,* you said. We make our own, you said. *One bad date* and you're going to give all that up?"

"Thanks for the pep talk."

"So we'll all be unmarried, one way or another," Luke went on. "We'll all be disappointed. My parents sent me this *incredible* brown suede jacket last month, and I looked so neat in it, then I left it somewhere. Well, I tore the campus apart but it's gone, and I felt just . . . so . . . sick. Then, three days later, I thought, Fuck, it's just clothes. I'm still here and that's what matters." Two beats, then: "So what's it like to get fucked?"

"Groovy and terrifying. It's lovely, really, yet you've got to sign yourself over to this . . . well, an overwhelming—"

"It sounds like our high-school graduation."

"No, *Luke*! I was so free that day. Free and myself."

"Feel better now?" he asked.

"No. But you talk sense. Give me a few days, because I am New York Woman, and I can take it!"

They each laughed a little, then Luke said, "Chris, I just flashed on the oddest picture of you, with some handsome guy and a cute little boy at a cottage door. And it's as if you were waving good-bye to me."

"Never," said Chris.

One of your closest friends meets a woman and moves in with her, and now you and your lover have to come to dinner. It does not go well. Perhaps the womanly intimacy that you and your lover so obviously share with your old friend threatens the fourth woman; perhaps she's simply a shit no matter who's in the room. In any case, she comes off as contentious, disdainful, and politically superior. You and your lover leave early. Heavy day tomorrow, sinus headache, workplace blues. Reasons and smiles. You and your lover exit the building in silence. On the street, waving at a cab, your lover says, "Loved her, *hated* him."

Auntie MacAssar is telling the audience what's wrong with her life— not only is the sex rotten, but there's so little of it—while Blue, wearing a red waiter's jacket, red shorts, and a collared red bow tie, passes with a tray.

"Another Kool-Aid with a wee spike of gin, young man," Auntie tells him. "And hold the Kool-Aid."

The Kid on stage. The Kid as Bombasta, Ramona Hagmore, the Contessa Dooit. The Kid coming on to Blue, who is now a sailor, now a delivery boy. The Kid singing "Indian Love Call":

When I'm balling you-oo-oo-oo, oo-oo-oo,
Will you ball me too-oo-oo-oo, oo-oo-oo?

It is the Act, the Kid, the Green Goddess, unreconstructed. Impervious. Impedient. "Another drink, handsome," he calls out, in spotlight, and slides into "Isn't It Romantic?," no spoof, no puns. That was always one of the Kid's most certain gifts, to blindside his commentary with sheer human feeling. Halfway through the verse, the Kid becomes aware of two women sitting up front, familiar, appreciative. Not till the second chorus does he realize that it's Lois and Elaine. *Jesus,* after all this time! He gives them a wink, meaning, Where the hell did you guys spring from?

Quick-change is the magic of the Act: turning upstage in a blackout to switch from Auntie to Bombasta while Blue crosses the stage in the nude as a ruse to catch the audience's eye.

Blue. Should I take him to San? He's heaven in the hay, but isn't he the reason why I never fell in love all these years? Too much risk in those boys, because they're too hot to pour it all into one receptacle.

The Kid is Bombasta now, hectoring, monitoring. "You think you're straight?" she rails at Blue, a lonesome cowboy in Stetson, chaps, and boots. "Who's Barbara Cook?"

Blue amiably retorts, "Say who?"

"Okay, you're straight."

I don't know, have I really been getting away with something all these years? They hounded Lenny Bruce to death but me they ignore. Of course, Bruce slashed away at their favorite lies. He was hard-core, religion and sex and the family. Next to that, I'm harmless, some faggot. We aren't real to them.

Now Bombasta is flirting with the cowboy; she is almost mild, yet still political, cultural. "Do you know any homos?" she asks the cowboy.

"Maybe my cousin Ricky Bob," Blue replies. "Because he likes to dress up in his mother's old fashions and parade around to the tune of 'Hello, Dolly!' You think that makes him a homo?"

"It could be a tip-off," Bombasta notes.

So Lois and Elaine are still together. I kind of expected that. Back in the old days, it was only the gay *men* that were out cruising all the time. The women would shack up and vanish together. I always wondered how they managed that.

The Kid has reached the finale, "As Time Goes By," which he sings to a sleeping Blue, stretched out nude on his stomach on a little cot. Toward the end, the Kid pulls a blanket over the man and sits next to him, gazing fondly upon . . . what? A fantasy? His lover? His son? As the music dies, the lights black out.

Backstage is a circus, as always on closing nights, as techies strike the set and the lights, and well-wishers throng the bitty dressing room. Glancing over at Blue, the Kid sees him doing his sleepy smile-and-nod at an older man in an impressive suit. East Seventies, the Kid guesses, with an ample beach house in—no, probably not the Pines. East Hampton or Montauk. Good enough: Blue deserves a feel of the real velvet after slumming it with the Kid for six weeks. Then Lois and Elaine came forward.

Lois says nothing as she shakes the Kid's hand, but she's smiling, and Elaine gives the Kid a kiss. "Johnny," she says, "it's beautiful to hear you sing again."

"We delayed starting our weekend," Lois puts in, "to stick around and catch your act."

"Heaven," the Kid says. "I'm in heaven."

"To see you on stage, Johnny!" Elaine tells him. "Still so young and lyrical! It makes me feel twenty and full of discovery about myself! How on earth do you do it?"

"It's all in the selection of moisturizers, enamels, and condiments specially prepared for me in Switzerland."

"Monkey glands," says Lois, nodding. She has read of the like in the *Reader's Digest*.

"Come to dinner," says Elaine. "We have twenty years to catch up on."

The Kid looks at Blue: He and his gentleman appear to have reached the bargaining stage.

"I'm free," says the Kid.

They went to that unmarked place on Bedford Street just below Christopher that, according to legend, was a speakeasy during Prohibition and somehow never got around to raising a signpost even after Franklin Roosevelt dismantled the government's implausible, unenforceable, and socially deconstructive ban on liquor.

"You have weekends, huh?" asked the Kid, savoring his scotch and settling in. "Patchogue? Amagansett?"

"Sea Cliff," said Elaine.

"You're a famous writer," said the Kid. "That's so neat. The noted chronicler of elegance and style. Rich people having fun." The Kid meant it genuinely.

"Except now I'd like to do what you do. Talk about it."

"The gay stuff?"

"Women stuff, more at."

"The Movement?"

"It's about people, not politics. Yet . . ."

"I say, Do it," Lois put in.

The Kid smiled. "The Mistress of Thriller Jill's."

"The Mistress of Kingdom Come, now."

"The dance palace?"

Lois nodded. "Saturday's gay night."

"Yeah? Men dancing with men?"

"Sure."

"Heavy. It's finally happening."

"Don't anyone look, please," said Elaine. "But there's a woman at the table against the wall to the left . . ."

Blunt Lois looked. "Dark hair, dark blouse?"

"You remember I told you I've seen the same person several times? That's the person."

Lois looked again. "She's just some woman drinking coffee."

"Johnny, come out to the house with us," said Elaine. "Let's have an all-gay weekend."

"Sounds pretty tense," said the Kid. "You have cats, right?"

"We're lesbians, aren't we? What about you, Johnny? Is there someone waiting for you back home?"

The Kid shook his head.

"He does seem young," said Lois, stifling an impulse to reach out and stroke his hair.

"He's the Kid," Elaine rejoined. "Johnny, do come out with us. I long to play hostess."

"Do you have Monopoly out there? I'm in the mood."

"Scrabble, and it's so dead with just two."

Lois put in, "Especially when your opponent keeps making up stupid words."

"And you challenge me every time, don't you?"

"Damn straight."

"Litanesque," the Kid invented. "Congenity. Apotestic."

"Quick," said Elaine, "let's get out of here—she just went to the ladies' room."

"Look, will you please?" said Lois, but Elaine was already heading for the door. "I'm *telling* you," she said, over her shoulder.

As it happened, the Kid's plane reservation left him free till Tuesday afternoon, and he felt confident that Blue had departed for a Major Weekend—last-minute jaunts to fey beaches in the company of a Fashionable Gentlemen were common then as now. So the Kid said yes, and Lois and Elaine dropped him off at his sublet so he could pack, and, though he promised to make it snappy, he turned on the radio to catch a weather reading. Flopping a few T-shirts and a jacket into his duffel, he heard the announcer usher in a musical selection, the instrumental hit of a few years earlier, "Love Is Blue."

The Kid had to laugh at that, for he was wise and love-free. "Yeah," he said aloud, closing up the place and opening the door. "Sure it is."

.   .   .

In a dingy little cinema on West Fifty-fifth Street, Frank watched the premiere of his debut film, *A Study in Power,* the title billed in the ads in capital letters except for the *y* as a hint to the cognoscenti, along with the helpful identification "all-male cast" and a photograph of shirtless, brooding Frank, a stud in power.

Frank didn't know what to expect from the audience, but was annoyed that so many of them were over-the-hill guys, totally unlike Frank's lean-and-mean coevals. Somehow he had thought the theatre might be filled with Henrys and Andys, as Hero's was; all Frank could see was Paul after Paul—and most of them weren't even looking at the screen. They spent the time seat-hopping and wandering the aisles. Probably covering the men's room, too, if Frank knew anything about these older gay characters.

One of them suddenly popped into Frank's row, two seats away, and started whispering to Frank. "Shitting, fucking," he said. "Piss and come. Hot licking all over you." After a few seconds' intermission, the man started it all over, so Frank got up, faced the guy, and said, "Get moving or I'll shove your head up your behind, right?" The guy got moving.

Slouching back into his seat, Frank felt really irritated. Why go to the movies except to *see* one? *A Study in Power* was no *Rio Bravo,* okay. The lighting was so haphazard that, even though it had been filmed entirely in one section of one loft, some of it was almost blindingly overbright and some of it was near black. Then, too, the sex itself seemed almost perfunctory, nothing like the expertly steamy combinations that Frank recalled from his week of filming. Was it because the story line was so phony? Because the whole thing lacked a structure?

I can do better than this, Frank was thinking. If there are going to be gay fuck movies, why can't they deal with gay life, fit the sex scenes into a statement? Like, maybe, what does *A Study in Power* really mean? What power does the stud have? Who responds to it? What's the stud like when he isn't having sex?

Frank groaned aloud when the painter came in and the camera veered toward him so sharply that it caught a glimpse of some of the lighting cables and a corner of the umbrella. Jumping up, Frank dodged a couple of importunate losers in the aisles and headed home for some heavy sulking and pondering.

Eric was sitting on Frank's stoop, glum as The Little Engine That Couldn't.

"Now what?" said Frank. "Paul throw you out, too?"

"I couldn't hack it any more. Sometimes he's nice, but mostly he just screams at me. Like I bought the wrong kind of carrots or something."

"Come on inside."

Upstairs, Eric immediately brightened. He did the boogaloo, then dropped onto the couch, mock-winded.

"Don't you ever pack up when you change addresses?" Frank asked, amused.

Eric shrugged. "What do I have to pack? Hey, can I come with you to the bar tonight? Maybe there's some job I can do."

"You aren't of age to enter a bar, short stuff. I don't know, maybe Henry's boy friend can use a stock boy in his store."

"Yeah!"

"Where do we put you meanwhile, though?"

"Can't I stay with you?"

"In this closet?" said Frank, pulling off his clothes for a shower. "You'd be on my nerves in two minutes. I'll give Henry a call, maybe he'll think of someone. Help yourself to the fridge."

Under the water, Frank ruminated over the movie and its lack of point. The director was all set to film another one, and he promised to build it around Frank. Frank wondered if the guy would let Frank put the show together, plot and cast it. Maybe do a version of Eric's life—the homeless kid knocking about the city, trying to find a place he belonged in.

Toweling off as he came out of the bathroom, Frank said, "Hey, you ever figure out whether you're a homo or a joe?"

Eric had taken off his shoes and thrown himself front-down on the bed with a smile of eerie contentment, like the model for a mattress ad.

"Who's Joe?"

"Straight, I mean."

Eric flipped over, his eyes on a tour of Frank's body. "Search me," he said.

"Who do you want to go out with, Faye Dunaway or Kirk Douglas?"

"I'll go out with you if you let me stay here."

"The hell you say." Frank sat in the armchair, the towel around his neck.

"Please, Frank." Eric got up and came over. "Come on, I'll give you a blowjob."

"Fuck."

"That, too," said Eric, trying to join Frank in the chair.

"Quit it," said Frank, taking hold of the boy. "There isn't room for two in this . . . Eric, you're too . . ."

"I'll tuck myself right in and you won't hardly know I'm even here," said the lad, ooching into Frank's lap and putting his arms around him. "We can just rest like this."

Frank stroked Eric's hair, and the boy purred.

"Tell me," said Frank. "What did you and Paul do for sex?"

"He'd just lick me up and down and blow me." Eric purred again. "Then he'd be nice to me for a whole fifteen minutes."

Frank liked the feel of the boy's body through his shirt, trim and trusting. It didn't arouse him; it calmed him, the touch of something innocent in Frank's restless, greedy life.

"It's funny about guys and their types," Frank said. "How some of us go for big virile guys and others like some grinning kid. So what's your type, anyway?"

"I like someone who is kind to me."

"Is that how you think of me? Kind?"

"You know you are," said Eric, holding Frank tight.

"No one ever calls me that, you know? All they ever see is Pleasure Daddy."

"I would do anything with you, Frank. Anything you asked, to make you like me."

"I already like you."

Shivering momentarily, Eric held Frank yet tighter, and Frank held the boy truly, wishing the best for him.

The two sat together for a while, silent, limp, resting.

Then Frank said, "This is what our movies should be about."

"I think 'When are you going to get married?' is my all-time favorite, though," Henry was telling his older brother, Tony. "You notice, not 'Are you getting married?,' implying that you have some choice in the matter. No—*when* is it going to happen, because marriage is inevitable, isn't it? Choice? There's a *choice*? This really *amazing* assumption that because I am given orders I am going to carry them out!"

"Yes, but," Tony told Henry, for perhaps the thousandth time in their lives. "They're conventional people, that's all."

"I could be lying on a couch making out with a boy friend, running my hands over his skin, our jeans bursting open with everybody-fuck hotness, and they'd be sitting there asking me when I'm going to get married."

"Well—"

"What's funny about it is, they only want me married so they won't be embarrassed when their friends ask about me. I'm supposed to placate their *friends'* idea of acceptable behavior? Do you realize how ridiculous these people are?''

"Still, telling your mother to . . . how did you put it?"

" 'Stick it up your flaming asshole, you stupid bitch.' "

Henry's brother laughed ruefully. That Henry. "I concede that they can be a terminal pain. But what does it accomplish to be rude to them?"

"It's part of the training. I make the penalty for nagging at me so expensive that they learn to hold it in."

"It didn't work, did it?"

"That's why I got rid of them."

Henry's brother laughed again, shook his head. "Henry," he said, "you can't get rid of your parents."

"You know," said Henry, keeping his voice low and looking at his brother spang on, "everywhere I turn there's some heterosexual telling me what I can and cannot do. I'm getting bloody fucking sick of it."

They walked on for a bit in silence. Beach, late April, a bit of a wind up, Jersey Shore, Henry's traditional first weekend in May with his brother's family. Who cares where they are? It's the words that matter.

Tony finally said, "Well, there's no law that says . . . Okay. But doesn't it feel funny?"

"Does it feel funny that I no longer have anyone in my life who nags and criticizes and hacks away at me? No, it doesn't feel funny. It feels great."

"You don't miss them at all?"

"They drilled away at me for some twenty-five years, and every time they struck I got a little more alienated. What would I be missing? I don't even *like* them any more."

Henry stopped walking. He said, "Look. Don't you realize what an infuriating nullification of everything I am that 'When are you getting married' shit is? You think it's just parents being bossy, don't you? No. Parents being bossy is 'Wipe your feet.' 'When are you getting married?' to a man who is gay and out is a deliberate assault on his very right to exist."

"Henry—"

"Don't you ever listen to anything, you?"

Henry's voice was still low but his face was savage. "You're like them," Henry went on. "Is that it?"

"Jesus, guy, calm down. I've always sided with you, haven't I?"

"Okay, okay, I'm sorry. *Damn.* But you see the passion this subject arouses? If I tell you I'm gay, then gay is what I am, and every observation you make about me from then on must take that into account. You can say, 'I hate you because you're gay' or 'I like you because you're gay' or even 'I have no opinion about your being gay.' But you *cannot* say, 'When are you going to get married?' I can deal with the bashers on one side of us and the cops on the other, because some of us are going to try to change the laws of the land so that people like me can enjoy a little live-and-let-live. But I will not deal with anyone who denies my very existence. Hear me, Tony—I *will not do it.*"

"Saved by the bell," said Tony, nodding up the beach at his wife and twin four-year-old daughters, Lee and Gemma, the kids scurrying delightedly toward the two men. "Here's Rebecca and all the little Szymanskis."

"What's your secret, anyway?" Henry asked. "How come they could never get to you?"

"I laugh at them. They're . . . What's that word you always use?"

"Dildo."

"No."

"Cock ring?"

"Henry, will you give it a rest? It's the word that means cheap and silly."

"Tacky?"

"That's it. Tacky."

The little girls swarmed over Henry and Tony, clamoring a report of the day's events and a preview of the evening.

"We're having popcorn for supper!" said Lee.

"And peas," Gemma added.

"Not to mention fried chicken," said Tony's wife, Rebecca.

"Henry," cried Lee, pulling on her uncle's arm, "let's go in the water."

"No," Gemma countered, on the other arm. "Sand castles *now*!"

Rebecca winked at Henry. " 'Happy families are all alike,' " she said.

It's eleven o'clock on a Saturday night at the Everard Baths, and the joint is jumping hot. A small horde waits in the little coffee bar till rooms become available, and word has it that many notorious circuit beauties have checked in tonight. The mood could be described as "feverish but worth it."

Insatiable Martin staggers in, towel around his waist, grimly dreamy. He has just had three of the best-looking men in town, one more or less after the other, and he's ready to leave. Just a little coffee to steady himself and

. . . Oh, was that Helmut Bettendorf who just passed the doorway? Is he here tonight, too?

"I've never had him even once," Martin reminds himself, leaving the coffee to cool as he slithers off.

The Kid so enjoyed his weekend in Sea Cliff that he canceled his return flight to San Francisco and stayed out at the house with Elaine while Lois returned to the city.

Seeing Lois off was a sentimental moment for the Kid. We're talking twenty years here; we're seeing glances over the shoulder at the F.B.I. turn into gay nights at a dance hall. Lois just grumbled away, however.

"She's convinced that, five minutes without Lois, and everything collapses," Elaine told the Kid.

"I just don't want those rascally bartenders robbing me blind."

It worked out well, because Elaine wanted time off, by herself, to ponder how best to traverse this crossroads she had reached in her career; and the Kid proposed to explore the local terrain on the house bicycle, a green Raleigh that Lois used for errands. Now and then over the week, Elaine and the Kid took walks, gave each other a cooking class ("You want to learn how to erect a cassoulet in two hours flat?" the Kid asked; and Elaine replied, "It's my dream come true"), and watched television like critics, drunk on their own commentary.

Saturday night was the big gay dance at Kingdom Come, and Elaine and the Kid were to train in that afternoon. Over lunch—chunks of homemade sourdough bread and the last of Elaine's chicken-carrot-mushroom soup—the Kid said, "You still do everything so beautifully. You react with affection and you observe so generously. I read *Love and Money*."

"Good God, a fan!"

"I was with a friend, and suddenly—this is on the street—he said, There's this book I can't go on living without reading, and he dragged me into City Lights and picked out this really *chic* piece of goods. And there's your name on it. I felt a shiver. As if something were beckoning to me from . . . I don't know. From some great force behind the scenes, combining us all. Like the way we're so famous for spotting each other? It's as if your book spotted me. So he bought it and *I* bought it."

"And read it, my Jerrett Troy?"

"Don't be shy, you know I loved it. You're a marvelous writer. But why are we all just . . . *suggested*? So many lines made me want to . . . You know? It's as if we *were* there but we *aren't* there."

"Well, we're in the next one," Elaine replied. "Except my publisher
. . . Oh, every author uses that word when what we really mean is *my
editor*. There's no great consortium atop you. It's one person, sink or
swim. Anyway, my editor isn't happy with the new Elaine Denslow.
What would you do if someone ordered you to . . ."

"Clean up the Act? Never."

Elaine smiled. "You live so purely."

"You want to know what's really youthful? You and Lois. You two
inspire me—one couple having sex for twenty years."

"But you men think there's nothing to our sex in the first place. I
imagine you: With no *member* going into her, what can it be worth? Ha,
you blind souls."

"Enlighten us."

"I will admit that Lo does *at times* operate with a rubber contrivance
shaped not unlike a penis. Even so, manipulation of this certain object
utterly outclasses anything comparable in the flesh and will of man, at least
as I experienced it."

"I always figured Lois for a top of death."

"A woman knows a woman's parts. So a woman can . . . well, 'fuck' a
woman . . . You heard my quote marks? . . . with an insider's perspective.
Remember, I was married. I've been with a man. The whole eight years,
I came perhaps ten times. Are you shocked, I hope?"

The Kid shrugged, smiled, played with his fork.

"Now," said Elaine, "I come ten times in a weekend."

"I used to think that, to the heterosexual corporation, the most terrifying aspect of the gay thing as a whole was this image they have of a man
screwing a man. Now I think a woman screwing a woman must terrify
them even more. It's such a merrily nonchalant nullification of their
power."

"Never. Those boardroom smoothies have no idea of what goes on in
the ladies' room. Now, Johnny." Elaine checked her watch. "We've perhaps four minutes left. *But*. What of you? Could some strong and handsome man be waiting around a corner? I ask if there's any lovely doom
written on your slate."

"Listen. I've had them top, bottom, and sideways. And *no one* ever
caught me. I'm uncaged. I *have* to be—I'm Pan, remember? The boy who
won't grow up?"

Elaine considered this.

"I knew you'd see it my way." The Kid looked at *his* watch. "Don't we
have a prom to get to?" he asked.

.   .   .

Henry was doing that open-closet and pawing-through-the-drawers routine, where one stares and stares at one's clothes, trying to hit on Just the
Thing that, combined with Just the Other Things, will transform one into
the invincible, irresistible Universal Type. Dress up? Dress down? Show
skin, feature the haircut, emphasize color, what?

Henry called Jim. "This is Sacred Acts' first dance," Henry said, "and its
officials have got to show class. What are you wearing?"

"Jeans and a white T-shirt," said Jim.

"You're so smart! Why didn't I . . . It's clean, it's fundamental. It says,
No one owns me. It says, Gay life is as basic as applehood and mother pie.
It's the boy next door. It's—"

"Actually, it's just more comfortable to dance in. Especially later on
when we go shirtless."

"Shorts would be even more comfortable," said Henry, wondering if
he dared.

"No," said Jim. "The look is construction worker, cowboy, trucker.
You never see them in shorts."

"Jeans and a T it is," said Henry.

Andy couldn't decide on the right tie. He wanted Henry to be proud of
him, to welcome him into the fraternity—particularly tonight, on the eve
of Andy's moving day.

Andy was elated, glowing with self-esteem. Henry had insisted that
Andy move on the sly, without telling his parents—the less they knew, the
less they could control, Henry said. Knowledge is a weapon, Henry said.
Andy decided to tell them anyway, but to face them down no matter what
they told him. Better to defy them than conceal from them.

And I *did* defy them!, Andy exulted, while balancing the green striped
silk tie against the solid red cotton tie. I can stand up to them now. Maybe
I shouldn't have given them the address—but how can you move without
telling your parents where?

Working a handkerchief into the pocket of his blazer, Andy thought, At
least my mother stopped mashing at me when I told her the address. In
fact, she got, well, almost quiet. Pleasant, even, and sort of thoughtful.
Maybe she's finally accepting that I am my own man.

.   .   .

No T-shirts or blazers for Jezebel: *This* night, he's going to *trip*!

Going to pick me up some sweet piece of bish, too, he thought, staring in the mirror, turning, adjusting. Some scared-ass white boy in the mood to slum. Cream him all night, then kick him out forever.

Louis buzzed from downstairs; at the apartment door, he gave Jezebel a quick up-and-down and said, "Man, you are tight this evening. You are going for action, I can see."

Jezebel had moored a black mesh shirt over white sailor's pants, topped off by a Greek fisherman's hat. Louis, however, had pulled on any old thing, and Jezebel said, "This your idea of party apparel? You need color, you need jive!"

Louis shrugged. "I'll probably end up with Lester, same as always. He doesn't care how I dress."

"Lend you my green silk shirt," said Jezebel, pulling open a drawer, "so you can upgrade your selection of sexual partner. Don't dance too much and get it all mildewed."

"Dance?" Louis snorted, trading shirts. "I'll proceed to a quiet corner with Lester and have our usual heart-to-heart grope."

"You let manager Lois catch you at it and you gonna get busted right out of the place. Wait, open up the top button on your pants. Yeah, and lower them a trifle. Let's see." Nodding approval at the effect, Jezebel went on, "Open-shirt look would be best with that green."

"How's this?"

"Gone have to graduate you past this egregious Lester to something more substantial."

"Like those white boys you're always chasing?"

"Not just chasing, catching. And *someone* around here has to promote harmony between the races, don't I?"

"How about a drink of the house water before we go?"

Filling a glass at the tap, Jezebel said, "Got to admit, I'm in the mood for a dance today. This fit right in with my plans. But what we *really* should be doing is marching through the city in organized might to demand reform, not dancing our asses off and scoring bish."

"Tasty water," said Louis, putting down the glass.

"That's it, don't listen. But someday it's got to happen. I can be poor and I can be loveless, but I ain't gone be no second-class citizen."

"So which would you take if you could choose—homo liberation or black equality?"

After a bit, Jezebel said, "Now, that's a funny question. I never looked at it so separate before."

"Let's go to the dance."

"No, wait a moment as I collect my thoughts."

"Talk as we go," urged Louis, pulling the door open.

Walking downstairs, Louis went on, "Or put it this way—which do you think we'll get first, if we get either? What do they hate more, the different race or the different sex?"

"One thing about haters," said Jezebel, "is they don't feel good unless they're *omnivorous*."

Chris, sharing a joint with Thompson and Chase in their dorm room, got a little giggly and asked them, "Who will dance a tango with me?"

"Not now," said Thompson.

"Not even later," said Chase. "It's a dance, not your high-school talent show."

"Oh, well," said Chris, deflated.

The two boys shared a look.

Fag hag, thought Chris. Well cast but in the wrong play. I should be with Ty. That would be miscast but in the *right* play.

Paul was so excited to be in on the shindig for once that he decided to splurge and pick up some beefcake on Third Avenue as his date for the dance. Let those contemptuous youths see him with a handsome devil on his arm. They'll change their tune! And wait till they see us leaving together. Ha!

Riding the bus up Third Avenue, however, Paul began to fret. What if the hustler cheated him—demanded cash up front and then absconded? What if he stabbed Paul? There were stories. Besides, what does one say to a hustler in the first place?

In the event, Paul stepped off the bus and found himself immediately face-to-face with the most *extraordinary* young chap, with an easy smile and wicked eyes. Overbite! Cheekbones! Shoulders!

"Nice night," said the young man.

It *can't* be this easy, surely. "Yes, it's . . . lovely," said Paul.

"Saw you lookin' me over."

"I . . . was?"

"My name's Blue." Extending his hand.

"I'm dance. No, I *mean,* I'm going to a dance and my name is Paul and I'd love to take you with me. It's called 'Revolutions.' "

"Sorry. Got to work."

"Of course. I *mean,* your work would be . . . squiring me to the dance." No, that sounds girlish. "I mean, I'll *pay* you to come with me."

"Where's the dance at, now?"

"Downtown."

"How long'll this take?"

"Till you . . . want to leave. . . ."

The boy nodded, thought, looked around, then back at Paul. "And date you after?"

". . . Date me?"

"That's right."

"Oh. I see. Yes. Well."

"Cost you extra."

"Yes, of . . . Well, how much?"

"All you can spare and then some, is my guess. 'Cause I'm special."

"Yes, I see that."

"I like fifty."

Paul's face told Blue that that was not to be, so Blue added, " 'Less you got a counteroffer."

Aching for this to work, Paul pulled out his money clip, counted his wad, and said, "All I have is forty-six dollars, and it's three dollars each to get in, plus drinks and carfare and—"

"Thirty'll do it for my time, all told."

"Dear me, that's cutting it so close."

Blue shrugged.

"Very well," said Paul. "We'll take the subway down, so speedy that way. Your name was . . ."

"Blue."

"You look so handsome and smooth in that vest. Wait till we parade in, I'll show those queens. I'll show them Revolutions!"

Frank was combing Eric's hair, trying to figure out what would be hot but not too alluring on an underage kid who was so starved for affection he'd go home with Godzilla.

"This is great," said Eric. "Me and big Frank at the dance. *Boy.*"

"Hold still. I'm going to give you a haircut."

Wrapping a towel around Eric's shoulders, Frank took up the trimming shears and snipped a bit off Eric's sides, leaving the top full, a look that only became common a generation later.

"I'm trying to give you a sophisticated kind of style," said Frank. "So people will think you're older."

"Yeah, you can trim me anytime, big boy."

Smiling as he brushed out the stray hairs, Frank said, "Where did you pick up that line?"

"Paul does stuff like that. He talks back to the TV. Like when some hunk shows up. Here's another one—this is during a western, and the hero comes in." Approximating Paul's slightly mincing air and snaky arm movements, Eric said, "Oh, cowboy, is it time for the roundup yet?"

Frank and Eric laughed together, then Eric turned and put his arms around Frank, silently entreating him for the hundredth time to let Eric stay in this magical haven where Frank lived. Gently disengaging, Frank said, "You look real sweet tonight. I bet you'll meet someone special at the dance, and your whole life will change."

The phone rang.

"Just give me two shakes, and we'll head out," said Frank, pulling up the receiver with "Yo."

"Frank?"

"Speaking."

"It's Larken."

Silence.

"Frank, I know you're startled. It's been years and everything, but I tried Information and there was only one Frank Hubbard. See, I met some friends for lunch and we decided to go to a movie. There's a porn house in the Tenderloin, and it was supposed to be this big joke-ez-vous kind of thing. But *you* were in the movie, Frank! And I was . . . I don't know, seeing you again. Frank, you look so great! I'm half-bald and my stomach hangs over my belt a little, but you're plain old godlike, as if you froze at thirty-two or something. And, Jesus, Frank, the muscles on you! I don't remember you like that. I told my friends how you were my first beau, and they laughed at me. So I said, 'Just wait till the credits and you'll see his name is Frank Hubbard.' Only now you're Rod Lockin. . . . Frank, are you there?"

"Shit, it's good to hear you talk to me, Lark." Frank sat in the armchair, as Eric stared, wondering what was happening.

"I don't remember how we lost contact," said Larken. "We didn't quarrel, did we?"

"No, your boy friends kept putting me off and irritating me, so I . . . Larky, how are you? Are you still living in—"

"Yes, it's so dandy here, Frank! It's so really open! I mean, in the Mission or Polk Gulch, everyone knows what you are and nobody cares. They say gay guys are literally crowding the town. We may even take over."

"I've missed you, Lark."

"Frank—"

"I don't think I can say how much. I don't think I realized until now."

"Gee, Frank, why'd we ever get out of touch? So many times something happened and I thought, If only I could tell Frank about it."

"Same here."

"Boy, you were some show in that movie. The way that guy—the painter?—was watching you while you were topping him. And the look on you, guy! I guess that's why my friends thought I was making it up about knowing you. They didn't want to believe that I had . . . felt what that's like. And it's funny, because way back then I didn't have anything to compare you to, so what did I know? It was just Larken and Frank to me, us two. And I've had so many beaux since then, some really good guys and some cads, I guess. Some for a week and some for longer. But, see, Frank . . . see . . . none of them ever . . . I mean, they weren't you. And that movie—Frank, I was awed. I kept thinking, I had that. That incredible man liked me once."

"Lark, I want to see you. I want to always talk to you. Nobody listens to me. I've got these plans about another movie, a better one. Something about what we are, right? But when I try to tell people, they say, Why don't you just have two guys fucking? Lark, that isn't all that our life is about!"

"I would listen to you, Frank."

"You always did." Frank was weeping. "You're the only guy in the world who knows me at all. Because you listened."

"I'm neater now, Frank. Carpenter—one of my old beaux—was like a drill sergeant. You should see me unpack the groceries. The flour goes *here,* and the milk goes *there.* . . ."

Frank wiping his eyes. "That didn't matter, anyway." More tears. "Lark . . ."

"I'm very organized about cooking, too. I've always got tubs of potato salad and chicken drumsticks in the fridge for noshing. Sometimes I nosh right through the day and never have to fix dinner or anything."

"Would the chicken be well done enough for me? Because I recall the way you—"

"All these years, Frank—*all this time*—and you're still the only guy I know who likes his meat incinerated. Gee, I'd have to store a special batch for you, I guess, taped with your name. That's how Carpenter made me handle everything. Name tapes on our special foods. Like, he loved day-old salad. Or if there was only one portion of rice pudding left."

"Listen," said Frank, getting up a smile now, nearly laughing. "I've got a dance to go to and a world of eyes to fascinate. They're looking for me, and I love it, you hear me, Lark? But give me a number so I can call you tomorrow, and we'll talk. Right?"

So they did that, and Frank took Eric to the dance; but on the way, Eric said, "I can't believe I saw you crying." Frank replied, "I'm like anyone else. I get scared by the size of my disappointments."

Kingdom Come lay on the Hudson River, in a rehabilitated warehouse south of Morton Street, a wide-open space that Lois had broken into one large central dance floor surrounded on the south and west by wet bars and on the north and east by bleachers. The building's original supporting pillars were left standing to mark out the geometry, and balconies over-hanging the side sections provided the offices, staff changing rooms, and spaces for private parties. These last proved an irritant on off nights, when couples would break in to neck and indulge in drugs of pleasure. The sight lines were awkward from downstairs, so these party spaces afforded genuine privacy whether one belonged there or not; but Lois could always sense when something fancy was going on, and would charge upstairs and throw everybody out.

Actually, Lois found it almost amusing how elaborate the sex could get up there in the darkness, especially on gay night; but the drugs outraged her. "Why can't they get high on dancing and beer?" she would ask. In the four years since she had opened Kingdom Come, it seemed as though the street touts would introduce some new and yet more unsavory delicacy every six months—"and fools rush in," said Lois, who in all her life had never touched anything stronger than wine and, once, a puff of weed, and who looked on with dour misgiving as, now and then, some gay brother had to be carried out of the place, babbling in narcotic delirium.

It was Elaine who suggested the vaguely Space Age motif of the décor—"so they'll know," she explained, "that they're not in the Peppermint Lounge or Arthur." They knew it, in fact, because of the clientele, younger and more simply dressed than the setters and toadies of trend who jammed the better-known discothèques. Lois had no desire to compete with those places, so often the living end this year and a morgue the next. Nor did she think Kingdom Come grand enough to deserve French. "Discothèque?" she'd say. "It's a dance hall!"

Gay night was her favorite, in part because there were never any fights, unless some joes slithered past the bouncer (a veteran with a practiced eye for Us and Them) to make trouble. Elaine liked gay night, too, because the boys struck her as pioneers, experimenting in the creation of a culture—unlike the habitués of Thriller Jill's, who willingly accepted rules that others had laid down. Jill's was so dark, gloomy but for the shrill banter of the warring queens. Gay night at Kingdom Come was colorful, like those handkerchiefs that some men wore in the back pocket of their jeans. The left pocket marked one as active, the right as passive, and the colors denoted one's particular sexual finesse. Blue, red, green, white, yellow: Who had originated this custom, and what did the colors mean?

And who was it who decided that certain songs were key items, slow dances for lovers, calmly radiant in each other's grip, and the rave-ups for narcissistic display, two men facing but never touching—confronting, perhaps, goading and reflecting? When the disc jockey chose an especially relevant title—the Tommy James ballad "Crystal Blue Persuasion," say, or the hectic "Grazin' in the Grass"—a great mass sigh would rise up and a people would stream onto the floor, finding identity in their anthems.

Nowadays, the lighting man is an essential element of disco technology, getting major billing on the flyers. In 1969, he was little more than an underling aiming a spotlight. Every now and then, as if making a gesture toward Kingdom Come's sci-fi atmosphere, Lois would flip a switch that threw a halo over the dance floor; there was as well an elaborate meteor-shower effect, made of countless tiny lights embedded in the ceiling. This was used most sparingly, because, as Lois put it, "The only one who gets anything out of it is the power company."

Another aspect of dancing culture that has evolved over the years is arrival time. In the late 1960s, the posted hours were respected as if for a dinner party: If the dance began at ten, ten was when the gang began to gather. By the mid-1970s, only the dolts poured in: The stars made entrances, the later the better. Years after, when the Flamingo and then the Saint were in their heyday, Chase and Thompson would think nothing of walking in well after two. But tonight at Kingdom Come they were at the door with Chris by ten-thirty, passing satiric comments as they pressed into the place.

"There's one," said Chase, noting an enticing yet shyly self-protected female dressed in the style of Arthur's Guinevere, all lace and fur.

"Don't point," said Thompson.

One drag queen, Chase meant, and so she was: in blue drag, meaning so flawlessly copied that idiot straight men—cops—wouldn't detect her. Uncompromising queens flashed red drag: deliberately androgynous and a bait to cops.

Blue drag, red drag, handkerchiefs, arrival times. The codes, the terminology, the system—you see how gay men and women have been working up a chart of behavioral style? In the 1920s, it was red ties. In the 1930s, it was wearing green on Thursdays. In the 1940s, it was a look in the eyes, a reality shoving itself forth. Now, in the 1960s, it's clothes and music and places to go.

Chase and Thompson are like tourists, Chris is thinking. They like to emphasize how different they are from all this, yet they want to be here. It's not honest.

So Chris says, "Now, *there's* a fetching young fellow."

Chase and Thompson turn to stare: at Blue, with whom Paul is proudly on parade.

"He's so blond!" says Chase. "It's too much!"

"Oh, it's just right," says Thompson. "Come on, Chase."

"I like you two better when you're open," says Chris.

"Open? About what?" asks Thompson, ever so blandly.

"About men's looks. What you find attractive."

Truly taken aback, Thompson stutters out, "Really, Chris, you're being a little pushy now."

"Well, you *are,* aren't you? I mean, why else are we at this dance?"

"*You're* not," Chase points out. "At least, not if torrid Ty is to be believed."

"So *pushy,*" Thompson repeats incredulously.

"What's Ty got to do with . . ." Chris begins, then switches tone. "Let's not fight this early in the evening, kiddos." Her pot high is melting away; it was one of those filmy, float-away highs, and she'll come down easily.

Thompson nods, but Chase is wary. Chris is blunt—that's dangerous in a friend.

.   .   .

Paul was having one of the few nights in his dreary life that he could call tip-top. During the walk from the subway, he watched men staring at Blue; some even glanced inquiringly at Paul, as if . . . Well, who can guess what they wanted to know?

Number, that's what they called an attractive man in Paul's youth. "Take a look at *that* number," a queen would say, poking you; or, "Who was that suit-and-tie number you picked up at Dreams?" Number: as if any man were but one of an endless series. Number: because affection was evanescent and that made you promiscuous. But were we?, Paul wondered. Wasn't the idea that gay people are unsteady invented by the state and its confederate witch cults, religion and psychiatry? *Number.* I never saw anyone as a number, Paul thought, forgetting Blue to travel back to the Other Side, as Paul so often did lately. I saw a handsome man as the great love I would never have.

And there was the Kid standing in front of them, crying, "Who's the heaven number in the deep eyes and true skin?"

Blue said, "Look who's here," with a hand on the Kid's shoulder.

"He's mine," Paul announced.

"He's no one's," the Kid replied, adding, "Why don't you go see about the drinks, Paul? I'll take a Bombasta—that's wit and raw nerve straight up."

Before Paul could answer, Blue said, "Look, it's okay, 'cause I'm with you. If I could just talk to him a little. . . ."

"Three beers," said Paul, vamoosing.

"Well," said the Kid. "Enjoy your weekend in Key West, or wherever it was?"

"He took me to a place up north a here. A country hotel. He showed me tennis playing, and there was a whole lotta food at every meal. But what I liked most was miniature golf. You ever try that?"

"I like you," said the Kid. "It'd be great if you liked me. You could come and stay with me in San. I wouldn't kill for it, mind you. But I think we'd get along really well somehow. Want my phone number?"

"Sure."

Instead of business cards, the Kid carried blank cardboard chits to fill out at will. He wrote:

JERRETT TROY
spare bedroom
San Francisco
(415) 626-0172

"Thanks."

"If it ever gets too tense for you here."

"Yeah," said Blue, watching the dancers on the floor. It was a slow one, couples swaying to the promise of a happy elegy with no penalty to pay. The Kid spotted Elaine at the edge of the crowd and, on impulse, went up and took her onto the floor. Till Lois cut in, they were the sole coed couple in sight.

Martin grabbed Henry and told him to get to the door fast because the bouncer wouldn't let Jezebel in. Before Henry had taken three steps, Jezebel (and Louis) sauntered up, Frank and Eric right behind them.

"It's cool," Frank told Henry. "I set the doorman straight on his racial policy."

"They already let in the three black peoples for the evening," said Jezebel, punctuating his rhythm with snaps in the face and snaps to the side, bellicose snaps like *so* at doormen, and slyer, somewhat ontological snaps at the world at large. "They met their quota, so—"

"One nice side effect," said Frank, "was, in the excitement, he forgot to card Eric. So we slipped in nice and easy."

"This is some setup," said Eric, looking around. "Man alive."

"Henry," said Jim, turning up—as one does at these dances—out of nowhere, "we just lost both our flyer hander-outers. Apparently, they fell instantly in love and . . ." Jim looking at Eric. "Well," Jim recovers, "so we need two guys to . . ."

"Eric," says Frank, with an eye on Henry, "help Jim with the flyers."

Jim protests, "I don't want to hand out flyers."

Frank and Henry shove the two of them in some direction, then nod.

"Oh, that's so pretty," says Jezebel. "That's smoother than Mary Worth. But what we gonna do about the racist *doorman* at our Sacred Acts dance? Because that is a *scandal,* you hear?"

"Jez—"

"You spare me your jive, Henry, because you ain't gonna have peace between straight and homo till you get peace between black and white."

Blue has appeared, smiling at Henry.

"That's right, don't heed the oracle," says Jezebel, bustling off.

"Blue," says Henry. They're shaking hands.

"Thanks for getting me that job," says Blue. "With Jerrett Troy."

"Good money?"

"Good exposure, certainly."

They laugh.

"Thought about you from time to time," says Blue. "Guess that sounds like I'm angling, but I did, just the same."

"You want to dance?"

Blue turns to survey the floor, the boys with the boys and the girls with the girls. Revolutions.

"Sure I'll dance," says Blue.

"Ty," said Chris, under her breath.

"Where?" said Chase.

"Oh, yes," said Thompson. "See there?"

"He just comes to this dance like that?" said Chris. "What's going on?"

Thompson looked inscrutable and Chase looked away.

"Spill it!" said Chris.

"He begged me, Chris," said Thompson. "He's been trying to bump into you all over campus. I told him we'd be here."

"Thanks a lot!"

"He says you haven't been taking his phone calls. That's not very up-standing, Chris."

Look who's lecturing me on morals, Chris thinks, keeping an eye on her searching ex–boy friend: wonderful, heartless Ty.

"The fuck of it is, there aren't enough women," said Lois, gazing upon the dance floor. "We're always the Who-let-*them*-in? group."

"Does our sexuality set us apart from the joes," the Kid asked, "or does it set gay men apart from gay women?"

"Everything in life gives us distance from straights, I should think," said Elaine. "Because we know them so well."

Just then Johnna Roberts showed up. Now, *she* had had no trouble at the door, in her conference-room blouse, touch-me-not skirt, and avant-garde silk scarf hanging open off her shoulders. She looked tough and sincere, and Lois was impressed.

"Alicia?" said Johnna.

"No, this is Lois," said Elaine. "She's always Lois, in fact."

"And I'm Jerrett Troy," said the Kid, "except when I become the Green Goddess of truth and desire, those essential elements of the sweet life, ever in love yet at war with each other."

Johnna Roberts wasn't smiling, so Lois said, "None of that Fauntleroy stuff. This is Elaine's editor, and the whole thing is to show her how we have this special world."

By then, Johnna was thoroughly insecure, suspicious, and irritated, so Elaine briskly took her off on a tour while Lois and the Kid shared an excuse-me-for-living shrug.

Paul pulled up before them like Diogenes with his lantern. "Have you seen my date, Johnny? That gorgeous southern cracker who—"

"Paul, you silly victim, why are you never in the useful places at the helpful moment? Blue was in my Act at Tremendo for six weeks. You're best friends with the owner, yet you never came to see us. But *that's* when you should have hooked up with him, say for a quiet dinner and the rest—not at a major party like this, with beauties rummaging through the crowd, hot to audition the new talent."

At this, Paul was worse than forlorn, deeper than crushed. He was totally dismantled.

"I only wanted everyone to respect me," he said quietly.

"Well, go find him, goofy!"

Way across the floor, Jim and Eric were sharing a cranberry juice after lasting out six consecutive dances and having managed to, uh, lose the flyers they were supposed to hand out. They felt mischievous and happy.

No doubt you've hardly noticed Jim. He's one of those "okay" people: okay looks, okay sense of humor, okay company. But he's in there, nevertheless. He knows his rights on earth and turns up in the useful places at the helpful moments, and that can take one far. It's the Jims of the world who sway elections, keep shows running, patiently argue causes with unbelievers. They're the bedrock of culture.

"I see a hot one," said Eric, as a couple brushed by them.

"Red T-shirt?"

"No, his boy friend. Look how's he's walking, like his legs are in charge of the whole place. He'll really plow Red T-shirt tonight."

Jim did a take. "Don't I keep hearing that you're straight?"

Eric made a face.

People were sailing by them, dancing, talking, kissing: It was like sitting in Café Florian or Quadri in the center of Venice and hearing, all about one, the gossip of Europe, of the world. Only connect. Jim put an arm around Eric's shoulder and Eric leaned into it. They shyly smiled at each other as the Kid and Blue came in sight, slow-dancing heart on heart, lost to care. Chris came tumbling past, Ty stalking her. Johnna Roberts circled the dance floor, with Elaine explaining, indicating. Henry was dancing with Andy. Jezebel was lecturing Louis. Gay girls and boys moved to the music, forgot their troubles, came on, got happy.

Paul ran into Andy, returning from the men's room.

"Paul," said Andy, "I'm moving tomorrow, have you heard?"

"Into Henry's place?"

"That's a nice shirt."

Paul made a little noise and preened. "Putting on the dog, don't you know. Oh, you haven't seen a big blond boy with devastating cornfed ways, have you? My date, dare I say?"

"No. . . ."

"All right, you found me," Chris told Ty.

"Darlin', darlin', I only want to talk to you. Didn't I come to see you here, like so?"

"God, don't charm me, please, will you?"

"What charm? It's just me, pretty one."

I hate this, Chris was thinking. He makes girls who are not natural beauties think they're irresistible, and I need that and he knows it.

"What are you doing here, anyway?" she challenged, "at a gay dance?"

"Look who's talking."

"I'm a fag hag—what's your excuse?"

"I *know,* darlin'. The mean old habits of our Ty here. He can't help himself. He gets . . . afraid of something in there."

"Don't dramatize yourself, play the reality of the scene."

"The lady directs."

"You're always forgiven, is that it? Everybody wants you to like them, so they'll always take you back." Chris is helpless, knowing that it's going to hurt again the next time he makes himself scarce. "God*damn* you handsome guys! Liberation for the girls!"

"Wish you'd sweeten up," he says, with a little hands-on and a dangerous-when-wet look. He's holding her; and Chris can't find it inside her to throw him away.

Elaine, with Johnna in tow, has just swept a cache of drugheads, neckers, and various kibitzers out of one of the balconies, and now author and editor stand at the front of it, gazing down on the scene. It's well after midnight and the place is packed and roaring.

"It's hard to believe," says Elaine, "that there was a time when such people had nothing of their own to go to but dingy demimonde saloons. Now they're dating and dancing like teenagers in July."

"Yes, it's been a reestablishing decade," Johnna responds. Her hand explains, vaguely. "Diversities."

"Will our lit reflect those diversities, I wonder?" A loaded question.

Johnna smiles. "Your book."

"My book and other books. Other writers' books."

Johnna shakes her head. "Who will buy?"

"Didn't I hear somewhere that most book buyers are women?"

"A very conservative group, though. They know their authors, and what they want from them."

Lois must have been feeling merry, for just then the meteor effect went off. The crowd cheered, and—it seemed—began to form patterns on the floor, star shapes, snakes and ladders, circles. A few of the men, overheated by nonstop dancing, pulled off their shirts, and the lighting man turned his follow spot upon them like some voyeur pointing There! *There!*

"It's like a fertility rite," Johnna observed. "Ironically enough."

Led by the roving spotlight, Johnna saw couples on every side, of every type: couples enamored and couples tersely courting, couples as aligned as the colors in ribbon candy and couples facing off, doing steps at each other.

"The genders are so separate," Johnna observed. "There's no—"

"Yes, that is strange. But every so often . . . you have to hunt for them—ah, there's a mixed pair."

The spotlight had caught Ty and Chris. Elaine and Johnna watched Ty coaxing his girl, nuzzling her, and Chris getting very into it, for all her misgivings. Young, free Ty and his fair maid is what Johnna saw.

"I don't call them mixed at all," she said. "They're so alike in their youth and joy, aren't they?"

She spoke fiercely. Elaine looked at Johnna, wondering what had suddenly troubled her.

"I *spy* them," said Johnna.

"What's wrong?"

"Is this liberation? It's all *youth* down there, Elaine. What's next, the confiscation of everyone over thirty?"

Johnna was looking hard at Ty and Chris, though the spotlight had moved on. Rooted to the spot, she was. Wounded to the nth and crabby to the core.

"Ask yourself what this *is*," Johnna demanded. "Is there a book in it? No."

Johnna is focused on Ty and that girl he was kissing. Ridiculous. To come here, chasing some misguidedly idealistic author who can't see that an unconventional way of living is not in itself a foundation for good writing. . . . To *come* here and *see* this!

"I've had enough," Johnna concluded. "Fiction is not about kinds of people, fiction is about people. If your characters are too limited—"

"Not limited," Elaine insisted. "*Pointed.* I would use the specific to address the general."

"Readership," said Johnna. "Movie deals. Clout and respect," she said. But she was thinking, That showboating little fuck and his coaxing act, and I bought it. I let him work me like a toaster.

"Look," Elaine urged. "Quick," as the spotlight hovered upon Henry, Andy, and Blue dancing with their arms around each other. "Now what do you see?"

"Three young men making fools of themselves."

But Henry was thinking, I've got it all with me now. Blue's hot and Andy's nice. If I could only combine them, *control* my life.

Henry pulled Andy and Blue closer, so tightly that the two looked up, surprised.

"Nice to be with friends," Blue commented; and Andy sighed.

Jezebel grabbed Henry from behind, shook him out of his reverie. "The *police*," Jezebel said. "They raided Hero's."

"What?"

Jezebel nodded.

Louis was with him. "A guy just came in with the whole report," said Louis. "They backed a truck up to the door of the house and loaded it up."

"You hear him, Henry?" said Jezebel.

"Jez, this isn't . . . It's not the time to . . ."

"*Henry.* We have *got* to do something *about* this."

"But now?" Henry looked about him, as if gesturing: On this night of nights?

"Henry, Henry, Henry. Think. Be smart, now."

Blue and Andy standing there watching. Louis melting away.

"Tomorrow it's names in the paper," Jezebel continued. "It's fired from their jobs, war with their families. How many times, Henry? When do we stop letting it happen?" Jezebel struggling for self-control, so angry and so right, yet unwilling to attack his own side. "We have to fight them," he almost whispered. "You gonna dance while Rome burns?"

Blue doesn't like this. Andy is uncomfortable.

"Have you ever asked yourself why they print those names after a raid?" Jezebel goes on. "You know why the *police* give them to the papers, sure. The *police* are hating beasts. But why do the papers go ahead and print the names? Is that news, Henry? Who's the guy at the paper who says, Yes, let's unmask the faggots, destroy their lives? Who's thinking that's good copy? Henry? Please . . . *please* let us do something now, tonight, while this is happening. They're probably still loading up the vans. They're taking us prisoner even now. Henry. Henry, listen. We have *got* to free ourselves of this *terrible* and *unnecessary* oppression."

"Henry," said Blue, "let's dance."

"You do and I'll kill you," said Jezebel.

"Nigger," said Blue; Henry got between them so fast that it was nothing but Jezebel shouting at Blue and Blue fisting up at Jezebel, as Henry ferried Jezebel off and away, to a dark corner where they squared off.

"What am I supposed to *do,* huh?" cried Henry. "Because this isn't a war rally and you *get off my back!*"

"What *you* are supposed to *do,* man, is you *lead* this crowd *out into the streets* to demand—"

"This crowd doesn't want—"

"They'll follow if you *show them how!*"

"Look, look"—grabbing Jezebel by the arms, because he was looking at Blue over Henry's shoulder and getting antsy—"I promise you, at the next meeting of Sacred Acts, we'll schedule a demonstration in front of the precinct house, and—"

"A demonstration! Wow, they gonna be so *peeved* at us for that! Heads will roll, huh, Henry boy?"

"Then what should I—"

"*Fight!* Not hang around! And not with your racist buddies! What should you? *That's* what!"

Shamed, Henry just stood there. At length, Jezebel walked away from him.

Andy came up and put a hand on Henry's shoulder.

"He's right, though," said Henry.

"Blue went off somewhere," said Andy.

"Yeah, he's an expert at that."

The music, big as apocalypse, drew the dance toward its climax. Everyone was on the floor, singing along with the Diamonds' hit, "It's So Cool":

You're gonna want me
And date me.
Oh, baby, don't accept me—
Create me.

I see Frank, a gleaming demon, dancing with Blue in an intricately sensual habañera; and Lois accepting a butch young fatale's "Dance, babe?" to hit the floor with purpose; and Henry trying to Forget About It as he circles the floor with Andy; and the Kid solemnly dancing by himself; and Jim, absurdly, teaching Eric the cha-cha; and Paul wandering around looking for Blue; and the girls and boys blasting off in this Kingdom Come; and furious Johnna Roberts striding through the middle of the dance floor—one side, all!—dogged by Elaine but unreachable, finished with it, unable to hear the history meter's ticking, the reinheriting of the earth. The name of the dance is Revolutions.

Frank got home after four, bundled Eric into bed, and dialed Larken's number.

"Frank, you gorgeous beast" was Larken's greeting. "You movie star."

Frank needed to tell of the dance, of the shocking sense of community that he had felt there. "Yet it was so natural, Lark," he said. "It didn't seem like something we were inventing. It's as if it had always been there somehow, just waiting for us to—"

"You actually go out dancing with men, now, huh?"

"God, it's so hot, Lark! How come we didn't know about this before? You fill a place full of our folks, and it's one great field of energy. Hey, any chance of your taking a trip here?"

"Any chance of your moving to San Francisco? We could use a leader. A 'role model,' they call it now."

"I'm just some guy, Lark."

"No, Frank. You're the top."

They went on for a bit in this vein, then Larken reviewed developments in his career as a cabaret master, putting acts together, booking clubs, and so on.

"You doing okay, buddy?" Frank asked. "Are you happy out there?"

"Frank, *you're* out there—we're Californians, remember? Yes, I'm happy. I'm doing well enough to feel free and I've got hope enough for the future to be intrigued with my own possibilities. What about you? Are you making another movie?"

"Oh, brother, yeah. This time the guy who runs the show is letting me take charge. Got some neat ideas, too."

"How do you cast something like that?"

"Call a few friends."

"Are you in this, too?"

"Sure."

Larken let out the hint of a sigh. "I have to tell you, I went back to that porn theatre twice. I guess I didn't appreciate you before. I didn't know . . . Gosh, Frank, if you came here, you'd be king of the Mission or something. You'd be a god."

Frank pulls away from such a notion. It embarrasses him—reproaches him, he thinks, with all that he was supposed to be that he cast out of his life.

"Anyway," said Larken, as they signed off, "if you ever want to come out here, I've got a spare room with your name on the door."

"Someday," said Frank.

Frank scarfed up some leftovers from the fridge, showered, and slipped into bed. Eric had seemed asleep, but as Frank pulled up the covers the kid turned around and folded himself around Frank, saying, "Who was that guy on the phone?"

"An old comrade."

"Were you boy friends?"

"Let's get to sleep now."

"Okay." Then: "Were you?"

"Yes."

"He still loves you, is that it?"

Frank didn't answer.

"You'll say I'm just a kid and I don't know beans. But I bet when someone falls in love with you they never get over it."

"How so, okay?"

"Because you can get over some guy who's incredibly handsome, or out-of-sight sex, or rich and gives you things, like. But you know what you can't get over?"

"Where did you find out so much about love, huh?"

"See? I'm just a kid. But Jim told me some things tonight, for instance. And you. And other people. I can hear ideas, you know."

"So what did you hear?"

Eric changed his grip, shifted the lay of his legs against Frank's, and rubbed his soft hair against Frank's cheek. "I heard that the guy you can't get over is the solid guy who's nice to you. Real solid and real nice. I heard that a guy like that will haunt you for all your earthly days."

"Bullshit," said Frank, putting an arm around Eric. "Go to sleep now, little one."

"Tough guy."

An hour or so later, the sun came up on Andy's moving day, and Andy was glad, and Henry was glad, and this was really happening.

"Good-bye, log cabin that my mother built for me," Andy told his apartment as he bustled around the movers, checking to see if he was leaving anything behind. He was. Subservience. Obedience. Apologies to unforgiving authorities.

I'm liberated, Andy thought in something of a daze as he rode uptown.

Henry joined Andy in his new place on East Fifty-sixth Street just as Andy was tacking up the framed poster of *Fiddler on the Roof* that he had bought a week ago. It was classy art, real Broadway theatre; Henry will appreciate it, Andy had told himself.

"Look!" Andy cried, as his boy friend walked in. "Look at my own place here! I was so pro at handling the movers, too! You would have—"

Henry pulled Andy close and squeezed him tight.

"Yow," said Andy.

"My hero," Henry called him then.

Andy gave Henry a tour, pointing out the special features—the bookshelves built into the wall, the twist locks on the metal window frames, the profusion of electrical outlets.

"You're easy to please," Henry observed. "You don't ask for much."

"Just the future," Andy replied.

Jim was giving a brunch in Andy's honor, and Andy was thrilled: Henry's friends were so fascinating. Henry felt restless at Jim's. I've done this too many times, he was thinking. He tried to take a lift from Andy's enthusiasm. He's so cute and trusting, so *enlivened* by everything. You'd have to be a tight-assed grouch not to respond to that.

Martin was going on about some guy he had tricked with three times in one week without realizing it (or something like that), and Jim was fussing with the records. Andy whispered to Henry, "I want to sleep with you."

"So I said, 'Do I know you?' " Martin was telling them. "He says, 'You're Jonesy, right?' And I said, 'Not only am I *not* Jonesy, but I—' "

"This," Andy whispered with a guilty smile, "is an unnecessary party. We could be having our own private liberation do, if you, uh, catch my drift."

That was Andy borrowing one of Jim's pet phrases, and Henry smiled. We learn from each other.

" 'You may not have a head for names,' " Martin continued, " 'but you can fuck like a—' "

"Hey, hey, hey," said Jim. "Aren't we supposed to be mapping out a husband sweepstakes for Eric?"

"Craig Woodruff said he'd try him out," said Martin.

"That drug lord?" said Jim, appalled.

"He's rich and sexy," said Martin, arms spread wide in reassurance.

"He's an evil piece of junk," Henry put in.

"Well, I'm *doing* my *best,*" Martin replied in mock-queen style, fanning himself with a limp wrist. "Oh, thorry, I forgot to lithp."

"I hate when you do that stuff," Henry said.

Andy flashed Henry a signal with his eyes: Let's go.

On the street, Henry said, "It almost worries me that you've gotten so confident, because then I wonder who's in charge here. But I love that wonder. I love seeing you inherit yourself. I love that."

"It's just . . . You have this marvelous circle of gay friends, you know? All I have is a few memories of people who were nice to me in high school. But sometimes I get tired of the gay part of your friends. Like when you get annoyed at something and Martin goes, 'Poor puss.' "

"That *is* irritating."

"They have these mannerisms, and we have each other."

"What a . . . lovely way to put it. I'd hug you if it weren't three-thirty in the afternoon in the East Fifties."

Jim lived four and a half blocks from Andy's new apartment, so our boys were back in no time—but when Andy unlocked his front door, they found Andy's mother cooking in the kitchen. The *Fiddler on the Roof* poster had been taken down, and plastic covers had been stretched over Andy's new leather couch.

"At last you come back, eh?" said Andy's mother, one eye on them and one on her work. "No invitation to visit from you, no phone call of, Mama, I'm in my fancy new place that I had to move to because where I'm from isn't good enough for me. *Ma che?* We forgive you. I got the key from your fancy doorman in the uniform. Your father's out getting copies made, and then we'll see, the fancy young apartment boy who thinks he knows more than his mama, eh? Who's this?"

Andy stood there, stricken.

"You were supposed to keep this address secret from them," said Henry, quietly. "This is the reason why."

"I never thought they would—"

"Of course you did. You hoped it."

"I said, Who *is* this, Adreiano?" Andy's mother repeated.

"Look at her giving me the Old Country evil eye," said Henry. "Look at you quaking. You're not man enough to be gay, Andy. You're not even man enough to leave home."

"Adreiano!" Andy's mother put down her spatula, left the stove. *"What does this mean, eh?"*

"Mama, what are you *doing* here?" said Andy, really upset. "I was going to ask you over when—"

"Tell your mother who I am, Adreiano."

Andy's mother took a step forward, eager for battle; then she halted, unsure of the stakes. It had just—this second—dawned on her that her son might be *anormale,* and she was willing to do almost anything to hear the idea exploded. Hastily, she regrouped. She wiped her hands on her apron, took another step forward, and smiled.

"I brought up a little pasta," she said, looking more at Henry than at Andy, "and the sauce is thickening in the pot. It's going right for the dinner, a boy and his mama and papa and his friend, to start up his new house." More smile, and a slight shrug. "Now, Adreiano."

Meaning, introduce us. Andy said nothing, though.

So Henry said, "I'm Andy's lover. I kiss him, fuck him, blow him, rim him, shrimp him, and am just beginning to hate him."

"Henry—"

"You may not be familiar with all my terms," Henry went on, addressing Andy's mother. "Fucking. Now, that's basic. All sex tends to fucking, because one demands to be top and one needs to be bottom, and gay men long to discover who of them was meant to play which—"

"I can soothe this out," Andy was saying, trying to take hold of Henry. Henry wouldn't look at him.

"You couldn't soothe a deck of Old Maid, Andy boy," said Henry. "Where was I? Blowing? Yes. Now, blowing is very different from fucking, because few agree as to which is the top and which the bottom in blowing. Is the top the icon who poses to be worshiped, or is *he* taken, his insides thwunked out into the—"

"Adreiano," in this dead voice, the sound of fat lies pierced by the arrows of what is true whether you like it or not.

"Mama, please leave. *Please*. You don't want to—"

"Rimming," said Henry, clearing his throat, "is the gay man's choice act because it is the most intimate, and most terrifying to straights." He spoke dreamily, a disembodied Henry, in tune with a philosophy but not with the scene at hand. He's even thinking, How much longer were Andy and I going to continue, anyway? Love is nice, but is it effective? "Now, as time blows on, you come to notice that each boy has his own unique taste, and Andy here . . . With Andy it's like dipping your tongue into a honey pot."

"You *dirty*!" Andy's mother screamed at Henry. "*Sporcizia!* You make delinquent my son!"

"Is that what I do, Andy?"

"Mama," Andy begged, "you don't know what this is about."

"I don't *know*? I don't hear what he says, the filth? The selfish? *God* doesn't hear? *Onta su noi!* To offend the way of God!"

"There is no God," Henry replied. "There is only rich white heterosexuals passing laws to consolidate their power."

"*Adreiano!* To even *know* him!" Andy's mother began to weep, quite genuinely. "To know such a person!"

She held out her arms to Andy, and he walked right in. "Adreiano," she warned, "to have a family is the most sacred thing to do on earth. To be raised in love and honor, so we go on to raise our own *bambini* in the same way."

"Don't ennoble it," said Henry. "You didn't raise a family out of choice. You raised a family because some guy with total power over you fucked your insides and made you bear children."

Andy's mother was stunned for about three seconds. Then she charged. Thrusting Andy aside, she stepped up to Henry and slapped him a good one just behind the right ear.

Henry looked at Andy.

Miserable Andy backed away. "Henry," he pleaded.

Henry smiled tensely at Andy's mother, then slowly walked over to the *Fiddler on the Roof* poster, leaning against the desk. "I was ten or eleven," said Henry, grasping the poster, raising it, showing it off. "And my father decided to punish me because I hadn't made shortstop on my Little League team. Both he and my older brother had been outstanding shortstops in their day, and I tried my best to make it, believe me. I just didn't have it. So my father revoked my television privileges, indefinitely, except for the pro baseball games, which I would in fact be forced to watch, for my edification and the greater glory of fathers."

Henry hefted the poster as if testing its weight, trying a grip or two.

"All this," he continued, "because I simply wasn't able to hold my own with the other, uh, chaps. So I piped up and said, I don't want to play softball from *any* position. I don't like softball. My father announced that he would *teach* me to like it by beating me. Not a strapping, you understand. My father liked to rock in there with fists flying and knocking you against the wall. A real hero, I'm sure you'll agree. Where was my mother during all this? She went upstairs to catch up on her sewing. Father knows best."

"Adreiano," said Andy's mother. "It's time for your friend to go."

"No, it was my brother who stood up for me. Something like, 'Dad, you can't punish him just because he didn't make—' And *crack!* across my brother's face, for daring to interfere. Now, I'm proud to say that *that* was what inspired me. Because suddenly there's this moment when you realize that everything your parents have taught you is garbage. They say, For Your Own Good, but they mean, For Our Endlessly Devouring Obsession with Convention."

"*Vergogna,*" said Andy's mother, dangerous but wary.

"As it happened, my brother had just come home from softball practice, bat and all. So I grabbed the bat and went for the windows. They were my father, and I was killing them. Now, he told my *brother* to stop me—and if my brother didn't, my father would go back on all his guarantees on his college scholarship. My brother then told my father what a fucking bastard he is. But me, I was jamming away at those glass windows. Like this."

Raising the *Fiddler on the Roof* poster, Henry aimed it at a corner of Andy's new desk—Andy cried *No!* as his mother gloated—and slammed it down with such force that the cardboard itself crumpled behind the shower of glass.

"*This* is your friend!" Andy's mother remarked.

Henry strode to the door, turned, and said, "Maybe it's too bad, Andy. But you love what they do to you and I cannot bear it."

"Henry," said Andy, low, beaten, a whimper floating past prison locks, "I don't love it."

"If you didn't love it, you wouldn't let them do it."

Henry left the apartment, and Henry and Andy did not speak again.

.   .   .

Dear Elaine,

What exactly do you say to the police—"A lunatic is following me and what if she's dangerous?" And how do you put it to Lois—"That woman I keep seeing is real, please save me"? Doesn't Alfred Hitchcock teach us that No One Believes You?

I was in the produce section of the Red Apple, and I heard "Hello, Elaine." So I turned and there she was: the woman who's always there. She was smiling and I was startled. I said something mild like "We've been seeing each other around the town, haven't we?," and her "Oh, yes; *yes*" was so fervent, so concentrated, that she might have been a fairy-tale stepmother responding to the question, Was it you who dipped the apple in the poison?

I was flustered, but I tried to move on in my assertively uninvolved New York style. I said, thumbing through the apples, "My roommate has a thing for Granny Smiths, but only the hard ones covered with freckles. They taste the best." I shrugged and walked. She followed. So I turned and asked, not pleasantly but inquiringly, "Is there something you want?"

"Yes," she replied. "I want what you have."

Elaine abruptly rose from her desk, fidgeting, shaking her head, crossing to open a window. Some writer, she thought: Cinderella and the Ritz I can do, but show me real life and my pencil breaks. *What I have,* she wants!

This weird city, Elaine thought, looking down on the street. Do I even want real life in my books? Because I surely don't want it in my life.

Oh, it's rich, Elaine. Rich it *is,* darling. One look at someone with the messy, terrible power of real human longing and you run like a child.

I have to step in here, because Elaine is wrong: She handled it well, actually. "What I have?" she asked the stranger, sensible, curious, bemused. Elaine in the role of Elaine. "What do I have?"

The woman who's always there brightened suddenly, as if the drugs had just kicked in.

"Love," she said. "It's always there for some of us, Elaine, and it can come and take us without warning. Love is anywhere. On a Broadway street, or in a moonlit ballroom, or right here in a store. Elaine, you are love to me."

The woman who's always there: youngish, short, trim, chopped-short hair, a hard mouth in a soft face. Scary, Elaine thinks. She's smiling to hide the anger.

"The creations of Elaine," the woman went on, making them sound like hats. "I have friends who would give anything to be talking to you now, like me. Maybe taking pictures—I brought a camera." This was an eager confidence, almost a plea. "There's always lunch."

Elaine turned and moved through the store, dodging the price checkers and the dodderers who go into a trance at the sight of the paper towels. Leaving her basket on an idle checkout counter—and thinking, Lois is going to have to do without her Granny Smiths—Elaine fled the place, hailed a cab, and rode away. Fifteen blocks south, she had the driver run east to Central Park West and back home again, leaping out and into her building in real jig time.

Music, she thought. I'll listen to something. *Calma, calma.*

Like many of her generation, Elaine had never quite adapted to the home stereo system. To plain folks raised in the Depression and the war years, home music meant radio; only aficionados and the pretentious bought records. As youth today automatically switches on MTV when entering a room, Lois and Elaine turned on the radio; you never knew what you'd get, but it was filled with personality. A world bubbled up in it: song, chat, sports, politics. It was like a hobby that cultivated itself as you sat there.

Music and coffee, Elaine thought, reheating and finishing off the pot. The wizards have replaced everything I'm used to with shortcuts—frozen instant coffee flakes and bottles of pre-mixed Mai Tais. Well, it *is* a young culture, eternally self-renewing, wanting new things of its own. Johnna was right about that.

"Far out," Elaine said aloud, as the radio played that *Hair* number about the Age of Aquarius. "Heavy. Groovy. Out of sight."

Someone knocked at the door; this almost never happened. New Yorkers maintain such strict codes of privacy that one shouldn't bang on a door to warn that the building is on fire without having buzzed up from downstairs first. To answer an unexpected knock—even to call out, "Who's there?"—can involve one in lurid, exotic plots.

Lois, of course, would storm right up to the door, pull it open, and grouch at whoever was there. Elaine was more reticent. Anyway, she'd had her fill of strangers today. She sat at the kitchen table, staring at the door, as the knocking grew louder.

"Elaine!" cried the woman who's always there. "I want to be inside with you! Elaine, I hear music! You didn't fool me with that taxicab,

Elaine. I know all about you, see? I was across the street when you came back, Elaine. You better open wide for me, now! I want to see what you're like!"

She wants what I have. What do I have? More curious than annoyed, Elaine switched off the radio, walked to the door, and spoke up: "If what you admire about Elaine Denslow is what you read in her books, then I am glad to inform you that the next one will be even more sharing than the others."

Elaine heard a rustling behind the door, nothing else.

"There will be more of me in this one," Elaine added. "Perhaps too much, even."

"No," came the voice. "There could never be too much of you, Elaine." After a moment she added, so softly she could scarcely have meant to be heard, "Let me see you. Let me feel you, Elaine."

"In my books."

"No, no, Elaine." Now she sounded happy. "Through the open door, a pathway to heaven."

I thought they only did this to movie stars, Elaine was thinking. How do they even find you?

"Elaine?" She knocked again. "I don't hear the music, Elaine! Please turn the music on!" Waiting, listening for it. Then: "Elaine, I need you to talk to me now! We've grown so close, then you shy away. It scares me at what I might do to you."

"I'm calling the police," said Elaine, calmly.

"Oh, no, *please*." Wheedling. "You mustn't." Forceful. "I only want to hear your sweet music, Elaine." Coy, now. "She's really nuts. "It's as if we were having coffee and tiny sandwiches at some posh Elaine-Denslow-sort-of place, discussing art nouveau, yet all I would think about is your body, Elaine, lying next to me."

Something was going on outside the door, some scratching or rubbing against the wood.

"I've had you on the page, Elaine, uhmm, yes. You're so available. You're forming a club, Elaine. The sorority of secret women. You may not—"

"What in the bleeding Herkimer is going on here?" said Lois, in the hall.

Elaine sprang to the door and pulled it open. "Save me!" she said.

Lois looked from Elaine to the women who's always there.

"All right, bangs," says Lois to the stranger. "What's this gig?"

Lois advances a pace, and the woman retreats. But her eyes—her face—reads, I'm not giving up. I am here. I read Elaine.

"Elaine and I," she says, "must make our beautiful music."

"Not on my carpet, you won't," says Lois, walking into the apartment. Holding the door and looking at the woman in the hall, she adds, "One more noise and I come out and kick a hole in you."

That was that. Elaine fell into Lois's arms, saying, "One, you are so handy, and, two, we have to move."

Lois enjoyed hearing Elaine praise Lois's valor, but she'd date a man rather than admit it. "I turn my back on you for one hour, and you've got women fucking our front door."

Lois walked to the mail pile, to pore and consider. "Hmm. Con Ed's overdue. Didn't you promise to—"

"I will, my king, I solemnly attend, but *please* can we think about how terrifying life has become? I mean, just—"

"Lord & Taylor?"

"I've an account now. Such lovely lines in Senior Misses."

"This bill is perfumed!"

"Lois, I want to get out of this city and we have to talk."

Lois thought it over a bit. "Was that one of your readers?"

"It would seem so."

"She likes your stuff so much she wants to . . ." Lois made a risqué little motion of the tongue.

"That and more, I fancy."

"Aren't they supposed to write through your publisher?"

"She probably did, and I never realized how . . ."

". . . deeply she was—"

"Yes, affected by what I managed to slip in about women loving women. I guess, after all, that you can only find us in fiction. In theatre, we don't exist. In movies, we're witches. Suddenly, there we are on the page, fair and true, and a lady goes ape to see her world affirmed."

"Magazines and bills," said Lois, finishing off the mail. "She'll be back, you know."

"I can be in Sea Cliff in two hours."

"She'll find you there, too, Miss. She wants contact. I saw."

"Lois, can't we move? *Have* we to be here indefinitely?"

Lois shrugged, then stopped, caught by something. "Chick," she said, "your books are that heavy?"

"It's not about heavy, it's about *honest*. Everyone's been lying about homos and lesbians for so long that even a veiled truth here and there can be incredibly energizing. I just . . . No, *what* is it?" Elaine thought. "*Yes.* I want to grow young. I need to see somewhere else and feel new again.

Somewhere totally novel to me. Mountains, dire swampland, suspicious locals."

"Where did you have in mind?" said Lois, smiling.

"Oh, that's how I especially like you. When you let me tell what I'm thinking of."

Ty said, "Maybe I'm just this vagabond kind of guy, can't be pinned down."

"Bull doody," said Chris.

Ty sighed, then grinned. "Here I am, taking you out for a lovely afternoon. It's Ty, it's spring, it's Central Park going way green for us. And you're not impressed."

Chris sighed, too, leaning back to look around them. They were sitting in the large crescent of grass in the center of the Rambles, and—though Chris had never heard anything about it before—it was clear that this was one of those meeting places that gays mysteriously mark out for themselves. All about were men, especially young men better-looking than they should be. They were athletic, but less in a recreational than a gymmy way, and their clothes seemed so . . . well, *aptly* chosen. They didn't look like guys taking it easy. They looked like models on a shoot.

"How come we're here and not somewhere else?" Chris asked.

Ty shrugged.

"I'm always here," Chris complained.

"Said you'd never been here before."

"Not physically. And why do you keep vanishing and then—"

"Because I always want more of you, darlin'."

Ty tried a combination or two of his various smiles, but Chris wanted information. This Ty could not give, because, frankly, he simply didn't know what impelled him. He reminds me of something I saw out on the beach at the Pines one summer: a great rough mutt of a dog who had laid claim to a piece of driftwood, which it would plop down in front of you. The dog would then bark insistently till you got up and threw the wood into the ocean for the dog to retrieve. Trotting back with the wood clamped between its jaws, it would drop the wood in front of the very next person sitting on the beach, and start over. In this manner it traversed the strand—yet, every so often, that dog would stop in an almost pensive way, look among the people it had already connected with, and trot back with the wood to urge someone to throw it a second, even a third, time.

That was Ty, eager to collect many fans, always worried that their passion might prove perfunctory. Always, Ty must test; and sometimes he fails. Johnna Roberts, for instance, never took a call from Ty again, and once, when he stopped by her apartment building and buzzed up, she told the doorman to get rid of him.

"How do I look?" said Chris, lying on her back, her head to the side, away from the sunlight. "Am I splendid in the grass?"

She's pretty darn okay, Ty thought, her hair flopping around and her eyes alight, and the tops of her very pretty breasts sort of strong and peeking out to say, Taste me. Ty was stirred; but a shadow passed over them, and Chris, glancing up, said, "You were at Kingdom Come last Saturday."

"Here," said Henry, handing her a flyer. "In case you want to stand with us to fight bigotry, oppressive laws, and the rest of the American way."

"Oh, a demonstration," said Chris, sitting up to examine the flyer. She's a veteran now. "Gay Liberation? That's my favorite kind." Ty was reading over her shoulder. Chris asked, "Do you welcome straights on the line?"

"You're not . . ."

"A lesbian. No. I'm sort of a gay man manqué. The right interests but the wrong biology."

Ty chuckled.

"A fellow traveler," said Chris, bold with her terminology. She smiled at Henry. "Hey, join us."

Henry looks around, checking out the lawn of sunbathers and conversationalists. A few loners reading the paper, a couple resting up from Frisbee, someone giving someone else a back rub.

"No," said Henry. "I've got a time problem." He's restless, tired of the whole thing. It's late in the day, no one cares—some of the men here simply laughed at him when they saw the flyer—and Henry has Blue in tow. Blue didn't laugh at the flyer: He shrugged, saying, "What's that gonna get you, man?"

Blue's sitting on a bench up by the main walkway, Thinking the Whole Thing Over. Henry's a good guy. He's got a nice place, small but comfortable. Good eating there, too; and the beer never runs out. Good beer, too, some German kind. Henry doesn't ask anything of you except sex, and with Blue you never have to ask in the first place. It's a good deal all around.

So why is the Whole Thing becoming a drag?

"Henry is serious," says Blue aloud, watching Henry as he approaches, head bowed and flyers largely wasted. "He is a very serious Henry."

Henry's idea of Blue is more textured: beautiful, obliging, exotic, amusing, full of pain that he so fiercely hides that he comes off to strangers as shallow. After that woebegone Andy, Blue is electric; but he's hidden. The sex is fine. It's not Henry's scene, exactly, but Henry has adapted to it; and, after climax, Blue waxes loving and humorous, and somehow this astounds Henry. Think of it: a Wild Boy growing fond.

So why is the Whole Thing beginning to feel unnecessary?

"Looks like no one's taking to yer papers," says Blue as Henry joins him on the bench.

"No one's around when you start a movement," Henry explains. "Twenty years from now, we'll be such a multitude there'll be a schism a week."

"Schism," Blue repeats.

"A division. A sundering."

"Yeah, they get cast asunder and suchlike in the Bible."

Henry looks at Blue.

"It might be time for our Blue to hit the road," Blue offers in a speculative manner, to see what Henry says to that.

Henry says nothing.

"Always been my intention to see up the world," Blue goes on. "Only been to West Virginia and New York so far. Thinking maybe of doing a spot of California, you know?"

Henry smiled wearily at Blue. "I bet you'd fit in wonderfully. You're Cal colors, aren't you? Yellow and gold. Smooth and young and almost carefree."

Henry looked at the lawn of gay folk, none of whom would take the slightest notice of the gay-lib demonstration he was promoting.

"What do you mean, 'almost'?" said Blue.

"It'll be fine," Jim told Eric, as they waited for the train to Sayville to take off. "Just don't talk a lot. Wait till *he* tells you what he wants from a boy. Then you fit into that."

"What am I, an actor?" Eric fumed.

Frank came into the car, and Eric waved him over, looking like a puppy about to tumble into his master's lap.

"The young man is up for a houseboy job in the Pines," Jim explained, as Frank joined them. "You know that palace they were building all last summer, way down toward Water Island? The one shaped like a giant Hershey's Kiss? That's the place."

" 'The Witch's Tit,' " said Frank. So the locals had dubbed it. "What's this guy like, besides rich?"

"He's a gent," said Jim.

Frank waited for a more explicit answer. He'd known many a gent to do unspeakable things to a kid like Eric.

"He's a good guy," Jim added. "A big wheel at the Joffrey Ballet and so on. He and Henry's older brother went to college together."

Frank nodded noncommittally.

"Don't worry, we've been screening them. Martin kept coming up with one velvet monster after another, but this one's legitimate."

"Yeah, if he pulls out the rubber mask and the handcuffs," Eric muttered, "I'm splitting."

Jim patted his shoulder. "I'll take you to my house first. If you're unhappy, come back to me and we'll put you up on the couch."

Frank liked that, guys looking out for each other. "There's always got to be a way out," he said. "A choice."

As the train pulled out of the station, Jim noted the attention they were getting from the other beach-bound gay men. It was a Friday-evening train in early June, with a heavy contingent of males wearing their ruts into the traditional route of the two trains, the van to the ferry slip, the boat over the bay to the Pines or Cherry Grove, and the exuberant arrival in a sandy ghetto without laws or clothing. To the professional gays like Frank and Henry and Martin, the men who worked only to amortize their leisure, who spent hours in the gym perfecting their appeal, and who spent winter waiting for summer and summer waiting for the weekend, the beach represented a fantasy made real. To the less devoted, like Jim, the fantasy was more glimpsed than experienced. To pass a prince in trunks on the boardwalk and nod hello was, to such as Frank, an invitation to the dance. To Jim, it was a highlight of the stay.

"I'm out for the whole two weeks," said Jim, enjoying the way the other guys in the car were staring at them and whispering. "A bagful of books, a clutch of *Times* recipes, and me, that's the trip."

"You've got the two muscle queens with the same name in your house, right?"

"Billy and Bill. They're ideal housemates. They're almost never around except to nap and sleep. What are you up to?"

Frank smiled. "I'm making a movie."

"What, a travelogue?"

"Sort of."

"I'm making a movie, too," said Eric. "It's about this heebie-jeebie boy who goes nuts and wrecks all the teepees in the Indian village. Yeah. So then he mocks the authorities and they try to throw him in jail. But he won't go, see? He's a runaway boy."

"Is that how you're going to talk at this rich guy's house?" said Frank. "Because forget it, okay?"

"Maybe he'll like it," said Jim. "I do."

There was little conversation after that. Frank read the *News,* Jim pulled out a paperback of *City of Night,* and Eric looked out the window. By the time they hit the ferry dock, Frank had fallen into company with some men Jim didn't know, and the trio broke up, Jim and Eric heading into the belly of the boat and Frank sitting on the roof to brave the heavy spray and watch the white of the houses gradually dot the trees as the boat approached the harbor.

Halfway across the bay, Eric came up and found Frank sitting alone. Eric said, "If I throw myself in the water, will you save me and take me home forever?"

"I'm no good for you, youngster."

"Sure you are. Why not?"

"Because I'm trash, okay?"

"No, you're some hero guy who rescues everyone."

"You're wrong about that, and I should know." The dog on the quicksand. "I don't rescue anybody, I just fuck around. You need some solid guy who'll give you ambition and a way to believe in yourself. That's why Jim is taking you out here. He's an upstanding guy."

"Yeah, he's okay," said Eric vaguely.

"Hey, would it knock you out to be nice to him? Because, I'll tell you, boy, Jim's your ace today."

Nearing port, the boat cut its speed to just above floating and wafted into the egg of water that the Pines called a harbor. It was near sundown, and tea dance at the Botel had reached its prime, the deck crowded with the blindsiding beauties, the deft arbiters, and the hapless followers of circuit life. Heads turned to examine the boat as it passed, and the ferry looked back. Frank was spotted; friend nudged friend and made remark.

"Are you ready for that?" Frank asked, nodding at the celebrants of the Mass that never stops. "Jailbait without a job or a friend?"

"I have a friend," Eric replied. "You're my friend." Eric was looking at Frank as a chipmunk looks at an oak: I'll believe in you.

"You go back down to Jim, now. Tell him thank you for his help."

"Okay."

By then, the ferry had landed, and Frank came down with Eric to find

Jim patiently waiting on the dock. They parted there, for Frank was heading west and Jim's house was so far to the east that his housemates kept a typical Pines red wagon locked up at the harbor to use in transporting groceries down the boardwalk.

"They're big as tanks," Jim explained to Eric as they walked, "but for some reason the idea of carrying bags of groceries . . ."

Eric wasn't listening, so Jim stopped talking. It was nearly a half mile to Jim's turnoff, but they took it in silence, till Eric grabbed Jim and whispered, "Look at that!"

It was a Pines deer, frozen still, not precisely looking at you but very aware of the traffic patterns in its vicinity.

"Can we feed it something?" asked Eric. "Animals are always hungry."

Jim took the second half of his train sandwich out of his overnight, pulled out the lettuce, and gave it to Eric. "Try that," Jim said.

Eric approached the deer with great care, holding the lettuce before him. Suddenly, the deer elegantly swung its head toward the food, sniffed, and turned away.

"He doesn't feature it," said Eric.

"Maybe it's the mayo from the sandwich. Try pulling off a branch from that tree there."

"Yeah!"

Eric backed up, pulled on a branch, and extended the freed leaves to the deer. It waited a long time, then finally turned to Eric, stretched forward, and calmly bit off a bit of green.

"Say!"

"Easy. Don't scare him."

Eric stood as the deer ate and, without warning, bounded off.

"Wow," said Eric. "The whole zoo's here."

"Come on," said Jim, leading off at the turn. "I want you to be sure of where it is in case you aren't happy with . . ."

Jim's house was one of those small, rudimentary rectangles—one bedroom on this side, one on that, combination kitchen–living room in the center, bathroom tucked in somewhere, and a deck running along three sides, the whole thing sitting on stilts and costing each shareholder maybe five hundred dollars for the season. It was Pines Basic, quite unlike the palazzo that Jim now took Eric to, the abode of his would-be gentleman, one walk over from Jim's and down to the ocean.

"I'm impressed," said Jim, looking at the place. "This guy is really loaded."

"Yeah," said Eric.

"You okay?"

Eric nodded.

"Maybe you better practice a smile."

Eric tried.

They started up the walk, then Jim halted. "Look," he said, "it's just an audition. If you don't want the part, come back to my place. You remember where it is?"

"You're real nice, aren't you?"

Taken aback, Jim said, "Well, I'm . . . I'm trying to . . ."

"No, you're really looking out for me. Helped me get this travel bag together, so I don't look like a doofus. And you wear those neat shirts, all striped and colored just right. You always know what to say. I make the dumbest jokes, and you laugh." Eric extended his hand. "Thank you," he said.

They shook, Eric said, "Here goes," and he abruptly turned and walked up to the house.

A moon of dire magic hangs over the Pines. *Careful!,* it warns, your dreams may come true! Some find the place dangerous, some seek out its romance, some deplore its rigid sense of style. To Frank, tonight, it was a workplace, as he trudged the beach, firming plans for his movie. He had, he was sure, a sound premise: A pleasant-looking but unerotic young man arrives on the island and strolls the walks, wrapped in trees and mystery. At intervals, strangers invite him into a house and the two of them have sex, each rendezvous more intensely physical than the last—and each time the young man leaves a house, he dons the clothes of his partner. Thus, he first exchanges his nondescript garb for the white T and slacks of his affectionate but undemanding first date; he later changes into the pastel Lacoste shirt, Speedos, and Mickey Mouse wristwatch of his second, somewhat more possessing date; and at last he mates with an infinitely forceful leather master (our own Frank), leaving in jeans and a leather jacket. The crescendo of the sexual quest, the building of the hotness, seemed to Frank to suggest the outline of a gay man's growth as a sensualist—and the tale could be told entirely in visuals, thereby forgiving the lack of an on-mike sound track. The cast was—let's just say—personable, and the locations ready. Frank could crank it out in two days, tops. But how, he wondered, was this story to end? Clearly, the third episode, with its dark lord of pleasure and its touches of S & M, marked a climax of some kind. But where did the young man go then?

. . .

The young man named Eric went to Jim's house a little after one A.M. that same night, but the place sat black and still, and Eric paused on the walk, wondering if he dared risk waking Jim up. At length, he decided to compromise: He'd knock, but quietly.

There was no answer. Listening at the door, Eric was sure he heard noises of some kind. People noises, sort of like talking, or very quiet singing.

Eric knocked a bit louder, then louder yet. He waited, heard heavy footsteps, saw a shape loom up in the black. He hoped it was Jim, but Jim didn't move that fast.

It was some big nude guy, his skin slick with sweat and his cock bobbing out hard and aching in front of him.

"What?" he said.

"I'm looking for Jim."

"Hey, *lawyer!*" the nude guy called out, letting the door bang closed as he turned and stamped back to his room.

Well, I can't get into any more trouble, Eric thought, slipping inside to look for Jim. And here he was, pulling on a sweatshirt over his shorts, drowsy yet smiling.

"Sorry I blew it with your roommate," said Eric. "Woke him up, I guess."

"It didn't work?"

Eric shook his head.

"Put your bag down. You can have the couch tonight and then we'll . . . You want something to drink? How about beer in a tankard? That ought to . . . Let's see what we have here." Peering into the fridge.

The sounds Eric had heard before poured out through the open door of Jim's housemates' room.

"What's the deal in there?" asked Eric.

"Sex."

"With noises?"

"Here."

Eric took the beer, hoisted it, and glopped a heavy first taste right through the foam.

"As long as I'm up," said Jim, "you want to talk about it?"

Eric hiccuped, wiping his mouth. He was a total teenager: rough, unformed, trying to figure things out.

"I don't want to get that big guy angry," Eric murmured, pointing at the other bedroom.

"Grab your sweater and we'll take a walk to the harbor. It's lovely at night."

Eric's sweater was an oversized horror of holes and patches, but the kid was clearly proud of it. "Big Frank gave this to me," he said.

The harbor makes a handsome vista at night, its oval ringed by bobbing pleasure cruisers, faced on the west by the lights of the Botel and other commercial establishments, and on the south by the vast line of wagons, some pristine and others weathered to rust.

"Wow, it's quiet," said Eric, as he and Jim parked themselves on a bench. "Look at all the wagons, though. It's as if nobody but little kids lived here."

"So what was this guy like?"

"Oh, he was all right. Tried to make me feel comfortable. He said, 'What music do you like?' What was I supposed to say? Yeah, sure, I dig minuets and opera singing. Hey, spin the platter and we'll all have a polka."

"What did you say?"

"Oh, then he goes, 'What would you like to wear?' I go, 'Sorry?' So he takes me to a closet of . . . costume clothes. Like, we're going to do a show, and here's your part, you know. He had, like, pirate, cop, cowboy . . . or, he says, would you prefer street boy? What's a *street boy*?"

Jim nodded. Nothing to say.

"I don't want to have to be what some guy expects," Eric went on. "How would I know what that even is?"

"It's like your parents all over again."

"You got that right," said Eric, looking up at the sky, then ahead of him, at the bay.

"Look," said Jim, "just tell me if I'm out of line. But do you miss your parents?"

"They kept shoving me around and throwing me out. Who'd miss that?"

"You like Frank, don't you?"

"Who doesn't?"

"Nobody doesn't. You want to know why?"

Eric smiled, a stray kid in a strange place with—luckily—a kind man.

"Frank is perfect hot," Jim explained. "He's got it all. And in bed he gets into some hungry-animal mode that fiercely possesses you yet never in any way would hurt you. So I've heard, at least. But it's more than that. He's this . . . this titanic authority figure. You know, he's very protective of the people he likes. Like you."

"Yeah?"

"He'd wreck anyone who did you harm."

"Really?"

"That's why some guys are afraid of him. He's not just a major beauty. He's an absolute. It's like trying to date . . . oh, Clark Gable or someone. There's too much there there."

"Tell me a story," said Eric.

"A story?"

"Isn't this a good time for one? With the boats dipping, and the moon. This big place with all these things in it, but the whole world is still. We're the only ones alive."

"A story, huh?"

Eric moved closer to Jim. "Yeah, something . . . where I can listen and don't have to *be* anything."

Jim shyly put an arm around Eric. "That okay?"

"Uh-huh."

"A story, now . . ."

"Tell me how you came to be here. Or how the place began. One of those legends."

"Would you like to hear how the bar Harry's Back East got its name?"

"Yeah."

"This is legendary," said Jim, warming to it. "There was this very hot guy named Harry, and he was breaking hearts up and down the city. Everywhere you went, there were guys keening and sighing for Harry."

"What's keening?"

"Getting all torn up."

"Was Harry like big Frank?"

"No, he was a mere mortal. One of those blonds with notable deltoids and nifty teeth. Now, Harry's best friend was . . . I don't know, *Tim*. Fine, good-natured fellow, crazy for Harry. They went everywhere together. But it was that typical gay thing, where Harry allowed Tim to worship him, but never responded in kind."

"Would Tim cry as he thought about it?"

Jim, chuckling, patted Eric's shoulder. "Tim accepted it as his debt to pay. But after a while it became so painful that when Harry announced that he was moving to Los Angeles to improve the quality of his promiscuity, Tim secretly rejoiced. With Harry out of his life, Tim made himself over. He joined a gym, started going to back-room bars—"

"What are they about?"

"Beer up front, sex in the rear."

"Woo."

"With Harry gone to the West, Tim became his own hero. Circuit beauties who once sneered at him were now lining up for a date."

"And he told them, 'Get lost'?"

"Are you kidding? He grabbed them, one after the other. This was the new Tim, and he wanted to enjoy it to the utmost."

"Yeah, he was in charge of what would happen to him."

"He was indeed," said Jim, daring to tickle Eric's ear.

"Then one day, a friend told him, 'I have good news and bad news— Harry's back east.' "

After a moment, Eric said, "I don't get it, but I like it."

"Let's start back."

At Jim's house, they drank some water, bathroomed, and set Eric up on the couch. The house was silent, except for the soothing pulse of the breaking Atlantic below them on the beach. But after a bit, those noises started seeping out of Jim's housemates' room again, and Eric decided this was reason enough to tiptoe into Jim's room, naked and nervous.

"Can I come in with you?" Eric whispered.

Jim made room, fitting his body against Eric's jigsaw-style, part to part. Then Jim whispered, "I don't know what I'm allowed to do with you."

"Let me be your boy friend," Eric replied, "and you can do anything."

Catching his breath as he held Eric by the sides of his torso, Jim said, "I'm not one of those rich Pines gays, you know. I'm just—"

"Does it have to be a millionaire?"

"No, I guess it doesn't. So . . . what do you like to do?"

"I don't know yet. Show me and I'll tell you. No—wait."

"Where are you—"

"Taking a peek at your roommates."

Eric slipped across the house to the muscle queens' open doorway, panoramaed, and slithered back to Jim.

"I don't know what that's called," he said, "but we're going to, like, save that one for next year."

·   ·   ·

Back in the city, Frank called Larken to crow over his new movie. The shooting had gone off without problems, the cast had surpassed itself, and this time they had a lighting man who seemed to know his craft. Best of all, Frank had finally thought up a fitting ending to his tale: After his high-octane experience with the leather daddy, the protagonist parades the boardwalk in his new uniform of S & M pleasure and—through a trick shot with the use of a double—passes his former self without the slightest recognition.

"And we fade on that."

"But, Frank, what does it mean?"

Frank laughed. "I'm not sure, Larky. Maybe that once you get deep into gay life, you become so changed that you lose all contact with the way you used to live?"

"You sound so proud, Frank. The last few times we've spoken, you've been kind of down."

"I've been down for a while, maybe."

"Anything wrong? Something specific?"

"Not that I'm aware of. But nothing's very right, either."

"Frank, did you ever think of moving out here?"

"No. . . ."

"I bet you'd really like it. So many of the guys I know say their whole way of looking at themselves is different because of this place."

"Tell me one thing, Lark. Who was in the theatre when you saw my movie?"

"A bunch of guys, I guess."

"Old guys? Cruising around?"

"No. Younger guys. And they were pretty wrapped up in what they were seeing. Why?"

"Just wondering, pal."

Frank had to go to work; but all the way to Hero's he was thinking about a San Francisco Frank, and what *he* might be like. He was thinking that nothing held him in New York, no great friendships, no responsibility. He was thinking that a new sphere of operations could invigorate his life. It was partly, I'd love to get used to a new neighborhood, and partly, I've had everybody in this town. Years before, Frank had walked out of California with a bus ticket and an overnight bag, and he could walk back in the same way.

So it was a distracted Frank who oversaw Hero's that evening. He even brought Henry the wrong drink—a bar-vodka Collins instead of Stoli on the rocks—and forgot Jim's beer altogether.

"Sorry, guys," said Frank.

"If all I have to worry about is the wrong drink," said Henry, "I'll be over the rainbow for the rest of my life."

"Oh, now, that was some *powerful* demonstration against the *police*," said Jezebel, a hand balancing on each head as he eyed Henry and Jim. "That was true liberation, wasn't it?"

"I'm doing my best, Jez," said Henry. "What do you want?"

"I want gays to stand forth and cry, We are the thing that is *just* as good as *you*!"

"I felt that power at the dance," said Jim.

"Maybe we should have dances," Henry suggested, "instead of demonstrations."

"We should," said promiscuous Martin, poking his nose in. "I took Robert Horneck and Ian Decker home for a threesome and, boy, did they—"

"You ain't gay," said Jezebel. "You just some jism machine. Why wasn't you at the demonstration?"

"Oh, please, these pathetic political games," said Martin. "As if anything—"

"You want the sex," Jezebel observed, "but you don't want the rights. You don't belong in this bar, in fact, because you some sly cheat taking advantage of the work that other folks do. And I sense I should throw your ass the hell out of the place. What you think of that, candybutt?"

"Jez—" Henry began.

"No, Henry. No, no, and Jezebel say no. We had enough of these opportunists who want to enjoy the secret benefits but not fight for the legitimization."

"I don't owe you anything," said Martin.

"You owe *yourself*, clownhead."

"Get your hands off me!"

"Get your *self* out of this bar!"

"Henry—"

"*Stay 'way!* I'm throwing this piece of scum out of my—"

"*Hey!*" said Frank.

"Jez, you can't—"

"Let go of me, you loony—"

"*They're rioting at the Stonewall!*" someone shouted in the doorway. "The police raided it and everyone fought back! Sheridan Square's a war zone!"

Jezebel, who had Martin by the hair and bent in two, pulled him up and released him.

Martin shook himself, feeling for broken pieces of ego.

"They're what?" Jim asked. "Rioting?"

The guy who had shouted in the doorway was gone, off to spread the word to other bars.

"Sure, the Stonewall," said Jezebel. "My, yes, the Stonewall. Isn't the drag queens of this world on the barricades twenty-four hours a time? Who better to make a demonstration—you listening, Henry? Ain't this the political event we been—"

"Don't get happy yet," said Henry, rising from the bar. "It could be just a—"

"It *could* be a statement striving to be made!"

"Call the bar," Jim urged Frank.

"What?"

"Call them and ask if—"

"Call the bar?" said Jezebel, advancing on Jim. "What they supposed to answer? Yes, we're resisting a *po*lice raid, no Pink Ladies served for the foreseeable—"

"Get your asses down to the Stonewall!" someone called into the bar from outside. *"It's happening!"*

Jezebel said, "That's about twelve blocks, which is, what?, seven, eight minutes at the rate I propose to travel at." He was already moving as he began to speak, and by the time he had finished he was gone.

Jim told Henry, "Hadn't we better . . ." They were starting to move, too, out the door and down the street in Jezebel's stormy wake.

"Big deal, a riot," said Martin, still smoothing himself out from Jezebel's assault. "So there's a raid. So there's a demonstration. So there's porn movies. So instead of 'homo' we call it 'gay.' So we all wear bomber jackets in winter. Does it change anything? *Really?*"

Frank was just looking at him, not speaking, not moving, just looking.

Years later, people would ask, Where were you when you heard about it?—as they also did for the assassinations of the decade, of the two Kennedys and King, comparably epic moments in our cultural history. In fact, most gay people took little notice of the riots at the Stonewall Inn bar in Sheridan Square on June 27, 28, and 29, 1969. They seemed isolated from The Life, so out, so aggressive, a drag-queen thing, a one-off. Let's take an informal poll of our friends and find out how they felt at the time.

.   .   .

Paul says, "Truth to tell, there had been *plenty* of bar riots in response to police raids. All through the sixties, if you knew anybody in another city, you'd hear about them. Chicago, New Orleans, Kansas City. But the newspapers never reported them. It was gossip, don't you see, not news. The public had no idea. Of course, the public had no idea we were there in the first place. There was a wonderful symmetry to it.

"So when the Stonewall Inn crowd fought back instead of letting the cops cart them away, I simply thought, So New York has had a riot, too, now. I had no idea it would be in the papers—and not only here but internationally!

"Where was I when I heard? Well, I remember that a friend, Kent Abrams, called to tell me, and it was so *very* late that I was quite peeved at him. He said he'd been calling people all night to talk about it, so there I was again, at the bottom of the list. And I must admit I rather chided him for waking me up and told him he could go right on with his calling. So I didn't hear about the riot till the next day, reading in the paper about "queen bees" defending their "nest." That's how they saw us in those days. If we weren't Commie spies, we were Joan Crawford."

"I just got this call from Jim," says Eric. "He says, 'Hey, something big's brewing, get your bod down here.' Oh, man, I was all settled in with the Yankees–Red Sox game and a giant bowl of popcorn that I had even gone and buttered by hand. And I knew that Jim could throw me out on the street if he got mad at me, and that would be zip for Eric, yet I kept saying, Come on, man, I don't want to, and like that. And Jim kept telling me I had to see this, it's history, and I'm saying, Look, I saw all the history I need in school. I was getting pissed off.

"Except, you know how most guys say things to make you feel bad? Like, it's supposedly your best friend, but sometimes he's harping on the one thing he *knows* you can't handle? Like your mom's a drunk or you had to do fifth grade twice? Well, Jim's the opposite. As soon as he knows your sore spots, he leaves them alone.

"So when he said, You come down here, I came."

Chris says, "The thing that hit me right up front was that it was the drag queens who pulled it off. Because the Stonewall was a red-drag spot, prob-

ably the most famous one in town. I don't know how I knew so much
about it. Thompson and Chase make a point of being very conversant
with the details of gay life, but even they were pretty confused about what
happened. But, oh, were they quick to rise above it! Chase called it 'vulgar,' and I called him 'smug,' and Thompson said, 'Apologize to Chase!,'
and I got kind of fierce with them, and I *think* I may have called them 'a
pair of high-hat faggots,' and we never had much to do with each other
after that."

Andy hardly knew of the riot. He was never a great reader of newspaper;
he followed the events of the great world by scanning headlines when he
passed a newsstand.

He says, "I didn't hear about that Stonewall thing till after the first
night. The rioting continued for several days, and at something like the
third night I was having family dinner, and while we were watching TV
the news came on. The newsman said something about it, and everybody
in the room made, you know, disgusted noises and groans. My mother
was looking at me as if she would tear me to shreds if I said anything.

"But what was I going to say? Those people who fought the police in
that bar weren't anything to me. It was Henry that I was connected to, just
him. I had never wanted to be political, even when I was handing out
flyers with him for some rally. I just wanted Henry to be my friend and
help me put a quiet life of my own together.

"I spent a lot of time walking streets that Henry might turn up on, near
his apartment and down by Hero's. I guess I could just have dropped into
the bar some night, but I was afraid he might hate me right in front of
everybody.

"I never did bump into Henry, and I never met anyone else like him.
Some days, someone would come into the store, and I'd try to signal him
in some way. But I guess I don't know what the signals are."

When Lois heard about it, all she said was "Good!" Elaine was more
rhapsodic: "It's historical. It is the Thing That Had to Happen, and I find
it touching and bizarre—one of my favorite combinations—that it was our
own outlaws who pulled it off, the drag queens we so love to disdain. For
they are the men-women of our days, the combiners. We needed that, to
remind us that we are not merely straights with different bed partners. I

distinctly remember putting down the realty ads that I had clipped from several New England papers to make a note to myself to write more about men in my fiction."

Louis says, "Do I remember where I was when I heard of it? Honey, I didn't *hear* of it, I was *in the bar*! But let me tell this for the record. Some folks started passing around this legend that the whole thing happened because Judy Garland had died a few days before, the picture being something like, The police troop into the Stonewall and we're muttering, First they take Miss Judy away, and now *this*! Well, that's a cute story, but, let's face it, some of us don't think the universe revolves around Judy Garland. The riots were about what the whole decade had been about, people's rights. I always preferred Rosemary Clooney myself.

"Tell you, if anyone was muttering when the cops pulled in, it was more like, Fuck these stupid police, and I'm not going to take this rough-up and getting called 'shitpacker' and loaded in that paddy wagon. *Not! This! Time!*

"Those cops were so stupid. Man, I've been in as many raids as they have, and I know what a raid's supposed to look like, the whole bar resentful and in despair. Well, *this* bar was *angry*. And there were just a few cops in the first place, like maybe they were getting overconfident. Didn't they *see* the whole of us staring at them and failing to give the usual pathetic cooperation?

"I mean, right away, the whole thing's wrong. One of the more flamboyant queens—no, let's face it, it was that obnoxious Puerto Rican bitch from the back alleys of San Juan, Chiquita La Mamba. Anyway, she starts screaming at one of the bartenders. She says, 'What is this, the Mafia shortcutting the cops again? With all you charge for a drink around here?' Then she turns to the cops and says—she's still shouting, you understand—'I guess you didn't get your bribes this week, so here's a little something on Miss Chiquita.' And she grabs a hunk of change from out of the tip bowl and throws it all right at some cop. I don't mean near him, I mean *at* him.

"Now, ordinarily, the cops would be on top of her with their nightsticks and she would be in the hospital. Because you know cops. Their third favorite thing's taking a freebie off a hooker. Their second favorite's pocketing Mafia hush-mouth money. Their favorite thing is beating up a fag. But, like I say, the mood of the bar was ugly, and, looking around, you could see everybody thinking, The cops are outnumbered, so if we all move *right now and together* . . . You see?

"Well, one cop caught on, and he grabbed the arm of the cop Miss Chiquita had offended—because he was going for her, of course—and said, 'Let's line 'em up outside.' You know, the Cool It, Man thing. Except now other guys were throwing change at the blues, and two of them made the fatal mistake of deciding that this was the ideal time to particularly arrest a pair of dykes and wrestle them out of the bar—because now there were only three cops left with all of us. You could hear the dykes screaming outside, trying to attract public attention—like in Russia, when the K.G.B. is trying to arrest you in Red Square and you holler so much that they melt away, because no one in Russia's supposed to know that there is a K.G.B. So, back in the Free World here, there's about forty of us and three fascists—and we're going to let *them* arrest *us*?

"Suddenly, everybody's moving. Not out of the bar, just around in it. There's kind of a mêlée around one cop and sort of a real fight with another, and unbeknownst to both of them one of the queens just took out the third with a bottle of something, simply grabbed it from behind the bar and smashed it on the cop's head and down he goes. So now all the queens are grabbing bottles and trying to brain the cops. I saw one guy trying to set the first cop on fire with his lighter. And what's funny is, for some reason I looked at the bartenders then, and they had these incredible expressions, like . . . *What the fuck is going on?*

"Then all you could hear was sirens, and like a flash we hightail it out of there, more or less passing the cops who are hightailing it *in*. Finally, we're all outside throwing stuff, and they're all inside hiding. Man, it was war.

"And this is what I keep asking myself: What jerk in the police department decided there hadn't been enough raids that month? What's inside the guys who do this to us? What do they get out of it? And how come the asshole blues who strolled into the Stonewall that night didn't see by the looks on our faces that we weren't going to be picked off like ducks this time? I saw it. How come they didn't? Because, I tell you, they got what they invented."

What they invented was a stew of fury that boiled out of the bar into the street and expanded so quickly that despite frantic calls for backup the police found themselves under siege in the bar. "*Torch* it!" some cried. "*Burn the fuzz!*" But the major urge of the event expressed itself in the deep, rolling bass of the chant "Gay *power*! Gay *power*!" Garbage cans were upended and browsed for suitable missiles, and bottles and such came flying every time the police opened the door.

The mob grew and grew and grew; Jezebel, Henry, and Jim were three blocks north of the bar when the density of the crowd forced them from a sprint to a shamble. Stonewall was a volcano, an eruption of noise and smoke. All around, they heard "Out of the closets and into the streets!"

"*Yes!*" Jezebel gasped out. "Oh, Miss Jesus, at last!"

Henry and Jim looked at each other in disbelief and exhilaration.

"Gay power!" Jezebel now shouted, trying to force a way through the press of bodies. "Make way for the ladies of the evening!"

"Hey, I'm just as fag as you are," said a man Jezebel was trying to get past, and Jezebel threw his arms around the guy.

"The night," Jezebel cried, "was made for love."

"Is that a definite offer?" the man asked, taking Jezebel in.

"No, no, this is *history,* comrade. Come on with us and make it."

What the hell is going on?, Blue was thinking as he came up West Tenth Street. Ahead, he could see and hear what looked like a city on fire, with a screaming mob and things flying through the air.

Working his way through the crowd to Seventh Avenue, Blue saw another something or other whizzing through the air . . . burning newspaper wrapped around something, it looked like, falling to earth at that drag bar.

"What's going on?" Blue asked the guy next to him.

"It's the graduation dance. We call it 'No More Harassment.' "

"No kidding."

"Ask those fucking pigs, if you think it's kidding." Then, in a hoarse shout, "*Kill* the bastards!"

Another load of burning paper flew overhead, this one crashing through the bar's plate-glass window, and a scream of contentment rose up.

"*Gay power!*"

"*No more raids! No more raids!*"

"*Civilian review boards now!*"

"*Sic semper tyrannis!*"

"*Kill the pig! Slit his throat!*" (This from a literary clique.)

"*We're people, too!*"

"*Up the drag queen!*"

Blue edged back from the fray, looking for a free phone booth.

.   .   .

"Shit, is that a TV news crew?" asked Henry, as a camera squad leaped out of a truck marked ABC.

"Oh, my Henry," said Jezebel, hugging him. "The politics is happening. *This* is the demonstration."

"Sacred Acts!" Henry declared.

"I been meaning to tell you, we *got* to change that name."

"How about the Union for Gay Liberation?"

"For Gay *Activism*," Jim corrected.

"The Gay Activist Union," Jezebel said, trying it out.

"No!" cried Henry. "How about the—"

"Hey!" Jim called out, for Eric had found them, and the boy sailed right into Jim's arms.

"Aw," said Jezebel, approvingly. "Look at the future there."

"It's scary," said Eric.

"No, my young friend, it's thrilling. Whoop, there go another firething in the air. If we burn this city down, will they start leaving us alone?"

The surge of people had pushed so far into the street that Seventh Avenue had become a parking lot. Cars that honked too aggressively or tried to drift forward were menaced by the crowd, turned over, a few even set on fire. One was commandeered with the intent of driving it straight into the front of the bar, but there were too many people in the way. The crush of bodies also handicapped sight lines for the impromptu show-girl parade (to bystanders' a cappella rendition of "A Pretty Girl Is Like a Melody") that some of the dressier queens performed around the tiny triangular block between Christopher and West Tenth Streets. But this was aberrant, for the rioting was no lark. There were injuries and arrests. Blue, of course, couldn't get away fast enough—just as well, for he didn't find an unoccupied phone booth till he was almost at Fourteenth Street. Pulling out his wallet, he found the card bearing the Kid's number, dialed for the operator, and placed a collect call.

The Kid was in a snappy mood. He had been reading yet another of Elaine's novels, hearing her voice in the words, enjoying her, admiring her. What if she did go ahead and write about the Other Side? It wouldn't seem quite so different or mysterious, then, would it?

Blue's timing was perfect. The Kid was in the mood for some on-site company, and delighted to hear that Blue was ready to blow into town.

"It's dangerous," Blue explained. "There's a riot goin' on a few blocks offa here."

"What kind of riot?"

"They're all the same, ain't they?"

"Do you need money? I could wire you some."

"Can I fly there? Never tried a plane before."

"Blue, *mon vieux,* this is on the level, yes?"

"Winter's too cold, summer's too wet, violence everywhere you turn. Sure, it's on the level."

"Okay, can do."

"Hey, you hold dances out there? Like the one a while back in Kingdom Hall?"

"*Come.* No, we don't, but you'll show us how."

"I'm gonna do that."

"*Revolutions.*"

"Huh?"

"Never mind."

One other telephone call of that night from New York to San Francisco interests us: Frank's, to Larken. Where so many saw in the Riot a promise of liberation, to Frank it only dramatized the might of oppression. He was well aware that his movies were more or less criminal acts, and that the law gave no protection even to his day-to-day work as a bartender in a gay hostel, and he was tired of living a totally illegal life. Larken's talk of San Francisco as the place where a Frank was not only possible but necessary had made a strong impression on him, and he became obsessed with the idea of moving out of New York and coming home.

"Well, it really is the place for us," Larken told him, with gentle certainty.

"Hell, I've picked up and never looked back before."

"Oh, Frank, it would be incredible to see you again, and have our talks and everything."

A few hundred yards from Frank's apartment, thousands of men and women had massed to express their disgust with state persecution; through his open window, Frank heard the sirens and the crashing and the upheaval of a forbidden people shouting their name.

"God, what a battle we have before us," he said.

"Are you coming, Frank? Really? Because this town is ready for you, boy."

Indeed, Frank was coming: because destiny wanted him to. Frank has a date with his future, which needs him in a certain place some years from now, to save the life of someone he has never heard of, a young man named Lonnie Ironword. Some of us float, some of us make choices, and a very few of us, like Frank, are Summoned.

PART V

Minneapolis, 1975

TOM DATED WOMEN but he thought about men. When he launched his business in renovating old houses, he started keeping a diary as a permanent record of all his transactions—notes on restructuring, decoration, materials; cost estimates and final tallies; reports on the subcontractors' work; and so on. He meant to set down his experiences for reference in future work. But he also wrote in this diary his thoughts on certain men he met, saw, even imagined. I quote at random:

This guy in the sandwich place next to the hardware. Twenty-nine, light brown hair cut short and smooth. Always gives me a smile and says, "Right you are, now." Sometimes he moves slow and dreamy, his eyes are half-shut. He can get the order mixed up, like his mind's on other things.

Mr. Larsson walked onto the site today. He was in a suit but you could see his arms swell through the coat, even his chest muscles inside his shirt. Well, he's in construction himself, so he knows what's doing, and he's real aggressive about asking questions. He took his coat off, and I was watching his ass, which is two melons doing a samba.

I see two guys, one very experienced and the other guy is young and not sure. The older one says, Come on, you'll like it once we get going. The young guy says no, but then they're locked up together, rolling and shouting. I don't know which guy is me.

There is nothing about women in the diary, though Tom is an energetic bachelor, dating up and down the Twin Cities and impressing the women he knows as thoughtful, pleasing, and scrupulous but never—in his whirling, moody way—committed. Women have always loved Tom and forgiven him; that's how he gets away with it, along with his looks and his thriving business. He's a catch. He's the Eligible Man of Urban Scandihoovia: tall, handsome, and unpredictable Tom Uhlisson, so isolated from what he is that he's leading two lives, one based on what he does and one based on what he won't admit he wants. This does not strike him as abnormal. It doesn't strike him at all: It's how he lives. If he did ponder it, he'd probably decide that many men live like this. What else can you do? Ask the guy in the sandwich place if he'd like to go out?

Does Tom ever think of Luke? He writes of him in the diary, in inconclusive vignettes that, like dreams, dissolve just before the climax. For instance:

Luke comes over with a six-pack, so he talks about college and dating. They are dates like I have. His women are similar, in every respect. I know this because we proceed to describe them, in detail—this is about the complexion of the skin that runs down the curve of the back, the taste of the nipples. Everything. So then it turns out that we are both seeing the same women. Luke is not really in college. He has been living in Minneapolis. This is strange but true.

There is a knock at the door. It is Sandy, a girl I was seeing. Now she is different. Her neat hair is braided and piled up top in a come-on way, cheap. And she is slinking around. She knows Luke, it seems. She says he has brought out the real woman in her. She wants to hold a pussy-stuffing contest and see who's best. Luke is already pulling off his shirt.

The diary sits locked in a desk in the "office" of Tom's house, a rambly Victorian on the west side of Minneapolis. It's a big place for a man alone, as many a daughter's mother would tell him; and I call it a gloomy place, because there is so little life in it. Tom never gives parties or dinners, though he goes to them. (He's a sociable fellow, in his disjointed way. That is, he'll come to your Saturday Night, then go into a trance and madden everyone.) Some of the rooms in Tom's house are empty. You wonder. But then, what's he supposed to do with them? He sleeps in the bedroom, relaxes in the living room, works in the office, eats in the kitchen. The rest of the place is redundant. When Tom bought and began renovating it, he thought of it as a show house, as a proof for wondering customers of the kind of work he could do. Then he thought, Fuck it.

This is why Tom's cousin Walt is coming, to help fill out the rooms. The two haven't seen each other since the autumn of 1968, when Tom moved to the Twin Cities, but it seemed that Walt got into some sort of trouble back home, and, in solemn conclave, the Uhlissons decreed that Walt shall join Tom in the metropolis and learn Tom's trade. Of course, now that Tom is on his own he has no need to obey any edict issuing out of Gotburg; but it immediately occurred to him that he could use some company around the house, and it might be nice to take a bit of family into the Uhlisson Company (Tom Uhlisson, Proprietor and Director).

Walt is coming by bus—the Orient Express of the Midwest—and Tom will drive down to the station to pick him up. It's a Saturday evening in early December, and Tom has long had the traditional survival kit for the Minnesota winter set up in the trunk. As a teen, Tom was playful, helter-skelter; as a man, he is orderly, prudent, assigning certain days of the week for chores, maintaining things-to-watch-for lists in his head for every current renovation project, keeping his diary locked in the desk even though he lives alone.

Walt's father made all the travel arrangements with Tom, as if Walt were a tot unable to read a timetable. Yet Walt is nineteen now, a bit taller than when Tom last saw him but, from the neck up, the same merrily serious little boy who was always cannonballing into the Dawsons' swimming pool.

"Say, Dexter, wait for me!" echoed in Tom's thoughts as Walt walked toward him, backpacked from the calves to the crown of his head, his hand stretched out to take Tom's and a great smile on his face.

"Cousin Tom!"

"Hey, pal!" as they shake. "How's that dog of yours?"

Walt's smile vanishes. "He died," Walt whispers. "It was very rough."

"I'm sorry."

There was an awkward pause; to fill it, Walt shook Tom's hand again.

"Come on," said Tom. "You must be hungry. Lucky for you Jeanette came today."

"Is that your girl friend?"

"The maid. She also cooks. She'll tend a casserole all day while she's cleaning, then fridge it for me to reheat later. I think there's a veal-and-sausage number in there now."

"I would love a hot dog."

"Same old Walt," said Tom, tousling the boy's hair.

They took a circuitous route homeward, so Walt could see some of Minneapolis, Tom occasionally playing guide. "There's supposed to be another city across the river," he said, with a wink. "But no one's ever been there."

"It is the City of the Twelfth of Never," said Walt. "Many of its doors can be opened only with special keys."

"Who has these keys?" asked Tom, playing along, as one always did with Walt.

"I might have a few," said Walt, carelessly.

In the house, Walt got out of harness in the kitchen, shucking off everything as a child does when he comes in from the snow.

"You're really filled out, pal," said Tom. "Shoulders and all. What did you play in high school?"

"Mostly the piano."

Tom put the casserole in the oven to warm and took his cousin on a tour of the house.

"You have a piano, Cousin Tom!" cried Walt, exultant in the living room.

"Well, it'll be nice to hear someone make use of it, I guess."

Walt sat at the keyboard and broke into the opening flourish of Grieg's Piano Concerto, then started rocking the music. Tom went into the kitchen to check on the food, pleased with the noise now filling his empty mansion. Walt joined him there, then picked up his gear as Tom led him to the room Walt would occupy.

"I ordered some furniture," Tom told him, "but the bed hasn't arrived yet. You can sack in with me."

Walt was unpacking, setting a few books and souvenirs on the fresh new bookcase and occupying the bureau. It's amazing how much a teenager can stuff into a backpack; among the T-shirts and Tolkien posters were four boxes of apple-cinnamon Pop-Tarts.

"You planning to open a concession?" Tom asked wryly.

"I wasn't sure if you stocked the right flavor."

"I don't stock any flavor of this stuff," said Tom, examining one of the boxes.

"Wasn't I smart to come prepared?" said Walt, taking out a stuffed bear.

"Golly," said Tom, "it's Claude! I haven't seen him in ages!"

"I don't usually need him any more, but if I left him behind my parents would have had him destroyed. They've moved me out for good, you know. I had to give my lifetime collection of Walt Disney comics to Harvey Oefnerling."

Walt turned to Tom.

"Cousin Tom," he said, "I really have to make good on this. Nobody approves of me back home now, so if I flunk with you, I'll really be in the seaweed."

"Don't worry, Walt. It'll all be fine. You'll like the business, too. I love what I do, and I do it well, and I'm going to teach you how to do it like me."

Right you are, now, but Walt started weeping.

"Shit," said Tom. "What's . . . what's wrong, Walt?"

"I'm in big trouble," Walt almost wailed.

Tom held the boy, patting his back. "No, you're not," he said. "You're in good hands here." Letting Walt go, he added, "Anything you want to talk about?"

Wiping his eyes, Walt shook his head.

"Well, come on downstairs," said Tom, guiding him with an arm around his shoulders. "I'm hungry."

It was a little like having a puppy, watching Walt hop through his pranks and worry his concerns. He did not burst into tears again or explain why he had done so, though it was clear that his being dispatched from Gotburg involved something more than his being apprenticed to a trade. But Walt threw himself eagerly into the business, accompanying Tom from site to site or staying home to run the office.

Walt was diligent at tending records and keeping Tom abreast of his phone messages. The boy was fascinated with the answering machine—there was none in Gotburg that he knew of—and he changed the taped greeting several times in his first week with Tom, trying, as he explained it, to "find the perfect greeting, which is trustworthy but also businesslike, and lets everyone know that Walt is here now."

The neighbors certainly knew it, for when the first snow fell, in a dense blanket that froze as it landed, Walt built a snow fort on the front lawn.

"This one's Gothic," he told Tom. "Last year in Gotburg I was working on a Camelot, but we ran out of cocoa for that after-snow pick-me-up, so I decided to stay inside."

Judith, Tom's current girl friend, thought Walt enchanting. "Is the whole town like that?" she asked. "Every minute you're around him, you sense his vulnerability. You want to shield him, almost."

Tom shrugged. "He's young."

"You're the finished product, then, because you're totally self-protected. You select what you show of yourself—no, don't make that silly face, because you know I'm right. Is that what Godsend does to people? Cause them to—"

"Gotburg. And it isn't your town that does things to you. It's your family. I had a rotten one. Walt had a nice one." How wrong Tom is about that we shall learn soon enough. "Besides, he was sort of the . . . the little doll of our group. We were always joking with him and looking out for him. So he's still playing out that kind of part."

"He's so sweet. Loving. He makes you worry that one day someone's going to be cruel and simply blast him away."

They were in Judith's kitchen. Before Walt arrived, Tom and Judith spent their overnights in Tom's house. But now Judith requested—modestly and, I think, quite appropriately—that Tom schedule his bed-sharing at her place. They were often in Judith's kitchen, for Tom routinely took a little something before bedtime, in what he and Luke, in the bygone days of staying over at each other's house so frequently that it was hard to tell where they slept from where they lived, termed a "midnight raid." This entailed standing in the insurrectionary freedom of the wide-open refrigerator door to consider the menu. Salami! Leftover spaghetti! Cherry pie to be hunked up in the hand and popped into the mouth!

Tom and Judith were enjoying a midnight raid, Tom working on a bologna sandwich and potato chips and Judith finishing off the last of a week's worth of split-pea-with-ham soup.

"Don't worry about Walt," Tom told Judith. "I'm taking real care of him."

"Who's taking care of you?"

"Well, no one has to, anyway."

Judith stirred her soup. She nodded.

"Huh. Well, I see the doctor is in," said Tom.

"And the lover is out."

"Look—"

"Tom, *you* look. You have it so together the whole town is agog. All my friends ask me, What is he like?"

"To know?"

"In bed, you dear fool."

Tom grinned. "So what do you say?"

" 'He has nothing to worry about.' "

Tom nodded.

"But that's not the point," Judith went on. "Who is Tom, and what is Walt telling me?"

"Judes, I don't know what that—"

"Who hurt you? Who did what to you?"

Tom said nothing.

"There's something in that town, isn't there?" Judith declared and asked. "Like in some horror movie."

"It was a beautiful place, Judith. It was green and wide and happy. It was a bunch of us all together, and we . . . It was our whole world, made by us. Snow fights and hamburgers and Walt's unbelievable dog." Tom's eyes were wet. "What a perfectly stupid time. I don't believe any of it happened."

This is what Tom wrote in his diary about Walt:

I am very fond of the young man. He likes to shower before bedtime, and since his bed still hasn't arrived he comes into my room toweling off, just naked and so trusting. I wouldn't hurt him for anything. I try to joke with him, wrestle him around. He yelps and runs away, then comes running back for more. But I wouldn't do anything with him. I just like the feel of him in my arms, and the way he melts and calls me Cousin Tom. But that's all. I worry because maybe if he wasn't my blood cousin I might really want him, not just sleep beside him. This is different from when you see a guy you like the looks of. This is Baby Walt. Look, I was there when he took his first steps in the back of the Lindstroms'. It was some grown-up shindig, where they drag the kids along. Suddenly, Walt reared up with this goofy grin and staggered around, chasing the Lindstroms' cat.

Well, finally they delivered Walt's bed, and he was so excited he said he'd put a notice to that effect in the next greeting he taped on the phone machine. I said to cool it, because who knows who's listening, anyway? Besides, he's still sleeping with me. I guess he just got used to it, or we both did, or something. Well, there's room for two there. He pours himself a can of V-8 most nights, and apparently he gets up and sips from it because by morning it's all gone. Sometimes he turns over real close to me and I can hear him breathing and I think about how he still calls me Cousin Tom after all these years of his life.

Judith gave a Christmas Eve party, inviting all her "friends away from their family," as she put it. Tom took Walt to Anthony's to pick out a new shirt, tie, and sport jacket.

"The girls'll love you like that," Tom told Walt when they got home and the boy tried everything on. "They'll want to eat you with a knife and fork."

"Won't I be young?" Walt asked, staring in the mirror. "They may seem a little racy for a country boy."

"You can handle them, pal. I'm counting on you."

"No, don't." Walt turned to the side. "Say, it's hard to look at your own profile."

"Why shouldn't I count on you?"

"I wonder if I should bring Claude."

"Aren't you a little big for Claude?"

"Yes. But he likes older men."

Claude stayed home, so Walt was by far the junior of the congregation. But Judith was attractive, smart, and generous, and such people tend to have comparable friends. So Walt was welcomed: respected by the men and adored by the women. Judith had a piano, too, and she played Christmas carols as the company hugged and sang, everything from "Good Christian Men, Rejoice" to "White Christmas," capped by a contest to see who knew the most verses to "Good King Wenceslas."

Then Walt took stage, accompanying himself in his own composition, "The Candy Corn Chorale," sung more or less to the tune of "God Rest You Merry Gentlemen":

Oh! Candy Corn went out to pray
And came back in the morning!
Candy Corn was then devoured
By all the merry folk!
Oh! Candy Corn went out to pray

And never did return!
For Candy Corn was et,
He was et!
Oh! Candy Corn was et!

Then everyone wanted to sing it, and Walt divided them by vocal type and built up a ringing choir fit to compete in an eisteddfod. Walt saw Judith smiling at Tom as they sang, and Walt loved that, and everyone was smiling; but everyone was a little sozzled by then, and it was time to part. Walt and Tom were the last guests to leave, staying to help Judith put her place in order. Tom and Judith took some minutes to themselves while Walt auditioned Debussy's *Children's Corner* suite on the piano. Then Walt joined them, saying, "That last piece was 'The Golliwog's Cake-walk.' "

"Let's cakewalk ourselves home," said Tom. "It's late."

Walt offered his hand to Judith, but she embraced him, saying, "I hope there will be many parties like this one, Walt."

In the car, Tom said, "Well, Judith really likes you."

"That was a nice crowd of people. They were quite turned on to 'The Candy Corn Chorale.' "

"It was quality music, pal."

Coming down from the high of a wonderful party, the two were silent for the rest of the ride. Once home, they separated on diverse errands. Walt pumped more carols out of the piano while Tom, in the office, took out his diary. He wrote:

I don't know how to proceed. I don't know what I want. I don't
know who I'm supposed to love. Could I screw Judith and hold
Walt, or should it be vice versa? I don't know what I'd do with Walt,
and yet I want to do it.

The phone rang; Tom glanced at his watch. It was a little after midnight.

"Don't answer it, Walt!" Tom called out. Some Christmas prank, probably. But the piano was silent, and Tom heard Walt talking and, then, suddenly, shouting.

"It's *Chris*, Cousin Tom! Chris is calling especially for us in a holiday spirit!"

Tom went as rigid as stone. *Chris?*

Walt, at the door, goes, "Hurry! It's the true voice of our past!"

Tom leaps up and follows the rushing Walt to the nearest extension, in the kitchen.

"Chris!"

"Oh, Tom, Merry Christmas, and I hope it isn't too late to call."

"No, it's . . . No, great to hear you! Chris!"

"This is Call Me Impulsive. I tried Information for Minneapolis, and there you—"

"Well, how are you, voice of our past? Walt is beside himself. Anyway, he *was*. He just wandered off again in the excitement."

"What's *he* doing there?"

"Living."

"Oh. Oh, that's so sweet, Tom. That's . . . Golly."

They did that for a while, then they did Chris's career, then New York, then Minneapolis—which fascinated Chris, who, like most Gotburgers, had never been there.

"I can't get over it," said Tom. "You're this big theatre lady now."

"One off-Broadway hit and nineteen dinner-theatre *Hello, Dolly!*s isn't big. It's promising."

"You'll have to come out to the Guthrie, I guess. It's this big theatre we have. Famous, Chris."

"Famous, right."

"Golly, Christmas, do you realize it? Old folks at home and all. We should hold a school reunion."

"What are you like, Tom? Would I recognize you?"

"Well, I'm the same. What about you?"

"I'm a little grander. My hair's different. My clothes. My work."

"Oh, Chris. All those years."

His tone sounded yielding, elegiacal, so Chris brought up Luke.

"No, Chris," Tom began—but Chris said, "Listen, boy, we three guys have some things to settle. You two do, anyway."

"It's bad old stuff, Chris. Leave it lay."

"I can't. Weeks'll go by, and it's all work. But then I have a thought, Tom, and it's us three. Right back there in the middle of the country."

"Oh, Chris. Yes. That was a beautiful time, I know. But something happened between Luke and me. Something I don't think about now. And you don't want to know."

"Luke told me."

Tom was quiet and Chris waited.

"I hurt him, Chris."

"Yes."

"Well, I wanted to and I did it. I hurt him bad. So bad I don't ever . . . I won't . . ."

"Tell me, Tom."

"Did he actually . . . Did he tell you what happened?"

"Tom . . ."

"Christ. To think about that now."

"Yes, but, Tom, everything we are came out of those years. Didn't it? We're all so full of choices, I guess, but our characters are formed then. So we play them out again and again, and we ruin our choices—"

"*Chris, I beat him up!* Isn't that bad enough? Shouldn't we leave it there?"

"Tom, do you want to talk to him?"

"*God,* no!" Then: "How is he?"

"Fine. He stayed in San Francisco. He's a . . . Don't laugh."

"Okay."

"A caterer. Parties and cakes and waiters with dip."

"What the hell kind of work is that?"

"He's happy, Tom."

"That's what he went to Berkeley for? To be a caterer? So everyone let me go walk, poor dumb Tom—and now I've got money in the bank and a growth operation."

"That's all it is to you? We lived on life, the three of us, for seventeen years! We rewrote the rules! We lived in each other's heads! We shared each other's pain so deeply that I get the chills recalling it. Everyone we knew had a pleasant childhood—we had a profound one. Every time I direct a love scene, I think of us. It was chivalrous, Tom! *Devotion!* Don't you ever think of that?"

"Of course I do," said Tom quietly.

"And miss it?"

"No! *Jesus,* never! I've got this straightened out here, and I'm not going back!'"

Walt walked into the kitchen, his face pale, Tom's diary in his hands.

"Tom?" said Chris.

"I'm in this, Cousin Tom," said Walt. "You wrote about me."

"Oh, *Christ in hell!*"

"Tom, what's wrong?"

"Chris, something . . . something just happened." Tom's eyes on Walt. "Things are out of control here, they really are." Walt standing there with the proof. "Chris, I have to go. I'm sorry."

"Of course, Tom."

"Chris," he said, starting to weep. "I couldn't be what anyone wanted. Don't you see that? That's what made me all mean and hard to people. I'm *nice* now."

"Don't cry, Cousin Tom."

"I'd better go, Tom."

"No, Chris, listen. I never knew what it was, but I knew somehow I couldn't handle it. I saw it coming, and it was Luke, and I . . . I . . ."

Walt was in his arms.

"Merry Christmas, Tom," said Chris, ringing off.

"You're my friend," Tom told Walt, sobbing as he held the boy. "You won't let me down, will you?"

Walt was weeping, too.

"Will you, pal?"

"Cousin Tom, please let me tell you why they sent me here. I have to for a reason."

"Yes. Yes."

Walt didn't say anything at first, as if he was assembling the parts of the story in their proper order. At last he began, "You know who this whole thing is really about?"

Wiping his eyes, Tom asked, "Who?," thinking, *Luke.*

"Dexter."

Jolted, Tom started to laugh.

"Well, it's true!"

"Come on, pal." Tom rose, guiding Walt to the living room. "After seeing your big-man cousin crying, you need a stiff drink and so do I."

"I want a Manhattan."

"Why?"

"Some ritzy people were drinking it in a movie on TV last week, and I want to try it."

"I don't know what's in that. How about a Bloody Mary, New York–style?"

"*Yes!* What's in it?"

"Besides the tomato juice and vodka, you put in horseradish sauce."

"It's a tangy treat," said Walt, "for us two weary adventurers."

Mixing the drinks, Tom told Walt how, years ago, he and Luke used to sample mixed drinks when their parents weren't around. "You know every grown-up in Gotburg had those really elaborate bars for parties, with carved figures on corks to stick in the opened bottles, and swizzle sticks, and cocktail onions, and so on? They always had a ton of drink recipe books, too. I guess the liquor stores gave them out. Well, Luke and

I spent one summer chugging through one of those books, anyway, sampling the different drinks. Golly, what a lot of shit! One part vermouth, one part gin, one part Angostura, one part marmalade, stir but do not shake . . . Cheers, pal!"

They drank.

"What happened to Luke now?" asked Walt. "You never mention him."

"Well, we got into some trouble. You don't want to hear about it."

They sat on the couch.

"Boy, that was some crying job, huh?" said Tom, his arm around Walt's shoulder. "But it's over now, and we don't have to speak about it ever—"

"Was the trouble with Luke just at the end of high school?" Walt asked. "When you were never around any more?"

"Yeah."

"Because I always meant to tell you that Luke came to me in a dream."

"Huh?"

"It is a very famous dream of mine, and I always recall it. He said to give you a message, and it was very important."

"What was the message?"

"That's the mystery section of the dream, because I don't remember."

"So why is the whole thing about Dexter?"

"Oh, my poor old dog. He was so vivacious and then he was ailing, and it got worse and worse. The vet said, He has lived a full and noble life, and now he can retire. But he was in misery all day long. He would lie around just groaning. The only time he came alive was when I gave him a bone from dinner, and he would chaw on it with gusto, just like the dog he used to be, and he would even growl if you came near him then."

"So you had him put to sleep?"

Walt shook his head. "They wouldn't let me."

"Aunt Frelinda and Uncle Harald?"

Walt nodded. "My sinister parents said Dexter was like one of us and you wouldn't kill one of *us* off if we were dying of cancer, would you?"

Tom grinned. "I bet you would."

"I'd kill *them* off anyway because of what they did. For poor Dexter got worse and worse, till he couldn't move without hurting, and I even went to the vet to ask for something to soothe Dexter forever, if you get my meaning. But that vet said, Only with my parents' consent."

Walt looked at Tom. "He was my dog, wasn't he? I always took care of him, so it should have been *my* consent."

Walt's voice shook a little. Regaining control, he went on: "So I did this awful thing. I took Dexter out in my old red wagon from the garage, and I went all the way out to the little woods. . . . Didn't Luke get beat up there once?"

"Yes."

"Who did it?"

"You tell your story, then I'll tell mine."

"So I wagoned Dexter deep in there where no one could see. This was just after Halloween, so the ground wasn't frozen hard yet, and I brought my snow shovel along."

Walt had turned away from Tom and his voice had lowered almost to a whisper.

"Dexter was whimpering all the way, because it's so rough in that forest, all up and down. Of course, he had no idea what this was about, I'm very sure of that. I got him out of the wagon very gently, and I petted him, and talked to him, and said how much I liked him and how he had always been my best friend despite a certain tendency to chase rabbits all the time. I was thinking of all the cute things he did, like when he would leap up at the table and snatch some spaghetti, and his mouth was all smeared up with noodles, and then he'd walk around with this puzzled look, as if he's thinking, I ate this but it's still there. I was behind him, just petting him and so on. 'Good dog,' I said. 'Good dog.' "

"You can look at me, Walt. It's not your fault, and you did the right thing."

"No, I didn't. I *didn't,* Cousin Tom. Because when I picked up the shovel to whack his head, he suddenly turned and saw me. What did he think of me, then?"

Walt began to cry again, tears pausing shyly at the crest of the cheek, then coursing down as Tom comforted him.

"Golly," said Tom. "This must be National Crying Week."

"At least I killed him with one blow. I made sure of that."

"You're a courageous boy."

"I didn't think so then. I felt so wicked. And I bet you think I cried, too, but I was too mad to. Because my parents made me do that. So I buried Dexter and put the shovel in the wagon and pulled it home, and I went right to my parents. They were watching the news on TV. Well, sir, I straight out told them that Dexter was dead and that I was a homosexual, and they were so shocked they forgot all about Dexter and made all these arguments about how I'm confused or it's just a phase and so on. Can you imagine not knowing what you are?"

"*That's* why they sent you here? Just because you . . . came out?"

"That is why, Cousin Tom."

"But . . . why here?"

"You're supposed to cure me. Let's have your story now."

All crying was behind them; they were curious, relaxed, ready to hear what this was. Tom told Walt about what had passed between himself and Luke, heartily revising certain discouraging details but presenting the saga honestly in the overall outline of its feelings.

"Golly!" said Walt, at last.

Tom nodded. "Golly," he agreed.

"But what happened to Luke in the little woods? Who did that to him?"

"Someone who was insecure and frightened and gay himself, and furious that Luke was . . . bringing the question up."

"Was it someone I know?"

"No. It's someone . . . long gone from the world."

"Cousin Tom, I have a confession to make. I have never had sex."

"Never, huh?"

"Well . . . I made out with Mary Sue McRoberts at her party after the Junior Prom. It was pretty famous in the class, too. Everybody teased me about it for weeks. Could I fix some Pop-Tarts in the toaster?"

"Sure, pal. I'll have one, too."

Readying the food in the kitchen, Walt said, "Nevertheless, I expect that everybody in the class knew I was a fairy."

Tom winced at the word.

"Did anyone know about you, Cousin Tom?"

"Just Luke, I guess. Maybe Chris . . . I don't know. But all my sex is with women, so how much of a fairy could I be, anyhow?"

"But which tells us more about you—what you do, or what you wish you were doing instead?"

"Are those Pop-Tarts ready yet?"

"See, we're always putting labels on people. You know—grind, jock, dookie . . ."

"What's a dookie?"

"A jerk."

"*Dookie?*"

"That's what everybody at Sawtooth High School calls it."

"Boy, they sure change the slang fast nowadays."

"How did your generation say it?"

"Dufo, I guess. Or klinker."

"Like, he's a real klinker?" Walt made a face. "That's *so* hip," he said, sarcastically.

"Well, what do you say? He's a real *dookie?*"

"We say, Cousin Tom is such a dookie, he chases girls."

Mock-threatening, Tom advanced on Walt, who got on the other side of the kitchen table, Tom growling and Walt giggling. Then Tom feinted left and lunged right, catching Walt and throwing him around a bit, till he realized that he had a hard-on and released the boy and retreated to the other side of the table.

"What's wrong, Cousin Tom?"

"How about just Tom from now on, huh?"

"Or just Dookie. *Oh,* the Pop-Tarts!" Walt ran to the toaster. "Yes, they're perfect! The ideal snack for young and old alike." Fetching plates and napkins, Walt added, "Remember our motto: 'When you're tired of Pop-Tarts, you're tired of life.' "

"We're going to have to find you a boy friend, aren't we?" said Tom quietly.

"We what?"

"Well, you're a grown man, Walt. What are you going to do about this aspect of your . . . this . . ."

Walt looked at Tom. "Do I have to do anything?"

"Well, which way are you going to go? Sexually, I mean."

"There's a choice?"

"Sure. You can try to find someone like yourself and . . . and so on, or you can do what I do."

"And lie?"

That stopped Tom, but momentarily. "It's not lying, Walt. It's the way I want to live."

"Okay."

"I have a right to."

"Let's eat our Pop-Tarts. You want butter on yours?"

"Look, Walt. You've met Judith. You see what fun she and I have. We just . . . fit together. Is that a lie to you?"

"Delicious," Walt enthused, holding his Pop-Tart on high and addressing an imaginary audience. "Yet so tasty, too."

"Walt—"

"Here's a quiz. Who would you rather do it with, Judith or Luke?"

Jolted again, Tom sputtered for a moment, then said, "Walt, that's *dumb.* Judith is beautiful in bed and Luke is someone I haven't seen in—"

"But if you saw him."

"It's crazy, Walt!"

"Okay."

"I mean, what a question."

"Can I have the rest of your Pop-Tart?"

"You're not off the hook yet, pal," said Tom, passing his plate. "I'm asking you, what are you going to do for . . . for dating?"

"Who says I have to do anything?"

"Well, you can't just . . . I mean—"

"You want to know what I did so far?"

Tom nodded.

"First, I made out with Peter Njelsted in ninth grade, in his basement. He talked me into it—he said we had to practice so girls wouldn't laugh at us."

"Well, how was that?"

"Sort of gooey. Then I did something with Thor Lundquist under the covers in his bed, when I had to sleep over during a snowstorm."

"Chris's little cousin?"

"He's not so little now. He's this well-known hero athlete and Student Government president, so of course he's always getting little guys like me into his bed where no one suspects a thing. Because suddenly I began to notice that every time a storm was coming, Thor would invite someone over for a study session."

"What exactly did you do?"

"I'm not sure. I had my eyes shut the entire time."

Tom smiled, then shook his head. "What are we going to do with you, pal?"

"Cousin Tom, are you mad at me for being gay?"

"Jesus, no! Do I look mad?"

"But you can't be happy about it—or you'd be dating a man yourself. Wouldn't you?"

"These thorny questions, Walt! I . . . Maybe everyone has secret longings for . . . you know, both men and women."

"I don't. I only long for men. I just don't know what to do about it."

"Have you ever been to a bar?"

"A gay bar?"

Tom nodded.

"Well . . . they don't have too many of those in Gotburg, you know."

Laughing, Tom said, "Well, they've got a few here. I'll take you, if you like."

Walt's eyes were wide. "You *would*?"

"Why not?"

"Do they have porn movies here, too?"

"Sure."

"Maybe that's where I should go—to find out what to do on a date."

"Maybe, if you met the right guy, he'd show you himself."

"Wouldn't he just get impatient with me for being a dookie about sex?"

"Well, not if he liked you, I guess." Tom glanced at his watch. "Golly, it's late anyhow. Come on, we'll finish talking about this tomorrow. Sack time."

As they left the kitchen, Walt said, "You know, it was really nice to discuss this, Cousin Tom. It feels very adult to me. Now I think I'll take Claude to bed and practice a few maneuvers on him."

They parted on the second-floor landing. Walt's light went out in minutes, but Tom didn't go right to bed. First he went back to the kitchen to retrieve his diary. Then he took it to the living room and read it from cover to cover, skipping some of the technical data but, in essence, reviewing the last eight years of his life. Here were men he had glimpsed, spoken to, somewhat known. Here were houses: resurfacing, extensions, estimates. You examine the structure, envision its potential, superintend its growth. Love could be like that, couldn't it? You sight, think about, develop someone. Chris made me cry. She lured me back into the old days. Of course, she thinks it was this great romantic trio we had, when the main thing was that they went off to college and left me behind. Now I'm as independent as they are, and I created that independence myself. When I build, I build sturdy. I make decisions to last, too. I am what I do.

Such belief in the course that he had chosen no doubt chaperoned Tom when he took Walt to the Magic Parrot on the first evening when the thermometer rose above ten degrees. "It's summer in the Twin Cities!" the Channel Four weatherman chortled. Low wind and a warm front. So Tom and Walt drove downtown and walked into a world. Those of my readers who savored the heady atmosphere of Thriller Jill's and Hero's might resent the plain-Jane air of the Magic Parrot: but this is the Midwest. We do things *basic* here, with none of your trendy angst, your East-versus-West-Coast anti-fashions. Instead of the Magic Parrot, they might have named this bar "A Night with the Guys."

Tom bought Walt a drink, then urged him to scout the place for a buddy. Walt mostly hung in the shadows, watching and trying to decide about things. But other customers noticed him and came up to talk. Moving to the rhythm of the jukebox and keeping an eye on Walt, Tom played the loner till he was surprised by a tall and very friendly fellow who came up out of nowhere and said, "What's cooking?"

Tom shrugged. Shrugging is the *nichevo,* the *shalom,* perhaps even the Esperanto of the Midwest; it can mean a thousand things, depending on the set of facial features, the motion of hands, the placement of legs. Tom's shrug said, Nothing's cooking, because I'm just here with a friend. He's gay and I'm his cousin.

Outlanders are entirely blind to this body language, but then midwesterners are constantly amazed at how many words they have to put together to express themselves in other sections of the land, even to say Nice evening, or Don't put cream in my tea. When Luke's parents took a trip to the East, Mrs. Van Bruenninger couldn't wait to get back and tell her friends how exhausting it was, trying to communicate. "Those New Yorkers," she told all and sundry, "don't hear anything that you say. You have to chew your cabbage twice in New York."

Reading Tom's shrug, the tall, friendly fellow looked around the room, checked Tom's gaze, and followed it to gaze at Walt, who was sipping his Kahlúa with milk as if it were the most intoxicating potion to be had in the land.

"Your brother?"

"Cousin."

"Cute boy."

"Well, he's a firm young man," and that doesn't make too much sense, but Tom was a little flustered. The bar and all: the dense gayness of it. He's right there in the center, more uncomfortable than intrigued. The jukebox rang its music through the great open room. It was "Indian Giver," the month's top single, by Tommy Woods. Remember?:

You gave all your heart to me,
Couldn't have been bolder.
And I'll admit I took you at your word.
Now you're going out with guys,
Giving me the shoulder.
And who thought it could ever have occurred?

"He's a little young," said the tall fellow to Tom. Then he said, "You, uh, do threesomes?"

"Huh?"

"You and the cousin. You take a guy home all together, you?"

"A . . . threesome? Well, *no*. I mean, we don't even . . . We're not . . ."

"I like a threesome. There's so much more you can do."

No, Tom's shrug said, I do twosomes with a woman named Judith; and the tall fellow shook hands and said so long.

Tom glanced over at Walt. He was talking to two right-looking young men. Fine boys, like Walt. Boy friends, Tom imagined. They come here to hang out.

In the corner near the jukebox there was this guy. He was smiling at Tom. Just standing there, smiling.

Someone bumped Tom from behind, he turned, and the man who had bumped him said, "Sorry," belligerently. Then he caught a look at Tom and brightened.

"So, hey, man!" he said. "Let me buy you a beer."

"Got one."

"So you'll got two." Turning to the bar, this guy called out, "Hey, George!"

"I don't want a beer," Tom told him.

"No problem, man. It's no *problem*."

"Yes, it is," said Tom quietly. "Because I am extremely happy with the beer I have and I don't want any other beer. Got me?"

Shrugging to say, Well, excuse *me*, the guy sauntered off.

The smiling man at the jukebox nodded as if supporting Tom and defending Tom's space. He was a big guy, ruggedly handsome, black hair going gray, poised and very easygoing in his dark cords and Irish fisherman's sweater. Tom liked the look.

Walt was talking to a blond kid.

A nondescript guy, older than seemed to be usual for this place, was staring intently at Tom, and Tom stared back, out of curiosity and irritation rather than welcome. Still, the guy came up and said hello.

"Hello, yourself," Tom answered.

"You're new here, aren't you?"

"First time."

The man nodded. "I know all the faces here. Perhaps you're new in the Twin Cities as well?"

Tom said, "Nope."

"Ah. Yes. Then either you just broke up with your lover, or you only just came out."

"You know a lot," said Tom. "Is that it?"

"Yes, you may be offended. That's your feeling, and it's healthy for us to show our feelings."

Walt and the blond are at the jukebox, discussing the selections, as the Eagles' "One of These Nights" comes on. The smiling man in the Irish fisherman's sweater has vanished.

"Can I give you my card?"

Tom wanted to say, What for?, but in his business, people were always trading cards and he reached for it automatically. All the card said was

> The Gay Discussion Group
> Allen Taylor
> 660-8931

and Tom quickly handed it back to the man.

"Don't you want to think about it?" Allen Taylor asked. "We are all in search of the life-affirming experience. We have hurdles to leap, goals to reach. But the question I always ask is, Are we maintaining our *selfness*? The men in my group use the discussions to open up the doors to self-ness."

Walt was shaking hands with the blond.

"We meet every Monday night, and I'm just about to start a second group on Wednesday, because of the raging demand, ha-ha. Why don't you consider it, and perhaps drop in on a Monday just for a look-see? A quick phone call, over before you know it, will advise you on the convenient place and time."

Walt was coming over.

"I think a man like you would benefit from our—"

Tom said, "You don't know me from a Clark bar."

"Yet I see that you are closed off from your selfness, by the tension with which you—"

"That was Danny, Cousin Tom. He's a pianist, too. We traded phone numbers."

Like business cards, Tom was thinking. He said, "Ready to split, pal?"

"Sure," said Walt, accepting the card that Allen Taylor offered him. "What's this about?"

"Cousin Tom will explain it to you."

"Like fish," said Tom.

Allen Taylor's little shrug, as Tom and Walt turned to go, said, See you Monday. Tom felt a little disgusted with the place and he was really ready to get through that door, but he gave a start when he saw the smiling man in the sweater leaning against the wall near the door. Walt was studying the card and didn't notice Tom nod at the man as they walked out into the frozen city night.

In the car, Walt announced that he had had a great social success at the Magic Parrot.

"Did anyone ask you home?" Tom asked.

"Danny did, but I told him you were my lover."

"Wow."

"Do you mind?"

"Well . . . it's funny . . ."

"About this discussion group . . ."

"No."

"No?"

"That guy is phonus balonus. You pay money for the right to open up your most painful thoughts to people you don't even know, then they all pick you apart and make you feel even worse."

"How do you know about it?"

Tom laughed grimly. "That's not the first time someone tried to get me to go to one of those things." And *"Selfness!"* he added, with a snort of contempt.

They drove a few blocks. Then Walt asked, "Is there an age thing that you have to be for this group?"

"I think he said fifty."

"Ha."

"Look, it's only for—"

"I want to try it, Cousin Tom."

Tom wrote in his diary about the smiling man in the bar:

> Very tall and in charge and watching me as if he knew some joke
> about me I'm not supposed to get. I don't know whether he would
> be the great guy kind of friend, the kind who's there for you no
> matter what. Or he could be the tricks up the sleeve kind that always
> tests you. Women are easier to get along with than men, because
> they're honest about what they want from you. With men, there's
> always some angle.

Tom told Judith about Walt's being gay.

"Well," she said, "I think I always thought so."

"Really?" Tom was surprised. "He's such an outgoing kind of guy, though."

Judith was at the piano, playing Chopin's E Major Prelude. Tom was hovering over her.

"Somebody wrote words to this," said Judith. "It's supposed to be atmosphere, but they made it a love song." She broke off. "Pianists like this piece because the main theme is very easy to get through."

Tom took her hands in his, stroked them. He was smiling and concerned. "You don't seem to care about what I just said. About Walt."

"What should I care?"

"Well, you accept it, then?"

"It's not up to me. God must accept it. All I have to do is live with it."

"Would that be a problem for you?"

Judith examined the music in front of her, pulled out this piece and that. "Tom, I like Walt. Are you asking me anything else?"

Tom was taken aback. He said, "No, I . . . Play some more."

Judith played "Serenade for the Doll," another piece from *Children's Corner,* and, around the middle of it, Tom said, "I'm not asking you anything."

Walt enrolled in Allen Taylor's discussion group and Tom visited a gay porn theatre, a run-down antique that had known mild glory as host to plays on national tour in the 1920s and then became a cinema during the Depression, a big-band dance hall during the war, and a movie house thereafter, including a season or two of "art" revival bookings before declining into its present state. Tom found a seat in an empty section and locked eyes with the screen. A feckless short entitled *The Merry Baker* inspired his contempt; but this was followed by a strangely compelling film called *The Stranger.* It proposed a businessman of some sort, all vested up in his suit and armed with his square-cut attaché, who is haunted by sightings of this really sexy older guy in T-shirt, jeans, and black leather jacket. *Really* sexy guy, with shoulders too wide for a doorway and arms out of some cartoon. Scary, serious, staring guy, this is, following the businessman on the street or just appearing in rooms, in and out of his clothes. The businessman is pretty okay-looking himself; you can see that they picked a guy who shows off well in a suit. It doesn't hide the build; it outlines it.

And there was this scene where the businessman comes home and unlocks his desk to open a secret drawer filled with porn. Straight porn. A secret drawer like Tom's; a diary, pictures, thinking. You see someone, and your hand moves to your cock. Now, what is sex—merging with someone you're fond of, or beating off to a fantasy?

This scene in the porn. This guy is paging through his magazine, but all the women are turning into the hunk in the leather jacket. Different views of him. Now his shirt's off, now the pants. He's standing, watching, looming. Help. Because then comes this trick shot where the guy seems to walk right out of the magazine into the businessman's room. One second it's your real life and the next second it's *suddenly*. The leather hunk isn't wearing leather any more, or anything, and he's taking hold of the businessman and feeling him up, right through his clothes. You can see the leather guy talking, but the sound track is just music. *What is he saying?*

They're getting down to business. The hunk takes forever stripping the businessman, as if he's observing a ritual procedure, maybe establishing one. It's Frank, of course; you knew that, though he's a stranger to Tom. The stranger dogging a guy with questions he not only has to answer but *ask*. The hunk has the businessman real close now, stroking his hair and whispering. A jump cut, and the businessman's stretched out on his stomach with the hunk on top of him, the two of them bucking away like tomorrow won't matter. But then the businessman happens to glance down at the open magazine, and the camera quickly closes in again on the woman porn. Camera pulls back: The hunk is gone, and the businessman, apparently hearing something, is hiking up his pants. The door opens, and a woman walks in, radiant, youthful, desirable. A smooth case. She says, "How was your day, honey?"

Tom scrambled up and out of there, away from the stranger; but where do you go? Who do you explain what to?

Walt said, "You should come to the group, Cousin Tom. You can really speak about things."

That sounded far too dangerous for prudent Tom. Speak about things to strangers?

But Walt said, "It's easier to talk deep to people who don't know you. Because they are not the true people in your life."

Tom brushed this away. But Walt kept hymning the joys of the group, and after a few weeks he actually got our Tom to give it a shot. It was a stormy session: The group members ganged up on Tom as a wolf pack trails a stray house pet. They knew what they were up to, all right.

One said, "You and this Judith are playing out some game."

Another, a little jerk with a scraggly beard, said, "It's a cop-out."

Tom turned to Allen Taylor and asked, "Are they allowed to do this to me?"

"How do you feel about what they're doing?" Allen replied.

"Well, so you're on their side?"

The bearded jerk said, "What a cop-out."

Tom looked at Walt. "Is this some initiating thing, pal? They always treat new guys this way?"

"The group can be rough on newcomers," said Allen. "Not least if they sense dishonesty."

"They don't know me," said Tom.

"The new guy is handsome," said an older black man who had been silent till now. "He's young, too, yet he has the mature and successful man's self-confidence. I think everyone in the room is threatened by that."

"George?" said Allen, to one of the others. "How do you react to what Jeff just said?"

George stirred unhappily.

"Ollie?"

This was the bearded jerk. "Who says he's handsome?" said Ollie. "He doesn't do anything for me."

"Look who's talking," said Tom. "Guy goes around with dogpatch all over his chin."

"That's a cop-out!"

"Walt, you ready to go?" said Tom.

"Now, you haven't said anything yet, Walt," Allen observed.

"And I won't."

Allen turned to Tom. "Why doesn't Walt want to talk about you, Tom? Could he be protecting your resistance to selfness? It was a break-through for you to join us, I know, a breakthrough to selfness. Yet as soon as you arrived, you fought and closed up."

Tom got up and went for his coat. "Your ride's leaving, Walt," he said.

As Walt got up, Ollie said, "Next time, bring your diary. You can read us from the hot parts."

Tom stepped menacingly toward Ollie, but Walt got in the way, flailing around as he wrestled with his coat. "We better go now, Cousin Tom," he said.

In the car, Tom said, "How much did you tell them, buddy?"

"I'm real sorry, Cousin Tom."

"Look, drop the 'Cousin' thing, will you?"

"They pried it out of me! That's how it works, you know. They keep accusing you until you tell them a story. Maybe I should just have made one up. It's a good thing Harvey Oefnerling wasn't there—I gave away plenty of his secrets, too." After a bit, Walt added, "Allen says it's very hard to be honest, but then you feel better, because it hurts to keep secret."

"Well, it doesn't hurt me."

"Allen says it does, but you don't know it."

"Who made him God?"

They were silent for a long time. Then Tom said, "Well, I don't think you should go to that group any more. You can go to the bar instead."

"Okay."

Catching Walt's miserable tone, Tom said, "Unless you really want to."

"I won't do anything that makes you mad at me."

"I just can't understand . . . Why is everyone always trying to figure me out? What happened to Live and Let Live? These nosy critics, always! If their lives are in such good shape, how come they all look like a bunch of losers?"

Walt giggled. "That was funny, what you said about Ollie's beard."

"Well, that is one fucking mess, I can say."

"He's always telling us about his lover Peter, who is very beautiful and kind and all those things. And how they have the perfect relationship and never fight and make love every night like two porn stars."

"Bullshit."

"Last week, everybody started turning on him, and he must be exaggerating, and Peter's not so hot as that. And Allen was questioning Ollie and Ollie was getting his answers crossed. You know, like one thing he said contradicted another thing. So finally Ollie said he had made the whole thing up. There was no Peter. And then he cried in front of us."

Tom was pulling into the driveway, enjoying a silent chuckle, as he always did, at the sight of Walt's snow fort, a little sickly but still standing.

Walt said, "When I first started going, I didn't like Ollie, either. But after I saw him crying I couldn't hate him any more, no matter what he said to me."

"Because he showed what a zero he is."

"No. Because the group took away the one thing he had that made him feel good, this magical story about a wonderful man who loved him. It was a lie, but he liked it and now he has nothing. It's funny how a fake story could be so important to you, isn't it, Tom?"

"Come on, we're home."

The phone was ringing when they got inside, and Tom picked it up in the kitchen.

"It's for you," he told Walt. "Who's Danny?"

"Oh!" Walt cried, running to the phone.

Danny, the blond from the bar, was inviting Walt to a party, and Tom, heating up some cocoa for them both, listened approvingly to Walt's enthusiasm. It was good for him to get out and make friends of his own kind, Tom thought.

Hanging up, Walt said, "Danny told me I have to bring my lover to the party."

"Well, maybe it's time to tell him the truth about that."

"Okay. Can I have two marshmallows in mine?" Spooning his cocoa around and dunking the marshmallows, Walt observed, "Of course, your parents and various grown-ups are always telling you to tell the truth. But there are times when it is necessary to fib."

"Do you need to let Danny think that I'm your boy friend? What if you called me Cousin Tom in front of him?"

"I don't violently need to. But it would ease it up for him and me to become friends, wouldn't it? Otherwise, he'll think I don't like him the way he wants me to."

"I remember him from the bar. He's a good-looking sort of guy, in his way. Maybe he'd be a good boy friend for you."

"Cousin Tom, the lonely-hearts expert."

"Walt, you're nineteen. You can't carry Claude around forever."

"Claude's retired. He hardly ever comes out of his room now."

"You know what I mean."

"Will you come to Danny's party?"

"I'd be out of place there, pal."

"Danny said it'll be a very mixed crowd."

"Yeah—blonds and brunets. Look, this is *your* party, Walt, not mine."

Tom promised to drive Walt over on the night and to pick him up if he couldn't cadge a ride. "Maybe we should fix you up with some party togs."

"We already did that, for Judith's Christmas party. Remember?"

"Well, this is a different kind of party."

Walt gave Tom a funny look. "How come you're so big on what to wear, all of a sudden? Danny says the worst people in the gay world are the ones who are always fussing around with their wardrobe."

"Well, clothes are important when you want to make an impression."

"I thought I would make an impression with my fine manners," said Walt, opening his mouth to show Tom a mush of cocoa and marshmallow.

"Very funny," said Tom; and the next day he took Walt to the store right after work. The boy sustained not the slightest reaction to anything Tom pointed out. To Walt, clothes existed for decency's sake and to keep warm in. So Tom made an executive decision: dark wool pleated slacks and an Irish fisherman's sweater. It was, of course, the same sweater that had hung so definitively on the shoulders of the big smiling man in the bar, and Tom really liked that style. He said, "Walt, you're going to make out like a bandit."

"Every time, you make this big deal about how I'm going to do. Why don't *you* go to parties and *you* make out like a bandit?"

"Because I already did that, pal. We all go through that . . . that social thing of—"

"We all do that?" said Walt. "Do you think Ollie does it?"

Tom made a noise. "He doesn't count."

"Oh, Tom," said Walt. "Everybody counts."

Riding with Tom to Danny's party, Walt became a little apprehensive at being a stranger in a crowd of friends, but, some hours later when he called Tom to say that he had a ride home with someone named Winthrop, he sounded chipper.

"Okeydokes," said Tom, picturing Winthrop as an amiable pixie who dresses in Necco wafer colors. When Tom heard a car arrive outside some forty minutes later, he went to the kitchen to turn on the outside light, and looked out of the window to see a tall man in a down coat helping Walt drag the garbage into the street for the next morning's pickup. As they came back up the driveway, Tom saw the man's face: It was the guy from the Magic Parrot, the smiler in the sweater!

"Was that Walt?" asked Judith, joining Tom in the kitchen.

"Someone's with him," said Tom.

Judith went to the window even as the door opened and Walt came in. Throwing off his coat, he cried, "That was a dandy party, and this is Winthrop."

"Win," said the man, smiling as he extended his hand.

Well, just don't you be knowing, now; don't think you've figured me out, rough-and-ready Tom was thinking as they shook hands. I've got my woman here, anyhow.

"And that's Judith," said Walt, in his curious habit of giving only first names in a culture whose every social act was predicated upon a very complete knowledge of one's family background. The only places in the Midwest where you don't use last names are kindergarten and prison.

"I promised Win some cocoa for taking me home," said Walt, crossing the room.

Win smiled and said, "Walt really took over at Danny's. The two of them played piano duets and everyone sang."

"*You* didn't," Walt noted, as he heated the milk.

"I guess I don't recall the words to anything. How come everybody else can sing right through *Oklahoma!* word by word? You guys just appear in the show or something?"

"Let me take your coat, Win," said Tom. And of course there was the sweater, and Walt was wearing his sweater, too, and as she sat at the kitchen table Judith commented on how nicely Win and Walt looked as a set.

"You could be father and son," she said.

That stopped Walt, who turned to them from the kitchen range, a mug in each hand. "How old are you?" he asked Win.

"Thirty-eight."

"Golly!" Walt looked at Tom, then Judith, as if taking age into account for the first time in his life. "Boy, I'm really young here," he said.

"Who's Danny?" asked Judith—but Tom didn't relish hearing Walt and Win chatting away about a gay party, so Tom said, "Danny's a friend of Walt's," and immediately followed it up with "What do you do, Win?"

"I'm a sex therapist."

Silence.

"Yes, that usually stops traffic," he went on. "Some people are curious about it, but they're afraid of being forward. Some people are plain shocked. I guess most of them never guessed there even was such a person."

"Well, *I'm* curious," said Judith.

"It's like many other things," said Win. "People have a problem and need the expert to help them solve it."

"You're the expert," said Judith, clearly fascinated. "But what are . . . well, the credentials, after all?"

Win smiled and said, "I don't supply a hot time—I help my patients conquer the emotional tangles that interfere with a sane sex life. I'm not a boy friend for hire. I'm an adviser."

"But do you . . ." Judith began. "I mean . . ."

"Serve as a sexual partner?"

Judith nodded.

"Yes."

Walt brought over a tray of four mugs of cocoa and a plate of cookies.

Tom said, "Walt's the only guy I know who comes home from a party and starts eating."

"I was so busy making music and meeting people that I didn't have time to eat. Besides, all Danny served was green peppers and hay."

"Hay?" said Judith.

"That California stuff."

"Sprouts?"

"Danny's a vegetarian," said Win. "He's always trying to get me to give up hunting."

Walt said, *"What?"*

"Well, I'm with Danny on that," said Judith.

"You're a hunter?" asked Walt.

"Somehow," said Win, wryly, "everything that I am upsets people. Yes, I'm a hunter, and a sex therapist, and bisexual, and Russian."

"Zdrasvitye, moi drug"—Hello, my friend—said Tom, who had done a lot of business with the Russian community in St. Paul.

"Bisexual?" said Judith. "How does that affect your therapy?"

"I know about you hunters," Walt put in. "You just go around shooting Bambi."

Win replied with the hunter's usual argument, that animals raised in the captivity of the agro-business are much worse treated than animals killed as food in the wild, citing chickens forced to spend their entire lives in body-tight cages, and so on. But Walt wasn't buying any of it, and neither am I. Free the chickens, stop the hunting, and collect all the guns, is my view.

"In answer to your question," Win told Judith, "I counsel both men and women, but if the therapy reaches a point of mutual physical involvement, I generally refer women clients to women colleagues."

"Why?"

"Women are less inhibited when discussing their problems with another woman. With a man, they feel they have to portray themselves."

"Claude feels that way," said Walt, "when there's another bear in the room."

Win and Tom reached over at exactly the same moment to tousle Walt's hair; their hands touched, and both immediately withdrew.

"Especially another cuddly yet somehow insecure bear," Walt continued, "like himself."

"This therapy," said Judith to Win. "How far does it go?"

"As far as necessary."

"But would you . . . would you actually . . . "

"Therapy really isn't about what you do in bed, Judith. It's about how you see yourself. I'm not giving the dos and don'ts of know-how. I'm soothing and developing the self-image."

"Claude could use your help, I expect," said Walt. "He's terribly naïve about sex." Dunking one of his cookies, he added, "Unless you would try to hunt him, and in that case I couldn't possibly introduce you."

"Oh, I wouldn't hurt Claude," said Win.

The next day, running an errand to the Stockman job on Colfax, Walt told Tom that he had liked the kitchen conversation—he called it a "quartet"—even more than Danny's party. "It was very grown-up," Walt said.

Walking to the car, Tom asked, "What did you think of Win?"

"He's nice, except for the hunting part."

"Really virile guy, isn't he? He kind of takes over."

"Danny has a crush on him. He says everyone does."

"Does Win have a . . . "

"Lover," Walt filled in, looking at Tom as if he had spelled "cow" with a *k*. "And he doesn't."

His tone careful, Tom said, "What would you think about taking a shot at Win's therapy?"

"Why?"

"Because maybe . . . you need it?"

They got into the car, and Tom gunned the motor and the subject, full speed ahead. "Look, Walt, it has to do with you telling Danny that I'm your . . . all right, *lover*, just out of, I don't know, shyness? You're old enough to be dating."

"Well, Claude wanted to go out dancing, but what if all his stuffing fell out? He has holes all over, you know, from Dexter getting excited and biting him."

After a bit, Tom said, "Well, okay."

Then he said, "Don't you want to at least *try* it?"

"Yes."

"*Yes.*"

"I like Win. Everyone says he's the hottest guy around. I just think it's funny that I was sent here so you could cure me of being gay, and instead you want to sign me up for lessons. Except I bet Win has a rule against therapy with anyone he already knows."

"I expect he'd break it for you, anyhow."

"How do you know?"

"I just know. I can tell when one guy digs another guy."

"But *why* do you know?"

"Because . . ."

"Because *why*?"

"Because I saw what it looks like."

"When?"

"A long, long time ago."

Win said, "I usually begin by asking the client why he wants to undergo therapy. But since you were really sent here by your cousin, why don't I skip that and ask you what you would like to do?"

"Do when?" Walt replied.

"Now. With me. If I'd met you in the Parrot, say. Took you home, got you here. We're talking. And I say, 'Walt, what do you want to do?' "

Walt didn't answer.

"Okay," said Win. "A little relaxing exercise first, okay?"

They were in the "client room," a nook in browns and navy blue with an impressive desk that was rather overshadowed (Walt thought) by the deceptively unassuming little bed.

Walt would rather have been exploring Win's house, a most friendly-looking Victorian tucked away between Hennepin and McAllin—pricey if you bought it, but Win had inherited it from his parents. He was raised in it, in fact, even (this is a little shocking) born in it. He's only half Russian, on his mother's side.

Win had Walt lie on his stomach on the bed; both were fully clothed except for their shoes.

"Okay, now. Listen up, Walt. This is to reassure you that nothing in the session is going to be out of your reach or in any way challenging." Straddling the boy, Win gently massaged his back and neck. "No one is going to ask you to do any more than you want to. I won't assign you any activities. I just want to help you get in touch with the activities you have already imagined in your daydreams."

Walt felt safe in his cords and sweater. But Win's patter had a slightly shopworn quality, as if he'd sold this massage to many, many a client.

"The main thing," Win went on, "is to relax. There is a flow in the pressure of my hands. Do you feel the flow?"

". . . yes . . ."

"You sound tentative."

"Only because I'm not sure."

"Right, then. Let me turn you over. Don't be afraid. . . . Walt, you really shouldn't grip the sides of the bed like that."

"In case of earthquake."

"All right, then, I won't turn you over."

Walt relaxed, the fool, and Win with loving determination flipped him onto his back.

"You cheated!" Walt cried.

"Don't fight me," said Win, continuing the massage. "Walt . . ."

"If only Claude were here."

"Claude," said Win, his hands working on Walt's sides, "is Walt."

"Win," said Walt, "is Tom."

Well, that struck truly. For about two seconds, Win was frozen, his hands without grip and his expertise baffled. He smiled down at Walt and said, "You aren't going to be easy, are you?"

"I'm the easiest boy in the Land of the Ten Thousand Lakes."

"Okay, slugger." Win got off the bed and motioned to Walt to sit up. They were next to each other now, Win's arm around Walt's shoulders. "Would you like to lean your head against me?"

"No."

"So you're fighting me."

"I can be shy and secret."

"You said I'm Tom. Are you attracted to Tom?"

"Who isn't? He's a great guy."

"That's your type, then? Older men, big guys? Protective, loving, and a little bossy?"

"Is that you or Cousin Tom?"

"Is that Cousin Tom?" Win insisted.

"He's not so bossy. And who says I *have* a type? I just want someone to like me."

"Someone to like you. Okay. Let's say you spot a guy you're really hot for. And this guy asks you out. You're going to end up at his place, spend the night together. Can you imagine this?"

"Yes."

"Now—what do you see the two of you doing?"

"Having breakfast."

Win was silent.

"I'm a big flop at therapy," said Walt. "Right?"

"No one is a flop at therapy, Walt, because it's not a test. But some clients do resist it." Win stood up. "Let's take a shower."

"Isn't my time up now?"

"Walt, I'm trying to help you."

"Allen Taylor said that at the discussion group. And then everybody was screaming at me."

"You went to Allen Taylor's group? He's a fraud, Walt."

"That's what Tom said. You know, I already took a shower once today."

Win propelled Walt to the bathroom with a hand on the back of his neck.

"I'm just trying to ease your shyness," Win explained. "You can't trust me till you feel secure with me."

"And maybe not even then."

Once the two of them were under the water, Win said, "Give yourself to this sensually, Walt, but don't feel you have to do anything in particular. Don't try to understand it, just enjoy it. Feel my hands on you? See? Think of this as an innocent pleasure. Just . . . drifting. There. The water is pleasant, refreshing. I'm holding you safe. Just holding you. Relax into it."

"How come there's no soap?"

"*Walt*. It's not a cleaning shower, it's . . . All right, I'll get some—"

"Oh, I'm all done."

"You stay *right there*."

Win popped back into the tub with a cake of soap. "This was a very good idea," he said. "Let me soap you up and you'll . . . Yes . . . lean into it. Arch your back a bit . . . Right . . ." Win worked on the boy in silence for a while, then murmured into his ear: "I just want you to relax, now. You can close your eyes if you want to, and I'm going to hold you close. You're just some very tempting little boy who's going to give it up for Daddy."

Instantly, Walt squirmed away, crying, "Give for *what*?"

"Walt, will you please relax?"

"But who's *Daddy*?"

Win shut the water off and handed Walt a towel. He said, "You think you're a clever case. But I'm a nutcracker, and I'm going to open you right up." He said it in an amiable manner.

.   .   .

After a while, Walt started to cooperate, though he was uncomfortable with Win's rule that, while Walt didn't have to do anything involuntarily, he did have to state a reason why. Win promised to accept the reason, whatever it was; he merely demanded that Walt come to terms with the things that intimidated him—not necessarily conquer them, but certainly identify them.

And Win said this: "Gay men who are inexperienced can be apprehensive about sex because they feel they're being judged on their sexual performance before they've mastered it. I always say, this is like reviewing a movie while it's being filmed. One thing I try to work on in my therapy is that you don't have to be good at everything, or even *do* everything. What you want is to find something you like to do and work on that till you're expert."

"How do I know what that is?" Walt asked.

"We're going into the bedroom right now to find out."

"Uh-oh."

Working with Walt, Win learned, was a bit like playing football. Now you're upfield, now you're driven back, and while you may score a goal here and there, the other side is running the ball just as hard as you are. Win gave Walt a course in fellatio, Win active and Walt passive, then Win got Walt to try it as the active party.

So Walt retaliated by bringing Claude to the next session. Win upped the stakes by teaching Walt the art of frottage—French for "rubbing," which is basically intercourse without penetration—with Win on top and Walt as the bottom. Then Win wanted to see Walt try it as a top, and Walt dutifully took over: but Claude was the bottom.

Win said, "Walt, you just want to have sex with yourself."

"It's hard to break old habits," Walt replied.

Tom, who had set the whole thing in motion, was very amused by all this. He took to asking Walt, "What did you learn in school today?" when Walt returned home; and Walt would say things like, "I finger-painted and Claude fucked Win," which Tom thought was screamingly funny.

Judith was a list maker. Every Sunday evening, with a week of work and leisure behind her, she went through a ritual of reflection, analyzing her life in ways large and small. She would remove her contacts and don her old tortoiseshells, pour out a small glass of fruit wine, light a cigarette—she seldom smoked—and compile her lists: of things to do, ideas to consider, changes she might make.

Tonight she wrote:

1. Tell landlord *2nd time* about getting heating units unclogged
2. What does William want for his bday prsnt?
3. Ask Tom

Then Judith paused, noting that the list was all about men—or, no, all about Judith but necessitating contact of some kind or other with men . . . the landlord, her brother William, Tom. This, she reflected, is a woman's life: having to cajole men into giving things one shouldn't even have to ask for, such as a reasonable source of heat in winter; and tiptoeing around men's fragile egos even in something as trivial as a birthday present, because last year William was so unhappy with the Mickey Mouse travel alarm that she gave him—"I already *have* a travel alarm!" he almost wailed—that he sulked right through the surprise party she had thrown for him; and ask Tom what?

"Tonight," Win told Walt, "I want you to fantasize."

"Okay. We're on a spaceship headed for Venus, the mysterious planet of flame and terror."

"No, Walt, let me finish. I want you to share one of your sexual fantasies with me."

"Never."

"We all have them, it's perfectly normal. But most of us are too embarrassed to tell anyone."

"And let's keep it that way."

"Look. Walt, I'm like your psychiatrist. You confide in me because I keep your secrets. Besides, the point of therapy is to free you to relate to what you want out of your erotic life. You see? You don't have to fall into anyone's idea of the established patterns. You make the patterns for yourself."

"But one problem is, I don't want to be here," said Walt sadly. "I'm afraid of all this."

"Why, Walt?"

Walt said nothing.

"Is it me?" Win asked. "Don't you like me?"

Walt nodded.

"We get along well, don't we?" said Win.

"It's interesting when you talk to me about how gay life works, and the bars, and your friends. It helps me understand what Danny is talking about sometimes, because he's so worldly, and I don't want him to be impatient with me. So you and I can have these nice conversations, and everything's fine, but then you start taking off your pants."

"Walt, what are you going to do if you meet someone you really like and he wants to take you home? A poor first night can close a good show."

"Yes, but isn't it really Tom you should be working with? At least I know what I am. But he's, like, this big mystery cousin. He's two shows at once."

"Do you know why Tom sent you to me?"

"Do you?"

Win smiled. "Let's try something so tame even you won't mind it. I'll even keep my pants on for this, okay?"

Taking off his shoes, Win lay on the bed faceup.

"Now, you get your shoes off, too. Okay. I want you to pretend that you've just come down the hall and looked in this room and seen a man lying on the bed, asleep. I'm the man."

"Whose house is this?"

"Any house. Now, think—who is the man you'd most like to see lying like that? Someone you know? A movie actor? A stranger you saw some-where one day? A figure you've imagined? Anyone you want—asleep, unthreatening, just quietly lying here, Walt. Who is the man?"

"Uncle Gustav."

"Why Uncle Gustav?"

"Because he once found me biting my nails and slapped me, and now that he's asleep I'm going to pour an entire jar of Bosco on him and—"

"No, Walt. This man is someone you like. Someone you want to be very close to. Lie down with."

"But then what?"

"You tell me."

Walt thought it over, but "Hmm" was all he said.

Win waited him out.

"I don't know who it should be," Walt finally added. "Except maybe Cousin Tom, because I'm getting kind of used to him by now."

"Okay. I'm Tom, asleep. You come in . . ."

"Yes."

"And you . . ."

"What?"

"You tell me."

"I do a funny dance?"

Win sighed. "Walt, Walt, Walt."

"All right. I lie down beside him. Is that the right answer?"

"It'll do for now. . . . Well, come on."

Walt lay next to Win, saying, "I should have Claude with me now to sit between us, only Cousin Tom hid him and he won't say where."

"Okay, you're lying next to Tom, and I'm asleep. Now what?—and, Walt, please play along with me for once."

"I put my arms around you and rest my head on your chest."

"Do it."

Walt did, and the two of them lay so for many minutes, listening to each other's breathing. Walt occasionally shifted position. Win never moved.

"This is nice," Walt admitted. "Now, don't say anything, because you're asleep."

Another minute, then Walt added, "But in your sleep you kind of turn this way and hold me a little, and then you say, 'I love you, Walt.' "

Judith made a second list, headed, "What Does a Woman Want from a Man?":

1. To be admired
2. Of course to be loved
3. To be protected, not controlled

Then, impulsively, Judith drew lines through these citations and wrote:

1. To be mystified
2. To be flattered
3. To be comprehended

No, she thought, I'm being too creative. What a woman wants from a man is her father. A commanding presence, intimately involved yet remote—respectful, really, if you think about it—and inspiringly powerful without being dangerous. Tom is like Judith's father, perhaps: humorous, though he never says anything funny; and very tolerant; and often distracted, except when on the job. Judith spent a weekday afternoon with Tom once, just for the heck of it, and she was impressed by how keenly he attended to detail, examining the finish of a built-in breakfront as if it were the rarest ivory, or heeding a subcontractor's report as a police detective takes a suspect's confession. Judith thought, He's never like that on a date.

Yet he was a wonderful lover. With other men, Judith had the feeling that their lovemaking was exactly the same with every woman they bedded. That must be wrong, she thought, because every woman is different, and the right man would not contain but—surely—*investigate* his partners. One of the problems with men is that they're the ones with the penis. Now, Tom was not only attentive to Judith but a constant surprise. He liked to hear her gasp, and he smiled at the oddest times. He would seek her out, *learn* her. Sometimes, as they made love, he was silent, and at other times he would tease her with lurid patter. "Here and there you'll hear me hum when I'm about to make it," he told her; but he never hummed. He was a box of riddles, which was no doubt why he fascinated women: because when the riddles weren't pestering you, he was kind and fair and strong.

Ask Tom *what*?

Win and Walt followed the fantasy session with some more massage practice and a shower. Then Win lectured Walt on anal intercourse, during which Walt occasionally held his hands to his ears and sang, to drown Win out.

Win said, "Walt, I just want you to know about this. I'm not advocating it or—"

"No, I can see it's like hunting, where you pin your victim down and shoot."

"No, Walt. That's rape."

"So you're saying that I could be a full-fledged member of gay society and never be fucked?"

"Walt, that's exactly what I've been—"

"That's keen news for Claude, because he *really* hates it."

"Maybe he had a bad experience," said Win, very gently, meaningfully.

"He did," said Walt, as gently and meaningfully as Win. "He went out with Winnie-the-Pooh. And I guess you've heard he likes it rough."

Win laughed, shaking his head, mock-rueful. "Walt, you're relentless. Where did you hear about rough, anyway?"

"Danny told me."

"Okay, Walt, you come here to me now."

"Why?"

"So I can give you a good, solid hug."

"But don't stick your tongue in my ear, okay?"

Win held Walt for a long time, and Walt held tight back, because in his desperately facetious way he was in fact looking for something that he felt unable to connect with: someone who would show him what he wanted from sex. "Why am I here?" Walt would ask Win, over and over. He asked it now, and now Win answered him: "Tom is using you to get to me."

Shocked, Walt broke the embrace.

"No, that's okay," Win went on. "Because, ashamed as I deserve to be to have to admit it, I'm using you to get to Tom."

I'm in the seaweed for sure, Tom thought, beating off to a vision of Win. A crowded vision—Win and Luke and Walt and the guy at the sandwich place and a whole lot of men Tom had seen shirtless on television, and the doings were racy, copious, thoughtcrime. Tom actually passed out—or dozed off—in the living room, a blanket pulled tight around himself, to ward off the devils.

Boys and girls, you can't. You are what you want.

Walt came down then. He had got up to pee and saw a light on, grabbed a blanket, and wandered downstairs. Tom was asleep on the couch, faceup, naked, for he had been tossing about and his defenses had slipped. Walt gazed upon his cousin for a while, letting his eyes rove and rove as he would never have dared do if Tom had been awake. Walt tried to figure out if Win's therapy had prepared him to take a step or two at this moment. Win was always coaching Walt to decide on that fundamental concept in the gay identity, What You Like To Do. But they had never covered What You Are Permitted To Do With Your Cousin.

Walt sat cross-legged on the floor, now staring up at Tom. I'm not good at this, he thought, but he laid a hand on Tom's stomach, gently rubbed the flesh a bit, took his hand away, watched to see what Tom would do.

Tom was still.

Walt moved over a bit and rubbed Tom's thigh and calf. Walt wondered if he should become a foot fetishist, because you could get away with doing very little yet no one would chide you. He pictured himself lying with Tom, each one's head at the other's foot, simultaneously sucking on each other's toes. That might be nice.

"What's up, slugger?" said Tom, slowly pulling himself up, his hair a chaos and his eyes half-closed. He looked wonderful.

"Aren't you cold?" asked Walt.

"Come up and sit with me. Talk to me."

Big Tom hefted Walt into his lap, blanket and all, pulling his own blanket around them.

"What did you learn in school today?"

"Do you like Win, Tom?"

"Sure I like Win," Tom replied, holding Walt close. "I like everybody." Tom rubbed his cheek against Walt's. Walt enjoyed that. "What do you do with Win?" Tom went on. "This is dangerous, but I don't care. Is it like Judith and me?"

"No, because Win's the older man and I'm the ephebe, like in old Greece."

"Who told you about Greece?"

"Danny. He knows a lot."

Walt smoothed out Tom's hair, just looking at him. Then he pushed the blanket back off Tom's shoulders and ran his hands over him. Tom was watching Walt, half smiling.

Walt said, "Am I going to have this hair on my chest when I'm older, too?"

"I guess so. Most guys do."

"Win is almost as hairy as Claude."

Tom laughed.

"Danny gave me a reading list to take to the library, so I could learn more. He's curious about what I do with Win, too. Danny's always got crushes on everybody."

"Have you done anything with Danny?"

"No. One of the books he put me onto, in the library? This novel? It was called *The City and the Pillar,* and it was about this young gay man and his travels. And how he never got over his first experience, with his best friend, on a camping trip. It was all about how he was always trying to get back to that."

"But you can't ever go back, Walt."

"No, that's not the point. Because when I got the book home, I saw all this writing inside the back cover. All this different handwriting of guys describing themselves and saying when they would be in the library at a certain spot, so they could meet other men. They give the dates, and this was going on for years in this one book. What do you think of that?"

"Walt, I love you so much."

Surprised, Walt was silent.

"Walt, I would even . . . well, take you to bed, if things were different."

"What things?"

"Everything in my life, I guess."

"Do you love Win, too?"

"Well, he's a very attractive guy. But if you change direction in the middle of it all, it wouldn't be just for a night, would it? You don't stop with Win—you *start* with Win, and then it's . . . Danny, or whoever. Then someone else, and someone after that."

"Why couldn't it be just one forever?"

"Because . . . there's so much of it, Walt."

"Why did you send me to Win, Cousin Tom?"

"Because I hoped . . . I hoped you would save me."

Walt put his arms around Tom and they rubbed cheeks some more. Then they started kissing. It was the most natural thing in the world.

"Do you do this with Win?" Tom whispered.

"No, because when he starts in, I just run under the bed and won't come out till he promises not to."

"Do you like it with me?"

"Yes."

More. Then Walt said, "Why don't you invite Win to dinner and tell him about this? He's my therapist and he should know. And maybe he'll suggest something."

"Sex for three?" said grinning Tom.

"No. I think it should be you and Win. I can go to Danny's and play Sorry. We've been holding a tournament."

"You really like Danny, huh?"

"Look, why don't we go to your room and I'll give you a massage? Win and I do that a lot."

"That's all I get? A massage?"

"Sometimes he tries to show me other maneuvers, but then I'm right under the bed again."

"Is that what I pay Win for? So you can hide and refuse to do anything?"

"Look who's talking."

Tom smiled and took Walt's hand. "Come on," he said, and up they went.

What a major step for Tom! Now I'm thinking of Judith and her surprise, when, soon enough, she hears of this. But that is an experience that the reader must undertake along with Judith. For we are not only your sons and daughters: We are your fathers and mothers, husbands and wives, fiancés and fiancées. We are everywhere, trapped by your social pressures, religious witchcraft, and suffocating laws. Free us! For Tom is not the only victim in the case: Judith is a victim, too.

Of Tom and Walt in Tom's bed, sincerely I blush to tell. Is it enough to report that Tom got less than he wanted and Walt more? Now, maybe Tom was indeed using Walt to address Win; but maybe Tom wants to use Win to address Luke. One of the curiosities of gay life is that we often turn, in our twenties and thirties, back to romances that we suffered—yes, that's the word—in our teens.

It is certainly enough to report that Tom immediately bounced from Pepperidge Farm sex with Walt to an all-the-way with Win, and nothing could have seemed more logical to all three of them. Sometimes getting from hello to bed can be awkward, confusing, a shambles. Sometimes it's sleek and easy. Tom invited Win over, and, from talking about Walt's progress in sex therapy, they moved to talking about sex. Tom said, "I really don't know anything about how it works out with two guys," and Win said, "You could use some therapy yourself," so Tom said, "How about now?"

Sleek and easy. The two of them went upstairs and had such an invigorating time together that they launched an affair, the very busy kind that, at least in its first few days, utterly encircles everything else in one's life, causing Win to cut back on his therapy schedule and Tom to become a bit sloppy in his work. All of this greatly amused Walt, who recounted every detail of it to Danny. Of course Danny put in his oar, especially when the two discussed who would be doing what to whom. Leninist Russians call this *"kto kovo,"* French deconstructionists call this *"analyse du texte,"* and gays call it "dishing."

Tom had never been happier or more worried in his life. The sex was gripping but it connected to awful truths, and Tom had been living with such perfect falseness that he scarcely knew what a lie was. Now Win said to him, "When are you going to confront Judith?"

So now she must hear of this. Tom is a responsible man, and he will, as he puts it in his business dealings, "assess the reality of the situation." But, as I say, how does he even know what the reality is? How is Judith to understand what's there if even Tom can't quite see it?

"You say you *do* love me," she says. "I hear this thing that you say, and *yet*. And yet you say that there is a . . . a man."

"Yes."

"You're tossing this at me, and I . . . Sorry, but I'm just trying to . . . This man . . . You're telling me that you love him, too?"

"No."

"Oh, good. So you're just . . . toying with him?"

"Well, we toy with each other, really. We don't pretend it's love."

"So you pretended with me?"

"Well, no. No, I—"

"You toyed with me, surely? 'Toyed,' but I just love that word . . ."

"Judith . . ."

"Or what *am* I to think? I knew you went from woman to woman. Now it turns out you go from woman to man."

Each one looks away.

"Well, I *wonder!*" Judith says. "And how much does this have to do with Walt?"

"It won't help if you get angry. . . ."

"Nor will it hurt! So just what have you been *doing*? I . . . Tell me! Who is real, Judith or this man? Who's real? Is he a . . . girlish man? Sorry, I don't know the term. . . . No, don't take my hand and . . . Just talk to me, please."

"The term is . . . I think it's 'twinkie.' Walt's friend Danny keeps us up on the lingo."

"Walt's friend Danny. Yes. Now, this man you're seeing—is he a twinkie?"

"He's a man, like any other."

"Like you?"

"Well, you've met him. Win. Remember? The sex therapist who drove Walt home from Danny's party last February."

"Win."

"That's right. Short for Winthrop."

"Classy name. You know, I have to tell you, in all candor, and I hope this won't offend you, but right at the minute I really feel like breaking something. Such as your head."

"If it makes you happier to get mad at me, then—"

"Tom! I'm not *mad* at you! I'm *amazed* at you! All those nights with me—I mean in bed, of course—just what was going through your mind, if I may?"

"Just . . . what a wonderful time I was having."

"This doesn't make any sense!"

It went on like that, in Judith's living room, for hours, the typical inconclusive (because apparently inconsistent) I'm-sorry-but-I'm-not-heterosexual-after-all announcement with question-and-answer period. The problem, for the woman on the receiving end, is that these scenes burden her with two problems at once: one, she just got jilted; and, two, she has to figure out what it says about *her* that she turned out to be perfect for the man who wasn't really looking for a woman after all.

I'll say this for Judith: Despite her exasperation, she retained her sense of humor and, at length, her generosity, realizing that it simply couldn't be in Tom to hurt her on purpose.

Of course, he had faced her alone, without reinforcements. But I wish he had brought some, for any other gay man—even fledgling Walt—could have done a better job of relieving Judith's concerns. For instance, Win would have said:

All sex is pleasurable, and, for a homosexual male attempting to convince himself that he's heterosexual, physical congress with a woman would be doubly pleasurable—for, besides the sensual stimulation, there's the psychological victory of having "proved" oneself. Now, this partially explains Tom's success with women, and I expect it also tells us why he kept moving from one woman to another—he never connected with any of them emotionally. But give him this—he did not, as many closeted men do, let Judith think he was simply breaking it off. He did not reject her, he disqualified himself. That's gallantry.

Walt would have said:

Cousin Tom didn't know how to be gay, but everyone who grows up in America learns how to be straight, because that's all they'll teach you. So that's what Tom had to be. It's just that now he's changed his mind. Maybe I had something to do with that, because I'm one of the mysterious few who grow up in America but don't know how to be straight. Not if it means being like Thor Lundquist, who captains the football team and calls guys homos when everyone's looking and then lures innocents into bed when no one's around.

Danny, a short, thin, slightly effeminate blond—the kind who always gets harassed in high school for the greater glory of heterosexual virtue—would have said:

Fuck *Tom* and fuck *Judith*! I'm sick forever of these closet cases and the women they fool so, so very easily! Why do all these guys have such a hang-up about what they are? I don't, and I'm no hero. Walt keeps trying to get me to come visit, instead of him having to come to me all the time, but I just won't hang around closet freaks and their girl friends.

Walt says the closet is "a desperate place." You know what I say? They're phonies, and you can't believe a thing about them. Not anything. Straights think the whole world is them, and everything else is unbelievable. They think gays are people you never see, on the fringes of everything, like vampires. Or maybe like me, who was the class fruit, the last guy picked when the captains chose up sides in gym and a big disappointment to my parents, as they never tire of telling me. But maybe my parents are a big disappointment to me, did you ever think of that? How would they like it if everything in society favored gays and they had to pretend to be like us or get bullied and fired and jailed? How about if I told them they *shame* me, just because they're not like me? Boy, if straights knew what we know, they'd realize that this ten percent of the population we supposedly represent is only the totally out gays, like me. There's this huge other group, like Walt's cousin, sneaking off to the bars and clubs and bathhouses and even toilets, leaving their girl friends or wives just so high and dry. That's what happens when you don't let people be what they are. So now Tom's girl friend is going to feel rejected—but how could she ever have felt accepted in the first place? She wasn't accepted. She was used.

To all of which, I believe, Judith might have said:

Sorry, I'm still mystified. If Tom is gay, what on God's earth is he doing dating women and *why the heck is he so good at it?* I suppose this explains his moody nature—being in the wrong place can be distracting, I'm sure. But even with these three, uh, experts affirming Tom's story, I find it hard to reckon. He enjoyed my company—that much I'm certain of—and for over a year. If he was gay then, wouldn't he still enjoy my company *now?* I'm not suggesting that a gay man should marry. But exactly how gay is he if he can be such a . . . well, such an *intimate* lover? Not that I want to keep seeing Tom. On the contrary, we both need time off now. We'll give it thought. Because I don't get it yet. And what I especially don't get is, How come suddenly half the men you know are gay? Where did they all *come* from?

PART VI

Minneapolis, 1977

"WIN IS LIKE the oldest brother," Walt was telling Danny, "who is a little fearsome but secretly you adore him. And Tom is the middle brother, who sees your side of it and makes up alibis for you and things."

"They're not that cute together," said Danny.

"You thought so last month."

"They're just another selfish half-closeted couple who think they're so straight-looking that they can get away with it, so all the poor faggots like me can screw themselves. I'm so sick of that, Walty!"

Danny had a second-floor rear near the famous conjunction of Emerson, Lake, and Palmer streets, with a little porch overlooking a garden, and now that spring was almost here he was always dragging Walt out there. Walt didn't dare say no. Danny would make them coffee—instead of the cocoa that for those raised in Gotburg was second only to water as the liquor of life—and out the two of them would go, Walt freezing in his coat and Danny making airy jokes one minute and fulminating the next.

"Those right-wing gays!" Danny went on. "Don't you so *love* that? Win even reads *National Review*!"

"I can't believe it!" cried Walt, wondering what *National Review* was.

"I'll bet your cousin's a Republican, too!" Danny pursued. "Maybe even you are. Who were you for in the last election—Nixon?"

"I favored Claude on a write-in ticket, though I knew it was virtually hopeless."

Danny hunched his shoulders tensely at this irrelevant whimsy. Real life is about real things. "How are we ever to achieve gay liberation," he asked, "if people like Win keep thinking they don't need it? Do you realize we have no political cohesion in any way, not even as a voting bloc? If some Ku Klux guy ran for office, you can bet your sweet bippy the blacks would know how to stop him. But people like Win actually vote *for* bigots. Even the anti-gay men."

"But you *like* Win. This here is where I met him—at your party."

"I like him as a *man,* Walty. Because he's so big and sexy and I'm crazy about that type. I get all warped inside me just standing near him, so how could I not like him? I just hate him as a person. I hate what he believes in."

"Well, what's that?"

"What do you *think*?" Danny snapped, irritated at Walt's high level of tolerance. "He believes in playing straight, and identifying with straights, and collaborating with them in their plot to rule the world. And this bisexual crap! Oh, ho! That's like the guns he collects—it's to remind you how virile he is, just in case the *gay* thing makes him seem a little nelly."

"Nelly?"

"Minty."

"Minty?"

"Oh, for Judas' Shame, Walty! Don't you know anything?"

"Danny, please don't be frustrated with me. I'm learning as fast as—"

"I'm sorry," said Danny angrily. "I could never be mad at you. I'm just venting my rage at Win and everything he represents."

"This coffee is nice."

"The *women* have a movement going, don't they? They're coming to an understanding of how they've been forced into a servile position. They're *organizing*."

"Fem lib?"

Danny made a face. "The *women's movement,* Walty. Oh, you're such a pre-political!"

"That's because I'm a small-town boy."

"Actually, it's small-town women who are building the movement, because they've the most limited lives of all. All they do is pay dues. *Kirche,*

Küche, Kinder. That's how my grandmother described it. You go to church, you cook the refreshments, you breed and nurture. Ha!"

"What dues?" asked Walt.

"Gender dues. Power dues. When a straight man says, I want to fuck you, you have to say yes. When a straight man says, I want a ham sandwich, you make it. When a straight man says, You can't have an abortion, because I will not let you nullify my seed, you say, Hallelujah. So he'll let you take the Pill sometimes, sure. Of course they don't publicize the medical risks involved in taking it, because guess who controls the mediums of—"

"But, Danny, why are you so busy with the problems of women?"

"Oh, Walt, don't you see they're our most obvious allies? The straight man is the ultimate partner-oppressor of women, right?"

Walt just blinked at Danny. Partner-oppressor?

"Look," said Danny. "He's the partner in his indicated role as boy friend, husband, and so on. But the system is designed to exploit her in order to exalt him. See?"

"No."

"I'll ignore that. And who's the partner of the gay man?"

"His boy friend."

"No, Walty, that's later. *If* he comes out at all. No, the gay man's partner is the straight man he *pretends* to be *like*. His father. His brothers. His schoolmates—and none of them know about him, right? His business associates. Yet who keeps us down, tells us what we can and can't do, smacks us when we're out of line?"

"Uncle Gustav."

After a long moment, Danny sadly said, "Walty, we're talking about people's lives here."

"I'm sorry, Danny."

"Do you know what they used to do to women who refused to participate in the straight man's society? Refused to accept the role he assigned her? Do you? They'd call them witches and burn them alive. Just because they refused to be used and fucked."

"Golly."

"I'm telling you, women are our allies. We should be building our politics with them."

"Okay. But how come you don't know any lesbians?"

"Tell me who you'd rather be with," said Tom to Win, "a man or a woman."

"I'd rather be with you."

"Come on and answer the question!"

It was quite early on a morning after; Win and Tom were stirring in bed, still in the stage of getting used to each other, both wondering if Walt had started the coffee.

" 'Who would you rather be with?,' " Win offered, "is not the right question. Because maybe you'd always rather be with someone else. Who would *you* rather be with, since you're asking?"

"A man, I guess."

"Yet you enjoyed your women?"

Tom shrugged: I enjoyed sex. Moreover—he's grouchy and sometimes thoughtless but he does have perspective—he spoke up to add, "They weren't *my* women. They were women who happened to be my friends."

"Coffee's ready!" Walt called, from downstairs.

"Shower first?" said Win.

"I would like to see you with a woman," Tom told him, his arms around him, moving against him, staring at him. "Just sit there and watch you."

"Would you like to see me with Judith?"

Tom slid back as if slapped. "Well, Jesus, what a thing to say!"

Win smiled. "I'm inside you, my friend," he remarked.

It took a bit of a while, but Judith made up with Tom, just friends now; and Walt and Danny "fooled around" (the culture's official term for sexual activity somewhat north of a peck on the cheek and considerably south of screwing with such abandon that the wallpaper peels and the lightbulbs explode); and Tom and Win broke up. It was Judith's observation that she had too much invested in Tom emotionally to cut him out of her life; and Walt and Danny's discovery that once they had sampled each other on the physical level they didn't need any repeats and could return to being side-kicks; and Tom and Win's realization that they were both born tops and thus sexually incompatible. There was little they could do that both en-joyed—one of them was always unsatisfied, even densely vexed. Tom did not want Win inside him, did not want to be possessed, known. He would hardly have uttered an endearment before he regretted having shown himself, and he ceaselessly worried about how fairly Win was coming to perceive him.

For Tom had never wanted to be perceived. Admired, liked, and en-vied, most certainly. This, after all, was the energy that drove his friendship

with Luke and Chris when they were growing up: A relationship so serenely solid made other friendships of the day seem coarse and banal. No
doubt Tom's affairs were also predicated upon this need to enhance his
legend, for he chose his partners well. They were women of class and style.
They reflected glory upon Tom. Even Win, when Tom came out, was of
this kind.

Glamorous Tom, the opportunist. But perhaps his character was per-
verted by the comprehensive subterfuges of the closet. At least he has
finally thrown off the most substantial of his masks; that should ease him
up somewhat. Certainly, Tom relaxed to the point of allowing Win to
lure him into a camping trip in late September, when the blackfly and
no-see-um season was over and the cold not yet set in. Win and Tom
were friends, like Tom and Judith and Walt and Danny, and now that Win
no longer had sexual control of Tom, he was amused at the notion of
carting him into the wilderness, where Win would still be master.

Tom felt dared. He wanted to accept the challenge, but only with Walt
along—and Walt wouldn't hear of it, even when Win promised not to
hunt anything.

"I went camping once," Walt told Tom. "It was terrible. There's no
bathrooms or toaster ovens."

"How will you get around while I'm gone, though?"

"Danny will take care of me."

Walt was adamant, so off went Tom and Win on their journey through
the wild. Alone in their tent in the northern night, they tried some heavy
fooling around—as both had known they were bound to—and it was
pleasant enough but no more, a certain sign that their little era of intensity
was over. They could now relax into that second stage in the gay social
structure, Friends for Life.

Something else occurred as a result of the trip: Walt faded out of this
curious triangle, therapy and all, and the two Uhlisson boys broke slightly
apart, Tom to pal around with Win, and Walt to grow closer to Danny.
The two younger men solidified their bond by putting an act together,
Walt on piano and Danny on one of his several instruments, the violin, to
offer themselves as a salon duo for work in restaurants and at parties and
weddings. The gay population of the Twin Cities still remembers this
incomparable team—trim, delighted Walt and lanky, "artistic" Danny—
running through medleys of old show tunes, and a miniature version of
Gershwin's *Rhapsody in Blue,* and the ragtime pieces that had been popu-
larized in the movie *The Sting* a few years before. Oh, they made wonderful music, the thumping piano and elegantly wailing violin coaching

listeners back to ancient times of the Gershwins and Cole Porter. Who dared speak when these two were on? They billed themselves as "Hot Broadway," holding forth at the Magic Parrot's special Sunday brunch, at wealthy Magnus Gleason's sixtieth birthday bash, and at various boîtes of the day. Danny would drive over and pick Walt up. Walt would be waiting in the kitchen, the loose-leaf notebooks of their music piled on the table. Danny would honk and Walt would come running out, and these were some of the happiest times in Danny's short life.

Tom was out and dating all this while. It was nothing much. Nobody he found was as hot as Win—including, at this point, Win himself. Sometimes Tom called Chris and poured himself into her ear; and she loved that. Her Tom, at last coming out. Her poignant boy, tender and defiant and crestfallen, trying to pull himself into one sensible piece with her help.

Chris had moved to San Francisco, somewhat because she had won a director-in-residence job with the major repertory company there but mainly, I believe, because a city full of gay men deserved to be a city full of Chris. She already knew the style, the feelings, and even the politics. Lesbians baffled her, because they didn't care much about clothes or show music—but, you know, most gay men don't, either. Tom and Luke, for instance, wore whatever their right hand connected with in the drawer, and they could sing their way through Oklahoma! about as well as the average American can sing through the third verse of "The Star-Spangled Banner."

But the gay men whom Chris knew were what she termed "cabaret gays"—generally somewhat knowledgeable about but in any case vastly interested in music and theatre and Hollywood. Some of them would, upon occasion, produce boy friends who were utterly at sea in conversations about Renata Scotto, or would tease men who didn't know Maria Callas from Maria Montez—and, Chris sensed, adore them for it. There seemed to be a belief that the less one knew about showbiz and art, the more virile one was: the more powerful, wonderful, straight.

Chris construed this as a form of gay self-hatred, and she would reproach those of her friends who traded in it. She would tell them of Tom and Luke, of their love for each other, shattered by Tom's self-hatred. But all these friends would say in reply was "Oo, set me up with the rough one!" or "Is either of them free this Saturday?" Then they'd realize that the Luke of the tale was their own Luke Van Bruenninger, and they'd laugh and dismiss the whole thing with "Oh, she's just another queen," or some such.

Chris would tell Tom of all this, and Tom was utterly bewildered,

much as Frank was, some pages ago, when Todd explained to him the
Science of Types.

"It's almost like jobs," said Tom. "You know, where there are plumb-
ers, or waiters, or lawyers. So the gay world has your cabaret gays,
or . . ."

"Rough trade, or actor-models, or . . . It's a little nutty, isn't it?"

"So what's Luke's job?"

"Oh, he's a cabaret boy, I guess."

"And what's my job?"

Chris laughed. "We'd have to invent one for you, my Tom. You'd be
something new here."

"Wouldn't fit in, huh?"

"Oh, Tom, that's just my crowd and their jokes. Everyone fits in. The
gay world has probably the most heterogeneous population there is. It's
like a million refugees, starting out from scratch in a new place."

"Well, refugees from what, anyhow?"

"From the job of being a fake straight, you might say."

How very different San Francisco must be from Minneapolis!, Tom
thought. "She's just another queen" haunted him as he tried to picture
what Luke's life was like. Luke as a queen? Luke, who loved the respect of
his peers almost as much as Tom had?

How about Tom as a queen? He had been dropping in on the gay porn
theatre again, but, as with that first time some months before, the art
excited terrible visions in him. He didn't know where to station himself.

One film in particular caught Tom's eye: *The Night Town*. It started
with this ordinary guy, nice-looking but unassuming, totally unlike the
smoldering beefcake you usually got in gay porn. There he was in his
office, obviously ending his day, packing up, saying good-bye to his secretary, doing that pointless elevator chatter with another woman, marching
briskly out into the street, where a long shot caught him and a hundred
other professional types stepping high in the sun. It was a bemusing start
for a porn film; most of them were nothing but Guys Doing It from opening to close.

Now the guy takes a shortcut through an alley, and he comes upon a
place called Club Night Town. He looks surprised, and quizzically examines the signs out front. "Featuring the musico-comic sensation, Bombasta," the hoardings read. The man is thinking this over. There is a
photograph of Bombasta, and it winks at him. Charmed and uncertain, he
enters the club.

Club Night Town. It is all men, sitting stonily at their tables. They could be statues, puppets. They *are* puppets!: When they clap for Bombasta's entrance, you can see the strings. The hero of the piece is looking around, wondering about this. A drink materializes at his table. Bombasta performs. She is one of those drag queens, and she pitches her act entirely at the hero guy. She even comes down off the stage and tries to kiss him, and he is so shocked he runs out of the club as the puppet audience slaps out an emotionless ovation.

Outside the club, the terrain has changed. Black night, a maze of paths, men lurking, watching, kissing, feeling each other. The hero rounds a corner: A teenager fucks a eunuch, who grins at the hero. Panicked, the hero starts running, but at every turning he encounters more drag queens or sex men, grabbing at him. Two men capture him and force him to his knees. For all his struggles, he is forced to blow them. Now Bombasta appears, to apply makeup to the poor guy's face and fit her turban onto his head. He is screaming for help, and everyone is laughing at him. Bombasta performs a charleston in time to the hero's cries.

Suddenly, this mighty new character appears out of nowhere: tall, straight dark hair and bushy mustache, so gymmed up his skin's like armor. He pulls the hero inside somewhere and comforts him, holds him. The guy is actually crying.

Tom wonders if this is acting.

The dark-haired man starts stripping the hero, who keeps saying no while the dark-haired man says *yes*. Over and over. Over and over again in this film of gay porn. No: as he's greasing him up. *Yes.* No: as he's grabbing his legs by the ankles and shoving them back and up. *Yes. Yes.* Please: as he slides in deep and solid, and of course it's that same porn actor from *The Stranger,* our own Frank, forty-seven and two months the week he made this film but, thanks to opulent genetics, a never-say-die fitness schedule, and gigantic aplomb, still formidable. *Yes,* Frank insists, moving to the beat of You Have To as the guy weeps and groans and the camera, which has been studying the two men's interlocking as a medical intern peruses a triple bypass, pulls back, so far back that we see that the two men are on some kind of stage, and the puppet audience is clapping, and Bombasta has reappeared to sing an old favorite:

Mister Sandman!
Please make me cream!

That was when Tom left the theatre, somewhat shaken—as Frank, artist of the erotic puzzle, meant him to be. I am in that film, Tom was thinking.

That's about me and my many ghosts. He started the car in the direction of Win's house, then thought, No, and headed for Judith's place.

It was late on a Sunday evening, and Judith was home, working on her lists for the coming week, and the month in general, and the rest of her life. In her mind, as she let him in, was Ask Tom what?

"I'm getting lost," he said.

She nodded, leading the way to the kitchen—the patio, coffeehouse, and Vatican City of midwestern life.

"Where to, now?" she asked.

He couldn't say. Didn't know.

"My poor Tom," she called him. "Would you ever have wanted to marry me?"

"You were the closest. The nearest thing to it."

"But you don't want that."

He said, "The first time I laid eyes on Win, I said, that's for me. Not that I made any attempt to speak to him. But when he turned up in my life anyway, I let it happen. I *helped* it to happen. I thought it would solve everything. Just to be . . ." He watched her, but he said, straight out, "To be held by him. So tight I'd never break free. Lend me that *passion*, I thought."

"What are you planning on, Tom? The same thing as marriage, but with a man? Domicile, friends of the same type, dogs instead of children, an all-gay Christmas party?"

"I don't know if that's how it works out. Danny . . . Walt's friend . . . Well, he's sort of the policy maker for this . . . kind of life. . . ."

Bringing over the reheated coffee, she tilted her head wryly. "Oh, there's a policy?" she asked.

"Danny thinks so. He lectures Walt, and Walt reports back to me."

"So. What's the policy?"

"Well, according to Danny, gay life isn't supposed to mirror the rest of the world. They invent their own social customs."

"They."

"It's just . . ." he began. "It's . . . Where do I go to find out who I am?"

"Now, that's simple," she said. "You go back to where it started."

"Where's that on earth?"

"It's where you were before you started renovating."

"*Selfness*," he muttered.

"*Luke*," she said. "That boy back in . . . back in your life somewhere. Ask him. He'll know."

So it wasn't Ask Tom. It was Tell him.

.   .   .

Tom tried staying away from the porn theatre and talking to Danny, but Danny exasperated easily, especially at men who Didn't Know What They Wanted.

"Who do you like to fuck?" Danny asked Tom. "Judith or Win?"

"I . . ." Tom started to say; and *"Bullshit!"* was Danny's opinion of that.

Walt was amazed at all this backing and filling. "I guess there really are bisexuals," he informed Tom. "Only don't tell Danny."

Ask Luke, Judith had said. It sounded right. Had Tom buried some honest feeling so deeply that it was as good as dead in him?

He had no intention of asking Luke anything. But, early in spring, Tom telephoned Chris in San Francisco, and from the moment he heard her voice he felt better. Lighter, anyway.

"It works out wonderfully that you've called," Chris said, "because *maybe* I am now facing heavy renovation on this building so I need your advice. *Maybe.* Like if I buy it."

"Well, Chris, you must be solvent, huh? Life is paying off."

"I've got a partner. Or two partners. The Ironwords. She's the costume designer at the theatre, and he's something in realty that they keep re-minding me of but . . . *Anyway.* It's a big building, in this, la, rather up-and-coming location, thank you all, with a floor for me and a floor for them and we'll rent out the rest to pay off the mortgage. You know, that middle-class thing."

"Neat," said Tom. "The wave of the future."

"Only the building is really a wreck, which is why we got such a good deal, and we need to . . . Well, can I question you? I've got a list. . . ."

"Shoot, Chris."

But almost all of Chris's questions involved what Tom termed "calls on the site": inspections of the property.

"So what do I do?" she asked.

"Well, by California law you've got to hire someone to give the place a once-over. So why don't you invite us out there?"

"Us?"

"Me and Walt. He's my partner, you know."

"You would come all the way out here just to . . . I mean, I'd love to see you after all these—and what's Walt like as a grown-up?"

"We'll never know. He and Claude are frozen at the age of twelve."

"The *bear?* Is he still—"

"Yeah, he's . . . Chris, what's wrong?"

"Oh, I'm crying. I've been crying a lot. I cry every morning, and then I pull myself together and run a rehearsal, and when I get home I cry some more."

"But—"

"Never mind. This girl gets over it."

"Okay."

Long pause.

"Well, what is it, Chris?" Tom says. "We always told each other everything."

"Not everything."

"Almost."

"This is past almost."

"*You* crying morning and night? It can't be some guy, I know that."

"Oh, Tom." She sounded warm and wonderful, the girl he grew up with and probably the person he least feared on earth. "How do you know that?"

"Because of how strong you are. It won't be a sour date that drags Chris down. It'll be something real heavy like . . . well, history."

"Shit, Tom, you even know that! Well, it is, I think. History. I had an abortion and I feel like a pioneer and meanwhile everyone loathes me."

Nothing.

"You, too?" she said.

"Hell, no. It's just . . . Golly. You went ahead and . . ."

"Got rid of the product of some man's sperm in my insides. Don't I have the right? If he wants a child out of it, let *him* carry it!"

"Chris, Chris! Don't give *me* the commercial. It's none of my opinion what goes on in your body. But . . . Holy cow! That's . . . daring. How are they taking it back home?"

"They don't know. I told a few friends around here, and most of them were so judgmental or icy or just embarrassed that I . . . Jesus, am I some man's *incubator*?"

"Well, hold on, Chris. It's just me here, another third of our famous slow dance at the prom. Chris, I love you, and I don't . . . I guess I don't care about the . . . morality?"

"The politics, Tom."

"Okay."

"Now that I've really pulled my guts out, in various ways."

"*Chris.*"

"I can see men getting upset, because they're afraid they'll lose their power over women if any woman can . . . well, and so on. But why even women would—"

"Chris, we're out of Gotburg and we don't have to take orders any more. I see that. I really do."

"Tom, if I could be anywhere now, it would be in your arms, holding on."

"I'll come out there and hold you."

She laughed.

"Well, I *could*," he said. "Walt has never seen San Francisco."

"Nor have you, if memory serves."

"I haven't seen anything but Minnesota. It would be cool to take off."

"If you come next month, you can see my new show. It's Shakespeare."

"Ugh. Poetry plays."

"But I do it with punks and nudity. You'd like it."

"What's the piece?"

"*All's Well That Ends Well.*"

"Well, I draw a blank, anyway, but if it's Shakespeare, I'm coming."

"Look, I'm serious about the house. I mean, this really needs an expert to—"

"Chris, I believe this is going to happen. I haven't taken a vacation in . . . Golly. . . ."

"Not *any* vacation?"

"Except for this completely hideous camping trip last fall way up near the Red Lakes, walking around wearing 6-12 like a wet suit."

"My intrepid Tom."

"Chris. Did it hurt? The operation?"

"Oh, my unspeakable *découpage*? No, I was under and out the entire time. The hurt is social. I mean, why legalize it if your friends' reaction is like a jail term?"

"I'll bet your boy friend was wild," Tom said, trying to make it a joke.

"My boy friend? My *drug dealer* couldn't handle it. Tom, you just don't . . . Well, you're a man, *enfin*. It's hard for you to—"

"Chris, I want to see you. I want to show Walt something special. Is it special there?"

"Oh, it's . . . it's a place that everyone ought to experience at some time in their life. It's either the ultimate American city or the aberrant American city, no one here knows or cares which. *End's Well*'s first night is May twenty-third, if you're in the mood for a gala."

"I don't know what I'm in the mood for. I thought a change of scene, as they say . . ."

"Well, this is a change from Scandihoovia, I'll say that. May twenty-third, Tom, if you mean it."

The first thing Walt said about this was that they were likely to meet Luke in San Francisco, because of Chris and all, and Luke would surely ask Walt if he had remembered to deliver his message to Tom.

"And I *don't* remember it, is the thing," said Walt. "You know, in my dream."

"Dreams don't count," said Tom.

"Boy, will Danny be pleased. He says San Francisco is the city of the future, especially for gays. He says it is 'socially inspiring.' Those very words."

"So how come he's in Minneapolis?"

It's odd how congenitally sedentary people like Tom suddenly develop an urge to travel. Men and women whose idea of a holiday is staying home to sleep late and repaint the kitchen mildly announce that this year they're going to Australia. When friends asked Tom why he was going to San Francisco, he simply said, "To help a friend with renovs on a house," but we know there's more to it. He needs to revisit his youth—not where it was located but how it felt, so he must bring Chris and Luke back into his life. He is elated and apprehensive; he doesn't know if Luke will speak to him. Worse, what if Luke is friendly but uncommunicative? What if Tom no longer matters to him?

Win predicted that Tom would find San Francisco jarring, a city full of gay men not just out but showing off, irritating the rest of the world. "I say anything goes as long as you don't scare the horses," Win told Tom. "But it's hard enough to get the average citizen to tolerate gay people. So if gays keep shoving themselves in everyone's face, well . . . That's how you get backlash. Look, what's on most people's minds? Meet the mortgage, keep the kids clean, shoot that noisy dog in the lot next door. They're not really interested in what some citizens do in their bedrooms. But you take that bedroom stuff out on the street—"

"Wait a minute," said Tom. "On the street like how?"

"Like a horde of sexy, muscular men wearing as little as possible stroll the city looking every hot guy up and down with a smirk. Or they're kissing in public. You know, as if they owned the place."

"I've been sitting listening to this," said Danny, "just in disbelief at what a rotten son of a bitch you are."

Alas, this was Tom and Walt's eve-of-the-trip dinner party: Tom and his friend Win, Walt and his friend Danny, and Judith and her brother William, all grouped around a good old Minnesota dinner of walleyed pike, hot potato salad, and creamed corn, with a green salad and the holiday brandy.

"Your opinion stinks," Danny went on. "San Francisco's gays aren't shoving anything in anyone's face, they're just living openly. Anyway, isn't that what straights do to us? *They* kiss in public! Who's pushier in cruising than the heterosexual male, huh, Mr. Smug?" Danny turned to Judith. "Aren't they? Pushy?"

"Some men can be. . . . It really might be a class thing rather than—"

"No, it's *not* class!" cried Danny. "It's *sexual politics!*"

"I'd say this is the kind of hysteria," Win told Danny, "that turns moderate people against your cause."

"*Who's* moderate," Danny countered, "you Republican freak?"

Before Win could respond, Walt broke in with "I just wish I could remember Luke's message to Tom."

"What message?" Judith asked.

"Oh, in my famous dream of long ago. Luke came to me the night before he left for college. He came in the dream and said—"

"William," said Tom. "You've been so quiet."

"Yes," said William. "Oh, yes."

"I hope we haven't shocked you with our . . . well—"

"I knew everyone would be fighting, from what Judith told me. All this trading of beds among a tight coterie is bound to create tension. Then you have the politics," a limp hand waving from Danny to Win, "and the spurned lady," taking in Judith. "Then the mystery guest." William smiled at them all. "Yes, why is *he* here?, you're thinking. Because Judith invited me. But why did she? Judith?"

"I would have felt odd without . . ."

"Support, of course. *That's* not why. Tell, Judith. Tell."

Even Danny, fuming at Win, turned to Judith and William to hear what this was.

Judith shrugged: It's your scene, apparently, so *you* play it.

"Dear," said William. "Dear me, it would seem that our Judith was hoping that, once ensconced in the company of merrily out-and-about

homosexuals, I, too, would be inspired to . . . now, this lovely term . . .
come out. Yes, Judith?"

"Wow," Danny uttered.

Tom said, "Well, no kidding."

"It's quite some party here," noted Walt.

"A moment of honesty" was Win's observation. "Sudden, but very timely, really."

Judith looked helpless.

"And yet," said William. "Oh, and yet. For what happiness has this honesty of yours brought you all? Nobody here seems to have what he wants. Everyone's uprooted, in flux. Is this fraternity that I see before me? Or lost souls?"

"Listen, you—" Danny began.

"I merely ask for information," said William.

"*I'm* happy," said Walt.

"And our rigid friend here," said William, turning to Danny with the devil's grin. "Are you happy?"

"What about if *anyone's* happy?" said Judith. "Maybe it should be, Are you more happy or less happy?"

"Now, that's a fair way to put it," said Win.

"The giant stirs," said William, "and all are still."

"Okay," said Judith. "Tom. Are you happy now that you've come out?"

"Yes," he answered. Two beats, then he added, "In fact, I have to say this, I don't know how I managed all those years when I lived . . . well, against my inclinations."

"Whatever they are," Judith added.

"Dear, dear," said William. "Well, *dear*. Because everyone's in love, it appears, yet no one's getting any."

"It doesn't have to be that kind of love," said Walt. "It only has to be friendship."

"Piffle," said William.

"We'll be in San Francisco for only a week," Walt went on, "yet I already know how much I'll miss Danny, to be able to tell him about things and see how he feels."

"What if you never come back from San Francisco?" said William. "It's the familiar story—midwestern boy sees the great city of do-as-you-like and promptly adopts it. After years of wondering and wishing, he has come home."

"I couldn't do that," said Walt.

"I was thinking of our handsome Tom. Young men like him are flocking to San Francisco by the horde, their heads turned by their comrades' greedy looks. They are claiming the city. Why, history is being made!"

"How do you react to this, Tom?" said Win, the therapist.

"Well, how could I just pick up and move, whatever I saw in San Francisco? I've got a business here. I know this town, and its people, and the subcontractors."

"San Francisco, the arriving city," said William. "Money's flowing in, the gentry are claiming whole sections to reconstruct and divide among themselves. You'd be in demand for many reasons, one has no doubt."

"You *pig,*" said Danny. "Goading us, mocking us, you smug stupid closet case. You're laughing at the thought of Walt moving away and leaving me alone."

"I never," said William, gloating.

"Are we moving, Cousin Tom? Because I didn't hear about this."

"We're just going on a trip," said Tom.

"It's the familiar story," William sang out. "It's Mecca, and Cousin Tom is a pilgrim."

"What about our music, Walty?" Danny pleaded. "We've got bookings for the next three months."

"But, Danny, we're not moving."

"They will," cried William. "They *will.*"

"Walty—"

"William, *stop* it!" said Judith.

"You wanted me out, my dear. This is out."

"Danny," said Tom, "it's no call to be upset about something that isn't even likely to happen."

"Yet who can say?" William put in, mock-horrified. "Yes, the familiar story."

"Danny," said Walt, "I will leave Claude with you as a pledge that I will come back. Because I would never abandon Claude."

"Would you really leave him with me?" asked Danny.

"You wait here," said Walt, leaving the kitchen.

Judith broke the pause that followed, telling William, "I hope you're satisfied."

"Oh, yes. *Yes.* Are you, who brought me? Did I perform as hoped?"

Judith gave him a black look, as Win said, "Now, come on, Danny," because Walt's friend was weeping.

"I don't have so many people I can rely on," said Danny, wiping his eyes.

"Mecca," said William. "Story. Gays are moving."

. . .

Tom and Walt docked at the St. Francis Hotel and cabbed right to Chris's in Cow Hollow.

"Oh, golly!" they all said, hugging and kissing. And "Look at Walt!," and "Look at Chris!"

"So when do I see this palace you're buying?" said Tom. "And how come you're not scurrying around the theatre if your opening's tonight?"

"Oh, we've been previewing for a week. It's all frozen now, trim and ready to run even if I say it as shouldn't. A bit moderne, a bit stoned, a bit traditional. The Bertram wears tights and a cape. Did I warn you that my style is early-middle eclectic? But the cast is lovely and the music's Gregorian rock, so we should have, at the least, a *succès de* controversy. And the Ironwords and I are taking you to the house tomorrow afternoon. Is six okay?"

"Anything's okay," said Tom, touching her as if touch were a charm by which each of them could forget all that he and she knew and start all over.

Walt, examining Chris's record collection, said, "You have four different recordings of *Carousel*."

"It's my favorite thing on earth."

"Is that because it says that people die but true love lasts forever?"

"I . . . Maybe. I thought I just liked the music." To Tom, behind Walt's back, she mouthed, "How'd he get so smart?"

"Listen," said Tom. "Do we get a tour of this town or are we on our own?"

"This particular girl is going right flat on her back in a nap before the grand event, so the Ironwords will squire you around. You'll like them— although why does anyone say that? Because how do I know what you like? Especially as Philip's really rather stiff; but Neville's a doll, nothing like her name, and they have a just-barely-teenage son who makes you want to go out and have . . ." Chris stopped. "Well. Anyway, he's Lonnie. Thirteen and just the finest young man. Clean-cut and tolerant, which I find increasingly rare among heterosexual males." She looked at Tom. "Except you?"

"I'm not . . . well . . . heterosexual."

"Ah, that's my Tom."

"I'm not, either," said Walt. "Not even sometimes."

The Ironwords arrived. They were all heterosexual, although—like many a San Franciscan—they were intimately acquainted with gay life, partly through their gay friends but also through the simple day-to-day of a city swelling with a gay population. As Chris had warned, Philip (never Phil) Ironword said little and asked less. He drove. His wife, Neville, led the tour, pointing out places of interest (such as the precise spot on Sacramento where she saw over a hundred hippies in a conga line during the Summer of Love), Lonnie affably amending his mother's very personalized spiel with notes on the more traditional sites—Chinatown, Coit Tower, the Robert Louis Stevenson Memorial, Mission Dolores, Nob Hill, the Haight.

Walt asked many questions. Tom was mostly silent, enjoying the ride but distracted by the realization that he would likely meet up with Luke that night at the theatre. Well, that's the history meter ticking out its jukebox romance, isn't it? That's fate. You're going to get it, one way or another. Chris has not mentioned Luke to Tom yet. But the guy lives here. He's Chris's friend. He won't miss her opening.

The Ironwords dropped Tom and Walt off at their hotel after the tour, promising to pick them up for the show.

"The theatre's just a few blocks away, but first nights are wonderful mob scenes," said Neville. "*Real* mob. We'll pick you up at seven-thirty. Right here? Outside?"

"Can do," said Tom.

As the car pulled away, Walt told Tom, "Lonnie's nice and you were quiet."

Tom put his arm around Walt's shoulder, knowing and unconcerned at once. Fuck 'em. This is my young cousin and I own him and love him and if you can't handle it . . . "I'm thinking," Tom told Walt, "about Luke."

Upstairs in the room, Walt expressed a life's dream of seeing what hotel room service was really like, so the two ate in, Walt poring over his volume of *What To See in San Francisco,* with insistent consultation of the enclosed map. Showered and changed, the two met the Ironwords downstairs and drove to the theatre, Tom's stomach going loop-the-loop while Walt and Lonnie discussed the movie *Carrie.*

"I didn't like it," Neville said, when the boys took a pause. "It had too many villains."

"Yeah, but, Mom, the good people more than evened it out," Lonnie explained. "The good guys are stronger than the bad guys."

"I suppose," said Neville.

"Yeah," said Lonnie. "The witch always melts."

"In movies," said Philip. "And here we are."

"Wow," said Walt, looking out the window. "This is my first premiere."

Philip drove off to park as the four others went inside, Tom both looking and trying not to look for Luke. As costume designer for the show, Neville knew a lot of the first-nighters, and it took quite a while to work down the aisle to the seats. So they had scarcely settled in before the houselights went down and the curtain shot up on a view of the household of the Countess of Rousillon in full ceremony, the men clad in mesh tunics and black leather pants and the women in black prom dresses.

Deep in thought, Tom saw little of the show. He was preparing a diary entry in his head, something synoptic, to take him from his youth to now, an autobiography of feelings. He knew this much: that everything that happens in your life depends on the company you keep. Wrong company, wrong life. He knew this, too: that whether anyone in Gotburg liked it or not, Walt had not been sent to Tom to be cured. Walt had been sent to cure.

Tom was still in his thoughts as the lights came up for intermission and the others rose to stretch their legs.

"I see Luke," Walt whispered to Tom.

"Where?"

Walt pointed him out, way down front in the middle of a row, alone, standing, waiting for the people ahead of him to move so he could come up the aisle. He would pass right next to Tom and Walt.

"He looks wonderful," Walt whispered.

He looked, in fact, like a man who had been enjoying life to fulfillment yet was retaining something of value to look forward to: a man with achievements behind and hope before him.

"Your boy friend, after all this time," Walt whispered, as he and Tom stared at Luke's slow yet steady progress toward them.

"A little risqué, what?" said Neville to Tom. "But that's Chris, and it's why she's popular here. Everything in San Francisco is a little bit . . . Tom, you look white."

Tom nodded.

"Are you . . . What's wrong?"

Walt said, "The past is coming at us."

"It's . . . well, an old friend who I haven't . . ."

Neville looked around. "Where?"

Walt pointed.

Lonnie, next to Neville, leaned over and said, "You guys waiting for a bus, or something?"

Following Tom's and Walt's eyes, Neville scanned the aisle. Luke was about fifteen feet ahead of them, moving with the traffic, minding his business, unaware.

"Well, who is it?" asked Neville. "Not Luke? Do you . . . Or didn't Chris *say* that you three grew up together? Silly me, then. But how long . . . Oh."

With pardon and excuse me, two couples from the middle of their row edged past them into the aisle. Luke was almost within arm's reach now, Tom, Walt, and Neville watching and waiting.

Tom's heart was drumming. "We haven't spoken in ten years," he murmured to Neville.

"Good gravy."

"Hello, Luke," Walt piped up. "Remember me?"

It took Luke a few seconds to place Walt. Breaking into an incredulous smile, he reached out to shake Walt's hand, then—involuntarily but inevitably—Luke quickly turned to see what force of nature had invited this piece of his sorrowfully inconclusive past into his amiable present, and there was Tom.

Tom nodded.

For a long moment, Luke stood blinking at Tom. Then Luke nodded, too.

"Oh!" Walt cried. *"Now I remember the message!"*

PART VII

San Francisco, 1985–1988

"FINE, JOHNNY, IT'S your choice. You can stick with your script and have another of those evenings with the Jerrett Troy we know and enjoy, or you can let me direct your rewrite into a startling and worthy act of theatre. You choose," Chris concluded.

"You couldn't just stage the play," the Kid asked, "without becoming my Svengali?"

Chris shook her head.

"Say why."

"Because," she told him, "what you have now is a sketch. Sixty minutes of spoof on soap operas. And they'll clap, they'll laugh, and they'll forget it. If you develop the *backstage* of the soap, the way it caters to American hypocrisy yet, in strange ways, tries to reeducate it, and the way the real lives of the actors war with the roles they take on . . . well, you might make the audience think about the world, and that's what theatre should do to its audience."

The Kid sighed; but the Kid had, I have to say, written another of his parodies with music about nothing much. Chris was right; this one had potential. *The Truth of Our Lives Through the Guides of Our Light* featured

Auntie MacAssar, one of the Kid's cabaret avatars, as a suburban Ms. Fixit, derailing the haughty and bringing—really, slamming—young lovers together. There were the usual Jerrett Troy touches—Auntie's virginally lubricious tea with St. John Lord Ramsbottom, during which she pulled his zipper down, stuck a giant rubber dildo into his fly, then feigned horror as the other other tea ladies took notice. ("Sinjin Lawd Rayamsbotteum!" Auntie would proclaim, trapping the pretensions of an entire culture in a Name.) Or there was Auntie's duel for the title of Ultimate Hostess of Riverrun with Suspicia Pushmore, when both ladies attempt to ensnare that unanimously esteemed musician, Professor Fleshgobaldi, for their competing "evening soirées," and when Auntie counters one of Suspicia's sorties with a remote-operated whoopee cushion, deftly placed and replaced to haunt Suspicia no matter where she lights.

"Another thing," said Chris.

"Hell . . ."

"Well, if you want me to direct it, Johnny . . ."

He did. Chris had become not only one of San Francisco's most popular stage directors but an uncanny judge of material and a sound coach of actors.

"I don't like the use of old songs," Chris told the Kid. "What you've got here is a mini-musical. So *write* it. Get a composer and—"

"I've got a composer. *Maybe.* A young man is on his way over to—"

"Fine, now write the score with him. 'Someone to Watch Over Me' and 'Blue Room' are from another age. Johnny, this play is *new*. Don't hit-parade your public. Challenge them."

The Kid was silent, sulking. He hated being corrected. Still, this could be his chance at Major Work, evening-length, stimulating, innovative.

"How much nudity can I get away with?" the Kid asked.

"Mr. Troy?"

This was Walt, walking down the aisle of the theatre. "I'm Walt Uhlisson, we spoke on the phone about my doing the incidental music and so on for—"

"Well, well, well," murmured Chris.

"Young," the Kid rejoined. "They're always so *young* now."

"So I've brought some of my music to play, if you want to audition my—*Chris is here!*"

"You *know* this?" the Kid asked Chris, as she and Walt shared a hug.

"We're from the same hometown," Chris explained. "Gotburg, Minnesota."

"Luke and Chris and my Cousin Tom were pretty much the social arbiters of the place," Walt added.

The Kid said, "Let's skip the reminiscing about Mooseturd and hear some music." As Walt moved to the piano, the Kid stopped him, a hand on his arm. "Tuneful," he said. "I want tuneful above all."

Walt plays. His stuff is stylish, a bit derivative but certainly tuneful. It reminds Chris of *The Boy Friend,* and that might be just what the show needs—"Heavy characters," she muses, "but a lighthearted score."

Finally, the Kid says, *"Good."* He takes Walt to lunch to talk about it. Walt listens well, smiles easily, and speaks with disarming, even battling, honesty. This is the Kid's third favorite kind of person. The first is the Hunk Who Whams and Slurps You All Night, the second the Big Macho Top Who's on His Back in Three Seconds.

"So, tell me, do you think you and I can write a score?" the Kid asked Walt over the coffee. "I mean, how do we know where the songs come?"

"They come where the feelings are. Where you *need* music."

"Hmm, yes, well. We have this character, the music professor Doctor Fleshgobaldi. So he gets a solo, I presume, and it's . . . what? About how he's this big fake, with jokes about Beethoven's Tenth and quotes from . . . What's that look on your face?"

"That's what they expect, Mr. Troy."

"Johnny."

"The songs should please them with surprise—tell them what they hadn't imagined, not what they suspected."

Johnny, corrected once too often this morning, was about to say something stifling, but suddenly—who knows why?—he reached out and brushed Walt's hair.

"Come on to my place," said the Kid, "and we'll look through it."

When they got there, the Kid offered Walt "some real coffee." In the kitchen, he went into a little number on the declining quality of that basic, all-American cup, on how easy it used to be to get good coffee anywhere. He was just about to reach When I Was Young—had his mouth all set, his head right into that Then versus Now mode—when he pulled back and shut up, because he's the Kid, and he's not ready to admit of a time when he was "young": for that means Now He Isn't.

Then Blue wandered in, nude and drowsy even after his shower, a towel over his shoulder, smiling at Walt as he passed on to another part of the house.

"Yes," said the Kid. "That's my live-in psychopath."

"I saw him in a movie," said Walt, quietly.

"*Rodan Devours Harrisburg,* probably. They're talking of an Oscar, you know. Though I feel his performance in the title role of *Megalon Eats Gidget* . . ." The Kid saw the awe in Walt and trailed off.

"It was a serious movie," said Walt. "He was on top of every man in the film, and I could see he knew what he was up to."

"He's a pro, all right."

"Is he always here?"

"He lives with me."

"You must be content about that." Walt was walking around, nosing into things. "These are great theatre posters you have. I've never been to New York."

Blue came back. This time the Kid introduced them, and there followed a bit of conversation.

"Porn movies," Walt observed, "make you feel like a feeb if you can't have the same sex that the actors have. My political friends say that having very good sex is part of the Movement. They say every time we come it's a defiance of heterosexist oppression."

Walt had been addressing these remarks to the Kid, but now he turned to Blue. "Do you feel politically motivated in your work?"

Blue smiled. "It's just fucking."

Walt gravely nodded, as if they had agreed on an enucleation of a passage in Goethe. "Is it a torment, always getting hard on cue?"

Sleepy Blue looked as if Walt had asked, Is it a torment, always putting ketchup on your steak? But the Kid came in with "They keep fluffers on hand for emergencies."

"Fluffers?"

"To urge on their virility. Cocksuckers. Ready-men."

Walt smiled. "They do?"

Blue shrugged.

The Kid went on, "The trouble is, those two incorrigibles, Burger Queen and Flatterbox, have monopolized the calling. Let some anxious beauty take two or three seconds to get it up, and out rush Burger Queen and Flatterbox, mouths agape, throwing the studio into a tizzy. Yea, betimes they may hide behind a prop tree, crying, 'Fluffers on the set!' And out they pour."

"Do the other actors ever fall in love with you?" Walt asked Blue.

Blue, stirring honey into his coffee, looked inquiringly at the Kid.

"He's a very gifted young composer," the Kid explained. "We're working on a show."

Blue looked at Walt.

"I know I should fill out a little more," said Walt, as if rejoining some observation that Blue might be thinking of making. "And maybe a mustache to give me age."

"I think you look real sweet just like so," said Blue.

"I don't want to be a feeb," Walt told him.

Not long after, Walt took a bus home, went upstairs, and knocked on a door.

"This is the house detective," he announced. "Do you have a woman in your room?"

He threw the door open: Tom and Luke were lying one-on-one, Luke's arms around Tom and the two of them grinning.

"*Two* women!" Walt exclaimed. "Here comes the cannonball!" as he dove on top of them, to cries of "Hey!" and "Walt, darn it!"

"Don't pretend you were napping," said Walt. "But, listen, I think this is really going to work out about the job. And it's my *own* music! I'm a composer now!"

"Well, get that briefcase off my leg, anyway," said Tom.

Luke kissed Walt's ear and said, "Congratulations."

"Someday you're going to have to let me watch," said Walt, thoughtfully. "I need pointers."

"I sent you to a therapist," said Tom, getting up. "And what did you do? Hide under the bed!"

"I wasn't ready then."

Luke said, "You got a letter from Danny."

"*Wow!* Where is it?"

"I left it in your room. And get your laundry together, because tomorrow's . . ."

Walt was already out of there. Letters-from-Danny days were serious business.

Dear Walt:

Danny is still trying to find a pianist so he can start up the act again, but nobody's as good as you were. It makes Danny impatient. He was auditioning this one guy on the *Show Boat* medley, and when they got to "Can't Help Lovin' Dat Man," the guy started jazzing it up and contorting it, so Danny put down his fiddle and shouted, "Did that come out of you?"

Your last letter worried Danny a little, because you sound really heavy about trying to have "ultimate sex." What even *is* that? I wish I knew. But Danny remembers all the nights he said he would do everything and get all blissed out. Then somehow it never felt all that great. I always tell him he shouldn't have let you move away. He should have begged you to stay or gone with you. Then we could all be together.

The letters would start with Walt-Danny things, then wander into local doings and chance tidbits such as "Win is dating Tom's old girlfriend Judith" or "Danny calls me 'Peanut.' " They always ended

Love, Claude

Evan was wearing the tight black skirt and the black leather lace-up bodice that shoved her breasts up and emphasized her long waist. "Looks should kill" was her motto. Two galoots drilling in the street gave her a whistle and the eye, so Evan stopped and said, "You like to fuck women?"

One was startled, wary; the other unraveled a smile and said, "Sure, honey, I like to fuck women."

"So do I," Evan told him, moving on, her heels clacking so loudly on the pavement they drowned out whatever the two guys were muttering after her.

Frank walked into the house just behind Evan, so of course he had to say hello in that amused way of his—because he knows she can't stand him. All right, at least he's gay, but will you give me a break from the he-man haircut and the cowboy drag? Christ, the guy must be fifty. That's one thing all men, straight and gay, have in common. They *never* give it up.

Letting Frank get ahead of her—Jesus, he's walking slow—Evan paused to light a cigarette till she saw Mr. Ironword come out of the second-floor apartment, walking the Ironwords' Highland white, Barkis. Cheese it, the landlord, Evan thought, ditching the butt and lighter in the hefty wallet she carried, held by a chain to a sort of watch pocket at the bottom left front of her lace-up. Tailor-made to her specifications, one hundred eighty-five bucks and worth it.

"Miss Zane." Old Ironword nodded as he passed; Barkis ignored her. Straight males, fuck the two of them. Evan lit her cigarette, inhaled deeply, head back on arched neck, like some goddamn dying swan. Lonnie Ironword suddenly appeared on the landing above her, but Evan played it cool. She and Lonnie are solid; he's about the only man she can stand. Believe it?—a *kind* male? But then, he's only twenty. Give him a few years and it'll be File my nails, bitch; and Swallow it, cunt; and Get on your knees and worship, squeeze.

"Hey, Evan," said Lonnie, heading downstairs. "How was the day?"

"Ha!" said Evan, which was about as pleasant as she could get right after work. Reaching the third floor, across the hall from Frank's door, Evan keyed in, gave Alice the minutest of glances, plopped down and said, "Disgusted."

"I have a reading tomorrow," said Alice, looking up from her book. "For Chris Lundquist."

"Oh, him."

"I didn't expect you to be excited for me."

"So? When are you ever excited about what I do?"

"Nightly, in that bed."

"That's what's holding us together? The sex? That's all it is?"

"That's all it is," said Alice mildly, putting down her book. "Come over here."

"No."

"Mmm, that soft voice. Sit in my lap. Rub my cheek and lick my ear. Open my clothes and make me wet. Whisper to me. Love me, do."

"Later."

Evan sighed. "What's that you're reading?"

Alice glanced down at the cover.

"What, you have to read me the title?" Evan challenged. "You don't know the name of the book you're reading?"

"It's a story collection. The title doesn't matter."

"What kind of stories?"

"Stories about women like us."

"They're writing dyke stories now? What's it called?"

"Women Who Love."

"Come here."

"Later."

Silent now, looking at Alice in a mischievous peering manner, Evan crossed her legs, swinging the top one heavily. "Actress, huh?" she finally said. "You actress."

"It threatens you."

"No, it doesn't *threaten* me. I just don't see why you have to . . . I don't know—"

"Meet people. Make comparisons. Enter someone else's world."

"I don't figure why you would be named Alice. You're such a . . . such a dear little piece, folding into my arms. So lovely. Why aren't you Darla? Or Caprice?"

"You don't want me free."

"I want you over here, now."

This time Alice came.

"Oh yes," said Evan. "At last to hold you. Kiss me, Miss. That's it. . . . Yes, women who love, the feel of you. Your skin. I'm going to fuck you so beautiful tonight. You'll be a happy love slave, won't you? Oh, we're kissing . . . oh, yes. Mmm, more, Allie, more, because it's you and me. Say it."

"You and me."

"Like it."

"I like it."

Evan kissed Alice so deep and long she had to gasp for breath. "My Chinese bride," Evan said.

Across the hall in Frank's apartment, Larken—first-floor front—was heating up the soup he had brought upstairs to feed the exhausted Frank.

"I don't know what it is," Frank was saying. "I'm so tired all day long. I mean, it couldn't be . . . Skip it."

"Face it, Frank, we're old-timers."

"Yeah, well . . . God knows, it's almost impossible to keep your shape no matter how much gym you . . ." Frank groaned.

"What?" Larken asked.

"A funny pain somewhere. You know, Larky, I think I ought to give it up and let my body structure slide." He shifted position in his chair, groaned, shifted again. It couldn't be AIDS, Frank had started to say, though AIDS had overwhelmed many of the men Frank knew—men similar to Frank in their ruthless devotion to pleasure. But I don't have night sweats, or nausea, or those other things that you start out with. And I never got fucked. Besides, it just couldn't happen to me, right?

"I've been thinking maybe I'll give up producing porn," Frank concluded.

Larken, ladling the soup into bowls, said nothing.

"They don't need my kind of porn, Lark, and that's fact. It's not hulking daddies any more, it's little blond kids. Porn used to be about the imagination. Now it's an order of cute to go."

"Gee."

"At least video makes the tech easier. Used to be, you'd get whole scenes in the dark. Now it's just Turn on the light switch. This is good soup."

Larken, spooning up his share, just looked at Frank, as he invariably did now, in awe. *This man,* his eyes read. There's no one else like him. And I don't even care that I've been in bed with him. *Scored* him. I just care that I've known him. If he puts his arm around my shoulder and knocks his head against my head, I can beat off on that for a week. This man is so true, he could simply ask for the time and then walk into your dreams as long as you live.

"Frank," Larken began.

"What are these things floating in the . . ."

"Show me."

Frank did.

"Escarole."

"They taste healthy. I feel better already."

I love you, Larken continued, thinking it.

So, we have met most of the house on Hyde Street: top floor, Frank across from Evan and Alice; second floor, Lonnie Ironword and his parents, Philip and Neville; first floor, Larken in the little studio overlooking the street and, in three rooms at the back, Chris, who co-owns the building with Philip and Neville.

Chris is out tonight, having dinner with her boy friend, David J. Henderson. She calls him J. because she thinks his initial looks silly in the middle of such a weighty name; and he calls her Christine because he thinks she's too womanly to go by a boy's name.

They're at David's place, a smallish two-roomer on Russian Hill that revels in a state-of-the-art kitchen. David likes to cook. It always smells wonderful in his kitchen, aired-out and vegetable-ish, with the bowls of green and red peppers and tomatoes and shallots, and the file box of house-specialty recipes, and the industrial-strength spice rack. It's a real *place.*

"Someday I'll live like this," says Chris. "With spotless surfaces and little bowls of things."

"You won't have the time," David observes as he peels an onion. "If you aren't directing, you're out drinking with the actors. Or you're holding a script conference or playing mother hen to some chap whose boy friend jilted him."

"There's a part for you in Johnny's play. A good one. It'll stretch you a bit."

"The soap-opera thing?"

"I have this idea that he'll finally slug a homer for once in his career if he fills in the backstage of the show. You know: Is the man-eating vixen a homebody devoted to her three children and utterly content with her husband? Is the good father in real life a loveless monster? Do these essential American families reflect or distort the truth of our lives?—which is Johnny's title, by the way. He *has* the concept, he just didn't take it far enough."

"That's my girl."

"I'm going to cast the whole thing with outsiders. Black, Hispanic, Asian, and so on. Exactly the way soap *isn't* cast, exactly what it's leaving out. So of course we've got to have a slice of white bread in there."

"Me?"

"There's something wonderfully medieval about Johnny's writing for a company of players, matching the parts to the talent. I think that's so . . . What are you smirking at?"

"Christine. You are such an idealist." Slicing the onion now, evenly, firmly, commandingly. "You know what theatre is? Theatre is lunatics trying to straighten themselves out."

"Except you."

"The only sane actors, Christine, are the ones who are in it for the money. It's work, like carpentry. Pure work."

"Anyway, I want you for the hero, this visiting English aristo. Hunk city."

David nods absently as he takes out the steaks.

"In the soap," Chris continues, "he's sort of bookish and inhibited. In real life, he's the ranking couch artist of the soap world, sleeping his way through the greenroom, or whatever they have in television." Mischievous Chris pauses, then: "Ask me if he's bi."

David sighs. "Christine, you're all junked up on fantasies, you know that?" He seasons the steaks: crushed garlic, pepper out of an antique wooden mill, parsley, paprika. Funny how much he knows about cooking, Chris thinks. "I'm going to have to shake those fantasies out of you."

She says, "No, you don't, Lohengrin." But one of her several interior voices says, Maybe I should listen to him, because I usually fall for gays and fakers, while this guy is totally legit. He redeems me. He is the first lover in my entire life who doesn't remind me of Luke and Tom. He is himself, just a man.

·   ·   ·

Some gays study bars. Some shop them. Tom and Luke hang out in one, that big new one—trendy this week—right in the center of the Castro. Sometimes they bring Walt along. They run into friends, they dish the talent, they keep in touch. It's the gay version of a swap meet. But you know what? Walt is not shy any more. He walks right up to guys and says, How do? As his politics inform him that all gay people are his comrades, socializing is an act of love. Then a guy will suddenly say, "Let's cut the bullshit—are you interested or not?" And Walt is stunned silent.

But *this* night, Blue is in the bar; and Walt is interested. From the moment Walt saw Blue in that porn movie, Walt was transfixed by Blue, by not only his looks but his sexual authority. Blue became his Number One, and we seldom meet up with our Number Ones, somehow, especially parading nude through a colleague's kitchen, or, now, leaning against the wall, passing his beer bottle across his forehead for a freshening chill, then smiling amiably as Walt approaches.

"Johnny's music boy," says Blue.

"You're the man in the movie."

They shake hands.

Now Walt doesn't know what to say. He turns from Blue to look around the crowded bar as if he were here to conduct a survey and had only paused to say hello. But Blue reaches with his free hand to pull Walt close to him, and, as if such things happened all the time, Walt leans his head on Blue's shoulder, and Blue says, "Yeah, that's real peaceful."

"Walt's gotten loose again," Tom told Luke, nodding at Walt and Blue across the room.

"Who is that guy?" asked Luke.

"Bad news for sure. Probably a drug dealer, big-time."

"How can you tell?" Then, doing Tom in a Bre'r Bear voice: " 'I know his kind. I'm gonna walk right over there and tell that piece of trash where to go. Well, you just watch me, pal.' "

"Is that supposed to be me?" Tom asked, amused.

" 'Coming on to my cousin, *huh*.' "

"When do I get to talk, Mr. Know-it-all?"

Back in his own voice, Luke said, "Don't break it up, because that'll only encourage Walt. Revolutionology. Remember when he introduced us to that guy with the dumb name? The one in the spandex shorts?"

"Spider."

"You did a very impatient number on his name, and Walt immediately made Spider his best friend."

"You live with Jerrett Troy," Walt was saying. "Would he be your lover, then?"

"Johnny uses me as a defense against lovers. That whole love world that tears you up. All that hungry, and that Where have you been all night or I'll kill you? He doesn't want to be a prisoner. But when they say, Are you gettin' it each day, as a man should?, he can point to me and say, Yes, I am Johnny and I'm gettin' it. Which he really has to be able to say, I tell you true. It's a social thing. Been happenin' for quite some years now, us two like so."

"But do you ever . . ."

"You don't see it yet," said Blue. "And that's sweet, because yer the wonderin' kind that a guy can do anything to. I'd get nested inside you, deep and full, and we could get to know each other real nice, I guarantee."

"I've been yearning to experience just how that works," said Walt. "But I'm afraid to go that far, at the same time."

Blue had his hand under Walt's chin—gently, gently—and Walt grew still.

"The hottest thing," Blue said, "is some young kind of kid who's afraid of it and wants it. Now, I would be really careful about you, work you open and ease into you with the deep breath thing, where I hold on to your shoulders and you just let it happen. You shouldn't worry none. You got Blue for a friend tonight."

"It's reassuring to hear," said Walt, feeling like a non-swimmer treading water in the deep end, "because I want to feel at one with my brothers and maximize the gay experience. Everyone says getting fucked is the ultimate thing, and I have to know about that. I have to. Of course, we'll do it safe-style, won't we? I've been going out with condoms and spermicidal for so long now, night after night, with no reason except who knew if . . ."

Blue put a hand on Walt's shoulder, and Walt looked up at Blue with alarm. This was the moment when it comes together, and Blue said, "I won't hurt you, my friend."

.   .   .

"Look, it's not my job to police him," Luke was saying. "He's got to—"

"I *told* you—"

"Uh-oh, take a gander."

Tom took a gander. Walt was gone and so was Blue.

"Well, *shoot*," said Tom. "Think they went back to the house? We could beat them there and—"

"Walt's not that dumb. He went home with the trash. *If* he's trash."

"Trust me, he's trash. He was all over Walt as if this was a back-alley sex club."

"What's made us so conservative?" Luke asked, thoughtfully. "Monogamy?"

Tom made no reply. Luke strongly suspected that Tom had sex with other men, easy to arrange in a building contractor's unstructured workday. And Luke had his moments, though few and seldom. Even in this medically dangerous age, it was absurd to expect an attractive and dynamic man in his mid-thirties to turn down opportunities that came his way. The bond, Luke felt, was what counted, the uniquely steadfast quality of their lifelong friendship. He just hoped Tom was well supplied with a sound brand of condoms.

"You know," said Tom, "there's nothing conservative about wanting the best for Walt."

"Maybe this is the best. He can get the slumming out of his system, and then it'll be good-bye to Spider and those rallies and the lectures. I pray."

"I know one thing. If we don't handle him right, he could be a very rebellious problem on our hands. You know?"

Luke nodded. "I know."

In Blue's room in Johnny's house, Blue and Walt got undressed watching each other, Blue with his easy smile and Walt serious. Then Blue took charge, kissing and stroking Walt till they were both full-mast, and Walt whispered, "If you're going to possess me, I have to say that this is my first time."

"How come yer whisperin'?" Blue asked, kissing Walt.

"Okay."

"First-time fuck is the most beautiful trim of all. I'm gonna score yer cherry tightness, and that will certainly content me."

"I'm always missing out on things," Walt explained, as they held and caressed each other, Walt aping Blue's movements because Blue was sheer porn and porn teaches how. "I hated myself for missing the riot last year, when Dan White was released. I was a coward, I have to admit that. And most of the time, when I go home with someone, I don't stay hard for very long. I must be this total gay flop."

"Shh," said Blue, moving Walt to the bed.

"I'm just wondering if this will hurt at all," said Walt.

"It's love, ain't it?" Blue replied, as he set Walt up on all fours. "Love hurts."

"Please don't hurt me, Blue."

Greasing the boy up, Blue said, "This is called the dog, fer clear reasons. It's proper fer a newcomer like you, 'cause you can back onto me bit by bit, and that'll ease the pain. No, don't tighten up, now. You give it all up fer me. First-time tightness, yeah. You tempting fine boy. I'm gonna pleasure-fuck you just right, okay?"

Evan was eating out Alice's cunt deep-dish style, whispering her usual litany all the while. "Go ahead, baby. Let me taste, baby. This is you, baby." Alice liked to be silent during sex and to hear nothing, but Evan was a sound track. "Oh, so licious," she goes. "Oh, tasty. My girl. My love one. Nipples. Thighs. Your lips," like a demented tour guide. "How deep can I go? Tell me."

"Deeper," says Alice, between sighs.

"So ordered," licking away, strong tongue, feasting on the wetness there, gripping her girl by the sides, the legs, the hair, always on her, never a pause. Evan likes it breathless. She likes it with Alice's legs over her shoulders, eating like that and stroking Alice's thighs. Alice emits a high-pitched moan then, pulls away, gets pulled back, sees the rough smile on Evan's mouth, fears and kisses it. Evan likes, especially, the fear in love. Evan likes forcing Alice. Alice turns onto her stomach in defense, but Evan licks Alice's back, biting her shoulders, licking then to salve the wound, biting again, lying atop, grasping all of Alice at once.

"You're like a man," Alice breathes out, and Evan loves that most of all.

Blue took a while greasing Walt up, telling him of the other positions they'd be sampling—the alligator, with Walt flat on his stomach; and the kiss-and-come, with Walt on his back.

"This is part of liberation," said Walt. "This is how I earn my wings."

"No, you got to talk about how it feels to be doing the dog with Blue. Love stuff and such. Yeah, yer workin' loose now. One finger, two fingers, three fingers, and turn. Doing the dog. Fingers here . . . Tell Blue how it feels. Speak to me, boy."

"Arf."

"Spoilin' my mood, huh?" said Blue; but he was laughing.

Evan is shrimping Alice, sucking on her lover's toes one by one, making the greedy noises of a child attacking the cookie jar as Alice, head thrown back, black hair flared behind her, paws the bedclothes as if she'd like to crawl through her body and become one with Evan's hunger.

Evan's delight is to take Alice too far, and make her weep and want it. Evan calls this "the tingles." She tells Alice, "You've got the tingles, and the only cure for the tingles is a very heavy fuck. Come on, now."

"No," says Alice.

"I can't help it if you're always getting the tingles," says Evan, moving Alice into position, kissing her tenderly to emphasize the violence that is coming, mooning over Alice's breasts, sucking on them with a brisk innocence.

"I don't have the tingles," Alice protests.

"I can feel it in your skin," Evan replies, running her hands along the curve of Alice's hips. "Your buttons are up," she adds, massaging Alice's nipples as if making an inspection. "It's the tingles, all right."

"No," Alice moans.

"Let me test your kisses," Evan suggests, looming over Alice, pulling her up, loving the way Alice's arms wind around Evan's neck. They meet, these two, passionately, perfectly. "Oh, yes," Evan gasps. "It's the tingles, to be sure. Lie back, babe, it's time."

"It's too much sex," Alice cries.

"Dykes are the women who have sex," Evan explains, her hand reaching for the truth of Alice, her centerpiece.

Gentle as he was, Blue did hurt Walt at first, but Walt was determined to stick it out, and after a bit the pain leveled off somewhat. "You okay?" Blue asked, several times, and Walt breathed out, "It's beautiful."

No, it was uncomfortable. This, Walt wondered, is the ultimate thing? Turning Walt on his side, Blue ran his hands over Walt in a teasing way as he pumped the boy's ass, and Walt really did try to *undergo* it, discover the magic. It should have been working: Blue was Walt's Dream Man, after all. But "Blue!" Walt cried. "It's hurting again!"

Blue pulled out, put his arms around Walt, and rested there with him.

"I'm sorry, Blue."

" 'S'okay, now."

Blue rolled Walt onto his back and gazed down on him.

"I told you," said Walt. "I'm just this big gay flop. It never used to bother me, but now . . ."

"Hold on a bit." Slipping off the condom, Blue got up, went to the stereo, and put on an LP of some big orchestra cooing through an easy-listening program.

"Mantovani," said Blue.

Woeful Walt announced, "It's my funeral music."

"You ain't givin' yerself a chance," said Blue, holding out his arms. "Come dance with me."

"What?"

"Come along, lad."

Walt obeyed the summons, and he and Blue went into a box step, Blue leading.

"Slow dance is my fave," said Blue. "Hold me closer, though. Relax. No one's gonna know about it but us."

As they danced, Walt's cock, which had gone soft a good while before, began to harden again.

"Uh-huh," Blue remarked. "I feel you now."

So they danced, and Blue whispered, "Pretend we're boy friends. We do it every day and we're crazy about each other."

They danced, Blue tracing lines along Walt's back. "I play this record on special occasions," he said. "I knew you were special the second I hit eyes with you, watchin' you look all around and pretend you weren't lookin' at all. You saw me, certainly. Did you think I was special, too?"

"I was very struck by you, Blue."

"I like the way you talk."

Well, they danced, and when the cut ended, Blue took Walt back to bed, working himself up, then softly guiding Walt down to him by the back of the neck, saying, "Get sweet on my piece, now."

"It's not safe, Blue."

"A minute or so won't hurt. Do it to the music."

Poor Walt: so eager to reach Gay City, so well equipped with maps and charts—yet so unhappy when he reads them.

.   .   .

"Oh, so *licious*," Evan breathes out. "Such lovely fuck with you." Kissing
Alice as she thrusts her hand into her, curing the tingles, working around
the soft edges of Alice's cunt with a steady pull. Alice is helpless, damp,
wild, and rising for more, torn out of herself. "Oh, *sin!*" she cries; and
Evan gloats at her power over her lover. Licking the love cream off her
fingers, leaning over Alice, holding her down, strong with her, kissing her,
loving her, and knowing Alice fears and needs her—which is all Evan
wants on earth—Evan whispers, "I want to fuck you in hell."

Blue is back inside Walt now, probing to the utmost, and Walt is weeping.
Nothing works for him, and nothing, he feels, ever will. If this incredible
big blond Blue cannot draw him to a climax, who ever can?

"You crying now?"

"No," Walt quietly wailed.

"Shit," said Blue, pulling out again. "Tell me what's wrong."

"*I'm* wrong, Blue."

"Let's rest a spell." Cuddling the boy, heartening him. Blue reads and
wants to soothe his worry. "Wonder what we'll do with a boy like you."

"Everybody gets sore at me when I go home with them, which isn't all
too often, for that very reason. I liked dancing with you, though."

"Well, I say *one* of us has to shoot. Get your legs up for that ol' Blue
kiss-an'-come."

Blue was very close to creaming by now, and, quickly burrowing into
Walt, he started to move his ass off, sailing to the moon.

"Yeah, now, that's for me," says Blue. "That's my ass, baby."

Blue went on in that vein, pounding and sighing and chanting, head
high and eyes bright; and Walt was very taken. "Oh, Blue," he said.

"Got to *go* with it. Hear me, now."

"Blue . . ."

"Now we're gettin' there."

"Oh, golly, Blue, I'm—"

"Sure, it's almost—"

"Wait, Blue!"

"Fixin' to come, boy! Here goes Blue!"

"*Yikes!*"

Walt's body shook as he exploded, Blue joining him a second or so
after, heads together, arms entwined.

"Blue!"

"Oh . . . oh, honey kid . . . you're . . ."

"No . . ." Panting. "Blue on top of me . . ."

"So damn right like that."

"I . . . Blue, I *came*. . . ."

"Yeah . . ."

Wet, hot, and emptied, the two held on to each other as Mantovani played through the gay San Francisco night. Up and down the town, women and men were out and wandering, calculating the possibilities. But here in a bedroom of the Kid's home, two men lay at peace, having achieved the dream.

I have to say something about this. It sometimes happens that two people of disparate backgrounds and hopes meet and fall almost instantly in love; it's happening now, for these two. If I had to rationalize it, I'd say that Walt desperately needs a man who will empower his sexuality, and that Blue is—unbeknownst to all—a softie who strongly responds to the emotionally wounded. But who can rationalize such needs? Love is Blue; that's all.

Upstairs, the Kid and Chris sat at his desk, talking over his script, *The Truth of Our Lives*. Chris was right: Setting the absurdly suave yet turbulent soap-opera plotting against the real life backstage was like cutting a cross section into American social life, sifting its hypocrisies for some sad, lovable truths.

"This is a gentle play," Chris told the Kid. "It wants to understand, even to forgive."

"I forgive no one."

"How you wish that were true."

Oh, Chris was right: The onstage scenes were all the more fun when they erupted in songs concocted specifically for these characters. "Every song should be a little off," Chris warned the Kid. "As if the character doesn't know why he or she is singing these lyrics, but the audience does."

"Whew, grammar," said the Kid. But Chris had good ideas. The Kid was especially amused by her determination to cast the show in a broad cultural mix, to explore a more comely authenticity than television's soaps ever did.

"Every role a different race!" Chris decreed, but half in jest. "Except for Auntie and the hunk, I don't want to see a white man on that stage."

"Speaking of the hunk," said the Kid, "how are you and David J. getting on?"

"Fervently."

"I approve. He's strong, sensible, and even tolerant. A woman's dream guy."

"Not a man's?"

"I like a little fire with my ice."

Chris nodded. "Like that strange blond boy you live with."

"He isn't strange. He just wears his cock ring a bit tight."

"What do you think of that black girl with the deep, deep voice for Suspicia?"

The Kid shrugged. "Good reading, I guess. And she's a hot visual. But can she be ruthless?"

"She can play it."

"She's gay, you know."

Chris paused. "I didn't, actually. Silly me."

Smiling, the Kid said, "You always know the gay men, but you miss the women. Why is that?"

"No idea."

"Figure it out, boss. The director of a soap-opera spoof should know gender presentation technique."

"Look, it's gays who are supposed to know who's gay on sight, not me."

"That's a myth, you know. It grew up back when everybody was closeted, and we had to sniff each other out. Like dogs meeting on the sidewalk. After you got the procedure down, you started to feel omnipotent if you pulled the mask off maybe four people a year. That's what we called it—'pulling the mask off.' But it was easy then, you know, because so many people *wanted* to be out. Nowadays, closeted gays usually fool everybody, at least in the short run. I sometimes wonder how tolerant we should be of that. Think of how useful it would be if the twenty percent or whatever it is all came out at once."

"Make sure you get J.'s shirt off somewhere in there, if possible without any pretext whatsoever. It's a soap tradition."

"Oh, it wouldn't be a Jerrett Troy production without skin. Do you think your Suspicia would go topless?"

"She seems game."

"Gamer than our hunk, I'll bet. Doesn't he have a problem with the beefcake stuff? Feels a bit penetrated?"

"Don't be wicked, Johnny. He'll do his job."

"Are you going to marry him?"

That stopped Chris for a while. "Golly, what a question."

"He's going to ask you." To Chris's scoffing look, the Kid offered, "I know men. I know love. I know yearning."

"Didn't you once tell me that never in your life have you allowed yourself to yearn for someone?"

"I didn't say 'allowed myself.' I said it never happened. And I wouldn't have it any other way. My idea of safe sex is the guy doesn't ask for your phone number."

Chris made a gesture: *See?*

"But I've observed," the Kid insisted. "The detective knows crime without committing it."

Smiling and vanquished, Chris asked, "Meanwhile, how's the score coming?"

"Heaven. That boy's a cool breeze in a New York August—eager, gifted, charming, and vulnerable. I'd stub my toe to avoid hurting him. So tell me—is the play *good*?"

"So far, Johnny, it's terrific."

"Fine," said David J. Henderson. "I could use a hit. No, Christine, *easy* strokes, and always up and down. Otherwise, the surface will look all crisscross when it dries."

They were painting David's apartment.

"It seems so odd to me that there's a system for painting walls," said Chris. "I mean, it's just painting. It's just walls."

"It's my home," said David, imperturbably.

"You're so strangely conventional in your worldview."

"No, Christine, *slow* brush, full paint . . . Right. Haste makes a mess. Conventional . . . maybe. If it means I prefer going home to my loved ones instead of trying to lead my entire life inside a theatre."

"You want kids," said Christine, resignedly. They'd been through this before.

"I want kids, Halloween candy, father-son athletic banquets . . ."

Chris made a retching noise. "Don't you realize how dreary those people are?"

"Chris, what do you think *I* am? My looks don't make me an exciting personality; you just think they do because . . . I don't know. It's glamorous or whatever." He had stopped painting, holding the brush, telling her something for the first time. "But I'm not glamorous. You see me as the captain of the something team in their legendary all-state season. Class President and Most Popular. I was never anything like that. I was . . . Well, just don't mistake the packaging for what's inside."

"I wouldn't, because in fact I was very close to two boys very much as you describe. Yet I saw how troubled they were."

"I was never troubled. I was boring." David started painting again. "You're probably misled because our sex is so good."

"Jesus, J., how could I be misled about something that basic? Someone at the theatre asked me what you were like in bed. I called you 'thorough.' It's the highest praise, believe me. I've known wilder men and more sensitive men. But I've never met anyone as skillful as you. You're some kind of fabuloso for sure."

"I guess I just love women." He's smiling.

"Maybe you'll always be out chasing skirt. Men who make love like that don't want to waste it, I've learned."

"No, I'll be home so much you'll be sick of me."

"I just hate that whole pregnancy thing," said Chris, with surprising force. "All the medical stuff—and I'm almost thirty-seven, which is risky. Though I guess we could adopt. . . ."

"I want my *own* kids. And thirty-seven's not so risky. We'd have to consult with a—you're splashing me with paint—uh, a doctor or two, obviously, and—"

Chris threw her brush down and cried, "*Damn* you for sounding so reasonable about it! Why aren't you some redneck who grabs me by the hair and bangs my head against the wall and calls me bitch?"

David stared at her, his chambray work shirt and oldest jeans daubed with paint, his face atilt, eyebrows up and wondering.

"Shit," said Chris, picking up her brush. "Why are you so *handsome?*"

The more they worked on the score for the play, the more the Kid respected Walt's talent and, more important, enjoyed Walt's company. The tales he told! Scandihoovia, Dexter, mean Uncle Gustav, Claude, Win, and Danny.

"You've had some life," said the Kid. "Did you ever do sex with those two uncles you live with, or whatever they are?"

"Not entirely," said Walt. "But you know what? They can be very parental at times."

"We're all parental about the people we love. I once saw a very young gay fellow fussing at his boy friend—some huge hunk old enough to be his father—because he had brought a chicken to eat during a showing of *Citizen Kane*."

Walt didn't grasp the nature of the offense. "Was it a live chicken?" he asked.

"No, but you are. Am I wrong, or do you have to beat them off with a plowshare?"

Walt blushed. "I don't have all that much time for romance. It can interfere with your career goals."

"Don't try to kid the all-knowing Green Goddess, lovey boy. I know your kind. When you fall—and you will—you'll fall heavy."

Walt said nothing, his expression even, his manner patient. Then he said, "I brought the music for Auntie MacAssar's big solo."

"Let's hear it."

"Get ready, it's got a wide range."

"So do I, Walt."

The Kid didn't own a piano, but he had rented one for him and Walt to work on, and Walt played the new music, singing the lines in his light baritone as the Kid looked over his shoulder, occasionally singing along.

"Play it again," the Kid ordered. A third time. Then he said, "Now me," and sang the number faultlessly as Walt expanded the accompaniment, flowing under the Kid's vocal with countermelodies and a touch of clashing harmonies.

"I love it," said the Kid at last.

"Golly, you really *can* sing!"

"Never underestimate a goddess. I was holding them spellbound at Thriller Jill's when I was barely old enough to shave."

"What's—"

"Wait here."

Returning from another room, the kid showed Walt the photograph of the young Johnny that he had kept all these years.

"Wow," said Walt. "You look so young and happy."

"I'm still happy," the Kid corrected, a bit crossly.

"What songs did they sing then? Show tunes? The rare stuff?"

"No, it wasn't . . . it wasn't all that gay then, the scene. We didn't have our music mapped out for us. I used to do some wicked parodies, though—pop tunes with fiddled-up lyrics just for us. Can you play 'Mr. Sandman'?"

"I don't know that one."

"A cappella, then."

And the Kid went into his lubricious version of the Chordettes' old hit, to Walt's delight. "Teach me that!" he begged.

They were still at it when Blue breezed in.

"You remember my housemate," the Kid began—but he stopped abruptly at the gladsome familiarity with which Blue and Walt greeted each other.

"Wondered when we'd cross paths some more," said Blue. "Didn't trade no phone numbers, sure, but a good mix like us tends to want to come together somehow or other, you know?"

Walt nodded solemnly.

"Well," said the Kid. "Well, well, well, well, well."

"You're morose and uncomplimentary just because I got the part," Alice told Evan over dinner, a Niçoise salad that the two had playfully—lovingly, really—collaborated on. They'd had the world on a yo-yo string till Alice broke her news.

"You're so smug about it," said Evan.

"I'm happy about it, and stop flicking anchovies into my plate."

"Not flicking, tossing. Like this, see?"

"I hate the way you argue. It's just word games. It settles nothing. Ha, *you're* the smug one."

"And suddenly *you're* Sarah Bernhardt? You think you're an actress? One role in some slimy—don't you get up from the table when I'm fighting with you!"

"I'm not fighting. You won, hooray for Evan."

"Damn you for a leech and a pansy! This is what I deserve for going with the silky-slim type!"

"What would suit you better?" asked Alice, washing her plate at the sink.

"A stone bitch, like me. And don't *dare,* don't you *dare* try to make peace by humoring me, Miss Muffett. I found you in the gutter and I can throw you back any day I choose."

"You found me," said Alice, going on to do the rest of the dishes and thus further infuriating Evan, "in the gourmet cheese boutique on Polk. I have never been in the gutter. My father is a Ph.D. in—"

"Fuck your Chink father and *stop doing the housework!*" A plate flew past Alice's head and smashed against the kitchen wall. *"There!"* cried Evan. "Wash that! And how about the salad bowl, you want to clean that, too?"

The salad bowl thudded against the sink, spilling food all over.

"I think I'll skip Monday-Night Wrestling," said Alice, going for her bag. When she turned, Evan was barring the door, a smile of victory over crossed arms. "You," she said, "are skipping nothing."

"Please let me pass."

Evan shook her head. "And don't tell me, for the hundredth time, that I'm fighting over nothing."

"On the contrary, you are very seriously threatened by my new job. You're afraid I'll break free of your stranglehold on me. There's another lesbian in the cast, a statuesque black woman. Perhaps I'll fall for her in a big way."

Roaring with fury, Evan grabbed for Alice, caught her hand on the strap of Alice's bag, lunged as Alice pulled the door open, and dove for Alice before she could reach the stairs.

"Let *go* of me!" Alice cried, knocking into Evan, breaking free, and dashing downstairs. Evan followed, shouting for joy, and she caught Alice again on the second-floor landing. This time they toppled, right onto Frank, who had been sitting by the banister, head down, in deep trouble.

"Evan, *stop*," Alice cried. "He's hurt!"

Evan had already stopped. "Frank?" she said.

All three of them were panting, Alice reaching for Frank but afraid to touch him in his distress. "What's wrong, Frank? Can you talk?"

Frank raised his head and pointed at his throat.

"What?" asked Alice. "Frank, *what?*"

The two women shared a look: What else could this be but . . . It?

Neville Ironword joined them, attracted by the noise. "All right," she began patiently, "the landlord's here."

"Frank's in trouble," said Evan.

"Frank?" said Neville, leaning down to him and taking his hand.

"I . . ." Frank began, gasping for breath. "I . . . can't . . . breathe."

"Evan, call an ambulance," Neville ordered. "Use our phone, it's quicker. Alice, what do we . . . Put him on his back or something?"

Alice said, "I'm worried and I don't know."

"Don't I have some authority," said Tom, "as your not only cousin but surrogate parent for the last ten years or so?"

"No one has authority over me," answered Walt, getting up from the table, "for I am a free-living gay man who will make his choices."

"Walt," Luke began.

"No."

"Can't you at least talk to us about it?"

"I'm not talking to anyone about who I get for a boy friend."

"Luke," said Tom. "Reason with him!"

Walt turned to Luke as Scarlett turned to Mammy. "You love me and my silly antics, so I always got away with everything. Why don't you look on this as another antic?"

"Walt," said Luke, "this guy is . . . just . . . not . . . good enough for you."

"You mean he isn't good enough for *you*. He's fine for me. Now, I've had a very tiring day of writing songs with Mr. Troy and having my ass reamed out by Blue, and I'm going to bed."

"You got a letter from Danny today," Luke went on, holding it aloft. Walt, who had left the kitchen, came charging back to claim it, but Luke backed up, holding it out of reach.

"Give it to me!"

"Not till we talk," said Luke, dodging around the table and handing the letter off to Tom.

"That is my sacred mail, and you have no right to play games with it!" Walt had ceased chasing the letter; he was still, he was mad, he was shouting. "You give me that *now*!"

Tom handed it over, shrugging at Luke. As Walt left, he muttered, "Don't you use Danny against me." Then he stopped at the doorway, turned, said, "The more you push, the less you get," and left.

"Well, he's tough, anyway," said Tom.

"It's that piece of trash," Luke offered, "hopping him up with sex. I always thought he was immune to it."

"He was," said Tom, "in Minnesota."

The odd side of it, however, was that Walt and Blue maintained a very touchy relationship. It looked solid to outsiders, as so many love affairs do in their first weeks, the gay honeymoon. Yet when the two were alone they fought when they weren't fucking, and sometimes when they were. For Walt was very into the Issues, and Blue couldn't have cared less. Then there was Blue's conventional good-ol'-boy racism, violently offensive to Walt's delicately awakening sense of tolerance. Worst of all was "Blue's Republican," as Walt thought of him—one of those blue-blooded mandarins whose partnership in the Corporation is not imperiled by his sexuality as long as he keeps it invisible. Every American city counts a subculture of these men with two lives, one that of the respectable courtier, and the other moated, not to be entered or even glimpsed except by the others of his kind. The more confident (or powerful) of these men are bachelors;

many others balance their Secret with a wife and children. But all must find some outlet for their sexuality, their true taste, the fools in rash visits to some park or men's room, the smart (and, if possible, wealthy) ones by hiring a companion.

This was the choice of Blue's Republican, Mason Crocker. Where they met, I do not know. They did not attend the same parties, and Mason Crocker was never to be seen in a gay bar. True, Blue ran an ad in the classified pages of *The Advocate,* under "Models and Masseurs." But Mason Crocker read the *Atlantic Monthly,* not *The Advocate.* I suspect that one of the more adventurous of Mason's inner circle had encountered Blue on a jaunt to the Castro, fell into conversation with him, and offered him money for sex. Feeling well served, the friend recommended Blue to Mason, and a meeting was arranged; or so I guess.

Certainly, Mason and Blue combined well. In due course, Mason's entire sex life comprised masturbation and visits from Blue; and Blue's entire livelihood was based upon Mason's velvet premiums—cash in an envelope lying on a table in the hall, to the right as you left the house.

Walt had no opinion about Blue's career in the sex industry, but Danny and, now, Walt's local friends were quick to point out the decadence in having any traffic with the Enemy, or with those who trafficked with them. Danny's letters were filled with outraged reports on the sayings and doings of Win, who had voted for Ronald Reagan even though Reagan had still not so much as mentioned the epidemic. "It isn't just that he pretends to be oblivious," Danny wrote once. "You can see that he's contributing to a climate of homophobia that encourages crimes against us. Every gay man struck down by a vicious straight with a baseball bat is Reagan's victim. And Win's, too."

Walt's political friends loved prodding Walt about this; they seemed to enjoy making him uneasy. Shreve said, "Everyone who isn't out is straight." Carson said, "Secret sex is counterrevolutionary." Spider said, "You can serve one master or ten masters, but not two."

Upstairs in his room, Walt put Danny's letter on his desk and tried to compose himself. He thought, I am shouting all over the place, so I must be unhappy. But love should make you carefree. Maybe I am not in love.

Creeping out to the stairwell, he caught a floating murmur of the voices of Tom and Luke going on about Blue. He *isn't* trash, Walt thought. Homophobes were the true trash of the world.

Back in his room, Walt opened Danny's letter. Guilty and angry is all I am now, he was thinking. I'm in the wrong mood to read this letter, he was thinking. Maybe I should wait till tomorrow. But you can't soothe bad news by stalling it: Claude had written to say that Danny had been diagnosed with AIDS, and Claude was really worried, because there hadn't been many cases around the town as yet, and the doctors were probably too inexperienced to treat it properly. Danny's doctor had said as much to him, in fact, as Claude quoted:

> We're still learning about this thing on a day-to-day basis, unfortunately. Sometimes the patients know more than we do.

Walt stopped reading. He lay back on his bed, holding the letter. He thought, Was there something I could have done to make this different? He went over his relationship with Danny, trying to find some moment when Walt could have interceded in Danny's life and saved him from this. He picked up the letter again and finished it:

> I'm doing all I can to cheer Danny up, but it is hard because he doesn't want to tell anyone yet, except he told his parents, and they are so worried they make Danny worried. He is crying all the time now, so maybe you should give him a cheer-up call.
>
> Love, Claude

Walt tore downstairs to the kitchen, waving the letter, showing Tom and Luke. "First Dexter and now Danny!" he cried. "This is what comes of being invisible and not having power as a voting bloc!"

Tom tried to put his arms around Walt, but Walt refused to be comforted. "What help are you?" he said.

"First," said Luke, "don't shout at us, and, second—"

"I *will* shout," Walt shouted. "People are dying, and I'm not to shout?"

"Well, you're shouting at the wrong people, young man," said Tom.

" 'Young man'?" Walt echoed. "Who are you today, Uncle Gustav?"

Well, they calmed Walt down and got him to call Danny. Walt was as light and helpful as he could be, but as soon as he hung up he ran up to his room, closed the door, and walked aimlessly around, weeping and wringing his hands. When Luke knocked on the door a bit later, Walt called out, "I'm a bad boy, so don't come in!" Luke came in, all the same.

The next day, Walt fussed and scowled all over the house, and he was very hard on Blue that night. The two had had many a spat before now but never a Major Fight, and for once Blue dished out more than he took, shoving Walt against the wall and telling him off just as straight as she goes. Hurt and furious, Walt tried to leave, but Blue held him down on the bed till he promised to behave. Then Blue apologized to Walt so lovingly that Walt wondered if he might be getting into some S & M thing because he so enjoyed the petting after the violence.

"I even bought you a present," said Blue, pulling out a gaily wrapped box.

"I hate it already," Walt groused. "I don't want presents when Danny is in trouble."

"But Danny's far away, and it's just us, now. Go on and open yer box."

"Okay, out of sheer scientific curiosity."

It was a sweater, vastly polytoned and overdesigned, with a tiny shawl around the back collar and fringelike threading overlaid upon the sleeves. It was so hopelessly ugly and Blue seemed so proud to be giving it that Walt was touched to the quick: Here, after all, was Blue's one vulnerability, his lack of class.

"Picked it out maself," said Blue, with a grin.

"But why? We never give each other presents."

"It's because I'm fond of you, and because I don't want us fightin'. And how about because . . . well, maybe because yer the only smart guy I ever been with who didn't talk to me like I'm too dumb to understand anythin'."

"I feel awful," Walt wailed. "Guilt is my passport!"

Blue chuckled. "Come on, youngster." He took Walt in his arms. "What *you* got to be guilty of?"

"Danny's sick, too, now," Walt explained, pulling back slightly. Why was everyone always grabbing him, as if a hug were a cure for major pain? "Everywhere you turn, your friends come down ill."

"So what makes you guilty?"

"Well, how come *I* don't?"

"You want to go visit Danny? I'll take you. Never seen the Midwest, anyways."

"I don't need to be taken. I'm not a helpless little kid, I just act like one. *Sometimes.* Besides, I can't leave, because of the show."

"After the show, then?"

"I don't know when that will be. I'm not just the composer, I'm the orchestra. Maybe Chris will let me take a few days off during the run. Or maybe it won't run."

"That'd be bad news, wouldn't it?"

"Well, sir, I guess it would."

Blue smiled. "Want to try on yer sweater and be a little nice to me?"

It was Walt, now, who hugged Blue, thinking that never in their thus far brief but intense relationship did the older man seem so goofy, unknowing, and secretly wonderful.

"I love you, Walt," said Blue. "I hope you know that."

"Well, he's smart enough not to bring that trash around here, anyway," said Tom, carrying mugs of coffee to the table.

"Tom," Chris said, "you sound a bit like a snob."

"He's very class-conscious," Luke agreed.

"It's not about class," said Tom. "It's about style. I know that kind of guy. Fancy-dan, no line of work, just sex and sleeping till what hour and wearing T-shirts to everything and that stupid redneck way of talking, which happens to drive me crazy."

"Walt *could* do better, actually," said Luke.

"What did you have in mind?" asked Chris.

"Well, how about someone like me," said Tom, "who worked his butt off building a business—which is more than can be said for you rising-above-it college types. Or, tell me, Luke, who pays the mortgage on the house while you're doing all that folderol with your catering?" Now to Chris: "And all you do is put on plays and have fun."

"Who runs the house chores?" Luke countered, mildly. "Who does the cooking with a serene professional touch?"

"Who crams your ass till even you stop begging for more?"

"Boys, boys," said Chris.

"For that matter, catering is a service industry," Luke went on, stirring milk and sugar into his coffee. "It's no different from construction." Now he slipped into his deep-voiced imitation of Tom. " 'And will you *please* stop banging that damn spoon around in that damn—' "

"All of this is beside the point," said Tom. "The point is Walt, because he's worrying me. Demonstrations and zaps and . . ." He looked at Luke. "Tell her."

Luke sort of grimaced, but he told her: "Walt got arrested. An AIDS march got out of hand."

"Good for him!"

"Chris!" said Tom. "That is *not* good!"

"You don't admire his commitment?"

"How do you think I feel when he lights into me, asking me how come

I pretended to be straight? Calls me a hypocrite, too. Didn't I practically raise him?"

"Maybe Blue will soften that side of him," said wise Chris. "Blue is not too keen on the issues, I'd say."

"You know him?" asked Luke.

"I meet him now and again at Johnny's. He's sort of a nonfunctioning houseboy there—has been, for as long as anyone remembers. Those two go way back."

"Well, that doesn't surprise me, anyway," said Tom. "That piece of trash has been fucking since he was eight."

"Tom's met Blue," said Luke. "Walt brought him back after a dance. I was working the Donnell party that night, so I missed it all, and of course Tom had nothing to say about it."

"What is there to say? He's trash and that's it."

Luke shrugged: It takes all kinds, including not only Blue but Tom.

Chris said, "Is there another slice of that cake with the . . . Oh, chivalry!"—because both men had jumped up to serve her. "Thank you." To Luke: "Did you really just *make* this?"

"Flour, eggs, almonds, cherries," said Luke.

Chris tasted, gave a little thrill, threw up her head, and cried, *"Incroyable!"*

"I don't think it's so terrible that Walt is political," said Luke.

"He's too relentless, though," Tom replied.

"Maybe we should all watch our politics nowadays. Did anyone see the TV program a few weeks ago about the White Aryans? On that afternoon show that follows—"

"Some of us are at work at that time."

"Tom, will you give it a break?"

Tom looked at Chris, and she shrugged a good, solid, midwestern he's-right-so-you-shut-up shrug; and Tom did.

"I mean," Luke went on, "these guys are really Nazis. They show you what hatred looks like. They don't disdain anyone different from them, they want to *kill* anyone different from them. They're so on fire that a fight broke out right on the show, real-life stuff. You should have seen the twisted faces. All right, they're a lunatic fringe, but they're killers. Killers, Tom."

"Well, golly, they're not my fault, are they?"

"They're not your target, either." To Chris: "He actually calls himself a Republican."

Appalled, Chris turned to fix Tom with perhaps the one gaze in all the world that he couldn't face down.

"It's a matter of taxes," said Tom. "Nothing else."

"It's a matter of women's rights," Chris replied. "And fighting racism. And preventing gay men from being beaten to death in the street for sport. It most surely is not a matter of taxes!"

"Whose side are you on, Tom?" Luke added.

"Damn the both of you!" Tom shouted.

There was a silence; Luke broke it. "He and I made it a rule a long time ago," he told Chris, "never to talk politics."

"Never to challenge your preconceptions?" Chris replied—to Tom, mainly. "Never to consider your obligations to others?"

Tom was silent, watching her.

"The problem with you middle-class gay guys is, you pass for white. You move to the metropolitan gay centers, and you're more or less closeted—'private,' you'd call it—when you step outside the ghetto. You assimilate yourselves, and suddenly you've got property to protect and money invested. I ask you, what impelled the militants of the civil rights movement of the sixties? You know what impelled them? They had nothing to lose. That's how they could brave the police dogs and the fire hoses. Even torture and death. Could you have done that?"

"You're as bad as Walt," Tom grumped.

"Walt is *good*."

"White Aryans," said Luke. "Such an insistent name."

Chris was still staring at Tom. He tried a smile and asked, "What's new on the David J. Henderson front?"

Chris shrugged: Nothing's new, he still appreciates me for the wrong reasons.

"Well," said Tom, "are you in love with him?"

"I might be."

"Light love, very-truth love, or die-without-benefit-of-the-touch-of-him love?" asked Luke.

"Hard to say."

"Light love, you feel like the heroine of a musical comedy. Very-truth, you turn pastel colors at the mention of his name but do not evaporate if he rejects you."

"And what's the last one?"

"You evaporate."

"I'm going to establish a new category, where you aren't mad for any of the candidates, but you have to vote for *somebody*. Meanwhile, what kind of love are you two in?"

Tom looked over at Luke.

"It's tricky to classify," Luke returned, "when you've been in it all your life."

Chris nodded. "It's funny to think of us lasting all this while together. Do you . . . do ever think back to the old days?"

"Sometimes," said Luke.

"Never," said Tom.

"I get very caught up in my work," said Chris. "During pre-production and rehearsal, there's only the play. It opens. And before the next one starts, there's a little space in there of vapid peace. J. likes me best then. It's the only time, he says, when I most truly get into the sex—because I'm not distracted by anything. He's wrong—because that's when I go back to our memories. I go back to that purity. That fantasy. That time of knowing that we could only go higher from here."

"That time," added Luke, "when we made our choices. We invented our liberty."

"That time when you both were so cruel to me," said Tom, "that I still could gladly kill you both."

After a moment, Chris asked Luke, "Is he like that in bed, too?," and Luke replied, "Even better."

I must intrude here to express a certain curiosity about how our once so dynamic Luke has, to quote Congreve, dwindled into a wife.

Yes, I say it. *Wife.* He runs the house, masterminds the food, turns the empathic ear upon Tom's occasional rants, gives more forgiveness than he gets, and seems content to let all the great events in his life be Tom's events.

Let's let Luke himself tell how he came to be so humbled:

I majored in English Lit at Berkeley, partly because I didn't know *what* to major in, but also to please my parents, because they were such big readers. I tell you, a book a day. *Each.* So it shouldn't surprise that I do the same. Feet up, a bowl of warm-washed apples, and something to read. *Ragtime.* Oz books. That Gaddis novel that no one else got through; I'll get through it.

But you want to know how I ended up living in Tom's shadow. He's the master, you feel. He works; I cater. Listen. There are no wives in gay marriages. Anyway, Tom is very easy to get along with as long as the house runs itself; and I never wanted anything but this. What was I supposed to hope for, a political career? The law? I have no talents. Look, this is my life: I wake at whim, chore around a bit, chide the defiant Walt if he's handy, then stretch out in the backyard listening to Puccini. And so on. Wouldn't you like a schedule that easy? That's life as I see it.

Auntie MacAssar, with the aid of Maestro Fleshgobaldi, has dropped a libido enhancer into Suspicia Pushmore's cup at the tea party welcoming St. John Lord Ramsbottom to Riverrun. Luring the other guests out of the room on the pretext of wanting to display her lovely new set of doilies illustrating scenes from the life of Admiral Zumwalt, Auntie leaves Lord Ramsbottom alone with Suspicia. As the aphrodisiac takes hold, Suspicia helplessly begins loosening Lord Ramsbottom's tie, then fondling his crotch, and, at last, ferociously tearing his clothes off and falling upon him—just as Auntie leads the ladies of the Riverrun Tea and Tatting Sodality back into the room. Whereupon the humiliated Suspicia and the bewildered Lord Ramsbottom abandon the stage to the first-act finale, "A Beautiful Day in the Neighborhood," as Auntie—once again the invincible queen of all her survey—directs a chorus in praise of suburban life.

"No," Chris called up from the fifth row. "No, hold the music. That button business isn't working. Fay!" The actress playing Suspicia came out from the wings, followed by the Lord Ramsbottom, David J. "The button stuff is too aggressive," Chris went on. "She's doing this *in spite of herself.* It's what she wants to do but doesn't dare to do."

"It's his buttons," Fay explained. "They're, like, you can't get them open easily."

"The laundry went wild with the starch again," said David.

"Neville?" asked Chris, turning to her costume designer.

"I'll resew them. Give you more maneuvering room."

"I didn't like the crotch stuff, either," said Chris, returning to Fay.

"Too heavy?"

"Too shy."

Fay laughed. "I guess I don't have much experience with men's crotches."

"The three of us, private workout, later," said Chris, moving aside to get a better view of the stage. "And, townspeople, all the blocking is wrong for the start of the number. Watch your marks. Alice, aren't you supposed to be to the right of the . . . Yes. Robert, you're totally off. You should be . . . Yes, but more . . . Okay, don't move. Donald, didn't I set you up stage right of Alice? Well, get there, please. I love the way the Caucasians bunch up together, because I positively remember a *highly integrated blocking*. Who's directing, me or the White Aryans?"

Blue was in the house, sitting in the third row, vacantly taking it in. At the break, he talked with Walt for a bit, each of them occasionally eyeing the Kid as they spoke. They're going to ask if Walt can move into my house, the Kid thought, watching them. Blue's trying to gauge my mood. They've probably been planning this for days, the little sneaks.

So Blue and Walt came over, and, indeed, asked if Walt could move into Blue's room.

"Hmm, arresting proposition," said the Kid, treading water. "I mean, maybe, but what if?"

"Those cousins of his are given' him a hard time," said Blue. "They don't like me much."

"This has happened awfully fast, hasn't it?"

"When it's right, you know it's right," said Walt.

"Look, short stuff," the Kid told him, "when it's right, *I'll tell you it's right*."

"My friend Shreve says it's the correct politics for gay men to live together and build lives. And my friend Carson says that makes them holy. And my friend Spider says a nation of gay lovers will shock the world."

"Your friend *Spider*?" said the Kid.

"Blue and I are buddies now."

I don't want this enchanting boy in the house, the Kid was thinking. But what objection could he, fairly, offer?

"You could see it like this," said Blue. "You've got money, and folks've heard a you, and you know everybody in town. You *have* what you want from life. So what would interfere with this boy comin' into yer house?"

"What are you saying, that I have no future?"

"I'm sayin' that you could be generous."

"All right," the Kid told Blue, as Walt took his lover's hand in excitement. "Make sure he knows the rules about saving water."

Blue pulled Walt's hand up and kissed it. You fine young fellows; how you tease. This is what love looks like—I see it now. Blue fucks me, I say, Nice, stud. Blue fucks Walt, and it's You are my dream of life, forever that I live.

But that is so *ridiculous*. To think that the emergence of one person in your life will change anything. Nobody changes anybody's life. We *are* what we *are*.

After the rehearsal, Alice and Fay walked out of the theatre together and, quite naturally—that is, with no one's saying, Are we doing this?, but the two doing this all the same—walked west down Sacramento.

"It's changey, being black and lesbian in such a mixed cast," said Fay.

"Chris Lundquist is famous for interracial casting," said Alice.

"It's not like real television, though, is it? Chris says soap opera is the fundamental American art form—I say it's video games."

Alice always speaks quietly. "They're from Japan."

"Yeah. . . . Oh, is that what you are? Japanese?"

"Chinese."

"Sorry."

"Never fear," said Alice. "It's a dread war between the two races, but nobody else is supposed to know or care about it."

They walked in silence for a while.

"How about a coffee stop?" Fay asked, at length. "We can do that actory thing and complain about the director."

"I adore her."

"Or the other actors."

"Oh yes, let's."

They went to Kaffee Klatsch, a trendy, "fern bar" version of a coffee-house, which Alice haunted for the cucumber sandwiches and which Evan refused to set foot in. It was handy—just two blocks from the house—and wonderfully deserted in the afternoons, when Alice liked to have a bite, and think, and ready herself for Evan's Return.

"Actually," said Alice, after they had ordered, "I find it interesting, the way Chris manages the natural tension of rehearsals. Most directors I've worked with—in college, mainly—kept trying to bottle it up, so it would build and explode. Chris tolerates it. Because you can't bottle it up. It's *there* and you *can't*."

"She's quirky," Fay agreed.

"Well, this is what I notice: As soon as the tension builds, she'll give it a shove and release it. Things never get out of hand, you see? With other directors, I've seen some terrifying . . ."

" 'Geschrei,' they call it."

"I have enough geschrei at home. The woman I live with. A real stone bull."

"Tell me everything."

Alice laughed. "No, it sounds too grim and decadent when you talk about it. And I hate the fighting. But there's something oddly appealing in the lovemaking. We go in for rough style, I have to say. I enjoy being . . ."

"Dominated?"

"More than that. Evan does the heavy things to me in such a loving way, it's a kind of higher bliss." Alice smiled. "That must sound terribly nuts to you."

"I've always wondered what it would be like with a stone bitch. I keep hearing the la-di-da about women tops, but all I've known is the push-me-pull-you type. You know, you do this to me, I'll do this to you. A round of kissing. Then we'll both do that . . ."

"I'm sure it's heaven with the right woman," said Alice. The food had arrived, but the two went right on, oblivious of the waitress. "Still, so many times before Evan, I found myself merely acting aroused out of politeness."

"Mmm, like marriage."

"With Evan, I never act. It's cards straight up on the table."

"I don't mind acting," said Fay. "I've been acting all my life."

Alice nodded. "Playing hetero."

"Not just that. In high school, I acted white. I was Barbie. I quit the Pep Squad because they developed a cheer based on a ghetto street rhyme." Fay shook her head ruefully. "I may still have a little white piece in me somewhere."

"That's why you're such a wonderful Suspicia. The village bitch scheming to jeer her rival and own the town—that's the whitest part going."

A moment, then: "You think I'm wonderful, *really?*"

"Everybody does. Oh, it's you versus Johnny, day after day, and we can see him hating you for being so sharp, and loving you because it's for the good of his play."

"He's an odd boy," said Fay. "Sometimes it's like he's seen it all and sometimes he could have just stepped off the bus from Yuba City."

"He's one of those amazing people who were out when they were twelve or something. Can you imagine, in those days?"

"Someone's staring at you on the street."

Alice turned to look through the plate-glass window at Evan, standing on the sidewalk, expressionless.

"That's Evan," said Alice calmly. "She'll probably kill me for this."

"Invite her in."

But Evan had proceeded on her way. She preferred to fight at home.

In the house on Hyde Street, Lonnie Ironword was sitting in front of Evan's door, rock cackling out of his headphones. He smiled and rose as Evan came upstairs. "Can I talk to you?" he asked.

"Exhausted. But all right, especially if it's parents-bashing."

"Not to bash them exactly," said Lonnie, pushing the headphones down to his neck. "But they're really in my crack about Dana. My girl friend?"

Dropping the mail onto a table and pulling off her jacket, Evan let out a snort. "Mr. and Mrs. Permissive?"

"Oh, it's all what-do-you-call-it . . . nuances. And, like, they suddenly go so radically *silent* on you. Look at us, we're doing the brood about you. Your future, your potential. I mean, give me a, will they please?"

"So Neville and Philip are parents after all," said Evan, enjoying the idea.

"It's Dana's family. Like, she lives in Daly City and her brother's in jail."

"For what?"

"Does it make a difference?"

"Don't get New Age on me. Could have been a drug bust. Could have been rape. You think that doesn't make a difference?"

"And they're always signaling how proud they are of me. Because I turned out clean. It's like they're daring me to get into trouble."

"So you're going to? *Smart.*"

"It's just . . . Dana's like an adventure. She's so *unlike,* you know? She puts danger into my life."

"She's lez," Evan decided.

Lonnie smirked. "No, I couldn't say that."

"You *animal!*" Evan cried, in fake disgust. Seriously, then: "You're doing it safe, right?"

Lonnie made a vague gesture.

"*Reckless.* Don't you straight trash ever listen to anything?"

"Well, I'll, like, mosey along . . ."

"You just hold your horses," said Evan, advancing on Lonnie. "Are you boning without protection?"

"No."

"Yes, you are!"

"That's so quacked, Evan! I'm not even in love with her, I just—"

"What's *that* got to do with it? *Ignorant!*"

The door opened, and Alice walked in. "Hello, Lonnie," she said, looking pretty pleased.

Evan grabbed Lonnie by the shoulders, saying, "Listen up, kitten. You get smart and wear a sock or you'll be killing women and then I won't like you. At *all*. Got it?"

Lonnie nodded.

"Now, you skedaddle, because Alice and I are going to have a fight and then I'm going to throw her la-di-da faggot ass out of my apartment."

Lonnie, Evan's hands still heavy upon him, looked at Alice.

"She's always throwing me out," said Alice, heading for the bathroom. "My parents joke about it. As in, Could Evan possibly throw you out next weekend, so you can come dog-sit while we're in Lake Placid?"

Lonnie looked at Evan.

"On your way," she told him.

"All right, I'll be safe with Dana," said Lonnie, moving to the door. "But how do I outzip my parents?"

"Bring Dana home for dinner, in her Daly City finery. Keep bringing her home, after a date or something. *Expose* them to Dana—and of course you keep bringing up her brother." Evan opened the door. "Then, suddenly, you stop. No Dana—program's over. They'll be so relieved, they'll give you all the room you need."

"Sounds good," said Lonnie, with a grin.

"Trust Uncle Evan."

Lonnie went out and Alice returned.

"Pack," said Evan.

"I was hoping this time I could just slip out with an overnight and then slip back after."

"This time, no after."

Alice sat, elegantly, as always, so catlike that one felt soothed to see it. Oh, what art.

"Well," said Alice. "Well, yes, I will. If I have to."

"You have to."

Alice went into the bedroom, into drawers there, selecting, refolding, all so orderly. Evan waited a bit—good timing is the difference between a hot movie-type scene and a mere scream session—then charged into the bedroom with "Who was that dyke in the restaurant?"

Alice didn't answer, so Evan grabbed her arm. They were eye to eye for a second or two, then Alice pulled away, observing, "That's good in sex, but when I'm being forced out it's supererogatory."

"Crypto-femme bitch," said Evan.

Alice continued packing. Oh, she's so patient. Evan stares at her. Evan's monumental.

"You don't want to love," says Alice. "You want to war."

"Was that my replacement? The black bitch?"

"She is my friend," as Alice holds up the white lace middy blouse that Evan gave her; Evan snatches it back.

"You venom," says Alice.

Evan slaps her, not *that* hard.

"What's her name?" Evan demands.

"Fay Cullenmore."

"Oh, way *down* upon the Swanee *River*," Evan annotates, in a Mae West manner. "Swear allegiance to the once and future me and you can stop packing."

"But I want to move out. Theatre. Women. The unknown."

Of course Evan smites Alice across the cheek once again, and Alice is glad.

She says, "I will learn what is true."

Across the hall, Larken was virtually screaming at Frank. "You *have* to see a doctor, Frank! You *have* to!"

Frank, sitting on the edge of the bed, rubbing his sore arms and shoulders, was half listening. Just now returned from the hospital—he had had P.C.P., the "AIDS pneumonia"—Frank felt strangely healthy. Yes, his joints were stiff and his body walked heavy, as if the whole construction were just about to sag. And he had lost some weight, especially around the lower half of his face. Without question, he had been altered, in the first stage of the decline that he had seen in many another man, gradually becoming a skeleton topped by screaming eyes in a death's-head.

Yet a stranger, never having known the other, the real Frank, would not have guessed a thing. "I could pass for alive," Frank said, taking a long look in the mirror after Larken had brought him home.

"Come on, you look fine," said Larken, with impressive conviction. "You'll fight this thing."

"No, Lark. I'll go down helpless in blood and shit, like everyone else. You looking forward to it? When I start pissing myself, and go barking mad in a pool of my own barf?"

"Jeez Louise, Frank! Don't—"

"Don't talk truth? You want me like the guys on the TV specials, saying, I'm going to lick this, you'll see! Then they show him six months later, a beanbag with purple sores all over. One order of death to go. Fuck, what an *end* to me, Lark! But, you know . . . maybe I deserve it."

Larken was too astonished—and angry—to reply.

"I'm not talking about God's revenge on gays, like the professional Christians," Frank went on, sitting there, feeling himself, looking evenly at Larken. "The other guys who have this, they're just unlucky. It's like cancer, or a car accident. But me . . . Why *should* I live? What have I ever done to deserve a miracle? And why should I prolong my torture? The quicker I go, the easier it'll be, right?"

That's when Larken started in about Frank's seeing a doctor regularly, and hanging on while science probes for a cure, or at least a treatment; and that was when Frank stopped listening. He hadn't been listening to much of anything on AIDS from the start—a few years before, when one of Frank's porn actors asked if he and his partner could use a condom during a fucking scene, Frank was more amused than anything else, and immediately figured out a sexy way the two could work the thing into the act. "I go back so far," Frank told them, "that I remember when men used these with women."

Soon enough, Frank was the first in the porn business to make condoms mandatory on the set. Yet, like many men, he didn't want to hear about AIDS, whether medically, socially, or politically. His attitude was, It's here and we're dying and nobody else cares, so it's all bad news: Why harp on it? Frank would shrug when men speculated on where the virus came from, scoff when someone suggested it might have been a government laboratory. Just two months ago, in March, the Mobilization Against AIDS group actually voted on how to deal with any attempt to round up those who were ill, and decided to fight it, if necessary, with armed resistance.

Now, there's an idea, Frank thought. Maybe I should make some statement, maybe take out one of those famous homophobic bigots. What could they do, put my corpse in jail?

"Frank, will you please listen?" Larken cried.

"Hey, you think I might have got this from blowing?"

"From . . . huh?"

"Yeah, I really got into that way back when, turned into a real cock eater. It's a great way to bring a guy off after you've screwed him." Frank smiled. "You know I like my partners satisfied."

"Frank, promise me you'll start seeing a—"

"Look—"

"No, *you* look, Frank, because this is . . . It's *stupid*, finally! All *right?*"

Frank just sat there, the magnificent warrior of the fight for sexual freedom now so wounded that—for the first time in their thirty-six-year association—Larken saw Frank as defenseless. Terrified, Larken moved to Frank, fell on his knees before him, and took his hands. "Please don't give up, Frank," Larken begged. "Please try to hang on. Remember . . . remember all those years ago, in L.A., when you came to my apartment? After the arrest? And I didn't want to speak to you? You pleaded with me, you said, 'I don't have anyone else to talk to about *who I am.*' Remember, Frank? Because if you merrily drop dead, I won't have anyone to talk to about who *I* am. And I don't mind sticking by you through the hard parts. Just don't die on me. Please?"

After a moment, Frank said, "I wish I could pull off one great act before I go. Something . . . redeeming."

"I know a good doctor. He's gay himself, and he really keeps up on the new treatments. Doctor Sorkin."

"So people would read about me and say, What a fine guy that was!"

"Frank, will you see Doctor Sorkin?"

"Doctor . . . Right. See a doctor. Okay."

"You *will?*"

"Sure."

Blue's Republican, Mason Crocker, decided it was time that he presented Blue to his circle, and he planned a party. It would be closeted—dressy and reserved, a banker's idea of fun, with a bartender and a pianist suavely trotting out the Gershwins and Rodgers and Hart and Cole Porter (not too much Porter) and perhaps a taste of Sondheim and *La Cage aux Folles*.

"I'm intrigued at the prospect of seeing you in a suit," Mason told Blue. "A dark pinstripe, I expect. You'll look like a half-tame tiger."

"Hope this doesn't throw you out, but I don't have a suit a any kind. Don't even own a tie."

Mason was relieved—much better to pick out the clothes himself than to trust Blue's taste. He took his protégé to Wilkes Bashford, where, Blue noticed, most of the information was conveyed through gesture and murmurs, Mason very slightly nodding or shaking his head as the salesman— old Mr. Bashford himself, Blue gathered—made his presentations. Mason bought Blue an entire outfit, from the shoes on up.

"Cuff links," said Blue later, in Mason's house, examining the pair, made of gold and shaped like watchworks. "This is getting serious."

"I want that," said Mason, as a servant cleared away the lunch things. Silence till they were alone again. Then: "I'm tired of using services and opening my door to strangers, trying to accommodate these . . . one-night fellows. I want a relationship, and I want it with you."

"Suits me, long as you don't mind that I got me a friend livin' in that I feel real tender about."

"Yes, of course. Jerrett Troy, the satiric entertainer. But you've been with him for years now. Hasn't the erotic aspect of your alliance . . . well, cooled down?"

"I don't mean Johnny. I got a new friend, special-close."

"More coffee?"

"Thank you kindly."

Refilling Blue's cup, Mason said, "I'm not one of those . . . sponsors? . . . who behaves like a boss. In truth, I prefer that we live apart and keep our schedules flexible. My feeling is that you are a very giving kind of chap, with room for more than one . . . what was that, 'special-close'? . . . man in your life. Am I right?"

"Never heard anyone describe me just like so," said Blue, with that slow smile. He can't help it; he's a natural man.

"May I ask how old you are?"

"Thirty-three and a bit."

Mason nodded. "I presume . . . well, I hope . . . that you've gotten all that youthful running around out of your system."

"Never ran around that much. I always hooked up with someone. Like Johnny, and now my boy Walt."

"Very, very good," said Mason. He put his hand on top of Blue's. "I think this is going to work out quite well for all of us."

Across town, in the Kid's house, he and Walt were playing over a song they had just written, a torch number for Suspicia Pushmore. Though she's the villain of the piece, they decided to empathize with her: At the next-to-closing spot, when the audience expected an eleven-o'clock song from the Kid, the spotlight would lock on the also-ran, singing "Collecting Friends":

Rememb'ring men can get awfully bleak.
You try to hold on,

Keep the dike-burstings mended—
But if ten were splendid
Can one be unique?

The Kid was fiercely proud of his lyrics and delighted with Walt's jazzily loitering melody. "I can hear Libby Holman!" the Kid declared. The pair were so stoned on success that they ran the piece over and over, the Kid singing to Walt's accompaniment, and, at the last repetition, they fell into each other's arms.

Startled by how good Walt felt, the Kid broke the embrace immediately, asking, "How do you like living with Blue?"

"Oh, he's so nice to me. And thank you for letting me move in here."

The Kid waved this away. "It makes our work easier. And I love company. It's so cute watching you wrestling every morning with Miss Coffee."

"That machine hates me, I know."

Now the Kid is smiling at Walt, fresh out of things to say, staring at the boy's eyes to keep from being seen looking at the rest of him in a hungry manner; and there is this pause.

"I need a shower," says Walt, and off he goes.

The Kid, who has never glimpsed Walt undressed, and is dying to, retires to his bedroom, seeks out some conversation piece—yes! the Davy Crockett bubble-gum trading cards that he collected in the 1950s, the second, green-backed series. Walt will be amused. Craftily timing his reappearance, the Kid stalks Walt in Blue's room just as Walt, having toweled off, stands nude and open.

"Oh, sorry," the Kid smiles, as Walt anchors the towel around his waist. "I thought you'd be agreeably amazed by the innocent pursuits of postwar youth." The Kid babbles on, and Walt is dutifully impressed; but it is all the Kid can do to keep his hands to himself, and soon enough he flees the room with his Davy Crockett cards thinking, *Fuck,* that boy is cute all over.

Luke said, "He's twenty-nine years old, Tom. We can't tell him what to do any—"

"We never told him what to do. We gave him all the choices in the world."

"Which proves that kids outfox you whether you're strict or easygoing. They just have their ways."

"I resent us having to get up a fancy meal to bribe him home for—"

"Tom, *I* cooked it, first off, and what you resent is playing host to Blue."

"Well, I was right about *him,* anyway. What kind of man calls himself a color?"

Luke, checking the oven, said, "If you push Blue away, you'll push Walt away. Welcome Blue and you welcome Walt."

"What did you make? Is it his favorite?"

"It's stuffed cabbage and bow ties, which is one of his eight hundred favorites. He changed them by the month, if you were listening."

"Golly, it's like we raised a kid."

"Besides," said Luke, "we've got a bonus on our side." He pointed to an envelope lying on the sideboard. "He got a letter from Danny today."

Dear Walt:

Danny wouldn't let me come with him to the hospital, he thinks I'm too *sensitive!* Ha, I'm much tougher than Danny. Anyway, I've been getting reports from his friends. Thank heaven for them, they really cheer him up, though it looks eerie with everyone but Danny wearing mouth masks. The nurses are mostly okay, except a few of them who treat Danny as if he was in prison for some terrible crime. He can't complain about them or even ask them to be more polite, though, because one of the other patients said then they don't come to see what's wrong if you buzz them at night. Even if the bed is wet and you're shivering.

But at least Danny has his visitors, and they bring strawberries and things. I guess he always knew that the main thing is to have fine friends, but times like this really make you know it.

The rest of the letter meandered into local gossip, as always, and there was not a word about Danny's condition, or what ailment had brought him to the hospital in the first place. Walt felt frustrated, especially at the closing paragraph:

I said maybe you should come out and see Danny, he likes you best of all. But Danny said he doesn't want you to see him like this. He was very fierce when he said it, so I know he means business.

Love, Claude

Luke had expected the letter to thrill Walt; instead, he spent the dinner now distracted, now morose, leaning his head to the side, ear to shoulder, taking little interest in anything. So the dinner became a trio, Luke and Tom entertaining Blue; and that was strained as baby's prunes.

"Bad news from Danny, it seems," said Luke, closing the door as Walt and Blue departed.

"Tell me, are we going to have to go through this regularly? Because I can't take another minute of that Pride of the Ozarks noise he makes. Guy sounds like a fucking folk song or something."

" 'The Ballad of Whitey Blue,' " Luke imagined, rendering it while he mimed the plucking of a banjo:

Goin' up by Jonesville,
Mountains mighty steep.
Wavin' at the purty belles,
Screwin' all the sheep.

Tom barked out a laugh and Luke put a hand on his shoulder, saying, "Walt is doing a phase. A year from now, you'll say 'blue' and all he'll think is 'sky.' Trust me."

Blue can be so dumb sometimes! Mason invites him to an intimate dinner, "so you can break in your new suit." It's a table for four, with two of Mason's oldest friends (both Stanford '66, like Mason)—and can't Blue see through this charade? Break in his suit? Oh, please. Isn't this a cautionary run-through for our Blue, a last-minute cram session in table manners, small talk, and how not to be too much larger than life?

Blue catches none of this. He thinks the event is just more of Mason, more relationship, a surer grounding in what is to be the source of Blue's revenue. He cannot hustle forever. He has heard of men like himself hooking up with men like Mason on such lucrative terms that they are more or less fixed for life, so this matters a lot to Blue. It has to work.

The evening goes well. Blue drinks Johnnie Walker Black with the other three—he's had scotch before—and evades mishap by ignoring the high-tech hors d'oeuvres. Yet he doesn't realize that he is under suspicion, utterly missing the highly pointed way in which the two guests ask after Blue's opinion on a host of subjects. He cannot divine the intentions of Mason's friend Sutter Morgan, who, during a discussion of the potential candidates in the 1988 presidential election, and favoring Baker over Bush, announces, "Everyone can be replaced," with his inflection and eyebrow raised in Blue's direction.

Indeed, all three men appear to aim their considerations at Blue in this moment, as if to ask, Are you going to pan out as Mason's protégé, or will you fail the final cut?

What a relief to get home and out of the fancy duds to Walt and his piano playing!

"What do you want to hear?" asks Walt, as Blue settles on the couch.

Blue says, "I like everythin' you play me."

"No, you're supposed to be in the mood for a certain thing. Like, I'm so maxed out, nothing less than Chopin will do. Or, Shoot me some ragtime."

"Either a those."

"How about ragtime Chopin?"

"Sure, it's my favorite."

Walt pounds into the opening of the twelfth Etude, in C Minor, *Allegro con fuoco,* suddenly ragging it when the harmony goes into the tonic and the melody leaps in. After a bit, he breaks off and joins Blue on the couch.

"What's wrong?" Blue asks, shifting his weight to make room and take hold of the boy.

"I want to sit with you and think how happy I am. What was that dinner like?"

" 'S'okay."

"Does this guy have one of those old San Francisco mansions?"

"He does, certainly."

"Is it bigger than Tom and Luke's house?"

"A mite. 'S'more a matter a what's in it than how big."

"Statues? Marble? Mahogany built-ins? Old family retainers?"

"Guess so."

"What's this guy like? Is he cute?"

"Well, he's old-fashioned. Always dress-up. Makes these little bows, kinda. Handsome guy, good shape."

"What do you talk about?"

"He talks. I smile."

"You know what? You can be sure it's true love if you never run out of anything to say. Because lovers keep being interested in each other."

"My man Mason is not about love, now."

"I meant us."

Blue folds his arms behind his head, slowly nodding at the fascinated Walt. "Yeah, so you really like me, huh?"

"Yes, Blue."

. . .

"You're my first black woman," Alice told Fay.

"You're my first Asian," Fay replied, in the drolly lingering tongue of the South. "Wonder how you'll taste."

The women laugh as they undress. To Alice, it feels like mischief. To Fay, it feels dangerous, compelling but slippery. Alice is so relaxed that she unnerves you. How calmly, sweetly, she said, "I would love to do it with you." Fay is playing along with bravado, but she's nervous: about showing her body, about needing to be appreciated, about what happens to them after this one time.

Alice doesn't throw her clothes off. She finds a correct place for them, folds them, confident in her rosy-white beauty. She tells Fay, "I wish Evan could know about this. She'd think I'm cheating on her. She owns me, she thinks."

Fay, stepping out of her panties, says, "I wish you hadn't said that."

"I wonder why not."

Fay is immobile, uncomfortable in her own apartment. "It's just . . . Who wants to be an episode in the saga of Alice and Evan?"

Alice goes to her, laughing. "I couldn't mean it like that."

Fay says, "One, I think you could, and, two, am I supposed to compete with Evan?"

Alice tastes of Fay's nipples, left, then right, her head emphasizing the circular, closing-in-on-you motion, her eyes wide, rapt. Alice smiles at Fay.

Fay backs up a step or two. "No, I'm very unhappy about this," she announces.

"Maybe it's racial anxiety?"

"Maybe I don't get what you're up to!"

"Oh no, Fay, please," Alice tells her. "It was going so sweetly, too. I only want what you want."

Fay has retrieved her panties. She's thinking it over—no, she puts them on, and her hand touches her chin as she regards Alice. "I *wanted* to come a little closer," Fay says. "To you, I mean. But now it seems you want to make a point with me."

"No—"

"*Yes!*"

"I'm finished with Evan. Come now, didn't she throw me out of her life?"

"You're one of the kind who never says, The End. It's always—"

"Never, babe." Pulling at Fay now with a delicious touch, wheedling her with caresses and kisses. "It's now, with me, Fay. Please, Fay. Yes, Fay?"

Drawing Fay to the bed, waxing passionate to envelop her, but Fay retreats, says no, not that, which drives Alice wild. She explodes upon Fay's body, seeking her most tender parts to invade them, drive Fay out of her cool, or her fear, make her cry *yes!* "Heavenly quim," Alice murmurs, lapping away as Fay's legs, dangling on Alice's shoulders, stretch forth to assist. Fay is happy—Alice makes sure, asking, "Are you a happy girl, my Fay?" as she turns her over to finger-ass her. And now Fay is fearful again, wondering what Alice will find, what Alice will then know of her. Fay's fear makes Alice wetter than ever.

"You don't understand," Chris was telling David J. "Walt was this cannonballing little boy, all over the place, and we were in charge of him, because his parents were busy with golf and canasta. So now when he—"

"Christine, did you ever consider going lesbian?"

"One doesn't *go* lesbian any more than one goes Irish. Anyway, as I've told you a thousand times, I'm a gay man manqué. Right taste, wrong biology. I know what gay men know, so I wanted to . . . Do you really care about this?"

"Yes."

"I wanted to share their amazing romantic notions about sex. Like when they saw some great-looking guy and imagined how their life would change if only they could get close to him. I always knew about that and I wanted to be part of it. I did. I did, J." She smiled. "So now what?"

"Could a man be that amazing?"

"Gay men think so. Women . . . women want something else—to be held and assured and protected."

"I can do that," he said, and he's right.

"I grew up with two of the most beautiful boys who ever lived. Which did I love? I loved both. Yet neither of them could have assured me. Of what? Protected me? From what?"

"Christine, what are you saying?"

"Women love ideals of men, not men themselves. Gentle Father, Deep Brother, Dangerous Boy from Across the Tracks . . ."

"So what am I?"

Chris put her arms around him, leaning her head against his shoulder. "I think you're my father with abs and tolerance."

"Okay." David put down the freshly washed head of Boston lettuce he was about to pull apart for the salad and took Chris in his arms, squeezing her right up into him, and he got hard instantly. She sighed.

"So," he said, "are you mine or not?"

Frank had his good days, when he felt as if the whole blame thing had been wondrously siphoned out of him during the previous night and he had become whole again, unhaunted. This could last for four or five days. Then everything would start to break again. He would be visited by terrible headaches. His insides would heave out oceans of bloody shit, vomit back even chicken broth and unbuttered toast.

Larken, tending Frank during the bad days, checking with the doctor and watching the clock for the next pharmaceutical feeding, bore it all as a kid bears homework. But what did Frank hate more than being helpless?

Blue, trying to be sophisticated, pulled a line he had heard one of Mason's friends use, "Everyone can be replaced"—and Walt, thinking of Danny, blew up at him. So they had another fight, a hasty and very nearly perfunctory one, flaring up and dying down inside of a minute.

Blue said they'd better take some fresh air.

It was a beautiful day in June, on the chilly side on Russian Hill and hazy, gusty, in the Mission, but sunny, all jackets off, in Golden Gate Park, where Blue and Walt went for their walk.

After a long silence, Blue said, "You think you like me, I know, but you only like some a me. The parts you don't like you get angry at, so you whip away at me, and that hurts my heart. Now, I got to tell you, youngster, I can't feature goin' through that forever."

Walt, sullenly pulling at tree leaves, said nothing.

"You want me to be different, and care about the things you care about. That's not right. I don't ask you to shift around fer me. Why do I have to fer you? Who'm I hurtin' if I don't run along to your rallies and demonstrations? Okay, I'm not yer avant-garde type. Can't you respect me for what I am? Maybe you should say somethin' now."

Walt was murdering leaves.

"I try to look after you, give you your proper space, understand you . . ."

"You *don't* understand me," said Walt. "If you did, you would join me at the rallies. You would see how it all connects. Every gay who doesn't work for liberation is as bad as a thousand straights who oppose it."

"Walt, you don't even know a straight!" Blue laughed. "So how can you talk about them? I never been to Paris, now would I try to say what it's like?"

"I was raised by straights!"

"Paid 'em no mind, too, just like me. Didn't you?"

"Oh, is *that* irrelevant."

"Well, now, you got the whole world figured out. Okay. But could you do me one favor and get the fuck off my case? 'Cause, right now, you're sittin' so heavy on me, my hair's kissin' grass."

"I love you, Blue!" Walt replied, as if that explained—or forgave—anything.

"I know that." Blue was amiable, slow to judge. He leaped high to place a slam dunk into the curve of a tree branch. "But you got jealous gods afore me, and they eat away at your love. I swear, sometimes you get so stern with me, Walt, if you were anyone else I'd punch his head off."

The two stopped walking and looked at each other then, a long look. Blue said, "I'm not gettin' through, am I?"

"I hear what you say," Walt grudged out.

"What do you want, Walt? What could I grant to make you happy and stop pickin' on folks?"

"I want Danny free of AIDS."

"No, somethin' I can give you with my mortal powers. Somethin' possible."

"That's all I want on earth."

"Nothin' fer Walt?" Blue asked, starting to move again and drawing Walt along.

Walt thought for a long time as they walked along the paths in the sunlight of this perfect anyone-for-tennis? day. "Yes, there's something. I want to be the top man, for once. I want to be the guy who—No, don't say you can give me that. It's my own failing, and I admit it. I'm the flop man."

Blue put an arm around Walt. "I know some sly ways," Blue told him, "where we might arrange this. Course, I never wanted to be the bottom, but I could make an exception fer you."

Walt shook his head. "I know I can't do it. I don't have the power."

"You come on back with me, now."

We have to remember that Blue had seen quite a variety of sexual accommodations in his career. He'd been with royalty and the handicapped, randy intellectuals and impotent athletes, the savage, the exhausted, the true, and the experimenting. So Blue was well trained, not only in the artillery of lovemaking but in its many several field expedients, the emergency measures some of us need if we are to take the hill. Here is what Blue did: He stretched Walt out on his stomach and gave him a long and intricate massage. Then he blew Walt till the boy was throbbing hard. Then Blue lay down and had Walt grease him up, urging Walt to take his time and "let the feelin' run all through you." But Walt wailed that he had gone down.

"I *told* you I can't," he said.

Blue turned over. "That ain't no problem," he whispered, "so will you come on and trust me, now?" Holding Walt, kissing him, taking his time now. "I'm gonna show you," he says, getting Walt to lie down on his stomach again and beat off while rocking to and fro along the length of the bed, right hand stroking his member and left hand running over his skin. "This is the most successful way," Blue assures Walt. That it proves to be: Walt gets heavy hard, his cock bouncing around as he gets the condom on, and he stays hard even as he makes his first wondering entry into his boy friend.

"Blue!" Walt cries. "This is *me* now!"

Blue, on all fours, says, "Just go easy on me, youngster. It's my first time since I was a yearlin'."

"Wow," says Walt. It's his first time ever. He feels he should patter a bit, the way Blue can, the hot stuff; but he fears he will make himself a fool.

"Whoa, don't bang me, pardner," Blue suggests. "Take it sure and slow."

"Blue, I want to turn you over. I want to have you the way you have me."

Blue is afraid that Walt might drop his erection if he loses a single stroke, so he says, "Just stay with it, youngster."

Now Walt is silent, building his load; and Blue braces himself at the crescendo of Walt's panting; and Walt gasps and thrusts forth his essence with a rush of power so pure that if Blue had not already been the love of his life, he must become so now.

In fact, when the exhausted, ecstatic Walt tumbled off Blue onto his back, he said, "At last I'm a man." Perhaps some of you find these strange words. What defines a man? But Blue understood Walt—could not, perhaps, have articulated precisely what Walt meant by equating virility with the top man's sense of command, but did at any rate feel a kinship with

Walt's feelings without actually sharing them. And Walt, I assure you, was wildly grateful for Blue's understanding. This is what love is, boys and girls: succor.

These two had the habit of watching television after making love, on Blue's secondhand black-and-white. It was news time, and they were treated to a feature on the White Aryans, who had burned a cross on some black family's yard and had been shot at. No one was hurt, and no arrests had yet been made. On any other night, Blue might have let drop some less than compassionate remark to which Walt might have responded in a somewhat apocalyptic manner. But this night the feature passed in silence, for our couple were contemplating each other on a spiritual plane. They were too thoughtful to fight.

Next time.

Four days later, the Kid's play opened; and our Blue was so proud of Walt that he invited Mason Crocker to help fill out his complimentary pair. Blue kept opening his program to the credits to pleasure himself in reading "Music by Walt Uhlisson" and running his finger over the line of type as if sealing a little package with Walt inside; and he openly doted upon Walt's bio, which, because of a lack of professional credentials, concentrated on a list of Walt's "extended family,": including not only Tom and Luke (and one Blue Gadsden) but Danny and Claude. It ended, "With warmest thanks to Jerrett Troy for liking me."

Neville Ironword, as always Chris's designer, joined Philip in the audience after a last-minute backstage visit, ignoring the empty third seat where Lonnie should have been. Philip did not ignore it. "What do you bet he won't show up?" he said.

"All right, he can be a few minutes late."

"Late? Your son is boycotting your premiere."

Neville decided to become fascinated with the program. "They misspelled Aeschylus," she observed.

"That boy," said Philip, "has had much liberty and little responsibility."

"Another line like that and I'll have to rent you out to a sitcom."

It had been Chris's idea that Walt play the show not in the pit but at an elegant console at the side of the stage, in front of the curtain. As Walt serenely took his place at the keyboard, Blue told Mason, "That's my boy, right there."

"Handsome," said Mason. "Authoritative."

"He's from the Midwest," Blue helpfully added.

Luke and Tom shared the glow of two parents at the first-grade Christmas pageant, one of those "It was all worth it for this" looks that explains why happy families are all alike. Luke even grabbed Tom's arm, as one catches one's breath. See! Our miniature human has become a young man, sterling in a suit.

"Boy, I love this," Tom agreed.

The houselights dimmed as Chris slipped into a seat at the rear and Philip stared first at Lonnie's empty place and then at Neville.

"Okay, okay," she whispered, as the curtain rose:

TABITHA, JENNIFER, AND SUSPICIA (PUSHMORE) DISCOVERED.

TABITHA: But, Suspicia, what do *you* think of that *dangerous* eyeful, St. John Lord Ramsbottom, so comely yet so rugged, so ruthless yet debonair, who has come to our own town of Riverrun on mysterious business that has yet to be disclosed?

I most proudly admit that the audience was warm and the applause was thunderous, almost from that first line. They loved the jokes, the score, the Kid. The curtain fell on an ovation, and everybody crowded backstage to fawn and rave, a good sign. They don't crowd for a flop. There was Walt, beaming in his blue serge, and Philip Ironword, very possessive of and sticking close to his Neville, both hoping no one would ask where Lonnie was. There was Tom and Luke, comprehending for the first time that their boy had talent, and Blue with Mason Crocker, who was pleased to meet Walt but troubled to say that he found some of the material "on the lurid side." Walt took it calmly. Then came the cast party, at Chez Panisse—the Kid sprang for it—so most of the backstage had decamped by the time that Evan dropped in on Alice.

"I'd like to have you back with me," Evan told her, neither apologetic nor commanding. It's what she wants, that simple.

"There's Fay to consider," said Alice, mooching around with her makeup.

"Serious, huh? I don't blame you, she's stacked."

"Though I'd love to come back. It isn't fun, living with my parents. Fay's place is just—Oh, Fay, here's Evan, at last you two meet! Dear me"—as Fay pulls back a step—"it's daggers at Evan. So deserved, too."

Evan extends her hand to Fay. "Totally bummed out, but hanging in there."

Fay takes the hand, sorry to have seemed unsporting.

"The rivals at bay," Alice captions it.

"She wants to make us enemies," Evan tells Fay. "We won't let her."

"I have to say," Fay puts in, "that my loyalty is to Alice."

"Will she come home? To me, I mean?"

Evan and Fay look at Alice.

"I'll have to ponder, won't I?" as she shifts from costume to party clothes. Oh—Evan thinks—that unbearably white skin, so cool to my touch till I reach the C-thing, when Alice girl goes crazy. "It's so troublesome . . . decisions, decisions," Alice goes on, enjoying the scene, the two damsels who want her. "Grandmother Lee had a phrase, 'Pressing the orange peel against the lichee nut.' Yes, Fay's place *is* too small for two. And Evan has all those wonderful clothes I occasionally borrow."

Alice turned to Fay and said, "Evan's offer is so very tempting, you see."

Returning home, the Ironwords found a message from Lonnie on the machine: Sorry he missed Neville's opening night, but Dana's car broke down, so Lonnie was going to overnight it in Daly City and hitch back to town tomorrow.

Neville looked at Philip.

"I'm grounding him when he turns up," said Philip. "And don't tell me not to."

"He's already passive-aggressing because of our reaction to his girl friend. You'll only—"

"He's out of control."

"He has been a sharp, affectionate, and generous boy all his life, Philip. Don't we owe him something for that?"

"What do you suggest?"

"Patience."

Larken, Larken's friend Sam Weaver, Evan, and Neville took turns keeping Frank company, for now that he was a Person with AIDS something could go wrong at any moment and render him helpless. Frank bristled at the fuss, but he liked the company. He had never been much for reading or listening to music or watching television. He wasn't "an apartment type of guy," as he always put it. He had lived his life *outside,* on the job or cruising or playing ball, whatever. Now that he was often homebound, companions at least helped pass the time.

Evan was great at it. She didn't worry like Larken or talk nonstop sex like Sam. Evan would read the newspaper to Frank—with droll commentary—and thus open the world to him.

"It's funny," Frank told her. "I never bothered with that start-your-day-with-the-paper thing, or reading up on the news after work. I figured, if anything happened, someone would tell me about it. Or . . . I don't know, maybe it's because I never had a day job like everyone else. I was always on odd hours—bartending, porn, law enforcement . . ."

"Law enforcement?"

"I was a cop. A long, long time ago."

"Fascinated," said Evan, putting down the paper. "Where was this?"

"L.A."

"What were you doing there?"

"I'm from there."

"And here I took you for one of those transplanted New Yorkers who come here because they've had everybody back home."

Frank shook his head. "New York was an excursion on my way to here."

"You know where my excursion was? New Orleans."

Frank smiled. "Where's your accent?"

"Oh, I was raised in Iowa. Mason City. But I always had this dream of living in a wild place, you dig? Like some women do the fantasy of imagining a racy older woman seducing them so they can come out? For me that was a city. But the place is so male-dominated. Like the police spend all their time arresting prostitutes, not the real criminals. And every time you shut the lights to go to sleep, some jackass starts playing a trumpet."

Evan laughed quietly, with a wry thinking-back look that softened her eyes and made her better than hot. Pretty.

"You'll think this is some scream, but I had plans of becoming a real slut. Different date every night, sure. And I *tried.* But I kept getting interested in my partners. I couldn't wait to see them again, check them out to see if they were as beautiful as I remembered. That Alice, now, she's got me *sharing* her with some jill from that play. *Nerve* of her!"

Perhaps feeling that she was becoming too confidential, Evan picked up the paper, opened it—then put it down. "It's so quaint how surprising people can be, isn't it?" she asked. "*Quaint,* I say. I took Alice for a shy little princess, and here she's cracking a whip . . . and you're a cop."

"Ex-cop. But some of it stays with you, I guess. In the way you see the world."

"Like what?"

"Like . . . well, every cop knows there are three kinds of people. The first kind is decent and fair. The second kind is basically okay, but can go weak under temptation, or if they've been drinking, or in extreme circumstances. The third kind is born scum, and they will stay scum no matter how many programs you stick them in. Civilians think the really bad crooks must be crazy—guys who pour Drāno down someone's throat, or beat children to death. They're not crazy. They're vicious. Vicious isn't crazy. It's just another human quality, right? Some people are generous and some people are garbage. Just because someone will do something you wouldn't doesn't make him crazy. I wouldn't climb Mount McKinley. Does that make the team that summits it crazy?"

Evan was smiling.

"What?" asked Frank.

"You really are a cop," she said. "But aren't you scum in the eyes of the law? You're a pornographer."

Frank shrugged. "Some laws are wrong, that's all. You know, I have a few friends who are cops. I don't see them often, but—"

"Gay cops?"

Frank shook his head.

"Do they know you're gay?"

"I've said as much, but they probably don't believe it. Somewhere in every cop's head is a vision of a guy putting on plays or getting into a state over a flat tire. *That's* the gay, see? Everyone else is straight."

"Can they be that out of touch? In San Francisco?"

"Cops are the same in every city, and it's not out of touch. It's stripping the world to its essentials."

Checking her watch as she nosed around in the paper, Evan said, "Fifteen minutes to Sam. You've got a choice of Herb Caen, sports, or a shoot-out between cops and White Aryans in Walnut Creek."

"Skip the bad news, okay?"

Walt was playing through his piano solo version of Rimsky-Korsakov's *Scheherazade* when the Kid sauntered in, dressed as Bombasta.

"Yikes!" said Walt, cutting off.

"Hey, fullback," the Kid emitted. "You a top or a bottom?"

"I think you scared me."

In his own voice, the Kid said, "You see me in drag every night."

"Not like this. Auntie MacAssar is a caricature. But now you really look like a woman. It's so devilish!"

Bette Davis exhaling smoke: "Thatdt petta pe a complimendt!"

"Surely it is," Walt replied. "Drag is revolutionary."

Ava Gardner, contralto, oozing through the room: "Yet enticing."

"I know that it is."

Ingrid Bergman in *Casablanca*, approaching the piano, tragic yet visionary: "I begged Paul Henreid not to go to the Underground meeting tonight. But he's so reckless, so noble." Leaning against the piano: "Play it, Sam."

"Play what?"

"All right, let's have a drink," said the Kid, himself again, a man in a getup, leading Walt to the kitchen. "What luck, the bar's still open. What'll it be?"

"I want a tomato cocktail."

"What's in that?"

"Tomato juice, pepper, and sauce of horseradish."

"Look, kid, the Hansel and Gretel Hour's been and gone. We'll have Bloodies and get smashed."

The Kid made strong ones, and, back in the living room, he asked Walt to play "that great old music of Broadway."

Walt started in on "Try to Remember," as the Kid stood, silent and watching. Admiring. Innocent Walt just plays. Finishing the number, he says, "When I was young, I had this ambition to go to New York and accompany *The Fantasticks* right there in the off-Broadway theatre with the harp and percussion. And Brenda Olafson was going to play the girl. She may have done it, for all I can say. She was very talented."

" 'When I was young,' " the Kid muttered. Then: "You're neglecting your drink."

As Walt took a sip, the Kid asked, "How would you like to go to New York and play *my* show? After the run here, I'm going to hit the big town. If they want me."

"Will Blue come?"

"Blue hates New York. He'd as soon set foot in Tanganyika."

Walt sighed. "I know he has flaws, but he's terribly kind to me. I just wish he'd stop trying to bring me together with his Republican. Have you met him?"

"I stay out of that side of Blue's life. Drink, boychick."

"Blue even told me—ha!—that this major party the Republican gave was disgustingly dull. But then Blue wants me to have lunch with the Republican—*and* I have to go to his fancy annual New Year's Eve party."

"New Year's Eve with all the guys in suits, imagine."

Walt nodded. "What do they wear where *you* go on New Year's Eve?"

"Chest hair."

"Anyway, this is a . . ." Walt got the joke and giggled. "This party isn't gay. It's everyone the Republican knows, straights and their wives and such."

"That's not New Year's Eve, that's Arbor Day in Topeka. With ties. Well, let's freshen our drinks."

Following the Kid to the kitchen, Walt said, "Blue told me how important this connection is. The Republican. He says he's just about broke, and this could . . . You don't give him money?"

"I used to. But only men who fall defenselessly, hopelessly, and utterly in love with the Blues of the world do that forever. No, I just let him live here and eat out the fridge. Otherwise, he's on his own."

"I lent him fifty dollars yesterday."

"*Walt!* Don't you realize what a trap that is?"

"Not with Blue, because—"

"Oh, Walt, you *didn't!*"

"No, he's honest and he truly loves me. Besides, think of how I owe him. He made San Francisco the place where I came into my own true time."

"Here," handing Walt his glass. "And let me tell you about San Francisco and its Blue boys."

Back in the living room, next to Walt on the couch, the Kid said, "Historically, this was always a tolerant place, easier to be . . . oh, let's say *nonconformist* in. That included sexual nonconformists. And, over the years, it developed a unique attraction for gay servicemen who were posted here. Sailors on leave, that kind of thing. The key event was the end of World War Two, when much of the Pacific Fleet was demobilized here. Many men elected to stay in San Francisco, because they could be themselves as they couldn't back home. That's really when the place gets its identity as a gay town."

"Wow."

"But ho. We're not talking about artists, writers, composers, and all the rest of our gifted gay brethren. We're talking *uncomplicated.* Farmers, working-class guys, the unambitious. Plus, this was hardly the cultural capital. *That* was—and is—New York. And New York is where the ambitious gays went—Truman Capote, Tennessee Williams, Leonard Bernstein, Montgomery Clift, even James Dean, before Hollywood. And it's that assembly of creative genius that electrifies a place. And the money, the power. San Francisco is for men like Blue: free but unimportant—no, don't interrupt with some touchingly loyal defense of your boy friend.

Blue is worthless. He's a dreamboat, but he's a no-account. That's what my mother called it. *No-account,* like my father. Blue is San Francisco without the politics. A lotus-eater. This is where college graduates come to turn into janitors and caterers. New York is the place of ambition, creation, achievement."

"So how come you're here?"

"You want truth?"

"Probably not."

"I left New York because I wasn't big enough to handle the competition. Besides, I couldn't compromise my . . . my craft. There was no way for me to become major on my terms—and no way I was willing to do it on theirs. Oh, I have regrets. That's why I want to take the show to New York. It could be my last chance."

"Let's freshen our drinks," Walt suggested.

"My, you're starting to inhale them, aren't you?" In the kitchen, the Kid said, "I love a man who knows his liquor."

"It's so way out, hearing gay history from a man in a crazy spangled dress with a turban on his head."

"Someday I'll show you my closet," as the Kid handed Walt his drink. "In fact . . . why not now?"

They went upstairs. It was Walt's first visit to the Kid's suite—a sitting room, bath, and dressing area, besides the bedroom.

Walt was impressed. "All this space!" he said.

"Now *see!*" cried the Kid, as he threw open the doors of the dressing room.

"It's so big you could go in there and no one would know!" Walt observed. "What a place for hide-and-seek!"

"Yes, but admire the *clothes.* A tradition stands before us." The Kid grabbed Walt. "Stay—wouldst thou not like to try crossing over thyself?"

"What?"

"Aren't you tempted to try something on?"

"You mean . . . go *transvesto?*"

"Don't play shocked, if ever you so please. Anyway, it's just a prank. A mind fuck. We must live up to the revolution, hmm?"

"Yes. Spider says—"

"Spider's here, darling," the Kid's hands on Walt's waist, "and you're Fly. Let's decide. Maiden, whore, grande dame . . . oh, yes, the schoolgirl! Sneaking a bit of Tangee onto her lips in the girls' lavatory, I imagine. And I bet we're the same size, what fun!"

"I don't want to, Mr. Troy."

"*Johnny,* you bossy little toy—and doing what we don't want is what wonderful adventures are all about. Imagine sex with Blue doing only what you want. That's not how he works, is it? He's surprise."

"He's very gentle when I'm fearful."

"Dear one, when boys like you are fearful, cocks get hard, not gentle."

Well, the Kid prodded and teased and soothed the sozzled Walt till Walt said okay, he'd try a taste of drag. Then the Kid brought out a two-tone green finishing-school outfit and helped Walt strip.

"Right down to the skin, now," said the Kid, reaching for the matching panties and stockings. "Legs a little wider," he urged, stroking the befuddled boy's thighs, feeding him the costume piece by piece, positioning him before the mirror, holding him, feeling him. The Kid was ruthless; but the Kid was desperate, for he had fallen for Walt as Jericho fell for Joshua. How could this have happened?, one asks. The Kid, we know, has had his passing passions, but he has never suffered the tormenting penetration of emotional need. Sex and friendship were always within his control. Now *he* is controlled: by a desire for sex and friendship with Walt so potent, so stirring, that it is consuming him. He cannot sleep, cannot eat, wanders lonely as a clod. For the first time in his life, the Kid is defenselessly, hopelessly, and utterly in love.

Across town, in an old walk-up just off Mission Street, Blue was visiting a colleague, Eddie Swindon, celebrated under his nom de porn of Drew Stoker and, like Blue, one of Frank's most constant video stars in the late 1970s and early '80s. You remember him—the big, ardent cornfed boy with the chestnut hair and the green eyes who always came on smiling? Eddie hadn't made a film in . . . well, it could have been years by now; and whenever Blue asked about him he heard conflicting rumors. So one day—this day, while the Kid was making his move on Walt—Blue dropped in on Eddie.

One of the rumors was true: Eddie was ill. When he opened the door, he seemed so thin and desolate, so *robbed* of life, that Blue was startled, and his face, for a moment, must have reflected a certain horror.

Because Eddie nodded, as if confirming Blue's opinion. "That's what happens," Eddie said, inviting Blue in. "I guess someone told you."

"How . . . how long have you known?"

"It's been a year now, officially. But I knew long before I went to the doctor. I kept waking up at night so sweated that the bed was like a swimming pool. Headaches all the time. Yeah, I kept thinking, if I resist hard enough, it'll go away."

Eddie indicated the kitchen counter, a school of pill bottles.

"It didn't," Eddie concluded.

He had been transformed from a merry Viking into a gloomy wraith, and the conversation did not flow. Like many men no longer fighting the affliction but rather helplessly succumbing to it, Eddie could focus on nothing other than his death, yet refused to talk about it. Blue spoke of Walt, the Kid's play, movies, the Raiders—anything to redeem the misery of this visit. All the while, he kept thinking of the Eddie he had known, of his energy and power and sense of fun. He recalled the time the two of them performed a sixty-nine scene in some video and had gotten so aroused that after the shooting stopped they went down the hall to fuck in private.

Blue hadn't been taking strong notice of the epidemic, for while he knew of many men who had been swallowed up in it, he didn't really know them. They were people in passing, friends of friends, those one bumped into but never sought out. Even Frank, a good friend if not a close one, usually sounded chipper on the phone and could be seen strolling the town with that notorious take-no-prisoners blaze in his eyes. To Blue, plague was something one heard tell of, no more. Now, at last, in Eddie's room, Blue was made to feel sorrow for an impending personal loss, and had to conceive of his own mortality.

"They tell me guys still go out," Eddie said. "Guys who have it. Not as bad as me, because who wouldn't run from them in terror? is my guess. But the new ones. They go out and give it to others. They say, If I have it, you should have it. Or they say, There won't be a cure till everybody has it. But then, why don't they fuck Reagan? They say they can't use condoms because they don't want to offend their new boy friend. Or condoms interfere with the fuckness. Remember when Frank made us wear rubbers on the set, no matter what? Pete Verlaine made a film for that HardPack outfit in San Diego, and he says they won't let you wear one even if you want to. Did you get fucked a lot, Blue?"

Blue shook his head.

"Did you do a lot of blowing, all-the-way style?"

"Not so much."

Eddie nodded. "You're probably okay, then."

Blue went over to Eddie and put his arms around him.

"I won't cry," said Eddie, holding on real tight. "No matter what they do to me. I promised myself I wouldn't break down for them."

Blue wondered who "them" referred to.

Outside, on Mission Street, a million lights greeted Blue: a candlelit AIDS march. Blue was never a one for religious exercises, and that's what this looked like, a great Mass of flickering light weaving through the darkness. Still, Blue stood and watched the long line of men and women as they passed him, and after a while he walked along, not joining the parade but keeping pace with it, watching it. The calm, the people. Such serenity in the face of such humiliation and loss. The patience. It was what Blue's people down home called "prayerful." Blue thought back to his youth, when he would complain to his mother that he had prayed to God and gotten no answer.

"Well, sure, you was answered," Blue's mother relished saying. "God said no."

Blue came home just as the Kid was helping Walt, dressed as a schoolgirl, down the front stairs. The Kid saw Blue and froze, and drunken Walt mumbled something; Blue advanced with a set look on his face, took hold of Walt, and asked the Kid, "How could you do this to him?"

"We're just—"

"I thought you were made a better stuff," Blue added, helping Walt to their room.

"It's a joke!"

"It's a mean thing that you did to hurt him and hurt me. Someday a guy should set you in front of a mirror so you could see how stupid you look in those lady clothes."

"Oh, grow up! We've all got a streak of girl somewhere in us, my he-man Blue!"

Still supporting the fuddled Walt, Blue turned to the Kid and said, "He-men are dyin' all over the place," a remark the Kid was not able to fathom.

Safe in their room, Blue tore the costume off Walt, put him into bed, got some aspirin, and made him down it.

"To save you from a headache tomorrow."

Walt was barely conscious, and he raved a bit about Real Men and what Real Men do. Then he dropped off, and Blue did, too; sometime later, both were awake again, Walt confused and spent and Blue soothing.

"Did you really see me like that?" Walt asked. "What did you think?"

"You were Johnny's puppet, is all. I'm surprised at him."

"It was a fantasy. Like the one I have of fucking you all tied up."

"You wouldn't get much fuckin' done if yer all roped like that, though."

"Not me, *you*."

"You want me tied? You really do, slick?"

"Or you would be clinging to a fence and I would whip your bottom."

"This isn't my Walt boy talkin'."

"Yes, I am."

"You want to control me? Like Johnny tried to control you just now?"

"Is that what it was?"

"It's somebody always tryin' to get a leg up on somebody else, and I don't know why that should be," said Blue. "You want to hear a joke?"

Walt hugged Blue close and said, "I feel so safe with you. I want to be always like this."

"I'd kiss you, except you got makeup all over."

"I was controlled."

"This Jewish guy meets this Catholic guy. The Jewish guy says, 'My father's the president of the Amalgamated Matzoh Biscuit Company. You don't get no higher than that in this man's world. What's yer father do?'

"The Catholic guy says, 'My father's a priest.' "

Acting the parts, turning his head now this way, now that. " 'A priest? That's all?'

" 'Well, if he works real hard, he could become a bishop.'

" 'Huh, a bishop.' " Waving this away.

" 'Or even a cardinal!'

" 'You'd compare this to the president of Amalgamated Matzoh?'

" 'Well, shit, what do you want, Jesus Christ?'

" 'Why not?' " says Blue, smooth and confident. " 'One of *our* boys made it.' "

This was a test, because Walt often chided Blue for his apparently limitless repertory of ethnic jokes, his "A Polack, a Chinaman, and a Jew" scenarios that treated offensive stereotypes. Blue wanted to see how far he could go tonight—but he also wanted to offer Walt a touch of compromise, dropping the word "Jew," which for some reason Walt held to be anti-Semitic, in favor of "Jewish," which was the term they used back in Gotburg: a Jewish family, a Jewish synagogue, a Jewish person.

So Blue got away with it. Walt laughed a little, then gently asked Blue how a Catholic priest could have a son.

"What, do they only have daughters?" asked Blue, stroking Walt's hair.

"They're bachelors. They can't marry or procreate. It's Protestants who have the family ministers."

"Live and learn," said Blue.

"Yet you were aware that Our Lord was Jewish, because the whole—"

"Got to admit, that had to be explained to me when I first heard the joke. Bet you think ol' Blue is one dumb guy, huh?"

"I think you're a wonderful man."

"Yeah? Well, so are you."

"No. I'm always this little boy, and I know it. I'm just never in charge."

"You were in charge a Blue not long ago, topped him clean and fair— and the first to do so since I was a teenager back home. Besides, that's not what a man is. You got all that lovin'ness in you, and fairness fer others. Those are a man's qualities."

"You would just cheer me up, no matter what."

"Ain't I always been honest with you?"

"Yes, Blue."

"Bein' honest now, too," said Blue, pulling Walt close to him so Walt could rest his head on Blue's chest. "There, now. I like to lay with you like this."

Upstairs, the Kid slept fitfully, tossing as he dreamed: of being young and desired by acclamation at Thriller Jill's. Joan Crawford was in the audience, and suddenly the Kid was Joan, calling some sailor "you gorgeous lug" as he slapped him. Then they were in bed, then flying, then they were both sailors, breaking the rules with a jukebox romance. They were having science-fiction sex, as aliens with bodies made entirely of holes and genitalia. Walt was watching. He said, "How could I have a faggot for a son?" Chris was the Kid's mother, worried and ineffectual. Except she looked like Lois. No, she *was* Lois, in Claire Trevor fuck-me-soon-I-beg-of-you wedgies, slapping a whole line of sailors. Some of them started stripping, in a late-night club with a back room. Walt was somewhere around, crying for help, and Derek Archer did his number in panties and Linda Darnell pump-me-till-I-pop heels; but everyone rushed the stage to get to the sailors. Walt said, "I want to go home," but one of the sailors had gotten hold of him. They were kissing. It was true love. The Kid kept saying, "We have to go home," but now Walt was a sailor, too, utterly regulation but for his footgear, David Manners now-I-lay-me-down-to-ream slippers. Everyone was chasing Walt, and the Kid was fifty-three years old. The past is coming at us.

We can measure the passage of time by vacations and Sundays, like kids mindful of a School Night. Or by the progress of the seasons, or our advancement in the workplace. Parents can mark the developments in a teenage son's romances, as the dubiously libertarian Philip and Neville did, hoping that Lonnie's fascination with Dana of Daly City would dwindle just as autumn falls before winter. "I'm not a snob," said Neville one night in her bright, bustling manner. "I just don't quite understand her attitude."

Philip replied, "She has no manners, she dresses like Dracula's daughter, and she is an idiot. It isn't snobbish to resent that. It's sensible."

Storytellers can chart time entirely by the yeses and nos of a touchy relationship—the triangle plotted by Evan, Alice, and Fay, for instance. This week, Evan and Alice are smooth and close; next week, they're at war; by Wednesday, Alice is back to living with Fay; two Sundays later, the three are brunching in a neutral part of town.

These many several choices. Nevertheless, to write of gay life in the mid-1980s is to navigate mainly from one medical crisis to the next, to note the onset of symptoms, the diagnosis, the treatments, the decline, the funeral. One man wanes as another remains provisionally intact. There is news of holistic tranquilization, clarified diets, restorative drugs that are banned at home bought over the counter in Mexico and France. A close friend dies; at the memorial service, another friend confides that he, too, is of the doomed brotherhood. Or, for example: Frank is doing fine and Danny is rapidly sinking.

In fact, Frank made his friends give up their watches and let him carry on with his life; he had Larken to look after him, when he needed it. Frank had sold his video business—backlog, equipment, studio lease, and all—to a rising young porn entrepreneur, and Larken persuaded Frank to put a little money into his lifestyle for a change. "You're always so Spartan and everything," said Larken. "A bed, a table, a chair, and the bottles of Beck's Dark in the fridge—that's your whole apartment!" Under Larken's supervision, Frank bought a CD player and some discs (weird things that Larken selected, plus *Victory at Sea,* which Frank said was the only classical music he really liked), and they instituted Listening Hours, stretched out together on the bed, resting and dreamy.

One rule Frank laid down: no talking about the disease. No clipping of articles from the *Chronicle* or *The Advocate*. "Just let it be," Frank ordered. "I don't want to get gnarled up about a hundred breakthroughs that won't change a thing in the end. Let me go peacefully, in my own way."

There came a day, however, when Frank wanted to talk about it. He knew that many gay men, both ill and hale, had taken up a spiritual viewpoint, considering reincarnation, meditation, and such ontological questions as Why me? Frank thought this ridiculous. "What keeps beating at me," Frank said, "is, How did it happen? I never got fucked, so—"

"Why did you never get fucked, Frank?"

"Are you reproaching me?"

"I'm just curious. You never tried it even once?"

Frank shook his head.

"Why? Some of the most virile guys I've known—big, rough mothers, I mean. Even *they* tried it from time to time. Maybe they were reticent about owning up to it, but at least they . . . No, I don't mean *at least,* because that's a value judgment. But you *are* the only guy who never, ever."

Frank shrugged.

"No, Frank. Say why."

"Because I couldn't give another man that kind of control over me."

"Control?"

"Yeah."

"Boy, I never felt that way about it. All that time ago, when you were on top of me, I just gloried in how turned on you got in getting down with me. I didn't feel controlled, I felt flattered."

"It's funny where we end up. Some guy goes from log cabin to president. Another is a cowboy one day, a movie star the next. Then there's a guy who starts as a cop and ends . . . how?"

"I don't know if this is a compliment or what, Frank. But never, in the thirty-odd years I've known you, did you not seem like a cop to me for a single second. It's always there in you, somehow."

The dog on the quicksand.

For Walt, the age set its rhythm in Danny's letters, coming more frequently now, and sometimes written out by Danny's mother to his dictation, because he had retinitis. It was odd to have to adjust to the alien strokes bearing the familiar voice—and annoying that Luke and Tom refused to forward the letters to Walt at the Kid's address.

"The only time we see you is when you pick up your mail," Luke explained. "Can't you look on it as a free dinner?"

"I don't like going where I can't take Blue," Walt replied.

"I'd be glad to see him. It's Tom who makes the rules."

"You let him boss you around, I see."

"Walt, one day you'll meet someone very special to you, and you'll learn that a few rules are—"

"I *have* met someone special, and his name is Blue, so *you* can just get *used* to it!"

"Okay, Walt, I got it. I'll make that meat loaf you love and you'll come get your letter. Peace?"

There was no peace in Danny's letters, I have to say. More and more, they were all hospital, wasting away, and dying. But this letter was suddenly nostalgic, about a childhood Danny, wondering and wishing:

Dear Walt:

Danny is fine on this Sunday. His mom made him his favorite breakfast, French bread à la French toast, with bacon and authentic maple syrup, served with milk coffee, and Danny's eyes have cleared till he can almost tell who everyone is when they come into his room. His mom is so cute, too, jumping up at all the commercial breaks to turn the sound off the TV. And Danny's hearing is fine. I always run about the house mornings, to keep it all quiet so he can sleep late. The others in the house smile as I go by, because well what is a bear doing in our house and so on. But they obey. Danny's dad even gave up smoking. I know he already wanted to give it up but it's kind of sweet that he could only do it now, when he thinks he might help Danny fight the ailment.

That's what they call it. They are afraid to say its name, as if that would lure up a devil to take Danny away. They are only thinking of what happens next, while Danny is thinking of his past.

This is what Danny told me: When he was fourteen, he went up to summer camp in the north woods. It was one of those fishing camps. Ugh, how terrible they are. Thousands of innocent fish die just so your dad can tell his friends that you're a man, you hooked a fish.

But the thing on Danny's mind is his little brother Gene was so darling when he was young that he was the mascot of the camp. Everyone was hugging him all the time and saying how cute he is. He was exempt from any bullying or hazing. And one day, after breakfast, two of the older kids just kind of followed Danny and Gene back to Danny's bunkhouse, and Gene had his little pal with him, Ronny Miller. And

Ronny was going on about something and one of the big kids decided to make a show of himself, how he's the boss of things, and he banged his hands against Ronny's ears very hard. You know, like saying, Shut up you little spaz. But Ronny really started to cry, one of those soundless sobs that really bounces off the walls because he is so hurt in his feelings.

Well, the other big kid didn't like this much. He knew what an obvious culprit his friend really was. But it was Danny who should have done something, or said something, and he didn't. He was afraid.

I keep telling him he shouldn't dwell on the past, but he keeps talking about it, how he should have acted in a strong way to defend the weak. He curses himself, because a gay man should know about protecting minorities from violence. And Danny didn't know, because he was afraid. Danny doesn't want to be afraid any more.

Love,
Claude

"They don't just kill us!" Walt raged. "They rip us apart, limb from limb!"

Shreve said, "Your boy friend socializes with the enemy." And Walt replied, "Oh, he takes their money, that's all. Blue doesn't care what a Republican thinks."

Carson said, "You're always fighting with Blue now. But you're always forgiving him." And Walt replied, "The fights are mostly my fault."

Spider said, "You are correct to fight. Everyone who doesn't work with us works against us." And Walt replied, "I'm trying to convert him." But Spider snapped right back with "What if he converts you?"

Poor Walt: so happy with Blue, and so frustrated. Why do we always seek to change the people we love? Reform them, cure them? Sure, there's tension when two don't agree. But is it not more advisable to learn to live in peaceful disagreement than to war over who shall be brought to book, forced to "agree"?

Listen to something that David J. Henderson told Chris, when he pointed out that he had, in effect, been proposing marriage to her for nearly a year and began to press her for an answer. At first perplexed, then flattered, and at length as captivated with him as when she had first laid eyes on him (and thought, What a handsome, virile, probably intelligent, and in any case absolutely *heavenly* man!), Chris officially responded, "Yes, but."

"No buts, Christine. Yes or no."

"Golly. Well, what are the terms?"

"You *know* the terms, we've been negotiating for months. I'm the husband, you're the wife."

"You mean, You're the man, so I'm the employee."

"I mean, I'm the worker, we're the partners."

"Do we have to . . . Can't we just marry and then work it out? Let it evolve?"

He shook his head.

She said, "I thought love conquers all."

"That's the mistake battered women make. They think love is the primary ingredient in marriage."

"So it's *not?*"

"It's one of several. What about responsibility, trust, understanding? Frankly, I think respect is more important than love. Loyalty, too."

"But love is . . . It's . . ."

"A bird, Christine. It's here, it flies away. You know what is the most important thing in a marriage?" It is this next statement, reader, that I wish to emphasize. "The most important thing is Getting the Rules Down in Advance and Holding to Them. You know my rules, Christine. Accept them or release me."

"Release you? Who am I, Guinevere?" Chris struck a Camelot pose. "Go, Lancelot, and never darken my towels again."

"You're joking because you're scared."

"All right, what are your rules again?"

"I make the money, you mother the children, we share the chores."

"What about my rules? My *career?*"

He shook his head. *No.*

"You prick."

"Christine, you *know* these live-together-work-separately showbiz relationships never work. Because there's no home in them, wouldn't you say? That's what I say. One of us has to give it up."

"Why not you?"

"Because I'm doing better than you. Do you know how much I made those two years on—"

"The soap-opera king! Right! So why aren't you a movie star?"

"I'm idealistic. I wanted my year of rep."

"J., this isn't rep, it just calls itself that. Rep is, like, you play Laertes on Monday, Cyrano on Tuesday, a Restoration cameo on Wednesday, and the youngest Tyrone in *Long Day's Journey* that night. It's not for people who are in it for the money, J."

He shrugged.

Enough of this. Now I want to ask Walt and Blue a comparable question: You think this is love? One fight after another, and always the same fight? You think you can go on indefinitely without getting some rules down, as J. suggests? Without trying to respect each other's differences instead of whacking away at them, the way Walt mashes Blue with politics and Blue scorches Walt with his many varieties of intolerance?

They'll be wiser when they're older, you think: but I'm not certain they'll last that long, the way they tear into each other. Naturally, Tom and Luke dote on Walt and Blue's fights. Already, Walt has moved out on Blue and back to Tom and Luke's several times, once for two straight weeks. Walt was very determined that time. "I'll never, never, *never*," he was saying. "Never in a *million*." Tom and Luke said nothing, afraid it was too good to be true. The Kid, too, held his peace, throwing up his hands at the theatre whenever Walt went into a dithyramb about how impossible Blue was. "I've been very forgiving of Blue in the past," Walt announced. "But this time I'm made of ice."

Then Blue visited backstage after the show one night, and Walt melted immediately if not sooner.

"Check-in time is first thing in the morning," the Kid cracked out; but Walt and Blue went right to Tom and Luke's and moved him back in with Blue that same night.

Okay, boys, now stop re-creating vicious patterns and *get the rules down*.

They didn't, alas. Blue is thirty-three and Walt is twenty-nine going on twelve, and both still think that life is for winging it. For instance, as the New Year approaches and Blue's Republican asks if Blue's "fine young lad" will be attending the party, Blue doesn't stop to consider how Walt might feel—and act—when surrounded by the people he believes he loathes. Blue is so dependent upon the stipend his Republican disburses that Blue fears to protest. And Walt wants to stand by Blue. Blue says it's important for Walt to come, so Walt says he will come.

That, of course, was their fatal mistake.

Listen. Just after Christmas, during intermission at the theatre, the Kid told Walt that they were definitely taking the show to New York—his replacement was stepping in in early January, and the Kid and Chris would fly out for auditions that weekend. There was room for Walt if he wanted to see the big city.

"Blue is my savior," said Walt. "I will not leave him."

Then came the package from Danny. Not a letter this time—a box. Luke phoned Walt, and Walt was very excited, absurdly so, as if he thought that Danny himself might be inside. "Don't anyone open that box till I get there," he warned Luke and Tom.

"Sauerbraten, mashed, and red cabbage?" Luke asked.

The box stood on the kitchen table and Walt went right for it. "Golly!" he said. "This is some ultimate thing, I know!"

"Maybe we should wait for Tom," said Luke.

"But how could I wait?" Walt sitting at the table, clutching the box. He examines the mailing label, written out in Danny's mother's now-familiar curlicue. "It's incredible of Danny to send me a present," said Walt. "Christmas. With all he has to worry about."

Tom came home soon enough, and the two older men stood by as Walt cut the strings and slit open the cardboard. Pulling away the wrapping, he reached in, touched something, and drew back, his face clouding as fast as a Kansas sky.

"Claude is in the box," he said.

Luke peered over and pulled out the bear. "Gosh, he must be as old as we are. Our life is in this box."

"Why would Danny send him to me, though? Claude was always a hometown sort of bear."

"Well, here's a letter, anyway," said Tom, fishing it out.

Walt took heart at the same old Danny envelope, light gray and square-cut, with a 4-H club stamp sealing the flap.

"Maybe Claude got into trouble," said Walt, "and Danny sent him here till it blows over."

"Open it," said Luke.

"I'm just about to," said Walt, beginning to weep. "I will really read this letter, only . . . What if it is not a *good* letter?"

Tom moved the box to the floor and sat at the table. He said, "Come on, now, Walt."

Luke put his arm around Walt's shoulders, sat him at the table, then sat himself. "We're all with you, Walt."

Walt wiped his eyes, opened the letter, and read aloud:

Dear Walt:

This is not a long letter, because most of the time I am not in my "full capacity," as Doctor Jeros says it. He told me that I should put my affairs in order before I go into the hospital again, and this is part of that. This letter. I hope you always believe that our friendship and our music act and conversations about so many things were all the best time of my life. I have not said that before, but okay I'm saying it now.

Walt flashed through the rest of the letter in silence, then put it down. "I should have known," he said. Luke reached for the letter, but Walt grabbed it back. "No," he insisted. "No, sir. I can do it."

Walt read:

I am asking Mom to send Claude back to you if it turns out that I don't come out of the hospital. You know how bossy and starved for affection Claude can be, and Mom has enough distractions. Please don't tell Claude that I died, because he has become so sensitive and unpredictable.

If you should see a ghost, well it's probably me, trying to say hello or just watching over you or something.

Love, Danny

Walt refolded the letter and put it in the envelope. "Don't look at me as if I'll explode," he said. "I've been doing that so much lately, I'm all exploded out. And, much as I would love to pick Claude up by a paw and use him to smash every glass and plate and head in this kitchen room, I won't do so."

"I should hope not," said Tom.

"I will just go home, now, and—"

"You *are* home," Tom told him.

"This is *your* home. My home is where Blue is."

Tom shot a glance at Luke.

"Uh, Walt, maybe you shouldn't be going anywhere just now," said Luke.

"I'll be going home," said Walt, almost airily. "With Claude. I'll tell Claude that Danny is dead. I will. And if he can't handle it, he can fuck himself."

"Walt—"

"Oh no, you don't!" cried Walt. He rose, and Tom and Luke did, too. "I'm not your victim! You just hate Blue and my freedom!"

"Walt, that's not it at—"

"So let go of me! I'll *kick* you! I'll never come here again!"

Tom had been about to subdue Walt; Tom backed off.

"You think I'm bluffing?" Walt cried. "I'll smash the place up and start to hate you!"

"Walt—"

"Don't try to force me around!"

"All right, then. Go back to your . . . to Blue," said Luke.

Walt went to the phone and called Blue. "Could you please come and get me here? . . . Because . . . Oh, I got some bad news and . . . Right now? Okay. Bye."

Then it was like Gary Cooper facing off the *High Noon* gunmen in that kitchen. "This is class war," Walt told them. "It's the decadent bourgeoisie against Blue and me together."

Tom said, "Honey, you're just as bourgeois as we are. Remember, I knew you when you and that teddy bear were peeing in *both* your pants."

"Tom!" said Luke. "For Christ's sake!"

"Well, who does he think he is, anyway?" growled Tom, as he stomped out.

"He just doesn't get it," said Walt, with withering scorn.

"His vision has been blurring lately," said Luke, no shading, just saying it. "He has terrible night sweats and weird headaches and a purple spot on his right foot."

It took Walt a second or two to absorb this.

"It isn't just Danny, Walt. Everyone who isn't dead is dying."

Walt and Luke were talking quietly at the kitchen table when Blue arrived. "What's goin' on?" he asked.

Walt said, as he rose, "Danny is dead and now even Tom is sick and I want to go home with you," bursting into tears on the last words as Blue took hold of him. That good, strong, there-for-you Blue, as Luke so clearly saw. Luke thought, we were ridiculous to hope to separate those two. "The trouble is," Walt wailed, "I have to play the show tonight, in my tragic mood."

"Can't they—"

"No, it has to be me. But could you stay with me there and then take me home?"

"Anythin' you want, youngster."

Then there was a funny pause, till Blue released Walt and said, "What's the bear?"

"Oh, that's Claude," Luke replied.

Blue nodded as if that explained everything.

When Luke got upstairs, Tom was already in bed, sliding through the paper while the television silently reverberated with news.

"So early?" asked Luke.

"Tired."

Luke nodded, sitting on the edge of the bed. "I told him," Luke said.

Tom shrugged.

"Well, he should know."

"Who's that?" asked Tom, staring at the television screen.

Luke turned to see a Polaroid of a young man who looked intensely familiar. "Undo the mute," said Luke.

". . . have made no comment as yet," said the announcer. "Now this." A commercial.

"Wasn't that . . . you know," said Tom. "Chris's partners' son? Who own the house together?"

"Oh, the Ironwords? Golly."

Tom switched to another news show—no, they were on the commercials, too. A third channel was stuck on—wait, here it was again. A Polaroid of a hostage alleged to be held in Daly City by the White Aryans, who have threatened to kill him unless a policeman agrees to substitute for him.

"We are attempting to substantiate the story, though neither the police nor the—"

Tom jumped back to the show that hadn't carried the story yet: There was the same Polaroid.

"That's Lonnie Ironword," Tom said.

"Zeus golly Jesus," said Luke. "You're right!"

"I love it like this," Walt told Blue, "miserable though I be. Under the covers with you, so secure and toasty."

"You want to talk about Danny now?"

"It will take me time to deal with that, Blue."

"I understand."

"Will you be so understanding if I ask not to go to the party tomorrow night?"

"Yeah, but I kind of need you to be there. All those New Year's people that I don't know, and tryin' not to embarrass Mason."

"I'm afraid of it."

"Who isn't? But I'll be with you, certainly."

This is Abbott and Costello saying they'll be with you on the Bataan Death March.

"I'll only go if I have to," said Walt.

"You have to," said Blue. "Because we got to help each other out at the problem times."

• • •

Evan was watching the late news, and there it was, for by now the television people had pieced it together: A young male San Francisco native was being held hostage in a residential block of Daly City by a member of the White Aryans in retaliation for an alleged "genocide of my people by the police." The hostage taker had promised to kill his hostage unless the police traded one of theirs for him, the policeman then to suffer White Aryan judgment. In fact: He "would pay for his Christian sins against the movement." The hostage taker was unnamed, because unknown, but the hostage was one Lonnie Ironword, ambushed while hitchhiking home.

So Evan shouted *"Shit!"* and ran across the hall to bang on Frank's door.

"Did you see what—" she began.

"We saw," said Larken. "What about . . . ?" He indicated the Ironwords' floor.

"Don't anybody worry," said Frank, looking astonishingly fit as he came up behind Larken. "Doctor Hubbard's on the case."

"Frank's been calling his cop friends. He thinks—"

"Lark, I asked you not to—"

"Well, Jeez, Frank, where's your white horse and everything?"

"You're going somewhere?" asked Evan, backing up as Frank came through the door. "Somewhere . . . momentous? Because what's that fixed and manly look on your face?"

"Somewhere unbearable. Daly City."

"Frank," Larken cried, "they need a SWAT team for this!"

"No, Larky," as Frank marches downstairs, so proud that, today at least, he has the power to move as easily as anyone in perfect health. "They need someone like unto a cop who has nothing to lose."

"This is the unbelievable part," said Larken, and *"Frank!,"* Evan shouted.

"I'm a ghost already," Frank called over his shoulder. "So who are you trying to reach?"

"I have to apologize for what I did to you," the Kid told Walt. "You're vulnerable and I'm ruthless. Blue's content and I'm jealous. We're all thieves and I'm we're." He took Walt's outstretched hand. "Yes, of course you'd be unbearably forgiving as well. Blue is furious with me, you know."

"He protects me so much that sometimes I sit on the bed and cry for joy. He makes me feel better than I am, because he respects me, and I don't even know why."

"They call that love," said the Kid.

Frank and the police, the following day. His cop friends—detectives, mostly—telling their superiors about this guy. The news media on the prowl, sensing a Break in the Story. Frank thinking, I've got two, three good days in me. Perfect days, then back to the living death. You think Frank is way off base, but he is not far from what the situation calls for—trained (if stale), credible, experienced in playing bait from his days on the Vice Squad, and, though unschooled in the necessary techniques, fearless and formidable.

Still, there was the "insurance" problem. If the chief of operations let Frank stand in and Frank was hurt, the city of San Francisco would be vulnerable in a multimillion-dollar lawsuit by any of Frank's relatives, no matter how distant.

Frank had an answer for that: He was the only child of only children, and all his relations had predeceased him. The chief would refer to a possible eighth cousin in Bakersfield—nobody has *no* relatives, right? But there might be professional pride in it as well. A big city like San Francisco can't field its own experts? It has to borrow a gay pornographer to protect the citizenry?

"But I *know* Lonnie Ironword!" Frank insisted. "We live in the same building, okay? It would help anyone trying to rescue him to be able to ascertain just how Lonnie is reacting to developments."

"Ascertain," the chief repeated. "Yeah, let's *ascertain*."

We're in Daly City at the site of the crisis, a quiet-looking little house in red with white trim. Hours have passed as the negotiators performed the obligatory first act in dealing with a hostage taker—exhaust him with talk. One reason why is to wear him down; another is that some of these characters are more interested in advertising their grave quarrels with the way of the world than in killing anybody. You let them unburden themselves, then let them surrender.

By now, it's well after dark of the next day, and Frank is getting nowhere in his windbreaker with the Smith & Wesson .38—a souvenir of his days on the force—tucked into the back of his waistband. The dog's on the quicksand and Frank's ready to spring, but the chief says no, they're going to talk the subject down, fit him into their sharpshooter sights, gas the place, whatever. And whatever doesn't involve Frank. Look, guy, thanks for the offer, but now you're wasting my time, so walk.

Frank walks, all right—into the army of cops and cop cars and television news teams ringing the floodlit street. Frank walks through all this and up to the subject's house; and Frank hears the shouts of the cops behind him, as with his hands in the air, Frank strides up to the fatal door, bawling out, "I'm the cop you wanted for the trade-off! Don't shoot, I'm coming in, okay?"

"Open the door *slow!*" a voice responds. "Slow, now, boy! Don't worry, I've got the drop on the kid here, so you'll soon see."

"God *fuck* the shit to *hell!*" remarks the chief, when he hears of it. "Happy new year!" Too late—Frank is inside, floating atop the quicksand, bringing himself back to life, sheer kismet.

At that moment, Blue and Walt were dressing for Mason Crocker's party, Walt presenting one reason after another why he should stay home.

"What kind of New Year's party starts at seven-thirty?" Walt groused, as Blue tried to straighten Walt's tie.

"Stop this fussin' all about, will you?"

"I *know* this is a mistake."

"It ain't . . . It's not a mistake fer you to accompany me to a society party. Do us both good, maybe."

"Blue, don't you see that these selfish Republicans are the reason that Danny is dead, and everyone else? They pretend that it's out of their hands, but secretly they're *glad*. They *want* us dead."

"Now why would they—"

"I've *told* you, and you never listen and that's why I'm always reproaching you. Because we keep bringing up the truth, the sex truth, which probably contains all the other truths combined. And most people build their whole lives on lies—but they get away with it because everyone else is lying, too. It's a lying society. So then the gays come forth to shatter these lies and—"

"Quit fiddlin' so I can neaten you up."

"I believe *you're* the one who needs advice on how to dress!" cried Walt, taking offense. "You rustic goof!"

At the look of hurt on Blue's face, Walt, pained at his own impatience, turned away. "You see why I shouldn't go. You see how this drives a wedge between us."

Blue gently pulled Walt around to face him, put his hands on Walt's shoulders, and said, "I need you with me tonight, because I'm no good at fancy socializin'. I know I'm trash, certainly. But I'm hopin' that you'll stay by my side and guide me from sayin' too many wrong things and losing the gig with Mason. He's real, real big on . . ."

"Style."

Blue nodded.

"The trouble is," Walt reasoned, "when you say that, you are giving me power over you, and I am not worthy of it. I betray everyone I love. I know I mash at you, and I hate myself for it, but then I mash you some more. I say horrible things to Tom and Luke, who are my fathers. And I let Danny die. I am disloyal and without honor, and I can't figure out how to be a better boy, and that just makes me madder. Don't force me to come to this party, Blue. Please don't do that."

Blue was weeping.

"Oh, no," said Walt, touching the tears. "Did I do this to you?"

"I went and saw Eddie Swindon again today. He's trash, just like me. Tennessee. He's goin' pretty fast now, and he was sayin', 'Just remember me, Blue, that's all I ask. Keep me in mind, and mention me from time to time. Maybe go to one of those meetin's where you get up one after the next and talk about a friend who's passed on. Speak his name and tell of his qualities.' He said that to me. And he said, 'How's it goin' with yer new beau?' I told him, 'It's the most beautiful thing when he's honest and true with me. But when he's hard, I know that love is the most painful thing of all.' "

They held each other for a long time. Then they went to the party.

"Incoming," said Frank coolly, as he entered the front room of the little Daly City house. The subject was a wild-looking working-class loser—early middle age, collapsed stomach, hair that had vastly thinned yet grew scraggling to his shoulders, tattoos leering beneath the sleeves of his T-shirt, jumpy and eager with his .45. The hostage, of course, was Lonnie, wan and exhausted, a bundle tossed on the broken-down couch with his hands tied in front of him at the wrists and his eyes wide at this unexpected visit. He's smart enough to be silent but his eyes read, *Frank?* Are you going to save me?

"Yeah, incomin'," says the subject, holding Frank right in the line of fire, wary yet curious. "You a vet? The 'Nam, could be?"

Frank shakes his head slowly.

"Now close the shittin' door, I'm no fool," says the subject. Door closed, he adds, "Move over here," using the gun to edge Frank deeper into the room. "Move it! Out of the—"

"You know what I call a man?" says Frank, confidentially more than rhetorically. Turning on the charm. "A man is as good as how many of the other side he has brought down. That's a man."

"More this way," edging him.

Frank does move a bit, but he's fixing the guy with his eyes. "Am I wrong?"

"Don't give me no shittin' spiel, Mr. Police, because you're already on the way out. What's a man? I brought you in here, see my power?" His head nods at the outside. "TV, attention. What I'm shittin' up to, it's news, you see that?"

Bravado. The guy's nervous, bought himself a deal he can't handle. Didn't think it through.

"I shittin' brought you in here, and you ain't walkin' out, got me?"

"It's a trade," says Frank, philosophically.

The subject giggles.

"What's a man?" Frank again asks. "Who's renowned? Who survives? Who watches? I'd call these worthy questions."

The subject's moving about, trying to keep his mind on Frank but distracted by the usual ephemera, all his favorite injuries. The 7-Eleven clerk who didn't show respect. The cop who stopped his car for no reason and hit him with six tickets and a sneer. The world that stood him in the corner, made him say *Sir*. Christ, Frank thinks, the pathetic *smallness* of scum! The concentration with which they harp away on *nothing!*

"I don't want a talkin' cop," the subject tells Frank. "I want a dead one."

"Looks like we'll have that," Frank replies, giving Lonnie a sign to rise. "I'm in, he's out. White Aryans honor their agreements, right?"

Lonnie rises and the subject gets anxious. "You're not the in-charge guy here!" he cries. "Shittin' . . . 'Cause no one'll tell me *what*, so hold your shittin' *horses*, see?"

"Deal's a deal," Frank murmurs, trying to signal Lonnie to move toward the door. I'm not God, right? We have to make our miracles for ourselves.

"*I'll* make the shittin' deal!"

"Stay put," Frank tells Lonnie. "Be cool."

The subject says, "Don't give orders."

Frank shrugs and holds it, limp, agreeable, unthreatening.

"You're too tall," the subject tells him.

.   .   .

Walt wouldn't leave Blue's side, though Mason kept trying to separate
them. Nor did Walt have much to say.

"So *serious*," said Mason, putting on an earnest face to match Walt's.
"Are you depressed or profound?"

"Worried," said Walt, as Blue gave him a heartening caress along the
back of the neck, and Mason, with a flicker of the eyes, censoriously rose
above it. *Be discreet*, he silently warned; *I don't want to*, Walt replied.

Walt managed to drag Blue off to a corner of the cavernous living room,
but even there Mason pelted them with friends and associates to meet and
conversations to fabricate, all about nothing—because when two gay men
are forced to delete the gay from their rap they have to leave out whom
they know, how they live, and where they've been. What's left?

"Mason wants you to play the piano sometime er other," Blue told
Walt, when they were alone.

"Ugh."

"At least then you won't have to talk."

"I need a drink."

"What's all this drinkin' you've suddenly took to?" Blue asked as he
waved at a waiter. "Used to be, you'd pass out halfway through a V-8."

"Johnny taught me the pleasures of the festive cup."

Blue said nothing, as he invariably did now when the Kid's name came
up. Walt asked the waiter for a Bloody Mary. Then Blue made an announcement: "If this Mason thing works out, I'm goin' to get us a real
place of our own."

"I like Johnny," said Walt.

Mason brought over a sparklingly pointless couple, some banker and his
wife, he inquisitive and she vivacious on any topic. Yet they lacked content. Naughty Walt kept addressing them as "Mr. and Mrs. Banker," and
they left soon.

"Don't get into trouble, now, youngster," said Blue.

Frank said, "The problem is that cops basically think like you do. But
we're not allowed to say so."

"I'll frisk you," said the subject. "Pat you down, that's the way."

"But it's tricky, balancing one action with another action. One life with
another life, say. I'm totally passive here, right? Still, it's my training
against your gun."

"I'm in charge of this," said the subject, quite furious.

"Oh, I see that."

"And you get down!" the subject screamed, pushing Lonnie back onto the couch. "You *move* when I *say,* you hear, now?"

"I don't do small talk," Walt, on his third Bloody Mary, was explaining to yet another of Mason's couples. "I only do topics."

"The economy," said the man.

"Choosing the right school," his wife put in.

"AIDS," said Walt.

Challenged, not deflated, the couple aired their sympathies. Then the wife said, "The ones I really feel sorry for are the infants. The innocents."

Walt froze.

Blue jumped in, quoting Walt: " 'All victims of AIDS are equals.' " But that didn't stop Walt from attacking this couple's heterosexist view of the plague. "They're innocent and I'm guilty, is that it?" he cried. "What am I guilty of, you loathly disgusting idiot?"

The woman looked at him as if, at any moment, a sign would appear, reading that Walt was a psycho and therefore not responsible.

"You lurid bitch," Walt added.

"That's enough," said her husband.

"Go fish," Walt told him.

The couple walked away.

"You better stop," Blue told Walt.

"Let the innocents stop! Let their straight phobo *parents* stop! Let the right-wing Nazis stop! *I'm* not going to stop!"

Walt was moving, Blue trying to grab him, and suddenly Mason was there, absolute consternation in a black pin-striped suit.

"The Howards told me . . ." Mason began. "I really feel—"

"Your mother blows dead rats in hell," Walt observed.

"I'm takin' him home."

"No, I really feel sorry for the infants," Walt insisted, resisting Blue's grasp. "You can't know how much, the infants. It's so—" Even Mason put out a hand to restrain the vivid Walt, but he backed away from them. "No, I'm at the piano. I'm entertaining, remember?"

The whole room was watching.

"Hello, boys and girls," Walt predicated, taking stage. "Walty is eager to—" He glanced at a dowager with a ferocious bodice and emeralds enough to outfit a Ziegfeld-size Oz pageant. "Yes, madam? What, your pet goose is ailing? He suffers from what the Catholics call sexagesima? Meaning his shithole is too tight? Never fear, the doctor is in. Just put him on the examination table, loosen him up, and let's have a gander."

Casing the joint like a pro—like the Kid doing his Act, come to say it—Walt spotted a particularly handsome man, winked, and stared at him, saying, "And now for my next trick."

The party stood in its tracks, drinks in hands, faces set, bearing it. Mason was looking at no one, and it was out of Blue's hands. "Music, ho," said Walt, moving to the piano. The Kid would have popped out another one-liner here, but Walt was a novice at cabaret. He jumped into a piano version of the vocal break to "Mr. Sandman," then sang the lyrics that the Kid had taught him:

Mister Sandman!
Please make me cream!
Send me a hunko,
'Cause I need to ream!
Give him a bum
Like melons in season.
I'll rim him promptly
'Cause I can't bear teasin' . . .

"They've been throwin' stuff in here all the day long," said the subject. "Telephone, food, you. Tryin' to distract me, ya see. Tire me out. So I'm done with the talkin'."

"The trade," Frank reminded him.

"You," said the subject, sending it to Lonnie but holding his gun and his gaze on Frank. "Who told you to get up?"

Move fast, Frank thought. The subject's tired and punchy.

"I told you to sit down," said the subject, turning his aim upon Lonnie, as Frank pulled up the back of his windbreaker with his left hand and drew with his right. Smooth, swift, silent; yet the earth turns over.

The subject and Frank are barrel to barrel. "Let the boy go and you'll have me, okay, we know that," said Frank, edging around to stand between the subject and the hostage, both hands steady on the piece, ever ready, our Frank. "Go, Lonnie," he says. "Slow and easy."

The subject was silent, no doubt reconsidering his choices as Lonnie, with great misgivings, went to the door and awkwardly fumbled it open through the rope around his wrists. "Close it after you," Frank ordered. "Tell them to stay put and wait."

Without a word, Lonnie left them alone.

"There it is," says Frank.

"Shit, I shoulda frisked you right off."

"You didn't handle this well."

"You got your trade, didn't you? Aren't you goin' to surrender to me?"

"Let's talk first."

"Fuckin' cheater is how I see it."

"You wanted a dead cop, right? You'll have one, I assure you."

"So stop holdin' the drop on me!"

"I'm curious to know what leads a man to this moment in his life. Two men, to this moment. We must have something in common, you and I. Something in our character. Right?"

"You gonna put your shittin' gun down, or what?"

"True, I don't see anything in you that I could share. You're a real dumb fuck, for starters—my Aunt Matilda could take a hostage more efficiently than you did. You're a mean fuck, too—what's that kid guilty of for you to put his life in jeopardy?"

Strange how quiet it was outside. There had been no noise when Lonnie left the house—no cheers, no stampede of media people, no splurge of light for the cameras. It was keenly still in the whole world.

"If you'll allow me some philosophizing," Frank went on, "the trouble with the world is, nobody's guilty of crimes any more. Guy sneaks into the city offices and murders two men out of personal revenge, then claims candy made him crazy. The jury doesn't say, Cut the bullshit, you killed two men because you wanted to, you disgusting slimebag. The jury says, Oh, okay."

Frank spoke with cold precision, but his eyes were on fire and he held the gun jutting out almost up the subject's nose. Frank was right, of course: The subject was incompetent by even amateur standards and had vaguely expected to pull off a publicity coup and then surrender, not be cornered by an angry angel of death.

"So what's your excuse?" Frank asked him. "Bad home background? Incomplete sex life? Maybe you're just a rotten piece of scum who doesn't deserve to live. Why trouble the state to try you? You're guilty. You know it and I know it."

Worrying, the subject said, "That phone thing they threw in here works both ways, remember. It's pickin' up every word you—"

"In the movie of this, my next line is 'Say your prayers.' "

The subject slowly lowered his hands and dropped the gun. He was shaking. "I give up," he said.

Frank lowered his gun, too, slightly, and let off five rounds into the subject's stomach.

Walt finished his song and stood at the piano, smiling at everyone. Walt smiled at Blue, who silently and slowly shook his head, the anger rising in him from deep, deep in the bone. Walt smiled at Mason, who also shook his head. "Thanks for the use of the hall," said Walt, already on his way out.

He was content. He took no notice of Blue, took his time retrieving his coat, said nothing as he strolled out into the wonderfully crisp and vital Nob Hill nightscape, where Blue, coatless, caught up with him and sorely taxed young Walt for his disloyalty and ingratitude and selfishness. Walt didn't respond. He kept walking.

Roughly pulling him around, Blue cried, "You stand and listen when I'm talkin' to you, Mister!"

But Walt turned again and kept walking. "We're quits, Blue," he called over his shoulder, still content.

The phone thing was cackling, and Frank heard the voice of the chief of operations furiously trying to find out where things stood.

Watching the subject writhing in his death throes, Frank said, "Hurts, right?" He picked up the receiver and said, "This is Frank Hubbard. The position is excellent. Give me one minute and I'll be home free."

There was static and the chief for reply, but Frank simply repeated, "I'll be home," and put the phone thing down. He sat on the couch, trying to keep his mind clear. He, too, was shaking. "You have your good days and bad days," he said aloud. "Tomorrow I could wake up a neurological wasteland, but this was a good day. The dog is off the quicksand."

He carefully fitted the .38 into his mouth, opening wide so he could aim the muzzle as close to straight up as makes no nevermind, and pulled the trigger. He was peaceful then. And now he is out of the story.

Who is the hero of this novel, I wonder? There have been moments when the Kid, Lois, Tom and Luke and Chris (triadically), and perhaps especially

Frank could each have emerged as the protagonist. But perhaps our saga lacks what Stonewall culture has, largely, lacked: a leader. Yet other oppressed peoples thrust forth their Spartacus, Boudicca, Wat Tyler, Margaret Sanger, Lech Walesa. It sometimes seems as if the sole unifying figure in gay culture is the current major male porn star.

Nevertheless, with the passing of Frank—who made the most ambitious voyage in these pages, from a dupe of the authoritarian régime to a progenitor of the rebellion's supremely mutinous characteristic, its sexuality—a hero does leave us. After the power of this man's self-assertion, the comings and goings of these people seem less vigorous by comparison, just so much gossip. Imagine a scandal sheet relating how a certain young musician and his love-for-sale boy friend threw a Major Scene at the New Year's "do" of the scion of an old Nob Hill family, how a certain drag artiste of local renown helped the musician move out on his boy friend on the sly, lock, stock, and cock ring. Rumor hath it that the scion has crossed the hustler off his party list and that the musician and the drag hag have run off together to Baghdad-on-Hudson.

Or what about that lady director and her hunk-of-the-month actor lover? The whole town's talking—seems the two are suffering tie-the-knot blues, because he wants her to end her career to concentrate on layette technique and the P.T.A. Sources close to the pair say it was a frosty February indeed when the couple separated, temporarily, so *she* could fulfill an engagement helming *She Stoops to Conquer* for the New York Shakespeare Festival. But the Town Crier hears that *he* flew in last weekend for a surprise visit, and all New York swears that *they* were the Couple of the Year—in the few moments, that is (we blush!), when they left the bedroom.

Tongues wagged when an Asian actress of our acquaintance dumped first one girl friend, then another, within a week, apparently in hopes of becoming San Francisco's gayest divorcée. Now the dish queens are exploding with the news that the ladies have erected a ménage à trois. It's Beach Blanket Bedlam!

As for that well-heeled, well-featured, and oh-so-contemporary family whose teenage son recently played a starring role in the suburban hostage drama that swept the ratings late last year: Looks like the generation jitters are over at last. Says the chastened son of this brush with death, "No more Daly City for me!" He's free again and eligible as ever, girls, so form a single line.

It was a quiet New Year's, though, for Larken Young, cited as the Sole Survivor and Longtime Partner of the late Frank Hubbard, who got his

Fifteen Minutes of Famous the hard way in that same Daly City extravaganza. Larken spent the end of the holiday clipping the newspapers and pasting up the final pages of the scrapbook he had been secretly keeping for twenty years on the life and works of big Frank. And now he, too, is out of the story.

Walt did indeed pack up and leave San Francisco for the East in the company of the Kid, though both diplomatically avoided trying to verbalize exactly how their relationship would work. The love-struck Kid was of course eager to make Walt his lover, but Walt was sore and tender just now, furious at Blue yet terrified of the determination with which he had tossed Blue out of his life and cut himself off from his home and family. The house of Tom and Luke had been Walt's sanctuary, the two men Walt's protectors. To flee was dangerous, serious, grown-up. Oh, Walt was curious about New York, full of wonder at the career he might forge in the nation's cultural capital. But he was afraid of the touchy people of the town, afraid of the unknown, and afraid, even, of the Kid.

Should Walt be leaving Tom just when he, too, had come down with It? Oddly, both Tom and Luke supported Walt's move, on the grounds that he ought to see what he could make of his music. Unspoken was their hope that a stay of a few months away from Blue would finish off that disagreeable episode; and their fear, too, that if Tom had It, Luke must have It as well. That was the way now, often: One man would care for his lover through his death, then follow him, cared for in turn by others.

"I should stay by their side," Walt had told the Kid.

"But this is your chance, young Walt," the Kid insisted. "Your *break*. If they have to die, won't it ease their pain if they can see you on the rise as a composer?"

"They do encourage my music," Walt conceded.

"There!"

Walt wanted to get away, and I know why: Blue. What a cinch it is to be hurt and angry at your lover for six or seven days. Then we think, Maybe I was wrong. Two weeks, three, and it's How do I clean up the mess I made? By then, however, Walt would be on the other side of the continent from Blue and redemption.

Redemption. Some of us fear it, you know. Loveless and inattentive parents can create deep inside us the belief that we are unworthy, and when someone inadvertently tries to reeducate us, we feel denuded and we balk. So Walt went with the Kid to New York. He went, poof! When

Blue rang Tom and Luke's to talk to Walt, Tom abruptly told him that Walt was out of his life, that's all she wrote, good-bye. Of course, the Kid checked in with his tenant Blue by phone from the East, as one does, and Blue asked where Walt might be.

"Oh, the young man's back in Minnesota. Something about a nice, long family visit."

"Why'd he do a thing like that?"

"You know these midwesterners, never happy if they're more than a mile from the haymow."

This is tricky. What if Blue called the Kid in New York and Walt answered? The two had settled into a tight little furnished two-bedroom walk-up on East Twenty-fifth Street, the best they could do in a squeezed market. Sooner or later, surely, Blue would have reason to call the Kid—some plumbing problem, some legal matter with the city. Then, too, over the months of their friendship, Blue and Walt had unveiled themselves to each other in detail, and Blue knew that Walt had no desire to see his Minnesota relations again. Many a time, Walt had said that Tom and Luke—and Blue—were all the family he cared to count. Besides, for how long would Blue be unaware that Walt was playing the Kid's show in New York? True, Blue didn't hobnob with the Kid's theatre crowd; nor did he follow the Kid's career. He's doin' the show in New York? Okay, that's fine, don't tell me more. Still, *eventually,* wouldn't someone, somehow, let it slip that Walt and the Kid were together in the East?

It almost happened, three weeks after Walt and the Kid had left San Francisco. Aching to speak to Walt, Blue rang Tom and Luke again, and this time he got Luke, a guilty man, uncomfortable about his and Tom's manipulation of Walt's love life. "Tom, it's got to be *his* decision, doesn't it?" he had said. Tom answered, "Well, it *is* his decision, anyway. He moved thousands of miles to get away from that jerk. If that's not a decision, tell me what is!"

Now, talking to Blue on the kitchen phone, Luke wondered if he should tell Blue the truth, even give him Walt's phone number in New York and let the two of them shape their relationship free of interference. I think Luke might well have done so—but Tom was in the room, dark-eyed, watchful behind the newspaper. Floundering, Tom turned to him. "Tom?" he pleaded.

"Hang up on him," Tom ordered.

.   .   .

A two-bedroom walk-up on East Twenty-fifth Street. Dirty city, callous folk, rowdies and zanies and thugs cascading through the streets.

"I'll probably never get used to life here," says Walt, idly looking out the windows, first one, then another, as if each glass might present a different Walt, all of them secure that no one would ever be certain who he was. "In this place, everyone wants something from you."

"We have to talk, my young friend," says the Kid. "I've made some coffee."

"I should have brought along my mug collection," says Walt as he joins the Kid at the miniature table in the kitchen. "My favorite had Prince Charles and Princess Di on it."

"You needn't be nervous, Walt. We'll be honest with each other, but we'll do it in a kindly manner."

"Okay."

"I'm fifty-five years old. I've kept trim and I still have my hair. Still, I'm no Blue. What I am is, one, good company, two, smart, funny, and rather well heeled, and, three, crazy about you. Maybe in . . . in l. with you—it's hard to say, you see? Hard to hear, too, I expect. But you're taking it well."

The Kid looked at Walt, fighting the urge to touch him, to personalize this almost businesslike appeal.

"It was a ghastly thing I did to you that night I dressed you up. I passed it off as mischief, but it was more or less a rape, because I deliberately got you wet in order to seduce you."

Walt pensively sipped his coffee.

"The only thing that stopped me from taking you to bed that night was . . . well, I must have had some seizure of guilt. But, mainly, you had got so sozzled that I was afraid I had poisoned you."

"I know I'm not one of your sturdy drinking-man types."

"You dear, dear boy. Is that well-meaning innocence and trust utterly natural?"

"Partly utterly."

"Well. Since that fateful night, I've kept my hands off you. I've *respected* you, is what it is. But you must understand that I'm out of my mind with longing for you. You see that, surely?"

Walt nodded.

"This is what I propose. A trial period, like taking a show out of town. This is our shakeout week in Boston. One week—during which you will allow me to assume a lover's rights. You needn't treat me with false enthusiasm, but you will let me . . . have you. When I was young, I enjoyed letting my partners run riot over me, especially what we called 'rough trade.' It was . . . I don't know, there wasn't all the choice of partners we have today, and it was smart, at times, to let it happen to you, come who may. Now I like to be in charge. So. We'll try that for a week, and, at the end of it, you will tell me how much of me you can handle, and I feel it best to warn you straight out that even if you don't ultimately want a physical relationship with me on any level—if you should tell me, in fact, that the very sight of me nauseates you beyond Thackerayan description—I'll still want you near me. That's . . . love? Just give me a week, Walt. Who knows? Maybe seven days of pleasuring myself with you will be all I'll ever require."

"Is this how you worked it out with Blue, when he moved in with you?" Walt asked.

The Kid sighed. "Blue is a sex machine. When he isn't fucking, he's cruising. And he's not all that fastidious about whom he fucks, either. Note my grammar, *whom*."

"I feel he loved me, though."

After a moment, the Kid gently said, "I know he did."

"Do you suppose he still does?"

Tell him the truth, said a piece of the Kid, his better side; but he feared losing Walt to the first plane heading west unless the boy was, uh, assisted in putting that business behind him.

That *business!*—a love so needful that each half of the couple felt ennobled by the other? A love so intense yet so bashful that Walt would weep with the force of their yearning? That *business!*

The Kid pulled his chair closer to Walt and put an arm around his shoulder.

"Say to me one thing," the Kid said. "If you could be back with Blue now—"

"No," said Walt firmly. "We are wrong for each other. We would just quarrel and shout." The Kid patted Walt's back sympathetically, but Walt said, "I'm not always this helpless little boy. You think I got swept up in your gala romantic gesture, running off with you to see the world or so, and now I'm supposedly having worries about it." Walt shook his head. "The truth is, I thought it over very strong, and I have no worries now. I feel as adventurous as you, and I put my past in a coffin."

Walt raised his mug, and the Kid joined him in toast.

"Now we just need to find a bigger place," Walt concluded.

"That's possible. I'm thinking of selling the house. Or perhaps renting it to a family."

"Golly."

"The more I've visited New York, the more I've longed to move here. If the play is a hit . . . Well, who knows?"

"Blue will have to move out, then, won't he?"

"So you *are* worried about him."

Walt shrugged.

"Listen to the Green Goddess. Blue has only to walk down Castro Street to shop his pick of the available talent—some lawyer, belike, with a spare room and a needy heart. The Blues of the world never end up on the street."

Walt nodded.

"Look, I'm not saying that Blue has no feelings. But they *are* pretty fluid. He could fall in love on a dare."

Walt stared into his coffee.

"Never fret. He'll land right side up."

On the contrary, Blue was in torment. He could not understand why Walt hadn't called by now—relationships as deep as theirs just don't end like this. Did they? Could Walt so . . . so happily . . . walk away? No letter or phone just to ask how Blue was? To say Walt was fine, in case Blue was wondering? Just to talk? Where, even, was he?

When the Kid called to give Blue notice that he was handing the house over to a realtor for commercial reassignment—Blue had a month to find other lodgings, two months if necessary, no reason to be unfeeling, is there?—Blue said, "Johnny, in all our years I've never pushed at you or lied er done anythin' vicious, have I?"

"No, of—"

"I've been a straight fellow with you."

"A fiasco of a word, but yes."

"So now I'm askin' you one question, and I'd like a straight answer back."

"He's with me. He wanted it that way."

"Can I speak to him?"

"Surely you realize that would make it difficult for him as well as me. He wants it quits with you."

"If he wants that, he can have it. But can't I just talk to him? Is that so wrong?"

"I think it is," the Kid lied. "He's hurt and angry and determined. You know what an obstinate little cuss he can be."

"It's not like him not to—"

"Has he called you? He may, in time. I place no ban on that. But right now, you really must leave him alone."

The phone would ring and ring and ring, and Walt never answered. He loved Blue still, but he resented Blue and hated himself for resenting him. Face it, the boy is a mess of injured feelings and conflicted wishes. He's raw. He's hurt. He's launching an affair with a man nearly twice his age whom he admires and likes but does not love and never will. He's in a new world, cut off from his family, scarred by all the death around him. His last act before leaving San Francisco was to go into the yard behind the house and bury Claude, bury him alive—just as, years before, he had carted Dexter into the little woods to kill him. Walt is one of those people who cannot enjoy what they want and end up having what they cannot use.

Blue kept ringing the Kid's New York number, hoping for Walt and getting the Kid or nothing. He was stonewalled. Then he was angry. Then he was considering flying to New York. Then he was picturing himself knocking on their door, and Walt not opening up, just leaving him out in the hall like that. Then Blue was very outraged. At length, he gave up, found a new boy friend, and moved out of the Kid's house. Blue traveled from man to man, lining up the next stay just as the present one was ending. He hustled some, took on the odd job of a physical kind, usually freelancing for moving companies. He gave his Republican suit away. He opened a savings account. One day, he ran into an ex-lover who was heading for his night job at an AIDS hospice, and Blue let this man take him along. "We can use an extra hand," the man said. He was amazed that Blue didn't know what "P.W.A." meant. "Person with AIDS," the man told him gently. Blue nodded. He followed the man on his rounds, holding things, conversing, being patient, listening. He was good at this work. "Beats haulin'," Blue explained.

"They're looking for new people all the time, okay," said the man. "Yes, because there's a lot of burnout around here. You have that fresh approach."

"It's not for me," said Blue.

"Yes, well," said the man, a former icon of the bars and baths who was now H.I.V.-positive, chaste, and given to prayer and good works. "Keep it in mind, perhaps. Because you're what they need."

Blue had to laugh at that. "Nobody needs me," he explained.

What Blue had been keeping in mind was Walt, to a painful degree. We all know that exquisitely hollow ache. Thinking it vain and girlish to succumb to it, Blue decided to keep busy with distractions, and he asked his friend if he could work at the AIDS hospice on an improvised schedule, without signing up big-time. "That's possible," said his friend. Blue showed up the next day, the day after. Long days, too—but Blue buried himself in them, smothered his loss in the soothing of other people's greater loss. Listening to them, he heard himself large.

Walt did call. The Kid's play had opened to reasonably good reviews and was doing nice business in the modest off-Broadway manner, the Kid and Walt had found a nicer apartment in the East Eighties, and he and Walt had settled into a pleasantly manageable relationship as vaguely erotic exes, past the heavy stuff and now into light make-out-and-blowjob sessions. Okay. Now Walt felt it time to reposition himself emotionally in his San Francisco family. He planned a late-summer visit and launched a search for Blue, calling Blue's friends to follow a trail from one boy friend to the next. One day in late June, Walt finally connected.

"Blue's at the hospice," said the current boy friend. "Who's this?"

"It's Walt Uhlisson."

After a moment: "Oh. Right. So you're the one."

"I can call back when—"

"No, I'll take your number. I'll tell him you called."

Hanging up, Walt thought, Boy, he sounded funny.

Funny, yes—but the current boy friend was no fool. He knew who Walt was—for who of us does not plague our latest with encomiums to his or her most distinguished predecessor? When Blue got home, the guy said, "I've asked the phone company to change our number. Too many of your old tricks are hassling us."

"Guess so," said Blue.

"I'm glad you're back, anyway. I've been hot for you all day. Let's hit the sack, huh?"

"Got this piece to read first," said Blue, pulling a homemade newsletter out of the run-down attaché he had bought for fifteen bucks on Sacramento one afternoon, from a guy in a hurry. Blue was in need of a briefcase, because there was so much that he had to carry around now. Articles, records, notes he had taken. There was so much news. Just as many P.W.A.s had grouped to test uncertain drugs on themselves, free of the obstructive meddling of government agencies, so had many afflicted gay men begun publishing their own AIDS magazines, reporting news that the city papers ignored and emphasizing anecdotal treatments adopted by others in their circle. In his brief but heady experience caring for P.W.A.s, Blue discovered that the ailing were best stimulated by reports of novel treatments. It was the *Star Wars* approach to AIDS care: if not doomsday, then flags, gold, majesty.

"You'd rather read than fuck, is that it?" asked Blue's current boy friend, a glorious gym bunny with a single flaw, a slightly Hogarthian nose.

Blue looked at him, thinking, What am I here for?

"Are you just a visual?" Blue's current boy friend went on. "All right, you're paying your share of the rent and so on, but your name isn't on the lease. I wanted a lover, not a roommate. We haven't scored since I don't know *fuck that,* Mister Health-Care Worker of the Year! *Will* you? *Huh?*"

Blue moved out the next day, and, the day after, Walt called.

"The number's going to change this afternoon," said Blue's current ex–boy friend, "so you can stop annoying me."

"I just want to—"

"He's gone. Permanently."

"Well, can you tell me—"

"Go fuck yourself," said the guy, holstering the receiver.

Tom died in late 1988, directly after coming home from the hospital and suffering a relapse of another of those bizarre diseases unknown to humans till now. Bird cancer. Monkey dropsy. These insanely *asinine* deaths. Walt returned to San Francisco for Tom's funeral, a discontented but quiet Walt, who stood between Chris and Luke holding their hands, watching the long box drop as if he were now one third an orphan.

Luke, paradoxically, seemed in robust health. He refused to be tested, partly for the usual reason—If I'm to die, tell me later—and partly out of distrust of the political meaning of such a test and a misgiving at how intensely the medical establishment embraced the H.I.V. cult, furiously rejecting opposing theories without probation.

"It isn't science to ignore alternative explanations without testing them," Luke told anyone who asked. "It's flat-earth geology."

Chris was around a lot; she even brought David J. Henderson over to watch Luke prepare Ten Thousand Lakes stuffed cabbage and wild rice, and J. got so engaged in the cuisine shoptalk that Luke said J. would make a passable gay guy.

"Another Stone Age stereotype," said Walt, who had dug Claude up and was giving him a bath in the kitchen sink. "I'm gay and I can't cook. I never even saw a quiche."

"For all that," said Chris, "I can't cook, and I'm a gay man manqué."

"That's where the manqué comes in," said Luke, clarifying the gravy.

Walt had planned to spend his free hours tracking Blue—but this time there was no great hunt, no trail to piece together. Blue was no longer one of the urban gay world's more or less anonymous beauties, to be spotted on the street, made legend in the discos. He had become prominent, a real person with a name and an occupation. Indeed, he worked for a California-based association that sent him nationwide from city to city, organizing gay hospices.

Walt couldn't believe it; he kept insisting that those he spoke to were confusing Blue with someone else. But too many unconnected sources verified the story. Walt marveled and pondered and left his name and phone number at the switchboard of Blue's firm, though the person who took it warned that Mr. Gadsden gets so many messages that he doesn't even try to keep up with them.

"He used to, you see. But so many of them were from relatives of people who died, always wanting to know more about it, you see. But who *does* know about it? Do you? Do I?"

"This is a personal message from an old friend of his," said Walt.

"Except our Mr. Gadsden is kind of like that river in the folk song—just keeps rolling along, you see. You might try a letter, though we can't seem to forward the mail fast enough. It's as if he didn't *want* to hear from anyone, see what I mean?"

"Thank you," said Walt. "I won't try any more."

Not long after Walt had returned to New York, Chris went out for a "thinking walk," a long, distracted hike during which she would run over her choices and try to remember not to move her lips when she rehearsed what she'd say to the various major characters in her life. Often, she would stop on the way for rest and refreshment; while sitting in Kaffee Klatsch, nursing an omelet and mint tea, she noticed a tense and rather attractive young woman staring at her from the next table.

"So you're the director," said the stranger.

Chris waited.

"Of that play. The soap opera?"

Chris slightly nodded.

"I lost my lover in your theatre. Alice Chen?"

"Oh. Oh, I see. Ah. Yes. Well, I think I'm losing my lover in my theatre, too," said Chris. "Unless I lose my theatre and absolutely surrender to my lover."

"Huh."

" 'If the sparrow flies, the hawk goes hungry.' "

"What's *that* the fuck?"

"A Swedish proverb. It sort of means that for everyone who gets something, someone else loses something. You could call it the arch-individualistic view of life. As opposed to the tribal or communistic."

The stranger thought this over, then picked up her grilled cheese deluxe and coffee and plonked herself down at Chris's table.

"Evan," she said.

"Chris."

"*Terribly curious.* I mean, your lover and so on."

Chris shrugged. "I've been trying to figure it out all day. J. wants a home-kind of wife—"

"Me, too."

Chris smiled. "Alice Chen was your—"

"She still is, except now we have one of those open relationships of the ultramodern lesbianic code, which says, Thou shalt not control thy girl friend's cunt." Evan took a bite of her sandwich. "Too much like het marriages, apparently."

"Alice seemed so demure, though. Anything but a couch artist, I would have thought."

"Lady, that's her *act*. She's a manipulative little bitch with a gate of stone. Some love and leave 'em, am I right? I am right. Alice collects 'em. Keeps us on a string, wet and panting."

"I should sign up for lessons."

"So what's a smart dame like you doing with one of these man-is-the-center-of-the-universe punks?"

"Oh, but there's the rub—he's incredibly thoughtful and generous. He's ideal."

"Do you want your fiber?"

"My . . ."

"The sprouts. Looks like you're skipping them."

Chris offered her plate and Even claimed the sprouts. "Go on," Evan urged. "Thoughtful, ideal . . ."

"Intellectually invigorating . . ."

"And built like a Percheron?"

Chris blushed. "You saw the show. He played the visiting English lord."

"Oh, lady. Those dreamboat straight men are death on a woman, you don't know that? They take what they want—just like my Alice."

"Except he's right, in a way. Showbiz marriages don't work unless the partners are always together, like the Lunts or Julie Andrews and Blake—"

"So how come *you* give up *your*—"

"Yet why should *he* give up for *me*? It's a stalemate."

"If he loved you, he wouldn't give you up!"

"He says we'd tear each other to shreds."

"Isn't that the fun part?"

"Not for me," said Chris.

"Fascinated." Evan polished off her sandwich, pointed at the last of Chris's omelet, and, at Chris's nod, scooped it onto her plate. "Hate wasting food," Evan explained. "So now what?"

"I give in or he walks."

"The toad."

"Well, he did offer a compromise—I can take off once every year for a single project."

"Pretty shitty."

"Except . . ." Chris began, then stopped.

"Come on, you can tell me."

"Well, I haven't really made it in a big way, have I? I'm not sure how important the theatre is to me now. It was more exciting when I was young and nobody was dying."

"That hasn't stopped Alice, I assure you."

"She's a wonderful actress, actually."

"Defter than you know."

"So what's *your* choice? Give her up, or—"

"Oh, I can't give Alice up, and I can't match her. I'm her slave and I hate it. She's breaking all the rules."

Chris smiled. "I always thought gay life didn't have rules."

"We don't have standard rules—we each make our own. And Alice . . . She just isn't *combining,* you know?"

"She seemed very close to Fay."

"Another slave. Good sex makes us all so demented!"

"My problem isn't sex," said Chris, deeply pensive, as if just figuring something out. "It's love. I want to go home. You know? I want a place that *is* home. With people waiting for me there, worrying if I'm late. Somewhere they can't have Christmas without me."

"Is this guy worth giving up the theatre?"

"No one's worth giving up something you live for. I just don't know how much I live for that . . . marvelous imaginary world now. I've seen a lot of life, haven't I? I've had my wild twenties, my invigorated thirties. I could . . . settle down?"

"Huh."

"What are you going to do? About Alice?"

"Go on suffering. Waiting for her call. Reinventing the rules in my mind, of what a woman's entitled to—you know, trying to remember to forget everything this society taught me about what I'm allowed to hope for."

"Hope for," Chris mused.

"Yeah. Because I hope that she'll see *me* as home and move back in. Come on *home,* I'll say, and she'll go . . ." Blushing, Evan quickly said, "Fuck all that—what are *you* going to do?"

Chris sipped her tea as the history meter ticked away. We need to know what she does. Chris Predicts.

"Flip a coin?" says Chris.

PART VIII

Lenapee,
New Hampshire,
1990

"ALL RIGHT, SHOW me," said Lois, putting on her horse trader's smile, which reads, I'm honest and I pay cash, but I drive a *tight* bargain.

"Got these flintlocks, now," said the guy.

"Hell, is this the Spirit of '76?"

"Heh, maybe just about."

"Well, those are some pieces. Estella, come and see."

"Tha's okay," says Estella, hanging back by the register. She doesn't care for this give-and-take with the customers. She wants only to add the prices and take the money. Fair enough.

"I like the style of that stuff," Lois tells the man. "Though who knows what's the market for these old—"

"They all say that. Drop in the store a week later—it's all sold."

"No kidding," says our Lois, unconvinced.

"Got these Glidden vases, fine things," the guy goes on, ladling out the art pottery, and now Lois is glad. "This'll put meat on the plate," she says.

"Heh, stuff'll jump right out of the store."

The store is Lois's antiques shop, where she has arrived after nearly two decades of opening and closing two taverns, a restaurant, and even a sedate little dance hall in various parts of Hillsborough County, just north of New Hampshire's Massachusetts borderline. Nothing seemed to work; the gelid, unadventurous clientele depressed her and the authorities hemmed her in with ordinances.

"There's not much bohemia to draw on here," said Elaine at some point in all this. "You've always catered to the nonconformists, after all."

"I thought New England was the land of the individualist," Lois had gruffed.

"It is, but they're all individualist in exactly the same way. How about opening an antiques store?"

"What?"

"Think of the larks you'd have, exploring the countryside for ware. And at least you'd be running something—that's your forte. Being in charge, keeping the keys, lacing into the staff, telling off the customers . . ."

Lois grunted with pleasure.

"Besides," Elaine went on, captivated by the picture of her Lois doling out bud vases and quaint fans to tourists, "it's the ultimate completion of the lesbian experience—two grannies retiring to the outback, where one writes novels and the other sells antiques."

"Yeah, but what do I know about antiques?"

"You'll learn by watching the customers. They spot the object of desire, their eyes light for the flash of a moment, they assume a disinterested pose—but you have caught them, and, quick!, the price shoots high. Come, you know you'd love haggling. And doesn't the whole idea remind you a bit of Thriller Jill's—the browsers and bargainers spilling into the place of magic where they may find something to make them feel loved?"

"What would I call this place?"

" 'Bull in a China Shop,' of course!"

In fact, Lois loved the work. Tooling around the crisp green land on her "hunts" for merchandise made her feel liberated of cares and responsibilities, even of age. Sixty-seven when she opened the store in 1987, she felt as tough and confident as when she had taken over Jill's, and though Bull in a China Shop looked like any other New England antiquery along the tourist trails, Lois delighted in her unique touches, such as stocking plenty of men's items like canes and hunting gear, and hiring the only Hispanic woman in a six-town radius, Estella Vargas. The building that Lois opened her store in was so antique itself that none of the locals could remember who had put it up or for what purpose: a small clapboard rectangle sitting by itself just outside of Lenapee, where Lois and Elaine had been living for eighteen years.

"Okay, what's *that* thing?" says Lois, already adding up what the buy is going to cost. Probably break three hundred, but she'll unload half the haul inside of a week for twice that, easy.

"Now *that,* lady," says the guy, "is a bear trap."

"Vicious mother."

"This here's a tricky proposition. An't even legal to own, but for on your personal property. I wouldn't have brung it, 'cept I know you got a specialty in items of the kind."

"How's it open?" asked Lois, examining the huge metal crescent, its halves bit closed in a murderous embrace of serrate teeth.

"See this safety latch here?" The guy indicated a lever with the toe of his boot. "Warn, now, you don't go near this bitch except you're in the heaviest footwear you own. All righty-roo. The whole thing's done with the edge of the boot. The tip edge, watch. First, hit the safety," as he did. "Second—carefully avoiding any contact with the teeth, break the jaws open, secure the bottom line with your foot, and very steadily—no, it's sort of like a jerking—pull the top line up and up till you hear it . . ." With a click, the bear trap held open, one great ready yawn of terror for when the time comes.

"Any ground rules?" Lois asked.

"Don't open it unless you want to kill something."

"I want to, all right. Just can I get away with it?"

The guy broke into a waterfall of laughter. "Ma'am, do you know what a pleasure of business it is to conduct with you, after the nonsense they give me upstate?"

"Always told you, come to me first."

"No, I paw the lazy Susans and sheet music over to them. I hand those right over, say it's Lois wants the *real* stuff."

"Close up that bear trap and let's talk money."

"Got something you don't need any more of?"

Lois handed him one of her hundred Souvenir of New Hampshire paperweights, a miniature metal tray in the shape of the state.

"Watch this," he said, tossing the piece at the open trap, which sprang closed on it with the bite of a kraken.

"*Shoot,* that thing takes off!" said Lois.

.   .   .

When Lois and Elaine first moved to Lenapee, Elaine decided that she needed something to take her out of the house every so often; all writers do. Lois, who—long, long before—had put in a stint as a grade-school teacher, suggested that Elaine fill in as a "teacher's assistant," the Other Woman who assists in kindergarten, directs the Thanksgiving Pageant, and rides along on field trips.

"You'll like the work," Lois told her. "Kids are wonderful, because they're still enchanted. They haven't got mean yet."

"Oh, yes! It would be so lovely to go among people who couldn't possibly say, 'So you're the one who writes those frightful books.' "

Elaine eventually became the Lenapee School System's field-trip assistant, helping to squire the Third Grade to the Hagerford textile mill, the Fourth Grade along a length of the Merrimack River, and the Fifth Grade to the fish hatcheries just beyond Grasmere. As we speak, while Lois was making her best offer on the bear trap, Elaine was riding with the Fourth Graders to Grasmere when the back half of the bus erupted in groans, jeers, and cries of "Get him off!"

The teacher, by herself in the front seat behind the driver, turned, seemed to assess the event, and turned back again, ignoring it.

The noise continued, and Elaine, herself turning, saw a boy way at the back who was obviously the target of the activity. He was crying, yet he appeared not frustrated and hurt, as children so often do when persecuted by their fellows, but rather scared, as if oppressed by more than ridicule.

"Shouldn't you do something about that?" Elaine asked the teacher, whom she didn't like.

"Why don't you try?" asked the teacher, neither unpleasantly nor helpfully. Neutral.

Elaine made her way down the aisle into a sea of kids holding their noses or pretending to vomit.

"Save us from Diarrhea Donny!" one cried.

"He's the end of the world!"

"Eeughw, I can't breathe!"

"Off the bus," the chant began, and most of the kids joined in. "Off the *bus*! Off the *bus*!" The teacher remained in her seat, looking straight ahead.

Elaine went up to the sobbing boy in the hindmost seat. It was obvious that he had befouled his clothes, and his classmates were grinning like ghouls as they sang away. "Off the *bus*!"

"That's enough," Elaine told them. "How would you like being mocked if you'd had an accident?"

"I wouldn't *have* an accident!" one boy snickered.

"He's always doing this!"

"Yeah, he's such a sick mess!"

"Stinkball Donny strikes again!"

"The teacher hates him."

"All of you be quiet!" Elaine roared, and, in the ensuing silence, one little girl quietly said, "My mommy says he has the AIDS epidemic."

Elaine stared at her.

"Because he is getting thin day by day," the child added.

Another moment, and Elaine sat next to Donny and put an arm around him. He was shivering, like a small animal surprised under a tree. "Just hang on," Elaine said. "We'll stop somewhere and get you cleaned up. Okay?"

Crushed with humiliation, Donny wouldn't look up.

"The rest of you leave him alone," said Elaine as she got up. "It's ignoble to laugh at someone in trouble."

At the front of the bus, the teacher was gazing out the window.

"And you just sit here, Scheherazade?" Elaine asked her.

The teacher turned a bland face to Elaine.

"We have to stop and remedy the situation," Elaine said. "Immediately."

"We can't stop the whole bus just because—"

"There's a filling station," Elaine told the driver. "Up on the right."

"Lady, nobody . . . Look—"

"Pull over and shut up." To the teacher, Elaine said, "What you are doing could easily lose you your job. It may be illegal, too."

"I do my job!"

"I believe we should let the authorities decide that one," said Elaine, adding, to encourage the driver, "That goes for you, too."

The driver pulled into the station; Elaine took Donny into the washroom and fixed him up as best she could. She was very frightened, because he had a few purplish spots on his skin, and, like most people, she wasn't clear on where the risks lay. Was the child ill? But then how could his parents send him to school without . . . Well, what does an ailing child go to school *with*? I'm sixty-eight and a tower of health, Elaine thought. I've never suffered anything but the usual childhood stuff and the annual cold or two. I can chance it.

Elaine used up the paper towels and decided to abandon Donny's soiled underpants in the garbage can.

"Please don't tell my mother" was all that Donny said at this time.

When they came out into the serene New England spring morning, a busload of young faces was watching them through the windows. Still faces, no song. Kids don't know the terminology, but they ken what's happening.

"It's quite some day," Elaine told Donny. "We'd best get you home now."

"My mother doesn't like it when they send me home."

The driver played a game of "not seeing" Elaine, and she had to bang on the door to get it open. Two steps into the bus, Elaine told the teacher, "We're going to turn around and go back to school. I'll drive this child to his home."

Wearily officious, as if this were some bureaucratic squabble late on a Friday afternoon, the teacher began, "I happen to be in charge of—"

"Or I'll call the police here and now," Elaine said calmly. "A bluff? Ah, check her eyes."

The driver looked questioningly at the teacher. "Oh, do what she says," said the teacher, shrugging. The ride back was pretty quiet.

At school, Elaine took Donny to the nurse, who agreed that Donny needed a doctor. At this, Donny became frantic, though he quieted down when Elaine said she would talk to his mother herself.

"Do you have any brothers or sisters?" Elaine asked him in the car. "Do you like video games? What sport do you play?" But conversation was fitful, Donny clearly dreading what was to come at home. The only full-out sentence he uttered was "I don't know why this is happening to me."

Donny lived in a part of Lenapee that Elaine had seldom seen, a residential section just off the Goffstown Road that was known as Backtown for reasons that the locals typically kept as obscure as possible. Hemidemisemi-lapsed working-class, Elaine thought, driving through it. Welfare checks and blighted elms, denial and anger. I should write about it.

Donny wouldn't get out of the car when they reached the address that the nurse had written out, so Elaine went alone to the door to confront Donny's mother.

"Sent him home again, eh?" she said, glancing at and then dismissing Elaine's car, child and all. "He says he's sick, is that it? I know, sure."

"He *is* sick. I was going to ask you what medical care he's getting. Because his condition . . . Well, I was—"

"It's none of your beeswax, is my guess." She called out, "Well, come on, why dontcha? Got another holiday fer yerself!"

Donny came reluctantly; when he reached the doorway, his mother slapped him so hard he went down.

"That's fer givin' me yer trouble," she said calmly.

Speechless, Elaine helped Donny up. She loathed this woman so much that she couldn't bear to address her by name. "This child isn't faking. He's helpless. He needs a doctor."

"You need to take your nose out of other folk's lives, Missus Fancy Fluff. You an't his teacher, I know that much. You from the county? An't seen you before."

"Who I am doesn't matter. This boy is your responsibility, not your rag doll. What you just did to him is . . . Don't any of you disgusting people have any respect for human *feelings*? His classmates jeer at him, his teacher ignores him, and meanwhile he's shitting his guts out on the school bus, with his skin turning purple, and his mother—his *mother!*—doesn't even . . ."

Why am I doing this? She's not listening. Nobody's listening to this at all, anywhere. It's not real to them. So nature's found a new way to mug people, so what?

The woman was looking at Elaine, just looking; now she spoke. "Purple skin's all the rage, din't you hear so?" she said, rolling up a sleeve of her blouse. "It's the new look in Lenapee, they all agree."

Her arms were dotted with purple lesions, some small, others quite large.

"I could show you some real pretty ones on my paps," she went on. "Right where he sucked as a tad. Medical care, is it? I'm sure you got some doctors in mind. Some fancy fluff doctor from the other side of town who works for potatoes?"

She pointed the boy inside, staring Elaine down as he passed, then closed the door behind her.

Driving home, Elaine worried it over and over. What was she supposed to do? She saw herself appealing to some authority and finding the same cold Who Cares What You Think? that she had found in the teacher and bus driver. Donny's mother haunted her, too, because she was . . . well, let's say it: not unlike Lois, without the smarts and gumption and hidden kindness. A plain woman, blunt, unaware of the seemly dressings and disguises mothers teach daughters in this world, to make them safe for men. But something saved Lois—or Lois saved Lois, and Lois saved Elaine, for surely those who attempt to wear the disguise when honesty is their only proper fit must go insane in the end.

"Peter Smith is in the spare room," said Lois, when Elaine got home. "He's had another fight with his . . . What's that black look about?"

"A bad day."

"Huh? On a class trip? What, did Polly Pigtails grow a hangnail or something?"

"One of the children is . . ."

"Chick, you need a sample of the teapot. It's that spearmint flavor you like so much." Pouring it out. "There. Steaming away. You're wondering why I'm home in the middle of the day. Well, I made a buy that you would not—"

Elaine burst into tears.

"Well, what's this, now?"

"I'll be fine, just let me—"

"I could use some tea myself," said Peter, coming into the kitchen.

"Thought you were napping it off," replied Lois as she watched Elaine.

"Yeah, then I heard all the excitement down here and I couldn't keep away."

Peter was seventeen, funny, weird, and gay: slim and handsome to warm the heart and so desperate for affection that he made you feel a saint if you said, "Lovely tie."

Actually, it was Elaine who would say it. Lois would say, "You wear stuff like that around here, they'll run you out on a rail."

Peter wore stuff like that, to school, a cookout, the store. He grew his hair long. He got on better with girls than boys. His father beat him for sport—not whenever he was drunk; whenever he was around—and Peter's mother would leave the room. That is: She allowed it.

"I need advice," said Peter, sitting at the kitchen counter.

"Then write Dear Abby," said Lois, pouring his tea.

"I shall advise you," said Elaine, joining Peter. "That's precisely why we obviously contented and self-respecting old lezbies and queens are here in the first place, to make it easier for—"

"I don't know about that Tennessee Williams character on Merrimack Road," said Lois. "Wilbur Cummings or whatever his name is, with his snuffbox and his vapors and his Saturday nights in Manchester. I don't know why that old queen is here. Comes into the store now and again, picking at everything. One of these days—"

"Wilson Enters is he, first off," said Elaine, as Lois and Peter shared a confidential look. "*And* on those pathetic Saturday nights, I expect, he may go as far as to buy a cheese sandwich for some toothsome young chap at the Bon Ton Salon, but—"

"Is that how I'll end up?" asked Peter. "Some quaint old fairy? Everyone laughing at me and I don't even know it?"

"No," said Elaine. "Because it's much easier for gays of your generation to accept themselves as they are. You won't have to create an artificial persona to match some ridiculous belief in yourself as something out of . . ." Elaine shrugged. "*Suddenly Last Summer?*"

"Then how come all those gay kids commit suicide? That's the new statistic."

"It isn't new," said Lois, rinsing the odd cup and plate in the sink. "It's just getting mentioned now."

"You'd think parents would . . ." Elaine began. "Would what? Would rather their children were happy? They always say so. But it's never the children's idea of happiness: It's the parents'. I met quite a parent today, I can tell you. A real Mother of the Year."

"Dressed in black, rides a broomstick, and a house just fell on her sister?" asked Peter.

"No."

"Not mine, obviously."

"Peter wants us to tell him," said Lois, inhaling her spearmint tea, a rare—for her—sensual exercise, "if he should run away."

"The city!" Peter cried.

Elaine said, "Oh, dear."

"I'm ready for it," Peter assured her. "I realized it suddenly last samba."

"But you haven't been graduated from high school yet! Surely you need that to . . . No. What do you want to be?"

"An MTV announcer."

"It's not his job and it's not his school," said Lois. "It's how does he escape from his piece-of-shit father, who may well kill him with beatings."

"My sister's gay, too."

Lois was startled silent.

Elaine said, "How ever did we get into this?"

"I started hanging around the China Shop," Peter explained. "Because I scoped Lois out as this sympathetic granny, and then—"

"No, I meant, How come we're caught up in the misadventures of a teenager we hardly know?"

Peter looked at her as if she'd asked where babies come from. "Because you're these, like, major-league advisers to a poor scared gay kid with murder for parents."

One of the cats, Zuleika, came running in, worrying a ball of tinfoil.

Then the other cat, The MacQuern, scurried in to intercept the foil and race off with it, Zuleika on his tail.

"Cats are a scream," Peter remarked. "They think they're so fabulous. Just like straights, you know?"

"Why does your father . . . He really beats you?" Elaine asked.

"Yeah, well, first he gets on my case about some parent thing, like, Your grades stink, or, Why aren't you on the football squad, like, or, What the shit are you dressed up as? So he gets really into it, it's building, and he's shouting and shoving me, and he *really* gets into that, so then he grabs me by the hair and he—"

"Stop," said Elaine. "Parents." She looked at Lois. "Yet he's so calm in the telling of such brutality. I . . . I don't recall anything like that when I was young. Do you?"

"I'm telling you, it never got mentioned. Brutal families were a big secret then. Like we were."

"Maybe I shouldn't have come out at the age of eleven," said Peter, mock-pensively. "It was a good, bold career move, but it kind of, like, *polarized* the *world*. Still, what choice did I have? One look and you *know* I'm gay. Why should I pretend? I didn't choose it, it chose me."

"So what does he do?" Elaine asked Lois.

"Hey, I love this, with you two making my plans."

"Your sister's gay, too?" Lois asked.

"Yeah, but she's hiding it. Successfully, so far."

"That proves it's genetic," said Elaine.

"Oh sure," Peter agreed. "Even my dog, Pet Shop Boy, is gay. He's got a thing for the Scottie puppy next door. Pet Shop Boy likes 'em young. Chicken meat."

Lois was staring at Peter. She asked Elaine, "You know who he reminds me of?"

Elaine nodded. "Johnny."

"Who's that?" asked Peter. "Some suave stylemeister who's seen it all, huh?"

"He's as fresh as Johnny ever was," Lois pointed out.

"But he has innocence. Johnny was always so knowing."

"Cute?" asked Peter.

"Devastating, actually. A child's sweetness and a man's self-assurance. A Pan, perhaps. So youthful. We called him 'the Kid.' Even now—"

"Where is this dude?"

"Here, as of tomorrow. He and Walt weekend here so often they're almost—"

"Walt? Some powder puff of a kept boy, whom I deftly replace with my innate grooviness?"

Lois chuckled. "No one will replace Walt in Johnny's life."

Elaine was thinking. "Is there some way," she asked, "that we can connect Peter to the local gay culture?"

"I *am* the local gay culture," Peter protested. "That's why I need to go to New York."

"They'll only cart you back here," said Lois. "Or whack the law at us for corrupting you. And who'll look after your sister?"

"Oh, she can handle my father. Besides, he likes her." After a moment, he added, "I think they're making it on the sly."

Lois shrugged. Fathers, who knows what they'll do?

"Maybe Peter should go to the police," said Elaine. "Assault is assault, even if it's your father."

"Yeah, the police'll be real receptive to a long-haired kid in a fag tie," said Lois, "swearing a complaint against his father."

"I'm doomed," said Peter.

"We'll bring you over to meet Johnny," said Lois. "Maybe he'll have an idea. Heck knows, he started out just like you. . . . What's that word for a kid who's smart?"

" 'Precocious,' " said Elaine.

"Ha!" said Peter. "Gay boys are *born* precocious. It's in our contracts."

"Where does he get that stuff from?" asked Lois, bemused.

Estella's brother Jose worked in Lois's store one afternoon a week, mostly hauling objects up from the basement and helping Lois load up and transport a buy. Lois liked Jose because he earned his dough with good hard labor and neither put her on with phony humility nor vexed her with brinkmanship Attitude, that let's-see-how-rude-I-can-get act that Lois kept running up against when she and Elaine made their annual New York trip in midsummer. Jose did his job neat and true and impersonal, and that's what counted, especially when he made the occasional delivery within the county. Though Lois's prime constituency was the town trade up from the "South"—Boston, Connecticut, and New York—her shop enjoyed a certain cachet among socially tenacious local women. One could create a pleasurable stir (or even disrupt a bridge-club Monday) with a reference to some piece or other "due in from Miss Lois's wonderful store in Lenapee."

Miss Lois. Miss Elaine. Such delicate locutions lead us to wonder just how Lois and Elaine's fellow citizens saw the pair. Was there a suspicion they were lovers? Perhaps their advanced age and natural dignity (in Lois's case, it was more an energy) protected them. Then there was Elaine's repute as a novelist. True, she was a dangerous one, outspoken. But, in Lenapee, they knew only that she was famous: They didn't know what for. In the end, the two were viewed, perhaps, as the world often views independent women living together, as a tiny nunnery, a place where flesh is hidden and passions suppressed.

Peter Smith's father viewed them as a challenge to his authority: as father and tyrant, lover and king. These two women and their damn-shit interference! So, late that afternoon, he swaggered into the China Shop, planted himself before Lois, and bawled out, "You fucking lady-men are trying to recruit my son!"

Jose, who had been setting up a display of antique baseball bats imprinted with the stars' names (including two Stan Musials, very rare of this kind), went on red alert. But Estella put a hand on his arm as Lois just stood there, calmly staring Mr. Smith down. She snacks on his kind.

Unaccustomed to a total lack of groveling and surrender, Mr. Smith tried to raise the stakes with some physical intimidation. He picked up one of those dear old fans—was this one moiré? velvet? Lois was never sure—and began twirling it in the air by its beaded black-string stem. Okay, that's it, and Jose stepped forth—but Lois signaled him back. The town wouldn't think anything of a Latino's getting jailed, but Lois was white, a woman, old (and thus perceived as helpless), and, most important, a proprietor. She held the ace on this deal.

"I want your faggot claws off my family," said Mr. Smith, letting the fan fly to hit the wall and drop.

Lois replied, "Get out of my store. What, you're still here? That's trespassing, and it's my citizen's duty to call the police. Oh. Here's my tea, fresh-poured and steaming hot from my famous China Shop samovar. Let's have a cup as I dial."

And Lois threw the tea into Mr. Smith's face, thinking, Burn in hell, baby.

"It was an accident, obviously," Lois told the police a bit later, as they led Mr. Smith off in handcuffs. "He was throwing the merchandise around and made me skittery all over. After, I tied his hands while he was wriggling around on the floor there. He was *so* out of control, officer," Lois added, thinking, That's cute. That's a cute, helpless-lady kind of touch. Lois the actress.

"That what you saw?" the officer asked Estella.

"Tha's right."

"He's a criminal," Jose put in.

Lois shrugged; and off went the cops with Mr. Smith.

"Recruiting his son?" Lois bit out then. "*He's* doing the recruiting. *Straights* recruit you with their churches and laws and their hatred. Well, the war's on now, I expect." She looked at Estella and Jose. "Anyone who wants to quit, that's fair by me."

"Tha's okay," said Estella. "Nobody else hire us, probably."

"What are Hispanics doing in New Hampshire, anyway?" asked Lois.

"I'm *born* here."

"Me, too," said Jose, flashing a winning smile.

Elaine, just then, was meeting the Kid and Walt's train in Manchester. Oh, it's kisses, exhilaration, and that wonderfully safe feeling we enjoy with oldest, truest friends, the ones who never pick at our raw spots or fail to empathize when we're in straits. There's a fine transaction in these visits: The boys give the girls city excitement, dish and something *doing*, while the girls give the boys a chance to relax.

What elaborate treats the hosts would prepare! And what delight at the unveiling of the arcane gourmet products the guests had brought!—for the only thing Elaine missed about New York was shopping for jars of imported antipasto, unheard-of chutneys, newfangled biscuits in the specialty shops. But I'm going to skip all that, for the history meter is ticking more loudly than ever before and I have many plot strands yet to bind. Time is all, the sole element in life that is absolutely spent. You can make more money or find another love—right?—but you can't reclaim spent time.

Let's cut to late that afternoon, when Lois took the Kid on a drive to New Boston while Elaine and Walt strolled along the mystery paths of the Lenapee woods.

"We had a forest like this in the middle of Gotburg," Walt noted. "It seemed so big and ferocious, but you know what? Once I was fifteen years old, I could tell it was a tidy little place. On an autumn day, you could stand in the middle and see clear to all the edges of it."

"Everything loses power as we age," said Elaine. "Adults seem less wise, even ridiculous. Authority is exposed as corrupt. By my age, what's left that's awesome?"

"Destiny. You know why? Because the older you get, the more you suspect that we're all part of some intense program. We influence each other without even knowing it. We can change the course of a life!"

"Tell me what's happening in New York. How are the men adjusting sexually to the Age of High Risk, pray?"

Walt shook his head. "It's like you know ten people. One or two are playing it extra-safe. Another three or four think safe sex means Don't touch anyone over twenty-nine."

"No!"

"Two more fuck all over the place, with a condom if you insist. The rest of them act as if there were no AIDS at all."

"I can't—"

"One guy told me that his new boy friend is making him fuck without protection in order to make a political statement."

"Oh, Walt!"

"So we herd into Central Park, and there's three girls from *City of Angels* with pom-poms, no less, and, I don't know, Woody Allen and so forth. On one of those diamonds on the Park's west side, near about Sixty-third Street. Been there since Pieter Stuyvesant, for all I know. So we're in our bleachers watching the *City of Angels* pom-pom girls revive those ridiculous high-school cheers, and the other team's in *their* bleachers watching their wives recalling *their* pep cheers. And it's the gays versus the cops at *baseball,* do you believe it?"

"Who won?"

"Ah, Lois, always striking at the heart of the thing. Doesn't the very act of gays and cops meeting on the sporting field impress you? Isn't it a relief from what we knew?"

"Any girls on our side?"

"The meanest second baseman I ever saw. She was scoring them out with bow and arrow."

Lois chuckled.

"We lost, but 16–14."

"Respectable," said Lois, braking as a Volkswagen ran a red light. "Any feeling that some air had been cleared with this game? I recall when cops didn't think we were human."

"Well, twenty years ago you couldn't have imagined this game. Now it's like the Yankees play the Dodgers."

"Huh."

"Granted, the die-hard haters don't show up, so it's a misleading picture. But a voice in you says, Could maybe some of them have switched over from loathing to tolerance? Did someone come out to them—a brother, a son, a colleague? Hell, a father? And did they suddenly realize how common this thing is, how right-around-the-corner? Gays are . . . We're . . ."

"Gays and lesbians."

"Gay *is* lesbian."

"Elaine says you have to say both words now. 'Gay' is just men."

"It used to be coed. Like first grade."

"Elaine likes 'queer.' It covers everything."

"Terms!" the Kid cried. "Remember when there wasn't a word for what we were—I mean, a real one? The only people who could speak of us were psychs and sociologists. Jesus, we weren't there! And now we hold parades."

"Looking real forward to the next one," said Lois. "All those bold young women, nipples straight out and everyone stand clear. That's *my* queer nation."

"Amen, brother," said the Kid.

"What's so strange," said Elaine, "is that they harp so on this family thing just when the news breaks out that the American family is the great repository of sinful secrets. Fathers seduce daughters, mothers scream their sons into catatonia or serial killing, and, through it all, the nation's First Family, those unbelievably disreputable Reagans, turns out to be practicing every lunacy and vanity available. Family values? That must mean Screw the kids and fuck the country."

Elaine and Walt walked along, now under the trees, now under the sun.

"It makes me so angry," Elaine went on, "that it's just as well I live off and away. I'd be shouting all day at people, reforming them."

"I made up a cure for being too angry," said Walt. "I call it Taking a Left Turn. It's where you would usually get mad, but you do nothing. You wait and think it over. You can always yell later. But, if you consider the whole thing, maybe you won't need to."

"Interesting."

"That's why I broke up with Blue—because I was yelling so much. And the more I yelled, the more I wanted to. Now that I know how to create deep inner peace, it's too late. But, you know?, all these three years I have been thinking about the word 'home.' Because my original home wasn't a great place to be, except for Tom and Luke and Chris watching out for me. So then my home was with them, but now it's kind of broken up because . . . well, you know."

"Isn't home what you have with Johnny?"

"I suppose so. . . ."

"Believe me," said the Kid, sharing a Rome apple with Lois on a bank of the Merrimack, "I've tried and tried. It's as if he vanished. You know these marginally socialized gay boys—they change addresses the way Madonna changes her pubic hairdo."

Lois guffawed.

"Thank God for a woman who doesn't go *Shame, shame!* at gay humor."

"Could this guy be dead?" Lois asked.

"I hunch otherwise. He's out there, somewhere or other. I kept thinking he'd call us one day: Hey, it's Blue, can I talk to Walt? Back when we moved to New York, I wouldn't let him—and I still dread it, because . . . Well, think what I'd lose."

"You love Walt that heavy?" asked Lois. "Yet you're scared he'd leave you?" She was trying to picture herself and Elaine on that level, couldn't see it. Leave for what?

"It's my neediness that scares me. I can blow an evening standing by the window watching the street if he's out late. I can read his mind by the way he eats his soup. I can feel the cream slowly filling his dick as he's fucking me, stroke by stroke. He doesn't know it, of course, but he's utterly in charge of me. No feeling is authentic until I share it with him. No personal or professional triumph is secured till he hears of it and congratulates and admires and maybe even likes me a little for it. I live . . . entirely within his compass."

"That's love, sucker."

Raising the core of the eaten apple, the Kid said, "This is me, the day Blue shows up and takes Walt away. But, you know, I'm a smart lover, give the boy plenty of room. That was the trouble with Blue—those two were so all over each other they were strangling." The Kid tossed the apple high, into the water. "Recycling," he explained.

"You really think Blue shows up and Walt walks? Just like that?"

The Kid shrugged. "The thing is, I always used to go around as Jerrett Troy, and if Blue's trying to find us, that's who he'd ask for. But nowadays I'm using my real name, and all he knows of that is 'Johnny.' "

"What's the rest of it, come to that?"

"It doesn't matter, because I'm the Kid—ever was and will be. It's not the name that matters, it's the me I invent. Dig, old pal?"

.   .   .

The late-afternoon wine flowed freely, and all were in a merry mood for dinner, giggling (Elaine), chuckling (Lois), crowing (Walt), and holding the stomach to roar uncontrollably (the Kid) at a fanfaronade of camp and satire. The Kid's main contribution was an improvisation on *Gone With the Wind* with Bombasta as Scarlett O'Hara, Lois as Rhett Butler, George Bush as Ashley, and Candice Bergen—"the woman every lesbian loves!" the Kid noted; and he's not far off—as Melanie, with Transvesto, every so often, trying to sneak his Sondheim cabaret act into the narrative.

The Kid had never been sharper; some of his uses of Lois-as-the-world's-most-virile-man were so persuasive that Elaine's eyebrows rose in awed alarm. Should parody be so perceptive? At the end, the other three gave the Kid an ovation, and Elaine said, "Johnny, you're ready for the world stage!"

"No, because straights still don't get it. Some of them hate us, some of them don't care, and some are probably trying to figure out and befriend us. But even they don't see what we see."

"What do we see?"

"Them."

The phone rang.

"At last they'll hear it," Lois told Elaine.

"Oh—our greeting tape. Yes, Lois stamps right over and picks up when it rings, but I'm always afraid that another of my intense fans . . ." She halted as the tape switched on. "Hello," came Elaine's voice. "This is Elaine. We're not in right now, but if you'd kindly leave a message . . ."

Lois's voice cut in, from some distance away: "Don't tell anyone, but I'm here, too!"

"Lois," said the Kid, "your sense of nuance!" He blew her a kiss.

"I'd redo it," said Elaine, "but it feels so true to life like that."

The caller had come on—a man's voice, rough, beery, possibly disguised through a handkerchief: "I'm going to firebomb your lives, you shit-fag queers. You lesbos." A pause, some rattling. Then: "You won't know it's coming, you hag fuck bitch-kill, but you'll be burning. I'll blow you away to your bones!" More rattling, a click, the dial tone.

Elaine looked at Lois; Lois shrugged.

"Late with the gas bill again?" the Kid asked.

Walt said, "Has that happened before?"

Elaine shook her head.

"I cut Peter Smith's father down to size in the store today. Got him arrested and what all. This is his idea of revenge—threatening women with anonymous phone calls. There's a straight man for you, every time. Sneaks, rapists, and pieces of shit."

"Oh, my God," said Elaine. "What if he comes around some night and—"

"I surely *hope* he comes around. Because tomorrow I'm buying the biggest, fiercest German shepherd I can find, and he can tear Peter Smith's father's balls off right here on my property, and then it'll be over."

"Who's Peter Smith?" asked the Kid.

"I'll get some lights for outside. Floodlights."

"For the store, too," Elaine put in.

"Already got night-lights there, front and back. All-nighters."

"You do?" Elaine asked, feeling safer.

"You didn't know that? You don't think I can protect my stuff? My people?"

"Isn't she wonderful?" Elaine asked—told—the men. "I'm no good for battle. I can't even deal with tragedy in art now. Every time the *Grapes of Wrath* movie comes on television, Lois pulls up a chair and I run upstairs to hide."

"I like that mother," said Lois. "No fancy stuff—just hangs in there and gets it done."

The guests were impressed with Lois's cold-blooded response to the hate call, and the weekend went on unimpeded. But Lois decided to move quick and cool, to counter any possible attack. Heck knows, such things were happening more and more, as church leaders and family fascists eagerly stirred up youthful daredevils while dressing themselves in masks of blameless reason.

"No time," Lois cried the next morning, waving customers away as she pored over the ads. "Estella will help you."

"I was wondering about that bear trap," said a man.

Lois looked up. "It came in with a buy. It's not for sale."

"Well, I just wondered. Does it work?"

Lois looked at him. "You ever see a bear trap that didn't?"

"I've never seen a bear trap. I was curious about this one. I mean, does one dare even open it?"

"*One* might not," said Lois. "But I sure can. Stand way back." Yet, as she moved, Lois hesitated. "No, heck that. I've got a dog to buy."

"I breed dogs," said the man.

"Sure."

"Really."

"Shepherds? Or a pinscher, maybe? I need a guard on my place. Intruder comes on the property, dog goes wild, jumps at his throat if necessary."

"I don't breed attack dogs, but I don't think you could do better than one of my Labs. Smart, loving, alert, and they'd jump the Lord Himself if He pulled a piece on you."

"Always saw them as placid animals."

"Well, they're house pets. Friendly's their style. But you declare war on them and they fight. Fast, sharp fighters, I'd say. Shepherds and pinschers are terrifying but they're unpredictable. A Lab'll stick."

"Hmm."

"I'd give you a look at my puppies if you'll trade me a look at this here trap."

"Don't want a puppy," said Lois, warming to this. "I want a full-grown. I could have trouble *tonight*."

"Got those as well. I could let you have Rock Hudson, though he'll cost you some."

Lois considered the guy. "Now, Rock Hudson could be just what I'd use."

"You willing to show me that trap, now?"

Lois had to follow the man's car all the way to New Boston for the dog, but she was happy with him: a big, dignified animal with bossy eyes and a formidable bark.

"How's he going to feel about separating here?" Lois asked the man.

"We have a few tricks," said the man, tying a red handkerchief around Rock Hudson's neck, as the dog preened. "They only get the bandanna on special occasions, so it makes them proud. Proud dog's an independent dog, you know. Then"—the guy stood up and picked through a box of dog toys—"we set him up with the red ball he used to chase when he was a tad." Noting the ball, the dog tensed a bit. "You'll find him easy to manage with the ball around. It's like the clock we put into the puppy basket to soothe them on their first night in the world."

"The ticking," said Lois, remembering. "They still do that?"

"Well, I do."

"Funny how some things in life are totally permanent and other things totally change, huh?"

"Hmm. Yeah, well. But I always say, it's not that things change so much as that we see them different. They're the same. We're just better informed."

"Well, how true that is," said Lois, shaking hands.

"Been a pleasure, ma'am. Really liked that bear trap."

Coming back into Lenapee, Lois was tooling down the Post Road when she saw Peter up ahead, walking home, followed at a slight distance by a gang of boys, presumably his schoolmates. Slowing as she neared, Lois could tell that Peter was nervous and the boys were laughing and shouting at him.

Wish I had one of those ball bats, Lois thought, getting out of the car. Peter looked as if he were lost in the desert and she were a Coke, but she signaled him to keep moving along right past her, to continue on home. They'll get him today, she was thinking, and me and Elaine tomorrow, as she strode up to the boys looking like an order of bloody murder to go. No, not up to them—into them, forcing them to fall back in surprise as she grabbed two heads by the hair and banged them together.

"Who else?" she said, as the boys made the usual outraged noises of the truly guilty. Move quick, keep at it, they'll back off. "Oh, you?" she asked, crashing two more skulls, this time in cymbal style, glancing off each other. *"Nice,"* she said. "Now, get the fuck *back*"—shoving one of them—"in *that* direction"—shoving another—"or what are you gonna do, strike a *lady?*"

"Who the shit are you, Batwoman?" cried one of the boys. Handsome, Lois noted, with Casanova hair and sensitive eyes. What gets inside such nice-looking people that they want to hurt others?

"Yeah, you should mind your fuckin' business, will ya?" said one of the boys.

"Yeah, because who the *fuck* she thinks she—"

Lois grabbed this one by the hair and collar and threw him into the parked car next to them with such triumphant vehemence that he momentarily passed out. Her father, long before, had a favorite piece of advice: "If the pie's so good, eat the whole thing."

Again, Lois asked, "Who else?" Seventy as she was, she had strength and commitment. The boys saw that she had made a very certain choice and was going to up the stakes by the second until they gave in to her will and retreated. One of them tried to hold his ground; him she slammed against one of the car windows, hoping it would break and disfigure him.

It didn't, but the other boys backed farther away and, oddly, were suddenly silent, lurking and staring and shaking themselves.

"Get in the car," Lois called over her shoulder, knowing that Peter had to be there. "We're going to call the police."

The enemy immediately dispersed, because the first thing a New Hampshire cop does when summoned to a scene of any kind is to find out who has Substances on his or her person.

Alone with Peter, Lois said, "Let's get our stories straight."

"Hey, there's a dog in there."

"Were they after you or what? Were you in fear of bodily harm?"

"Yeah, they were after me. I don't know if they were going to do anything. I mean, don't get a boy wrong, I'm really glad you—"

"*If* they were going to do anything, huh? What, do they have to lug a cannon around for you to get the picture? It always starts with nothing. Walking behind you and calling out things. But it ends with killing you. And how about looking at me when I—"

"I'm sorry, I'm sorry."

"Like that guy in Maine a few years back. Not much older than you, and it started like nothing with him. High-schoolers doing a little bullying. Suddenly, he's screaming that he can't swim but they're throwing him in the river. Why, Peter? For sport! *We die for their fun!*" Had she been literary, she might have added, " 'As flies to wanton boys.' " Of course, then she wouldn't have been my Lois.

She was scarcely Peter's, at that. He had never heard her yell before, never seen her furious. In the car, he stared at her. They weren't talking.

Because Lois was deep in thought. No, it's not sport, is it? It's serious business. Because it's always started by the big secret gay. He's so crazed to convince the world that he's hetero that it's not enough to *appear* straight. He's got to organize defensive expeditions. So when he's a teen, he's leading his friends in jump-the-faggot assaults. When he's older, he's heading up Parents With Christian Values groups. Because, let's face it, the real straights are busy running car pools and coaching Little League and making love. The fake straight is the one obsessed with getting the gays.

"Your father," Lois said suddenly. "Did he ever seem gay to you?"

"He . . . Did he what?"

"Okay, I don't mean gay like belonging to our kind of life. But did you ever notice him . . . looking at another man? Trying not to cruise? Maybe getting all alert when one of those hunk-in-the-shower soap commercials comes on television?"

Peter thought it over. "I can't say I ever did. You think it's funny that he's so gung ho about hetness?"

"Everyone else in the country is worried about the economy. He's worried about who's having sex with who else where no one can even see it. I think it's funny, yeah."

"So who's the dog in the backseat?"

"Rock Hudson."

"Oh, that's no name! He looks like a Winston to me."

"Winston?" Lois echoed, laughing.

"Hey, Winston." Peter extended his hand, and the dog nosed shyly forward. "Here, boy. Winston, dog. Yeah, that's the way." Peter petted the dog. "Good boy. Good dog." To Lois, he said, "He knows who he is."

After dropping Peter off, Lois brought Winston home and announced that she was starting right in on building a doghouse. Walt wanted to help, as long as he didn't have to get too close to the power saw, and Elaine and the Kid went upstairs to schmooze in his favorite part of the house, a semi-finished attic room with a great sunny dormer window that had been fixed up with a bench running along its length. There the Kid and Elaine ensconced themselves and watched Lois and Walt starting Winston's doghouse.

"Isn't she amazing?" said Elaine. "Who else would have the lumber and tools right where she wants them—not to mention knowing how to do it in the first place?"

"Do you ever . . . stray?"

"Oh, Johnny!"

"Well . . ."

"What woman would stray from Lois? She's my goddess, my secret, my red Delicious apple. She's everything."

"But do you never see some young creature with the dear velvet skin and full-blooming breasts and think . . ."

"Well . . . hmm. Last year. During our annual New York visit for, la!, Gay Pride. I did see this youngish blond woman hurrying up Third Avenue. She had one of those new haircuts where it's thick atop with a brush cut along the brow and very thin around the ears, and she was walking with such a heavy tread—and her eyes! Glowing with comment and judgments. I thought, That's the new young Lois. Twenty-three, twenty-four, and, oh, so dishy! But did I follow her? Surely never."

"You're content."

"Lois and my books, that's it for me. And some socializing work. Some reason to feel that I have done something for someone before I depart."

"That's your writing."

"No, the only way to do something is to *do something*. There's a little boy in this town who may have . . . Well, some ill condition. And he's so scared and so unknowing and so unloved. Can I do something for him? For the blind? For the lame, the dispossessed? I've had a successful life, excellent love and work. I owe—surely I owe—sharing something of that with those who haven't what I have."

"No, you're crying! Jesus . . ."

"It's that boy and his fear. What I saw. No, I'm all right. Look. . . ."

Elaine indicated the window, through which the Kid saw Lois measuring two-by-fours with a T square while Walt gamboled with Winston.

"Natural people," said Elaine.

"Not Walt. He created himself, just like me—but there're a few kinks in his system. He built the maze, yet he doesn't know the way home."

Elaine was gazing out the window.

"He's joyful," she noted. "Innocent. There is so little of that. Do you know, I'm now phone pals with my old editor? Johnna Roberts? Gloomy and jaded—yet somehow I sense that that is New York's version of joyful and innocent. It's the things you are when you're feeling good. Oh. No, not good. Sensible. Profound. The average American's idea of a good time is a six-pack, no speeding ticket, and some girl gets fucked. The New Yorker's idea of a good time is Israel retaliates for a terrorist attack."

"I could use that line in the Act."

"Anyway, Johnna Roberts. Nowadays she's very into novels by uncompromising young women. She tells me, 'How did I ever let you go?' "

"How did she?"

"She wasn't ready then. I don't even know how it happened that *I* was. Oh . . . I think of writing about how it feels to be a dyke the way I felt about Lois the day I met her: *This has to occur.* That's it, Johnny. That's all there is."

The Kid, too, gazed out the window. Lois had defined her doghouse framework and was starting to fill out the sides. Walt, who had painted (red) what structure there was, was now painting the spare two-by-fours, just in case, while playing ball with Winston.

"Such wonderful people I've known," said Elaine. "Such lovely, caring, lovely people. If a fairy had come and said, 'Go straight and I'll grant you a million dollars,' I'd have turned it down. Wouldn't you?"

"Well . . . A million I'd have to think about."

.   .   .

Lois had a buy scheduled for that evening, way up in Contoocook. But she was so busy that day that she didn't take off till after nine o'clock, and it was nearly midnight that she got back to Lenapee. Still, she decided to head straight for the store and unload then and there.

Wonder how much it costs me keeping these lights on all night?, she was wondering, though of course by now Elaine was earning enough for them both to live in the most heedless luxury, had either wanted to. Lois always paid her own way, covered her share; it wouldn't even have occurred to her not to do so. Elaine's money was Elaine's. She gave some of it to good, solid charities like Lambda Legal Defense Fund and frittered some of it away on froufrou like that English book club with the fancy editions: Agatha Christie bound as tasty as Shakespeare, when Elaine had Lois's own collection of Christie paperbacks to choose from. But, if it made Elaine happy, it was good.

How easy to find happiness, Lois mused. Whatever else they toss at you, it's there, just ask for it. Oh, there's a line? So line up. It's waiting, it happens. Lois's parents had no trouble hooking up. They lived quietly and joyfully together, never a tough word in a month of Sundays. And when one died, the other died, too. And think of me, now. I saw Elaine and her flat tire and I just . . . stopped.

Going to have to take this display of baseball bats downstairs, make room for the new stuff: a shelf of Oz books in early editions with color plates and such to sting the collectors right in the quick, a pile of song sheets in the pre–World War I king size, a series of British royalty mugs, an antique German Monopoly set, a silver business-card caddy, maps, prints, sporting equipment . . . I must be the queen of what's irrelevant.

Lois's eye fell on the bear trap, and she impulsively decided to open it. Fit it up for the kill. Maybe she had spent one hour or so too long with maps and prints, not to mention moiré fans. Maybe she was fascinated, as some are, by WET PAINT or DO NOT ENTER. Anyway, Lois carefully set the jaws of the trap apart and ready to spring, then stood back and stared at it.

Shoot, what a hefty piece, she thought.

The dog breeder had likened it to a self-administered test. He said, "Everyone has to face their own particular trap—set it out and bait it themselves. Then they have to conquer it. You know? We make our own traps."

"What if you don't know what your trap is?" Lois asked.

"Ma'am, that would be as bad as falling into it."

Life as a *boutiquière*. Lois phoned Elaine to say she was going to be home late, did the receipts, priced some of the new stuff, and decided to carry all but one of the bats downstairs herself and set up some of the new merchandise. In a cash-down industry like this, delays of a day or two could send business to your competitors—like that sneaky Penny Koster in Goffstown, with her Penny's From Heaven (which Elaine referred to as "Doilies From Hell"). Lois loved getting a new buy priced and on the shelves within a day.

As she was about to come upstairs, she heard something, a noise from outside, maybe a car. Quickly, silently, Lois mounted the stairs and paused in the doorway. More noises—car doors? No, a trunk. Someone grunting—carrying something heavy? The sounds were coming from the back, so there was no window to look out of.

Place is all lit up, and I'm downstairs, so it looked deserted. And someone's here to make trouble. Okay, let's do the camera. Lois grabbed the Polaroid, listened, heard nothing, then pulled the back door open.

There in the night was Peter Smith's father, huffing around with a big rough stained can of something; and Lois snapped his shot.

"One more," she told him. "Say 'cheese.' "

He didn't seem startled. "Well, there's the lezbin, I see," he said, putting down the can. "Didn't notice you in the light of the store."

"Went downstairs," said Lois, taking him from another angle. "What's in the drum?"

"Gasoline."

Another photo. "Nice of you to do the store and spare the house."

"The house is next." He laughed. "Now, here it's so late I thought you'd left the car overnight. Guess I shoulda known, but that is not gonna matter. You and me, we're gonna settle up now and here, see." And he came forward, with the gasoline, into the store.

"If you have to talk in clichés, it's *here and now*," said Lois, snapping away and passing the pictures from the camera to the counter quite, quite calmly, thinking, There's the Stan Musial bat and the open bear trap. He's so slow and stupid, he probably isn't armed, but if he moves for a piece, I push him into the trap. Fact, I'd kind of like to.

"Ayuh, clichés you say" was the response of Peter's father.

The lug. Thinks he's got me just by his bulk and his manner. By his testosterone. The helpless granny shaking away here. Christ, what a jackass! Doesn't even take a look around, maybe warn himself about the jaws of death just behind him. Smirking at me. Enjoying himself.

"Oh, clichés," he sang out. "But you'll be Fainting Fanny when I get done." His face hardened, all wrapped up in itself. "You can't have children the Christian way, so you witch our sons to your cult."

I could lunge forward. One good push and he'd fall straight back into the trap. The world would be a better place for everyone with scum like this out of the picture. And how many times am I supposed to repel this invader? The house is next? Oh, the *house* is *next,* huh?

Simple as dough, Peter's father pulls up on the lid of the gasoline can, grins at Lois, and tips the can over, to let the liquid saturate the wooden floor.

"Place'll go up like a fifty-year-old *Guardian,*" says Peter's father.

"Thing is," says Lois, ready to move the instant he reaches for a match, "people like you aren't just dangerous to gays. You're dangerous to everyone. Because there isn't a thing you don't hate except yourself, and I've had it clear to Herkimer with the likes of you!" Staring at him, she takes one step back. "All my life," she says, "I've been ignoring you." One more step back. "And that was my dumb mistake." One more step. She's even with the bat. She grabs it, moves forward. "Well, no more," and now he's reaching for something in his pocket, but Lois feints left, then hefts the bat up, right, and solid, smashing down on his shins with a crack you could hear in western Vermont. Peter's father goes down screaming, missing the bear trap by a foot and a half.

Fuck, I got the angle wrong.

Lois gives Peter's father another taste of the bat, right in the crotch. "One to grow on," she tells him, as he goes into a wild gasping thing, like *Hgnuuuuuuh.*

"The house is next?" she asks him, delivering one more blow to his genitals. I mean, why fool around, you know?

Lois calls the police. Then she calls Elaine to say she'll be home even later than she thought with a really interesting story. As the cops pull up, she tosses another Souvenir of New Hampshire miniature tray at the trap, which springs closed momentously.

Peter visited the next day, clearly worshipful of these brazen, bracing New Yorkers. And, lo, one of them turned out to be Jerrett Troy!

"You're famous!" cried Peter, first thing. "Just like Elaine. And my father's in jail and I'm this more or less wild gay boy who's eager to learn and anxious to please. I'm sort of cute, by the way."

The Kid decided to get that old picture of himself that he's always dragging around, to show to all and sundry the glory of Johnny in youth, opulent and irreproachable in his plundering, consciousless joy. But Elaine said, "No, Johnny! That daguerreotype again, oh please!" and the Kid held back. "My youth is officially over," he announced, with a grand bow.

"No," Walt observed, "your youth is over when you feel that your one true love has . . ." Walt stopped, unwilling to offend the Kid. "When something goes terribly wrong in your whole existence."

"You New Yorkers always know life," said Peter. "I want to come with you to the Great City of the Western World." He pronounced it with capital letters; I heard him. And he was fast and funny, and, I thought, He has possibilities.

"You're too young to go anywhere," said Lois.

"Are you *sure?*" Elaine asked him.

"We can put him up till he finds a place," said Walt.

"City life is hard on a new boy," said the Kid. "I'm afraid they'll beat you down."

"They're already doing that here," Peter replied. "That's why I want to get out." He turned to Lois. "I could be the gay Dick Whittington. Where's my cat?"

"There are cats here," said Walt. "But now it's mainly Winston the dog."

"Sure, he's my protégé."

Hearing his name, the dog ambled over to sample the affections of the company.

"Enjoy it while you can," Lois told him, " 'cause, come bedtime, you'll be out in the yard, guarding the homestead."

"No, I *have* to come to New York," said Peter. "Don't I?"

The Kid said, "I warn you, it's a tough gig."

"I'd be splendid there," said Peter, pacing and camping. "Note my characteristic poses: *thus,*" as he struck one. "Or *thus,*" another. "Then I—"

"It's not just style," the Kid insisted. "It's determination. And what about money?"

"I'll bankroll him," said Lois.

"Lois!" Elaine cried. "My J. P. Morgan!"

"Heck, I've been laughing at Johnny's nun-and-blind-man joke for forty years. Maybe Peter's the next—"

"What nun-and-blind-man joke?" the Kid asked.

" 'Nice tits, lady. Now, where do you want the blinds hung?' "

"God, I'd forgotten that! It stayed with you all this time? *That?*"

"Something about that nun showing off in such delight," said Lois. "Then she's so embarrassed. But what happens *after* the joke? Doesn't she snap back? She says, I am stronger now."

Elaine added, "She says, We have to fight. We have sneaked through and paid no price. We think we're safe. But that little boy in Backtown isn't safe, and I don't feel I've sneaked through any more. Who's safe? George Bush is safe. No one else is safe."

"Wow, it's history here!" Peter exclaimed.

"No," said Lois. "It's self-defense."

"It's about going home," said Walt. "You aren't given a home, you find one. You make one."

"Oh, I've got to be a part of this," said Peter. He was so inspired that his eyes were tearing.

"You remembered that ridiculous old joke," said the Kid, moving to Lois. "Those nights in Jill's, Lois. *That* was *home*."

"Huh."

"Home is where your friends are," said Elaine.

"Where your kind is," said the Kid.

"What you fight to protect," Elaine insisted. "We utterly mustn't back off now. The biological family is rotten. It's made of hateful mothers and molesting fathers. Trust me, I've seen their children! Up the new family!—the one you choose!"

"Yes!" cried Peter. "*Yes!* I'm ready to choose!"

"God, the things we've known!" cried the Kid, taking the hands of Lois and Elaine, drawing Walt along with him, and Peter as well. "Home? Going home? *This* is home. This is my church. This is community and truth. This is our style, our very gay life. It's made of us, you see."

Elaine and Peter were in tears, and everyone was clutching each other, except Lois, who disengaged herself with the words "Fancy stuff," and moved to one side to pet the dog.

PART IX

New York City, Gay Pride Week, 1991

ON A SULTRY Monday evening, three men and a woman walk out of the weekly ACT UP meeting in appalled silence. Standing on the sidewalk, not ready to move on just yet, they look at each other in disbelief.

Finally, one of the men—mid-twenties, slim and effeminate, earring and savage haircut, Silence = Death T-shirt—says, "There are three places where I, as a gay man, feel truly in danger—a suburban mall, an Irish bar, and an ACT UP meeting."

Another of the men, physically much like the first, says, "Did I actually hear that black woman demand that we change the name of the group because 'ACT UP' has become gay-identified?"

"Why was it *founded*, for Christ's sake?" says the first man. "Moms have the P.T.A., little boys have the Little League. Don't we get one fucking group of our own?"

The third man—big, black, much older than his friends, a volatile personality who shifts from flamboyant queen to stately collegiate within a phrase . . . it's Jezebel, in fact—said, "The trouble *began* with this town-meeting style of congress, is what. The idea that all opinions are created equal. *Some* opinions are worthless diatribe specially *designed* to call attention to the o*pin*ion holder and mess *up* on everybody *else!*"

"I heard that!"

"Amen!"

"What they keep pushing all this leftist agenda on us? Ain't they enough piss-shit *leftist* groups they can join? They got to infiltrate ours?"

"Because we let them speak," said one of the other men. "Anywhere else, these lunatics would be told to shut up. We give them a stage."

Now the woman spoke up. "What do you think of the notion that some of these spoilers are F.B.I. moles?"

"No way," one of the white men replied. "Even the F.B.I. isn't as disgustingly destructive as the commissars we've welcomed into our midst. The quota police. Every committee has to have ten black women. *Ten black women, ten black women.*" Noting the company now streaming out of Cooper Union, signaling the meeting's end, he shouted, *"What the fuck do ten black women have to do with gay men dying of AIDS, you blithering idiot bitch cunts?"*

"Come on," his friends said, pulling him away. "We'll go to Eats and chill."

"Luke is fine, I *told* you. It's some miracle, I guess. Oh, here it is."

Chris fished a worn leather account book out of her shopping bag.

"Cousin Tom's journal," said Walt.

"Luke wants you to have it. It's worthy reading—it made the plane ride seem like a trip on the trolley." Chris performed a stage shiver. "Lots of purple passages. Tom always was brutally direct."

"How's your baby?"

"Timothy is ideal. Ebullient, ravingly healthy, and he's utterly and breathlessly mine, mine, mine—and don't think J. doesn't know it."

"Is J. jealous?"

"No, it's what he wants. Mother-baby bonding is part of his plan. I believe he hopes to be discovered as some marvelous repository of male lore and wisdom when Timothy is fourteen or fifteen, and then he'll wean him from me. But I carried that tiny being for the better part of a year. He *grew* in *me,* and that baby knows it."

"Boy, you're not a gay man manqué nowadays."

"Will you drop me from the club?"

Walt, so often quiet and self-absorbed lately, smiled and gave Chris a hug.

"Hey, boys and girls!" the Kid called from the living room. "Come quick and see!"

"We have such a big classy apartment now," said Walt, leading Chris, "that you can stay in shape just by walking from room to room."

"Gaze!" cried the Kid, indicating an old movie playing on television.

"At what?" asked Chris. "Oh, Anne Baxter?"

"It's Denise Darcel, and, no, I mean the man."

"I couldn't spot Denise Darcel?" said Chris. "That surely proves I'm no longer a gay man of any kind."

"Will you *please* look at the *guy*?" said the Kid.

All three watched as a stiff and savorless yet arrestingly handsome man remonstrated with the obdurate Darcel, told her off, and stormed—mildly—out of the scene.

"That's Derek Archer," said the Kid. "My first movie star."

Denise Darcel prowled around the room, then threw a vase against the wall for a fade-out, and a commercial came on.

"Mute the set, Johnny," said Chris. "We have to talk."

"Aren't you going to ask me what he was like?"

"I saw. Steamy but stolid. A fancy-pants who'd sell his mother to make it."

"That's not the point. He was one of those gays who were destroyed because he lived too soon. Twenty years later, he could have come out and enjoyed life, but instead he was forced to cushion himself inside the role of the elegant joe. He fooled no one, of—"

"Joe who?" asked Walt.

"Post–World War Two parish lingo," Chris explained, "meaning 'heterosexual male.' "

"You're back in the club."

To the Kid, Chris said, "All right, now, this actor you were so thrilled to see across the arc of the years. Did he leave a mark on you? Influence you?"

The Kid was wary. "So how come you ask?"

"So how come he's not in your play? Your first movie star? Was he a benefactor? A mentor?"

"I have *selected* from my many occasions. This a play script, not *Sixty Minutes*. I have boiled my days down. I have reinvented, crystallized."

At a look from Chris, Walt left the room, closing the door behind him.

"Johnny, I only get into the theatre once a year, so it has to be a *hot* show. *A Gay Life* is epic and sharp and funny and touching—but what have you left out?"

"Plenty, but as usual your Piscatorian epic style has added in everything but the Barry Sisters doing 'Matchmaker, Matchmaker,' so perhaps—"

"You've left out a Great Love. You've got gay history and showbiz tattle and T-rooms and arrests and Stonewall and disco and politics, not to mention birth, death, and infinity. But the protagonist only has sex and friendships, never an all-encompassing romance that would . . . well . . ."

"What? Make him miserable every time he thinks of it, like Walt? Or march him at gunpoint from his chosen field of endeavor, like you? Or a thousand other examples I can name of love's walking wounded."

"Low blow, Johnny. I'm happy with J. and Tim. And Walt was always a moody boy, always . . . questing and disappointed. Besides, I'm not talking real life, I'm talking art. Your play needs a love story."

The Kid stared at the silent television (where Derek Archer was leaning out of a stagecoach to call up to the driver), then remoted the power off.

"I want it hard stuff," said the Kid. "No sentiment."

"The tale needs feelings."

"It's too late, besides. We start previews in two weeks."

"You've got seventeen days till previews, and, anyway, you could slip this in in a night's work. It's six terse scenes—the meeting, the stirrings, the seduction, the honeymoon, the catastrophe, the last meeting years later, when each man is so much further along in his life that rapprochement is—"

"Fucking Jesus!" the Kid screamed. "Don't you *ever* run out of ideas? Are you always this *theatre genius*? Why don't you write your own play?"

He paused, embarrassed at his atrocious manners.

"All right," he said. "I'll add it in."

"Don't do me any favors."

"I'm sorry," he snapped. "Don't I ever get to create something on my own?"

"This *is* your own, Johnny. Somewhere in you is a Great Love that you're trying to hide on the back burner. Now, bring it forward and let it boil up."

"All right."

"And kindly stop growling."

"Can I make it the movie star? That way he can die early on."

"Is that who your Great Love was?"

The Kid was silent.

"Whatever works best, Johnny."

· · ·

Eats is a scum-glam-rock bar way down on Second Avenue, where the East Village sort of ends and nothing sort of begins. It gets a mixed crowd—gays and straights in indistinguishable underworld uniforms, transvestites in full kit, skinheads, grungeboys in Mohawks that would terrify an Indian, dopers, sellers, and the odd group of N.Y.U. students talking semiotics. The jukebox is unpredictable—new-wave punk groups one moment, classic Motown or Delta blues the next. When "Stop! In the Name of Love" comes on, a horde of boys will rise to sync along, complete with the ritual hand motions.

Jezebel and his friends fall into a booth, still enervated from the evening's meeting.

"How far we've come," says one of the men. "That's what I keep telling myself. Imagine pollsters asking about 'the gay vote' in 1950 or something? We've gotten *somewhere* fast, anyway. Am I not right?" he asks Jezebel.

"Do tell."

They order a pitcher and wave over a colleague, a high-energy character big on the 'zine scene, editor in chief of *Boys Just Want to Suck Jock,* one of New York's most adorably ratty homemade newspapers.

"So who're we outing this week?" asks someone.

"If you can't feed me, at least read me," says the editor, passing out copies from his backpack. "Our double-special Gay Pride and New Kids on the Block issue." He wears a baseball cap that reads "Straights to Hell."

"One of our few mainstream pundits down in D.C. did a number on outing a few months ago," says the woman. "He feels that denouncing our own is political suicide."

"Closeted queers who collaborate with homophobes aren't our own," says someone else.

"Hey, politics," says the editor, sitting with them. "I'll take random notes."

"To understand who the enemy is, is to seize the revolutionary moment," says one of the boys.

"Be easier to understand who *ain't* the enemy is," Jezebel remarks.

"Two hundred thousand AIDS deaths," says the woman, "and not a single AIDS assassination. There's something wrong with that statistic."

Screaming noises erupt at the other end of the bar—laughter or anger, hard to tell which.

" 'To understand who the enemy is,' " murmurs the editor, taking it down in a tiny notebook.

"I'll say you who the enemy is," Jezebel offers. "I'll give it in plain

English, too. It's this stupid fighting among ourselves, all this boycotting of our own agencies, and schisms within our ranks, and assholes detecting racism with a magnifying glass. We need *leaders! Unity! Clear-cut goals!* We have to be a *national bloc* or *that's all!*"

"Fine," says the woman. "Now just tell me—if there were no plague, and women were fighting for a cure for breast cancer, how many men would hit the streets with us?"

"CURE FOR BREAST CANCER CONSIDERED," murmurs the editor, scribbling away.

"What do you bet," the woman continues, "that if men got penis cancer all over the place, the entire medical establishment would be working for a cure night and—"

"Don't pull the righteous-sister act on me, do you please," says Jezebel.

"Haven't we had enough angry lesbians on our cases tonight?" says someone else.

"Don't offend my people," says the woman.

"Honey," Jezebel replies, "they're my people, too."

The next afternoon, Tuesday, Henry sits dreaming at his desk in the office of the fifth magazine in his editorial career. It has been a long slide downhill, from the trendy and sophisticated to the eccentrically practical—a hobby-crafts rag catering to the kind of people who erect Victorian birdhouses and open-sided carports in the Sun Belt. Once, Henry was a features editor, chronicling the high life; now he's the copy person, rebuilding decrepit punctuation and clarifying obscure phraseology.

Well, as they say, It's a living—and that's astounding in itself, for Henry spent the 1980s burying people. Six years ago, Jim was nursing Eric through his death, then went home to his parents in Chicago to be cared for in turn. His family didn't want to take him in, and he died in the street. Was it that long ago now? Six years? But I hear him yet. The phone rings, and I think, That's Jim. Why didn't he call me when it happened? He knows—knew—I would have flown out to get him, though the airlines were always shoving P.W.A.s off planes then. And Jim of all people: so prudent, even before the Big Death was identified. How did he get it? And how did *I* walk through this hail of bullets?

Henry's desk is covered with blueprints and galleys and fresh copy, but he's staring out the window, gliding from memory to memory. Gay Pride Week always affects him enormously, as the countdown of days to the climactic Sunday Parade stimulates his old dreams of contributing to the raising up of a gay nation. Even at direst times, when it feels as if everyone is Positive or dead, Henry still sees the Parade as a day of rebirth, a pageant on the one thing gays have always excelled in, socializing.

It was at the Parade, in 1987, that Henry met Bobby, a good-natured yet dangerous-looking Polish boy from New Jersey who was fascinated by Henry's intellectual take on everything from movies to the importance of junior college in getting a decent job. Bobby was sweet but Bobby had power; Henry, too, was fascinated. They finished off the Parade at the Village fair, packed into the post-fair dancing on the pier, and went to Henry's apartment, where Bobby, on his third beer, admitted that he was "probably gay" but didn't know anything about it, had never even had sex with a man. In fact, he had come to the Parade precisely to, as he put it, "break into this lifestyle thing."

Bobby turned out to be a natural, raw but committed—and, in his appetitive yet loving approach, a blend of Henry's two types, the Wild Boy and the Sweetheart. Carefully hiding his new life from his relations, Bobby became Henry's lover, balancing Henry with his studies and a very full family life at home.

The two years with Bobby were the happiest—well, let's say the most serene—in Henry's romantic career. Never before had he so delighted in the sheer physical appeal of his partner; never had he felt so in control while being swept away. For Bobby, Henry knew that rare love that moves past fine sex and strong emotional support into ecstasy. He didn't mind that he was by far the more involved of the two, that Bobby was, in a way, using him, as a mentor teaching the dos and don'ts of gay life. Henry liked being the know-all. Besides, when Bobby would tell him, "You're neat to talk to because you understand about things," Henry rejoiced—as intellectuals will—that he could have impact on this beautiful beast. And when Bobby left for Los Angeles in late 1988, Henry wept but never blamed. Bobby would drop in on his occasional trips east, and when he walked into Henry's place Henry would hold him and hold him, and Bobby would laugh and pat Henry's back and say, "It's okay, Henry guy. It's okay."

Neatening his desk to check out for the day, Henry thought of himself as the crocodile from *Peter Pan,* haunting the Parade for more of what he had tasted, for another Bobby. Hopeless, of course: Who gets more than one in this life? Anyway, it was all no-fault cruising now for Henry, look but don't touch. Terrified of that mortifying death, Henry had become an onanist, endlessly running porn video and beating off, to drain himself of hunger.

Coming home, Henry pulled off his clothes, grabbed the last of yesterday's Heinekens from the fridge, and turned on the rest of last night's video. A Latino man was fucking a white man who had a huge handlebar mustache; the camera stared at the bottom, on all fours, as he raised his head and calmly stared back. Yes, he seemed to mean, I'm doing this, and nothing on earth—neither law, nor hatred, nor plague—is going to stop me.

If we had only put that energy into our politics, Henry thought, we would have built that gay nation.

Across the river, in a backyard in Brooklyn, a group of old friends is enjoying a barbecue, all straights but for one man, who remarks that the categories of Trivial Pursuit are strangely weighted toward specialized interests. Sports, for instance. Half of the population—women—doesn't follow sports either as history or current event, and gays—

"Come on," says one of the straights. "Sports are part of life. Wallpaper. Everyone knows who . . . well . . ."

"Who pitches for the Yankees?" says our gay friend. "I don't."

"*History*'s the killer," says a woman.

"No, because history is F.D.R. and 1848 and Weimar. It's supposed to be part of our education. *Sports* is the killer, because its inclusion says that we're all supposed to have some take on it, whereas—"

"Well, everyone—"

"No, *not everyone!* Many people don't *know* about it and don't *care* about it! What would you say to a category in musical comedy? Would you know who wrote *Kiss Me, Kate*? Or who played Reno Sweeney and Annie Oakley?"

The straights were mystified. "But nobody knows that stuff," said one of them.

"Nobody I'm friendly with knows about sports. Except you."

"So?"

"You straight men think the whole world is you. What you like is liked. What you know is known. It never occurs to you that there are people on the planet who don't see the world through your eyes."

Everyone's quiet.

Says our gay friend, "You just don't get it. You're so used to yourselves, you don't know that anyone else is there."

·   ·   ·

Back in Manhattan, at a Village piano bar during a rendition of "Over the Rainbow," a woman tells her male friend, "I always feel left out when they play this!"

"Are you kidding? This number is *universal!*"

"Oh? So how come it's the *gay* national anthem?"

The next morning—Wednesday of this Gay Pride Week, 1991—an old woman makes her way into the offices of the Gay Men's Health Crisis.

"Who do I speak to about this?" she demands, banging an envelope against her open palm. "This disgusting mail you keep sending me. Right here, this . . . this . . . I don't want it in my mailbox. I'm not giving you people any money and I'm not taking any more mail from you!"

The woman is imperious, and the G.M.H.C.ers, wanting no problems—that's their problem—take the woman's name and assure her that she'll be pulled from the computer.

"Pulled?" she says. "Computers?"

"You'll never hear from us again."

"Starting when, I'd like to know!"

But hold. A G.M.H.C. officer, told of what's going on at Reception, says, "She *what?*"

His co-workers try to calm him.

"She said *what?*" he screams. "And you gave in to her fucking *what?*"

Moments later, he is in Reception, screaming at the woman.

"You disgusting stupid bitch!" he explains. "People are dying by the thousands and *you* don't want *mail?*"

His colleagues combine to head him off, though the woman, strangely, doesn't seek cover or seem to react in any way.

"I'll give you the fucking *mail*," the man cries, struggling to throw a paperweight at the woman as his friends try to drag him back into the offices. "You screaming stupid *bitch!* You *hating Nazi* dried-up *filth!* Loveless . . . Let *go* of me, you fucks! *She's* the one you should be after!"

"You'd better leave," a young woman urges the visitor.

"Don't shove *me,*" the old woman cried. "I've had—"

"*Move,*" says the young woman, firmly taking the visitor out of the offices, into the elevator, and downstairs to the lobby, where she eyes the old woman and says, "You know when you've taken a really major dump and your ass is *really* browned up?"

The old woman stares at her.

"I mean, when the johnny paper is just *smeared* brown."

"You kids must think you own the world!"

"The paper isn't you. The smear isn't you. But think of some freak in the night, rummaging through garbage, tenderly licking up the smear. The freak is you. And if I thought I could get away with it, I'd kick your fucking cunt in. Now, get out of the office building of the Gay Men's Health Crisis, you demented vicious idiot."

The young woman turns and walks away.

Henry's having lunch with one of his former writers—from his feature-editor days—and, suddenly, the guy comes out to Henry. Last year they were closeted; this year they're rigging up for the Green and Orange Party.

"It was Elaine Denslow's books that did it," the writer tells Henry. "She inspired me to . . . to talk about my life. But you must know about this, don't you?"

"Yes, I—"

"Now I need to hear about the adventures, the *origins*."

"It's not that—"

"The back-room bars!"

"Will you *please*?" Henry nearly shouts. "It's a whole life. It's not just fucking."

"Yes, of course. It's Liza Minnelli, too."

"No. No, it's some kid in Racine or Dallas who doesn't know how his or her friends will react when they learn that he or she wants *this* instead of *that*. It's people who have been so lied to that they don't know who they are, and people who have been born to a higher comedy, because growing up having to fake it makes them sharp and sassy."

"Well, you'll like this," says the writer. "Because I figured I was ready to put my byline right out on the gay table for all to see. Maybe try a novel."

Henry made the tiniest of wry faces.

"It's a dirty job, but somebody's got to do it," said the writer. "Anyway, my agent shopped it around, and one editor—a woman, who should know about prejudice . . . Well, she says, 'Oh, who cares about a gay novel, it'll be nothing but sex.' Then she adds, 'I certainly hope your author won't call the rest of us "breeders." I hate that habit of reducing people to what they do in bed.' "

Lady, you can go bald at high noon in Macy's window.

.   .   .

Peter Smith was having a bad week. Both of his part-time waiter jobs fell apart at the same time, he was subsisting on graham crackers and Velveeta, and no way would he be able to make the rent. I could call Johnny and Walt, he thought. Or Lois and Elaine. But I don't want to be known as a flop and a moocher. I don't want them to lose their faith in me.

Some of my readers might call this pride, as if naming a sin; but it's just a desire to retain one's self-respect. Peter's roommate, an unassuming—all right, dreary—man who worked in the billing department of Roosevelt Hospital, said that if "things didn't improve" for Peter it would really be necessary for him to move out by Sunday, it really, really would. Peter agreed, thinking, Something's got to come through by then.

Now we're on line at the box office for *Grand Hotel*. This couple isn't buying tickets, they're moving in. The man—white-haired, lined mouth, wearing a leisure suit (remember those?) and bearing a shoulder bag—is looking off, as if to say, They can't give us fifth row center when we *ask* for it? His wife, doing all the talking, turns to him, saying, "They got fourteenth row side orchestra for the sixteenth, or twentieth row center for the twenty-eighth."

"They got, they got," the man echoes.

"So which?"

The man shrugs, looks away, doesn't care to know from this. He wants fifth row center.

"Shaney, so what night do I get it for?"

"Ask if they have fifth row for the sixteenth."

"We don't," says the box-office man, amazingly patient—as are the people in the line. Wouldn't you be pulling out your can of Mace at this point?

"He already said they don't have fifth row for any night this or next month."

"Don't shout at me, Eva!"

"I'm not shouting, Shaney."

"So buy the ones you said."

"Which ones?"

At that point, a man standing directly behind them turned to the man he was with and said, "Now you know why *we're* the ones who are known as gay."

·   ·   ·

The Kid was revising his play, writing in the character of the protagonist's Great Love that Chris has asked for. It needn't be a big part, the Kid told himself. Just evocative. Imposing. Some exquisitely sad and wonderful memory.

So who is it? Autobiography is the easy way out—you don't have to invent anything. But it is hurtful to present oneself defenselessly. "One guy naked from the knees up," the Kid muttered as he made notes. I could base it on Derek Archer—the shattered icon, Hollywood, closeted, a bi wanna-be. Then the terrifying death. It's romantic with political over-tones. I could remodel Blue—the cast is pretty hot but we could always use another hunk, because gay life is looks, no matter what the militant left-outs contend. I could set Walt on stage—hell, maybe Walt should play him.

Suddenly the Kid crumpled his notes and socked them into the waste-basket with such *ping!* it fell over. What the fuck do I have to put love on the stage for? Isn't this the tale of a man who lives without it? Man can, you know. I recall Blue in our first days together in San, how easily we fit together, whether it was You feel like a little somethin' tonight? or Goin' out and see you later. It wasn't love, yet it was creamy smooth. I have to say, when that boy was on, he was *prime*. But it never had to be love and never was. And Walt is . . . He's your stuffed zebra named Plonky. He doesn't ask for much and he's always there.

Idea: Make the Great Love a stuffed animal?

No, asinine.

Make the Great Love a straight? That happens. Some lifelong buddy who . . . Oh, that's so poky.

A sailor? A playwright? A model? A suit gay, a clone, a street boy?

Walt came in, having seen the Walt Disney *Beauty and the Beast*.

"How was it?" the Kid asked, joining Walt in the kitchen.

"I don't respond to cartoons," said Walt, making cinnamon toast and tea. "But Claude made us sit through it twice."

He's still doing it, the Kid thought. After all these years, the bear and the silly, tenderly injured idealism.

Well, it's got to be Walt, then. He's too theatrical to waste. So sweet to comfort, so wonderful to encourage. So dear.

Besides, he really is my

Thursday noon, Walt is rehearsing a new piece with his violinist partner, Glen Adelson, a medley of tunes from *Follies*. "Baby, you really get into that," says Glen. "You play like someone who's madly, sadly, and *badly* in love."

"I'm not, though," Walt answers, taking a drag on his Yoo-Hoo.

"Now, what *I'm* looking forward to is the day they outlaw smoking in restaurants. Why do they have to concentrate all the tobacco right where *we* are?"

"We're not together on the rhythm on 'The Road You Didn't Take.' "

"Gays are the only ones still smoking, anyway."

Walt glanced inquiringly at Glen.

"Well, haven't you noticed?" Glen went on. "All my straight friends have given it up or never started. Didn't yours?"

"I don't have straight friends," said Walt.

"Why ever not, you silly bitch?"

"I used to be so political, I was boycotting them."

"Eek, how *twisted*!"

Shrugging, Walt turned a few pages of music. "Right here," he said. "On the words 'Chances that you miss.' "

"Yes, but some of my closest friends are straight," Glen insisted. "And they're, like, totally supportive. They're all urging me to march in the Parade this year."

"Don't you always?" asked Walt, mildly, surprised but ready to forgive. The new Walt.

"Of course I always," said Glen. Then: "I mean, I've always wanted to."

"I've always wanted to eat an apple," said Walt.

Glen looked at him, bewildered.

"You pick up the apple," Walt explained, "you bite into the apple, you take more bites, you have eaten the apple. The Parade's the apple. What's the big deal?"

Glen nodded, a little uneasy, for there was nothing he wanted more than Walt's good opinion. Glen said, "I'm afraid of it."

"Why?"

"It's so big and full of everyone knowing each other and feeling secure."

"I thought you were the famous master of the revels at Boybar and those places."

"Yes, in a little room surrounded by friends. Then I'm *such* a giddy bitch, like, totally heav."

"So march surrounded by friends."

"Mine don't march."

"That's what you get for knowing straights."

"Walt, no, the straights watch the Parade and cheer their little hearts out. It's my *gay* pals who have better things to do."

"That's so strange to me."

"Could I march with you?"

"Sure."

"Well. Well, *right.*" Glen brightened. "That's the way," he said. "Now, when do I set up?"

"The easiest thing would be to wait by the Plaza Hotel and join in when you see us coming around the corner."

"Yes! Yes, Walt, I will!"

The Lesbian Zappers have prepared it, through leaks about the Republicans' schedules from—shall we say?—friends of the family. The Zappers confer, moments before Point Zero, with a handsome and vigorous young man who nevertheless will be, for all he can expect, dead in months. The president's spokesman is having dinner in a hamburger joint, and this is a Confrontation. There's no television, no coverage. It's an act all for its own sake. The gay man strides into the restaurant toward the president's big fat fuck, crying, "I'm dying and you're having *dinner,* you vicious piece of *shit!*"

The big fat fuck recognizes the young man, who has enlivened many of his dinners, and the big fat fuck screams, *"I don't owe you people anything!,"* at which the young man pulls the tablecloth and sends the big fat fuck's dinner flying into his lap.

"Why don't you eat my *blood* while you're at it?" the young man cries; but the Secret Servicemen have grabbed and cuffed him. They're all old acquaintances, for this has happened many times before. Not that this or any other action will change anything in the head of the big fat fuck, for he was raised hating gays, Jews, blacks, women, artists, writers . . . anyone who isn't a rich straight white Christian conformist male. But pulling his dinner off his chin and onto the floor feels good. It's a release to finger the men who relish your death.

As the Secret Servicemen are about to lead the young man off, one of them stands before him, looks him heavy in the eyes, and, apparently oblivious of his colleagues or any camera-news team that might have rushed in, says, "I need to tell you how much I admire what you are doing."

. . .

Right, it's Pride Week: So of course Public Television suddenly trots out its gay programming, with a Daring Foreign Film (especially *Maurice*) on Monday, a documentary about people who were gay in the 1930s and are still alive (mostly in wheelchairs) on Tuesday, a ballet on Wednesday, and, on Thursday—tonight—another documentary.

Two women are watching, their arms around each other, their free hands holding glasses of Evian with lime.

They see a black woman saying, "There was so much of it around, oh my dear. So it was hard to believe that *anyone* was straight."

They see a blonde who must have been a beauty in her prime saying, "It was difficult, but we found each other because we had to. *We had to.*"

They see a woman who says she is Jewish and "that could complicate things," because, often, she would connect with a woman who would say something horribly anti-Semitic. "The country," this woman says, "was still very divided into sections. One section wouldn't know anything about the other sections. You would sleep with another woman, and that might be wonderful. But the next morning, she'd be a southern Baptist or whatever. The night before, she was just an accent. Suddenly, she's a person. And a bigot. Not a vicious, mean bigot, but a product of her section. You know, Jews have horns and so on. I'd say, 'Well, I'm Jewish.' She'd be flabbergasted. 'But you don't have horns.' " After a moment, the woman adds, "I'm not kidding, you know."

They see a woman saying, "I was fat and black and I wanted to sing opera. Well, who would be friendly to me except the gays of the world? I kept trying to force myself to have affairs with lesbians, but what I really wanted were the gay boys. They were so cute."

One of the lesbians asks the other, "Do you relate to any of this?"

"It's not us," says her partner. "But it's something. It's history."

"Maybe it'll make sense later on."

"It makes sense to me now."

Dead-hearted yet calm, a man of about thirty-five paces through his apartment, not especially listening to the Police's *Synchronicity,* his late lover's favorite record. "Murder by Numbers." "King of Pain." "Every Breath You Take." "O My God."

It's all gone, his peace—and just then his late lover's two older brothers key their way into the apartment without a knock. They give the man a look of contempt and immediately start unfolding cardboard boxes and filling them with objects from the apartment—whatever attracts them, especially technical equipment, CDs, and anything else that can be resold. The two speak to each other as if the bereaved survivor of their brother's death were not in the room—even: as if he had never existed. They take and take and take, so the man calls the cops. When they arrive, they immediately start in on the man. "Why don't you let them bury their dead?" says one cop. "You probably killed him with AIDS," says the other. He asks the brothers, "This guy attack you physically?," encouraging more than inquiring.

Hmm. "Well, yeah." Brother looks at brother.

"He threatened us and everything."

"With what?" asks the cop. "A kitchen knife?" He all but nods his head at the kitchen, but this is unnecessary. One brother marches into the kitchen, opens a couple of drawers, while the man protests and the cops tell him to shut up. The brother finds the cutlery, singles out something suitable, and brings it to the cops, saying, "He used this."

The man is handcuffed and led away as the two brothers go on looting the apartment. The Police CD runs to its close and one of the brothers grabs it, snaps it into its case, and tosses it into one of his cartons. Synchronicity.

Later that night, at Eats, a well-known comedienne and actress who stands somewhere between Notoriously Rumored and Definitively Outed is telling off a bunch of lesbians. "Stop acting like pigs," she advises. "That isn't *style*. You think that's style? You behave like a bunch of straight men, trying to push everyone around. And it's just your inadequate bullshit. Maybe show the world our class and tact, how about? This dingy Roller Derby approach really turns me off."

The lesbians are silent and unhappy.

"You can be bold and free without throwing your weight around and making everybody disgusted with you," says the comedienne, an utterly uninhibited cultural phenomenon.

It's Friday. Peter Smith has heard about a possible job opportunity with a "buyer's club," one of those organizations that import drugs sold over the counter in foreign lands, for use by American P.W.A.s who don't have the two hundred years to wait while the F.D.A. makes its teasingly fastidious tests.

Peter runs down an address on East Twenty-second Street and investigates. Well, yes, there's a slot; but have you the nerve? This is borderline-legal, cutting-edge stuff. It sounds trendy and cool but it's basically suicide missions.

"I will fight to live!" Peter sang out; the guy just looked at him. "I mean, if I have to do battle . . ." The guy still looking. Wrong approach. "I'm game, I'm young, I'm spunky," Peter announced. "I'm real, too."

"This isn't lip-synching in some drag act," the guy said. "People are dying. We're looking out for and buying contraband medicine to ease their pain. I don't believe you're right for this."

"Look," said Peter. "I'm cut off from everyone I know and I'm about to be thrown out of my apartment because I can't make the rent. I can't even make lunch today. Don't you think someone desperate for work would be the best worker?"

"Desperation isn't a credential. We already get that from our clients. What we need is experience and smarts."

His look clearly told Peter to go, and Peter did.

Dear Elaine,

Well, it's our annual Parade trip. Scowly Lois says the Parade gets longer and slower every year, but she also says it's ours and that's it.

We're back in the Plaza, same room (over the Park) and so snazzy. "This is how they lived in the books you *used* to write," says Lois, so apparently she approves that I have Gone Political.

We saw a very rough rehearsal of Johnny's new play, *A Gay Life*. So honest! His director, Chris Henderson, would be in great demand, I should think, but Johnny says she is devoted to her family and rarely works. Even: She used to be Chris Lundquist, but took on her husband's name in midcareer. This is serious marriage. Wary Lois asked me, "Would you have changed your name for me?," and I said, "I'd change my name for a bird on the wing, a newsboy, a stiletto. I *am* change." Normally, my Lois would grunt at such, but this time she brushed my lips with a scavenger's kiss. Oh, what a thought!—Lois as a corsair, her head kerchiefed in vermilion, brandishing a cutlass and ordering prisoners to the plank. A certain lurid cardinal tries to recant. He reveals that he has been gay—in secret!—all this time. "That makes it worse!" Lois thunders. She paddles him along the plank with the flat of her sword, and he plunges. When I think of all the Catholic youth he has urged to go after gays with baseball bats, I wonder why he couldn't have been burned alive instead.

We called Peter Smith, but there was no answer, just a tape of his roommate. This is the fourth or fifth time this month, and we are a little worried.

Walt and Glen were playing their third set in Fluke of the Day, a tony seafood restaurant. At the end of their *Show Boat* medley, a white-haired man tipped them twenty.

"My son is a musician, like you," he explained. "In Berkeley, California. He's studying there, set to be the next Heifetz. But just as yet he's playing weekend brunches in a restaurant. Yes, like you. I'd like to think that someone's appreciating his playing sometime around now, just as I have appreciated you young fellows."

"Thank you," said Walt, and for a minute it looked as if he and the old guy were going to hug.

Three members of Queer Nation march into an Irish bar in deepest Queens on a mission of Cultural Integration. They order beers and talk quietly among themselves, though on this defensively intolerant turf their chatty T-shirts (such as one woman's "I'm not gay but my girl friend is") resound like cannon fire. And when one of the locals gets nosy and stares at them, the gays chant, "We're here, we're queer, get used to it!"

The bar resents it but, tonight at least, nobody starts shoving and swinging, either.

Saturday morning, Blue wakes up on a couch. Shower's running, smell of coffee brewing, low table of soft-porn magazines . . . Where is he? Oh, right. Sam Something. Another of the many men stationed along the informal AIDS network of political activists, P.W.A.s, news reporters, and volunteers who put Blue up in his travels from town to town.

Where was he? Portland, Boston, Hartford, Baltimore, and Hartford again (the hospice director suffered a nervous collapse and Blue was subbing). Where's he off to? Des Moines, Kansas City, then (he hopes) home. He was due in Des Moines last week, but the Hartford emergency perplexed his schedule, so Blue decided to stop over in New York and see the Parade.

Sam comes out in a bathrobe, toweling his hair. "Hey, you're up."

Blue gives him a drowsy smile.

"There's coffee."

"Much obliged. Plain black fer me."

Sam is brisk and friendly, more like a guy hosting a long-lost cousin than a single gay man alone in a room with a glorious hunk. Three months shy of forty now, Blue has topped his Wild Boy and Hot Daddy phases with a unique type unknown to gay taxonomy, something reassuring and fraternal, even clerical, the slit eyes gone kind and the grin tightened up, solemn: a Byronic sandman, perhaps? He is as fair, fit, and loving as ever, but less ready now. In any case, Sam is bound to keep it strictly hands-off, according to an unwritten law along the network that Blue is to be treated with chastity and a little awe.

Blue likes it so. For twenty years, he could rejoice in the knowledge that with the exception of a few fiercely heterosexual men, everyone he met wanted him. It was exhilarating but exhausting, especially when it was coming at him even when he didn't want it, couldn't possibly use it, would rather die than do it. Or: would rather live than risk it. So many men, so much suffering. It was Death by Fucking, and by then Blue's looks seemed irrelevant to him, even shameful at a time when his brothers were being turned into scarecrows. Sometimes he wanted to feel invisible.

"Sleep well?" asked Sam, setting a steaming mug on the table by the couch.

"Okay, I guess. One couch is plumb like another these days. Seems I'm never in bed any more." On anyone else, that might carry a double meaning, but Blue delivers it as lean and true as a CAT scan.

"Are you always on the road?"

"Pretty much." Idly glancing at his coffee, Blue notices a gay magazine with a famous face on the cover, a showbiz figure once rumored to be gay and now most thoroughly outed. The star, and thus the news, are both so big that the straight media have taken up the story.

Nodding at the magazine, Sam says, "There's one less heterosexual in America this week."

"Funny how there's no privacy nowadays. I mean for anybody."

"Well. Yes. But. If we keep silent about our hypocrites, are we observing their privacy or honoring their shame?"

Blue hesitated. Then: "I don't know about shame er pride, I guess. I'm just tryin' to get from this day to the morrow keepin' sane and doin' what I can to help out. It's like with this Pride Week a ours. Now, isn't pride somethin' yer entitled to when you done somethin' fine? Climbed a mountain, say. Composed a great orchestra symphony. Set a swimmin' record. But why would you be proud a somethin' that's just a matter a chance? Like some guy says he's proud to be Irish, or proud to be from Texas, or even proud to be American. He didn't do anythin' to be those things, did he? I'm not ashamed to be gay, but am I proud? It's not any achievement, just what I am. I'm *proud* of what I *do,* see?"

"You've taken on the system simply by coming out. You fight the bigots just by being what you are. I'd say that's worth being proud of."

"Maybe so." Blue dared a sip of his coffee, still simmering in the mug. "This tastes special."

"I make it with chicory."

"Got a need in me to go out talkin' with folks tonight, hear a few things from the cuttin'-edge crowd. What's a good place to meet them? You know, ACT UP members and the like."

"There's a bar called Eats down on Second Avenue. That's about as edgy as it gets."

"I'll give it a try."

Peter Smith was facing his last day as a person with an address. He had agreed to vacate the apartment by midnight tomorrow; his roommate had already signed up with a share service and was muttering about the registration fee that Peter has cost him.

Peter was undaunted. He had come to New York for liberation from virtually everything that had tried to shape him—religion, sexism, and unquestioning obedience to the patriarchy, the rule of the fathers—and release from such pervasive tyrannies is not bought on the cheap. In fact, Peter was making a game out of his incipient homelessness, preparing a huge cardboard sign he would carry in the Parade. It read:

YOUNG, CUTE, AND HOMELESS

ADOPT ME?

ALL SERIOUS OFFERS CONSIDERED

If worse came to worst, he could always appeal to Lois and Elaine. They wouldn't let him rot in the street; anyway, that sort of thing just didn't happen to middle-class boys like Peter.

.   .   .

At the Del Vecchios', Andy's mother is washing up in the kitchen, Cecilia drying, while Andy and his wife, Brenda, take turns reading to Bridget, their youngest (of three). The television runs in the background, as it does all day at Mrs. Del Vecchio's, even when she goes to the grocery. As it is just after six, the news is on, and Cecilia occasionally darts into the living room to take in the more arresting stories.

Things have not gone well for Andy's mother. Her husband suffered a stroke in 1982, and though she moved the family-dinner day from Sunday to Saturday to allow everyone more time for propitiating acts of piety on the holy day—time that only Andy's mother put to devotional use—Mr. Del Vecchio died all the same. Worse yet, Andy's mother saw her power structure immediately crumble. Both her sons-in-law announced that they would no longer be attending the weekly dinner, and then Gianna and her children stopped coming. Cecilia's kids had already drifted away from the family rituals—"That's right," Andy's mother had remarked, "send them to a college and what do you get? Disobedience from the children, *that's* what you get!"—and Gianna's son Keith, who had been graduated from Georgetown a year ago, had elected to stay in D.C. and seek a political career.

Andy was trouble, too, with that headstrong wife, a real little know-it-all. Too young for him, too—Andy was thirty-two and Brenda twenty-one when they were married. And not even Italian—*Czech* she is, with a name no one can pronounce and relatives who look like they came out of a cuckoo clock. *Rosponetta* is what Andy's mother called her daughter-in-law, in private, to her confidantes and in prayer: Little Toad. She begged God to whisper enticements into the ear of this Brenda, to lure her into adulteries, to destroy her marriage and take her out of the Del Vecchio world—of course, leaving the three children behind.

"And there's a parade in town," said the television news reader, perking up after a sordid report on White Aryan activities in the Northwest. "Lauren has the story."

"That's right, Bill. This is Gay Pride Week, and, as always, the week will climax with the Gay Pride Parade tomorrow, as gay groups from all over the eastern half of the country gather to march down Fifth—"

"Turn it off!" Andy's mother shouted, coming into the living room as she dried her hands in a dish towel. "Bridget shouldn't know about such filth!"

"It isn't filth," said Brenda. "We're taking Bridget to see the Parade for herself."

Andy's mother gasped in horror.

". . . and only the Saint Patrick's and Thanksgiving Day parades attract more—"

"Turn the television off, Cecilia!"

"If anyone touches the set," said Brenda quietly, "we're leaving."

Andy's mother stared not at Brenda but at Andy. Useless. Her power had lost its tang long before, when her Carlone passed on; and when Andy's mother went to the mat on the naming of Andy's third baby, insisting on "Elvira" (after her own mother), and Brenda pinned her for the count with this stupid "Bridget," like some Irish slime from Hell's Kitchen; and when Andy informed his mother that if she told Brenda to shut up once more, they would never set foot in her house again.

Weeping didn't help. Screaming didn't help. Dying in agony was tempting as sheer revenge, because it would scar Andy for life; but then she wouldn't be around to enjoy it. Without a word, Andy's mother went back into the kitchen.

"What's going on in this room?" Bridget asked her mother, as a commercial came on.

"Not a thing, darling," said Brenda, and she shrugged out a smile at Andy.

The doings at Eats get going early for a gay bar, but then it is as much a social club as a cruise parlor, and they flip a good burger there.

Seven-forty or so, and the gang is in gear: booth-hopping, digging the jukebox, hanging out on the sidewalk to check out the fashions. A boy named C.J., shirtless in suspendered jeans, is voguing to Elton John's "Crocodile Rock," mouthing the words and raising his chin whenever John reaches for a high note. Blue's at a table with the 'zine editor.

"Tell me your life story," the editor says, pulling out his notebook. "The next issue's short a column."

"This an interview?" asks Blue, amused. "Here?"

"What's your favorite pie? How do you spend Christmas? How big is your dick?"

Blue pensively strokes the editor's hair and says, "I once knew someone who looked like you."

"Did you like him?"

"I surely loved him."

"Def. Totally def, here."

A man and woman join them, both young, vital, and dressed for the *quartier* in oversized Ts and bandannas around the neck. It isn't clear whether or not they know the 'zine editor—they certainly don't know Blue—yet they plop down like a comic duo in a movie who have the director's confidence.

"We have decided," says the male, "that my boy friend is the second biggest slut in the world."

"I'm the first," says the editor, looking at Blue.

"No, my girl friend," says the female. "Open her purse, and what do you find?"

"Lovely new mittens?" says the editor, as Blue takes his hand.

"Disgusting sex toys and slips of paper—*Linda* and a phone number, *Claire* and a phone number, *Maddy* and a—"

"I thought only aging straight men on the Upper West Side carried purses. That seventies look, for making a hip entrance into Zabar's."

"Love is such a bitch," says the male. "Because men are too easy."

"I'd say men are hard," Blue offers, yanking his attention away from the 'zine editor. "They're perfectionists. Sure, they're quick to buddy up. But the second you fall short a their demands, yer out in the hall, sayin', What happened?"

"I bet you don't fall short," says the 'zine editor. "Hot stuff."

"Now, women," Blue goes on, taking the editor's hand again. "Women are more patient. Once they like you, you don't have to be so marvelous every second."

"Shit, another bisexual," says the female.

"They're better than sheep," the editor points out.

The jukebox has switched to the Clash: "Career Opportunities." C.J. is still voguing.

"Never been with a woman, actually," Blue admits. "I just know how they are, somehow."

Jezebel pulls up, trying to figure out where he knows Blue from. Blue doesn't recall him.

"Well, anyway," says Jezebel. "This joke. A black guy wants to visit the African homeland, travel agent quotes the fare at a thousand even. Black guy goes out and mugs everyone in sight, comes back and dumps his haul on the travel agent, who counts it and says, 'You're five cents short.'

"Black guys says, 'Be right back,' hits the street, sees a little old Jewish man approaching. Says, 'Hey, rabbi, can I have a nickel to go to Africa?'

"And the Jewish guys says, 'Here's a quarter, my son. Take four friends.' "

Silence.

"Def," the 'zine editor pronounces it, at length. He's fixed on Blue. "You've got to admit it's def."

Jezebel looks at Blue.

"It points up a truth about race relations, maybe," Blue concedes. "But it makes us a tad uncomfortable because it—"

"*I'll* say," the woman puts in. "Those old stereotypes. It's like hearing 'faggot' and 'nigger' and—"

"Shit, it's the word police!" says Jezebel. "Ain't we, as sheer gay people, had enough of others telling us how to be? We got to do it ourselves? I'm sick of it. Looksism. Privileging. Waitron. Scorched animal corpses. Stolen products. Dead white males. Who's *that*? Thomas Jefferson, Franklin Roosevelt? I'm supposed to have contempt for them because a bunch of ignorant assholes decides so?"

The woman was about to answer, but Blue shook his head. "What he says is fair," Blue pointed out.

"Tell you my concern," Jezebel goes on. "Do I wear drag or shorts-and-muscles to the shindig tomorrow?"

"Well, *I'm* sick of Old Gay," says the woman's companion. "Drag, and opera, and Fire Island. *Gyms!* Making fun of women!"

"That icky Lypsinka," the woman notes.

"Define 'icky,' " says the 'zine editor. "Define 'Lypsinka.' "

"Think we ought to work harder to get along," says Blue. "That's a strange and antagonizin' idea, of New Gay versus Old."

"All you need is love," the 'zine editor remarks. "Love with the proper stranger."

"I've been off love fer years now," says Blue. "I'm a loner. I hurt somethin' all fierce at times, wantin' someone to hold on to. Some buddy of the special-close variety. Hug him when he aches, pat him when he's in his glory. Sweet-talk him at night, maybe tell him a my troubles, set aside the cares of the day. I miss that, certainly. And it was took from me, too. I didn't give it up. I would do anythin' to remake it, get a second chance. But I don't even know where it got to. Sex? I scarcely lay a hand on anyone now. But sometimes I think, if someone showed up in the right style, I could fit him up for love for a night er two. Rough his hair and soothe him up, and it would feel most rightly like the real thing."

The jukebox switched to Buddy Holly—"It's So Easy to Fall in Love"—and Blue said, "Funny, all these old melodies I'm hearin'. Like my whole life is on parade before me. All my days of what I been, both helpful and negative. All the times I was intolerant as well as bein' kind and Christian.''

Blue had been gazing off into the ozone for all this; now he turned to the 'zine editor.

"You're a fine, hot-lookin' young fellow," Blue told him. "I would really like to date you tonight."

"Let's go," said the 'zine editor.

Later that night, the Kid came home from a long, heated, and very stimulating conference with Chris. Rehearsals were still a shambles (a very good sign), but the new scenes on the Great Love were going in on Thursday. Chris said they were terrific.

"You've done it, Johnny," she had said. "He's magic and doom and what we know and fear to believe in, all at once. He's beautiful."

"I made him up entirely."

Chris's eyes flickered for, at the longest, a millisecond. "Of course."

When the Kid got home, Walt was still up, in his room, reading by the light of his Jiminy Cricket lamp.

"How's it going, slugger?" asked the Kid, looking in on him.

"Okay."

"What a tone! You sound like a fluffer who got fired five minutes before Jeff Stryker was due on the set. What's the book?"

Walt held it up.

" 'The Shlong of Bernadette,' " the Kid pretended to read.

"It's The Song—"

"Christ, take a joke, will you?" said the Kid, soothingly, as he sat on the edge of the bed. "Shlong Without End. A Shlong to Remember. Pagan Love Shlong."

Walt was unable to laugh.

"Aw, come on, Walty," the Kid urged.

"Danny called me that," said Walt, very quietly. "How is the play going?"

"Holding at par. Why are you reading that particular novel? Are you hoping for a miracle?"

"I was just thinking—what if Blue was searching for me and didn't know where to look?"

After a moment, the Kid asked, "Is that what you're hoping?"

"It's what I'm wondering."

I will never really lose him because he is in my play now. He's more than a person—he's a theme, my Great Love. Trusting and earnest, sweetness to die. He's what I never was: Honest. Pure. Undefended. All the things I adore but never believed in. I've admired some men and been hot for others, and there are many I've liked. But Walt is the thing I love in this vale of missed chances and making do and at least now I will always have him on my stage.

The Kid said, "I'm all for bed. It's been a heavy day of *ars longa*." He patted Walt's blanketed thigh. "Don't worry. You're young enough to correct your mistakes. Besides, tomorrow's the Parade. Your favorite day."

"You know why?" said Walt. "Because I always think that all up and down it, people are having adventures that change their lives forever."

The Kid got up. "Tomorrow, sport," he said.

On Sunday morning, Walt's violinist, Glen Adelson, awoke in one of those today's-the-awful-day moods. All those handsome men stripped to Speedos and Reeboks, all the friendships in holy communion, all the wonderful commotion of an oppressed people celebrating the deliverance that must come—this can seem overwhelming to an insecure young man with no strong affiliation to the Parade in the first place.

Cutting strawberries and a banana into a bowl of Corn Flakes, Glen bucked himself up with the thought that Walt and the Kid would ease him into the throng. They would spot him and throw their arms wide, and he would belong.

Yes, he thought, reaching for the milk. That is how it will be today.

Up in the Plaza Hotel, Lois was showering and Elaine was tuned in to the Weather Channel. She was shaking her head with misgiving as Lois came in, a towel wrapped around her waist, like a man. Well, that's her way.

"They always say it never rains on Gay Pride Day," said Elaine. "And here's a thirty-percent warning of thundershowers."

"You get through to Peter?"

"I got his roommate. He said Peter's moving out today."

"Where to?"

"He didn't know. He'll give him the message, he said, but by then we'll all be at the Parade."

Lois shrugged.

"Well, we're partly responsible for him," said Elaine.

"We saved his life, now we owe him?"

"I don't like having to worry on Pride Day."

"If you cheer up, I'll let you order breakfast from room service."

"I already did. Two deluxes."

"Chick, these hotel breakfasts cost more than a night at the opera!"

"And they don't last nearly as long," Elaine admitted—but Lois, thinking back to the weekend or so that she'd spent at *Die Walküre,* brightened considerably.

Blue was washed and dressed by the time the 'zine editor got back with coffee and doughnuts from the corner. He lived simply: mattress on the floor, books and papers all over, empty fridge, dead stove.

"I hope you like it with milk," the editor said, stamping in. "Good, you're up. Who's Walt?"

"Huh?"

"That's what you called me all night. Well, all the latter part of the night." Unpacking at the rickety table. "The doughnut roll call is one chocolate, one sugared, one glutenwheat, or whatever they . . . What?"

Blue smiled. "Just tryin' to keep up."

"Yeah, that's very winning, that hayseed style. It's, like, *the* def. You're really some armful of trouble. That was my first marathon, by the way. I've been fucked by experts, but not all night long at twenty-minute intervals. Did you just escape from a monastery?"

"Could I have the sugared doughnut?"

"Monster, you can have the skin off my back. Where do you go to learn . . . What's in you, pardner, is what I mean?"

"I had a good time with you," said Blue, seriously. "I've been off sex because of all the death, but every so often a fella cuts loose."

The editor nodded.

"I had you whimpering," Blue went on. "Walt whimpered, too, because he loved me so. I always liked it when guys fell in love with me, but Walt was the only guy I loved maself."

"You're dangerous."

"Only now, instead of fucking guys, I take care of them."

"Are you marching today?"

"Who'd I march with? I'll watch, certainly."

"That's cool. Actors need an audience."

"Much obliged for the coffee."

"For you, monster, anything."

"Why do you call me that?"

"Because you're so light in the street and so deep in bed. When you came, my life passed before my eyes. I bet Walt was afraid of you."

"More like I was scared a Walt."

"Where's Walt now?"

Blue shrugged. "No one seems to know."

The city is dotted with pre-Parade parties this morning; let's drop in on one on the Upper West Side: all-male, mostly late thirties and early forties, six or seven old friends and a new boy friend or two, casual but sporty dress, mimosas all round, remains of a cheese-mushroom omelet and new-potato salad cooling on the coffee table, host and current ex-lover clearing away plates and napkins.

Bob says, "The one problem with the Parade is, they don't leave *anyone* out."

"Yeah," Grey agrees. "Three guys carrying a cardboard sign saying, 'Gays of Bayonne.' "

" 'Gay Vegan Pre-op Transvestite Nuns Who Underneath Their Wimples Wear Curlers in Their Hair,' " Greg invents.

"Who do you know who's gay," asks Bob, "every other day of the year? Your dentist. Your lawyer. Right? Your old high-school buddy, your neighbor down the hall, your . . . just *people*. Suddenly, on Parade Day, we're nothing but a lunatic fringe. Everyone's nude and dancing and a drag queen."

"Who wants to see dentists and lawyers marching?" asks Noel. "Give me those floats with the shirtless go-go boys. Can't get enough. Gym and skin tone—that's my Parade."

"That's your life," says Bob.

"In my dreams."

"I think there should be comics," Grey offers. "You know, riding in cars doing routines. 'Cause aren't we famous for our humor?"

Allen says, "I'd like to see a float of porn stars in action."

"No, a variety show with porn stars!"

"Who'd host?"

Grey raises a silencing hand. "*The Rod Garetto Show,*" he presents, naming a particular favorite.

"That should be on television," says Greg.

Bob hums the start of the overture to *Gypsy* as Grey intones, announcer-style, "And now, direct from Television City in Hollywood, *The Rod Garetto Show,* with Rod's guests—Peter Allen's houseboy, David Geffen's houseboy, Barry Diller's houseboy . . ."

"And Liza Minnelli," Greg adds.

"Rod comes out and does his monologue, introduces his guests—"

"Then one of them says, 'Let's have a rimming contest.'"

"The studio audience is hooked, America is awed. . . ."

"In the White House, the president touches a button, scrambling the signal—"

"Wait," Grey cuts in. "Is Rod the biggest dick in porn, or is—"

"No, Rick Donovan is surely—"

"I'd call them a tie," says Greg.

"*Major* boners," Noel observes. "I mean, who's bigger than that?"

"I remember a guy," says Oliver. "Not that I ever had him. But he was sort of legendary in the 1970s. A bartender or mover or something. One of those overgrown clones. Unforgivably handsome and gymmed to kill, and on top of it all he was—"

"Oh, right," says Noel. "At Hero's."

"*Yes!*"

"Big Frank. Sure."

"Tell," Greg urges.

"Yeah, big Frank. He was the ultimate clone in those years. When he showed up at tea dance, it was, like, head for the hills, because God just walked in and you can't have Him. Let me tell you, he wrecked many a summer for many a Pines beauty. No matter how good you were, he was better. And what he had . . . Well, it was like The Dread Secret of Harvest Home"—here Oliver went into a Bette Davis voice—"what no woman sees and men shudder to tell of."

"Did he have a lover?" Greg asks. "I mean, who's fabulous enough to deserve *that?*"

"I don't think he even had a friend. He was sort of a loner."

"So where is he now?" Bob asks.

"Probably rocking on the porch of a ranchero somewhere. He always had a western air, sort of."

"Like a marshal," Noel agrees, "cleaning up the town."

"Gosh," says Greg. "He must have had the world on a string."

"Gentlemen," the host announces, "the Parade awaits us." He raises a glass. "To pride!"

"To tolerance!" says Bob.

"To a really dependable designer astringent!" says Noel.

"To freedom," says Greg.

They drink.

It was Walt's fond quirk, every year, to wander through the groups and floats lining up along Central Park West, to attach the Kid and himself to whatever attracted him—Yale alumni one year (Walt admired the bulldog), a huge caucus of disco boppers another, even the Twisted Lesbians (because he liked their banner). Walt and the Kid would amble across the Park—silent, pensive, thinking large thoughts on this Day of Days—and bend south to the mêlée of bodies and conveyances and vendors and cops and yellow-shirted Parade monitors, where Walt would browse and select.

"This year, we'll march with a really zonky group," Walt promised.

"Ye gods, not those dancers again, I hope," said the Kid.

Two lost but implacably facetious drag queens were conferring with a monitor, his eyes frozen on his clipboard. A cop watched two women smooching. Three sailors, a whirling dervish (who was whirling), two Mounties, a cowboy contessa, and an Indian brave with a tambourine passed, singing "Seventy-six Trombones" in pig Latin. And a drab older man in a blue-and-white seersucker suit and a blue bow tie was looking at the Kid as the Kid was trying to place him.

The man smiled as the Kid approached.

"Desmond?" said the Kid, incredulously.

"Hello, Johnny."

"My God, what in the *hellness* of *ever* are you *doing* here?"

"Oh, Johnny, I live here now. An *affaire d'amour* went bad for me back home some years ago, and, somehow, everywhere I went reminded me of . . . him. The Pizza Hut on Coronado, where we met that first unforgettable night. The gas station at La Cienega and Evans where, bowing to an uncontrollable impulse and noting the absence of the service personnel, I stole my first kiss from—"

"Desmond!" cried Johnny, grabbing him, charmed and in marvel. "You're just the same! You're—"

"This year we're marching with the Gay Writers," said Walt, "because they have photos of great novelists on poles and they said I could carry one."

"Walt, this is Desmond, the deaf pianist of Thriller Jill's."

"I'm a pianist, too," said Walt, as they shook hands.

"Is this your young protégé, Johnny? I know you're a celebrity now, perhaps with an entourage."

"No, it's just Walt and me. Desmond, it's *fine* to see you again! You know, I still see Lois and Elaine. They'll probably be somewhere in the crowd."

"Oh, Johnny, those great old times and our sweet music!"

"Desmond, Desmond," the Kid cried, pulling him close. "You're the most adorable square! Just hearing your rap again . . ." Releasing him, the Kid said, "This is going to be one of those *wonderful* parades! It's a sign, I know it!"

"Johnny, the famous Jerrett Troy! I always tell them, I knew him when!"

"Oh, Desmond. Were even *we* young once?"

"Oh, surely. At least, you were."

Chaos, skin, music, were all about them. Signs—"I Love My Gay Father!," "Free Burt Reynolds," "It's Not Sexual Preference, It's Sexual Orientation: I Don't *Prefer* Women, I *Only* Like Women, and That's Why God Made Lesbians!"—were being hefted. Groups were swelling, monitors waving people from there to here, pennants were getting a last-minute shaking out, late arrivals were breathlessly pulling in.

"It's Parade time," said Walt, with a gulp.

"Desmond."

"Johnny."

They kept looking at each other and smiling and waving as Walt pulled the Kid halfway down Sixty-second Street. A band struck up and whistles went off. Walt grabbed the Kid's hand, and, up ahead, the first groups lurched into step and the Parade took off. Bob and Greg had lost their fellows in the confusion of lineup, so they had simply taken position at the head of the show, just to see what that might feel like. At the cheers that greeted them as they turned onto Central Park South, Bob leaned over to Greg and said, with a sigh, "We're here, we're queer, they're used to it."

Glen Adelson was at Fifty-sixth Street as the Parade swung onto Fifth Avenue. He was thinking that all his friends were so far downtown that they couldn't help him now. Walt could, but Walt was not unlike a spelling test when you were eleven and could hardly get through "diamond," much less "aerial."

Walt, Glen thought, please be proud of me.

.   .   .

Paul was in his element, chatting up the boys on the Parade's many pauses. He was marching with ACT UP, apparently without embarrassment, though almost all of them were twentysomething and Paul was seventy-one. It was exhilarating to be with the most popular group in the whole Parade, cheered to the tens at every intersection. True, Paul was aware of his disadvantages. Gay life—even on Parade Day, even in the thick of a political organization—has to do with how you look, so many of Paul's companions would nod absently at his sallies and move off to the side. But some—blackmailed by their politically correct disdain for "ageism"—attended to his aperçus. All that Paul wanted was: a little attention.

"Now, in the old days," he was telling some trim, dark-haired youth in a razor cut, "if you saw someone you knew and he wasn't alone, it was *absolutely understood* that you were to pass him by as if you were strangers."

At Paul's weighty vocal pause, the young man looked inquiringly at him.

"Well, to protect his *cover,* you see."

"Wow."

"Pass him by, even if he was your best friend. Just *pass* him right *by.* Oh, you can't imagine what is was like then. Why, if you simply wore a black leather jacket, the cops would nab you on some unheard-of law or other."

"Like what?"

"Loitering. Jaywalking. Inciting to riot. Obstructing an officer. Oh, and if you didn't give them the humble *sir* routine . . . well, they'd beat you bloody and call it 'resisting arrest.' "

"They still do that."

"Oh, they couldn't possibly," Paul replied. The kid stared darkly at him, and Paul knew that he'd once again inefficiently crashed the generation gap.

Henry ran into Jezebel at Forty-fifth Street just as the Parade began to trundle past them. They were grabbing each other and what all.

"Henry, you fiend!"

"Jez, it's our day!"

"It's *everyone's* day, man. This the day of the civil rights for all the chillun of *God.* You know what I'm saying here? It ain't gays versus straights, it's the free peoples of *all* kinds against the church Nazis. It's the *do it* sort versus the *you can't* police."

"Jez, talk plain English, I beg of you. I'm nursing the hangover of the age."

"Sex last night?" Jezebel as Anne Baxter's confidante in *All About Eve*.

"I wish. No, just all keyed up about this." Henry extended an arm at the marchers. "Drag queens and politics," he remarked.

"Drag queens *is* politics," said Jezebel, spotting friends in the Parade and moving out to join them. Henry watched. Directly behind Jezebel's group was a convertible surmounted by Sybil Bruncheon, the drag persona of a handsome and extremely well built young man whose low-cut gown emphasized his powerful arms and shoulders. As he passed, waving and thrilling and blowing kisses, two cops looked at each other in amazement: Why would a good-looking guy *do* that?

Blue was surprised that the 'zine editor was skipping the Parade. "Isn't this the major event in gay life?" Blue asked. "Don't you need to cover it? History and such? Community?"

"Define 'community.' "

So Blue walked uptown alone, taking in the people already crowding the sidewalks, though the Parade was not even in sight yet. The enthusiasm, nonetheless, was overpowering. Are *all* these folks gay?, Blue wondered.

Glen, waiting for Walt to show up, was fascinated by a dance float bearing gorgeous, prancing boys wearing only white shorts, white socks, and white sneakers.

Oh, my heaven, Glen thought, staring at one boy in particular: straight red hair, easy smile, slim with one of those really long waists tightening down to a pinprick navel. Twirling and bumping about, the boy smiled at Glen. It was a siren's smile, for Glen immediately began walking south along with the float, keeping the boy in view.

So Glen missed Walt and the Kid, who curled onto Fifth Avenue just eleven minutes later, as a Tinker Bell–ish drag queen on roller skates rolled by, blessing the cheering crowd with her fairy wand.

Peter Smith was heading toward the Parade from the east, in the Thirties. He had his "Young, Cute, and Homeless" sign and high hopes. This day, he decided to imagine, would change his life. Who knew whom he might meet? Whom; it's classy. Some millionaire dealer in antiques. A suave movie producer. Maybe some easygoing older guy with a spare room and a wondering heart.

Coming at you!, Peter thought.

I say the great moment of the Parade is when ACT UP reaches Saint Patrick's Cathedral and the Hasidic Jews and other professional bigots behind police barriers, waving signs reading, "AIDS for Gays," and "God Made Adam and Eve, Not Adam and Steve." There is something inspiring in the way the mighty activist host, lean and dauntless in black T-shirts and jeans, turns to confront the enemy with a mass kiss-in. Paul suffers a pang at this; he feels obliterated by this act of self-empowering boys and girls who feel free to make their own history. In Paul's day, history did all the making.

There is a lot of stop-and-start in the Parade. Whenever the disco floats have to wait while automobile traffic crosses Fifth Avenue, everyone goes into his or her dance; but Glen just stood and stared at his redhead.

How bold am I allowed to be?, Glen worried—that eternal question—but the redhead grinned at him, and, thus encouraged, Glen stepped closer. Now the redhead was whirling, throwing his arms out and pulling them in as if summoning some demon power. The Parade picked up again, and the redhead froze as the float heaved into motion. He gave Glen a shrug and a smile.

I don't have to have sex with him, Glen was thinking, hurrying along, staring at the boy. I just want him to like me.

Henry, rummaging through the banks of spectators looking for old and perhaps new friends, paused to groan as a bisexual group paraded by. There were many groans from the crowd, even boos. Gays find it hard enough to fight for their rights without having to carry these freeloaders on their backs as well.

"You're just trying to *in* yourselves!" shouted a woman, from the sidewalk.

"Into the closets and off of the streets!" cried another woman, revising the famous gay war cry.

"Henry?" came a voice behind him.

Henry turned.

"It's Bobby."

Henry gaped.

"Hey, it's been years, hasn't it, pal?" said Bobby. Beaming, he held out a hand, but, as Henry took it, Bobby pulled him close, held him tight, and whispered, "I love you, guy."

Henry was so confused that he struggled to free himself. "Bobby . . ." he began. "Wait—"

"No, listen," said Bobby, still beaming. Proudly, he introduced Henry to "the new guy in my life." Jed? Jeff? Henry didn't catch it, for his hearing was blurred and his eyes were all on Bobby.

"What . . . what *happened* to you?" Henry finally got out. "You're a poster or something!"

Bobby had gone the route from top to toe. When Henry had known him, he was a mall jock, an oversized sweatshirt in a Kmart haircut. Now he looked like something in a catalogue that shatters your week: fifty-dollar hairstyle, giant bite-me teeth, ruthless mesh T, and just-barely running shorts.

"I know what it is," Henry went on. "You finally figured out that you're beautiful."

"Henry," said Bobby, touched but trying to bluff his way past it, "you always saw the best in me, pal."

"I'm seeing it now. Didn't you move to L.A.?"

"Yeah. But Jerr"—here a doting look at the New Guy in My Life— "got transferred and I've got a shot at starting a catering business."

"Bobby says you taught him everything he knows," said Jerr: who, now that Henry was focusing, seemed a second Bobby, big and dumb and so wonderful that you fear to come too close.

"Catering?"

"Yeah. I have this deal where I can specialize in Polish weddings. 'Cause I know that scene, but I give them a little extra style. Like canapés, French, you know? For dessert, tiramisù. Word gets around. You know, all the girls talking among themselves, who had the best wedding. 'Well, Marta had this really classy affair.' " (Imitating a woman, Bobby spoke her words in his voice; Henry thought, *this* is New Gay.) "Marta's friends ask, 'Who catered?' Answer—Bobby Koscievsky." Bobby laughed, then he took Henry in his arms. "*Mój dobry pan,* eh?"

Henry was shaking.

.   .   .

Peter Smith was walking along Thirty-sixth Street just west of Third Avenue. Five hetero-jocko thugs were walking east on the same block, all wearing gas masks. You know, to protect them from the Parade's AIDS fumes. Like all of Murray Hill, Thirty-sixth Street takes a dip on its eastern limits, putting much of it out of the sight of the many policemen o'er-watching Fifth Avenue—which is exactly what the gas masks were counting on. They went for Peter as Cardinal O'Connor goes after used condoms left on his one-holy-mother-church-except-excuse-me-Father-but-all-your-priests-are-child-molesters altar.

Peter sensed that the gas masks were trouble, and he tried to innocent his way past them: You look terribly harmless and move real fast. But one of them grabbed Peter's cardboard sign—grabbed it in a highly jocular manner, as if wishing to read and digest its message. Peter was trapped, because the sign was around his neck and the gas mask was holding on to it. The mask said, "Excuse me, do you know what time it is?," but he was already pulling back for a heavy right cross. Peter went down, and they all crowded in for a major stomp, about thirty-five seconds' worth, extra-heavy on the kicks to the sides of the midsection, because you can do truly lasting damage that way, and avoiding the head, because that way you kill: Whereas if you only injure a faggot, no matter how badly, and if you are convicted, they tend to let you off easy. Whereas if you kill, you might have to do a few months in jail.

As the dance float approached Forty-second Street, Glen's redhead borrowed a pair of castanets from a buddy and played them as he moved, played them—Glen was certain—about Glen and himself, enticingly, hypnotically.

Directly in front of the Library is the reviewing stand, where local celebs wave and survey, where the watching crowd is at its thickest, where the networks plant their cameras. And it was here that Glen, inching along with his redhead, staring and hoping and falling in love with him, finally made his move. Well, no: The redhead did the moving, luring Glen closer and closer with his capering exhibition. Finally, almost in tears, Glen was standing just below the redhead, looking up at him; and the boy in the shorts and sneakers put down the castanets, inclined toward Glen, and slowly extended a hand to him, saying. "Well, come on up, boy toy."

This can really happen?, Glen was thinking, as he took the redhead's hand and was pulled up onto the float. The redhead winked at him.

"My name's Glen."

"Clarence."

They shook hands.

"I like shy boys," said Clarence. "You're shy, right?"

Glen nodded.

"We're going to get on great," said Clarence. "It's going to be really nice, us two."

How Glen felt then was beyond description.

Elaine, having watched all this, pointed it out to Lois and said, "*That's what I mean. About this being a magical day—as long as it doesn't rain."

"Yeah, but they charge too much for an ice cream sandwich."

"Yet you ate two, plus half of mine, I couldn't help noticing."

"Watch the Parade, chick. You have the rest of your life to notice what I do."

"Well, hello," said an attractive woman somewhere between her mid-thirties and a frisky middle age. "You're . . . Lois? Oh, and . . ."

"Elaine," Elaine said.

"You're Johnny's play director," said Lois.

"Chris. We met at the rehearsal Friday."

"Nice work there. It's fun to see Johnny getting bossed around for a change."

"It's a lovely play," Elaine put in. "Johnny says you're quite wonderful with it. You inspire him."

"I love gay men," said Chris. "Being around them has made me . . . knowledgeable. I suppose I should feel left out here, a straight woman. A wife and mother, even. But I know that this is my day, too. This wonderful feeling of being unconventional not out of rebellion but because we simply don't need convention to order our lives around. Because we're special, whether we're straight or gay. There's a message in that, surely."

"Oh, that *must* be right," Elaine agreed. "It has a touch of the speech about it, but if the others heard it—"

"The others," Lois grunted. "I can recall when *we* were the others. Like spirits that fly around at night and explode in the sun."

"Why, Lois, you *poet!*"

"You know," Chris went on, a bit diffidently, "after meeting you, I kept thinking I knew you from somewhere. It's only just hit me—Kingdom Come."

"Yeah," said Lois. "I ran it."

"I used to dance there, when I was at N.Y.U. You threw me and my friends out of the balcony a few times."

"Probably for some good reason."

Chris and Elaine laughed, and Lois replied with one of her *Oh, yeah?* looks.

"It's funny," Chris continued. "All these people around us, of all ages. All these stories they carry . . . like her"—pointing out a woman bearing a sign reading, "I Wish I Had the Courage of My Beautiful Lesbian Daughter." Chris gazed upon the Parade for a moment. A long one, a deep gaze, surrendering to it in triumph as the parched traveler bends to the welling fountain, or the infant lips its mother's nipple. "Such stories," Chris finally said. "All interconnected. Like Johnny's play, except bigger. Epic."

"What are the play's chances?" Lois asked. "I mean, to be a hit or something."

"Five years ago, I would have said, it'll be admired by a few. Because it has an edge, you know. But now, things have opened up so, it might well be popular. Could get a lot of media spin."

"It's quite funny," Elaine observed.

"Oh, to be sure. Whatever happens to Johnny at any time, he never loses his laughter."

"Those scenes in the cabaret at the start of the show?" said Lois. "That was my place, too."

"Killer Mary's?"

"Thriller Jill's was the real name. Johnny started there before there ever was a Jerrett Troy. We called him the Kid."

A huge dance float glided past to the pounding of the disco and the exhilarating whoop-de-do of the boys and girls.

"There's another chick without a top," Lois remarked, nodding at her. "You get more of that each year."

"It's unruly public relations," said Elaine, regretfully.

"The Parade is not diplomacy," Chris pointed out. "It's celebration."

"Thing I don't get is how weird it turns, down at the end," said Lois. "That street fair's no different from any New York street fair—same vendors with the sausages and zeppoles. Then the gigantic crowds down at the pier."

"We always hotfoot it to the Plaza for tea," said Elaine, scanning the heavens for an update on the weather forecast.

"Come join us," Lois told Chris. "It's a treat and a half. They cut the crusts off the sandwiches and charge double, but, heck, it's only once a year."

"It sounds lovely," said Chris.

"There's Walt and Johnny!" cried Elaine, waving. Lois and Chris waved, too, calling to them. But pensive Walt and the protective Kid, one arm around Walt's shoulder, did not hear them.

Blue had gotten as far uptown as Twenty-seventh Street. Every so often he would roost on a hydrant and take in the show, but the Parade moved so slowly that he would get impatient and pace on. Besides, the spectators were as interesting as the marchers. Three young guys quarrel over a Frozfruit. Two women sway in each other's arms, weeping for joy. A mischievous six-year-old tears off as his parents call out, "Tyler! *Tyler!*"

Look at the cute-to-die dude strutting the sidewalk, shirtless, carrying a gym bag. Competition's so fierce these days of our lives that biceps and chest aren't enough; shoulder caps and formidable abdominals are essential.

What else is essential? Blue wonders. The gym bunny barely glances at the Parade. He sees someone not unlike himself on one of the floats, pauses to admire, then smilingly moves on.

He must think, This is not about me.

Peter Smith is struggling to get up. What about passersby, policemen? He's alone. He is made of a million bad pains; but he is relieved, as he edges up off the sidewalk, to see no dark red stains on the pavement.

It hurts very heavy, a deeply-inside-you hurt, and he knows he should find someone to help him. He can breathe. He can walk, slowly. He is holding on to fronts of buildings—handles, metalwork, piping—as he moves. Which way? East. Yes, that's where he . . . no longer lives. Where's home, now? A dim thought: I shouldn't have left New Hampshire, because this couldn't have happened to me there. (Oh yes, it could.) He tries to talk to people coming by, but they hurry along, faces set. No Peter for us. Peter tries to imagine what his face looks like—blood running out of his mouth, his nose. Who'd adopt him now? He can't even talk right. He says, "Would you kindly help me get an ambulance?" to this guy walking up from Third, but the guy is already shaking his head and tuning Peter out, as if he were another of the thousands pulling a dodge and asking for money.

Peter continues to inch his way eastward. Third Avenue has a lot of foot traffic. Surely someone will help him there.

By now, the front of the Parade was nosing into the Village, and Glen saw his straight friends waving and cheering as he and Clarence shared a long kiss.

Can I believe this? All you have to do is show up and cruise persistently and you get . . . *him*?

"Who're those guys shouting at you?" Clarence asked Glen, as he dipped and gestured and sighed, all to music.

"Friends."

"That's cool," said Clarence, as Glen got bold and hugged him from behind, licking his right ear.

"That's pretty," said Clarence, growling appreciatively. "Yeah, from such a shy boy, too."

Henry was marching with Bobby and Jerr, and all three were uproarious. "Solidarity, Henry!" Bobby cried at one point. "Just like in Poland!"

Well, yes—today, at least. Privately, Henry mused that probably no political movement in history counted as little solidarity as this one, with its separatists and integrators, its radicals and Log Cabin Republicans, its "gay" and "queer," its middle-classniks and drag queens and feminists and leather men and leather women and that disgusting lunatic fringe of six or seven pederasts that the media feature as if they were our Continental Congress.

Still, on this afternoon, the feeling was unity. This was the one day when everyone In the Life seemed part of a great striding giant of a history that would never cease its advance. Whatever else might be troubling your times, *this* day gave a bracing shock to the immune system.

That is, except for the Silent Moment, when the entire Parade, from Washington Square to Central Park, halts to consider our slain people. In earlier years, colored balloons were let fly in a kind of camp memorial; but it turned out that these would drop into the ocean and choke unwitting sea creatures. So now we simply raise our hands in salute to the fallen. Some recite the names of dead friends, some actually address them in prayer, and others wait, just stand and think and say nothing.

Henry was considering Jim and Eric: his best friend and the young fellow whose dogged and even pestering devotion turned Jim from a reasonably happy guy into a man of radiant contentment. He and Eric were literally living for each other; no wonder they died months apart.

Was I that happy with Bobby?, Henry wondered, stealing a look at him as they stood in the Silent Moment. Is he that happy with Jerr? And how much less than happy must I be if I never know what Jim and Eric knew? Oh shit, Henry thought, as a tear popped up in one eye. I miss Jim so much.

Quite a ways south of Henry, Glen and his new boy friend stood stock-still on the dance float; Glen sensed a strange seriousness in Clarence. He turned to him, and Clarence put his arms around Glen and held him tight. It was a serious holding, a keening-for-dead-friends hug, but Glen felt it as a belonging hug as well. A liking hug.

Back up at the Forty-second Street Library, Elaine was clutching Lois's hand, thinking of the little boy in Backtown, who had died in March, followed by his mother two months later. She had been arrested for causing a disturbance in a restaurant some few days before, and the disease had so dwindled and misguised her that the police had been afraid to touch her.

Chris was thinking of Tom, of how fiercely he fought to live even when everything had been taken from him—skin and brain and form— and only a husk was left. Chris thought of Luke, of how coolly he proceeded with his life, shrugging away questions. She wondered whom she would spare if she were Sophie and Nazis forced her to choose between J. and Timothy.

Walt, at Thirty-fifth Street—his right arm straight up in the air and the fingers splayed, ignoring the traditional crossing of the middle fingers— was thinking of Danny. Walt had this recurring dream in which he and Danny shared a place in New York. They never had sex, but they were always touching, and Danny was very happy. It was a night dream, but Walt could conjure it up by day, and did so now. Tom entered the dream, because he wanted Danny. He proposed to spank him, right across the knee; then they would really be close. Danny said okay, but he was looking at Walt to get him out of it.

"You may want to check out the cat on the sidewalk to your left," murmured a guy standing next to Walt. "He's cruising you like condoms become illegal tomorrow."

"This is not a correct time to cruise," whispered Walt. He was staring straight ahead.

"True, but this grade of hot you don't see every minute. I mean, the guy's a one-man mattress convention. Scope it out."

"I've decided to believe you," said Walt, refusing to turn and look.

"Suit yourself," said the guy.

Then the Silence was over, and the Parade jolted back into step; and Walt—just for the sake of the argument—looked over to see who was cruising him: a tall blond man somewhat older than himself, staring at him with such intensity that Walt was transfixed, and the others in his group had to step around him. Oh, this is the magic of the Parade, Walt thought to himself, his eyes never leaving the man, and he cautiously began to walk toward him. Soon enough, the two stood before each other like Abel confronting Cain. But wait, now. Who had killed whom? Who had suffered more, who been more profligate in the expressing of the tender cruelties, who had more stubbornly and consistently refused to understand that we must be gentle with our comrades and save our fury for our enemies? And what will these two say now? What will they decide to do?

Because, yes, of course it was Blue.

The Kid saw the entire thing with a rush of dismay, as you must surely imagine. Walt and his fucking Parade, he thought, watching as the two men, just across the street from him, shook hands and began to speak. Moving off to stand on the sidewalk behind the spectators, the Kid tried to figure out what they were saying to each other. Perhaps Blue was chiding Walt:

BLUE: How could you do that to me, Walt? Runnin' me off like so?
WALT: I was angry and afraid.
BLUE: Fer three years?

Or was Walt pleading and Blue playing it high-hat? For instance:

WALT: Why didn't you call me?
BLUE: I reckoned you'd had yer fill a me and moved on to other things. And that's okay, 'cause I did, too.

No, wait—it's small talk, nothing heavy:

BLUE: Well, yer lookin' real fine, youngster.
WALT: You've held up pretty well, too, Blue.
BLUE: Yeah, well, you know what a clean life I lead—don't drink, don't smoke, don't chase women . . .

Truth to tell, none of these scenarios quite fitted what the Kid saw. Walt and Blue were standing very, very close, as if each were trying to slip inside the other. They were touching hands and shoulders and eyes like blind men. They were feeling each other as if trying to prove something by their very contact. They had instantly connected, were gone from worldly concerns. They were flying through the heavens; they were flight itself. And, now that Blue was more generous and Walt more peaceable, they were what the Kid had never known: a perfect fit.

I will tell you what they said to each other:

Walt began, "I tried to replace you, but it didn't work very well."

Blue smiled down at Walt and replied, "Yeah, well, I guess you got to get back at ol' Blue for sayin' everybody could be replaced, once upon a time when I didn't know any better."

Then Walt looked up at Blue—for once, not critically or impatiently but with absolute trust—and Walt said, "You know why I liked you so much? Because you were the only one to make me feel that I could be in charge, instead of being this leprechaun doing a funny dance in the background. Cousin Tom and Luke and Chris . . . They all think I'm a professional little brother."

"Yeah," said Blue, tracing with his fingers the lines and angles of Walt's face, "but that funny talk and your wonderin' ways would always tantalize a guy. Oh, don't be cryin', now. Don't be cryin', Walt."

"I'm only crying because of all the times that I dreamed that you forgave me."

That was when Blue took Walt powerfully and irresistibly and permanently in his arms and Walt held and held and held on, because love is Blue.

And that was when the Kid left the Parade. He ran up the cross street, east through Murray Hill, trying not to think of much, not caring where he would end up. It was not long before he came to a kind of clearing in the urban wood, where all the streets give way to the feed-in to the Queens-Midtown Tunnel under a rare great looming of sky. There is a park there, benches and tables next to courts for handball and basketball, and the sportsmen of the day leaped and shouted, oblivious of everything but their score.

The Kid sat there for some time, wordlessly shaking off the street connivers and the homeless and the freaks who work these places, refusing even to look at them—but one of them spoke the Kid's name in a quavery, broken voice, and the Kid met his gaze.

"Peter?" he said, getting up. "What on earth happened to you?"

"I got beaten." Peter crumpled onto the bench. "Gas masks . . ."

"Hadn't we better call an ambulance?"

"I was crawling along the sidewalk and no one would help me. And now I don't . . . Johnny, listen . . ."

"No, I'm going to get a cab and—"

"Please sit down and let me talk to you. See, I'm the new homeless guy in town because . . . Oh, gee . . ."

Peter started crying and the Kid dropped back on the bench next to him. Hopeless. How can I comfort anybody when my own life has just gone through the shredder?

"Look," the Kid said. "It's ridiculous to cry, because your life is just under way." The Kid put an arm around Peter, who cried out in pain.

"They kept kicking me and laughing," he sobbed. "How could they do that?"

"We have to get you to a hospital."

"No. Please. Just . . . Where am I supposed to live now?"

"Why didn't you call me, Peter?"

"Oh, I would have. I wanted to solve it on my own and not be obliged to anyone. You know how that feels?"

"Yes." Oh, yes.

"But then I got hurt and no one would help me. I just don't get that."

Carefully shifting position, Peter leaned his head on the Kid's shoulder. "They walked past me," Peter went on. "Like, it's not *our* problem. Who cares if you die?"

Some moments passed. Then the Kid said, "You'll come home with me and we'll get you cleaned up and fed and rested and then we'll figure something out. You can stay with me, if you like. A vacancy just opened up in my life." Peter's head went up and he was about to say something, but the Kid hushed him with a gesture, saying only, "You'd be surprised," thinking of Walt and Blue on the sidewalk, of how they were tasting each other at the eyes, a pair of cannibals saying hello. Steam puffing out of their ears. Do-or-die love in their souls. So easy for them. So easy. "A vacancy, I say. Maybe we can . . . comfort each other. I'm old and past it, but I'm smart and funny and I can teach you things and take care of you. And if you would . . . well, if you'd want to . . . see, to work out a relationship, that would be heavenly for me at just this moment in my life. Because I'm in pain, too. I tell you this. But if that's not on the bill for you, I'll respect that. Because I never took advantage of anyone. Almost never. And I used to be a looker myself. Somehow I never quite stopped feeling like one. Decades would pass, but I kept thinking I was—"

"What's your last name?" asked Peter. "Your real one?"

"Smith," I told him. "Like yours. Not that I used it much. I always thought it was too joe and regular for a boy on the Other Side."

The sky went boom and, instantly, the heaviest rain since Genesis 7:11 poured down upon the city, and everybody scattered and grabbed all the cabs. So there we were. I helped Peter hobble across First Avenue to shelter under a storefront awning, and he started to cry again. So I very gently put my arm around his shoulders and said, "Don't fret, now. Think of all you're going to see. Think of the friends you'll make and the history that you'll be part of. Everything is possible now. Everything is you: with your ideals and energy and your youth. I would have given anything to have come along now instead of when I did. Come on, Peter."

Peter wiped his eyes. "Will I be famous? Will I be loved? Will I get my heart's desire?"

"Most have to settle for being famous *or* loved, it would seem."

"Which would you say you were?"

"I never quite made it to either. But I got my heart's desire, I think."

"What was that?"

"Liberty."

The rain was beating the streets with such ferocity that everyone had vanished from sight. A few cars passed carefully by; all the cabs were full.

"This can't last long," I said. "Whatever they throw at us, we'll come back ten times stronger." I laughed. "Even if I do sound like an ACT UP poster. Right?"

Peter nodded.

"Right," I said. "Don't worry, because you're safe now, I promise. You're free. Yes, and Blue is safe. And Walt is free. And I'm the Kid—I snap back and never go down, I swear to you. Oh . . . well, once, at the side of a pool, glorious young men were kind to me and I really lost it, because I couldn't bear it that the ones with all the power could be that nice. I thought it was either nice *or* power. I'll readily admit that I wept that day. But never since."

"I wept today," said Peter.

"Well, you've made quota, and you can't weep again. You're going to work on your fame and love, and your heart's desire, too, and as soon as this terror of nature stops we're going to start laughing. We'll pull absurd stunts and break each other up. I know all the stories—I'll tell you of the Mistress of Thriller Jill's and the Saint of Christopher Street and me, the Green Goddess."

"Do I have to choose between being famous and being loved? Or—"

"It gets chosen for you."

A man ran by, fast as hell, his clothes plastered to his body.

"You can be the new Kid," I told Peter. "It's probably time."

"I won't be much trouble. I'll be full of whimsy, like a panda. Whenever Miss Tybogen would say, 'All right, Richie Mallinson, you march right down to the principal's office and tell *him* what was so important that you had to whisper it to Lester Steranko during Home Room Quiet Time,' all the boys would do the *Dragnet* theme. Dum-de-*dum*-dum. So one day Miss Tybogen said, 'Class, because Marcia Ellsmere has received three A's in a row, she will be the new class monitor,' and I went, 'Dum-de-*dum*-dum,' and got a big laugh."

He gulped on the last few words and broke into sobs again; and, as I did not appear to have it in me to soothe his pain, I did nothing. You reach a point at which you cannot control the event, so you stand aside and let the hurt flow free.

"Just tell me this," Peter choked out. "Why were the gas masks having fun when they did that to me? I see that they hate me, but why do they *love* to hate me?"

We listened to the roar of the rain on the city, and to the history meter, ticking in our time. Peter, shivering in the sudden cold, moved closer to me.

"This will be over soon," I said. "And then we can go home."

ABOUT THE AUTHOR

ETHAN MORDDEN was born in Heavensville, Pennsylvania, and raised there, in Venice, Italy, and on Long Island. An alumnus of the Locust Valley Friends school and the University of Pennsylvania, Mr. Mordden worked as an editor of romance comic books and a musical director of off-Broadway productions of opera and musical comedy before launching his writing career. He is the author of twenty-four books, including the more-or-less celebrated *Buddies* trilogy; a novel, *One Last Waltz;* and the pseudonymous story cycle *A Bad Man Is Easy to Find,* under the byline of M. J. Verlaine.